JOHN DOS PASSOS

JOHN DOS PASSOS

NOVELS 1920–1925
One Man's Initiation: 1917
Three Soldiers
Manhattan Transfer

THE LIBRARY OF AMERICA

———

First Printing
The Library of America–142

Townsend Ludington
WROTE THE NOTES FOR THIS VOLUME

Contents

ONE MAN'S INITIATION: 1917

To the memory of those with whom I saw rockets in the sky, on the road between Erize-la-Petite and Erize-la-Grande, in that early August twilight in the summer of 1917.

Chapter I

IN THE huge shed of the wharf, piled with crates and baggage, broken by gang-planks leading up to ships on either side, a band plays a tinselly Hawaiian tune; people are dancing in and out among the piles of trunks and boxes. There is a scattering of khaki uniforms, and many young men stand in groups laughing and talking in voices pitched shrill with excitement. In the brown light of the wharf, full of rows of yellow crates and barrels and sacks, full of racket of cranes, among which winds in and out the trivial lilt of the Hawaiian tune, there is a flutter of gay dresses and coloured hats of women, and white handkerchiefs.

The booming reverberation of the ship's whistle drowns all other sound.

After it the noise of farewells rises shrill. White handkerchiefs are agitated in the brown light of the shed. Ropes crack in pulleys as the gang-planks are raised.

Again, at the pierhead, white handkerchiefs and cheering and a flutter of coloured dresses. On the wharf building a flag spreads exultingly against the azure afternoon sky.

Rosy yellow and drab purple, the buildings of New York slide together into a pyramid above brown smudges of smoke standing out in the water, linked to the land by the dark curves of the bridges.

In the fresh harbour wind comes now and then a salt-wafting breath off the sea.

Martin Howe stands in the stern that trembles with the vibrating push of the screw. A boy standing beside him turns and asks in a tremulous voice, "This your first time across?"

"Yes. . . . Yours?"

"Yes. . . . I never used to think that at nineteen I'd be crossing the Atlantic to go to a war in France." The boy caught himself up suddenly and blushed. Then swallowing a lump in his throat he said, "It ought to be time to eat."

> "*God help Kaiser Bill!*
> *O-o-o old Uncle Sam.*

3

> *He's got the cavalry,*
> *He's got the infantry,*
> *He's got the artillery;*
> *And then by God we'll all go to Germany!*
> *God help Kaiser Bill!"*

The iron covers are clamped on the smoking-room windows, for no lights must show. So the air is dense with tobacco smoke and the reek of beer and champagne. In one corner they are playing poker with their coats off. All the chairs are full of sprawling young men who stamp their feet to the time, and bang their fists down so that the bottles dance on the tables.

"*God help Kaiser Bill.*"

Sky and sea are opal grey. Martin is stretched on the deck in the bow of the boat with an unopened book beside him. He has never been so happy in his life. The future is nothing to him, the past is nothing to him. All his life is effaced in the grey languor of the sea, in the soft surge of the water about the ship's bow as she ploughs through the long swell, eastward. The tepid moisture of the Gulf Stream makes his clothes feel damp and his hair stick together into curls that straggle over his forehead. There are porpoises about, lazily tumbling in the swell, and flying-fish skim from one grey wave to another, and the bow rises and falls gently in rhythm with the surging sing-song of the broken water.

Martin has been asleep. As through infinite mists of greyness he looks back on the sharp hatreds and wringing desires of his life. Now a leaf seems to have been turned and a new white page spread before him, clean and unwritten on. At last things have come to pass.

And very faintly, like music heard across the water in the evening, blurred into strange harmonies, his old watchwords echo a little in his mind. Like the red flame of the sunset setting fire to opal sea and sky, the old exaltation, the old flame that would consume to ashes all the lies in the world, the trumpet-blast under which the walls of Jericho would fall down, stirs and broods in the womb of his grey lassitude. The bow rises and falls gently in rhythm with the surging singsong of the broken water, as the steamer ploughs through the long swell of the Gulf Stream, eastward.

"See that guy, the feller with the straw hat; he lost five hundred dollars at craps last night."

"Some stakes."

It is almost dark. Sea and sky are glowing claret colour, darkened to a cold bluish-green to westward. In a corner of the deck a number of men are crowded in a circle, while one shakes the dice in his hand with a strange nervous quiver that ends in a snap of the fingers as the white dice roll on the deck.

"Seven up."

From the smoking-room comes a sound of singing and glasses banged on tables.

> "*Oh, we're bound for the Hamburg show,*
> *To see the elephant and the wild kangaroo,*
> *An' we'll all stick together*
> *In fair or foul weather,*
> *For we're going to see the damn show through!*"

On the settee a sallow young man is shaking the ice in a whisky-and-soda into a nervous tinkle as he talks:

"There's nothing they can do against this new gas. . . . It just corrodes the lungs as if they were rotten in a dead body. In the hospitals they just stand the poor devils up against a wall and let them die. They say their skin turns green and that it takes from five to seven days to die—five to seven days of slow choking."

"Oh, but I think it's so splendid of you"—she bared all her teeth, white and regular as those in a dentist's show-case, in a smile as she spoke—"to come over this way to help France."

"Perhaps it's only curiosity," muttered Martin.

"Oh no. . . . You're too modest. . . . What I mean is that it's so splendid to have understood the issues. . . . That's how I feel. I just told dad I'd have to come and do my bit, as the English say."

"What are you going to do?"

"Something in Paris. I don't know just what, but I'll certainly make myself useful somehow." She beamed at him provocatively. "Oh, if only I was a man, I'd have shouldered my gun the first day; indeed I would."

"But the issues were hardly . . . defined then," ventured Martin.

"They didn't need to be. I hate those brutes. I've always hated the Germans, their language, their country, everything about them. And now that they've done such frightful things . . ."

"I wonder if it's all true . . ."

"True! Oh, of course it's all true; and lots more that it hasn't been possible to print, that people have been ashamed to tell."

"They've gone pretty far," said Martin, laughing.

"If there are any left alive after the war they ought to be chloroformed. . . . And really I don't think it's patriotic or humane to take the atrocities so lightly. . . . But really, you must excuse me if you think me rude; I do get so excited and wrought up when I think of those frightful things. . . . I get quite beside myself; I'm sure you do too, in your heart. . . . Any red-blooded person would."

"Only I doubt . . ."

"But you're just playing into their hands if you do that. . . . Oh, dear, I'm quite beside myself, just thinking of it." She raised a small gloved hand to her pink cheek in a gesture of horror, and settled herself comfortably in her deck chair. "Really, I oughtn't to talk about it. I lose all self-control when I do. I hate them so it makes me quite ill. . . . The curs! The Huns! Let me tell you just one story. . . . I know it'll make your blood boil. It's absolutely authentic, too. I heard it before I left New York from a girl who's really the best friend I have on earth. She got it from a friend of hers who had got it directly from a little Belgian girl, poor little thing, who was in the convent at the time. . . . Oh, I don't see why they ever take any prisoners; I'd kill them all like mad dogs."

"What's the story?"

"Oh, I can't tell it. It upsets me too much. . . . No, that's silly, I've got to begin facing realities. . . . It was just when the Germans were taking Bruges, the Uhlans broke into this convent. . . . But I think it was in Louvain, not Bruges. . . .

I have a wretched memory for names. . . . Well, they broke in, and took all those poor defenceless little girls . . ."

"There's the dinner-bell."

"Oh, so it is. I must run and dress. I'll have to tell you later. . . ."

Through half-closed eyes, Martin watched the fluttering dress and the backs of the neat little white shoes go jauntily down the deck.

The smoking-room again. Clink of glasses and chatter of confident voices. Two men talking over their glasses.

"They tell me that Paris is some city."

"The most immoral place in the world, before the war. Why, there are houses there where . . ." his voice sank into a whisper. The other man burst into loud guffaws.

"But the war's put an end to all that. They tell me that French people are regenerated, positively regenerated."

"They say the lack of food's something awful, that you can't get a square meal. They even eat horse."

"Did you hear what those fellows were saying about that new gas? Sounds frightful, don't it? I don't care a thing about bullets, but that kind o' gives me cold feet. . . . I don't give a damn about bullets, but that gas . . ."

"That's why so many shoot their friends when they're gassed. . . ."

"Say, you two, how about a hand of poker?"

A champagne cork pops.

"Jiminy, don't spill it all over me."

"Where we goin', boys?"

> *Oh, we're going to the Hamburg show*
> *To see the elephant and the wild kangaroo,*
> *And we'll all stick together*
> *In fair or foul weather,*
> *For we're going to see the damn show through!*

Chapter II

BEFORE going to bed Martin had seen the lighthouses winking at the mouth of the Gironde, and had filled his lungs with the new, indefinably scented wind coming off the land. The sound of screaming whistles of tug-boats awoke him. Feet were tramping on the deck above his head. The shrill whine of a crane sounded in his ears and the throaty cry of men lifting something in unison.

Through his port-hole in the yet colourless dawn he saw the reddish water of a river with black-hulled sailing-boats on it and a few lanky little steamers of a pattern he had never seen before. Again he breathed deep of the new indefinable smell off the land.

Once on deck in the cold air, he saw through the faint light a row of houses beyond the low wharf buildings, grey mellow houses of four storeys with tiled roofs and intricate ironwork balconies, with balconies in which the ironwork had been carefully twisted by artisans long ago dead into gracefully modulated curves and spirals.

Some in uniform, some not, the ambulance men marched to the station, through the grey streets of Bordeaux. Once a woman opened a window and crying, "Vive l'Amérique," threw out a bunch of roses and daisies. As they were rounding a corner, a man with a frockcoat on ran up and put his own hat on the head of one of the Americans who had none. In front of the station, waiting for the train, they sat at the little tables of cafés, lolling comfortably in the early morning sunlight, and drank beer and cognac.

Small railway carriages into which they were crowded so that their knees were pressed tight together—and outside, slipping by, blue-green fields, and poplars stalking out of the morning mist, and long drifts of poppies. Scarlet poppies, and cornflowers, and white daisies, and the red-tiled roofs and white walls of cottages, all against a background of glaucous green fields and hedges. Tours, Poitiers, Orléans. In the names of the stations rose old wars, until the floods of scarlet poppies seemed the blood of fighting men slaughtered

8

through all time. At last, in the gloaming, Paris, and, in crossing a bridge over the Seine, a glimpse of the two linked towers of Notre Dame, rosy grey in the grey mist up the river.

"Say, these women here get my goat."

"How do you mean?"

"Well, I was at the Olympia with Johnson and that crowd.
They just pester the life out of you there. I'd heard that Paris
was immoral, but nothing like this."

"It's the war."

"But the Jane I went with . . ."

"Why didn't you spend the night with her?"

"I got sort o' disgusted, and then I began to sober up."

"You'd better take precautions."

"You bet. . . . It's sort o' disgusting, though, isn't it?"

"Looks like every woman you saw walking on the street
was a whore. They certainly are good-lookers though."

"King and his gang are all being sent back to the States."

"I'll be darned! They sure have been drunk ever since they
got off the steamer."

"Raised hell in Maxim's last night. They tried to clean up
the place and the police came. They were all soused to the
gills and tried to make everybody there sing the 'Star Spangled Banner.'"

"Damn fool business."

Martin Howe sat at a table on the sidewalk under the
brown awning of a restaurant. Opposite in the last topaz-clear
rays of the sun, the foliage of the Jardin du Luxembourg
shone bright green above deep alleys of bluish shadow. From
the pavements in front of the mauve-coloured houses rose
little kiosks with advertisements in bright orange and vermilion and blue. In the middle of the triangle formed by the
streets and the garden was a round pool of jade water. Martin
leaned back in his chair looking dreamily out through half-
closed eyes, breathing deep now and then of the musty scent
of Paris, that mingled with the melting freshness of the wild
strawberries on the plate before him.

As he stared in front of him two figures crossed his field of
vision. A woman swathed in black crepe veils was helping a

soldier to a seat at the next table. He found himself staring in a face, a face that still had some of the chubbiness of boyhood. Between the pale-brown frightened eyes, where the nose should have been, was a triangular black patch that ended in some mechanical contrivance with shiny little black metal rods that took the place of the jaw. He could not take his eyes from the soldier's eyes, that were like those of a hurt animal, full of meek dismay. Someone plucked at Martin's arm, and he turned suddenly, fearfully.

A bent old woman was offering him flowers with a jerky curtsey.

"Just a rose, for good luck?"

"No, thank you."

"It will bring you happiness."

He took a couple of the reddest of the roses.

"Do you understand the language of flowers?"

"No."

"I shall teach you. . . . Thank you so much. . . . Thank you so much."

She added a few large daisies to the red roses in his hand.

"These will bring you love. . . . But another time I shall teach you the language of flowers, the language of love."

She curtseyed again, and began making her way jerkily down the sidewalk, jingling his silver in her hand.

He stuck the roses and daisies in the belt of his uniform and sat with the green flame of Chartreuse in a little glass before him, staring into the gardens, where the foliage was becoming blue and lavender with evening, and the shadows darkened to grey-purple and black. Now and then he glanced furtively, with shame, at the man at the next table. When the restaurant closed he wandered through the unlighted streets towards the river, listening to the laughs and conversations that bubbled like the sparkle in Burgundy through the purple summer night.

But wherever he looked in the comradely faces of young men, in the beckoning eyes of women, he saw the brown hurt eyes of the soldier, and the triangular black patch where the nose should have been.

Chapter III

A T EPERNAY the station was wrecked; the corrugated tin of the roof hung in strips over the crumbled brick walls.

"They say the Boches came over last night. They killed a lot of permissionaires."

"That river's the Marne."

"Gosh, is it? Let me get to the winder."

The third-class car, joggling along on a flat wheel, was full of the smell of sweat and sour wine. Outside, yellow-green and blue-green, crossed by long processions of poplars, aflame with vermilion and carmine of poppies, the countryside slipped by. At a station where the train stopped on a siding, they could hear a faint hollow sound in the distance: guns.

Croix de Guerre had been given out that day at the automobile park at Châlons. There was an unusually big dinner at the wooden tables in the narrow portable barracks, and during the last course the General passed through and drank a glass of champagne to the health of all present. Everybody had on his best uniform and sweated hugely in the narrow, airless building, from the wine and the champagne and the thick stew, thickly seasoned, that made the dinner's main course.

"We are all one large family," said the General from the end of the barracks . . . "to France."

That night the wail of a siren woke Martin suddenly and made him sit up in his bunk trembling, wondering where he was. Like the shriek of a woman in a nightmare, the wail of the siren rose and rose and then dropped in pitch and faded throbbingly out.

"Don't flash a light there. It's Boche planes."

Outside the night was cold, with a little light from a waned moon.

"See the shrapnel!" someone cried.

"The Boche has a Mercedes motor," said someone else. "You can tell by the sound of it."

"They say one of their planes chased an ambulance ten miles along a straight road the other day, trying to get it with a machinegun. The man who was driving got away, but he had shell-shock afterwards."

"Did he really?"

"Oh, I'm goin' to turn in. God, these French nights are cold!"

The rain pattered hard with unfaltering determination on the roof of the little arbour. Martin lolled over the rough board table, resting his chin on his clasped hands, looking through the tinkling bead curtains of the rain towards the other end of the weed-grown garden, where, under a canvas shelter, the cooks were moving about in front of two black steaming cauldrons. Through the fresh scent of rain-beaten leaves came a greasy smell of soup. He was thinking of the jolly wedding-parties that must have drunk and danced in this garden before the war, of the lovers who must have sat in that very arbour, pressing sunburned cheek against sunburned cheek, twining hands callous with work in the fields. A man broke suddenly into the arbour behind Martin and stood flicking the water off his uniform with his cap. His sand-coloured hair was wet and was plastered in little spikes to his broad forehead, a forehead that was the entablature of a determined rock-hewn face.

"Hello," said Martin, twisting his head to look at the new-comer. "You section twenty-four?"

"Yes. . . . Ever read 'Alice in Wonderland'?" asked the wet man, sitting down abruptly at the table.

"Yes, indeed."

"Doesn't this remind you of it?"

"What?"

"This war business. Why, I keep thinking I'm going to meet the rabbit who put butter in his watch round every corner."

"It was the best butter."

"That's the hell of it."

"When's your section leaving here?" asked Martin, picking up the conversation after a pause during which they'd both stared out into the rain. They could hear almost constantly the grinding roar of camions on the road behind the café and the slither of their wheels through the mud-puddles where the road turned into the village.

"How the devil should I know?"

"Somebody had dope this morning that we'd leave here for Soissons to-morrow." Martin's words tailed off into a convictionless mumble.

"It surely is different than you'd pictured it, isn't it, now?"

They sat looking at each other while the big drops from the leaky roof smacked on the table or splashed cold in their faces.

"What do you think of all this, anyway?" said the wet man suddenly, lowering his voice stealthily.

"I don't know. I never did expect it to be what we were taught to believe. . . . Things aren't."

"But you can't have guessed that it was like this . . . like Alice in Wonderland, like an ill-intentioned Drury Lane pantomime, like all the dusty futility of Barnum and Bailey's Circus."

"No, I thought it would be hair-raising," said Martin.

"Think, man, think of all the oceans of lies through all the ages that must have been necessary to make this possible! Think of this new particular vintage of lies that has been so industriously pumped out of the press and the pulpit. Doesn't it stagger you?"

Martin nodded.

"Why, lies are like a sticky juice overspreading the world, a living, growing flypaper to catch and gum the wings of every human soul. . . . And the little helpless buzzings of honest, liberal, kindly people, aren't they like the thin little noise flies make when they're caught?"

"I agree with you that the little thin noise is very silly," said Martin.

Martin slammed down the hood of the car and stood upright. A cold stream of rain ran down the sleeves of his slicker and dripped from his greasy hands.

Infantry tramped by, the rain spattering with a cold glitter on grey helmets, on gun-barrels, on the straps of equipment. Red sweating faces, drooping under the hard rims of helmets, turned to the ground with the struggle with the weight of equipment; rows and patches of faces were the only warmth in the desolation of putty-coloured mud and bowed mud-coloured bodies and dripping mud-coloured sky. In the cold colourlessness they were delicate and feeble as the faces of children, rosy and soft under the splattering of mud and the shagginess of unshaven beards.

Martin rubbed the back of his hand against his face. His skin was like that, too, soft as the petals of flowers, soft and warm amid all this dead mud, amid all this hard mud-covered steel.

He leant against the side of the car, his ears full of the heavy shuffle, of the jingle of equipment, of the splashing in puddles of water-soaked boots, and watched the endless rosy patches of faces moving by, the faces that drooped towards the dripping boots that rose and fell, churning into froth the soupy, putty-coloured mud of the road.

The schoolmaster's garden was full of late roses and marigolds, all parched and bleached by the thick layer of dust that was over them. Next to the vine-covered trellis that cut the garden off from the road stood a green table and a few cane chairs. The schoolmaster, something charmingly eighteenth-century about the cut of his breeches and the calves of his legs in their thick woollen golf-stockings, led the way, a brown pitcher of wine in his hand. Martin Howe and the black-haired, brown-faced boy from New Orleans who was his car-mate followed him. Then came a little grey woman in a pink knitted shawl, carrying a tray with glasses.

"In the Verdunois our wine is not very good," said the schoolmaster, bowing them into chairs. "It is thin and cold like the climate. To your health, gentlemen."

"To France."

"To America."

"And down with the Boches."

In the pale yellow light that came from among the dark clouds that passed over the sky, the wine had the chilly gleam of yellow diamonds.

"Ah, you should have seen that road in 1916," said the schoolmaster, drawing a hand over his watery blue eyes. "That, you know, is the Voie Sacrée, the sacred way that saved

Verdun. All day, all day, a double line of camions went up, full of ammunition and ravitaillement and men."

"Oh, the poor boys, we saw so many go up," came the voice, dry as the rustling of the wind in the vine-leaves, of the grey old woman who stood leaning against the schoolmaster's chair, looking out through a gap in the trellis at the rutted road so thick with dust, "and never have we seen one of them come back."

"It was for France."

"But this was a nice village before the war. From Verdun to Bar-le-Duc, the Courrier des Postes used to tell us, there was no such village, so clean and with such fine orchards." The old woman leaned over the schoolmaster's shoulder, joining eagerly in the conversation.

"Even now the fruit is very fine," said Martin.

"But you soldiers, you steal it all," said the old woman, throwing out her arms. "You leave us nothing, nothing."

"We don't begrudge it," said the schoolmaster, "all we have is our country's."

"We shall starve then. . . ."

As she spoke the glasses on the table shook. With a roar of heavy wheels and a grind of gears a camion went by.

"O good God!" The old woman looked out on to the road with terror in her face, blinking her eyes in the thick dust.

Roaring with heavy wheels, grinding with gears, throbbing with motors, camion after camion went by, slowly, stridently. The men packed into the camions had broken through the canvas covers and leaned out waving their arms and shouting.

"Oh, the poor children," said the old woman, wringing her hands, her voice lost in the roar and the shouting.

"They should not destroy property that way," said the schoolmaster. . . . "Last year it was dreadful. There were mutinies."

Martin sat, his chair tilted back, his hands trembling, staring with compressed lips at the men who jolted by on the strident, throbbing camions. A word formed in his mind: tumbrils.

In some trucks the men were drunk and singing, waving their bidons in the air, shouting at people along the road, crying out all sorts of things: "Get to the front!" "Into the trenches with them!" "Down with the war!" In others they sat quiet, faces corpse-like with dust. Through the gap in the trellis Martin stared at them, noting intelligent faces, beautiful faces, faces brutally gay, miserable faces like those of sobbing drunkards.

At last the convoy passed and the dust settled again on the rutted road.

"Oh, the poor children!" said the old woman. "They know they are going to death."

They tried to hide their agitation. The schoolmaster poured out more wine.

"Yes," said Martin, "there are fine orchards on the hills round here."

"You should be here when the plums are ripe," said the schoolmaster.

A tall bearded man, covered with dust to the eyelashes, in the uniform of a commandant, stepped into the garden.

"My dear friends!" He shook hands with the schoolmaster and the old woman and saluted the two Americans. "I could not pass without stopping a moment. We are going up to an attack. We have the honour to take the lead."

"You will have a glass of wine, won't you?"

"With great pleasure."

"Julie, fetch a bottle, you know which. . . . How is the morale?"

"Perfect."

"I thought they looked a little discontented."

"No. . . . It's always like that. . . . They were yelling at some gendarmes. If they strung up a couple it would serve them right, dirty beasts."

"You soldiers are all one against the gendarmes."

"Yes. We fight the enemy but we hate the gendarmes." The commandant rubbed his hands, drank his wine and laughed.

"Hah! There's the next convoy. I must go."

"Good luck."

The commandant shrugged his shoulders, clicked his heels together at the garden gate, saluted, smiling, and was gone.

Again the village street was full of the grinding roar and throb of camions, full of a frenzy of wheels and drunken shouting.

"Give us a drink, you."

"We're the train de luxe, we are."

"Down with the war!"

And the old grey woman wrung her hands and said:

"Oh, the poor children, they know they are going to death!"

Chapter IV

MARTIN, rolled up in his bedroll on the floor of the empty hayloft, woke with a start.

"Say, Howe!" Tom Randolph, who lay next him, was pressing his hand. "I think I heard a shell go over."

As he spoke there came a shrill, loudening whine, and an explosion that shook the barn. A little dirt fell down on Martin's face.

"Say, fellers, that was damn near," came a voice from the floor of the barn.

"We'd better go over to the quarry."

"Oh, hell, I was sound asleep!"

A vicious shriek overhead and a shaking snort of explosion.

"Gee, that was in the house behind us. . . ."

"I smell gas."

"Ye damn fool, it's carbide."

"One of the Frenchmen said it was gas."

"All right, fellers, put on your masks."

Outside there was a sickly rough smell in the air that mingled strangely with the perfume of the cool night, musical with the gurgling of the stream through the little valley where their barn was. They crouched in a quarry by the roadside, a straggling, half-naked group, and watched the flashes in the sky northward, where artillery along the lines kept up a continuous hammering drum-beat. Over their head shells shrieked at two-minute intervals, to explode with a rattling ripping sound in the village on the other side of the valley.

"Damn foolishness," muttered Tom Randolph in his rich Southern voice. "Why don't those damn gunners go to sleep and let us go to sleep? . . . They must be tired like we are."

A shell burst in a house on the crest of the hill opposite, so that they saw the flash against the starry night sky. In the silence that followed, the moaning shriek of a man came faintly across the valley.

Martin sat on the steps of the dugout, looking up the shattered shaft of a tree, from the top of which a few ribbons of bark fluttered against the mauve evening sky. In the quiet he could hear the voices of men chatting in the dark below him, and a sound of someone whistling as he worked. Now and then, like some ungainly bird, a high calibre shell trundled through the air overhead; after its noise had completely died away would come the thud of the explosion. It was like battledore and shuttlecock, these huge masses whirling through the evening far above his head, now from one side, now from the other. It gave him somehow a cosy feeling of safety, as if he were under some sort of a bridge over which freight-cars were shunted madly to and fro.

The doctor in charge of the post came up and sat beside Martin. He was a small brown man with slim black moustaches that curved like the horns of a long-horn steer. He stood on tip-toe on the top step and peered about in every direction with an air of ownership, then sat down again and began talking briskly.

"We are exactly four hundred and five mètres from the Boche. . . . Five hundred mètres from here they are drinking beer and saying, 'Hoch der Kaiser.'"

"About as much as we're saying 'Vive la République,' I should say."

"Who knows? But it is quiet here, isn't it? It's quieter here than in Paris."

"The sky is very beautiful to-night."

"They say they're shelling the Etat-Major to-day. Damned embusqués; it'll do them good to get a bit of their own medicine."

Martin did not answer. He was crossing in his mind the four hundred and five mètres to the first Boche listening-post. Next beyond the abris was the latrine from which a puff of wind brought now and then a nauseous stench. Then there was the tin roof, crumpled as if by a hand, that had been a cook shack. That was just behind the second line trenches that zig-zagged in and out of great abscesses of wet, upturned clay along the crest of a little hill. The other day he had been there, and had clambered up the oily clay where the boyau had caved in, and from the level of the ground had looked for an anxious minute or two at the tangle of trenches and pitted gangrened soil in the direction of the German outposts. And all along these random gashes in the mucky clay were men, feet and legs huge from clotting after clotting of clay, men with greyish-green faces scarred by lines of strain and fear and boredom as the hillside was scarred out of all semblance by the trenches and the shell-holes.

"We are well off here," said the doctor again. "I have not had a serious case all day."

"Up in the front line there's a place where they've planted rhubarb. . . . You know, where the hillside is beginning to get rocky."

"It was the Boche who did that. . . . We took that slope from them two months ago. . . . How does it grow?"

"They say the gas makes the leaves shrivel," said Martin, laughing.

He looked long at the little ranks of clouds that had begun to fill the sky, like ruffles on a woman's dress. Might not it really be, he kept asking himself, that the sky was a beneficent goddess who would stoop gently out of the infinite spaces and lift him to her breast, where he could lie amid the amber-fringed ruffles of cloud and look curiously down at the spinning ball of the earth? It might have beauty if he were far enough away to clear his nostrils of the stench of pain.

"It is funny," said the little doctor suddenly, "to think how much nearer we are, in state of mind, in everything, to the Germans than to anyone else."

"You mean that the soldiers in the trenches are all further from the people at home than from each other, no matter what side they are on."

The little doctor nodded.

"God, it's so stupid! Why can't we go over and talk to them? Nobody's fighting about anything. . . . God, it's so hideously stupid!" cried Martin, suddenly carried away, helpless in the flood of his passionate revolt.

"Life is stupid," said the little doctor sententiously.

Suddenly from the lines came a splutter of machine-guns.

"Evensong!" cried the little doctor. "Ah, but here's business. You'd better get your car ready, my friend."

The brancardiers set the stretcher down at the top of the steps that led to the door of the dugout, so that Martin found himself looking into the lean, sensitive face, stained a little with blood about the mouth, of the wounded man. His eyes followed along the shapeless bundles of blood-flecked uniform till they suddenly turned away. Where the middle of the man had been, where had been the curved belly and the genitals, where the thighs had joined with a strong swerving of muscles to the trunk, was a depression, a hollow pool of blood, that glinted a little in the cold diffusion of grey light from the west.

The rain beat hard on the window-panes of the little room and hissed down the chimney into the smouldering fire that sent up thick green smoke. At a plain oak table before the fireplace sat Martin Howe and Tom Randolph, Tom Randolph with his sunburned hands with their dirty nails spread flat and his head resting on the table between them, so that Martin could see the stiff black hair on top of his head and the dark nape of his neck going into shadow under the collar of the flannel shirt.

"Oh, God, it's too damned absurd! An arrangement for mutual suicide and no damned other thing," said Randolph, raising his head.

"A certain jolly asinine grotesqueness, though. I mean, if you were God and could look at it like that . . . Oh, Randy, why do they enjoy hatred so?"

"A question of taste . . . as the lady said when she kissed the cow."

"But it isn't. It isn't natural for people to hate that way, it can't be. It even disgusts the perfectly stupid damn-fool people, like Higgins, who believes that the Bible was written in God's own handwriting and that the newspapers tell the truth."

"It makes me sick at ma stomach, Howe, to talk to one of those Hun-hatin' women, if they're male or female."

"It is a stupid affair, *la vie*, as the doctor at P.I. said yesterday. . . ."

"Hell, yes. . . ."

They sat silent, watching the rain beat on the window, and run down in sparkling finger-like streams.

"What I can't get over is these Frenchwomen." Randolph threw back his head and laughed. "They're so bloody frank.

Did I tell you about what happened to me at that last village on the Verdun road?"

"No."

"I was lyin' down for a nap under a plumtree, a wonderfully nice place near a li'l brook an' all, an' suddenly that crazy Jane. . . . You know the one that used to throw stones at us out of that broken-down house at the corner of the road. . . . Anyway, she lays down beside me an' before I am properly awake is all cuddled up an' ready for business. I had a regular wrastlin' match gettin' away from her."

"Funny position for you to be in, getting away from a woman."

"But doesn't that strike you funny? Why, down where I come from a drunken mulatto woman wouldn't act like that. They all keep up a fake of not wantin' your attentions." His black eyes sparkled, and he laughed his deep ringing laugh, that made the withered woman smile as she set an omelette before them.

"Voilà, messieurs," she said with a grand air, as if it were a boar's head that she was serving.

Three French infantrymen came into the café, shaking the rain off their shoulders.

"Nothing to drink but champagne at four francs fifty," shouted Howe. "Dirty night out, isn't it?"

"We'll drink that, then!"

Howe and Randolph moved up and they all sat at the same table.

"Fortune of war?"

"Oh, the war, what do you think of the war?" cried Martin.

"What do you think of the peste? You think about saving your skin."

"What's amusing about us is that we three have all saved our skins together," said one of the Frenchmen.

"Yes. We are of the same class," said another, holding up his thumb. "Mobilised same day." He held up his first finger. "Same company." He held up a second finger. "Wounded by the same shell. . . . Evacuated to the same hospital. Convalescence at same time. . . . Réformé to the same depôt behind the lines."

"Didn't all marry the same girl, did you, to make it complete?" asked Randolph.

They all shouted with laughter until the glasses along the bar rang.

"Not exactly, but we were once in a town where there was only one woman. Which amounted to the same. . . ."

"You must be Athos, Porthos, and d'Artagnan."

"Some more champagne, madame, for the three musketeers," sang Randolph in a sort of operatic yodel.

"All I have left is this," said the withered woman, setting a bottle down on the table.

"Is that poison?"

"It's cognac, it's very good cognac," said the old woman seriously.

"C'est du cognac! Vive le roi cognac!" everybody shouted.

> "*Au plein de mon cognac*
> *Qu'il fait bon, fait bon, fait bon,*
> *Au plein de mon cognac*
> *Qu'il fait bon dormir.*"

"Down with the war! Who can sing the 'Internationale'?"

"Not so much noise, I beg you, gentlemen," came the withered woman's whining voice. "It's after hours. Last week I was fined. Next time I'll be closed up."

The night was black when Martin and Randolph, after lengthy and elaborate farewells, started down the muddy road towards the hospital. They staggered along the slippery footpath beside the road, splashed every instant with mud by camions, huge and dark, that roared grindingly by. They ran and skipped arm-in-arm and shouted at the top of their lungs:

> "*Auprès de ma blonde,*
> *Qu'il fait bon, fait bon, fait bon,*
> *Auprès de ma blonde,*
> *Qu'il fait bon dormir.*"

A stench of sweat and filth and formaldehyde caught them by the throat as they went into the hospital tent, gave them a sense of feverish bodies of men stretched all about them, stirring in pain.

"A car for la Bassée, Ambulance 4," said the orderly.

Howe got himself up off the hospital stretcher, shoving his

flannel shirt back into his breeches, put on his coat and belt and felt his way to the door, stumbling over the legs of sleeping brancardiers as he went. Men swore in their sleep and turned over heavily. At the door he waited a minute, then shouted:

"Coming, Tom?"

"Too damn sleepy," came Randolph's voice from under a blanket.

"I've got cigarettes, Tom. I'll smoke 'em all up if you don't come."

"All right, I'll come."

"Less noise, name of God!" cried a man, sitting up on his stretcher.

After the hospital, smelling of chloride and blankets and reeking clothes, the night air was unbelievably sweet. Like a gilt fringe on a dark shawl, a little band of brightness had appeared in the east.

"Some dawn, Howe, ain't it?"

As they were going off, their motor chugging regularly, an orderly said:

"It's a special case. Go for orders to the commandant."

Colours formed gradually out of chaotic grey as the day brightened. At the dressing-station an attendant ran up to the car.

"Oh, you're for the special case? Have you anything to tie a man with?"

"No, why?"

"It's nothing. He just tried to stab the sergeant-major."

The attendant raised a fist and tapped on his head as if knocking on a door. "It's nothing. He's quieter now."

"What caused it?"

"Who knows? There is so much. . . . He says he must kill everyone. . . ."

"Are you ready?"

A lieutenant of the medical corps came to the door and looked out. He smiled reassuringly at Martin Howe. "He's not violent any more. And we'll send two guardians."

A sergeant came out with a little packet which he handed to Martin.

"That's his. Will you give it to them at the hospital at Fourreaux? And here's his knife. They can give it back to him when he gets better. He has an idea he ought to kill everyone he sees. . . . Funny idea."

The sun had risen and shone gold across the broad rolling lands, so that the hedges and the poplar-rows cast long blue shadows over the fields. The man, with a guardian on either side of him who cast nervous glances to the right and to the left, came placidly, eyes straight in front of him, out of the dark interior of the dressing-station. He was a small man with moustaches and small, goodnatured lips puffed into an o-shape. At the car he turned and saluted.

"Good-bye, my lieutenant. Thank you for your kindness," he said.

"Good-bye, old chap," said the lieutenant.

The little man stood up in the car, looking about him anxiously.

"I've lost my knife. Where's my knife?"

The guards got in behind him with a nervous, sheepish air. They answered reassuringly, "The driver's got it. The American's got it."

"Good."

The orderly jumped on the seat with the two Americans to show the way. He whispered in Martin's ear:

"He's crazy. He says that to stop the war you must kill everybody, kill everybody."

In an open valley that sloped between hills covered with beech-woods, stood the tall abbey, a Gothic nave and apse with beautifully traced windows, with the ruin of a very ancient chapel on one side, and crossing the back, a well-proportioned Renaissance building that had been a dormitory. The first time that Martin saw the abbey, it towered in ghostly perfection above a low veil of mist that made the valley seem a lake in the shining moonlight. The lines were perfectly quiet, and when he stopped the motor of his ambulance, he could hear the wind rustling among the beech-woods. Except for the dirty smell of huddled soldiers that came now and then in drifts along with the cool woodscents, there might have been no war at all. In the soft moonlight the great trac-eried windows and the buttresses and the high-pitched roof seemed as gorgeously untroubled by decay as if the carvings on the cusps and arches had just come from under the careful chisels of the Gothic workmen.

"And you say we've progressed," he whispered to Tom Randolph.

"God, it is fine."

They wandered up and down the road a long time, silently, looking at the tall apse of the abbey, breathing the cool night air, moist with mist, in which now and then was the huddled, troubling smell of soldiers. At last the moon, huge and swollen with gold, set behind the wooded hills, and they went back to the car, where they rolled up in their blankets and went to sleep.

Behind the square lantern that rose over the crossing, there was a trap door in the broken tile roof, from which you could climb to the observation post in the lantern. Here, half on the roof and half on the platform behind the trap door, Martin would spend the long summer afternoons when there was no call for the ambulance, looking at the Gothic windows of the lantern and the blue sky beyond, where huge soft clouds passed slowly over, darkening the green of the woods and of the weed-grown fields of the valley with their moving shadows.

There was almost no activity on that part of the front. A couple of times a day a few snapping discharges would come from the seventy-fives of the battery behind the abbey, and the woods would resound like a shaken harp as the shells passed over to explode on the crest of the hill that blocked the end of the valley where the Boches were.

Martin would sit and dream of the quiet lives the monks must have passed in their beautiful abbey so far away in the Forest of the Argonne, digging and planting in the rich lands of the valley, making flowers bloom in the garden, of which traces remained in the huge beds of sunflowers and orange marigolds that bloomed along the walls of the dormitory. In a room in the top of the house he had found a few torn remnants of books; there must have been a library in the old days, rows and rows of musty-smelling volumes in rich brown calf worn by use to a velvet softness, and in cream-coloured parchment where the fingermarks of generations showed brown; huge psalters with notes and chants illuminated in green and ultramarine and gold; manuscripts out of the Middle Ages with strange script and pictures in pure vivid colours; lives of saints, thoughts polished by years of quiet meditation of old divines; old romances of chivalry; tales of blood and death and love where the crude agony of life was seen through a dawn-like mist of gentle beauty.

"God! if there were somewhere nowadays where you could flee from all this stupidity, from all this cant of governments, and this hideous reiteration of hatred, this strangling hatred . . ." he would say to himself, and see himself working in the fields, copying parchments in quaint letterings, drowsing his feverish desires to calm in the deep-throated passionate chanting of the endless offices of the Church.

One afternoon towards evening as he lay on the tiled roof with his shirt open so that the sun warmed his throat and chest, half asleep in the beauty of the building and of the woods and the clouds that drifted overhead, he heard a strain from the organ in the church: a few deep notes in broken rhythm that filled him with wonder, as if he had suddenly been transported back to the quiet days of the monks. The rhythm changed in an instant, and through the squeakiness of shattered pipes came a swirl of fake-oriental ragtime that resounded like mocking laughter in the old vaults and arches. He went down into the church and found Tom Randolph playing on the little organ, pumping desperately with his feet.

"Hello! Impiety I call it; putting your lustful tunes into that pious old organ."

"I bet the ole monks had a merry time, lecherous ole devils," said Tom, playing away.

"If there were monasteries nowadays," said Martin, "I think I'd go into one."

"But there are. I'll end up in one, most like, if they don't put me in jail first. I reckon every living soul would be a candidate for either one if it'd get them out of this God-damned war."

There was a shriek overhead that reverberated strangely in the vaults of the church and made the swallows nesting there fly in and out through the glassless windows. Tom Randolph stopped on a wild chord.

"Guess they don't like me playin'."

"That one didn't explode though."

"That one did, by gorry," said Randolph, getting up off the floor, where he had thrown himself automatically. A shower of tiles came rattling off the roof, and through the noise could be heard the frightened squeaking of the swallows.

"I am afraid that winged somebody."

"They must have got wind of the ammunition dump in the cellar."

"Hell of a place to put a dressing-station—over an ammunition dump!"

The whitewashed room used as a dressing-station had a smell of blood stronger than the chloride. A doctor was leaning over a stretcher on which Martin caught a glimpse of two naked legs with flecks of blood on the white skin, as he passed through on his way to the car.

"Three stretcher-cases for Les Islettes. Very softly," said the attendant, handing him the papers.

Jolting over the shell-pitted road, the car wound slowly through unploughed weed-grown fields. At every jolt came a rasping groan from the wounded men.

As they came back towards the front posts again, they found all the batteries along the road firing. The air was a chaos of explosions that jabbed viciously into their ears, above the reassuring purr of the motor. Nearly to the abbey a soldier stopped them.

"Put the car behind the trees and get into a dugout. They're shelling the abbey."

As he spoke a whining shriek grew suddenly loud over their heads. The soldier threw himself flat in the muddy road. The explosion brought gravel about their ears and made a curious smell of almonds.

Crowded in the door of the dugout in the hill opposite they watched the abbey as shell after shell tore through the roof or exploded in the strong buttresses of the apse. Dust rose high above the roof and filled the air with an odour of damp tiles and plaster. The woods resounded in a jangling tremor, with the batteries that started firing one after the other.

"God, I hate them for that!" said Randolph between his teeth.

"What do you want? It's an observation post."

"I know, but damn it!"

There was a series of explosions; a shell fragment whizzed past their heads.

"It's not safe there. You'd better come in all the way," someone shouted from within the dugout.

"I want to see; damn it. . . . I'm goin' to stay and see it out, Howe. That place meant a hell of a lot to me." Randolph blushed as he spoke.

Another bunch of shells crashing so near together they did not hear the scream. When the cloud of dust blew away, they saw that the lantern had fallen in on the roof of the apse, leaving only one wall and the tracery of a window, of which the shattered carving stood out cream-white against the reddish evening sky.

There was a lull in the firing. A few swallows still wheeled about the walls, giving shrill little cries.

They saw the flash of a shell against the sky as it exploded in the part of the tall roof that still remained. The roof crumpled and fell in, and again dust hid the abbey.

"Oh, I hate this!" said Tom Randolph. "But the question is, what's happened to our grub? The popote is buried four feet deep in Gothic art. . . . Damn fool idea, putting a dressing-station over an ammunition dump."

"Is the car hit?" The orderly came up to them.

"Don't think so."

"Good. Four stretcher-cases for 42 at once."

At night in a dugout. Five men playing cards about a lamp-flame that blows from one side to the other in the gusty wind that puffs every now and then down the mouth of the dugout and whirls round it like something alive trying to beat a way out.

Each time the lamp blows the shadows of the five heads writhe upon the corrugated tin ceiling. In the distance, like kettle-drums beaten for a dance, a constant reverberation of guns.

Martin Howe, stretched out in the straw of one of the bunks, watches their faces in the flickering shadows. He wishes he had the patience to play too. No, perhaps it is better to look on; it would be so silly to be killed in the middle of one of those grand gestures one makes in slamming the card down that takes the trick. Suddenly he thinks of all the lives that must, in these last three years, have ended in that grand gesture. It is too silly. He seems to see their poor lacerated souls, clutching their greasy dogeared cards, climb to a squalid Valhalla, and there, in tobacco-stinking, sweat-stinking rooms, like those of the little cafés behind the lines, sit in groups of five, shuffling, dealing, taking tricks, always with the same slam of the cards on the table, pausing now and then to scratch their louse-eaten flesh.

At this moment, how many men, in all the long Golgotha that stretches from Belfort to the sea, must be trying to cheat their boredom and their misery with that grand gesture of slamming the cards down to take a trick, while in their ears, like tom-toms, pounds the death-dance of the guns.

Martin lies on his back looking up at the curved corrugated ceiling of the dugout, where the shadows of the five heads writhe in fantastic shapes. Is it death they are playing, that they are so merry when they take a trick?

Chapter V

THE THREE PLANES gleamed like mica in the intense blue of the sky. Round about the shrapnel burst in little puffs like cotton-wool. A shout went up from the soldiers who stood in groups in the street of the ruined town. A whistle split the air, followed by a rending snort that tailed off into the moaning of a wounded man.

"By damn, they're nervy. They dropped a bomb."

"I should say they did."

"The dirty bastards, to get a fellow who's going on permission. Now if they beaded you on the way back you wouldn't care."

In the sky an escadrille of French planes had appeared and the three German specks had vanished, followed by a trail of little puffs of shrapnel. The indigo dome of the afternoon sky was full of a distant snoring of motors.

The train screamed outside the station and the permission-aires ran for the platform, their packed musettes bouncing at their hips.

The dark boulevards, with here and there a blue lamp lighting up a bench and a few tree-trunks, or a faint glow from inside a closed café where a boy in shirt-sleeves is sweeping the floor. Crowds of soldiers, Belgians, Americans, Canadians, civilians with canes and straw hats and well-dressed women on their arms, shop-girls in twos and threes laughing with shrill, merry voices; and everywhere girls of the street, giggling alluringly in hoarse, dissipated tones, clutching the arms of drunken soldiers, tilting themselves temptingly in men's way as they walk along. Cigarettes and cigars make spots of reddish light, and now and then a match lighted makes a man's face stand out in yellow relief and glints red in the eyes of people round about.

Drunk with their freedom, with the jangle of voices, with the rustle of trees in the faint light, with the scents of women's hair and cheap perfumes, Howe and Randolph stroll along slowly, down one side to the shadowy columns of the

Madeleine, where a few flower-women still offer roses, scent-
ing the darkness, then back again past the Opéra towards the
Porte St. Martin, lingering to look in the offered faces of
women, to listen to snatches of talk, to chatter laughingly
with girls who squeeze their arms with impatience.

"I'm goin' to find the prettiest girl in Paris, and then you'll
see the dust fly, Howe, old man."

The hors d'œuvres came on a circular three-tiered stand;
red strips of herrings and silver anchovies, salads where green
peas and bits of carrot lurked under golden layers of sauce,
sliced tomatoes, potato salad green-specked with parsley,
hard-boiled eggs barely visible under thickness of vermilion-
tinged dressing, olives, radishes, discs of sausage of many different forms and colours, complicated bundles of spiced salt
fish, and, forming the apex, a fat terra-cotta jar of pâté de foie
gras. Howe poured out pale-coloured Chablis.

"I used to think that down home was the only place they
knew how to live, but oh, boy . . ." said Tom Randolph,
breaking a little loaf of bread that made a merry crackling
sound.

"It's worth starving to death on singe and pinard for four
months."

After the hors d'œuvres had been taken away, leaving them
Rabelaisianly gay, with a joyous sense of orgy, came sole hidden in a cream-coloured sauce with mussels in it.

"After the war, Howe, ole man, let's riot all over Europe;
I'm getting a taste for this sort of livin'."

"You can play the fiddle, can't you, Tom?"

"Enough to scrape out *Auprès de ma blonde* on a bet."

"Then we'll wander about and you can support me. . . .
Or else I'll dress as a monkey and you can fiddle and I'll
gather the pennies."

"By gum, that'd be great sport."

"Look, we must have some red wine with the veal."

"Let's have Mâcon."

"All the same to me as long as there's plenty of it."

Their round table with its white cloth and its bottles of
wine and its piles of ravished artichoke leaves was the centre
of a noisy, fantastic world. Ever since the orgy of the hors

d'œuvres things had been evolving to grotesqueness, faces, whites of eyes, twisted red of lips, crow-like forms of waiters, colours of hats and uniforms, all involved and jumbled in the melée of talk and clink and clatter.

The red hand of the waiter pouring the Chartreuse, green like a stormy sunset, into small glasses before them broke into the vivid imaginings that had been unfolding in their talk through dinner. No, they had been saying, it could not go on; some day amid the rending crash of shells and the whine of shrapnel fragments, people everywhere, in all uniforms, in trenches, packed in camions, in stretchers, in hospitals, crowded behind guns, involved in telephone apparatus, generals at their dinner-tables, colonels sipping liqueurs, majors developing photographs, would jump to their feet and burst out laughing at the solemn inanity, at the stupid, vicious pomposity of what they were doing. Laughter would untune the sky. It would be a new progress of Bacchus. Drunk with laughter at the sudden vision of the silliness of the world, officers and soldiers, prisoners working on the roads, deserters being driven towards the trenches would throw down their guns and their spades and their heavy packs, and start marching, or driving in artillery waggons or in camions, staff cars, private trains, towards their capitals, where they would laugh the deputies, the senators, the congressmen, the M.P.'s out of their chairs, laugh the presidents and the prime ministers, and kaisers and dictators out of their plush-carpeted offices; the sun would wear a broad grin and would whisper the joke to the moon, who would giggle and ripple with it all night long. . . . The red hand of the waiter, with thick nails and work-swollen knuckles, poured Chartreuse into the small glasses before them.

"That," said Tom Randolph, when he had half finished his liqueur, "is the girl for me."

"But, Tom, she's with a French officer."

"They're fighting like cats and dogs. You can see that, can't you?"

"Yes," agreed Howe vaguely.

"Pay the bill. I'll meet you at the corner of the boulevard." Tom Randolph was out of the door. The girl, who had a little of the aspect of a pierrot, with dark skin and bright lips and gold-yellow hat and dress, and the sour-looking officer who was with her, were getting up to go.

At the corner of the boulevard Howe heard a woman's voice joining with Randolph's rich laugh.

"What did I tell you? They split at the door and here we are, Howe. . . . Mademoiselle Montreil, let me introduce a friend. Look, before it's too late, we must have a drink."

At the café table next to them an Englishman was seated with his head sunk on his chest.

"Oh, I say, you woke me up."

"Sorry."

"No harm. Jolly good thing."

They invited him over to their table. There was a moist look about his eyes and a thickness to his voice that denoted alcohol.

"You mustn't mind me. I'm forgetting. . . . I've been doing it for a week. This is the first leave I've had in eighteen months. You Canadians?"

"No. Ambulance service; Americans."

"New at the game then. You're lucky. . . . Before I left the front I saw a man tuck a hand-grenade under the pillow of a poor devil of a German prisoner. The prisoner said, 'Thank you.' The grenade blew him to hell! God! Know anywhere you can get whisky in this bloody town?"

"We'll have to hurry; it's near closing time."

"Right-o."

They started off, Randolph and the girl talking intimately, their heads close together, Martin supporting the Englishman.

"I need a bit o' whisky to put me on my pins."

They tumbled into the seats round a table at an American bar.

The Englishman felt in his pocket.

"Oh, I say," he cried, "I've got a ticket to the theatre. It's a box. . . . We can all get in. Come along; let's hurry."

They walked a long while, blundering through the dark streets, and at last stopped at a blue-lighted door.

"Here it is; push in."

"But there are two gentlemen and a lady already in the box, meester."

"No matter, there'll be room." The Englishman waved the ticket in the air.

The little round man with a round red face who was taking the tickets stuttered in bad English and then dropped into French. Meanwhile, the whole party had filed in, leaving the Englishman, who kept waving the ticket in the little man's face.

Two gendarmes, the theatre guards, came up menacingly; the Englishman's face wreathed itself in smiles; he linked an arm in each of the gendarmes', and pushed them towards the bar.

"Come drink to the Entente Cordiale. . . . Vive la France!"

In the box were two Australians and a woman who leaned her head on the chest of one and then the other alternately, laughing so that you could see the gold caps in her black teeth.

They were annoyed at the intrusion that packed the box insupportably tight, so that the woman had to sit on the men's laps, but the air soon cleared in laughter that caused people in the orchestra to stare angrily at the box full of noisy men in khaki. At last the Englishman came, squeezing himself in with a finger mysteriously on his lips. He plucked at Martin's arm, a serious set look coming suddenly over his grey eyes. "It was like this"—his breath laden with whisky was like a halo round Martin's head—"the Hun was a nice little chap, couldn't 'a' been more than eighteen; had a shoulder broken and he thought that my pal was fixing the pillow. He said 'Thank you' with a funny German accent. . . . Mind you, he said 'Thank you'; that's what hurt. And the man laughed. God damn him, he laughed when the poor devil said 'Thank you.' And the grenade blew him to hell."

The stage was a glare of light in Martin's eyes; he felt as he had when at home he had leaned over and looked straight into the headlight of an auto drawn up to the side of the road. Screening him from the glare were the backs of people's heads: Tom Randolph's head and his girl's, side by side, their cheeks touching, the pointed red chin of one of the Australians and the frizzy hair of the other woman.

In the entr'acte they all stood at the bar, where it was very hot and an orchestra was playing and there were many men in khaki in all stages of drunkenness, being led about by women who threw jokes at each other behind the men's backs.

"Here's to mud," said one of the Australians. "The war'll end when everybody is drowned in mud."

The orchestra began playing the *Madelon* and everyone roared out the marching song that, worn threadbare as it was, still had a roistering verve to it that caught people's blood.

People had gone back for the last act. The two Australians, the Englishman, and the two Americans still stood talking.

"Mind you, I'm not what you'd call susceptible. I'm not soft. I got over all that long ago." The Englishman was addressing the company in general. "But the poor beggar said 'Thank you.'"

"What's he saying?" asked a woman, plucking at Martin's arm.

"He's telling about a German atrocity."

"Oh, the dirty Germans! What things they've done!" the woman answered mechanically.

Somehow, during the entr'acte, the Australians had collected another woman; and a strange fat woman with lips painted very small, and very large bulging eyes, had attached herself to Martin. He suffered her because every time he looked at her she burst out laughing.

The bar was closing. They had a drink of champagne all round that made the fat woman give little shrieks of delight. They drifted towards the door, and stood, a formless, irresolute group, in the dark street in front of the theatre.

Randolph came up to Martin.

"Look. We're goin'. I wonder if I ought to leave my money with you . . ."

"I doubt if I'm a safe person to-night. . . ."

"All right. I'll take it along. Look . . . let's meet for breakfast."

"At the *Café de la Paix.*"

"All right. If she is nice I'll bring her."

"She looks charming."

Tom Randolph pressed Martin's hand and was off. There was a sound of a kiss in the darkness.

"I say, I've got to have something to eat," said the Englishman. "I didn't have a bit of dinner. I say—mangai, mangai." He made gestures of putting things into his mouth in the direction of the fat woman.

The three women put their heads together. One of them knew a place, but it was a dreadful place. Really, they mustn't think that. . . . She only knew it because when she was very young a man had taken her there who wanted to seduce her.

At that everyone laughed and the voices of the women rose shrill.

"All right, don't talk; let's go there," said one of the Australians. "We'll attend to the seducing."

A thick woman, a tall comb in the back of her high-piled black hair, and an immovable face with jaw muscled like a prize-fighter's, served them with cold chicken and ham and champagne in a room with mouldering greenish wall-paper lighted by a red-shaded lamp.

The Australians ate and sang and made love to their women. The Englishman went to sleep with his head on the table.

Martin leaned back out of the circle of light, keeping up a desultory conversation with the woman beside him, listening to the sounds of the men's voices down corridors, of the front door being opened and slammed again and again, and of forced, shrill giggles of women.

"Unfortunately, I have an engagement to-night," said Martin to the woman beside him, whose large spherical breasts heaved as she talked, and who rolled herself nearer to him invitingly, seeming with her round pop-eyes and her round cheeks to be made up entirely of small spheres and large soft ones.

"Oh, but it is too late. You can break it."

"It's at four o'clock."

"Then we have time, ducky."

"It's something really romantic, you see."

"The young are always lucky." She rolled her eyes in sympathetic admiration.

"This will be the fourth night this week that I'll sleep without a man. . . . I'll chuck myself into the river soon."

Martin felt himself softening towards her. He slipped a twenty-franc note in her hand.

"Oh, you are too good. You are really galant homme, you."

Martin buried his face in his hands, dreaming of the woman

he would like to love to-night. She should be very dark, with red lips and stained cheeks, like Randolph's girl; she should have small breasts and slender, dark, dancer's thighs, and in her arms he could forget everything but the madness and the mystery and the intricate life of Paris about them. He thought of Montmartre, and Louise in the opera standing at her window singing the madness of Paris. . . .

One of the Australians had gone away with a little woman in a pink negligée. The other Australian and the Englishman were standing unsteadily near the table, each supported by a sleepy-looking girl. Leaving the fat woman sadly finishing the remains of the chicken, large tears rolling from her eyes, they left the house and walked for a long time down dark streets, three men and two women, the Englishman being supported in the middle, singing in a desultory fashion.

The girls had two rooms on the fourth floor. As soon as they got there the Englishman tumbled into the bed and went to sleep, snoring loudly.

The Australian took off his coat and opened his shirt. The girls began getting undressed, trying to turn their yawns into little seductive faces.

"Say, old man, have you got a . . ." the Australian whispered in Martin's ear.

"No, I haven't. . . . I'm awfully sorry."

"Never mind. . . . Come along, Janey." He picked his girl up under the arms and, pressing her to him, carried her into the other room.

"Well. . . ." The other girl, in corset and drawers, with her curly brown hair tumbled over one eye and new rouge on her lips, held out her hands. "There's only you and me."

"No, dearie. I must go," said Martin.

"As you will. I'll take care of your friend." She yawned.

He kissed her and stumbled down the dark stairs, his nostrils full of the smell of the rouge on her lips.

He walked a long while with his hat off, breathing deep of the sharp night air. The streets were black and silent. Intemperate desires prowled about him like cats in the darkness.

He woke up and stretched himself stiffly, smelling grass and damp earth. A pearly lavender mist was all about him,

through which loomed the square towers of Notre Dame and the row of kings across the façade and the sculpture about the darkness of the doorways. He had lain down on his back on the little grass plot of the Parvis Notre Dame to look at the stars, and had fallen asleep.

It must be nearly dawn. Words were droning importunately in his head. "The poor beggar said 'Thank you' with a funny German accent and the grenade blew him to hell." He remembered the man he had once helped to pick up in whose pocket a grenade had exploded. Before that he had not realized that torn flesh was such a black red, like sausage meat.

"Get up, you can't lie there," cried a gendarme.

"Notre Dame is beautiful in the morning," said Martin, stepping across the low rail on to the pavement.

"Ah, yes; it is beautiful."

Martin Howe sat on the rail of the bridge and looked. Before him, with nothing distinct yet to be seen, were two square towers and the tracery between them and the row of kings on the façade, and the long series of flying buttresses of the flank, gleaming through the mist, and, barely visible, the dark, slender spire soaring above the crossing. So had the abbey in the forest gleamed tall in the misty moonlight; like mist, only drab and dense, the dust had risen above the tall apse as the shells tore it to pieces.

Amid a smell of new-roasted coffee he sat at a table and watched people pass briskly through the ruddy sunlight. Waiters in shirt-sleeves were rubbing off the other tables and putting out the chairs. He sat sipping coffee, feeling languid and nerveless. After a while Tom Randolph, looking very young and brown with his hat a little on one side, came along. With him, plainly dressed in blue serge, was the girl. They sat down and she dropped her head on his shoulder covering her eyes with her dark lashes.

"Oh, I am so tired."

"Poor child! You must go home and go back to bed."

"But I've got to go to work."

"Poor thing." They kissed each other tenderly and langu

The waiter came with coffee and hot milk and little loaves of bread.

"Oh, Paris is wonderful in the early morning!" said Martin.

"Indeed it is. . . . Good-bye, little girl, if you must go. We'll see each other again."

"You must call me Yvonne." She pouted a little.

"All right, Yvonne." He got to his feet and pressed her two hands.

"Well, what sort of a time did you have, Howe?"

"Curious. I lost our friends one by one, left two women and slept a little while on the grass in front of Notre Dame. That was my real love of the night."

"My girl was charming. . . . Honestly, I'd marry her in a minute." He laughed a merry laugh.

"Let's take a cab somewhere."

They climbed into a victoria and told the driver to go to the Madeleine.

"Look, before I do anything else I must go to the hotel."

"Why?"

"Preventives."

"Of course; you'd better go at once."

The cab rattled merrily along the streets where the early sunshine cast rusty patches on the grey houses and on the thronged fantastic chimney-pots that rose in clusters and hedges from the mansard roofs.

Chapter VI

THE LAMP in the hut of the road control casts an oblong of light on the white wall opposite. The patch of light is constantly crossed and scalloped and obscured by shadows of rifles and helmets and packs of men passing. Now and then the shadow of a single man, a nose and a chin under a helmet, a head bent forward with the weight of the pack, or a pack alone beside which slants a rifle, shows up huge and fantastic with its loaf of bread and its pair of shoes and its pots and pans.

Then with a jingle of harness and clank of steel, train after train of artillery comes up out of the darkness of the road, is thrown by the lamp into vivid relief and is swallowed again by the blackness of the village street, short bodies of seventy-fives sticking like ducks' tails from between their large wheels; caisson after caisson of ammunition, huge waggons hooded and unhooded, filled with a chaos of equipment that catches fantastic lights and throws huge muddled shadows on the white wall of the house.

"Put that light out. Name of God, do you want to have them start chucking shells into here?" comes a voice shrill with anger. The brisk trot of the officer's horse is lost in the clangour.

The door of the hut slams to and only a thin ray of orange light penetrates into the blackness of the road, where with jingle of harness and clatter of iron and tramp of hoofs, gun after gun, caisson after caisson, waggon after waggon files by. Now and then the passing stops entirely and matches flare where men light pipes and cigarettes. Coming from the other direction with throbbing of motors, a convoy of camions, huge black oblongs, grinds down the other side of the road. Horses rear and there are shouts and curses and clacking of reins in the darkness.

Far away where the lowering clouds meet the hills beyond the village a white glare grows and fades again at intervals: star-shells.

*

41

"There's a most tremendous concentration of sanitary sections."

"You bet; two American sections and a French one in this village; three more down the road. Something's up."

"There's goin' to be an attack at St. Mihiel, a Frenchman told me."

"I heard that the Germans were concentrating for an offensive in the Four de Paris."

"Damned unlikely."

"Anyway, this is the third week we've been in this bloody hole with our feet in the mud."

"They've got us quartered in a barn with a regular brook flowing through the middle of it."

"The main thing about this damned war is ennui—just plain boredom."

"Not forgetting the mud."

Three ambulance drivers in slickers were on the front seat of a car. The rain fell in perpendicular sheets, pattering on the roof of the car and on the puddles that filled the village street. Streaming with water, blackened walls of ruined houses rose opposite them above a rank growth of weeds. Beyond were rain-veiled hills. Every little while, slithering through the rain, splashing mud to the right and left, a convoy of camions went by and disappeared, truck after truck, in the white streaming rain.

Inside the car Tom Randolph was playing an accordion, letting strange nostalgic little songs filter out amid the hard patter of the rain.

> "*Oh, I's been workin' on de railroad*
> *All de livelong day;*
> *I's been workin' on de railroad*
> *Jus' to pass de time away.*"

The men on the front seat leaned back and shook the water off their knees and hummed the song.

The accordion had stopped. Tom Randolph was lying on his back on the floor of the car with his arm over his eyes. The rain fell endlessly, rattling on the roof of the car, dancing silver in the coffee-coloured puddles of the road. Their bore-

dom fell into the rhythm of crooning self-pity of the old coon
song:

> "*I's been workin' on de railroad*
> *All de livelong day;*
> *I's been workin' on de railroad*
> *Jus' to pass de time away.*"

"Oh, God, something's got to happen soon."

Lost in rubber boots, and a huge gleaming slicker and
hood, the section leader splashed across the road.

"All cars must be ready to leave at six to-night."

"Yay. Where we goin'?"

"Orders haven't come yet. We're to be in readiness to leave
at six to-night. . . ."

"I tell you, fellers, there's goin' to be an attack. This concentration of sanitary sections means something. You can't
tell me . . ."

"They say they have beer," said the aspirant behind Martin
in the long line of men who waited in the hot sun for the
copé to open, while the dust the staff cars and camions raised
as they whirred by on the road settled in a blanket over the
village.

"Cold beer?"

"Of course not," said the aspirant, laughing so that all the
brilliant ivory teeth showed behind his red lips. "It'll be de-
testable. I'm getting it because it's rare, for sentimental
reasons."

Martin laughed, looking in the man's brown face, a face in
which all past expressions seemed to linger in the fine lines
about the mouth and eyes and in the modelling of the cheeks
and temples.

"You don't understand that," said the aspirant again.

"Indeed I do."

Later they sat on the edge of the stone well-head in the
courtyard behind the store, drinking warm beer out of tin
cups blackened by wine, and staring at a tall barn that had
crumpled at one end so that it looked, with its two frightened
little square windows, like a cow kneeling down.

"Is it true that the ninety-second's going up to the lines to-night?"

"Yes, we're going up to make a little attack. Probably I'll come back in your little omnibus."

"I hope you won't."

"I'd be very glad to. A lucky wound! But I'll probably be killed. This is the first time I've gone up to the front that I didn't expect to be killed. So it'll probably happen."

Martin Howe could not help looking at him suddenly. The aspirant sat at ease on the stone margin of the well, leaning against the wrought iron support for the bucket, one knee clasped in his strong, heavily-veined hands. Dead he would be different. Martin's mind could hardly grasp the connection between this man full of latent energies, full of thoughts and desires, this man whose shoulder he would have liked to have put his arm round from friendliness, with whom he would have liked to go for long walks, with whom he would have liked to sit long into the night drinking and talking—and those huddled, pulpy masses of blue uniform half-buried in the mud of ditches.

"Have you ever seen a herd of cattle being driven to abattoir on a fine May morning?" asked the aspirant in a scornful, jaunty tone, as if he had guessed Martin's thoughts.

"I wonder what they think of it."

"It's not that I'm resigned. . . . Don't think that. Resignation is too easy. That's why the herd can be driven by a boy of six . . . or a prime minister!"

Martin was sitting with his arms crossed. The fingers of one hand were squeezing the muscle of his forearm. It gave him pleasure to feel the smooth, firm modelling of his arm through his sleeve. And how would that feel when it was dead, when a steel splinter had slithered through it? A momentary stench of putrefaction filled his nostrils, making his stomach contract with nausea.

"I'm not resigned either," he shouted in a laugh. "I am going to do something some day, but first I must see. I want to be initiated in all the circles of hell."

"I'd play the part of Virgil pretty well," said the aspirant, "but I suppose Virgil was a staff officer."

"I must go," said Martin. "My name's Martin Howe, S.S.U.84."

"Oh yes, you are quartered in the square. My name is Merrier. You'll probably carry me back in your little omnibus."

When Howe got back to where the cars were packed in a row in the village square, Randolph came up to him and whispered in his ear:

"D.J.'s to-morrow."

"What's that?"

"The attack. It's to-morrow at three in the morning; instructions are going to be given out to-night."

A detonation behind them was a blow on the head, making their ear-drums ring. The glass in the headlight of one of the cars tinkled to the ground.

"The 410 behind the church, that was. Pretty near knocks the wind out of you."

"Say, Randolph, have you heard the new orders?"

"No."

A tall, fair-haired man came out from the front of his car where he had been working on the motor, holding his grease-covered hands away from him.

"It's put off," he said, lowering his voice mysteriously. "D.J.'s not till day after to-morrow at four-twenty. But to-morrow we're going up to relieve the section that's coming out and take over the posts. They say it's hell up there. The Germans have a new gas that you can't smell at all. The other section's got about five men gassed, and a bunch of them have broken down. The posts are shelled all the time."

"Great," said Tom Randolph. "We'll see the real thing this time."

There was a whistling shriek overhead and all three of them fell in a heap on the ground in front of the car. There was a crash that echoed amid the house-walls, and a pillar of black smoke stood like a cypress tree at the other end of the village street.

"Talk about the real thing!" said Martin.

"Ole 410 evidently woke 'em up some."

It was the fifth time that day that Martin's car had passed the cross-roads where the calvary was. Someone had propped up the fallen crucifix so that it tilted dark despairing arms against the sunset sky where the sun gleamed like a huge copper kettle lost in its own steam. The rain made bright yellowish stripes across the sky and dripped from the cracked feet of the old wooden Christ, whose gaunt, scarred figure hung out from the tilted cross, swaying a little under the beating of the rain. Martin was wiping the mud from his hands after changing a wheel. He stared curiously at the fallen jowl and the cavernous eyes that had meant for some country sculptor ages ago the utterest agony of pain. Suddenly he noticed that where the crown of thorns had been about the forehead of the Christ someone had wound barbed wire. He smiled, asking the swaying figure in his mind, "What do You think of it, old boy? How do You like Your followers? Not so romantic as thorns, is it, that barbed wire?"

He leaned over to crank the car.

The road was filled suddenly with the tramp and splash of troops marching, their wet helmets and their rifles gleaming in the coppery sunset. Even through the clean rain came the smell of filth and sweat and misery of troops marching. The faces under the helmets were strained and colourless and cadaverous from the weight of the equipment on their necks and their backs and their thighs. The faces drooped under the helmets, tilted to one side or the other, distorted and wooden like the face of the figure that dangled from the cross.

Above the splash of feet through mud and the jingle of equipment, came occasionally the ping, ping of shrapnel bursting at the next cross-roads at the edge of the woods.

Martin sat in the car with the motor racing, waiting for the end of the column.

One of the stragglers who floundered along through the churned mud of the road after the regular ranks had passed stopped still and looked up at the tilted cross. From the next cross-roads came, at intervals, the sharp twanging ping of shrapnel bursting.

The straggler suddenly began kicking feebly at the prop of the cross with his foot, and then dragged himself off after the column. The cross fell forward with a dull splintering splash into the mud of the road.

The road went down the hill in long zig-zags, through a village at the bottom where out of the mist that steamed from the little river a spire with a bent weathercock rose above the broken roof of the church, then up the hill again into the woods. In the woods the road stretched green and gold in the first horizontal sunlight. Among the thick trees, roofs covered with branches, were rows of long portable barracks with doors decorated with rustic work. At one place a sign announced in letters made of wattled sticks, *Camp des Pommiers.*

A few birds sang in the woods, and at a pump they passed a lot of men stripped to the waist who were leaning over washing, laughing and splashing in the sunlight. Every now and then, distant, metallic, the pong, pong, pong of a battery of seventy-fives resounded through the rustling trees.

"Looks like a camp meetin' ground in Georgia," said Tom Randolph, blowing his whistle to make two men carrying a large steaming pot on a pole between them get out of the way.

The road became muddier as they went deeper into the woods, and, turning into a cross-road, the car began slithering, skidding a little at the turns, through thick soupy mud. On either side the woods became broken and jagged, stumps and split boughs littering the ground, trees snapped off halfway up. In the air there was a scent of newly-split timber and of turned-up woodland earth, and among them a sweetish rough smell.

Covered with greenish mud, splashing the mud right and left with their great flat wheels, camions began passing them returning from the direction of the lines.

At last at a small red cross flag they stopped and ran the car into a grove of tall chestnuts, where they parked it beside another car of their section and lay down among the crisp leaves, listening to occasional shells whining far overhead. All through the wood was a continuous ping, pong, ping of batteries, with the crash of a big gun coming now and then like the growl of a bull-frog among the sing-song of small toads in a pond at night.

Through the trees from which they lay they could see the close-packed wooden crosses of a cemetery from which came a sound of spaded earth, and where, preceded by a priest in a muddy cassock, little two-wheeled carts piled with shapeless things in sacks kept being brought up and unloaded and dragged away again.

Showing alternately dark and light in the sun and shadow of the woodland road, a cook waggon, short chimney giving out blue smoke, and cauldrons steaming, clatters ahead of Martin and Randolph; the backs of two men in heavy blue coats, their helmets showing above the narrow driver's seat. On either side of the road short yellow flames keep spitting up, slanting from hidden guns amid a pandemonium of noise.

Up the road a sudden column of black smoke rises among falling trees. A louder explosion and the cook waggon in front of them vanishes in a new whirl of thick smoke. Accelerator pressed down, the car plunges along the rutted road, tips, and a wheel sinks in the new shell-hole. The hind wheels spin for a moment, spattering gravel about, and just as another roar comes behind them, bite into the road again and the car goes on, speeding through the alternate sun and shadow of the woods. Martin remembers the beating legs of a mule rolling on its back on the side of the road and, steaming in the fresh morning air, the purple and yellow and red of its ripped belly.

"Did you get the smell of almonds? I sort of like it," says Randolph, drawing a long breath as the car slowed down again.

The woods at night, fantastic blackness full of noise and yellow leaping flames from the mouths of guns. Now and then the sulphurous flash of a shell explosion and the sound of trees falling and shell fragments swishing through the air. At intervals over a little knoll in the direction of the trenches, a white star-shell falls slowly, making the trees and the guns among their tangle of hiding branches cast long green-black shadows, drowning the wood in a strange glare of desolation.

"Where the devil's the abri?"

Everything drowned in the detonations of three guns, one after the other, so near as to puff hot air in their faces in the midst of the blinding concussion.

"Look, Tom, this is foolish; the abri's right here."

"I haven't got it in my pocket, Howe. Damn those guns."

Again everything is crushed in the concussion of the guns.

They throw themselves on the ground as a shell shrieks and explodes. There is a moment's pause, and gravel and bits of bark tumble about their heads.

"We've got to find that abri. I wish I hadn't lost my flashlight."

"Here it is! No, that stinks too much. Must be the latrine."

"Say, Tom."

"Here."

"Damn, I ran into a tree. I found it."

"All right. Coming."

Martin held out his hand until Randolph bumped into it; then they stumbled together down the rough wooden steps, pulled aside the blanket that served to keep the light in, and found themselves blinking in the low tunnel of the abri.

Brancardiers were asleep in the two tiers of bunks that filled up the sides, and at the table at the end a lieutenant of the medical corps was writing by the light of a smoky lamp.

"They are landing some round here to-night," he said, pointing out two unoccupied bunks. "I'll call you when we need a car."

As he spoke, in succession the three big guns went off. The concussion put the lamp out.

"Damn," said Tom Randolph.

The lieutenant swore and struck a match.

"The red light of the poste de secours is out, too," said Martin.

"No use lighting it again with those unholy mortars. . . . It's idiotic to put a poste de secours in the middle of a battery like this."

The Americans lay down to try to sleep. Shell after shell exploded round the dugout, but regularly every few minutes came the hammer blows of the mortars, half the time putting the light out.

A shell explosion seemed to split the dugout and a piece of éclat whizzed through the blanket that curtained off the door. Someone tried to pick it up as it lay half-buried in the board floor, and pulled his fingers away quickly, blowing on them. The men turned over in the bunks and laughed, and a smile came over the drawn green face of a wounded man who sat very quiet behind the lieutenant, staring at the smoky flame of the lamp.

The curtain was pulled aside and a man staggered in holding with the other hand a limp arm twisted in a mud-covered sleeve, from which blood and mud dripped on to the floor.

"Hello, old chap," said the doctor quietly. A smell of disinfectant stole through the dugout.

Faint above the incessant throbbing of explosions the sound of a claxon horn.

"Ha, gas," said the doctor. "Put on your masks, children." A man went along the dugout waking those who were asleep and giving out fresh masks. Someone stood in the doorway blowing a shrill whistle, then there was again the clamour of a claxon near at hand.

The band of the gas-mask was tight about Martin's forehead, biting into the skin.

He and Randolph sat side by side on the edge of the bunk, looking out through the crinkled isinglass eyepieces at the men in the dugout, most of whom had gone to sleep again.

"God, I envy a man who can snore through a gas-mask," said Randolph.

Men's heads had a ghoulish look, strange large eyes and grey oilcloth flaps instead of faces.

Outside the constant explosions had given place to a series of swishing whistles, merging together into a sound as of water falling, only less regular, more sibilant. Occasionally there was the rending burst of a shell, and at intervals came the swinging detonations of the three guns. In the dugout, except for two men who snored loudly, raspingly, everyone was quiet.

Several stretchers with wounded men on them were brought in and laid in the end of the dugout.

Gradually, as the bombardment continued, men began sliding into the dugout, crowding together, touching each other for company, speaking in low voices through their masks.

"A mask, in the name of God, a mask!" a voice shouted, breaking into a squeal, and an unshaven man, with mud caked in his hair and beard, burst through the curtain. His eyelids kept up a continual trembling and the water streamed down both sides of his nose.

"Oh God," he kept talking in a rasping whisper, "O God, they're all killed. There were six mules on my waggon and a shell killed them all and threw me into the ditch. You can't find the road any more. They're all killed."

An orderly was wiping his face as if it were a child's.

"They're all killed and I lost my mask. . . . O God, this gas . . ."

The doctor, a short man, looking like a gnome in his mask with its wheezing rubber nosepiece, was walking up and down with short, slow steps.

Suddenly, as three soldiers came in drawing the curtain aside, he shouted in a shrill, high-pitched voice:

"Keep the curtain closed! Do you want to asphyxiate us?"

He strode up to the newcomers, his voice strident like an angry woman's. "What are you doing here? This is the poste de secours. Are you wounded?"

"But, my lieutenant, we can't stay outside . . ."

"Where's your own cantonment? You can't stay here; you can't stay here," he shrieked.

"But, my lieutenant, our dugout's been hit."

"You can't stay here. You can't stay here. There's not enough room for the wounded. Name of God!"

"But, my lieutenant . . ."

"Get the hell out of here, d'you hear?"

The men began stumbling out into the darkness, tightening the adjustments of their masks behind their heads.

The guns had stopped firing. There was nothing but the constant swishing and whistling of gas-shells, like endless pails of dirty water being thrown on gravel.

"We've been at it three hours," whispered Martin to Tom Randolph.

"God, suppose these masks need changing."

The sweat from Martin's face steamed in the eyepieces, blinding him.

"Any more masks?" he asked.

A brancardier handed him one. "There aren't any more in the abri."

"I have some more in the car," said Martin.

"I'll get one," cried Randolph, getting to his feet.

They started out of the door together. In the light that streamed out as they drew the flap aside they saw a tree opposite them. A shell exploded, it seemed, right on top of them; the tree rose and bowed towards them and fell.

"Are you all there, Tom?" whispered Martin, his ears ringing.

"Bet your life."

Someone pulled them back into the abri. "Here; we've found another."

Martin lay down on the bunk again, drawing with difficulty each breath. His lips had a wet, decomposed feeling.

At the wrist of the arm he rested his head on, the watch ticked comfortably.

He began to think how ridiculous it would be if he, Martin Howe, should be extinguished like this. The gas-mask might be defective.

God, it would be silly.

Outside the gas-shells were still coming in. The lamp showed through a faint bluish haze. Everyone was still waiting.

Another hour.

Martin began to recite to himself the only thing he could remember, over and over again in time to the ticking of his watch.

> "*Ah, sunflower, weary of time.*
> *Ah, sunflower, weary of time,*
> *Who countest the steps of the sun;*
> *Ah, sunflower, weary of time,*
> *Who countest . . .*"

"One, two, three, four," he counted the shells outside exploding at irregular intervals.

There were periods of absolute silence, when he could hear batteries pong, pong, pong in the distance.

He began again.

> "*Ah, sunflower, weary of time,*
> *Who countest the steps of the sun*

In search of that far golden clime
Where the traveller's journey is done.

"Where the youth pined away with desire
And the pale virgin shrouded in snow
Arise from their graves and aspire
Where my sunflower wishes to go."

Whang, whang, whang; the battery alongside began again, sending out the light. Someone pulled the blanket aside. A little leprous greyness filtered into the dugout.

"Ah, it's getting light."

The doctor went out and they could hear his steps climbing up to the level of the ground.

Howe saw a man take his mask off and spit.

"O God, a cigarette!" Tom Randolph cried, pulling his mask off. The air of the woods was fresh and cool outside. Everything was lost in mist that filled the shell-holes as with water and wreathed itself fantastically about the shattered trunks of trees. Here and there was still a little greenish haze of gas. It cut their throats and made their eyes run as they breathed in the cool air of the dawn.

Dawn in a wilderness of jagged stumps and ploughed earth; against the yellow sky, the yellow glare of guns that squat like toads in a tangle of wire and piles of brass shell-cases and split wooden boxes. Long rutted roads littered with shell-cases stretching through the wrecked woods in the yellow light; strung alongside of them, tangled masses of telephone wires. Torn camouflage fluttering greenish-grey against the ardent yellow sky, and twining among the fantastic black leafless trees, the greenish wraiths of gas. Along the roads camions overturned, dead mules tangled in their traces beside shattered caissons, huddled bodies in long blue coats half buried in the mud of the ditches.

"We've got to pass. . . . We've got five very bad cases."

"Impossible."

"We've got to pass. . . . Sacred name of God!"

"But it is impossible. Two camions are blocked across the road and there are three batteries of seventy-fives waiting to get up the road."

Long lines of men on horseback with gas-masks on, a rearing of frightened horses and jingle of harness.

"Talk to 'em, Howe, for God's sake; we've got to get past."

"I'm doing the best I can, Tom."

"Well, make 'em look lively. Damn this gas!"

"Put your masks on again; you can't breathe without them in this hollow."

"Hay! ye God-damn sons of bitches, get out of the way."

"But they can't."

"Oh, hell, I'll go talk to 'em. You take the wheel."

"No, sit still and don't get excited."

"You're the one's getting excited."

"Damn this gas."

"My lieutenant, I beg you to move the horses to the side of the road. I have five very badly wounded men. They will die in this gas. I've got to get by."

"God damn him, tell him to hurry."

"Shut up, Tom, for God's sake."

"They're moving. I can't see a thing in this mask."

"Hah, that did for the two back horses."

"Halt! Is there any room in the ambulance? One of my men's just got his thigh ripped up."

"No room, no room."

"He'll have to go to a poste de secours."

The fresh air blowing hard in their faces and the woods getting greener on either side, full of ferns and small plants that half cover the strands of barbed wire and the rows of shells.

At the end of the woods the sun rises golden into a cloudless sky, and on the grassy slope of the valley sheep and a herd of little donkeys are feeding, looking up with quietly moving jaws as the ambulance, smelling of blood and filthy sweat-soaked clothes, rattles by.

Black night. All through the woods along the road squatting mortars spit yellow flame. Constant throbbing of detonations.

Martin, inside the ambulance, is holding together a broken stretcher, while the car jolts slowly along. It is pitch dark in the car, except when the glare of a gun from near the road gives him a momentary view of the man's head, a mass of bandages from the middle of which a little bit of blood-soaked beard sticks out, and of his lean body tossing on the stretcher with every jolt of the car. Martin is kneeling on the floor of the car, his knees bruised by the jolting, holding the man on the stretcher, with his chest pressed on the man's chest and one arm stretched down to keep the limp bandaged leg still.

The man's breath comes with a bubbling sound, now and then mingling with an articulate groan.

"Softly. . . . Oh, softly, oh—oh—oh!"

"Slow as you can, Tom, old man," Martin calls out above the pandemonium of firing on both sides of the road, tightening the muscles of his arm in a desperate effort to keep the limp leg from bouncing. The smell of blood and filth is misery in his nostrils.

"Softly. . . . Softly. . . . Oh—oh—oh!" The groan is barely heard amid the bubbling breath.

Pitch dark in the car. Martin, his every muscle taut with the agony of the man's pain, is on his knees, pressing his chest on the man's chest, trying with an arm stretched along the man's leg to keep him from bouncing in the broken stretcher.

"Needn't have troubled to have brought him," said the hospital orderly, as blood dripped fast from the stretcher, black in the light of the lantern. "He's pretty near dead now. He won't last long."

Chapter VII

"So YOU like it, Will? You like this sort of thing?"

Martin Howe was stretched on the grass of a hillside a little above a cross-roads. Beside him squatted a ruddy-faced youth with a smudge of grease on his faintly-hooked nose. A champagne bottle rested against his knees.

"Yes. I've never been happier in my life. It's a coarse boozing sort of a life, but I like it."

They looked over the landscape of greyish rolling hills scarred everywhere by new roads and ranks of wooden shacks. Along the road beneath them crawled like beetles convoy after convoy of motor trucks. The wind came to them full of a stench of latrines and of the exhaust of motors.

"The last time I saw you," said Martin, after a pause, "was early one morning on the Cambridge bridge. I was walking out from Boston, and we talked of the Eroica they'd played at the Symphony, and you said it was silly to have a great musician try to play soldier. D'you remember?"

"No. That was in another incarnation. Have some fizz."

He poured from the bottle into a battered tin cup.

"But talking about playing soldier, Howe, I must tell you about how our lieutenant got the Croix de Guerre. . . . Somebody ought to write a book called *Heroisms of the Great War*. . . ."

"I am sure that many people have, and will. You probably'll do it yourself, Will. But go on."

The sun burst from the huddled clouds for a moment, mottling the hills and the scarred valleys with light. The shadow of an aeroplane flying low passed across the field, and the snoring of its motors cut out all other sound.

"Well, our louie's name's Duval, but he spells it with a small 'd' and a big 'V.' He's been wanting a Croix de Guerre for a hell of a time because lots of fellows in the section have been getting 'em. He tried giving dinners to the General Staff and everything, but that didn't seem to work. So there was nothing to it but to get wounded. So he took to going to the front posts; but the trouble was that it was a hell of a quiet sector and no shells ever came within a mile of it. At last somebody made a mistake and a little Austrian eighty-eight came tumbling in and popped about fifty yards from his staff car. He showed the most marvellous presence of mind, 'cause he clapped his hand over his eye and sank back in the seat with a groan. The doctor asked what was the matter, but old Duval just kept his hand tight over his eye and said, 'Nothing, nothing; just a scratch,' and went off to inspect the posts. Of course the posts didn't need inspecting. And he rode round all day with a handkerchief over one eye and a look of hero-ism in the other. But never would he let the doctor even peep at it. Next morning he came out with a bandage round his head as big as a sheik's turban. He went to see headquarters in that get-up and lunched with the staff-officers. Well, he got his Croix de Guerre all right—cited for assuring the evacua-tion of the wounded under fire and all the rest of it."

"Some bird. He'll probably get to be a general before the war's over."

Howe poured out the last of the champagne, and threw the bottle listlessly off into the grass, where it struck an empty shell-case and broke.

"But, Will, you can't like this," he said. "It's all so like an ash-heap, a huge garbage-dump of men and equipment."

"I suppose it is . . ." said the ruddy-faced youth, discover-ing the grease on his nose and rubbing it off with the back of his hand. "Damn those dirty Fords. They get grease all over you! I suppose it is that life was so dull in America that any-thing seems better. I worked a year in an office before leaving home. Give me the garbage-dump."

"Look," said Martin, shading his eyes with his hand and staring straight up into the sky. "There are two planes fighting."

They both screwed up their eyes to stare into the sky, where two bits of mica were circling. Below them, like wads of cotton-wool, some white and others black, were rows of the smoke-puffs of shrapnel from anti-aircraft guns.

The two boys watched the specks in silence. At last one be-gan to grow larger, seemed to be falling in wide spirals. The other had vanished. The falling aeroplane started rising again into the middle sky, then stopped suddenly, burst into flames, and fluttered down behind the hills, leaving an irregular trail of smoke.

"More garbage," said the ruddy-faced youth, as he rose to his feet.

"Shrapnel. What a funny place to shoot shrapnel!"

"They must have got the bead on that bunch of materiel the genie's bringing in."

There was an explosion and a vicious whine of shrapnel bullets among the trees. On the road a staff-car turned round hastily and speeded back.

Martin got up from where he was lying on the grass under a pine tree, looking at the sky, and put his helmet on; as he did so there was another sharp bang overhead and a little reddish-brown cloud that suddenly spread and drifted away among the quiet tree-tops. He took off his helmet and examined it quizzically.

"Tom, I've got a dent in the helmet."

Tom Randolph made a grab for the little piece of jagged iron that had rebounded from the helmet and lay at his feet.

"God damn, it's hot," he cried, dropping it; "anyway, finding's keepings." He put his foot on the shrapnel splinter.

"That ought to be mine, I swear, Tom."

"You've got the dent, Howe; what more do you want?"

"Damn hog."

Martin sat on the top step of the dugout, diving down whenever he heard a shell-shriek loudening in the distance. Beside him was a tall man with the crossed cannon of the artillery in his helmet, and a shrunken brown face with crimson-veined cheeks and very long silky black moustaches.

"A dirty business," he said. "It's idiotic. . . . Name of a dog!"

Grabbing each other's arms, they tumbled down the steps together as a shell passed overhead to burst in a tree down the road.

"Now look at that." The man held up his musette to Howe. "I've broken the bottle of Bordeaux I had in my musette. It's idiotic."

"Been on permission?"

"Don't I look it?"

They sat at the top of the steps again; the man took out bits of wet glass dripping red wine from his little bag, swearing all the while.

"I was bringing it to the little captain. He's a nice little old chap, the little captain, and he loves good wine."

"Bordeaux?"

"Can't you smell it? It's Medoc, 1900, from my own vines. . . . Look, taste it, there's still a little." He held up the neck of the bottle and Martin took a sip.

The artilleryman drank the rest of it, twisted his long moustaches and heaved a deep sigh.

"Go there, my poor good old wine." He threw the remnants of the bottle into the underbrush. Shrapnel burst a little down the road. "Oh, this is a dirty business! I am a Gascon. . . . I like to live." He put a dirty brown hand on Martin's arm.

"How old do you think I am?"

"Thirty-five."

"I am twenty-four. Look at the picture." From a tattered black note-book held together by an elastic band he pulled a snapshot of a jolly-looking young man with a fleshy face and his hands tucked into the top of a wide, tightly-wound sash. He looked at the picture, smiling and tugging at one of his long moustaches. "Then I was twenty. It's the war." He shrugged his shoulders and put the picture carefully back into his inside pocket. "Oh, it's idiotic!"

"You must have had a tough time."

"It's just that people aren't meant for this sort of thing," said the artilleryman quietly. "You don't get accustomed. The more you see the worse it is. Then you end by going crazy. Oh, it's idiotic!"

"How did you find things at home?"

"Oh, at home! Oh, what do I care about that now? They get on without you. . . . But we used to know how to live, we Gascons. We worked so hard on the vines and on the fruit-trees, and we kept a horse and carriage. I had the best-looking rig in the department. Sunday it was fun; we'd play bowls and I'd ride about with my wife. Oh, she was nice in those days! She was young and fat and laughed all the time. She was something a man could put his arms around, she was.

We'd go out in my rig. It was click-clack of the whip in the air and off we were in the broad road. . . . Sacred name of a pig, that one was close. . . . And the Marquis of Mont-marieul had a rig, too, but not so good as mine, and my horse would always pass his in the road. Oh, it was funny, and he'd look so sour to have common people like us pass him in the road. . . . Boom, there's another. . . . And the Marquis now is nicely embusqué in the automobile service. He is sta-tioned at Versailles. . . . And look at me. . . . But what do I care about all that now?"

"But after the war . . ."

"After the war?" He spat savagely on the first step of the dugout. "They learn to get on without you."

"But we'll be free to do as we please."

"We'll never forget."

"I shall go to Spain . . ." A piece of shrapnel ripped past Martin's ear, cutting off the sentence.

"Name of God! It's getting hot. . . . Spain: I know Spain." The artilleryman jumped up and began dancing, Spanish fashion, snapping his fingers, his big moustaches swaying and trembling. Several shells burst down the road in quick succession, filling the air with a whine of fragments.

"A cook waggon got it!" the artilleryman shouted, dancing on. "Tra-la la la-la-la-la, la-la la," he sang, snapping his fingers.

He stopped and spat again.

"What do I care?" he said. "Well, so long, old chap. I must go. . . . Say, let's change knives—a little souvenir."

"Great."

"Good luck."

The artilleryman strode off through the woods, past the portable fence that surrounded the huddled wooden crosses of the graveyard.

Against the red glare of the dawn the wilderness of shat-tered trees stands out purple, hidden by grey mist in the hol-lows, looped and draped fantastically with strands of telephone wire and barbed wire, tangled like leafless creepers, that hang in clots against the red sky. Here and there guns squat among piles of shells covered with mottled green cheese-cloth, and spit long tongues of yellow flame against the sky. The ambulance waits by the side of the rutted road littered with tin cans and brass shell-cases, while a doctor and two stretcher-bearers bend over a man on a stretcher laid among the underbrush. The man groans and there is a sound of ripping bandages. On the other side of the road a fallen mule feebly wags its head from side to side, a mass of purple froth hanging from its mouth and wide-stretched scarlet nostrils.

There is a new smell in the wind, a smell unutterably sordid, like the smell of the poor immigrants landing at Ellis Island. Martin Howe glances round and sees advancing down the road ranks and ranks of strange grey men whose mushroom-shaped helmets give an eerie look as of men from the moon in a fairy tale.

"Why, they're Germans," he says to himself; "I'd quite forgotten they existed."

"Ah, they're prisoners." The doctor gets to his feet and glances down the road and then turns to his work again.

The tramp of feet marching in unison on the rough shell-pitted road, and piles and piles of grey men clotted with dried mud, from whom comes the new smell, the sordid, miserable smell of the enemy.

"Things going well?" Martin asks a guard, a man with ashen face and eyes that burn out of black sockets.

"How should I know?"

"Many prisoners?"

"How should I know?"

The captain and the aumonier are taking their breakfast, each sitting on a packing-box with their tin cups and tin plates ranged on the board propped up between them. All round red clay, out of which the abri was excavated. A smell of antiseptics from the door of the dressing-station and of lime and latrines mingling with the greasy smell of the movable kitchen not far away. They are eating dessert, slices of pineapple speared with a knife out of a can. In their manner there is something that makes Martin see vividly two gentlemen in frock-coats dining at a table under the awning of a café on the boulevards. It has a leisurely ceremoniousness, an ease that could exist nowhere else.

"No, my friend," the doctor is saying, "I do not think that

an apprehension of religion existed in the mind of palæolithic man."

"But, my captain, don't you think that you scientific people sometimes lose a little of the significance of things, insisting always on their scientific, in this case on their anthropological, aspect?"

"Not in the least; it is the only way to look at them."

"There are other ways," says the aumonier, smiling.

"One moment. . . ." From under the packing-box the captain produced a small bottle of anisette. "You'll have a little glass, won't you?"

"With the greatest pleasure. What a rarity here, anisette."

"But, as I was about to say, take our life here, for an example." . . . A shell shrieks overhead and crashes hollowly in the woods behind the dugout. Another follows it, exploding nearer. The captain picks a few bits of gravel off the table, reaches for his helmet and continues. "For example, our life here, which is, as was the life of palæolithic man, taken up only with the bare struggle for existence against overwhelming odds. You know yourself that it is not conducive to religion or any emotion except that of preservation."

"I hardly admit that. . . . Ah, I saved it," the aumonier announces, catching the bottle of anisette as it is about to fall off the table. An exploding shell rends the air about them. There is a pause, and a shower of earth and gravel tumbles about their ears.

"I must go and see if anyone was hurt," says the aumonier, clambering up the clay bank to the level of the ground; "but you will admit, my captain, that the sentiment of preservation is at least akin to the fundamental feelings of religion."

"My dear friend, I admit nothing. . . . Till this evening, good-bye." He waves his hand and goes into the dugout.

Martin and two French soldiers drinking sour wine in the doorway of a deserted house. It was raining outside and now and then a dripping camion passed along the road, slithering through the mud.

"This is the last summer of the war. . . . It must be," said the little man with large brown eyes and a childish, chubby brown face, who sat on Martin's left.

"Why?"

"Oh, I don't know. Everyone feels like that."

"I don't see," said Martin, "why it shouldn't last for ten or twenty years. Wars have before. . . ."

"How long have you been at the front?"

"Six months, off and on."

"After another six months you'll know why it can't go on."

"I don't know; it suits me all right," said the man on the other side of Martin, a man with a jovial red rabbit-like face. "Of course, I don't like being dirty and smelling and all that, but one gets accustomed to it."

"But you are an Alsatian; you don't care."

"I was a baker. They're going to send me to Dijon soon to bake army bread. It'll be a change. There'll be wine and lots of little girls. Good God, how drunk I'll be; and, old chap, you just watch me with the women. . . ."

"I should just like to get home and not be ordered about," said the first man. "I've been lucky, though," he went on; "I've been kept most of the time in reserve. I only had to use my bayonet once."

"When was that?" asked Martin.

"Near Mont Cornélien, last year. We put them to the bayonet and I was running and a man threw his arms up just in front of me saying, 'Mon ami, mon ami,' in French. I ran on because I couldn't stop, and I heard my bayonet grind as it went through his chest. I tripped over something and fell down."

"You were scared," said the Alsatian.

"Of course I was scared. I was trembling all over like an old dog in a thunderstorm. When I got up, he was lying on his side with his mouth open and blood running out, my bayonet still sticking into him. You know you have to put your foot against a man and pull hard to get the bayonet out."

"And if you're good at it," cried the Alsatian, "you ought to yank it out as your Boche falls and be ready for the next one. The time they gave me the Croix de Guerre I got three in succession, just like at drill."

"Oh, I was so sorry I had killed him," went on the other Frenchman. "When I went through his pockets I found a post-card. Here it is; I have it." He pulled out a cracked and worn leather wallet, from which he took a photograph and a bunch of pictures. "Look, this photograph was there, too. It hurt my heart. You see, it's a woman and two little girls. They look so nice. . . . It's strange, but I have two children, too, only one's a boy. I lay down on the ground beside him—I was all in—and listened to the machine-guns tapping put, put, put, put, put, all around. I wished I'd let him kill me instead. That was funny, wasn't it?"

"It's idiotic to feel like that. Put them to the bayonet, all of them, the dirty Boches. Why, the only money I've had since the war began, except my five sous, was fifty francs I found on a German officer. I wonder where he got it, the old corpse-stripper."

"Oh, it's shameful! I am ashamed of being a man. Oh, the shame, the shame . . ." The other man buried his face in his hands.

"I wish they were serving out gniolle for an attack right now," said the Alsatian, "or the gniolle without the attack'd be better yet."

"Wait here," said Martin, "I'll go round to the copé and get a bottle of fizzy. We'll drink to peace or war, as you like. Damn this rain!"

"It's a shame to bury those boots," said the sergeant of the stretcher-bearers.

From the long roll of blanket on the ground beside the hastily-dug grave protruded a pair of high boots, new and well polished as if for parade. All about the earth was scarred with turned clay like raw wounds, and the tilting arms of little wooden crosses huddled together, with here and there a bent wreath or a faded bunch of flowers.

Overhead in the stripped trees a bird was singing.

"Shall we take them off? It's shame to bury a pair of boots like that."

"So many poor devils need boots."

"Boots cost so dear."

Already two men were lowering the long bundle into the grave.

"Wait a minute; we've got a coffin for him."

A white board coffin was brought.

The boots thumped against the bottom as they put the big bundle in.

An officer strode into the enclosure of the graveyard, flicking his knees with a twig.

"Is this Lieutenant Dupont?" he asked of the sergeant.

"Yes, my lieutenant."

"Can you see his face?" The officer stooped and pulled apart the blanket where the head was.

"Poor René," he said. "Thank you. Good-bye," and strode out of the graveyard.

The yellowish clay fell in clots on the boards of the coffin. The sergeant bared his head and the aumonier came up, opening his book with a vaguely professional air.

"It was a shame to bury those boots. Boots are so dear nowadays," said the sergeant, mumbling to himself as he walked back towards the little broad shanty they used as a morgue.

Of the house, a little pale salmon-coloured villa, only a shell remained, but the garden was quite untouched; fall roses and bunches of white and pink and violet phlox bloomed there among the long grass and the intruding nettles. In the centre the round concrete fountain was no longer full of water, but a few brownish-green toads still inhabited it. The place smelt of box and sweetbriar and yew, and when you lay down on the grass where it grew short under the old yew tree by the fountain, you could see nothing but placid sky and waving green leaves. Martin Howe and Tom Randolph would spend there the quiet afternoons when they were off duty, sleeping in the languid sunlight, or chatting lazily, pointing out to each other tiny things, the pattern of snail-shells, the glitter of insects' wings, colours, fragrances that made vivid for them suddenly beauty and life, all that the shells that shrieked overhead, to explode on the road behind them, threatened to wipe out.

One afternoon Russell joined them, a tall young man with thin face and aquiline nose and unexpectedly light hair.

"Chef says we may go en repos in three days," he said, throwing himself on the ground beside the other two.

"We've heard that before," said Tom Randolph. "Division

hasn't started out yet, ole boy; an' we're the last of the division."

"God, I'll be glad to go. . . . I'm dead," said Russell.

"I was up all last night with dysentery."

"So was I. . . . It was not funny; first it'd be vomiting, and then diarrhœa, and then the shells'd start coming in. Gave me a merry time of it."

"They say it's the gas," said Martin.

"God, the gas! Turns me sick to think of it," said Russell, stroking his forehead with his hand. "Did I tell you about what happened to me the night after the attack, up in the woods?"

"No."

"Well, I was bringing a load of wounded down from P.J. right and I'd got just beyond the corner where the little muddy hill is—you know, where they're always shelling—when I found the road blocked. It was so God-damned black you couldn't see your hand in front of you. A camion'd gone off the road and another had run into it, and everything was littered with boxes of shells spilt about."

"Must have been real nice," said Randolph.

"The devilish part of it was that I was all alone. Coney was too sick with diarrhœa to be any use, so I left him up at the post, running out at both ends like he'd die. Well . . . I yelled and shouted like hell in my bad French and blew my whistle and sweated, and the damned wounded inside moaned and groaned. And the shells were coming in so thick I thought my number'd turn up any time. An' I couldn't get anybody. So I just climbed up in the second camion and backed it off into the bushes. . . . God, I bet it'll take a wrecking crew to get it out. . . .

"That was one good job.

"But there I was with another square in the road and no chance to pass that I could see in that darkness. Then what I was going to tell you about happened. I saw a little bit of light in a ditch beside a big car that seemed to be laying on its side, and I went down to it and there was a bunch of camion drivers, sitting round a lantern drinking.

"'Hello, have a drink!' they called out to me, and one of them got up, waving his arms, ravin' drunk, and threw his arms around me and kissed me on the mouth. His hair and beard were full of wet mud. . . . Then he dragged me into the crowd.

"'Ha, here's a copain come to die with us,' he cried.

"I gave him a shove and he fell down. But another one got up and handed me a tin cup full of that God-damned gniolle, that I drank not to make 'em sore. Then they all shouted, and stood about me, sayin', 'American's goin' to die with us. He's goin' to drink with us. He's goin' to die with us.' And the shells comin' in all the while. God, I was scared.

"'I want to get a camion moved to the side of the road. . . . Good-bye,' I said. There didn't seem any use talkin' to them.

"'But you've come to stay with us,' they said, and made me drink some more booze. 'You've come to die with us. Remember you said so.'

"The sweat was running into my eyes so's I could hardly see. I told 'em I'd be right back and slipped away into the dark. Then I thought I'd never get the second camion cranked. At last I managed it and put it so I could squeeze past, but they saw me and jumped up on the running-board of the ambulance, tried to stop the car, all yellin' at once, 'It's no use, the road's blocked both ways. You can't pass. You'd better stay and die with us. Caput.'

"Well, I put my foot on the accelerator and hit one of them so hard with the mud-guard he fell into the lantern and put it out. Then I got away. An' how I got past the stuff in that road afterwards was just luck. I couldn't see a God-damn thing; it was so black and I was so nerved up. God, I'll never forget these chaps' shoutin', 'Here's a feller come to die with us.'"

"Whew! That's some story," said Randolph.

"That'll make a letter home, won't it?" said Russell, smiling. "Guess my girl'll think I'm heroic enough after that."

Martin's eyes were watching a big dragonfly with brown body and cream and rainbow wings that hovered over the empty fountain and the three boys stretched on the grass, and was gone against the azure sky.

The prisoner had grey flesh, so grimed with mud that you could not tell if he were young or old. His uniform hung in a formless clot of mud about a slender frame. They had treated him at the dressing-station for a gash in his upper arm, and he was being used to help the stretcher-bearers. Martin sat in the front seat of the ambulance, watching him listlessly as he walked down the rutted road under the torn shreds of camouflage that fluttered a little in the wind. Martin wondered what he was thinking. Did he accept all this stench and filth and degradation of slavery as part of the divine order of things? Or did he too burn with loathing and revolt?

And all those men beyond the hill and the wood, what were they thinking? But how could they think? The lies they were drunk on would keep them eternally from thinking. They had never had any chance to think until they were hurried into the jaws of it, where was no room but for laughter and misery and the smell of blood.

The rutted road was empty now. Most of the batteries were quiet. Overhead in the brilliant sky aeroplanes snored monotonously.

The woods all about him were a vast rubbish-heap; the jagged, splintered boles of leafless trees rose in every direction from heaps of brass shell-cases, of tin cans, of bits of uniform and equipment. The wind came in puffs laden with an odour as of dead rats in an attic. And this was what all the centuries of civilisation had struggled for. For this had generations worn away their lives in mines and factories and forges, in fields and work-shops, toiling, screwing higher and higher the tension of their minds and muscles, polishing brighter and brighter the mirror of their intelligence. For this!

The German prisoner and another man had appeared in the road again, carrying a stretcher between them, walking with the slow, meticulous steps of great fatigue. A series of shells came in, like three cracks of a whip along the road. Martin followed the stretcher-bearers into the dugout.

The prisoner wiped the sweat from his grime-streaked forehead, and started up the step of the dugout again, a closed stretcher on his shoulder. Something made Martin look after him as he strolled down the rutted road. He wished he knew German so that he might call after the man and ask him what manner of a man he was.

Again, like snapping of a whip, three shells flashed yellow as they exploded in the brilliant sunlight of the road. The slender figure of the prisoner bent suddenly double, like a pocket-knife closing, and lay still. Martin ran out, stumbling in the hard ruts. In a soft child's voice the prisoner was babbling endlessly, contentedly. Martin kneeled beside him and tried to lift him, clasping him round the chest under the arms. He was very hard to lift, for his legs dragged limply in their soaked trousers, where the blood was beginning to saturate the muddy cloth, stickily. Sweat dripped from Martin's face, on the man's face, and he felt the arm-muscles and the ribs pressed against his body as he clutched the wounded man tightly to him in the effort of carrying him towards the dugout. The effort gave Martin a strange contentment. It was as if his body were taking part in the agony of this man's body. At last they were washed out, all the hatreds, all the lies, in blood and sweat. Nothing was left but the quiet friendliness of beings alike in every part, eternally alike.

Two men with a stretcher came from the dugout, and Martin laid the man's body, fast growing limper, less animated, down very carefully.

As he stood by the car, wiping the blood off his hands with an oily rag, he could still feel the man's ribs and the muscles of the man's arm against his side. It made him strangely happy.

At the end of the dugout a man was drawing short, hard breath as if he'd been running. There was the accustomed smell of blood and chloride and bandages and filthy miserable flesh. Howe lay on a stretcher wrapped in his blanket, with his coat over him, trying to sleep. There was very little light from a smoky lamp down at the end where the wounded were. The French batteries were fairly quiet, but the German shells were combing through the woods, coming in series of three and four, gradually nearing the dugout and edging away again. Howe saw the woods as a gambling table on which, throw after throw, scattered the random dice of death.

He pulled his blanket up round his head. He must sleep. How silly to think about it. It was luck. If a shell had his number on it he'd be gone before the words were out of his mouth. How silly that he might be dead any minute! What right had a nasty little piece of tinware to go tearing through his rich, feeling flesh, extinguishing it?

Like the sound of a mosquito in his ear, only louder, more vicious, a shell-shriek shrilled to the crash.

Damn! How foolish, how supremely silly that tired men somewhere away in the woods the other side of the lines should be shoving a shell into the breach of a gun to kill him, Martin Howe!

Like dice thrown on a table, shells burst about the dugout, now one side, now the other.

"Seem to have taken a fancy to us this evenin'," Howe heard Tom Randolph's voice from the bunk opposite.

"One," muttered Martin to himself, as he lay frozen with fear, flat on his back, biting his trembling lips, "two. . . . God, that was near!"

A dragging instant of suspense, and the shriek growing loud out of the distance.

"This is us." He clutched the sides of the stretcher.

A snorting roar rocked the dugout. Dirt fell in his face. He looked about, dazed. The lamp was still burning. One of the wounded men, with a bandage like an Arab's turban about his head, sat up in his stretcher with wide, terrified eyes.

"God watches over drunkards and the feeble-minded. Don't let's worry, Howe," shouted Randolph from his bunk.

"That probably bitched car No. 4 for evermore," he answered, turning on his stretcher, relieved for some reason from the icy suspense.

"We should worry! We'll foot it home, that's all."

The casting of the dice began again, farther away this time.

"We won that throw," thought Martin to himself.

Chapter VIII

DUCKS QUACKING woke Martin. For a moment he could not think where he was; then he remembered. The rafters of the loft of the farmhouse over his head were hung with bunches of herbs drying. He lay a long while on his back looking at them, sniffing the sweetened air, while farmyard sounds occupied his ears, hens cackling, the grunting of pigs, the rou-cou-cou-cou, rou-cou-cou-cou of pigeons under the eaves. He stretched himself and looked about him. He was alone except for Tom Randolph, who slept in a pile of blankets next to the wall, his head, with its close-cropped black hair, pillowed on his bare arm. Martin slipped off the canvas cot he had slept on and went to the window of the loft, a little square open at the level of the floor, through which came a dazzle of blue and gold and green. He looked out. Stables and hay-barns filled two sides of the farmyard below him. Behind them was a mass of rustling oak-trees. On the lichen-greened tile roofs pigeons strutted about, putting their coral feet daintily one before the other, puffing out their glittering breasts. He breathed deep of the smell of hay and manure and cows and of unpolluted farms.

From the yard came a riotous cackling of chickens and quacking of ducks, mingled with the peeping of the little broods. In the middle a girl in blue gingham, sleeves rolled up as far as possible on her brown arms, a girl with a mass of dark hair loosely coiled above the nape of her neck, was throwing to the fowls handfuls of grain with a wide gesture.

"And to think that only yesterday . . ." said Martin to himself. He listened carefully for some time. "Wonderful! You can't even hear the guns."

Chapter IX

THE EVENING was pearl-grey when they left the village; in their nostrils was the smell of the leisurely death of the year, of leaves drying and falling, of ripened fruit and bursting seed-pods.

"The fall's a maddening sort o' time for me," said Tom Randolph. "It makes me itch to get up on ma hind legs an' do things, go places."

"I suppose it's that the earth has such a feel of accomplishment," said Howe.

"You do feel as if Nature had pulled off her part of the job and was restin'."

They stopped a second and looked about them, breathing deep. On one side of the road were woods where in long alleys the mists deepened into purple darkness.

"There's the moon."

"God! it looks like a pumpkin."

"I wish those guns'd shut up 'way off there to the north."

"They're sort of irrelevant, aren't they?"

They walked on, silent, listening to the guns throbbing far away, like muffled drums beaten in nervous haste.

"Sounds almost like a barrage."

Martin for some reason was thinking of the last verses of Shelley's *Hellas*. He wished he knew them so that he could recite them.

> "*Faiths and empires gleam*
> *Like wrecks in a dissolving dream.*"

The purple trunks of saplings passed slowly across the broad face of the moon as they walked along. How beautiful the world was!

"Look, Tom." Martin put his arm about Randolph's shoulder and nodded towards the moon. "It might be a ship with puffed-out pumpkin-coloured sails, the way the trees make it look now."

"Wouldn't it be great to go to sea?" said Randolph, looking straight into the moon, "an' get out of this slaughterhouse. It's nice to see the war, but I have no intention of taking up butchery as a profession. . . . There is too much else to do in the world."

They walked slowly along the road talking of the sea, and Martin told how when he was a little kid he'd had an uncle who used to tell him about the Vikings and the Swan Path, and how one of the great moments of his life had been when he and a friend had looked out of their window in a little inn on Cape Cod one morning and seen the sea and the swaying gold path of the sun on it, stretching away, beyond the horizon.

"Poor old life," he said. "I'd expected to do so much with you." And they both laughed, a little bitterly.

They were strolling past a large farmhouse that stood like a hen among chicks in a crowd of little outbuildings. A man in the road lit a cigarette and Martin recognised him in the orange glare of the match.

"Monsieur Merrier!" He held out his hand. It was the aspirant he had drunk beer with weeks ago at Brocourt.

"Hah! It's you!"

"So you are en repos here, too?"

"Yes, indeed. But you two come in and see us; we are dying of the blues."

"We'd love to stop in for a second."

A fire smouldered in the big hearth of the farmhouse kitchen, sending a little irregular fringe of red light out over the tiled floor. At the end of the room towards the door three men were seated round a table, smoking. A candle threw their huge and grotesque shadows on the floor and on the whitewashed walls, and lit up the dark beams of that part of the ceiling. The three men got up and everyone shook hands, filling the room with swaying giant shadows. Champagne was brought and tin cups and more candles, and the Americans were given the two most comfortable chairs.

"It's such a find to have Americans who speak French," said a bearded man with unusually large brilliant eyes. He had been introduced as André Dubois, "a very terrible person," had added Merrier, laughing. The cork popped out of the bottle he had been struggling with.

"You see, we never can find out what you think about

things. . . . All we can do is to be sympathetically inane, and *vive les braves alliés* and that sort of stuff."

"I doubt if we Americans do think," said Martin.

"Cigarettes, who wants some cigarettes?" cried Lully, a small man with a very brown oval face to which long eye-lashes and a little bit of silky black moustache gave almost a winsomeness. When he laughed he showed brilliant, very regular teeth. As he handed the cigarettes about he looked searchingly at Martin with eyes disconcertingly intense. "Merrier has told us about you," he said. "You seem to be the first American we'd met who agreed with us."

"What about?"

"About the war, of course."

"Yes," took up the fourth man, a blonde Norman with an impressive, rather majestic face, "we were very interested. You see, we bore each other, talking always among ourselves. . . . I hope you won't be offended if I agree with you in saying that Americans never think. I've been in Texas, you see."

"Really?"

"Yes, I went to a Jesuit College in Dallas. I was preparing to enter the Society of Jesus."

"How long have you been in the war?" asked André Dubois, passing his hand across his beard.

"We've both been in the same length of time—about six months."

"Do you like it?"

"I don't have a bad time. . . . But the people in Boccaccio managed to enjoy themselves while the plague was at Florence. That seems to me the only way to take the war."

"We have no villa to take refuge in, though," said Dubois, "and we have forgotten all our amusing stories."

"And in America—they like the war?"

"They don't know what it is. They are like children. They believe everything they are told, you see; they have had no experience in international affairs, like you Europeans. To me our entrance into the war is a tragedy."

"It's sort of goin' back on our only excuse for existing," put in Randolph.

"In exchange for all the quiet and the civilisation and the beauty of ordered lives that Europeans gave up in going to the new world we gave them opportunity to earn luxury, and, infinitely more important, freedom from the past, that gangrened ghost of the past that is killing Europe to-day with its infection of hate and greed of murder.

"America has turned traitor to all that, you see; that's the way we look at it. Now we're a military nation, an organised pirate like France and England and Germany."

"But American idealism? The speeches, the notes?" cried Lully, catching the edge of the table with his two brown hands.

"Camouflage," said Martin.

"You mean it's insincere?"

"The best camouflage is always sincere."

Dubois ran his hands through his hair.

"Of course, why should there be any difference?" he said.

"Oh, we're all dupes, we're all dupes. Look, Lully, old man, fill up the Americans' glasses."

"Thanks."

"And I used to believe in liberty," said Martin. He raised his tumbler and looked at the candle through the pale yellow champagne. On the wall behind him, his arm and hand and the tumbler were shadowed huge in dusky lavender blue. He noticed that his was the only tumbler.

"I am honoured," he said; "mine is the only glass."

"And that's looted," said Merrier.

"It's funny . . ." Martin suddenly felt himself filled with a desire to talk. "All my life I've struggled for my own liberty in my small way. Now I hardly know if the thing exists."

"Exists? Of course it does, or people wouldn't hate it so," cried Lully.

"I used to think," went on Martin, "that it was my family I must escape from to be free; I mean all the conventional ties, the worship of success and the respectabilities that is drummed into you when you're young."

"I suppose everyone has thought that. . . ."

"How stupid we were before the war, how we prated of small revolts, how we sniggered over little jokes at religion and government. And all the while, in the infinite greed, in the infinite stupidity of men, this was being prepared." André Dubois was speaking, puffing nervously at a cigarette between phrases, now and then pulling at his beard with a long, sinewy hand.

"What terrifies me rather is their power to enslave our minds," Martin went on, his voice growing louder and surer as his idea carried him along. "I shall never forget the flags, the menacing, exultant flags along all the streets before we went to war, the gradual unbaring of teeth, gradual lulling to sleep of people's humanity and sense by the phrases, the phrases. . . . America, as you know, is ruled by the press. And the press is ruled by whom? Who shall ever know what dark forces bought and bought until we should be ready to go blinded and gagged to war? . . . People seem to so love to be fooled. Intellect used to mean freedom, a light struggling against darkness. Now the darkness is using the light for its own purposes. . . . We are slaves of bought intellect, willing slaves."

"But, Howe, the minute you see that and laugh at it, you're not a slave. Laugh and be individually as decent as you can, and don't worry your head about the rest of the world; and have a good time in spite of the God-damned scoundrels," broke out Randolph in English. "No use worrying yourself into the grave over a thing you can't help."

"There is one solution and one only, my friends," said the blonde Norman; "the Church. . . ." He sat up straight in his chair, speaking slowly with expressionless face. "People are too weak and too kindly to shift for themselves. Government of some sort there must be. Lay Government has proved through all the tragic years of history to be merely a ruse of the strong to oppress the weak, of the wicked to fool the confiding. There remains only religion. In the organisation of religion lies the natural and suitable arrangement for the happiness of man. The Church will govern not through physical force but through spiritual force."

"The force of fear." Lully jumped to his feet impatiently, making the bottles sway on the table.

"The force of love. . . . I once thought as you do, my friend," said the Norman, pulling Lully back into his chair with a smile.

Lully drank a glass of champagne greedily and undid the buttons of his blue jacket.

"Go on," he said; "it's madness."

"All the evil of the Church," went on the Norman's even voice, "comes from her struggles to attain supremacy. Once assured of triumph, established as the rule of the world, it becomes the natural channel through which the wise rule and direct the stupid, not for their own interest, not for ambition for worldly things, but for the love that is in them. The freedom the Church offers is the only true freedom. It denies the world, and the slaveries and rewards of it. It gives the love of God as the only aim of life."

"But think of the Church to-day, the cardinals at Rome, the Church turned everywhere to the worship of tribal gods. . . ."

"Yes, but admit that that can be changed. The Church has been supreme in the past; can it not again be supreme? All the evil comes from the struggle, from the compromise. Picture to yourself for a moment a world conquered by the Church, ruled through the soul and mind, where force will not exist, where instead of all the multitudinous tyrannies man has choked his life with in organising against other men, will exist the one supreme thing, the Church of God. Instead of many hatreds, one love. Instead of many slaveries, one freedom."

"A single tyranny, instead of a million. What's the choice?" cried Lully.

"But you are both violent, my children." Merrier got to his feet and smilingly filled the glasses all round. "You go at the matter too much from the heroic point of view. All this sermonising does no good. We are very simple people who want to live quietly and have plenty to eat and have no one worry us or hurt us in the little span of sunlight before we die. All we have now is the same war between the classes: those that exploit and those that are exploited. The cunning, unscrupulous people control the humane, kindly people. This war that has smashed our little European world in which order was so painfully taking the place of chaos, seems to me merely a gigantic battle fought over the plunder of the world by the pirates who have grown fat to the point of madness on the work of their own people, on the work of the millions in Africa, in India, in America, who have come directly or indirectly under the yoke of the insane greed of the white races. Well, our edifice is ruined. Let's think no more of it. Ours is now the duty of rebuilding, reorganising. I have not faith enough in human nature to be an anarchist. . . . We are too like sheep; we must go in flocks, and a flock to live must organise. There is plenty for everyone, even with the huge growth in population all over the world. What we want is organisation from the bottom, organisation by the ungreedy, by the humane, by the uncunning, socialism of the masses that shall spring from the natural need of men to help one another; not socialism from the top to the ends of the governors, that they may clamp us tighter in their fetters. We must stop the economic war, the war for existence of man against man. That will be the first step in the long climb to civilisation. They must co-operate, they must learn that it is saner and more advantageous to help one another than to hinder one another in the great war against nature. And the tyranny of the feudal money lords, the unspeakable misery of this war is driving men closer together into fraternity, co-operation. It is the lower classes, therefore, that the new world must be founded on. The rich must be extinguished; with them wars will die. First between rich and poor, between the exploiter and the exploited. . . ."

"They have one thing in common," interrupted the blonde Norman, smiling.

"What's that?"

"Humanity. . . . That is, feebleness, cowardice."

"No, indeed. All through the world's history there has been one law for the lord and another for the slave, one humanity for the lord and another humanity for the slave. What we must strive for is a true universal humanity."

"True," cried Lully, "but why take the longest, the most difficult road? You say that people are sheep; they must be driven. I say that you and I and our American friends here are not sheep. We are capable of standing alone, of judging all for ourselves, and we are just ordinary people like anyone else."

"Oh, but look at us, Lully!" interrupted Merrier. "We are too weak and too cowardly . . ."

"An example," said Martin, excitedly leaning across the table. "We none of us believe that war is right or useful or anything but a hideous method of mutual suicide. Have we the courage of our own faith?"

"As I said," Merrier took up again, "I have too little faith to be an anarchist, but I have too much to believe in religion." His tin cup rapped sharply on the table as he set it down.

"No," Lully continued, after a pause, "it is better for man to worship God, His image on the clouds, the creation of his fancy, than to worship the vulgar apparatus of organised life, government. Better sacrifice his children to Moloch than to that society for the propagation and protection of commerce, the nation. Oh, think of the cost of government in all the ages since men stopped living in marauding tribes! Think of the great men martyred. Think of the thought trodden into the dust. . . . Give man a chance for once. Government should be purely utilitarian, like the electric light wires in a house. It is a method for attaining peace and comfort—a bad one, I think, at that; not a thing to be worshipped as God. The one reason for it is the protection of property. Why should we have property? That is the central evil of the world. . . . That is the cancer that has made life a hell of misery until now; the inflated greed of it has spurred on our nations of the West to throw themselves back, for ever, perhaps, into the depths of savagery. . . . Oh, if people would only trust their own fundamental kindliness, the fraternity, the love that is the strongest thing in life. Abolish property, and the disease of the desire for it, the desire to grasp and have, and you'll need no government to protect you. The vividness and resiliency of the life of man is being fast crushed under organisation, tabulation. Overorganisation is death. It is disorganisation, not organisation, that is the aim of life."

"I grant that what all of you say is true, but why say it over and over again?" André Dubois talked, striding back and forth beside the table, his arms gesticulating. His compound shadow thrown by the candles on the white wall followed him back and forth, mocking him with huge blurred gestures. "The Greek philosophers said it and the Indian sages. Our descendants thousands of years from now will say it and wring their hands as we do. Has not someone on earth the courage to act? . . ." The men at the table turned towards him, watching his tall figure move back and forth.

"We are slaves. We are blind. We are deaf. Why should we

argue, we who have no experience of different things to go on? It has always been the same: man the slave of property or religion, of his own shadow. . . . First we must burst our bonds, open our eyes, clear our ears. Now we know nothing but what we are told by the rulers. Oh, the lies, the lies, the lies, the lies that life is smothered in! We must strike once more for freedom, for the sake of the dignity of man. Hopelessly, cynically, ruthlessly we must rise and show at least that we are not taken in; that we are slaves but not willing slaves. Oh, they have deceived us so many times. We have been such dupes, we have been such dupes!"

"You are right," said the blonde Norman sullenly; "we have all been dupes."

A sudden self-consciousness chilled them all to silence for a while. Without wanting to, they strained their ears to hear the guns. There they were, throbbing loud, unceasing, towards the north, like hasty muffled drum-beating.

> "*Cease; drain not to its dregs the wine,*
> *Of bitter Prophecy.*
> *The world is weary of its past.*
> *Oh, might it die or rest at last.*"

All through the talk snatches from *Hellas* had been running through Howe's head.

After a long pause he turned to Merrier and asked him how he had fared in the attack.

"Oh, not so badly. I brought my skin back," said Merrier, laughing. "It was a dull business. After waiting eight hours under gas bombardment we got orders to advance, and so over we went with the barrage way ahead of us. There was no resistance where we were. We took a lot of prisoners and blew up some dugouts and I had the good luck to find a lot of German chocolate. It came in handy, I can tell you, as no ravitaillement came for two days. We just had biscuits and I toasted the biscuits and chocolate together and had quite good meals, though I nearly died of thirst afterwards. . . . We lost heavily, though, when they started counterattacking."

"An' no one of you were touched?"

"Luck. . . . But we lost many dear friends. Oh, it's always like that."

"Look what I brought back—a German gun," said André Dubois, going to the corner of the room.

"That's some souvenir," said Tom Randolph, sitting up suddenly, shaking himself out of the reverie he had been sunk in all through the talk of the evening.

"And I have three hundred rounds. They'll come in handy some day."

"When?"

"In the revolution—after the war."

"That's the stuff I like to hear," cried Randolph, getting to his feet. "Why wait for the war to end?"

"Why? Because we have not the courage. . . . But it is impossible until after the war."

"And then you think it is possible?"

"Yes."

"Will it accomplish anything?"

"God knows."

"One last bottle of champagne," cried Merrier.

They seated themselves round the table again. Martin took in at a glance the eager sunburned faces, the eyes burning with hope, with determination, and a sudden joy flared through him.

"Oh, there is hope," he said, drinking down his glass. "We are too young, too needed to fail. We must find a way, find the first step of a way to freedom, or life is a hollow mockery."

"To Revolution, to Anarchy, to the Socialist state," they all cried, drinking down the last of the champagne. All the candles but one had guttered out. Their shadows swayed and darted in long arms and changing, grotesque limbs about the room.

"But first there must be peace," said the Norman, Jean Chenier, twisting his mouth into a faintly bitter smile.

"Oh, indeed, there must be peace."

"Of all slaveries, the slavery of war, of armies, is the bitterest, the most hopeless slavery." Lully was speaking, his smooth brown face in a grimace of excitement and loathing. "War is our first enemy."

"But oh, my friend," said Merrier, "we will win in the end. All the people in all the armies of the world believe as we do. In all the minds the seed is sprouting."

"Before long the day will come. The tocsin will ring."

"Do you really believe that?" cried Martin. "Have we the courage, have we the energy, have we the power? Are we the men our ancestors were?"

"No," said Dubois, crashing down on the table with his fist; "we are merely intellectuals. We cling to a mummified world. But they have the power and the nerve."

"Who?"

"The stupid average working-people."

"We only can combat the lies," said Lully; "they are so easily duped. After the war that is what we must do."

"Oh, but we are all such dupes," cried Dubois. "First we must fight the lies. It is the lies that choke us."

It was very late. Howe and Tom Randolph were walking home under a cold white moon already well sunk in the west; northward was a little flickering glare above the tops of the low hills and a sound of firing as of muffled drums beaten hastily.

"With people like that we needn't despair of civilisation," said Howe.

"With people who are young and aren't scared you can do lots."

"We must come over and see those fellows again. It's such a relief to be able to talk."

"And they give you the idea that something's really going on in the world, don't they?"

"Oh, it's wonderful! Think that the awakening may come soon."

"We might wake up to-morrow and . . ."

"It's too important to joke about; don't be an ass, Tom."

They rolled up in their blankets in the silent barn and listened to the drum-fire in the distance. Martin saw again, as he lay on his side with his eyes closed, the group of men in blue uniforms, men with eager brown faces and eyes gleaming with hope, and saw their full red lips moving as they talked.

The candle threw the shadows of their heads, huge, fantastic, and of their gesticulating arms on the white walls of the kitchen. And it seemed to Martin Howe that all his friends were gathered in that room.

Chapter X

"THEY SAY you sell shoe-laces," said Martin, his eyes blinking in the faint candlelight.

Crouched in the end of the dugout was a man with a brown skin like wrinkled leather, and white eyebrows and moustaches. All about him were piles of old boots, rotten with wear and mud, holding fantastically the imprints of the toes and ankle-bones of the feet that had worn them. The candle cast flitting shadows over them so that they seemed to move back and forth faintly, as do the feet of wounded men laid out on the floor of the dressing-station.

"I'm a cobbler by profession," said the man. He made a gesture with the blade of his knife in the direction of a huge bundle of leather laces that hung from a beam above his head. "I've done all those since yesterday. I cut up old boots into laces."

"Helps out the five sous a bit," said Martin, laughing.

"This post is convenient for my trade," went on the cobbler, as he picked out another boot to be cut into laces, and started hacking the upper part off the worn sole. "At the little hut, where they pile up the stiffs before they bury them—you know, just to the left outside the abri—they leave lots of their boots around. I can pick up any number I want." With a clasp-knife he was cutting the leather in a spiral, paring off a thin lace. He contracted his bushy eyebrows as he bent over his work. The candlelight glinted on the knife blade as he twisted it about dexterously.

"Yes, many a good copain of mine has had his poor feet in those boots. What of it? Some day another fellow will be making laces out of mine, eh?" He gave a wheezy, coughing laugh.

"I guess I'll take a pair. How much are they?"

"Six sous."

"Good."

The coins glinted in the light of the candle as they clinked in the man's leather-blackened palm.

"Good-bye," said Martin. He walked past men sleeping in the bunks on either side as he went towards the steps.

At the end of the dugout the man crouched on his pile of old leather, with his knife that glinted in the candlelight dexterously carving laces out of the boots of those who no longer needed them.

Chapter XI

THERE IS no sound in the poste de secours. A faint green-ish light filters down from the quiet woods outside. Martin is kneeling beside a stretcher where lies a mass of torn blue uniform crossed in several places by strips of white bandages clotted with dark blood. The massive face, grimed with mud, is very waxy and grey. The light hair hangs in clots about the forehead. The nose is sharp, but there is a faint smile about the lips made thin by pain.

"Is there anything I can get you?" asks Martin softly.

"Nothing." Slowly the blue eyelids uncover hazel eyes that burn feverishly.

"But you haven't told me yet, how's Merrier?"

"A shell . . . dead . . . poor chap."

"And the anarchist, Lully?"

"Dead."

"And Dubois?"

"Why ask?" came the faint rustling voice peevishly. "Every-body's dead. You're dead, aren't you?"

"No, I'm alive, and you. A little courage. . . . We must be cheerful."

"It's not for long. To-morrow, the next day. . . ." The blue eyelids slip back over the crazy burning eyes and the face takes on again the waxen look of death.

THREE SOLDIERS

CONTENTS

"*Les contemporains qui souffrent de certaines choses ne peuvent s'en souvenir qu'avec une horreur qui paralyse tout autre plaisir, même celui de lire un conte.*"

STENDHAL

PART ONE
MAKING THE MOULD

I

THE COMPANY stood at attention, each man looking straight before him at the empty parade ground, where the cinder piles showed purple with evening. On the wind that smelt of barracks and disinfectant there was a faint greasiness of food cooking. At the other side of the wide field long lines of men shuffled slowly into the narrow wooden shanty that was the mess hall. Chins down, chests out, legs twitching and tired from the afternoon's drilling, the company stood at attention. Each man stared straight in front of him, some vacantly with resignation, some trying to amuse themselves by noting minutely every object in their field of vision,—the cinder piles, the long shadows of the barracks and mess halls where they could see men standing about, spitting, smoking, leaning against clapboard walls. Some of the men in line could hear their watches ticking in their pockets.

Someone moved, his feet making a crunching noise in the cinders.

The sergeant's voice snarled out: "You men are at attention. Quit yer wrigglin' there, you!"

The men nearest the offender looked at him out of the corners of their eyes.

Two officers, far out on the parade ground, were coming towards them. By their gestures and the way they walked, the men at attention could see that they were chatting about something that amused them. One of the officers laughed boyishly, turned away and walked slowly back across the parade ground. The other, who was the lieutenant, came towards them smiling. As he approached his company, the smile left his lips and he advanced his chin, walking with heavy precise steps.

"Sergeant, you may dismiss the company." The lieutenant's voice was pitched in a hard staccato.

The sergeant's hand snapped up to salute like a block signal. "Companee dis . . . missed," he sang out.

The row of men in khaki became a crowd of various individuals with dusty boots and dusty faces. Ten minutes later they lined up and marched in a column of fours to mess. A few red filaments of electric lights gave a dusty glow in the brownish obscurity where the long tables and benches and the board floors had a faint smell of garbage mingled with the smell of the disinfectant the tables had been washed off with after the last meal. The men, holding their oval mess kits in front of them, filed by the great tin buckets at the door, out of which meat and potatoes were splashed into each plate by a sweating K.P. in blue denims.

"Don't look so bad tonight," said Fuselli to the man opposite him as he hitched his sleeves up at the wrists and leaned over his steaming food. He was sturdy, with curly hair and full vigorous lips that he smacked hungrily as he ate.

"It ain't," said the pink flaxen-haired youth opposite him, who wore his broad-brimmed hat on the side of his head with a certain jauntiness.

"I got a pass tonight," said Fuselli, tilting his head vainly.

"Goin' to tear things up?"

"Man . . . I got a girl at home back in Frisco. She's a good kid."

"Yer right not to go with any of the girls in this goddam town. . . . They ain't clean, none of 'em. . . . That is if ye want to go overseas." The flaxen-haired youth leaned across the table earnestly.

"I'm goin' to git some more chow. Wait for me, will yer?" said Fuselli.

"What yer going to do down town?" asked the flaxen-haired youth when Fuselli came back.

"Dunno,—run round a bit an' go to the movies," he answered, filling his mouth with potato.

"Gawd, it's time fer retreat." They overheard a voice behind them.

Fuselli stuffed his mouth as full as he could and emptied the rest of his meal reluctantly into the garbage pail.

A few moments later he stood stiffly at attention in a khaki row that was one of hundreds of other khaki rows, identical, that filled all sides of the parade ground, while the bugle blew somewhere at the other end where the flag-pole was. Somehow it made him think of the man behind the desk in the office of the draft board who had said, handing him the papers sending him to camp, "I wish I was going with you," and had held out a white bony hand that Fuselli, after a moment's hesitation, had taken in his own stubby brown hand. The man had added fervently, "It must be grand, just grand, to feel the danger, the chance of being potted any minute. Good luck, young feller. . . . Good luck." Fuselli remembered unpleasantly his paper-white face and the greenish look of his bald head; but the words had made him stride out of the office sticking out his chest, brushing truculently past a group of men in the door. Even now the memory of it, mixing with the strains of the national anthem made him feel important, truculent.

"Squads right!" came an order. Crunch, crunch, crunch in the gravel. The companies were going back to their barracks. He wanted to smile but he didn't dare. He wanted to smile because he had a pass till midnight, because in ten minutes he'd be outside the gates, outside the green fence and the sentries and the strands of barbed wire. Crunch, crunch, crunch; oh, they were so slow in getting back to the barracks and he was losing time, precious free minutes. "Hep, hep, hep," cried the sergeant, glaring down the ranks, with his aggressive bulldog expression, to where someone had fallen out of step.

The company stood at attention in the dusk. Fuselli was biting the inside of his lips with impatience. Minutes dragged by.

At last, as if reluctantly, the sergeant sang out:

"Dis . . . missed."

Fuselli hurried towards the gate, brandishing his pass with an important swagger.

Once out on the asphalt of the street, he looked down the long row of lawns and porches where violet arc lamps already contested the faint afterglow, drooping from their iron stalks far above the recently planted saplings of the avenue. He stood at the corner slouched against a telegraph pole, with the camp fence, surmounted by three strands of barbed wire, behind him, wondering which way he would go. This was a hell of a town anyway. And he used to think he wanted to travel round and see places.—"Home'll be good enough for me after this," he muttered. Walking down the long street towards the centre of town, where was the moving-picture show, he thought of his home, of the dark apartment on the ground floor of a seven-storey house where his aunt lived. "Gee, she used to cook swell," he murmured regretfully.

On a warm evening like this he would have stood round at the corner where the drugstore was, talking to fellows he knew, giggling when the girls who lived in the street, walking arm and arm, twined in couples or trios, passed by affecting ignorance of the glances that followed them. Or perhaps he would have gone walking with Al, who worked in the same optical-goods store, down through the glaring streets of the theatre and restaurant quarter, or along the wharves and ferry slips, where they would have sat smoking and looking out over the dark purple harbor, with its winking lights and its moving ferries spilling swaying reflections in the water out of their square reddish-glowing windows. If they had been lucky they would have seen a liner come in through the Golden Gate, growing from a blur of light to a huge moving brilliance, like the front of a high-class theatre, that towered above the ferry boats. You could often hear the thump of the screw and the swish of the bow cutting the calm bay-water, and the sound of a band playing, that came alternately faint and loud. "When I git rich," Fuselli had liked to say to Al, "I'm goin' to take a trip on one of them liners."

"Yer dad come over from the old country in one, didn't he?" Al would ask.

"Oh, he came steerage. I'd stay at home if I had to do that. Man, first class for me, a cabin de lux, when I git rich."

But here he was in this town in the East, where he didn't know anybody and where there was no place to go but the movies.

"'Lo, buddy," came a voice beside him. The tall youth who had sat opposite at mess was just catching up to him. "Goin' to the movies?"

"Yare, nauthin' else to do."

"Here's a rookie. Just got to camp this mornin'," said the

tall youth, jerking his head in the direction of the man beside him.

"You'll like it. Ain't so bad as it seems at first," said Fuselli encouragingly.

"I was just telling him," said the other, "to be careful as hell not to get in wrong. If ye once get in wrong in this damn army . . . it's hell."

"You bet yer life . . . so they sent ye over to our company, did they, rookie? Ain't so bad. The sergeant's sort o' decent if ye're in right with him, but the lieutenant's a stinker. . . . Where you from?"

"New York," said the rookie, a little man of thirty with an ash-colored face and a shiny Jewish nose. "I'm in the clothing business there. I oughtn't to be drafted at all. It's an outrage. I'm consumptive." He spluttered in a feeble squeaky voice.

"They'll fix ye up, don't you fear," said the tall youth. "They'll make you so goddam well ye won't know yerself. Yer mother won't know ye, when you get home, rookie. . . . But you're in luck."

"Why?"

"Bein' from New York. The corporal, Tim Sidis, is from New York, an' all the New York fellers in the company got a graft with him."

"What kind of cigarettes d'ye smoke?" asked the tall youth.

"I don't smoke."

"Ye'd better learn. The corporal likes fancy ciggies and so does the sergeant; you jus' slip 'em each a butt now and then. May help ye to get in right with 'em."

"Don't do no good," said Fuselli. . . . "It's juss luck. But keep neat-like and smilin' and you'll get on all right. And if they start to ride ye, show fight. Ye've got to be hard boiled to git on in this army."

"Ye're goddam right," said the tall youth. "Don't let 'em ride yer. . . . What's yer name, rookie?"

"Eisenstein."

"This feller's name's Powers . . . Bill Powers. Mine's Fuselli. . . . Goin' to the movies, Mr. Eisenstein?"

"No, I'm trying to find a skirt." The little man leered wanly. "Glad to have got ackwainted."

"Goddam kike!" said Powers as Eisenstein walked off up a

side street, planted, like the avenue, with saplings on which the sickly leaves rustled in the faint breeze that smelt of factories and coal dust.

"Kikes ain't so bad," said Fuselli, "I got a good friend who's a kike."

They were coming out of the movies in a stream of people in which the blackish clothes of factory-hands predominated.

"I came near bawlin' at the picture of the feller leavin' his girl to go off to the war," said Fuselli.

"Did yer?"

"It was just like it was with me. Ever been in Frisco, Powers?"

The tall youth shook his head. Then he took off his broad-brimmed hat and ran his fingers over his stubby tow-head.

"Gee, it was some hot in there," he muttered.

"Well, it's like this," said Fuselli. "You have to cross the ferry to Oakland. My aunt . . . ye know I ain't got any mother, so I always live at my aunt's. . . . My aunt an' her sister-in-law an' Mabe . . . Mabe's my girl . . . they all came over on the ferry-boat, 'spite of my tellin' 'em I didn't want 'em. An' Mabe said she was mad at me, 'cause she'd seen the letter I wrote Georgine Slater. She was a toughie, lived in our street, I used to write mash notes to. An' I kep' tellin' Mabe I'd done it juss for the hell of it, an' that I didn't mean nawthin' by it. An' Mabe said she wouldn't never forgive me, an' then I said maybe I'd be killed an' she'd never see me again, an' then we all began to bawl. Gawd! it was a mess. . . ."

"It's hell sayin' good-by to girls," said Powers, understandingly. "Cuts a feller all up. I guess it's better to go with coosies. Ye don't have to say good-by to them."

"Ever gone with a coosie?"

"Not exactly," admitted the tall youth, blushing all over his pink face, so that it was noticeable even under the ashen glare of the arc lights on the avenue that led towards camp.

"I have," said Fuselli, with a certain pride. "I used to go with a Portugee girl. My but she was a toughie. I've given all that up now I'm engaged, though. . . . But I was tellin' ye. . . . Well, we finally made up an' I kissed her an' Mabe said she'd never marry any one but me. So when we was walkin' up the street I spied a silk service flag in a winder, that was all fancy with a star all trimmed up to beat the band, an' I said to myself, I'm goin' to give that to Mabe, an' I ran in an' bought it. I didn't give a hoot in hell what it cost. So when we was all kissin' and bawlin' when I was goin' to leave them to report to the overseas detachment, I shoved it into her hand, an' said, 'Keep that, girl, an' don't you forgit me.' An' what did she do but pull out a five-pound box o' candy from behind her back an' say, 'Don't make yerself sick, Dan.' An she'd had it all the time without my knowin' it. Ain't girls clever?"

"Yare," said the tall youth vaguely.

Along the rows of cots, when Fuselli got back to the barracks, men were talking excitedly.

"There's hell to pay, somebody's broke out of the jug."

"How?"

"Damned if I know."

"Sergeant Timmons said he made a rope of his blankets."

"No, the feller on guard helped him to get away."

"Like hell he did. It was like this. I was walking by the guardhouse when they found out about it."

"What company did he belong ter?"

"Dunno."

"What's his name?"

"Some guy on trial for insubordination. Punched an officer in the jaw."

"I'd a liked to have seen that."

"Anyhow he's fixed himself this time."

"You're goddam right."

"Will you fellers quit talkin'? It's after taps," thundered the sergeant, who sat reading the paper at a little board desk at the door of the barracks under the feeble light of one small bulb, carefully screened. "You'll have the O.D. down on us."

Fuselli wrapped the blanket round his head and prepared to sleep. Snuggled down into the blankets on the narrow cot, he felt sheltered from the sergeant's thundering voice and from the cold glare of officers' eyes. He felt cosy and happy like he had felt in bed at home, when he had been a little kid. For a moment he pictured to himself the other man, the man who had punched an officer's jaw, dressed like he was, maybe only nineteen, the same age like he was, with a girl like Mabe waiting for him somewhere. How cold and frightful it must feel to be out of the camp with the guard looking for you! He pictured himself running breathless down a long street pursued by a company with guns, by officers whose eyes glinted cruelly like the pointed tips of bullets. He pulled the blanket closer round his head, enjoying the warmth and softness of the wool against his cheek. He must remember to smile at the sergeant when he passed him off duty. Somebody had said there'd be promotions soon. Oh, he wanted so hard to be promoted. It'd be so swell if he could write back to Mabe and tell her to address her letters Corporal Dan Fuselli. He must be more careful not to do anything that would get him in wrong with anybody. He must never miss an opportunity to show them what a clever kid he was. "Oh, when we're ordered overseas, I'll show them," he thought ardently, and picturing to himself long movie reels of heroism he went off to sleep.

A sharp voice beside his cot woke him with a jerk.

"Get up, you."

The white beam of a pocket searchlight was glaring in the face of the man next to him.

"The O.D.," said Fuselli to himself.

"Get up, you," came the sharp voice again.

The man in the next cot stirred and opened his eyes.

"Get up."

"Here, sir," muttered the man in the next cot, his eyes blinking sleepily in the glare of the flashlight. He got out of bed and stood unsteadily at attention.

"Don't you know better than to sleep in your O.D. shirt? Take it off."

"Yes, sir."

"What's your name?"

The man looked up, blinking, too dazed to speak.

"Don't know your own name, eh?" said the officer, glaring at the man savagely, using his curt voice like a whip.—"Quick, take off yer shirt and pants and get back to bed."

The Officer of the Day moved on, flashing his light to one side and the other in his midnight inspection of the barracks.

Intense blackness again, and the sound of men breathing deeply in sleep, of men snoring. As he went to sleep Fuselli could hear the man beside him swearing, monotonously, in an even whisper, pausing now and then to think of new filth, of new combinations of words, swearing away his helpless anger, soothing himself to sleep by the monotonous reiteration of his swearing.

A little later Fuselli woke with a choked nightmare cry. He had dreamed that he had smashed the O.D. in the jaw and had broken out of the jug and was running, breathless, stumbling, falling, while the company on guard chased him down an avenue lined with little dried-up saplings, gaining on him, while with voices metallic as the clicking of rifle triggers officers shouted orders, so that he was certain to be caught, certain to be shot. He shook himself all over, shaking off the nightmare as a dog shakes off water, and went back to sleep again, snuggling into his blankets.

II

Ｊoｈｎ Ａｎｄʀᴇᴡs stood naked in the center of a large bare room, of which the walls and ceiling and floor were made of raw pine boards. The air was heavy from the steam heat. At a desk in one corner a typewriter clicked spasmodically.

"Say, young feller, d'you know how to spell imbecility?"

John Andrews walked over to the desk, told him, and added, "Are you going to examine me?"

The man went on typewriting without answering. John Andrews stood in the center of the floor with his arms folded, half amused, half angry, shifting his weight from one foot to the other, listening to the sound of the typewriter and of the man's voice as he read out each word of the report he was copying.

"Recommendation for discharge" . . . click, click . . . "Damn this typewriter. . . . Private Coe Elbert" . . . click, click. "Damn these rotten army typewriters. . . . Reason . . . mental deficiency. History of Case. . . ."

At the moment the recruiting sergeant came back.

"Look here, if you don't have that recommendation ready in ten minutes Captain Arthurs'll be mad as hell about it, Bill. For God's sake get it done. He said already that if you couldn't do the work, to get somebody who could. You don't want to lose your job do you?"

"Hullo," the sergeant's eyes lit on John Andrews, "I'd forgotten you. Run around the room a little. . . . No, not that way. Just a little so I can test yer heart. . . . God, these rookies are thick."

While he stood tamely being prodded and measured, feeling like a prize horse at a fair, John Andrews listened to the man at the typewriter, whose voice went on monotonously.

"No . . . record of sexual dep. . . . O hell, this eraser's no good! . . . pravity or alcoholism; spent . . . normal . . . youth on farm. App-ear-ance normal though im . . . say, how many 'm's' in immature?"

"All right, put yer clothes on," said the recruiting sergeant. "Quick, I can't spend all day. Why the hell did they send you down here alone?"

"The papers were balled up," said Andrews.

"Scores ten years . . . in test B," went on the voice of the man at the typewriter. ". . . Sen . . . exal ment . . . m-e-n-t-a-l-i-t-y that of child of eight. Seems unable . . . to either. . . . Goddam this man's writin'. How kin I copy it when he don't write out his words?"

"All right. I guess you'll do. Now there are some forms to fill out. Come over here."

Andrews followed the recruiting sergeant to a desk in the far corner of the room, from which he could hear more faintly the click, click of the typewriter and the man's voice mumbling angrily.

"Forgets to obey orders. . . . Responds to no form of per . . . suasion. M-e-m-o-r-y, nil."

"All right. Take this to barracks B. . . . Fourth building, to the right; shake a leg," said the recruiting sergeant.

Andrews drew a deep breath of the sparkling air outside. He stood irresolutely a moment on the wooden steps of the building looking down the row of hastily constructed barracks. Some were painted green, some were of plain boards, and some were still mere skeletons. Above his head great piled, rose-tinted clouds were moving slowly across the immeasurable free sky. His glance slid down the sky to some tall trees that flamed bright yellow with autumn outside the camp limits, and then to the end of the long street of barracks, where was a picket fence and a sentry walking to and fro, to and fro. His brows contracted for a moment. Then he walked with a sort of swagger towards the fourth building to the right.

John Andrews was washing windows. He stood in dirty blue denims at the top of a ladder, smearing with a soapy cloth the small panes of the barrack windows. His nostrils were full of a smell of dust and of the sandy quality of the soap. A little man with one lined greyish-red cheek puffed out by tobacco followed him up also on a ladder, polishing the panes with a dry cloth till they shone and reflected the mottled cloudy sky. Andrews's legs were tired from climbing up and down the ladder, his hands were sore from the grittiness of the soap; as he worked he looked down, without thinking, on rows of cots where the blankets were all folded the same way, on some of which men were sprawled in attitudes of utter relaxation. He kept remarking to himself how strange it was that he was not thinking of anything. In the last few days his mind seemed to have become a hard meaningless core.

"How long do we have to do this?" he asked the man who was working with him. The man went on chewing, so that Andrews thought he was not going to answer at all. He was just beginning to speak again when the man, balancing thoughtfully on top of his ladder, drawled out:

"Four o'clock."

"We won't finish today then?"

The man shook his head and wrinkled his face into a strange spasm as he spat.

"Been here long?"

"Not so long."

"How long?"

"Three months. . . . Ain't so long." The man spat again, and climbing down from his ladder waited, leaning against the wall, until Andrews should finish soaping his window.

"I'll go crazy if I stay here three months. . . . I've been here a week," muttered Andrews between his teeth as he climbed down and moved his ladder to the next window.

They both climbed their ladders again in silence.

"How's it you're in Casuals?" asked Andrews again.

"Ain't got no lungs."

"Why don't they discharge you?"

"Reckon they're going to, soon."

They worked on in silence for a long time. Andrews stared at the upper right-hand corner and smeared with soap each pane of the window in turn. Then he climbed down, moved his ladder, and started on the next window. At times he would start in the middle of the window for variety. As he worked a rhythm began pushing its way through the hard core of his mind, leavening it, making it fluid. It expressed the vast dusty dullness, the men waiting in rows on drill fields, standing at attention, the monotony of feet tramping in unison, of the dust rising from the battalions going back and forth over the dusty drill fields. He felt the rhythm filling his whole body, from his sore hands to his legs, tired from marching back and

forth, from making themselves the same length as millions of
other legs. His mind began unconsciously, from habit, working on it, orchestrating it. He could imagine a vast orchestra
swaying with it. His heart was beating faster. He must make
it into music; he must fix it in himself, so that he could make
it into music and write it down, so that orchestras could play
it and make the ears of multitudes feel it, make their flesh tingle with it.

He went on working through the endless afternoon, climbing up and down his ladder, smearing the barrack windows
with a soapy rag. A silly phrase took the place of the welling
of music in his mind: "Arbeit und Rhythmus." He kept saying it over and over to himself: "Arbeit und Rhythmus." He
tried to drive the phrase out of his mind, to bury his mind in
the music of the rhythm that had come to him, that expressed
the dusty boredom, the harsh constriction of warm bodies full
of gestures and attitudes and aspirations into moulds, like the
moulds toy soldiers are cast in. The phrase became someone
shouting raucously in his ears: "Arbeit und Rhythmus,"—
drowning everything else, beating his mind hard again, parch-
ing it.

But suddenly he laughed aloud. Why, it was in German. He
was being got ready to kill men who said that. If anyone said
that, he was going to kill him. They were going to kill everybody who spoke that language, he and all the men whose feet
he could hear tramping on the drill field, whose legs were all
being made the same length on the drill field.

III

IT WAS Saturday morning. Directed by the corporal, a bandy-legged Italian who even on the army diet managed to keep a faint odour of garlic about him, three soldiers in blue denims were sweeping up the leaves in the street between the rows of barracks.

"You fellers are slow as molasses. . . . Inspection in twenty-five minutes," he kept saying.

The soldiers raked on doggedly, paying no attention.

"You don't give a damn. If we don't pass inspection, I get hell—not you. Please queeck. Here, you, pick up all those goddam cigarette butts."

Andrews made a grimace and began collecting the little grey sordid ends of burnt-out cigarettes. As he leant over he found himself looking into the dark-brown eyes of the soldier who was working beside him. The eyes were contracted with anger and there was a flush under the tan of the boyish face.

"Ah didn't git in this here army to be ordered around by a goddam wop," he muttered.

"Doesn't matter much who you're ordered around by, you're ordered around just the same," said Andrews.

"Where d'ye come from, buddy?"

"Oh, I come from New York. My folks are from Virginia," said Andrews.

"Indiana's ma state. The tornado country. . . . Git to work; here's that bastard wop comin' around the buildin'."

"Don't pick 'em up that-a-way; sweep 'em up," shouted the corporal.

Andrews and the Indiana boy went round with a broom and a shovel collecting chewed-out quids of tobacco and cigar butts and stained bits of paper.

"What's your name? Mahn's Chrisfield. Folks all call me Chris."

"Mine's Andrews, John Andrews."

"Ma dad uster have a hired man named Andy. Took sick an' died last summer. How long d'ye reckon it'll be before us-guys git overseas?"

"God, I don't know."

"Ah want to see that country over there."

"You do?"

"Don't you?"

"You bet I do."

"All right, what you fellers stand here for? Go an' dump them garbage cans. Lively!" shouted the corporal waddling about importantly on his bandy legs. He kept looking down the row of barracks, muttering to himself, "Goddam. . . . Time fur inspectin' now, goddam. Won't never pass this time."

His face froze suddenly into obsequious immobility. He brought his hand up to the brim of his hat. A group of officers strode past him into the nearest building.

John Andrews, coming back from emptying the garbage pails, went in the back door of his barracks.

"Attention!" came the cry from the other end. He made his neck and arms as rigid as possible.

Through the silent barracks came the hard clank of the heels of the officers inspecting.

A sallow face with hollow eyes and heavy square jaw came close to Andrews's eyes. He stared straight before him noting the few reddish hairs on the officer's Adam's apple and the new insignia on either side of his collar.

"Sergeant, who is this man?" came a voice from the sallow face.

"Don't know, sir; a new recruit, sir. Corporal Valori, who is this man?"

"The name's Andrews, sergeant," said the Italian corporal with an obsequious whine in his voice.

The officer addressed Andrews directly, speaking fast and loud.

"How long have you been in the army?"

"One week, sir."

"Don't you know you have to be clean and shaved and ready for inspection every Saturday morning at nine?"

"I was cleaning the barracks, sir."

"To teach you not to answer back when an officer addresses you. . . ." The officer spaced his words carefully, lingering on them. As he spoke he glanced out of the corner of his eye at his superior and noticed the major was frowning. His tone changed ever so slightly. "If this ever occurs again you may be sure that disciplinary action will be taken. . . . Attention there!" At the other end of the barracks a man had moved. Again, amid absolute silence, could be heard the clanking of the officers' heels as the inspection continued.

"Now, fellows, all together," cried the "Y" man who stood with his arms stretched wide in front of the movie screen. The piano started jingling and the roomful of crowded soldiers roared out:

> "Hail, Hail, the gang's all here;
>   We're going to get the Kaiser,
>   We're going to get the Kaiser,
>   We're going to get the Kaiser,
>   Now!"

The rafters rang with their deep voices.

The "Y" man twisted his lean face into a facetious expression.

"Somebody tried to put one over on the 'Y' man and sing 'What the hell do we care?' But you do care, don't you, Buddy?" he shouted.

There was a little rattle of laughter.

"Now, once more," said the "Y" man again, "and lots of guts in the get and lots of kill in the Kaiser. Now all together. . . ."

The moving pictures had begun. John Andrews looked furtively about him, at the face of the Indiana boy beside him intent on the screen, at the tanned faces and the close-cropped heads that rose above the mass of khaki-covered bodies about him. Here and there a pair of eyes glinted in the white flickering light from the screen. Waves of laughter or of little exclamations passed over them. They were all so alike, they seemed at moments to be but one organism. This was what he had sought when he had enlisted, he said to himself. It was in this that he would take refuge from the horror of the world that had fallen upon him. He was sick of revolt, of thought, of carrying his individuality like a banner above the turmoil. This was much better, to let everything go, to stamp out his maddening desire for music, to humble himself into the mud of common slavery. He was still tingling with sudden anger from the officer's voice that morning: "Sergeant, who is this man?" The officer had stared in his face, as a man might stare at a piece of furniture.

"Ain't this some film?" Chrisfield turned to him with a smile that drove his anger away in a pleasant feeling of comradeship.

"The part that's comin's fine. I seen it before out in Frisco," said the man on the other side of Andrews. "Gee, it makes ye hate the Huns."

The man at the piano jingled elaborately in the intermission between the two parts of the movie.

The Indiana boy leaned in front of John Andrews, putting an arm around his shoulders, and talked to the other man.

"You from Frisco?"

"Yare."

"That's goddam funny. You're from the Coast, this feller's from New York, an' Ah'm from ole Indiana, right in the middle."

"What company you in?"

"Ah ain't yet. This feller an me's in Casuals."

"That's a hell of a place. . . . Say, my name's Fuselli."

"Mahn's Chrisfield."

"Mine's Andrews."

"How soon's it take a feller to git out o' this camp?"

"Dunno. Some guys says three weeks and some says six months. . . . Say, mebbe you'll get into our company. They transferred a lot of men out the other day, an' the corporal says they're going to give us rookies instead."

"Goddam it, though, but Ah want to git overseas."

"It's swell over there," said Fuselli, "everything's awful pretty-like. Picturesque, they call it. And the people wears peasant costumes. . . . I had an uncle who used to tell me about it. He came from near Torino."

"Where's that?"

"I dunno. He's an Eyetalian."

"Say, how long does it take to git overseas?"

"Oh, a week or two," said Andrews.

"As long as that?" But the movie had begun again, unfolding scenes of soldiers in spiked helmets marching into Belgian cities full of little milk carts drawn by dogs and old women in peasant costume. There were hisses and catcalls when a German flag was seen, and as the troops were pictured advancing, bayonetting the civilians in wide Dutch pants, the old women with starched caps, the soldiers packed into the stuffy Y.M.C.A. hut shouted oaths at them. Andrews felt blind hatred stirring like something that had a life of its own in the young men about him. He was lost in it, carried away in it, as in a stampede of wild cattle. The terror of it was like ferocious hands clutching his throat. He glanced at the faces round him. They were all intent and flushed, glinting with sweat in the heat of the room.

As he was leaving the hut, pressed in a tight stream of soldiers moving towards the door, Andrews heard a man say:

"I never raped a woman in my life, but by God, I'm going to. I'd give a lot to rape some of those goddam German women."

"I hate 'em too," came another voice, "men, women, children and unborn children. They're either jackasses or full of the lust for power like their rulers are, to let themselves be governed by a bunch of warlords like that."

"Ah'd lahk te cepture a German officer an' make him shine ma boots an' then shoot him dead," said Chris to Andrews as they walked down the long row towards their barracks.

"You would?"

"But Ah'd a damn side rather shoot somebody else Ah know," went on Chris intensely. "Don't stay far from here either. An' Ah'll do it too, if he don't let off pickin' on me."

"Who's that?"

"That big squirt Anderson they made a file closer at drill yesterday. He seems te think that just because Ah'm littler than him he can do anything he likes with me."

Andrews turned sharply and looked in his companion's face; something in the gruffness of the boy's tone startled him. He was not accustomed to this. He had thought of himself as a passionate person, but never in his life had he wanted to kill a man.

"D'you really want to kill him?"

"Not now, but he gits the hell started in me, the way he teases me. Ah pulled ma knife on him yisterday. You wasn't there. Didn't ye notice Ah looked sort o' upsot at drill?"

"Yes . . . but how old are you, Chris?"

"Ah'm twenty. You're older than me, ain't yer?"

"I'm twenty-two."

They were leaning against the wall of their barracks, looking up at the brilliant starry night.

"Say, is the stars the same over there, overseas, as they is here?"

"I guess so," said Andrews, laughing. "Though I've never been to see."

"Ah never had much schoolin'," went on Chris. "I lef' school when I was twelve, 'cause it warn't much good, an' dad drank so the folks needed me to work on the farm."

"What do you grow in your part of the country?"

"Mostly coan. A little wheat an' tobacca. Then we raised a lot o' stock. . . . But Ah was juss going to tell ye Ah nearly did kill a guy once."

"Tell me about it."

"Ah was drunk at the time. Us boys round Tallyville was a pretty tough bunch then. We used ter work juss long enough to git some money to tear things up with. An' then we used to play craps an' drink whiskey. This happened just at coan-shuckin' time. Hell, Ah don't even know what it was about, but Ah got to quarrellin' with a feller Ah'd been right smart friends with. Then he laid off an' hit me in the jaw. Ah don't know what Ah done next, but before Ah knowed it Ah had a hold of a shuckin' knife and was slashin' at him with it. A knife like that's a turruble thing to stab a man with. It took four of 'em to hold me down an' git it away from me. They didn't keep me from givin' him a good cut across the chest, though. Ah was juss crazy drunk at the time. An' man, if Ah wasn't a mess to go home, with half ma clothes pulled off and ma shirt torn. Ah juss fell in the ditch an' slep' there till daylight an' got mud all through ma hair. . . . Ah don't scarcely tech a drop now, though."

"So you're in a hurry to get overseas, Chris, like me," said Andrews after a long pause.

"Ah'll push that guy Anderson into the sea, if we both go over on the same boat," said Chrisfield laughing; but he added after a pause: "It would have been hell if Ah'd killed that feller, though. Honest Ah wouldn't a-wanted to do that."

*

"That's the job that pays, a violinist," said somebody.

"No, it don't," came a melancholy drawling voice from a lanky man who sat doubled up with his long face in his hands and his elbows resting on his knees. "Just brings a living wage . . . a living wage."

Several men were grouped at the end of the barracks. From them the long row of cots, with here and there a man asleep or a man hastily undressing, stretched, lighted by occasional feeble electric-light bulbs, to the sergeant's little table beside the door.

"You're gettin' a dis-charge, aren't you?" asked a man with a brogue, and the red face of a jovial gorilla, that signified the bartender.

"Yes, Flannagan, I am," said the lanky man dolefully.

"Ain't he got hard luck?" came a voice from the crowd.

"Yes, I have got hard luck, Buddy," said the lanky man, looking at the faces about him out of sunken eyes. "I ought to be getting forty dollars a week and here I am getting seven and in the army besides."

"I meant that you were gettin' out of this goddam army."

"The army, the army, the democratic army," chanted someone under his breath.

"But, begorry, I want to go overseas and 'ave a look at the 'uns," said Flannagan, who managed with strange skill to combine a cockney whine with his Irish brogue.

"Overseas?" took up the lanky man. "If I could have gone an' studied overseas, I'd be making as much as Kubelik. I had the makings of a good player in me."

"Why don't you go?" asked Andrews, who stood on the outskirts with Fuselli and Chris.

"Look at me . . . t.b.," said the lanky man.

"Well, they can't get me over there soon enough," said Flannagan.

"Must be funny not bein' able to understand what folks say. They say 'we' over there when they mean 'yes,' a guy told me."

"Ye can make signs to them, can't ye?" said Flannagan, "an' they can understand an Irishman anywhere. But ye won't 'ave to talk to the 'uns. Begorry I'll set up in business when I get there, what d'ye think of that?"

Everybody laughed.

"How'd that do? I'll start an Irish House in Berlin, I will, and there'll be O'Casey and O'Ryan and O'Reilly and O'Flarrety, and begod the King of England himself'll come an' set the goddam Kaiser up to a drink."

"The Kaiser'll be strung up on a telephone pole by that time; ye needn't worry, Flannagan."

"They ought to torture him to death, like they do niggers when they lynch 'em down south."

A bugle sounded far away outside on the parade ground. Everyone slunk away silently to his cot.

John Andrews arranged himself carefully in his blankets, promising himself a quiet time of thought before going to sleep. He needed to lie awake and think at night this way, so that he might not lose entirely the thread of his own life, of the life he would take up again some day if he lived through it. He brushed away the thought of death. It was uninteresting. He didn't care anyway. But some day he would want to play the piano again, to write music. He must not let himself sink too deeply into the helpless mentality of the soldier. He must keep his will power.

No, but that was not what he had wanted to think about. He was so bored with himself. At any cost he must forget himself. Ever since his first year at college he seemed to have done nothing but think about himself, talk about himself. At least at the bottom, in the utterest degradation of slavery, he could find forgetfulness and start rebuilding the fabric of his life, out of real things this time, out of work and comradeship and scorn. Scorn—that was the quality he needed. It was such a raw, fantastic world he had suddenly fallen into. His life before this week seemed a dream read in a novel, a picture he had seen in a shop window—it was so different. Could it have been in the same world at all? He must have died without knowing it and been born again into a new, futile hell.

When he had been a child he had lived in a dilapidated mansion that stood among old oaks and chestnuts, beside a road where buggies and oxcarts passed rarely to disturb the sandy ruts that lay in the mottled shade. He had had so many dreams; lying under the crêpe-myrtle bush at the end of the overgrown garden he had passed the long Virginia afternoons, thinking, while the dryflies whizzed sleepily in the sunlight, of the world he would live in when he grew up. He had planned so many lives for himself: a general, like Caesar, he was to conquer the world and die murdered in a great marble hall; a wandering minstrel, he would go through all countries singing and have intricate endless adventures; a great musician, he would sit at the piano playing, like Chopin in the engraving, while beautiful women wept and men with long, curly hair hid their faces in their hands. It was only slavery that he had not foreseen. His race had dominated for too many centuries for that. And yet the world was made of various slaveries.

John Andrews lay on his back on his cot while everyone about him slept and snored in the dark barracks. A certain terror held him. In a week the great structure of his romantic world, so full of many colors and harmonies, that had survived school and college and the buffeting of making a living in New York, had fallen in dust about him. He was utterly in the void. "How silly," he thought; "this is the world as it has appeared to the majority of men, this is just the lower half of the pyramid."

He thought of his friends, of Fuselli and Chrisfield and that funny little man Eisenstein. They seemed at home in this army life. They did not seem appalled by the loss of their liberty. But they had never lived in the glittering other world. Yet he could not feel the scorn of them he wanted to feel. He thought of them singing under the direction of the "Y" man:

> "Hail, Hail, the gang's all here;
> We're going to get the Kaiser,
> We're going to get the Kaiser,
> We're going to get the Kaiser,
> Now!"

He thought of himself and Chrisfield picking up cigarette butts and the tramp, tramp, tramp of feet on the drill field. Where was the connection? Was this all futile madness? They'd come from such various worlds, all these men sleeping about him, to be united in this. And what did they think of it, all these sleepers? Had they too not had dreams when they were boys? Or had the generations prepared them only for this?

He thought of himself lying under the crêpe-myrtle bush through the hot, droning afternoon, watching the pale magenta flowers flutter down into the dry grass, and felt, again, wrapped in his warm blankets among all these sleepers, the straining of limbs burning with desire to rush untrammelled through some new keen air. Suddenly darkness overspread his mind.

He woke with a start. The bugle was blowing outside. "All right, look lively!" the sergeant was shouting. Another day.

IV

THE STARS were very bright when Fuselli, eyes stinging with sleep, stumbled out of the barracks. They trembled like bits of brilliant jelly in the back velvet of the sky, just as something inside him trembled with excitement.

"Anybody know where the electricity turns on?" asked the sergeant in a good-humored voice. "Here it is." The light over the door of the barracks snapped on, revealing a rotund cheerful man with a little yellow mustache and an unlit cigarette dangling out of the corner of his mouth. Grouped about him, in overcoats and caps, the men of the company rested their packs against their knees.

"All right; line up, men."

Eyes looked curiously at Fuselli as he lined up with the rest. He had been transferred into the company the night before.

"Attenshun," shouted the sergeant. Then he wrinkled up his eyes and grinned hard at the slip of paper he had in his hand, while the men of his company watched him affectionately.

"Answer 'Here' when your name is called. Allan, B. C."

"Yo!" came a shrill voice from the end of the line.

"Anspach."

"Here."

Meanwhile outside the other barracks other companies could be heard calling the roll. Somewhere from the end of the street came a cheer.

"Well, I guess I can tell you now, fellers," said the sergeant with his air of quiet omniscience, when he had called the last name. "We're going overseas."

Everybody cheered.

"Shut up, you don't want the Huns to hear us, do you?"

The company laughed, and there was a broad grin on the sergeant's round face.

"Seem to have a pretty decent top-kicker," whispered Fuselli to the man next to him.

"You bet yer, kid, he's a peach," said the other man in a voice full of devotion. "This is some company, I can tell you that."

"You bet it is," said the next man along. "The corporal's in the Red Sox outfield."

The lieutenant appeared suddenly in the area of light in front of the barracks. He was a pink-faced boy. His trench coat, a little too large, was very new and stuck out stiffly from his legs.

"Everything all right, sergeant? Everything all right?" he asked several times, shifting his weight from one foot to the other.

"All ready for entrainment, sir," said the sergeant heartily.

"Very good, I'll let you know the order of march in a minute."

Fuselli's ears pounded with strange excitement. These phrases, "entrainment," "order of march," had a businesslike sound. He suddenly started to wonder how it would feel to be under fire. Memories of movies flickered in his mind.

"Gawd, ain't I glad to git out o' this hell-hole," he said to the man next him.

"The next one may be more of a hell-hole yet, buddy," said the sergeant striding up and down with his important confident walk.

Everybody laughed.

"He's some sergeant, our sergeant is," said the man next to Fuselli. "He's got brains in his head, that boy has."

"All right, break ranks," said the sergeant, "but if anybody moves away from this barracks, I'll put him in K.P. till—till he'll be able to peel spuds in his sleep."

The company laughed again. Fuselli noticed with displeasure that the tall man with the shrill voice whose name had been called first on the roll did not laugh but spat disgustedly out of the corner of his mouth.

"Well, there are bad eggs in every good bunch," thought Fuselli.

It gradually grew grey with dawn. Fuselli's legs were tired from standing so long. Outside all the barracks, as far as he could see up the street, men stood in ragged lines waiting.

The sun rose hot on a cloudless day. A few sparrows twittered about the tin roof of the barracks.

"Hell, we're not goin' this day."

"Why?" asked somebody savagely.

"Troops always leaves at night."

"The hell they do!"

"Here comes Sarge."

Everybody craned their necks in the direction pointed out. The sergeant strolled up with a mysterious smile on his face.

"Put away your overcoats and get out your mess kits."

Mess kits clattered and gleamed in the slanting rays of the sun. They marched to the mess hall and back again, lined up again with packs and waited some more.

Everybody began to get tired and peevish. Fuselli wondered where his old friends of the other company were. They were good kids too, Chris and that educated fellow, Andrews. Tough luck they couldn't have come along.

The sun rose higher. Men sneaked into the barracks one by one and lay down on the bare cots.

"What you want to bet we won't leave this camp for a week yet?" asked someone.

At noon they lined up for mess again, ate dismally and hurriedly. As Fuselli was leaving the mess hall tapping a tattoo on his kit with two dirty finger nails, the corporal spoke to him in a low voice.

"Be sure to wash yer kit, buddy. We may have pack inspection."

The corporal was a slim yellow-faced man with a wrinkled skin, though he was still young, and an arrow-shaped mouth that opened and shut like the paper mouths children make.

"All right, corporal," Fuselli answered cheerfully. He wanted to make a good impression. "Fellers'll be sayin' 'All right, corporal,' to me soon," he thought. An idea that he repelled came into his mind. The corporal didn't look strong. He wouldn't last long overseas. And he pictured Mabe writing Corporal Dan Fuselli, O.A.R.D.5.

At the end of the afternoon, the lieutenant appeared suddenly, his face flushed, his trench coat stiffer than ever.

"All right, sergeant; line up your men," he said in a breathless voice.

All down the camp street companies were forming. One by one they marched out in columns of fours and halted with their packs on. The day was getting amber with sunset. Retreat sounded.

Fuselli's mind had suddenly become very active. The notes of the bugle and of the band playing "The Star Spangled Banner" sifted into his consciousness through a dream of what it would be like over there. He was in a place like the Exposition ground, full of old men and women in peasant costume, like in the song, "When It's Apple Blossom Time in Normandy." Men in spiked helmets who looked like firemen kept charging through, like the Ku-Klux Klan in the movies, jumping from their horses and setting fire to buildings with strange outlandish gestures, spitting babies on their long swords. Those were the Huns. Then there were flags blowing very hard in the wind, and the sound of a band. The Yanks were coming. Everything was lost in a scene from a movie in which khaki-clad regiments marched fast, fast across the scene. The memory of the shouting that always accompanied it drowned out the picture. "The guns must make a racket, though," he added as an after-thought.

"Atten-shun!"

"Forwa-ard, march!"

The long street of the camp was full of the tramping of feet. They were off. As they passed through the gate Fuselli caught a glimpse of Chris standing with his arm about Andrews's shoulders. They both waved. Fuselli grinned and expanded his chest. They were just rookies still. He was going overseas.

The weight of the pack tugged at his shoulders and made his feet heavy as if they were charged with lead. The sweat ran down his close-clipped head under the overseas cap and streamed into his eyes and down the sides of his nose. Through the tramp of feet he heard confusedly cheering from the sidewalk. In front of him the backs of heads and the swaying packs got smaller, rank by rank up the street. Above them flags dangled from windows, flags leisurely swaying in the twilight. But the weight of the pack, as the column marched under arc lights glaring through the afterglow, inevitably forced his head to droop forward. The soles of boots and legs wrapped in puttees and the bottom strap of the pack of the man ahead of him were all he could see. The pack seemed heavy enough to push him through the asphalt pavement. And all about him was the faint jingle of equipment and the tramp of feet. Every part of him was full of sweat. He could feel vaguely the steam of sweat that rose from the ranks of struggling bodies about him. But gradually he forgot everything but the pack tugging at his shoulders, weighing down his thighs and ankles and feet, and the monotonous rhythm of his feet striking the pavement and of the other feet, in front of him, behind him, beside him, crunching, crunching.

The train smelt of new uniforms on which the sweat had dried, and of the smoke of cheap cigarettes. Fuselli awoke with a start. He had been asleep with his head on Bill Grey's shoulder. It was already broad daylight. The train was jolting slowly over cross-tracks in some dismal suburb, full of long soot-smeared warehouses and endless rows of freight cars, beyond which lay brown marshland and slate-grey stretches of water.

"God! that must be the Atlantic Ocean," cried Fuselli in excitement.

"Ain't yer never seen it before? That's the Perth River," said Bill Grey scornfully.

"No, I come from the Coast."

They stuck their heads out of the window side by side so that their cheeks touched.

"Gee, there's some skirts," said Bill Grey. The train jolted to a stop. Two untidy red-haired girls were standing beside the track waving their hands.

"Give us a kiss," cried Bill Grey.

"Sure," said a girl,—"anythin' fer one of our boys."

She stood on tiptoe and Grey leaned far out of the window, just managing to reach the girl's forehead.

Fuselli felt a flush of desire all over him.

"Hol' onter my belt," he said. "I'll kiss her right."

He leaned far out, and, throwing his arms around the girl's pink gingham shoulders, lifted her off the ground and kissed her furiously on the lips.

"Lemme go, lemme go," cried the girl.

Men leaning out of the other windows of the car cheered and shouted.

Fuselli kissed her again and then dropped her.

"Ye're too rough, damn ye," said the girl angrily.

A man from one of the windows yelled, "I'll go an' tell mommer"; and everybody laughed. The train moved on. Fuselli looked about him proudly. The image of Mabe giving him the five-pound box of candy rose a moment in his mind.

"Ain't no harm in havin' a little fun. Don't mean nothin'," he said aloud.

"You just wait till we hit France. We'll hit it up some with the Madimerzels, won't we, kid?" said Bill Grey, slapping Fuselli on the knee.

> "Beautiful Katy,
> Ki-Ki-Katy,
> You're the only gugugu-girl that I adore;
> And when the mo-moon shines
> Over the cowshed,
> I'll be waiting at the ki-ki-ki-kitchen door."

Everybody sang as the thumping of wheels over rails grew faster. Fuselli looked about contentedly at the company sprawling over their packs and equipment in the smoky car.

"It's great to be a soldier," he said to Bill Grey. "Ye kin do anything ye goddam please."

"This," said the corporal, as the company filed into barracks identical to those they had left two days before, "is an embarkation camp, but I'd like to know where the hell we embark at." He twisted his face into a smile, and then shouted with lugubrious intonation: "Fall in for mess."

It was pitch dark in that part of the camp. The electric lights had a sparse reddish glow. Fuselli kept straining his eyes, expecting to see a wharf and the masts of a ship at the end of every alley. The line filed into a dim mess hall, where a thin stew was splashed into the mess kits. Behind the counter of the kitchen the non-coms, the jovial first sergeant, and the business-like sergeant who looked like a preacher, and the wrinkled-faced corporal who had been on the Red Sox outfield, could be seen eating steak. A faint odor of steak frying went through the mess hall and made the thin chilly stew utterly tasteless in comparison.

Fuselli looked enviously towards the kitchen and thought of the day when he would be a non-com too. "I got to get busy," he said to himself earnestly. Overseas, under fire, he'd have a chance to show what he was worth; and he pictured himself heroically carrying a wounded captain back to a dressing tent, pursued by fierce-whiskered men with spiked helmets like fire-men's helmets.

The strumming of a guitar came strangely down the dark street of the camp.

"Some guy sure can play," said Bill Grey who, with his hands in his pockets, slouched along beside Fuselli.

They looked in the door of one of the barracks. A lot of soldiers were sitting in a ring round two tall negroes whose black faces and chests glistened like jet in the faint light. "Come on, Charley, give us another," said someone.

"Do Ah git it now, or mus' Ah hesit-ate?"

One negro began chanting while the other strummed care-lessly on the guitar.

"No, give us the 'Titanic.'"

The guitar strummed in a crooning rag-time for a moment. The negro's voice broke into it suddenly, pitched high.

"Dis is de song ob de Titanic,
Sailin' on de sea."

The guitar strummed on. There had been a tension in the negro's voice that had made everyone stop talking. The soldiers looked at him curiously.

"How de Titanic ran in dat cole iceberg,
How de Titanic ran in dat cole iceberg
Sailin' on de sea."

His voice was confidential and soft, and the guitar strummed to the same sobbing rag-time. Verse after verse the voice grew louder and the strumming faster.

"De Titanic's sinkin' in de deep blue,
Sinkin' in de deep blue, deep blue,
Sinkin' in de sea.
O de women an' de chilen a-floatin' in de sea,
O de women an' de chilen a-floatin' in de sea,
Roun' dat cole iceberg,
Sung 'Nearer, my gawd, to Thee,'
Sung 'Nearer, my gawd, to Thee,
Nearer to Thee.'"

The guitar was strumming the hymn-tune. The negro was singing with every cord in his throat taut, almost sobbing.

A man next to Fuselli took careful aim and spat into the box of sawdust in the middle of the ring of motionless soldiers.

The guitar played the rag-time again, fast, almost mockingly. The negro sang in low confidential tones.

"O de women an' de chilen dey sank in de sea.

O de women an' de chilen dey sank in de sea,

Roun' dat cole iceberg."

Before he had finished a bugle blew in the distance. Everybody scattered.

Fuselli and Bill Grey went silently back to their barracks.

"It must be an awful thing to drown in the sea," said Grey as he rolled himself in his blankets. "If one of those bastard U-boats . . ."

"I don't give a damn," said Fuselli boisterously; but as he lay staring into the darkness, cold terror stiffened him suddenly. He thought for a moment of deserting, pretending he was sick, anything to keep from going on the transport.

"O de women an' de chilen dey sank in de sea,

Roun' dat cole iceberg."

He could feel himself going down through icy water. "It's a hell of a thing to send a guy over there to drown," he said to himself, and he thought of the hilly streets of San Francisco, and the glow of the sunset over the harbor and ships coming in through the Golden Gate. His mind went gradually blank and he went to sleep.

The column was like some curious khaki-colored carpet, hiding the road as far as you could see. In Fuselli's company the men were shifting their weight from one foot to the other, muttering, "What the hell a' they waiting for now?" Bill Grey, next to Fuselli in the ranks, stood bent double so as to take the weight of his pack off his shoulders. They were at a cross-roads on fairly high ground so that they could see the long sheds and barracks of the camp stretching away in every direction, in rows and rows, broken now and then by a grey drill field. In front of them the column stretched to the last

bend in the road, where it disappeared on a hill among mus-
tard-yellow suburban houses.

Fuselli was excited. He kept thinking of the night before,
when he had helped the sergeant distribute emergency rations, and had carried about piles of boxes of hard bread,
counting them carefully without a mistake. He felt full of desire to do things, to show what he was good for. "Gee," he
said to himself, "this war's a lucky thing for me. I might have
been in the R.C. Vicker Company's store for five years an'
never got a raise. An' here in the army I got a chance to do
almost anything."

Far ahead down the road the column was beginning to
move. Voices shouting orders beat crisply on the morning air.
Fuselli's heart was thumping. He felt proud of himself and of
the company—the damn best company in the whole outfit.
The company ahead was moving, it was their turn now.

"Forwa-ard, march!"

They were lost in the monotonous tramp of feet. Dust rose
from the road, along which like a drab brown worm crawled
the column.

A sickening unfamiliar smell choked their nostrils.

"What are they taking us down here for?"

"Damned if I know."

They were filing down ladders into the terrifying pit which
the hold of the ship seemed to them. Every man had a blue
card in his hand with a number on it. In a dim place like an
empty warehouse they stopped. The sergeant shouted out:

"I guess this is our diggings. We'll have to make the best of
it." Then he disappeared.

Fuselli looked about him. He was sitting in one of the lowest of three tiers of bunks roughly built of new pine boards.
Electric lights placed here and there gave a faint reddish tone
to the gloom, except at the ladders, where high-power lamps
made a white glare. The place was full of tramping of feet and
the sound of packs being thrown on bunks as endless files of
soldiers poured in down every ladder. Somewhere down the
alley an officer with a shrill voice was shouting to his men:
"Speed it up there; speed it up there." Fuselli sat on his bunk
looking at the terrifying confusion all about, feeling bewil-

dered and humiliated. For how many days would they be in that dark pit? He suddenly felt angry. They had no right to treat a feller like that. He was a man, not a bale of hay to be bundled about as anybody liked.

"An' if we're torpedoed a fat chance we'll have down here," he said aloud.

"They got sentries posted to keep us from goin' up on deck," said someone.

"God damn them. They treat you like you was a steer being taken over for meat."

"Well, you're not a damn sight more. Meat for the guns."

A little man lying in one of the upper bunks had spoken suddenly, contracting his sallow face into a curious spasm, as if the words had burst from him in spite of an effort to keep them in.

Everybody looked up at him angrily.

"That goddam kike Eisenstein," muttered someone.

"Say, tie that bull outside," shouted Bill Grey good-naturedly.

"Fools," muttered Eisenstein, turning over and burying his face in his hands.

"Gee, I wonder what it is makes it smell so funny down here," said Fuselli.

Fuselli lay flat on deck resting his head on his crossed arms. When he looked straight up he could see a lead-colored mast sweep back and forth across the sky full of clouds of light grey and silver and dark purplish-grey showing yellowish at the edges. When he tilted his head a little to one side he could see Bill Grey's heavy colorless face and the dark bristles of his unshaven chin and his mouth a little twisted to the left, from which a cigarette dangled unlighted. Beyond were heads and bodies huddled together in a mass of khaki overcoats and life preservers. And when the roll tipped the deck he had a view of moving green waves and of a steamer striped grey and white, and the horizon, a dark taut line, broken here and there by the tops of waves.

"O God, I feel sick," said Bill Grey, taking the cigarette out of his mouth and looking at it revengefully.

"I'd be all right if everything didn't stink so. An' that mess hall. Nearly makes a guy puke to think of it." Fuselli spoke in a whining voice, watching the top of the mast move, like a pencil scrawling on paper, back and forth across the mottled clouds.

"You belly-achin' again?" A brown moon-shaped face with thick black eyebrows and hair curling crisply about a forehead with many horizontal wrinkles rose from the deck on the other side of Fuselli.

"Get the hell out of here."

"Feel sick, sonny?" came the deep voice again, and the dark eyebrows contracted in an expression of sympathy. "Funny, I'd have my sixshooter out if I was home and you told me to get the hell out, sonny."

"Well, who wouldn't be sore when they have to go on K.P.?" said Fuselli peevishly.

"I ain't been down to mess in three days. A feller who lives on the plains like I do ought to take to the sea like a duck, but it don't seem to suit me."

"God, they're a sick lookin' bunch I have to sling the hash to," said Fuselli more cheerfully. "I don't know how they get that way. The fellers in our company ain't that way. They look like they was askeered somebody was going to hit 'em. Ever noticed that, Meadville?"

"Well, what d'ye expect of you guys who live in the city all your lives and don't know the butt from the barrel of a gun an' never straddled anything more like a horse than a broomstick. Ye're juss made to be sheep. No wonder they have to herd you round like calves." Meadville got to his feet and went unsteadily to the rail, keeping, as he threaded his way through the groups that covered the transport's after deck, a little of his cowboy's bow-legged stride.

"I know what it is that makes men's eyes blink when they go down to that putrid mess," came a nasal voice.

Fuselli turned round.

Eisenstein was sitting in the place Meadville had just left.

"You do, do you?"

"It's part of the system. You've got to turn men into beasts before ye can get 'em to act that way. Ever read Tolstoi?"

"No. Say, you want to be careful how you go talkin' around the way you do." Fuselli lowered his voice confidentially. "I heard of a feller bein' shot at Camp Merritt for talkin' around."

"I don't care. . . . I'm a desperate man," said Eisenstein.

"Don't ye feel sick? Gawd, I do. . . . Did you get rid o' any of it, Meadville?"

"Why don't they fight their ole war somewhere a man can get to on a horse? . . . Say that's my seat."

"The place was empty. . . . I sat down in it," said Eisenstein, lowering his head sullenly.

"You kin have three winks to get out o' my place," said Meadville, squaring his broad shoulders.

"You are stronger than me," said Eistenstein, moving off.

"God, it's hell not to have a gun," muttered Meadville as he settled himself on the deck again. "D'ye know, sonny, I nearly cried when I found I was going to be in this damn medical corps? I enlisted for the tanks. This is the first time in my life I haven't had a gun. I even think I had one in my cradle."

"That's funny," said Fuselli.

The sergeant appeared suddenly in the middle of the group, his face red.

"Say, fellers," he said in a low voice, "go down an' straighten out the bunks as fast as you goddam can. They're having an inspection. It's a hell of a note."

They all filed down the gang planks into the foul-smelling hold, where there was no light but the invariable reddish glow of electric bulbs. They had hardly reached their bunks when someone called, "Attention!"

Three officers stalked by, their firm important tread a little disturbed by the rolling. Their heads were stuck forward and they peered from side to side among the bunks with the cruel, searching glance of hens looking for worms.

"Fuselli," said the first sergeant, "bring up the record book to my stateroom; 213 on the lower deck.

"All right, Sarge," said Fuselli with alacrity. He admired the first sergeant and wished he could imitate his jovial, domineering manner.

It was the first time he had been in the upper part of the ship. It seemed a different world. The long corridors with red carpets, the white paint and the gilt mouldings on the partitions, the officers strolling about at their ease—it all made him think of the big liners he used to watch come in through the Golden Gate, the liners he was going to Europe on some day, when he got rich. Oh, if he could only get to be a sergeant first-class, all this comfort and magnificence would be his. He found the number and knocked on the door. Laughter and loud talking came from inside the stateroom.

"Wait a sec!" came an unfamiliar voice.

"Sergeant Olster here?"

"Oh, it's one o' my gang," came the sergeant's voice. "Let him in. He won't peach on us."

The door opened and he saw Sergeant Olster and two other young men sitting with their feet dangling over the red varnished boards that enclosed the bunks. They were talking gaily, and had glasses in their hands.

"Paris is some town, I can tell you," one was saying. "They say the girls come up an' put their arms round you right in the main street."

"Here's the records, sergeant," said Fuselli stiffly in his best military manner.

"Oh thanks. . . . There's nothing else I want," said the sergeant, his voice more jovial than ever. "Don't fall overboard like the guy in Company C."

Fuselli laughed as he closed the door, growing serious suddenly on noticing that one of the young men wore in his shirt the gold bar of a second lieutenant.

"Gee," he said to himself. "I ought to have saluted."

He waited a moment outside the closed door of the stateroom, listening to the talk and the laughter, wishing he were one of that merry group talking about women in Paris. He began thinking. Sure he'd get private first-class as soon as they got overseas. Then in a couple of months he might be corporal. If they saw much service, he'd move along all right, once he got to be a non-com.

"Oh, I mustn't get in wrong. Oh, I mustn't get in wrong," he kept saying to himself as he went down the ladder into the hold. But he forgot everything in the sea-sickness that came on again as he breathed in the fetid air.

The deck now slanted down in front of him, now rose so that he was walking up an incline. Dirty water slushed about from one side of the passage to the other with every lurch of the ship. When he reached the door the whistling howl of the wind through the hinges and cracks made Fuselli hesitate a long time with his hand on the knob. The moment he turned the knob the door flew open and he was in the full sweep of the wind. The deck was deserted. The wet ropes strung along it shivered dismally in the wind. Every other moment came the rattle of spray, that rose up in white fringy trees to windward and smashed against him like hail. Without closing the door he crept forward along the deck, clinging as hard as he could to the icy rope. Beyond the spray he could see huge marbled green waves rise in constant succession out of the mist. The roar of the wind in his ears confused him and terrified him. It seemed ages before he reached the door of the forward house that opened on a passage that smelt of drugs and breathed out air, where men waited in a packed line, thrown one against the other by the lurching of the boat, to get into the dispensary. The roar of the wind came to them faintly, and only now and then the hollow thump of a wave against the bow.

"You sick?" a man asked Fuselli.

"Naw, I'm not sick; but Sarge sent me to get some stuff for some guys that's too sick to move."

"An awful lot o' sickness on this boat."

"Two fellers died this mornin' in that there room," said another man solemnly, pointing over his shoulder with a jerk of the thumb. "Ain't buried 'em yet. It's too rough."

"What'd they die of?" asked Fuselli eagerly.

"Spinal somethin'. . . ."

"Menegitis," broke in a man at the end of the line.

"Say, that's awful catchin' ain't it?"

"It sure is."

"Where does it hit yer?" asked Fuselli.

"Yer neck swells up, an' then you juss go stiff all over," came the man's voice from the end of the line.

There was a silence. From the direction of the infirmary a man with a packet of medicines in his hand began making his way towards the door.

"Many guys in there?" asked Fuselli in a low voice as the man brushed past him.

"Right smart . . ." The rest of the man's words were caught away in the shriek of the wind when he opened the door.

When the door closed again the man beside Fuselli, who was tall and broad shouldered with heavy black eyebrows, burst out, as if he were saying something he'd been trying to keep from saying for a long while:

"It won't be right if that sickness gets me; indeed it won't. . . . I've got a girl waitin' for me at home. It's two years since I ain't touched a woman all on account of her. It ain't natural for a fellow to go so long as that."

"Why didn't you marry her before you left?" somebody asked mockingly.

"Said she didn't want to be no war bride, that she could wait for me better if I didn't."

Several men laughed.

"It wouldn't be right if I took sick an' died of this sickness, after keepin' myself clean on account of that girl. . . . It wouldn't be right," the man muttered again to Fuselli.

Fuselli was picturing himself lying in his bunk with a swollen neck, while his arms and legs stiffened, stiffened.

A red-faced man half way up the passage started speaking:

"When I thinks to myself how much the folks need me home, it makes me feel sort o' confident-like, I dunno why. I juss can't cash in my checks, that's all." He laughed jovially.

No one joined in the laugh.

"Is it awfully catchin'?" asked Fuselli of the man next him.

"Most catchin' thing there is," he answered solemnly.

"The worst of it is," another man was muttering in a shrill hysterical voice, "bein' thrown over to the sharks. Gee, they ain't got a right to do that, even if it is war time, they ain't got a right to treat a Christian like he was a dead dawg."

"They got a right to do anythin' they goddam please, buddy. Who's goin' to stop 'em I'd like to know," cried the red-faced man.

"If he was an awficer, they wouldn't throw him over like that," came the shrill hysterical voice again.

"Cut that," said someone else, "no use gettin' in wrong juss for the sake of talkin'."

"But ain't it dangerous, waitin' round up here so near

where those fellers are with that sickness," whispered Fuselli to the man next him.

"Reckon it is, buddy," came the other man's voice dully.

Fuselli started making his way toward the door.

"Lemme out, fellers, I've got to puke," he said. "Shoot," he was thinking, "I'll tell 'em the place was closed; they'll never come to look."

As he opened the door he thought of himself crawling back to his bunk and feeling his neck swell and his hands burn with fever and his arms and legs stiffen until everything would be effaced in the blackness of death. But the roar of the wind and the lash of the spray as he staggered back along the deck drowned all other thought.

Fuselli and another man carried the dripping garbage-can up the ladder that led up from the mess hall. It smelt of rancid grease and coffee grounds and greasy juice trickled over their fingers as they struggled with it. At last they burst out on to the deck where a free wind blew out of the black night. They staggered unsteadily to the rail and emptied the pail into the darkness. The splash was lost in the sound of the waves and of churned water fleeing along the sides. Fuselli leaned over the rail and looked down at the faint phosphorescence that was the only light in the whole black gulf. He had never seen such darkness before. He clutched hold of the rail with both hands, feeling lost and terrified in the blackness, in the roaring of the wind in his ears and the sound of churned water fleeing astern. The alternative was the stench of below decks.

"I'll bring down the rosie, don't you bother," he said to the other man, kicking the can that gave out a ringing sound as he spoke.

He strained his eyes to make out something. The darkness seemed to press in upon his eyeballs, blinding him. Suddenly he noticed voices near him. Two men were talking.

"I ain't never seen the sea before this, I didn't know it was like this."

"We're in the zone, now."

"That means we may go down any minute."

"Yare."

"Christ, how black it is. . . . It'ld be awful to drown in the dark like this."

"It'ld be over soon."

"Say, Fred, have you ever been so skeered that . . . ?"

"D'you feel a-skeert?"

"Feel my hand, Fred. . . . No . . . There it is. God, it's so hellish black you can't see yer own hand."

"It's cold. Why are you shiverin' so? God, I wish I had a drink."

"I ain't never seen the sea before . . . I didn't know . . ."

Fuselli heard distinctly the man's teeth chattering in the darkness.

"God, pull yerself together, kid. You can't be skeered like this."

"O God."

There was a long pause. Fuselli heard nothing but the churned water speeding along the ship's side and the wind roaring in his ears.

"I ain't never seen the sea before this time, Fred, an' it sort o' gits my goat, all this sickness an' all. . . . They dropped three of 'em overboard yesterday."

"Hell, kid, don't think of it."

"Say, Fred, if I . . . if I . . . if you're saved, Fred, an' not me, you'll write to my folks, won't you?"

"Indeed I will. But I reckon you an' me'll both go down together."

"Don't say that. An' you won't forget to write that girl I gave you the address of?"

"You'll do the same for me."

"Oh, no, Fred, I'll never see land. . . . Oh, it's no use. An' I feel so well an' husky. . . . I don't want to die. I can't die like this."

"If it only wasn't so goddam black."

PART TWO
THE METAL COOLS

I

I T WAS purplish dusk outside the window. The rain fell steadily making long flashing stripes on the cracked panes, beating a hard monotonous tattoo on the tin roof overhead. Fuselli had taken off his wet slicker and stood in front of the window looking out dismally at the rain. Behind him was the smoking stove into which a man was poking wood, and beyond that a few broken folding chairs on which soldiers sprawled in attitudes of utter boredom, and the counter where the "Y" man stood with a set smile doling out chocolate to a line of men that filed past.

"Gee, you have to line up for everything here, don't you?" Fuselli muttered.

"That's about all you do do in this hell-hole, buddy," said a man beside him.

The man pointed with his thumb at the window and said again:

"See that rain? Well, I been in this camp three weeks and it ain't stopped rainin' once. What d'yer think of that for a country?"

"It certainly ain't like home," said Fuselli. "I'm going to have some chauclate."

"It's damn rotten."

"I might as well try it once."

Fuselli slouched over to the end of the line and stood waiting his turn. He was thinking of the steep streets of San Francisco and the glimpses he used to get of the harbor full of yellow lights, the color of amber in a cigarette holder, as he went home from work through the blue dusk. He had begun to think of Mabe handing him the five-pound box of candy when his attention was distracted by the talk of the men behind him. The man next to him was speaking with hurried nervous intonation. Fuselli could feel his breath on the back of his neck.

"I'll be goddamned," the man said, "was you there too? Where d'you get yours?"

"In the leg; it's about all right, though."

"I ain't. I won't never be all right. The doctor says I'm all right now, but I know I'm not, the lyin' fool."

"Some time, wasn't it?"

"I'll be damned to hell if I do it again. I can't sleep at night thinkin' of the shape of the Fritzies' helmets. Have you ever thought that there was somethin' about the shape of them goddam helmets . . . ?"

"Ain't they just or'nary shapes?" asked Fuselli, half turning round. "I seen 'em in the movies." He laughed apologetically.

"Listen to the rookie, Tub, he's seen 'em in the movies!" said the man with the nervous twitch in his voice, laughing a croaking little laugh. "How long you been in this country, buddy?"

"Two days."

"Well, we only been here two months, ain't we, Tub?"

"Four months; you're forgettin', kid."

The "Y" man turned his set smile on Fuselli while he filled his tin cup up with chocolate.

"How much?"

"A franc; one of those looks like a quarter," said the "Y" man, his well-fed voice full of amiable condescension.

"That's a hell of a lot for a cup of chauclate," said Fuselli.

"You're at the war, young man, remember that," said the "Y" man severely. "You're lucky to get it at all."

A cold chill gripped Fuselli's spine as he went back to the stove to drink the chocolate. Of course he mustn't crab. He was in the war now. If the sergeant had heard him crabbing, it might have spoiled his chances for a corporalship. He must be careful. If he just watched out and kept on his toes, he'd be sure to get it.

"And why ain't there no more chocolate, I want to know?" the nervous voice of the man who had stood in line behind Fuselli rose to a sudden shriek. Everybody looked round. The "Y" man was moving his head from side to side in a flustered way, saying in a shrill little voice:

"I've told you there's no more. Go away!"

"You ain't got no right to tell me to go away. You got to get me some chocolate. You ain't never been at the front, you goddam slacker." The man was yelling at the top of his lungs. He had hold of the counter with two hands and swayed from side to side. His friend was trying to pull him away.

"Look here, none of that, I'll report you," said the "Y" man. "Is there a non-commissioned officer in the hut?"

"Go ahead, you can't do nothin'. I can't never have nothing done worse than what's been done to me already." The man's voice had reached a sing-song fury.

"Is there a non-commissioned officer in the room?" The "Y" man kept looking from side to side. His little eyes were hard and spiteful and his lips were drawn up in a thin straight line.

"Keep quiet, I'll get him away," said the other man in a low voice. "Can't you see he's not . . . ?"

A strange terror took hold of Fuselli. He hadn't expected things to be like that. When he had sat in the grandstand in the training camp and watched the jolly soldiers in khaki marching into towns, pursuing terrified Huns across potato fields, saving Belgian milk-maids against picturesque backgrounds.

"Does many of 'em come back that way?" he asked a man beside him.

"Some do. It's this convalescent camp."

The man and his friend stood side by side near the stove talking in low voices.

"Pull yourself together, kid," the friend was saying.

"All right, Tub; I'm all right now, Tub. That slacker got my goat, that was all."

Fuselli was looking at him curiously. He had a yellow parchment face and a high, gaunt forehead going up to sparse, curly brown hair. His eyes had a glassy look about them when they met Fuselli's. He smiled amiably.

"Oh, there's the kid who's seen Fritzies' helmets in the movies. . . . Come on, buddy, come and have a beer at the English canteen."

"Can you get beer?"

"Sure, over in the English camp."

They went out into the slanting rain. It was nearly dark,

but the sky had a purplish-red color that was reflected a little on the slanting sides of tents and on the roofs of the rows of sheds that disappeared into the rainy mist in every direction. A few lights gleamed, a very bright polished yellow. They followed a board-walk that splashed mud up from the puddles under the tramp of their heavy boots.

At one place they flattened themselves against the wet flap of a tent and saluted as an officer passed waving a little cane jauntily.

"How long does a fellow usually stay in these rest camps?" asked Fuselli.

"Depends on what's goin' on out there," said Tub, pointing carelessly to the sky beyond the peaks of the tents.

"You'll leave here soon enough. Don't you worry, buddy," said the man with the nervous voice. "What you in?"

"Medical Replacement Unit."

"A medic, are you? Those boys didn't last long at the Château, did they, Tub?"

"No, they didn't."

Something inside Fuselli was protesting: "I'll last out though. I'll last out though."

"Do you remember the fellers went out to get poor ole Corporal Jones, Tub? I'll be goddamned if anybody ever found a button of their pants." He laughed his creaky little laugh. "They got in the way of a torpedo."

The "wet" canteen was full of smoke and a cosy steam of beer. It was crowded with red-faced men, with shiny brass buttons on their khaki uniforms, among whom was a good sprinkling of lanky Americans.

"Tommies," said Fuselli to himself.

After standing in line a while, Fuselli's cup was handed back to him across the counter, foaming with beer.

"Hello, Fuselli," Meadville clapped him on the shoulder. "You found the liquor pretty damn quick, looks like to me."

Fuselli laughed.

"May I sit with you fellers?"

"Sure, come along," said Fuselli proudly, "these guys have been to the front."

"You have?" asked Meadville. "The Huns are pretty good

scrappers, they say. Tell me, do you use your rifle much, or is it mostly big gun work?"

"Naw; after all the months I spent learnin' how to drill with my goddam rifle, I'll be a sucker if I've used it once. I'm in the grenade squad."

Someone at the end of the room had started singing:

> "O Mademerselle from Armenteers,
> Parley voo!"

The man with the nervous voice went on talking, while the song roared about them.

"I don't spend a night without thinkin' o' them funny helmets the Fritzies wear. Have you ever thought that there was something goddam funny about the shape o' them helmets?"

"Can the helmets, kid," said his friend. "You told us all about them onct."

"I ain't told you why I can't forgit 'em, have I?"

> "A German officer crossed the Rhine;
> Parley voo?
> A German officer crossed the Rhine;
> He loved the women and liked the wine;
> Hanky Panky, parley voo . ."

"Listen to this, fellers," said the man in his twitching nervous voice, staring straight into Fuselli's eyes. "We made a little attack to straighten out our trenches a bit just before I got winged. Our barrage cut off a bit of Fritzie's trench an' we ran right ahead juss about dawn an' occupied it. I'll be goddamned if it wasn't as quiet as a Sunday morning at home."

"It was!" said his friend.

"An' I had a bunch of grenades an' a feller came runnin' up to me, whisperin', 'There's a bunch of Fritzies playin' cards in a dug-out. They don't seem to know they're captured. We'd better take 'em pris'ners!'

"'Pris'ners, hell,' says I, 'We'll go and clear the buggars out.' So we crept along to the steps and looked down. . . ."

The song had started again:

> "O Mademerselle from Armenteers,
> Parley voo?"

"Their helmets looked so damn like toadstools I came near laughin'. An' they sat round the lamp layin' down the cards serious-like, the way I've seen Germans do in the Rathskeller at home."

> "He loved the women and liked the wine,
>   Parley voo?"

"I lay there lookin' at 'em for a hell of a time, an' then I clicked a grenade an' tossed it gently down the steps. An' all those funny helmets like toadstools popped up in the air an' somebody gave a yell an' the light went out an' the damn grenade went off. Then I let 'em have the rest of 'em an' went away 'cause one o' 'em was still moanin'-like. It was about that time they let their barrage down on us and I got mine."

> "The Yanks are havin' a hell of a time,
>   Parley voo?"

"An' the first thing I thought of when I woke up was how those goddam helmets looked. It upsets a feller to think of a thing like that." His voice ended in a whine like the broken voice of a child that has been beaten.

"You need to pull yourself together, kid," said his friend.

"I know what I need, Tub. I need a woman."

"You know where you get one?" asked Meadville. "I'd like to get me a nice little French girl a rainy night like this."

"It must be a hell of a ways to the town. . . . They say it's full of M.P.'s too," said Fuselli.

"I know a way," said the man with the nervous voice. "Come on, Tub."

"No, I've had enough of these goddam frog women."

They all left the canteen.

As the two men went off down the side of the building, Fuselli heard the nervous twitching voice through the metallic patter of the rain:

"I can't find no way of forgettin' how funny those guys' helmets looked all round the lamp . . . I can't find no way . . ."

Bill Grey and Fuselli pooled their blankets and slept together. They lay on the hard floor of the tent very close to each other, listening to the rain pattering endlessly on the drenched canvas that slanted above their heads.

"Hell, Bill, I'm gettin' pneumonia," said Fuselli, clearing his nose.

"That's the only thing that scares me in the whole goddam business. I'd hate to die o' sickness . . . an' they say another kid's kicked off with that—what d'they call it?—menegitis."

"Was that what was the matter with Stein?"

"The corporal won't say."

"Ole Corp. looks sort o' sick himself," said Fuselli.

"It's this rotten climate," whispered Bill Grey, in the middle of a fit of coughing.

"For cat's sake quit that coughin'. Let a feller sleep," came a voice from the other side of the tent.

"Go an' get a room in a hotel if you don't like it."

"That's it, Bill, tell him where to get off."

"If you fellers don't quit yellin', I'll put the whole blame lot of you on K.P.," came the sergeant's good-natured voice. "Don't you know that taps has blown?"

The tent was silent except for the fast patter of the rain and Bill Grey's coughing.

"That sergeant gives me a pain in the neck," muttered Bill Grey peevishly, when his coughing had stopped, wriggling about under the blankets.

After a while Fuselli said in a very low voice, so that no one but his friend should hear:

"Say, Bill, ain't it different from what we thought it was going to be?"

"Yare."

"I mean fellers don't seem to think about beatin' the Huns at all, they're so busy crabbin' on everything."

"It's the guys higher up that does the thinkin'," said Grey grandiloquently.

"Hell, but I thought it'd be excitin' like in the movies."

"I guess that was a lot o' talk."

"Maybe."

Fuselli went to sleep on the hard floor, feeling the comfortable warmth of Grey's body along the side of him, hearing the endless, monotonous patter of the rain on the drenched canvas above his head. He tried to stay awake a minute to remember what Mabe looked like, but sleep closed down on him suddenly.

The bugle wrenched them out of their blankets before it was light. It was not raining. The air was raw and full of white mist that was cold as snow against their faces still warm from sleep. The corporal called the roll, lighting matches to read the list. When he dismissed the formation the sergeant's voice was heard from the tent, where he still lay rolled in his blankets.

"Say, Corp, go an' tell Fuselli to straighten out Lieutenant Stanford's room at eight sharp in Officers' Barracks, Number Four."

"Did you hear, Fuselli?"

"All right," said Fuselli. His blood boiled up suddenly. This was the first time he'd had to do servants' work. He hadn't joined the army to be a slavey to any damned first loot. It was against army regulations anyway. He'd go and kick. He wasn't going to be a slavey. . . . He walked towards the door of the tent, thinking what he'd say to the sergeant. But he noticed the corporal coughing into his handkerchief with an expression of pain on his face. He turned and strolled away. It would get him in wrong if he started kicking like that. Much better shut his mouth and put up with it. The poor old corp couldn't last long at this rate. No, it wouldn't do to get in wrong.

At eight, Fuselli, with a broom in his hand, feeling dull fury pounding and fluttering within him, knocked on the un-painted board door.

"Who's that?"

"To clean the room, sir," said Fuselli.

"Come back in about twenty minutes," came the voice of the lieutenant.

"All right, sir."

Fuselli leaned against the back of the barracks and smoked a cigarette. The air stung his hands as if they had been scraped by a nutmeg-grater. Twenty minutes passed slowly. Despair seized hold of him. He was so far from anyone who cared about him, so lost in the vast machine. He was telling himself that he'd never get on, would never get up where he could show what he was good for. He felt as if he were in a tread-mill. Day after day it would be like this,—the same routine, the same helplessness. He looked at his watch. Twenty-five minutes had passed. He picked up his broom and moved round to the lieutenant's room.

"Come in," said the lieutenant carelessly. He was in his shirt-sleeves, shaving. A pleasant smell of shaving soap filled the dark clapboard room, which had no furniture but three cots and some officers' trunks. He was a red-faced young man with flabby cheeks and dark straight eyebrows. He had taken command of the company only a day or two before.

"Looks like a decent feller," thought Fuselli.

"What's your name?" asked the lieutenant, speaking into the small nickel mirror, while he ran the safety razor obliquely across his throat. He stuttered a little. To Fuselli he seemed to speak like an Englishman.

"Fuselli."

"Italian parentage, I presume?"

"Yes," said Fuselli sullenly, dragging one of the cots away from the wall.

"Parla Italiano?"

"You mean, do I speak Eyetalian? Naw, sir," said Fuselli emphatically, "I was born in Frisco."

"Indeed? But get me some more water, will you, please?"

When Fuselli came back, he stood with his broom between his knees, blowing on his hands that were blue and stiff from carrying the heavy bucket. The lieutenant was dressed and was hooking the top hook of the uniform carefully. The collar made a red mark on his pink throat.

"All right; when you're through, report back to the Company." The lieutenant went out, drawing on a pair of khaki-colored gloves with a satisfied and important gesture.

Fuselli walked back slowly to the tents where the Company was quartered, looking about him at the long lines of barracks, gaunt and dripping in the mist, at the big tin sheds of the cook shacks where the cooks and K.P.'s in greasy blue denims were slouching about amid a steam of cooking food.

Something of the gesture with which the lieutenant drew on his gloves caught in the mind of Fuselli. He had seen people make gestures like that in the movies, stout dignified people in evening suits. The president of the Company that owned the optical goods store, where he had worked, at home in Frisco, had had something of that gesture about him.

And he pictured himself drawing on a pair of gloves that way, importantly, finger by finger, with a little wave of self-satisfaction when the gesture was completed. . . . He'd have to get that corporalship.

> "There's a long, long trail a-winding
>   Through no man's land in France."

The company sang lustily as it splashed through the mud down a grey road between high fences covered with great tangles of barbed wire, above which peeked the ends of warehouses and the chimneys of factories.

The lieutenant and the top sergeant walked side by side chatting, now and then singing a little of the song in a deprecating way. The corporal sang, his eyes sparkling with delight. Even the sombre sergeant who rarely spoke to anyone, sang. The company strode along, its ninety-six legs splashing jauntily through the deep putty-colored puddles. The packs swayed merrily from side to side as if it were they and not the legs that were walking.

> "There's a long, long trail a-winding
>   Through no man's land in France."

At last they were going somewhere. They had separated from the contingent they had come over with. They were all alone now. They were going to be put to work. The lieutenant strode along importantly. The sergeant strode along importantly. The corporal strode along importantly. The right guard strode more importantly than anyone. A sense of importance, of something tremendous to do, animated the company like wine, made the packs and the belts seem less heavy, made their necks and shoulders less stiff from struggling with the weight of the packs, made the ninety-six legs tramp jauntily in spite of the oozy mud and the deep putty-colored puddles.

It was cold in the dark shed of the freight station where they waited. Some gas lamps flickered feebly high up among the rafters, lighting up in a ghastly way white piles of ammunition boxes and ranks and ranks of shells that disappeared in the darkness. The raw air was full of coal smoke and a smell of freshly-cut boards. The captain and the top sergeant had disappeared. The men sat about, huddled in groups, sinking as far as they could into their overcoats, stamping their numb wet feet on the mud-covered cement of the floor. The sliding doors were shut. Through them came a monotonous sound of cars shunting, of buffers bumping against buffers, and now and then the shrill whistle of an engine.

"Hell, the French railroads are rotten," said someone.

"How d'you know?" snapped Eisenstein, who sat on a box away from the rest with his lean face in his hands staring at his mud-covered boots.

"Look at this," Bill Grey made a disgusted gesture towards the ceiling. "Gas. Don't even have electric light."

"Their trains run faster than ours," said Eisenstein.

"The hell they do. Why, a fellow back in that rest camp told me that it took four or five days to get anywhere."

"He was stuffing you," said Eisenstein. "They used to run the fastest trains in the world in France."

"Not so fast as the 'Twentieth Century.' Goddam, I'm a railroad man and I know."

"I want five men to help me sort out the eats," said the top sergeant, coming suddenly out of the shadows. "Fuselli, Grey, Eisenstein, Meadville, Williams . . . all right, come along."

"Say, Sarge, this guy says that frog trains are faster than our trains. What d'ye think o' that?"

The sergeant put on his comic expression. Everybody got ready to laugh.

"Well, if he'd rather take the side-door Pullmans we're going to get aboard tonight than the 'Sunset Limited,' he's welcome. I've seen 'em. You fellers haven't."

Everybody laughed. The top sergeant turned confidentially to the five men who followed him into a small well-lighted room that looked like a freight office.

"We've got to sort out the grub, fellers. See those cases? That's three days' rations for the outfit. I want to sort it into three lots, one for each car. Understand?"

Fuselli pulled open one of the boxes. The cans of bully beef flew under his fingers. He kept looking out of the corner of his eye at Eisenstein, who seemed very skilful in a careless way.

The top sergeant stood beaming at them with his legs wide apart. Once he said something in a low voice to the corporal. Fuselli thought he caught the words: "privates first-class," and his heart started thumping hard. In a few minutes the job was done, and everybody stood about lighting cigarettes.

"Well, fellers," said Sergeant Jones, the sombre man who rarely spoke, "I certainly didn't reckon when I used to be teachin' and preachin' and tendin' Sunday School and the like that I'd come to be usin' cuss words, but I think we got a damn good company."

"Oh, we'll have you sayin' worse things than 'damn' when we get you out on the front with a goddam German aëroplane droppin' bombs on you," said the top sergeant, slapping him on the back. "Now, I want you five men to look out for the grub." Fuselli's chest swelled. "The company'll be in charge of the corporal for the night. Sergeant Jones and I have got to be with the lieutenant; understand?"

They all walked back to the dingy room where the rest of the company waited huddled in their coats, trying to keep their importance from being too obvious in their step.

"I've really started now," thought Fuselli to himself. "I've really started now."

The bare freight car clattered and rumbled monotonously over the rails. A bitter cold wind blew up through the cracks in the grimy splintered boards of the floor. The men huddled in the corners of the car, curled up together like puppies in a box. It was pitch black. Fuselli lay half asleep, his head full of curious fragmentary dreams, feeling through his sleep the aching cold and the unending clattering rumble of the wheels and the bodies and arms and legs muffled in coats and blankets pressing against him. He woke up with a start. His teeth were chattering. The clanking rumble of wheels seemed to be in his head. His head was being dragged along, bumping over cold iron rails. Someone lighted a match. The freight car's black swaying walls, the packs piled in the center, the bodies heaped in the corners where, out of khaki masses here and there gleamed an occasional white face or a pair of eyes—all showed clear for a moment and then vanished again in the utter blackness. Fuselli pillowed his head in the crook of someone's arm and tried to go to sleep, but the scraping rumble of wheels over rails was too loud; he stayed with open eyes staring into the blackness, trying to draw his body away from the blast of cold air that blew up through a crack in the floor.

When the first greyness began filtering into the car, they all stood up and stamped and pounded each other and wrestled to get warm.

When it was nearly light, the train stopped and they opened the sliding doors. They were in a station, a foreign-looking station where the walls were plastered with unfamiliar advertisements. "V-E-R-S-A-I-L-L-E-S"; Fuselli spelt out the name.

"Versales," said Eisenstein. "That's where the kings of France used to live."

The train started moving again slowly. On the platform stood the top sergeant.

"How d'ye sleep," he shouted as the car passed him. "Say, Fuselli, better start some grub going."

"All right, Sarge," said Fuselli.

The sergeant ran back to the front of the car and climbed on.

With a delicious feeling of leadership, Fuselli divided up the bread and the cans of bully beef and the cheese. Then he sat on his pack eating dry bread and unsavoury beef, whistling joyfully, while the train rumbled and clattered along through a strange, misty-green countryside,—whistling joyfully because he was going to the front, where there would be glory and excitement, whistling joyfully because he felt he was getting along in the world.

It was noon. A pallid little sun like a toy balloon hung low in the reddish-grey sky. The train had stopped on a siding in the middle of a russet plain. Yellow poplars, faint as mist, rose slender against the sky along a black shining stream that swirled beside the track. In the distance a steeple and a few red roofs were etched faintly in the greyness.

The men stood about balancing first on one foot and then on the other, stamping to get warm. On the other side of the river an old man with an oxcart had stopped and was looking sadly at the train.

"Say, where's the front?" somebody shouted to him.

Everybody took up the cry: "Say, where's the front?"

The old man waved his hand, shook his head and shouted to the oxen. The oxen took up again their quiet processional gait and the old man walked ahead of them, his eyes on the ground.

"Say, ain't the frogs dumb?"

"Say, Dan," said Bill Grey, strolling away from a group of men he had been talking to. "These guys say we are going to the Third Army."

"Say, fellers," shouted Fuselli. "They say we're going to the Third Army."

"Where's that?"

"In the Oregon forest," ventured somebody.

"That's at the front, ain't it?"

At that moment the lieutenant strode by. A long khaki muffler was thrown carelessly round his neck and hung down his back.

"Look here, men," he said severely, "the orders are to stay in the cars."

The men slunk back into the cars sullenly.

A hospital train passed, clanking slowly over the cross-tracks. Fuselli looked fixedly at the dark enigmatic windows, at the red crosses, at the orderlies in white who leaned out of the doors, waving their hands. Somebody noticed that there were scars on the new green paint of the last car.

"The Huns have been shooting at it."

"D'ye hear that? The Huns tried to shoot up that hospital train."

Fuselli remembered the pamphlet "German Atrocities" he had read one night in the Y.M.C.A. His mind became suddenly filled with pictures of children with their arms cut off, of babies spitted on bayonets, of women strapped on tables and violated by soldier after soldier. He thought of Mabe. He wished he were in a combatant service; he wanted to fight, fight. He pictured himself shooting dozens of men in green uniforms, and he thought of Mabe reading about it in the papers. He'd have to try to get into a combatant service. No, he couldn't stay in the medics.

The train had started again. Misty russet fields slipped by and dark clumps of trees that gyrated slowly waving branches of yellow and brown leaves and patches of black lace-work against the reddish-grey sky. Fuselli was thinking of the good chance he had of getting to be corporal.

At night. A dim-lighted station platform. The company waited in two lines, each man sitting on his pack. On the opposite platform crowds of little men in blue with mustaches and long, soiled overcoats that reached almost to their feet were shouting and singing. Fuselli watched them with a faint disgust.

"Gee, they got funny lookin' helmets, ain't they?"

"They're the best fighters in the world," said Eisenstein, "not that that's sayin' much about a man."

"Say, that's an M.P.," said Bill Grey, catching Fuselli's arm. "Let's go ask him how near the front we are. I thought I heard guns a minute ago."

"Did you? I guess we're in for it now," said Fuselli.

"Say, buddy, how near the front are we?" they spoke together excitedly.

"The front?" said the M.P., who was a red-faced Irishman with a crushed nose. "You're 'way back in the middle of France." The M.P. spat disgustedly. "You fellers ain't never goin' to the front, don't you worry."

"Hell!" said Fuselli.

"I'll be goddamned if I don't get there somehow," said Bill Grey, squaring his jaw.

A fine rain was falling on the unprotected platform. On the other side the little men in blue were singing a song Fuselli could not understand, drinking out of their ungainly-looking canteens.

Fuselli announced the news to the company. Everybody clustered round him cursing. But the faint sense of importance it gave him did not compensate for the feeling he had of being lost in the machine, of being as helpless as a sheep in a flock.

Hours passed. They stamped about the platform in the fine rain or sat in a row on their packs, waiting for orders. A grey belt appeared behind the trees. The platform began to take on a silvery gleam. They sat in a row on their packs, waiting.

II

THE COMPANY stood at attention lined up outside of their barracks, a long wooden shack covered with tar paper. In front of them was a row of dishevelled plane trees with white trunks that looked like ivory in the faint ruddy sunlight. Then there was a rutted road on which stood a long line of French motor trucks with hunched grey backs like elephants. Beyond these were more plane trees and another row of barracks covered with tar paper, outside of which other companies were lined up standing at attention.

A bugle was sounding far away.

The lieutenant stood at attention very stiffly. Fuselli's eyes followed the curves of his brilliantly-polished puttees up to the braid on his sleeves.

"Parade rest!" shouted the lieutenant in a muffled voice.

Feet and hands moved in unison.

Fuselli was thinking of the town. After retreat you could go down the irregular cobbled street from the old fair-ground where the camp was to a little square where there was a grey stone fountain and a gin-mill where you could sit at an oak table and have beer and eggs and fried potatoes served you by a girl with red cheeks and plump white appetizing arms.

"Attention!"

Feet and hands moved in unison again. They could hardly hear the bugle, it was so faint.

"Men, I have some appointments to announce," said the lieutenant, facing the company and taking on an easy conversational tone. "At rest! . . . You've done good work in the storehouse here, men. I'm glad I have such a willing bunch of men under me. And I certainly hope that we can manage to make as many promotions as possible—as many as possible."

Fuselli's hands were icy, and his heart was pumping the blood so fast to his ears that he could hardly hear.

"The following privates to private first-class," read the lieutenant in a routine voice: "Grey, Appleton, Williams, Eisenstein, Porter . . . Eisenstein will be company clerk. . . ." Fuselli was almost ready to cry. His name was not on the list.

The sergeant's voice came after a long pause, smooth as velvet.

"You forget Fuselli, sir."

"Oh, so I did," the lieutenant laughed a small dry laugh. —"And Fuselli."

"Gee, I must write Mabe tonight," Fuselli was saying to himself. "She'll be a proud kid when she gets that letter."

"Companee dis . . . missed!" shouted the sergeant genially.

> "O Madermoiselle from Armenteers,
>   Parley voo?
> O Madermoiselle from Armenteers,"

struck up the sergeant in his mellow voice.

The front room of the café was full of soldiers. Their khaki hid the worn oak benches and the edges of the square tables and the red tiles of the floor. They clustered round the tables, where glasses and bottles gleamed vaguely through the tobacco smoke. They stood in front of the bar, drinking out of bottles, laughing, scraping their feet on the floor. A stout girl with red cheeks and plump white arms moved contentedly among them, carrying away empty bottles, bringing back full ones, taking the money to a grim old woman with a grey face and eyes like bits of jet, who stared carefully at each coin, fingered it with her grey hands and dropped it reluctantly into the cash drawer. In the corner sat Sergeant Olster with a flush on his face, and the corporal who had been on the Red Sox outfield and another sergeant, a big man with black hair and a black mustache. About them clustered, with approbation and respect in their faces, Fuselli, Bill Grey and Meadville the cowboy, and Earl Williams, the blue-eyed and yellow-haired drug-clerk.

> "O the Yanks are having the hell of a time,
>   Parley voo?"

They pounded their bottles on the table in time to the song.

"It's a good job," the top sergeant said, suddenly interrupting the song. "You needn't worry about that, fellers. I saw to it that we got a good job. . . . And about getting to the front, you needn't worry about that. We'll all get to the front soon enough. . . . Tell me this war is going to last ten years."

"I guess we'll all be generals by that time, eh, Sarge?" said Williams. "But, man, I wish I was back jerkin' soda water."

"It's a great life if you don't weaken," murmured Fuselli automatically.

"But I'm beginnin' to weaken," said Williams. "Man, I'm homesick. I don't care who knows it. I wish I could get to the front and be done with it."

"Say, have a heart. You need a drink," said the top sergeant, banging his fist on the table. "Say, mamselle, mame shows, mame shows!"

"I didn't know you could talk French, Sarge," said Fuselli.

"French, hell!" said the top sergeant. "Williams is the boy can talk French."

"Voulay vous couchay aveck moy. . . . That's all I know."

Everybody laughed.

"Hey, mamzelle," cried the top sergeant. "Voulay vous couchay aveck moy? We, We, champagne." Everybody laughed, uproariously.

The girl slapped his head good-naturedly.

At that moment a man stamped noisily into the café, a tall broad-shouldered man in a loose English tunic, who had a swinging swagger that made the glasses ring on all the tables. He was humming under his breath and there was a grin on his broad red face. He went up to the girl and pretended to kiss her, and she laughed and talked familiarly with him in French.

"There's wild Dan Cohan," said the dark-haired sergeant. "Say, Dan, Dan."

"Here, yer honor."

"Come over and have a drink. We're going to have some fizzy."

"Never known to refuse."

They made room for him on the bench.

"Well, I'm confined to barracks," said Dan Cohan. "Look at me!" He laughed and gave his head a curious swift jerk to one side. "Compree?"

"Ain't ye scared they'll nab you?" said Fuselli.

"Nab me, hell, they can't do nothin' to me. I've had three

court-martials already and they're gettin' a fourth up on me."
Dan Cohan pushed his head to one side and laughed. "I got
a friend. My old boss is captain, and he's goin' to fix it up. I
used to alley around politics chez moy. Compree?"

The champagne came and Dan Cohan popped the cork up
to the ceiling with dexterous red fingers.

"I was just wondering who was going to give me a drink,"
he said. "Ain't had any pay since Christ was a corporal. I've
forgotten what it looks like."

The champagne fizzed into the beer-glasses.

"This is the life," said Fuselli.

"Ye're damn right, buddy, if yer don't let them ride yer,"
said Dan.

"What they got yer up for now, Dan?"

"Murder."

"Murder, hell! How's that?"

"That is, if that bloke dies."

"The hell you say!"

"It all started by that goddam convoy down from
Nantes . . . Bill Rees an' me. . . . They called us the shock
troops.—Hy! Marie! Ancore champagne, beaucoup.—I was
in the Ambulance service then. God knows what rotten service I'm in now. . . . Our section was on repo and they sent
some of us fellers down to Nantes to fetch a convoy of cars
back to Sandrecourt. We started out like regular racers, just
the chassis, savey? Bill Rees an' me was the goddam tail of the
peerade. An' the loot was a hell of a blockhead that didn't
know if he was coming or going."

"Where the hell's Nantes?" asked the top sergeant, as if it
had just slipped his mind.

"On the coast," answered Fuselli. "I seen it on the map."

"Nantes's way off to hell and gone anyway," said wild Dan
Cohan, taking a gulp of champagne that he held in his mouth
a moment, making his mouth move like a cow ruminating.

"An' as Bill Rees an' me was the tail of the peerade an'
there was lots of cafés and little gin-mills, Bill Rees an' me'd
stop off every now and then to have a little drink an' say
'Bonjour' to the girls an' talk to the people, an' then we'd go
like a bat out of hell to catch up. Well, I don't know if we
went too fast for 'em or if they lost the road or what, but we

never saw that goddam convoy from the time we went out of Nantes. Then we thought we might as well see a bit of the country, compree? . . . An' we did, goddam it. . . . We landed up in Orleans, soused to the gills and without any gas an' with an M.P. climbing up on the dashboard."

"Did they nab you, then?"

"Not a bit of it," said wild Dan Cohan, jerking his head to one side. "They gave us gas and commutation of rations an' told us to go on in the mornin'. You see we put up a good line of talk, compree? . . . Well, we went to the swankiest restaurant. . . . You see we had on those bloody British uniforms they gave us when the O.D. gave out, an' the M.P.'s didn't know just what sort o' birds we were. So we went and ordered up a regular meal an' lots o' vin rouge an' vin blank an' drank a few cognacs an' before we knew it we were eating dinner with two captains and a sergeant. One o' the captains was the drunkest man I ever did see. . . . Good kid! We all had dinner and Bill Rees says, 'Let's go for a joy-ride.' An' the captains says, 'Fine,' and the sergeant would have said, 'Fine,' but he was so goggle-eyed drunk he couldn't. An' we started off! . . . Say, fellers, I'm dry as hell! Let's order up another bottle."

"Sure," said everyone.

> "Ban swar, ma cherie,
> Comment allez vous?"

"Encore champagne, Marie, gentille!"

"Well," he went on, "we went like a bat out of hell along a good state road, and it was all fine until one of the captains thought we ought to have a race. We did. . . . Compree? The flivvers flivved all right, but the hell of it was we got so excited about the race we forgot about the sergeant an' he fell off an' nobody missed him. An' at last we all pull up before a gin-mill an' one captain says, 'Where's the sergeant?' an' the other captain says there hadn't been no sergeant. An' we all had a drink on that. An' one captain kept sayin', 'It's all imagination. Never was a sergeant. I wouldn't associate with a sergeant, would I, lootenant?' He kept on calling me lootenant. . . . Well that was how they got this new charge against me. Somebody picked up the sergeant an' he got concussion o' the brain an' there's hell to pay, an' if the poor buggar croaks, . . . I'm it. . . . Compree? About that time the captains start wantin' to go to Paris, an' we said we'd take 'em, an' so we put all the gas in my car an' the four of us climbed on that goddam chassis an' off we went like a bat out of hell! It'ld all have been fine if I wasn't lookin' cross-eyed. . . . We piled up in about two minutes on one of those nice little stone piles an' there we were. We all got up an' one o' the captains had his arm broke, an' there was hell to pay, worse than losing the sergeant. So we walked on down the road. I don't know how it got to be daylight. But we got to some hell of a town or other an' there was two M.P.'s all ready to meet us, . . . Compree? . . . Well, we didn't mess around with them captains. We just lit off down a side street an' got into a little café an' went in back an' had a hell of a lot o' café o' lay. That made us feel sort o' good an' I says to Bill, 'Bill, we've got to get to headquarters an' tell 'em that we accidentally smashed up our car, before the M.P.'s get busy.' An' he says, 'You're goddamned right,' an' at that minute I sees an M.P. through a crack in the door comin' into the café. We lit out into the garden and made for the wall. We got over that, although we left a good piece of my pants in the broken glass. But the hell of it was the M.P.'s got over too an' they had their pop-guns out. An' the last I saw of Bill Rees was—there was a big fat woman in a pink dress washing clothes in a big tub, an' poor ole Bill Rees runs head on into her an' over they both goes into the washtub. The M.P.'s got him all right. That's how I got away. An' the last I saw of Bill Rees he was squirming about on top of the washtub like he was swimmin', an' the fat woman was sittin' on the ground shaking her fist at him. Bill Rees was the best buddy I ever had."

He paused and poured the rest of the champagne into his glass and wiped the sweat off his face with his big red hand.

"You ain't stringin' us, are you?" asked Fuselli.

"You just ask Lieutenant Whitehead, who's defending me in the court-martial, if I'm stringin' yer. I been in the ring, kid, and you can bet your bottom dollar that a man's been in the ring'll tell the truth."

"Go on, Dan," said the sergeant.

"An' I never heard a word about Bill Rees since. I guess they got him into the trenches and made short work of him."

Dan Cohan paused to light a cigarette.

"Well, one o' the M.P.'s follows after me and starts shootin'. An' don't you believe I ran. Gee, I was scared! But I was in luck 'cause a Frenchman had just started his camion an' I jumped in and said the gendarmes were after me. He was white, that frog was. He shot the juice into her an' went off like a bat out of hell an' there was a hell of a lot of traffic on the road because there was some damn-fool attack or other goin' on. So I got up to Paris. . . . An' then it'ld all have been fine if I hadn't met up with a Jane I knew. I still had five hundred francs on me, an' so we raised hell until one day we was havin' dinner in the café de Paris, both of us sort of jagged up, an' we didn't have enough money to pay the bill an' Janey made a run for it, but an M.P. got me an' then there was hell to pay. . . . Compree? They put me in the Bastille, great place. . . . Then they shipped me off to some damn camp or other an' gave me a gun an' made me drill for a week an' then they packed a whole gang of us, all A.W.O.L's, into a train for the front. That was nearly the end of little Daniel again. But when we was in Vitry-le-François, I chucked my rifle out of one window and jumped out of the other an' got on a train back to Paris an' went an' reported to headquarters how I'd smashed the car an' been in the Bastille an' all, an' they were sore as hell at the M.P.'s an' sent me out to a section an' all went fine until I got ordered back an' had to alley down to this goddam camp. An' now I don't know what they're goin' to do to me."

"Gee whiz!"

"It's a great war, I tell you, Sarge. It's a great war. I wouldn't have missed it."

Across the room someone was singing.

"Let's drown 'em out," said the top sergeant boisterously.

> "O Mademerselle from Armenteers,
>   Parley voo?"

"Well, I've got to get the hell out of here," said wild Dan Cohan, after a minute. "I've got a Jane waitin' for me. I'm all fixed up, . . . Compree?"

He swaggered out singing:

> "Bon soir, ma cherie,
> Comment alley vous?
> Si vous voulez
> Couche avec moi. . . ."

The door slammed behind him, leaving the café quiet.

Many men had left. Madame had taken up her knitting and Marie of the plump white arms sat beside her, leaning her head back among the bottles that rose in tiers behind the bars.

Fuselli was staring at a door on one side of the bar. Men kept opening it and looking in and closing it again with a peculiar expression on their faces. Now and then someone would open it with a smile and go into the next room, shuffling his feet and closing the door carefully behind him.

"Say, I wonder what they've got there," said the top sergeant, who had been staring at the door. "Mush be looked into, mush be looked into," he added, laughing drunkenly.

"I dunno," said Fuselli. The champagne was humming in his head like a fly against a window pane. He felt very bold and important.

The top sergeant got to his feet unsteadily.

"Corporal, take charge of the colors," he said, and walked to the door. He opened it a little, peeked in; winked elaborately to his friends and skipped into the other room, closing the door carefully behind him.

The corporal went over next. He said, "Well, I'll be damned," and walked straight in, leaving the door ajar. In a moment it was closed from the inside.

"Come on, Bill, let's see what the hell they got in there," said Fuselli.

"All right, old kid," said Bill Grey.

They went together over to the door. Fuselli opened it and looked in. He let out a breath through his teeth with a faint whistling sound.

"Gee, come in, Bill," he said, giggling.

The room was small, nearly filled up by a dining table with a red cloth. On the mantel above the empty fireplace were candlesticks with dangling crystals that glittered red and yellow and purple in the lamplight, in front of a cracked mirror that seemed a window into another dingier room. The paper was peeling off the damp walls, giving a mortuary smell of mildewed plaster that not even the reek of beer and tobacco had done away with.

"Look at her, Bill, ain't she got style?" whispered Fuselli.

Bill Grey grunted.

"Say, d'ye think the Jane that feller was tellin' us he raised hell with in Paris was like that?"

At the end of the table, leaning on her elbows, was a woman with black frizzy hair cut short, that stuck out from her head in all directions. Her eyes were dark and her lips red with a faint swollen look. She looked with a certain defiance at the men who stood about the walls and sat at the table.

The men stared at her silently. A big man with red hair and a heavy jaw who sat next her kept edging up nearer. Someone knocked against the table making the bottles and liqueur glasses clustered in the center jingle.

"She ain't clean; she's got bobbed hair," said the man next Fuselli.

The woman said something in French.

Only one man understood it. His laugh rang hollowly in the silent room and stopped suddenly.

The woman looked attentively at the faces round her for a moment, shrugged her shoulders, and began straightening the ribbon on the hat she held on her lap.

"How the hell did she get here? I thought the M.P.'s ran them out of town the minute they got here," said one man.

The woman continued plucking at her hat.

"You venay Paris?" said a boy with a soft voice who sat near her. He had blue eyes and a milky complexion, faintly tanned, that went strangely with the rough red and brown faces in the room.

"Oui, de Paris," she said after a pause, glancing suddenly in the boy's face.

"She's a liar, I can tell you that," said the red-haired man, who by this time had moved his chair very close to the woman's.

"You told him you came from Marseilles, and him you came from Lyon," said the boy with the milky complexion, smiling genially. "Vraiment de ou venay vous?"

"I come from everywhere," she said, and tossed the hair back from her face.

"Travelled a lot?" asked the boy again.

"A feller told me," said Fuselli to Bill Grey, "that he'd talked to a girl like that who'd been to Turkey an' Egypt. . . . I bet that girl's seen some life."

The woman jumped to her feet suddenly screaming with rage. The man with the red hair moved away sheepishly. Then he lifted his large dirty hands in the air.

"Kamarad," he said.

Nobody laughed. The room was silent except for feet scraping occasionally on the floor.

She put her hat on and took a little box from the chain bag in her lap and began powdering her face, making faces into the mirror she held in the palm of her hand.

The men stared at her.

"Guess she thinks she's the Queen of the May," said one man, getting to his feet. He leaned across the table and spat into the fireplace. "I'm going back to barracks." He turned to the woman and shouted in a voice full of hatred, "Bon swar."

The woman was putting the powder puff away in her jet bag. She did not look up; the door closed sharply.

"Come along," said the woman, suddenly, tossing her head back. "Come along one at a time; who go with me first?"

Nobody spoke. The men stared at her silently. There was no sound except that of feet scraping occasionally on the floor.

III

THE OATMEAL flopped heavily into the mess-kit. Fuselli's eyes were still glued together with sleep. He sat at the dark greasy bench and took a gulp of the scalding coffee that smelt vaguely of dish rags. That woke him up a little. There was little talk in the mess shack. The men, that the bugle had wrenched out of their blankets but fifteen minutes before, sat in rows, eating sullenly or blinking at each other through the misty darkness. You could hear feet scraping in the ashes of the floor and mess kits clattering against the tables and here and there a man coughing. Near the counter where the food was served out one of the cooks swore interminably in a whiny sing-song voice.

"Gee, Bill, I've got a head," said Fuselli.

"Ye're ought to have," growled Bill Grey. "I had to carry you up into the barracks. You said you were goin' back and love up that goddam girl."

"Did I?" said Fuselli, giggling.

"I had a hell of a time getting you past the guard."

"Some cognac! . . . I got a hangover now," said Fuselli.

"I'm goddamned if I can go this much longer."

"What?"

They were washing their mess-kits in the tub of warm water thick with grease from the hundred mess-kits that had gone before, in front of the shack. An electric light illumined faintly the wet trunk of a plane tree and the surface of the water where bits of oatmeal floated and coffee grounds,—and the garbage pails with their painted signs: WET GARBAGE, DRY GARBAGE; and the line of men who stood waiting to reach the tub.

"This hell of a life!" said Bill Grey, savagely.

"What d'ye mean?"

"Doin' nothin' but pack bandages in packin' cases and take bandages out of packin' cases. I'll go crazy. I've tried gettin' drunk; it don't do no good."

"Gee; I've got a head," said Fuselli.

Bill Grey put his heavy muscular hand round Fuselli's shoulder as they strolled towards the barracks.

"Say, Dan, I'm goin' A.W.O.L."

"Don't ye do it, Bill. Hell, look at the chance we've got to get ahead. We can both of us get promoted if we don't get in wrong."

"I don't give a hoot in hell for all that. . . . What d'ye think I got in this goddamed army for? Because I thought I'd look nice in the uniform?"

Bill Grey thrust his hands into his pockets and spat dismally in front of him.

"But, Bill, you don't want to stay a buck private, do you?"

"I want to get to the front. . . . I don't want to stay here till I get in the jug for being spiffed or get a court-martial. . . . Say, Dan, will you come with me?"

"Hell, Bill, you ain't goin'. You're just kiddin', ain't yer? . . . They'll send us there soon enough. I want to get to be a corporal,"—he puffed out his chest a little—"before I go to the front, so's to be able to show what I'm good for. See, Bill?"

A bugle blew.

"There's fatigue, an' I ain't done my bunk."

"Me neither. . . . They won't do nothin', Dan. . . . Don't let them ride yer, Dan."

They lined up in the dark road feeling the mud slopping under their feet. The ruts were full of black water, in which gleamed a reflection of distant electric lights.

"All you fellows work in Storehouse A today," said the sergeant, who had been a preacher, in his sad, drawling voice. "Lieutenant says that's all got to be finished by noon. They're sending it to the front today."

Somebody let his breath out in a whistle of surprise.

"Who did that?"

Nobody answered.

"Dismissed!" snapped the sergeant disgustedly.

They straggled off into the darkness towards one of the lights, their feet splashing confusedly in the puddles.

Fuselli strolled up to the sentry at the camp gate. He was picking his teeth meditatively with the splinter of a pine board.

"Say, Phil, you couldn't lend me a half a dollar, could you?" Fuselli stopped, put his hands in his pockets and looked at the sentry with the splinter sticking out of a corner of his mouth.

"Sorry, Dan," said the other man; "I'm cleaned out. Ain't had a cent since New Year's."

"Why the hell don't they pay us?"

"You guys signed the pay roll yet?"

"Sure. So long!"

Fuselli strolled on down the dark road, where the mud was frozen into deep ruts, towards the town. It was still strange to him, this town of little houses faced with cracked stucco, where the damp made grey stains and green stains, of confused red-tiled roofs, and of narrow cobbled streets that zigzagged in and out among high walls overhung with balconies. At night, when it was dark except for where a lamp in a window spilt gold reflections out on the wet street or the light streamed out from a store or a café, it was almost frighteningly unreal. He walked down into the main square, where he could hear the fountain gurgling. In the middle he stopped indecisively, his coat unbuttoned, his hands pushed to the bottom of his trousers pockets, where they encountered nothing but the cloth. He listened a long time to the gurgling of the fountain and to the shunting of trains far away in the freight yards. "An' this is the war," he thought. "Ain't it queer? It's quieter than it was at home nights." Down the street at the end of the square a band of white light appeared, the searchlight of a staff car. The two eyes of the car stared straight into his eyes, dazzling him, then veered off to one side and whizzed past, leaving a faint smell of gasoline and a sound of voices. Fuselli watched the fronts of houses light up as the car made its way to the main road. Then the town was dark and silent again.

He strolled across the square towards the Cheval Blanc, the large café where the officers went.

"Button yer coat," came a gruff voice. He saw a stiff tall figure at the edge of the curve. He made out the shape of the pistol holster that hung like a thin ham at the man's thigh. An M.P. He buttoned his coat hurriedly and walked off with rapid steps.

He stopped outside a café that had "Ham and Eggs" written in white paint on the window and looked in wistfully. Someone from behind him put two big hands over his eyes. He wriggled his head free.

"Hello, Dan," he said. "How did you get out of the jug?"

"I'm a trusty, kid," said Dan Cohan. "Got any dough?"

"Not a damn cent!"

"Me neither. . . . Come on in anyway," said Cohan. "I'll fix it up with Marie." Fuselli followed doubtfully. He was a little afraid of Dan Cohan; he remembered how a man had been court-martialed last week for trying to bolt out of a café without paying for his drinks.

He sat down at a table near the door. Dan had disappeared into the back room. Fuselli felt homesick. He was thinking how long it was since he had had a letter from Mabe. "I bet she's got another feller," he told himself savagely. He tried to remember how she looked, but he had to take out his watch and peep in the back before he could make out if her nose were straight or snub. He looked up, clicking the watch in his pocket. Marie of the white arms was coming laughing out of the inner room. Her large firm breasts, neatly held in by the close-fitting blouse, shook a little when she laughed. Her cheeks were very red and a strand of chestnut hair hung down along her neck. She picked it up hurriedly and caught it up with a hairpin, walking slowly into the middle of the room as she did so with her hands behind her head. Dan Cohan followed her into the room, a broad grin on his face.

"All right, kid," he said. "I told her you'd pay when Uncle Sam came across. Ever had any Kümmel?"

"What the hell's that?"

"You'll see."

They sat down before a dish of fried eggs at the table in the corner, the favoured table, where Marie herself often sat and chatted, when wizened Madame did not have her eye upon her.

Several men drew up their chairs. Wild Dan Cohan always had an audience.

"Looks like there was going to be another offensive at Verdun," said Dan Cohan. Someone answered vaguely.

"Funny how little we know about what's going on out there," said one man. "I knew more about the war when I was home in Minneapolis than I do here."

"I guess we're lightin' into 'em all right," said Fuselli in a patriotic voice.

"Hell! Nothin' doin' this time o' year anyway," said Cohan. A grin spread across his red face. "Last time I was at the front the Boche had just made a coup de main and captured a whole trenchful."

"Of who?"

"Of Americans—of us!"

"The hell you say!"

"That's a goddam lie," shouted a black-haired man with an ill-shaven jaw, who had just come in. "There ain't never been an American captured, an' there never will be, by God!"

"How long were you at the front, buddy," asked Cohan coolly. "I guess you been to Berlin already, ain't yer?"

"I say that any man who says an American'ld let himself be captured by a stinkin' Hun, is a goddam liar," said the man with the ill-shaven jaw, sitting down sullenly.

"Well, you'd better not say it to me," said Cohan laughing, looking meditatively at one of his big red fists.

There had been a look of apprehension on Marie's face. She looked at Cohan's fist and shrugged her shoulders and laughed.

Another crowd had just slouched into the café.

"Well if that isn't wild Dan! Hello, old kid, how are you?"

"Hello, Dook!"

A small man in a coat that looked almost like an officer's coat, it was so well cut, was shaking hands effusively with Cohan. He wore a corporal's stripes and a British aviator's fatigue cap. Cohan made room for him on the bench.

"What are you doing in this hole, Dook?"

The man twisted his mouth so that his neat black mustache was a slant.

"G.O. 42," he said.

"Battle of Paris?" said Cohan in a sympathetic voice.

"Battle of Nice! I'm going back to my section soon. I'd never have got a court-martial if I'd been with my outfit. I was in the Base Hospital 15 with pneumonia."

"Tough luck!"

"It was a hell of a note."

"Say, Dook, your outfit was working with ours at Chamfort that time, wasn't it?"

"You mean when we evacuated the nut hospital?"

"Yes, wasn't that hell?" Dan Cohan gulped down half a glass of red wine, smacked his thick lips, and began in his story-telling voice:

"Our section had just come out of Verdun where we'd been getting hell for three weeks on the Bras road. There was one little hill where we'd have to get out and shove every damn time, the mud was so deep, and God, it stank there with the shells turning up the ground all full of mackabbies as the poilus call them. . . . Say, Dook, have you got any money?"

"I've got some," said Dook, without enthusiasm.

"Well, the champagne's damn good here. I'm part of the outfit in this gin mill; they'll give it to you at a reduction."

"All right!"

Dan Cohan turned round and whispered something to Marie. She laughed and dived down behind the curtain.

"But that Chamfort was worse yet. Everybody was sort o' nervous because the Germans had dropped a message sayin' they'd give 'em three days to clear the hospital out, and that then they'd shell hell out of the place."

"The Germans done that! Quit yer kiddin'," said Fuselli.

"They did it at Souilly, too," said Dook.

"Hell, yes. . . . A funny thing happened there. The hospital was in a big rambling house, looked like an Atlantic City hotel. . . . We used to run our car in back and sleep in it. It was where we took the shell-shock cases, fellows who were roarin' mad, and tremblin' all over, and some of 'em paralysed like. . . . There was a man in the wing opposite where we slept who kept laughin'. Bill Rees was on the car with me, and we laid in our blankets in the bottom of the car and every now and then one of us'ld turn over and whisper: 'Ain't this hell, kid?' 'cause that feller kept laughin' like a man who had just heard a joke that was so funny he couldn't stop laughin'. It wasn't like a crazy man's laugh usually is. When I first heard it I thought it was a man really laughin', and I guess I laughed too. But it didn't stop. . . . Bill Rees an' me laid in our car shiverin', listenin' to the barrage in the distance with now and then the big noise of an aeroplane bomb, an' that feller laughin', laughin', like he'd just heard a joke, like something had struck him funny." Cohan took a gulp of champagne and jerked his head to one side. "An' that damn laughin' kept up until about noon the next day when the orderlies strangled the feller. . . . Got their goat, I guess."

Fuselli was looking towards the other side of the room, where a faint murmur of righteous indignation was rising from the dark man with the unshaven jaw and his companions. Fuselli was thinking that it wasn't good to be seen round too much with a fellow like Cohan, who talked about the Germans notifying hospitals before they bombarded them, and who was waiting for a court-martial. Might get him in wrong. He slipped out of the café into the dark. A dank wind blew down the irregular street, ruffling the reflected light in the puddles, making a shutter bang interminably somewhere. Fuselli went to the main square again, casting an envious glance in the window of the Cheval Blanc, where he saw officers playing billiards in a well-lighted room painted white and gold, and a blond girl in a raspberry-colored shirtwaist enthroned haughtily behind the bar. He remembered the M.P. and automatically hastened his steps. In a narrow street the other side of the square he stopped before the window of a small grocery shop and peered inside, keeping carefully out of the oblong of light that showed faintly the grass-grown cobbles and the green and grey walls opposite. A girl sat knitting beside the small counter with her two little black feet placed demurely side by side on the edge of a box full of red beets. She was very small and slender. The lamplight gleamed on her black hair, done close to her head. Her face was in the shadow. Several soldiers lounged awkwardly against the counter and the jambs of the door, following her movements with their eyes as dogs watch a plate of meat being moved about in a kitchen.

After a little the girl rolled up her knitting and jumped to her feet, showing her face,—an oval white face with large dark lashes and an impertinent mouth. She stood looking at the soldiers who stood about her in a circle, then twisted up her mouth in a grimace and disappeared into the inner room.

Fuselli walked to the end of the street where there was a bridge over a small stream. He leaned on the cold stone rail and looked into the water that was barely visible gurgling beneath between rims of ice.

"O this is a hell of a life," he muttered.

He shivered in the cold wind but remained leaning over the water. In the distance trains rumbled interminably, giving him a sense of vast desolate distances. The village clock struck eight. The bell had a soft note like the bass string of a guitar. In the darkness Fuselli could almost see the girl's face grimacing with its broad impertinent lips. He thought of the sombre barracks and men sitting about on the end of their cots. Hell, he couldn't go back yet. His whole body was taut with desire for warmth and softness and quiet. He slouched back along the narrow street cursing in a dismal monotone. Before the grocery store he stopped. The men had gone. He went in jauntily pushing his cap a little to one side so that some of his thick curly hair came out over his forehead. The little bell in the door clanged.

The girl came out of the inner room. She gave him her hand indifferently.

"Comment ça va! Yvonne? Bon?"

His pidgin-French made her show her little pearly teeth in a smile.

"Good," she said in English.

They laughed childishly.

"Say, will you be my girl, Yvonne?"

She looked in his eyes and laughed.

"Non compris," she said.

"We, we; voulez vous et' ma fille?"

She shrieked with laughter and slapped him hard on the cheek.

"Venez," she said, still laughing. He followed her. In the inner room was a large oak table with chairs round it. At the end Eisenstein and a French soldier were talking excitedly, so absorbed in what they were saying that they did not notice the other two. Yvonne took the Frenchman by the hair and pulled his head back and told him, still laughing, what Fuselli had said. He laughed.

"No, you must not say that," he said in English, turning to Fuselli.

Fuselli was angry and sat down sullenly at the end of the table, keeping his eyes on Yvonne. She drew the knitting out of the pocket of her apron and holding it up comically between two fingers, glanced towards the dark corner of the room where an old woman with a lace cap on her head sat asleep, and then let herself fall into a chair.

"Boom!" she said.

Fuselli laughed until the tears filled his eyes. She laughed too. They sat a long while looking at each other and giggling, while Eisenstein and the Frenchman talked. Suddenly Fuselli caught a phrase that startled him.

"What would you Americans do if revolution broke out in France?"

"We'd do what we were ordered to," said Eisenstein bitterly. "We're a bunch of slaves." Fuselli noticed that Eisenstein's puffy sallow face was flushed and that there was a flash in his eyes he had never seen before.

"How do you mean, revolution?" asked Fuselli in a puzzled voice.

The Frenchman turned black eyes searchingly upon him.

"I mean, stop the butchery,—overthrow the capitalist government.—The social revolution."

"But you're a republic already, ain't yer?"

"As much as you are."

"You talk like a socialist," said Fuselli. "They tell me they shoot guys in America for talkin' like that."

"You see!" said Eisenstein to the Frenchman.

"Are they all like that?"

"Except a very few. It's hopeless," said Eisenstein, burying his face in his hands. "I often think of shooting myself."

"Better shoot someone else," said the Frenchman. "It will be more useful."

Fuselli stirred uneasily in his chair.

"Where'd you fellers get that stuff anyway?" he asked. In his mind he was saying: "A kike and a frog, that's a good combination."

His eye caught Yvonne's and they both laughed. Yvonne threw her knitting ball at him. It rolled down under the table and they both scrambled about under the chairs looking for it.

"Twice I have thought it was going to happen," said the Frenchman.

"When was that?"

"A little while ago a division started marching on Paris. . . .

And when I was in Verdun. . . . O there will be a revolution. . . . France is the country of revolutions."

"We'll always be here to shoot you down," said Eisenstein.

"Wait till you've been in the war a little while. A winter in the trenches will make any army ready for revolution."

"But we have no way of learning the truth. And in the tyranny of the army a man becomes a brute, a piece of machinery. Remember you are freer than we are. We are worse than the Russians!"

"It is curious! . . . O but you must have some feeling of civilization. I have always heard that Americans were free and independent. Will they let themselves be driven to the slaughter always?"

"O I don't know." Eisenstein got to his feet. "We'd better be getting to barracks. Coming, Fuselli?" he said.

"Guess so," said Fuselli indifferently, without getting up.

Eisenstein and the Frenchman went out into the shop.

"Bon swar," said Fuselli, softly, leaning across the table. "Hey, girlie?"

He threw himself on his belly on the wide table and put his arms round her neck and kissed her, feeling everything go blank in a flame of desire.

She pushed him away calmly with strong little arms.

"Stop!" she said, and jerked her head in the direction of the old woman in the chair in the dark corner of the room. They stood side by side listening to her faint wheezy snoring.

He put his arms round her and kissed her long on the mouth.

"Demain," he said.

She nodded her head.

Fuselli walked fast up the dark street towards the camp. The blood pounded happily through his veins. He caught up with Eisenstein.

"Say, Eisenstein," he said in a comradely voice, "I don't think you ought to go talking round like that. You'll get yourself in too deep one of these days."

"I don't care!"

"But, hell, man, you don't want to get in the wrong that bad. They shoot fellers for less than you said."

"Let them."

"Christ, man, you don't want to be a damn fool," expostulated Fuselli.

"How old are you, Fuselli?"

"I'm twenty now."

"I'm thirty. I've lived more, kid. I know what's good and what's bad. This butchery makes me unhappy."

"God, I know. It's a hell of a note. But who brought it on? If somebody had shot that Kaiser."

Eisenstein laughed bitterly. At the entrance of camp Fuselli lingered a moment watching the small form of Eisenstein disappear with its curious waddly walk into the darkness.

"I'm going to be damn careful who I'm seen goin' into barracks with," he said to himself. "That damn kike may be a German spy or a secret-service officer." A cold chill of terror went over him, shattering his mood of joyous self-satisfaction. His feet slopped in the puddles, breaking through the thin ice, as he walked up the road towards the barracks. He felt as if people were watching him from everywhere out of the darkness, as if some gigantic figure were driving him forward through the darkness, holding a fist over his head, ready to crush him.

When he was rolled up in his blankets in the bunk next to Bill Grey, he whispered to his friend:

"Say, Bill, I think I've got a skirt all fixed up in town."

"Who?"

"Yvonne—don't tell anybody."

Bill Grey whistled softly.

"You're some highflyer, Dan."

Fuselli chuckled.

"Hell, man, the best ain't good enough for me."

"Well, I'm going to leave you," said Bill Grey.

"When?"

"Damn soon. I can't go this life. I don't see how you can."

Fuselli did not answer. He snuggled warmly into his blankets, thinking of Yvonne and the corporalship.

In the light of the one flickering lamp that made an unsteady circle of reddish glow on the station platform Fuselli looked at his pass. From Reveille on February fourth to Reveille on February fifth he was a free man. His eyes smarted

with sleep as he walked up and down the cold station platform. For twenty-four hours he wouldn't have to obey anybody's orders. Despite the loneliness of going away on a train
in a night like this in a strange country Fuselli was happy. He
clinked the money in his pocket.

Down the track a red eye appeared and grew nearer. He
could hear the hard puffing of the engine up the grade. Huge
curves gleamed as the engine roared slowly past him. A man
with bare arms black with coal dust was leaning out of the
cab, lit up from behind by a yellowish red glare. Now the cars
were going by, flat cars with guns, tilted up like the muzzles
of hunting dogs, freight cars out of which here and there
peered a man's head. The train almost came to a stop. The
cars clanged one against the other all down the train. Fuselli
was looking into a pair of eyes that shone in the lamplight; a
hand was held out to him.

"So long, kid," said a boyish voice. "I don't know who the
hell you are, but so long; good luck."

"So long," stammered Fuselli. "Going to the front?"

"Yer goddam right," answered another voice.

The train took up speed again; the clanging of car against
car ceased and in a moment they were moving fast before
Fuselli's eyes. Then the station was dark and empty again, and
he was watching the red light grow smaller and paler while
the train rumbled on into the darkness.

A confusion of gold and green and crimson silks and intricate designs of naked pink-fleshed cupids filled Fuselli's mind,
when, full of wonder, he walked down the steps of the palace
out into the faint ruddy sunlight of the afternoon. A few
names, Napoleon, Josephine, the Empire, that had never had
significance in his mind before, flared with a lurid gorgeous
light in his imagination like a tableau of living statues at a
vaudeville theatre.

"They must have had a heap of money, them guys," said
the man who was with him, a private in Aviation. "Let's go
have a drink."

Fuselli was silent and absorbed in his thoughts. Here was
something that supplemented his visions of wealth and glory
that he used to tell Al about, when they'd sit and watch the

big liners come in, all glittering with lights, through the
Golden Gate.

"They didn't mind having naked women about, did they?"
said the private in Aviation, a morose foul-mouthed little man
who had been in the woolen business.

"D'ye blame them?"

"No, I can't say's I do. . . . I bet they was immoral, them
guys," he continued vaguely.

They wandered about the streets of Fontainebleau listlessly,
looking into shop windows, staring at women, lolling on
benches in the parks where the faint sunlight came through a
lacework of twigs purple and crimson and yellow, that cast intricate lavender-grey shadows on the asphalt.

"Let's go have another drink," said the private in Aviation.

Fuselli looked at his watch; they had hours before train
time.

A girl in a loose dirty blouse wiped off the table.

"Vin blank," said the other man.

"Mame shows," said Fuselli.

His head was full of gold and green mouldings and silk and
crimson velvet and intricate designs in which naked pink-
fleshed cupids writhed indecently. Some day, he was saying to
himself, he'd make a hell of a lot of money and live in a house
like that with Mabe; no, with Yvonne, or with some other
girl.

"Must have been immoral, them guys," said the private in
Aviation, leering at the girl in the dirty blouse.

Fuselli remembered a revel he'd seen in a moving picture of
"Quo Vadis," people in bath robes dancing around with large
cups in their hands and tables full of dishes being upset.

"Cognac, beaucoup," said the private in Aviation.

"Mame shows," said Fuselli.

The café was full of gold and green silks, and great brocaded
beds with heavy carvings above them, beds in which writhed,
pink-fleshed and indecent, intricate patterns of cupids.

Somebody said, "Hello, Fuselli."

He was on the train; his ears hummed and his head had an
iron band round it. It was dark except for the little light that
flickered in the ceiling. For a minute he thought it was a goldfish in a bowl, but it was a light that flickered in the ceiling.

"Hello, Fuselli," said Eisenstein. "Feel all right?"

"Sure," said Fuselli with a thick voice. "Why shouldn't I?"

"How did you find that house?" said Eisenstein seriously.

"Hell, I don't know," muttered Fuselli. "I'm goin' to sleep."

His mind was a jumble. He remembered vast halls full of green and gold silks, and great beds with crowns over them where Napoleon and Josephine used to sleep. Who were they? O yes, the Empire,—or was it the Abdication? Then there were patterns of flowers and fruits and cupids, all gilded, and a dark passage and stairs that smelt musty, where he and the man in Aviation fell down. He remembered how it felt to rub his nose hard on the gritty red plush carpet of the stairs. Then there were women in open-work skirts standing about, or were those the pictures on the walls? And there was a bed with mirrors round it. He opened his eyes. Eisenstein was talking to him. He must have been talking to him for some time.

"I look at it this way," he was saying. "A feller needs a little of that to keep healthy. Now, if he's abstemious and careful . . ."

Fuselli went to sleep. He woke up again thinking suddenly: he must borrow that little blue book of army regulations. It would be useful to know that in case something came up. The corporal who had been in the Red Sox outfield had been transferred to a Base Hospital. It was t.b. so Sergeant Osler said. Anyway they were going to appoint an acting corporal. He stared at the flickering little light in the ceiling.

"How did you get a pass?" Eisenstein was asking.

"Oh, the sergeant fixed me up with one," answered Fuselli mysteriously.

"You're in pretty good with the sergeant, ain't yer?" said Eisenstein.

Fuselli smiled deprecatingly.

"Say, d'ye know that little kid Stockton?"

"The white-faced little kid who's clerk in that outfit that has the other end of the barracks?"

"That's him," said Eisenstein. "I wish I could do something to help that kid. He just can't stand the discipline. . . . You ought to see him wince when the red-haired sergeant over there yells at him. . . . The kid looks sicker every day."

"Well, he's got a good soft job: clerk," said Fuselli.

"Ye think it's soft? I worked twelve hours day before yesterday getting out reports," said Eisenstein, indignantly. "But the kid's lost it and they keep ridin' him for some reason or other. It hurts a feller to see that. He ought to be at home at school."

"He's got to take his medicine," said Fuselli.

"You wait till we get butchered in the trenches. We'll see how you like your medicine," said Eisenstein.

"Damn fool," muttered Fuselli, composing himself to sleep again.

The bugle wrenched Fuselli out of his blankets, half dead with sleep.

"Say, Bill, I got a head again," he muttered.

There was no answer. It was only then that he noticed that the cot next to his was empty. The blankets were folded neatly at the foot. Sudden panic seized him. He couldn't get along without Bill Grey, he said to himself, he wouldn't have anyone to go round with. He looked fixedly at the empty cot.

"Attention!"

The company was lined up in the dark with their feet in the mud puddles of the road. The lieutenant strode up and down in front of them with the tail of his trench coat sticking out behind. He had a pocket flashlight that he kept flashing at the gaunt trunks of trees, in the faces of the company, at his feet, in the puddles of the road.

"If any man knows anything about the whereabouts of Private 1st-class William Grey, report at once, as otherwise we shall have to put him down A.W.O.L. You know what that means?" The lieutenant spoke in short shrill periods, chopping off the ends of his words as if with a hatchet.

No one said anything.

"I guess he's S.O.L."; this from someone behind Fuselli.

"And I have one more announcement to make, men," said the lieutenant in his natural voice. "I'm going to appoint Fuselli, 1st-class private, acting corporal."

Fuselli's knees were weak under him. He felt like shouting and dancing with joy. He was glad it was dark so that no one could see how excited he was.

"Sergeant, dismiss the company," said the lieutenant bringing his voice back to its military tone.

"Companee dis-missed!" said out the sergeant jovially.

In groups, talking with crisp voices, cheered by the occurrence of events, the company straggled across the great stretch of mud puddles towards the mess shack.

IV

Yvonne tossed the omelette in the air. It landed sizzling in the pan again, and she came forward into the light, holding the frying pan before her. Behind her was the dark stove and above it a row of copper kettles that gleamed through the bluish obscurity. She flicked the omelette out of the pan into the white dish that stood in the middle of the table, full in the yellow lamplight.

"Tiens," she said, brushing a few stray hairs off her forehead with the back of her hand.

"You're some cook," said Fuselli getting to his feet. He had been sprawling on a chair in the other end of the kitchen, watching Yvonne's slender body in tight black dress and blue apron move in and out of the area of light as she got dinner ready. A smell of burnt butter, with a faint tang of pepper in it, filled the kitchen, making his mouth water.

"This is the real stuff," he was saying to himself,—"like home."

He stood with his hands deep in his pockets and his head thrown back, watching her cut the bread, holding the big loaf to her chest and pulling the knife towards her. She brushed some crumbs off her dress with a thin white hand.

"You're my girl, Yvonne; ain't yer?" Fuselli put his arms round her.

"Sale bête," she said, laughing and pushing him away.

There was a brisk step outside and another girl came into the kitchen, a thin yellow-faced girl with a sharp nose and long teeth.

"Ma cousine. . . . Mon 'tit américain." They both laughed. Fuselli blushed as he shook the girl's hand.

"Il est beau, hein?" said Yvonne gruffly.

"Mais, ma petite, il est charmant, vot' américain!" They laughed again. Fuselli who did not understand laughed too, thinking to himself, "They'll let the dinner get cold if they don't sit down soon."

"Get maman, Dan," said Yvonne.

Fuselli went into the shop through the room with the long

oak table. In the dim light that came from the kitchen he saw the old woman's white bonnet. Her face was in shadow but there was a faint gleam of light in her small beady eyes.

"Supper, ma'am," he shouted.

Grumbling in her creaky little voice, the old woman followed him back into the kitchen.

Steam, gilded by the lamplight, rose in pillars to the ceiling from the big tureen of soup.

There was a white cloth on the table and a big loaf of bread at the end. The plates, with borders of little roses on them, seemed, after the army mess, the most beautiful things Fuselli had ever seen. The wine bottle was black beside the soup tureen and the wine in the glasses cast a dark purple stain on the cloth.

Fuselli ate his soup silently understanding very little of the French that the two girls rattled at each other. The old woman rarely spoke and when she did one of the girls would throw her a hasty remark that hardly interrupted their chatter.

Fuselli was thinking of the other men lining up outside the dark mess shack and the sound the food made when it flopped into the mess kits. An idea came to him. He'd have to bring Sarge to see Yvonne. They could set him up to a feed. "It would help me to stay in good with him." He had a minute's worry about his corporalship. He was acting corporal right enough, but he wanted them to send in his appointment.

The omelette melted in his mouth.

"Damn bon," he said to Yvonne with his mouth full.

She looked at him fixedly.

"Bon, bon," he said again.

"You. . . . Dan, bon," she said and laughed. The cousin was looking from one to the other enviously, her upper lip lifted away from her teeth in a smile.

The old woman munched her bread in a silent preoccupied fashion.

"There's somebody in the store," said Fuselli after a long pause. "Je irey." He put his napkin down and went out wiping his mouth on the back of his hand. Eisenstein and a chalky-faced boy were in the shop.

"Hullo! are you keepin' house here?" asked Eisenstein.

"Sure," said Fuselli conceitedly.

"Have you got any chawclit?" asked the chalky-faced boy in a thin bloodless voice.

Fuselli looked round the shelves and threw a cake of chocolate down on the counter.

"Anything else?"

"Nothing, thank you, corporal. How much is it?"

Whistling "There's a long, long trail a-winding," Fuselli strode back into the inner room.

"Combien chocolate?" he asked.

When he had received the money, he sat down at his place at table again, smiling importantly. He must write Al about all this, he was thinking, and he was wondering vaguely whether Al had been drafted yet.

After dinner the women sat a long time chatting over their coffee, while Fuselli squirmed uneasily on his chair, looking now and then at his watch. His pass was till twelve only; it was already getting on to ten. He tried to catch Yvonne's eye, but she was moving about the kitchen putting things in order for the night, and hardly seemed to notice him. At last the old woman shuffled into the shop and there was the sound of a key clicking hard in the outside door. When she came back, Fuselli said good-night to everyone and left by the back door into the court. There he leaned sulkily against the wall and waited in the dark, listening to the sounds that came from the house. He could see shadows passing across the orange square of light the window threw on the cobbles of the court. A light went on in an upper window, sending a faint glow over the disorderly tiles of the roof of the shed opposite. The door opened and Yvonne and her cousin stood on the broad stone doorstep chattering. Fuselli had pushed himself in behind a big hogshead that had a pleasant tang of old wood damp with sour wine. At last the heads of the shadows on the cobbles came together for a moment and the cousin clattered across the court and out into the empty streets. Her rapid footsteps died away. Yvonne's shadow was still in the door:

"Dan," she said softly.

Fuselli came out from behind the hogshead, his whole body flushing with delight. Yvonne pointed to his shoes. He took them off, and left them beside the door. He looked at his watch. It was a quarter to eleven.

"Viens," she said.

He followed her, his knees trembling a little from excitement, up the steep stairs.

The deep broken strokes of the town clock had just begun to strike midnight when Fuselli hurried in the camp gate. He gave up his pass jauntily to the guard and strolled towards his barracks. The long shed was pitch black, full of a sound of deep breathing and of occasional snoring. There was a thick smell of uniform wool on which the sweat had dried. Fuselli undressed without haste, stretching his arms luxuriously. He wriggled into his blankets feeling cool and tired, and went to sleep with a smile of self-satisfaction on his lips.

The companies were lined up for retreat, standing stiff as toy soldiers outside their barracks. The evening was almost warm. A little playful wind, oozing with springtime, played with the swollen buds on the plane trees. The sky was a drowsy violet color, and the blood pumped hot and stinging through the stiffened arms and legs of the soldiers who stood at attention. The voices of the non-coms were particularly harsh and metallic this evening. It was rumored that a general was about. Orders were shouted with fury.

Standing behind the line of his company, Fuselli's chest was stuck out until the buttons of his tunic were in danger of snapping off. His shoes were well-shined, and he wore a new pair of puttees, wound so tightly that his legs ached.

At last the bugle sounded across the silent camp.

"Parade rest!" shouted the lieutenant.

Fuselli's mind was full of the army regulations which he had been studying assiduously for the last week. He was thinking of an imaginary examination for the corporalship, which he would pass, of course.

When the company was dismissed, he went up familiarly to the top sergeant:

"Say, Sarge, doin' anything this evenin'?"

"What the hell can a man do when he's broke?" said the top sergeant.

"Well, you come down town with me. I want to introduce you to somebody."

"Great!"

"Say, Sarge, have they sent that appointment in yet?"

"No, they haven't, Fuselli," said the top sergeant. "It's all made out," he added encouragingly.

They walked towards the town silently. The evening was silvery-violet. The few windows in the old grey-green houses that were lighted shone orange.

"Well, I'm goin' to get it, ain't I?"

A staff car shot by, splashing them with mud, leaving them a glimpse of officers leaning back in the deep cushions.

"You sure are," said the top sergeant in his good-natured voice.

They had reached the square. They saluted stiffly as two officers brushed past them.

"What's the regulations about a feller marryin' a French girl?" broke out Fuselli suddenly.

"Thinking of getting hitched up, are you?"

"Hell, no." Fuselli was crimson. "I just sort o' wanted to know."

"Permission of C.O., that's all I know of."

They had stopped in front of the grocery shop. Fuselli peered in through the window. The shop was full of soldiers lounging against the counter and the walls. In the midst of them, demurely knitting, sat Yvonne.

"Let's go and have a drink an' then come back," said Fuselli.

They went to the café where Marie of the white arms presided. Fuselli paid for two hot rum punches.

"You see it's this way, Sarge," he said confidentially, "I wrote all my folks at home I'd been made corporal, an' it'ld be a hell of a note to be let down now."

The top sergeant was drinking his hot drink in little sips. He smiled broadly and put his hand paternal-fashion on Fuselli's knee.

"Sure; you needn't worry, kid. I've got you fixed up all right," he said; then he added jovially, "Well, let's go see that girl of yours."

They went out into the dark streets, where the wind, despite the smell of burnt gasolene and army camps, had a faint suavity, something like the smell of mushrooms; the smell of spring.

Yvonne sat under the lamp in the shop, her feet up on a

box of canned peas, yawning dismally. Behind her on the counter was the glass case full of yellow and greenish-white cheeses. Above that shelves rose to the ceiling in the brownish obscurity of the shop where gleamed faintly large jars and small jars, cans neatly placed in rows, glass jars and vegetables. In the corner, near the glass curtained door that led to the inner room, hung clusters of sausages large and small, red, yellow, and speckled. Yvonne jumped up when Fuselli and the sergeant opened the door.

"You are good," she said. "Je mourrais de cafard." They laughed.

"You know what that mean—cafard?"

"Sure."

"It is only since the war. Avant la guerre on ne savais pas ce que c'etait le cafard. The war is no good."

"Funny, ain't it?" said Fuselli to the top sergeant, "a feller can't juss figure out what the war is like."

"Don't you worry. We'll all get there," said the top sergeant knowingly.

"This is the sarjon, Yvonne," said Fuselli.

"Oui, oui, je sais," said Yvonne, smiling at the top sergeant.

They sat in the little room behind the shop and drank white wine, and talked as best they could to Yvonne, who, very trim in her black dress and blue apron, perched on the edge of her chair with her feet in tiny pumps pressed tightly together, and glanced now and then at the elaborate stripes on the top sergeant's arm.

Fuselli strode familiarly into the grocery shop, whistling, and threw open the door to the inner room. His whistling stopped in the middle of a bar.

"Hello," he said in an annoyed voice.

"Hello, corporal," said Eisenstein. Eisenstein, his French soldier friend, a lanky man with a scraggly black beard and burning black eyes, and Stockton, the chalky-faced boy, were sitting at the table that filled up the room, chatting intimately and gaily with Yvonne, who leaned against the yellow wall beside the Frenchman and showed all her little pearly teeth in a laugh. In the middle of the dark oak table was a pot of hyacinths and some glasses that had had wine in them. The odor of the hyacinths hung in the air with a faint warm smell from the kitchen.

After a second's hesitation, Fuselli sat down to wait until the others should leave. It was long after pay-day and his pockets were empty, so he had nowhere else to go.

"How are they treatin' you down in your outfit now?" asked Eisenstein of Stockton, after a silence.

"Same as ever," said Stockton in his thin voice, stuttering a little. . . . "Sometimes I wish I was dead."

"Hum," said Eisenstein, a curious expression of understanding on his flabby face. "We'll be civilians some day."

"I won't," said Stockton.

"Hell," said Eisenstein. "You've got to keep your upper lip stiff. I thought I was goin' to die in that troopship coming over here. An' when I was little an' came over with the emigrants from Poland, I thought I was goin' to die. A man can stand more than he thinks for. . . . I never thought I could stand being in the army, bein' a slave like an' all that, an' I'm still here. No, you'll live long and be successful yet." He put his hand on Stockton's shoulder. The boy winced and drew his chair away.

"What for you do that? I ain't goin' to hurt you," said Eisenstein.

Fuselli looked at them both with a disgusted interest.

"I'll tell you what you'd better do, kid," he said condescendingly. "You get transferred to our company. It's an A1 bunch, ain't it, Eisenstein? We've got a good loot an' a good top-kicker, an' a damn good bunch o' fellers."

"Our top-kicker was in here a few minutes ago," said Eisenstein.

"He was?" asked Fuselli. "Where'd he go?"

"Damned if I know."

Yvonne and the French soldier were talking in low voices, laughing a little now and then. Fuselli leaned back in his chair looking at them, feeling out of things, wishing despondently that he knew enough French to understand what they were saying. He scraped his feet angrily back and forth on the floor. His eyes lit on the white hyacinths. They made him think of florists' windows at home at Eastertime and the noise and bustle of San Francisco's streets. "God, I hate this rotten hole," he muttered to himself. He thought of Mabe. He made a noise with his lips. Hell, she was married by this time. Anyway Yvonne was the girl for him. If he could only have Yvonne to himself; far away somewhere, away from the other men and that damn frog and her old mother. He thought of himself going to the theatre with Yvonne. When he was a sergeant he would be able to afford that sort of thing. He counted up the months. It was March. Here he'd been in Europe five months and he was still only a corporal, and not that yet. He clenched his fists with impatience. But once he got to be a non-com it would go faster, he told himself reassuringly.

He leaned over and sniffed loudly at the hyacinths.

"They smell good," he said. "Que disay vous, Yvonne?"

Yvonne looked at him as if she had forgotten that he was in the room. Her eyes looked straight into his, and she burst out laughing. Her glance had made him feel warm all over, and he leaned back in his chair again, looking at her slender body so neatly cased in its black dress and at her little head with its tightly-done hair, with a comfortable feeling of possession.

"Yvonne, come over here," he said, beckoning with his head.

She looked from him to the Frenchman provocatively. Then she came over and stood behind him.

"Que voulez-vous?"

Fuselli glanced at Eisenstein. He and Stockton were deep in excited conversation with the Frenchman again. Fuselli heard that uncomfortable word that always made him angry, he did not know why, "Revolution."

"Yvonne," he said so that only she could hear, "what you say you and me get married?"

"Marriés . . . moi et toi?" asked Yvonne in a puzzled voice.

"We we."

She looked him in the eyes a moment, and then threw back her head in a paroxysm of hysterical laughter.

Fuselli flushed scarlet, got to his feet and strode out, slamming the door behind him so that the glass rang. He walked hurriedly back to camp, splashed with mud by the long lines of grey motor trucks that were throbbing their way slowly through the main street, each with a yellow eye that lit up faintly the tailboards of the truck ahead. The barracks were dark and nearly empty. He sat down at the sergeant's desk and began moodily turning over the pages of the little blue book of Army Regulations.

The moonlight glittered in the fountain at the end of the main square of the town. It was a warm dark night of faint clouds through which the moon shone palely as through a thin silk canopy. Fuselli stood by the fountain smoking a cigarette, looking at the yellow windows of the Cheval Blanc at the other end of the square, from which came a sound of voices and of billiard balls clinking. He stood quiet letting the acrid cigarette smoke drift out through his nose, his ears full of the silvery tinkle of the water in the fountain beside him. There were little drifts of warm and chilly air in the breeze that blew fitfully from the west. Fuselli was waiting. He took out his watch now and then and strained his eyes to see the time, but there was not light enough. At last the deep broken note of the bell in the church spire struck once. It must be half past ten.

He started walking slowly towards the street where Yvonne's grocery shop was. The faint glow of the moon lit up the grey houses with the shuttered windows and tumultuous red roofs full of little dormers and skylights. Fuselli felt deliciously at ease with the world. He could almost feel Yvonne's body in his arms and he smiled as he remembered the little faces she used to make at him. He slunk past the shuttered windows of the shop and dove into the darkness under the arch that led to the court. He walked cautiously, on tiptoe, keeping close to the moss-covered wall, for he heard voices in the court. He peeped round the edge of the building and saw that there were several people in the kitchen door talking. He drew his head back into the shadow. But he had caught a glimpse of the dark round form of the hogshead beside the kitchen door. If he only could get behind that as he usually did, he would be hidden until the people went away.

Keeping well in the shadow round the edge of the court, he slipped to the other side, and was just about to pop himself in behind the hogshead when he noticed that someone was there before him.

He caught his breath and stood still, his heart thumping.

The figure turned and in the dark he recognised the top sergeant's round face.

"Keep quiet, can't you?" whispered the top sergeant peevishly.

Fuselli stood still with his fists clenched. The blood flamed through his head, making his scalp tingle.

Still the top sergeant was the top sergeant, came the thought. It would never do to get in wrong with him. Fuselli's legs moved him automatically back into a corner of the court, where he leaned against the damp wall; glaring with smarting eyes at the two women who stood talking outside the kitchen door, and at the dark shadow behind the hogshead. At last, after several smacking kisses, the women went away and the kitchen door closed. The bell in the church spire struck eleven slowly and mournfully. When it had ceased striking, Fuselli heard a discreet tapping and saw the shadow of the top sergeant against the door. As he slipped in, Fuselli heard the top sergeant's good-natured voice in a large stage whisper, followed by a choked laugh from Yvonne. The door closed and the light was extinguished, leaving the court in darkness except for a faint marbled glow in the sky.

Fuselli strode out, making as much noise as he could with his heels on the cobble stones. The streets of the town were silent under the pale moon. In the square the fountain sounded loud and metallic. He gave up his pass to the guard and strode glumly towards the barracks. At the door he met a man with a pack on his back.

"Hullo, Fuselli," said a voice he knew. "Is my old bunk still there?"

"Damned if I know," said Fuselli; "I thought they'd shipped you home."

The corporal who had been on the Red Sox outfield broke into a fit of coughing.

"Hell, no," he said. "They kep' me at that goddam hospital till they saw I wasn't goin' to die right away, an' then they told me to come back to my outfit. So here I am!"

"Did they bust you?" said Fuselli with sudden eagerness.

"Hell, no. Why should they? They ain't gone and got a new corporal, have they?"

"No, not exactly," said Fuselli.

V

MEADVILLE stood near the camp gate watching the motor trucks go by on the main road. Grey, lumbering, and mud-covered, they throbbed by sloughing in and out of the mud holes in the worn road in an endless train stretching as far as he could see into the town and as far as he could see up the road.

He stood with his legs far apart and spat into the center of the road; then he turned to the corporal who had been in the Red Sox outfield and said:

"I'll be goddamed if there ain't somethin' doin'!"

"A hell of a lot doin'," said the corporal, shaking his head. "Seen that guy Daniels who's been to the front?"

"No."

"Well, he says hell's broke loose. Hell's broke loose!"

"What's happened? . . . Be gorry, we may see some active service," said Meadville, grinning. "By God, I'd give the best colt on my ranch to see some action."

"Got a ranch?" asked the corporal.

The motor trucks kept on grinding past monotonously; their drivers were so splashed with mud it was hard to see what uniform they wore.

"What d'ye think?" asked Meadville. "Think I keep store?"

Fuselli walked past them towards the town.

"Say, Fuselli," shouted Meadville. "Corporal says hell's broke loose out there. We may smell gunpowder yet."

Fuselli stopped and joined them.

"I guess poor old Bill Grey's smelt plenty of gunpowder by this time," he said.

"I wish I had gone with him," said Meadville. "I'll try that little trick myself now the good weather's come on if we don't get a move on soon."

"Too damn risky!"

"Listen to the kid. It'll be too damn risky in the trenches. . . . Or do you think you're goin' to get a cushy job in camp here?"

"Hell, no! I want to go to the front. I don't want to stay in this hole."

"Well?"

"But ain't no good throwin' yerself in where it don't do no good. . . . A guy wants to get on in this army if he can."

"What's the good o' gettin' on?" said the corporal. "Won't get home a bit sooner."

"Hell! but you're a non-com."

Another train of motor trucks went by, drowning their talk.

Fuselli was packing medical supplies in a box in a great brownish warehouse full of packing cases where a little sun filtered in through the dusty air at the corrugated sliding tin doors. As he worked, he listened to Daniels talking to Meadville who worked beside him.

"An' the gas is the goddamndest stuff I ever heard of," he was saying. "I've seen fellers with their arms swelled up to twice the size like blisters from it. Mustard gas, they call it."

"What did you get to go to the hospital?" said Meadville.

"Only pneumonia," said Daniels, "but I had a buddy who was split right in half by a piece of a shell. He was standin' as near me as you are an' was whistlin' 'Tipperary' under his breath when all at once there was a big spurt o' blood an' there he was with his chest split in half an' his head hangin' by a thread like."

Meadville moved his quid of tobacco from one cheek to the other and spat on to the sawdust of the floor. The men within earshot stopped working and looked admiringly at Daniels.

"Well; what d'ye reckon's goin' on at the front now?" said Meadville.

"Damned if I know. The goddam hospital at Orleans was so full up there was guys in stretchers waiting all day on the pavement outside. I know that. . . . Fellers there said hell'd broke loose for fair. Looks to me like the Fritzies was advancin'."

Meadville looked at him incredulously.

"Those skunks?" said Fuselli. "Why they can't advance. They're starvin' to death."

"The hell they are," said Daniels. "I guess you believe everything you see in the papers."

Eyes looked at Daniels indignantly. They all went on working in silence.

Suddenly the lieutenant, looking strangely flustered, strode
into the warehouse, leaving the tin door open behind him.

"Can anyone tell me where Sergeant Osler is?"

"He was here a few minutes ago," spoke up Fuselli.

"Well, where is he now?" snapped the lieutenant angrily.

"I don't know sir," mumbled Fuselli, flushing.

"Go and see if you can find him."

Fuselli went off to the other end of the warehouse. Outside
the door he stopped and bit off a cigarette in a leisurely fashion. His blood boiled sullenly. How the hell should he know
where the top sergeant was? They didn't expect him to be a
mind-reader, did they? And all the flood of bitterness that had
been collecting in his spirit seethed to the surface. They had
not treated him right. He felt full of hopeless anger against
this vast treadmill to which he was bound. The endless succession of the days, all alike, all subject to orders, to the interminable monotony of drills and line-ups, passed before his
mind. He felt he couldn't go on, yet he knew that he must
and would go on, that there was no stopping, that his feet
would go on beating in time to the steps of the treadmill.

He caught sight of the sergeant coming towards the warehouse, across the new green grass, scarred by the marks of
truck wheels.

"Sarge," he called. Then he went up to him mysteriously.
"The loot wants to see you at once in Warehouse B."

He slouched back to his work, arriving just in time to hear
the lieutenant say in a severe voice to the sergeant:

"Sergeant, do you know how to draw up court-martial
papers?"

"Yes, sir," said the sergeant, a look of surprise on his face.
He followed the precise steps of the lieutenant out of the
door.

Fuselli had a moment of panic terror, during which he went
on working methodically, although his hands trembled. He
was searching his memory for some infringement of a regula-
tion that might be charged against him. The terror passed as
fast as it had come. Of course he had no reason to fear. He
laughed softly to himself. What a fool he'd been to get scared

like that, and a summary court-martial couldn't do much to you anyway. He went on working as fast and as carefully as he could, through the long monotonous afternoon.

That night nearly the whole company gathered in a group at the end of the barracks. Both sergeants were away. The corporal said he knew nothing, and got sulkily into bed, where he lay, rolled in his blankets, shaken by fit after fit of coughing.

At last someone said:

"I bet that kike Eisenstein's turned out to be a spy."

"I bet he has too."

"He's foreign born, ain't he? Born in Poland or some goddam place."

"He always did talk queer."

"I always thought," said Fuselli, "he'd get into trouble talking the way he did."

"How'd he talk?" asked Daniels.

"Oh, he said that war was wrong and all that goddamed pro-German stuff."

"D'ye know what they did out at the front?" said Daniels. "In the second division they made two fellers dig their own graves and then shot 'em for sayin' the war was wrong."

"Hell, they did?"

"You're goddam right, they did. I tell you, fellers, it don't do to monkey with the buzz-saw in this army."

"For God's sake shut up. Taps has blown. Meadville, turn the lights out!" said the corporal angrily. The barracks was dark, full of a sound of men undressing in their bunks, and of whispered talk.

The company was lined up for morning mess. The sun that had just risen was shining in rosily through the soft clouds of the sky. The sparrows kept up a great clattering in the avenue of plane trees. Their riotous chirping could be heard above the sound of motors starting that came from a shed opposite the mess shack.

The sergeant appeared suddenly; walking past with his shoulders stiff, so that everyone knew at once that something important was going on.

"Attention, men, a minute," he said.

Mess kits clattered as the men turned round.

"After mess I want you to go immediately to barracks and roll your packs. After that every man must stand by his pack until orders come." The company cheered and mess kits clattered together like cymbals.

"As you were," shouted the top sergeant jovially.

Gluey oatmeal and greasy bacon were hurriedly bolted down, and every man in the company, his heart pounding, ran to the barracks to do up his pack, feeling proud under the envious eyes of the company at the other end of the shack that had received no orders.

When the packs were done up, they sat on the empty bunks and drummed their feet against the wooden partitions, waiting.

"I don't suppose we'll leave here till hell freezes over," said Meadville, who was doing up the last strap on his pack.

"It's always like this. . . . You break your neck to obey orders an' . . ."

"Outside!" shouted the sergeant, poking his head in the door. "Fall in! Atten-shun!"

The lieutenant in his trench coat and in a new pair of roll puttees stood facing the company, looking solemn.

"Men," he said, biting off his words as a man bites through a piece of hard stick candy; "one of your number is up for court-martial for possibly disloyal statements found in a letter addressed to friends at home. I have been extremely grieved to find anything of this sort in any company of mine; I don't believe there is another man in the company . . . low enough to hold . . . entertain such ideas. . . ."

Every man in the company stuck out his chest, vowing inwardly to entertain no ideas at all rather than run the risk of calling forth such disapproval from the lieutenant. The lieutenant paused:

"All I can say is if there is any such man in the company, he had better keep his mouth shut and be pretty damn careful what he writes home. . . . Dismissed!"

He shouted the order grimly, as if it were the order for the execution of the offender.

"That goddam skunk Eisenstein," said someone.

The lieutenant heard it as he walked away.

"Oh, sergeant," he said familiarly; "I think the others have got the right stuff in them."

The company went into the barracks and waited.

The sergeant-major's office was full of a clicking of type-writers, and was overheated by a black stove that stood in the middle of the floor, letting out occasional little puffs of smoke from a crack in the stove pipe. The sergeant-major was a small man with a fresh boyish face and a drawling voice who lolled behind a large typewriter reading a magazine that lay on his lap.

Fuselli slipped in behind the typewriter and stood with his cap in his hand beside the sergeant-major's chair.

"Well what do you want?" asked the sergeant-major gruffly.

"A feller told me, Sergeant-Major, that you was lookin' for a man with optical experience;" Fuselli's voice was velvety.

"Well?"

"I worked three years in an optical-goods store at home in Frisco."

"What's your name, rank, company?"

"Daniel Fuselli, Private 1st-class, Company C, medical supply warehouse."

"All right, I'll attend to it."

"But, sergeant."

"All right; out with what you've got to say, quick." The sergeant-major fingered the leaves of his magazine impatiently.

"My company's all packed up to go. The transfer'll have to be today, sergeant."

"Why the hell didn't you come in earlier? . . . Stevens, make out a transfer to headquarters company and get the major to sign it when he goes through. . . . That's the way it always is," he cried, leaning back tragically in his swivel chair. "Everybody always puts everything off on me at the last minute."

"Thank you, sir," said Fuselli, smiling.

The sergeant-major ran his hand through his hair and took up his magazine again peevishly.

Fuselli hurried back to barracks where he found the company still waiting. Several men were crouched in a circle playing craps. The rest lounged in their bare bunks or fiddled with their packs. Outside it had begun to rain softly, and a smell of wet sprouting earth came in through the open door.

Fuselli sat on the floor beside his bunk throwing his knife down so that it stuck in the boards between his knees. He was whistling softly to himself. The day dragged on. Several times he heard the town clock strike in the distance.

At last the top sergeant came in, shaking the water off his slicker, a serious, important expression on his face.

"Inspection of medical belts," he shouted. "Everybody open up their belt and lay it on the foot of their bunk and stand at attention on the left side."

The lieutenant and a major appeared suddenly at one end of the barracks and came through slowly, pulling the little packets out of the belts. The men looked at them out of the corners of their eyes. As they examined the belts, they chatted easily, as if they had been alone.

"Yes," said the major. "We're in for it this time. . . . That damned offensive."

"Well, we'll be able to show 'em what we're good for," said the lieutenant, laughing. "We haven't had a chance yet."

"Hum! Better mark that belt, lieutenant, and have it changed. Been to the front yet?"

"No, sir."

"Hum, well. . . . You'll look at things differently when you have," said the major.

The lieutenant frowned.

"Well, on the whole, lieutenant, your outfit is in very good shape. . . . At ease, men!" The lieutenant and the major stood at the door a moment raising the collars of their coats; then they dove out into the rain.

A few minutes later the sergeant came in.

"All right, get your slickers on and line up."

They stood lined up in the rain for a long while. It was a leaden afternoon. The even clouds had a faint coppery tinge. The rain beat in their faces, making them tingle. Fuselli was looking anxiously at the sergeant. At last the lieutenant appeared.

"Attention!" cried the sergeant.

The roll was called and a new man fell in at the end of the line, a tall man with large protruding eyes like a calf's.

"Private 1st-class Daniel Fuselli, fall out and report to head-quarters company!"

Fuselli saw a look of surprise come over men's faces. He smiled wanly at Meadville.

"Sergeant, take the men down to the station."

"Squads, right," cried the sergeant. "March!"

The company tramped off into the streaming rain.

Fuselli went back to the barracks, took off his pack and slicker and wiped the water off his face.

The rails gleamed gold in the early morning sunshine above the deep purple cinders of the track. Fuselli's eyes followed the track until it curved into a cutting where the wet clay was a bright orange in the clear light. The station platform, where puddles from the night's rain glittered as the wind ruffled them, was empty. Fuselli started walking up and down with his hands in his pockets. He had been sent down to unload some supplies that were coming on that morning's train. He felt free and successful since he joined the headquarters company. At last, he told himself, he had a job where he could show what he was good for. He walked up and down whistling shrilly.

A train pulled slowly into the station. The engine stopped to take water and the couplings clanked all down the line of cars. The platform was suddenly full of men in khaki, stamping their feet, running up and down shouting.

"Where you guys goin'?" asked Fuselli.

"We're bound for Palm Beach. Don't we look it?" someone snarled in reply.

But Fuselli had seen a familiar face. He was shaking hands with two browned men whose faces were grimy with days of travelling in freight cars.

"Hullo, Chrisfield. Hullo, Andrews!" he cried. "When did you fellows get over here?"

"Oh, 'bout four months ago," said Chrisfield, whose black eyes looked at Fuselli searchingly. "Oh! Ah 'member you. You're Fuselli. We was at trainin' camp together. 'Member him, Andy?"

"Sure," said Andrews.

"How are you makin' out?"

"Fine," said Fuselli. "I'm in the optical department here."

"Where the hell's that?"

"Right here." Fuselli pointed vaguely behind the station.

"We've been training about four months near Bordeaux," said Andrews; "and now we're going to see what it's like."

The whistle blew and the engine started puffing hard. Clouds of white steam filled the station platform, where the soldiers scampered for their cars.

"Good luck!" said Fuselli; but Andrews and Chrisfield had already gone. He saw them again as the train pulled out, two brown and dirt-grimed faces among many other brown and dirt-grimed faces. The steam floated up tinged with yellow in the bright early morning air as the last car of the train disappeared round the curve into the cutting.

The dust rose thickly about the worn broom. As it was a dark morning, very little light filtered into the room full of great white packing cases, where Fuselli was sweeping. He stopped now and then and leaned on his broom. Far away he heard a sound of trains shunting and shouts and the sound of feet tramping in unison from the drill ground. The building where he was was silent. He went on sweeping, thinking of his company tramping off through the streaming rain, and of those fellows he had known in training camp in America, Andrews and Chrisfield, jolting in box cars towards the front, where Daniel's buddy had had his chest split in half by a piece of shell. And he'd written home he'd been made a corporal. What was he going to do when letters came for him, addressed Corporal Dan Fuselli? Putting the broom away, he dusted the yellow chair and the table covered with order slips that stood in the middle of the piles of packing boxes. The door slammed somewhere below and there was a step on the stairs that led to the upper part of the warehouse. A little man with a monkey-like greyish-brown face and spectacles appeared and slipped out of his overcoat, like a very small bean popping out of a very large pod.

The sergeant's stripes looked unusually wide and conspicuous on his thin arm.

He grunted at Fuselli, sat down at the desk, and began at once peering among the order slips.

"Anything in our mailbox this morning?" he asked Fuselli in a hoarse voice.

"It's all there, sergeant," said Fuselli.

The sergeant peered about the desk some more.

"Ye'll have to wash that window today," he said after a pause. "Major's likely to come round here any time. . . . Ought to have been done yesterday."

"All right," said Fuselli dully.

He slouched over to the corner of the room, got the worn broom and began sweeping down the stairs. The dust rose about him, making him cough. He stopped and leaned on the broom. He thought of all the days that had gone by since he'd last seen those fellows, Andrews and Chrisfield, at training camp in America; and of all the days that would go by. He started sweeping again, sweeping the dust down from stair to stair.

Fuselli sat on the end of his bunk. He had just shaved. It was a Sunday morning and he looked forward to having the afternoon off. He rubbed his face on his towel and got to his feet. Outside, the rain fell in great silvery sheets, so that the noise on the tar-paper roof of the barracks was almost deafening.

Fuselli noticed, at the other end of the row of bunks, a group of men who all seemed to be looking at the same thing. Rolling down his sleeves, with his tunic hitched over one arm, he walked down to see what was the matter. Through the patter of the rain, he heard a thin voice say:

"It ain't no use, sergeant, I'm sick. I ain't a' goin' to get up."

"The kid's crazy," someone beside Fuselli said, turning away.

"You get up this minute," roared the sergeant. He was a big man with black hair who looked like a lumberman. He stood over the bunk. In the bunk at the end of a bundle of blankets was the chalk-white face of Stockton. The boy's teeth were clenched, and his eyes were round and protruding, it seemed from terror.

"You get out o' bed this minute," roared the sergeant again.

The boy was silent; his white cheeks quivered.

"What the hell's the matter with him?"

"Why don't you yank him out yourself, Sarge?"

"You get out of bed this minute," shouted the sergeant again, paying no attention.

The men gathered about walked away. Fuselli watched fascinated from a little distance.

"All right, then, I'll get the lieutenant. This is a court-martial offence. Here, Morton and Morrison, you're guards over this man."

The boy lay still in his blankets. He closed his eyes. By the way the blanket rose and fell over his chest, they could see that he was breathing heavily.

"Say, Stockton, why don't you get up, you fool?" said Fuselli. "You can't buck the whole army."

The boy didn't answer.

Fuselli walked away.

"He's crazy," he muttered.

The lieutenant was a stoutish red-faced man who came in puffing followed by the tall sergeant. He stopped and shook the water off his campaign hat. The rain kept up its deafening patter on the roof.

"Look here, are you sick? If you are, report sick call at once," said the lieutenant in an elaborately kind voice.

The boy looked at him dully and did not answer.

"You should get up and stand at attention when an officer speaks to you."

"I ain't goin' to get up," came the thin voice.

The officer's red face became crimson.

"Sergeant, what's the matter with the man?" he asked in a furious tone.

"I can't do anything with him, lieutenant. I think he's gone crazy."

"Rubbish. . . . Mere insubordination. . . . You're under arrest, d'ye hear?" he shouted towards the bed.

There was no answer. The rain pattered hard on the roof.

"Have him brought down to the guardhouse, by force if necessary," snapped the lieutenant. He strode towards the door. "And sergeant, start drawing up court-martial papers at once." The door slammed behind him.

"Now you've got to get him up," said the sergeant to the two guards.

Fuselli walked away.

"Ain't some people damn fools?" he said to a man at the other end of the barracks. He stood looking out of the window at the bright sheets of the rain.

"Well, get him up," shouted the sergeant.

The boy lay with his eyes closed, his chalk-white face half-hidden by the blankets; he was very still.

"Well, will you get up and go to the guardhouse, or have we to carry you there?" shouted the sergeant.

The guards laid hold of him gingerly and pulled him up to a sitting posture.

"All right, yank him out of bed."

The frail form in khaki shirt and whitish drawers was held up for a moment between the two men. Then it fell a limp heap on the floor.

"Say, Sarge, he's fainted."

"The hell he has. . . . Say, Morrison, ask one of the orderlies to come up from the Infirmary."

"He ain't fainted. . . . The kid's dead," said the other man. "Give me a hand."

The sergeant helped lift the body on the bed again.

"Well, I'll be goddamned," said the sergeant.

The eyes had opened. They covered the head with a blanket.

PART THREE
MACHINES

I

THE FIELDS and the misty blue-green woods slipped by slowly as the box car rumbled and jolted over the rails, now stopping for hours on sidings amid meadows, where it was quiet and where above the babel of voices of the regiment you could hear the skylarks, now clattering fast over bridges and along the banks of jade-green rivers where the slim poplars were just coming into leaf and where now and then a fish jumped. The men crowded in the door, grimy and tired, leaning on each other's shoulders and watching the plowed lands slip by and the meadows where the golden-green grass was dappled with buttercups, and the villages of huddled red roofs lost among pale budding trees and masses of peach blossom. Through the smells of steam and coal smoke and of unwashed bodies in uniforms came smells of moist fields and of manure from fresh-sowed patches and of cows and pasture lands just coming into flower.

"Must be right smart o' craps in this country. . . . Ain't like that damn Polignac, Andy?" said Chrisfield.

"Well, they made us drill so hard there wasn't any time for the grass to grow."

"You're damn right there warn't."

"Ah'd lak te live in this country a while," said Chrisfield.

"We might ask 'em to let us off right here."

"Can't be that the front's like this," said Judkins, poking his head out between Andrews's and Chrisfield's heads so that the bristles of his unshaven chin rubbed against Chrisfield's cheek. It was a large square head with closely cropped light hair and porcelain-blue eyes under lids that showed white in the red sunburned face, and a square jaw made a little grey by the sprouting beard.

"Say, Andy, how the hell long have we all been in this god-dam train? . . . Ah've done lost track o' the time. . . ."

"What's the matter; are you gettin' old, Chris?" asked Judkins laughing.

Chrisfield had slipped out of the place he held and began poking himself in between Andrews and Judkins.

"We've been on this train four days and five nights, an' we've got half a day's rations left, so we must be getting somewhere," said Andrews.

"It can't be like this at the front."

"It must be spring there as well as here," said Andrews.

It was a day of fluffy mauve-tinted clouds that moved across the sky, sometimes darkening to deep blue where a small rainstorm trailed across the hills, sometimes brightening to moments of clear sunlight that gave blue shadows to the poplars and shone yellow on the smoke of the engine that puffed on painfully at the head of the long train.

"Funny, ain't it? How li'l everythin' is," said Chrisfield. "Out Indiana way we wouldn't look at a cornfield that size. But it sort o' reminds me the way it used to be out home in the spring o' the year."

"I'd like to see Indiana in the springtime," said Andrews.

"Well you'll come out when the wa's over and us guys is all home . . . won't you, Andy?"

"You bet I will."

They were going into the suburbs of a town. Rows and clusters of little brick and stucco houses were appearing along the roads. It began to rain from a sky full of lights of amber and lilac color. The slate roofs and the pinkish-grey streets of the town shone cheerfully in the rain. The little patches of garden were all vivid emerald-green. Then they were looking at rows and rows of red chimney pots over wet slate roofs that reflected the bright sky. In the distance rose the purple-grey spire of a church and the irregular forms of old buildings. They passed through a station.

"Dijon," read Andrews. On the platform were French soldiers in their blue coats and a good sprinkling of civilians.

"Gee, those are about the first real civies I've seen since I came overseas," said Judkins. "Those goddam country people

down at Polignac didn't look like real civilians. There's folks
dressed like it was New York."

They had left the station and were rumbling slowly past interminable freight trains. At last the train came to a dead stop.

A whistle sounded.

"Don't nobody get out," shouted the sergeant from the car
ahead.

"Hell! They keep you in this goddam car like you was a
convict," muttered Chrisfield.

"I'd like to get out and walk around Dijon."

"O boy!"

"I swear I'd make a bee line for a dairy lunch," said Judkins.

"Hell of a fine dairy lunch you'll find among those goddam
frogs. No, vin blank is all you'ld get in that goddam town."

"Ah'm goin' to sleep," said Chrisfield. He stretched himself
out on the pile of equipment at the end of the car. Andrews
sat down near him and stared at his mud-caked boots, running one of his long hands, as brown as Chrisfield's now,
through his light short-cut hair.

Chrisfield lay looking at the gaunt outline of Andrews's
face against the light through half-closed eyes. And he felt a
warm sort of a smile inside him as he said to himself: "He's a
damn good kid." Then he thought of the spring in the hills
of southern Indiana and the mocking-bird singing in the
moonlight among the flowering locust trees behind the
house. He could almost smell the heavy sweetness of the locust blooms, as he used to smell them sitting on the steps
after supper, tired from a day's heavy plowing, while the clatter of his mother's housework came from the kitchen. He
didn't wish he was back there, but it was pleasant to think of
it now and then, and how the yellow farmhouse looked and
the red barn where his father never had been able to find time
to paint the door, and the tumble-down cowshed where the
shingles were always coming off. He wondered dully what it
would be like out there at the front. It couldn't be green and
pleasant, the way the country was here. Fellows always said it
was hell out there. Well, he didn't give a damn. He went to
sleep.

He woke up gradually, the warm comfort of sleep giving
place slowly to the stiffness of his uncomfortable position

with the hobnails of a boot from the back of a pack sticking into his shoulder. Andrews was sitting in the same position, lost in thought. The rest of the men sat at the open doors or sprawled over the equipment.

Chrisfield got up, stretched himself, yawned, and went to the door to look out. There was a heavy important step on the gravel outside. A large man with black eyebrows that met over his nose and a very black stubbly beard passed the car. There were a sergeant's stripes on his arm.

"Say, Andy," cried Chrisfield, "that bastard is a sergeant."

"Who's that?" asked Andrews getting up with a smile, his blue eyes looking mildly into Chrisfield's black ones.

"You know who Ah mean."

Under their heavy tan Chrisfield's rounded cheeks were flushed. His eyes snapped under their long black lashes. His fists were clutched.

"Oh, I know, Chris. I didn't know he was in this regiment."

"God damn him!" muttered Chrisfield in a low voice, throwing himself down on his packs again.

"Hold your horses, Chris," said Andrews. "We may all cash in our checks before long . . . no use letting things worry us."

"I don't give a damn if we do."

"Nor do I, now." Andrews sat down beside Chrisfield again.

After a while the train got jerkily into motion. The wheels rumbled and clattered over the rails and the clots of mud bounced up and down on the splintered boards of the floor. Chrisfield pillowed his head on his arm and went to sleep again, still smarting from the flush of his anger.

Andrews looked out through his fingers at the swaying black box car, at the men sprawled about on the floor, their heads nodding with each jolt, and at the mauve-grey clouds and bits of sparkling blue sky that he could see behind the silhouettes of the heads and shoulders of the men who stood in the doors. The wheels ground on endlessly.

The car stopped with a jerk that woke up all the sleepers and threw one man off his feet. A whistle blew shrilly outside.

"All right, out of the cars! Snap it up; snap it up!" yelled the sergeant.

The men piled out stiffly, handling the equipment out from hand to hand till it formed a confused heap of packs and rifles outside. All down the train at each door there was a confused pile of equipment and struggling men.

"Snap it up. . . . Full equipment. . . . Line up!" the sergeant yelled.

The men fell into line slowly, with their packs and rifles. Lieutenants hovered about the edges of the forming lines, tightly belted into their stiff trench coats, scrambling up and down the coal piles of the siding. The men were given "at ease" and stood leaning on their rifles staring at a green water-tank on three wooden legs, over the top of which had been thrown a huge piece of torn grey cheese-cloth. When the confused sound of tramping feet subsided, they could hear a noise in the distance, like someone lazily shaking a piece of heavy sheet-iron. The sky was full of little dabs of red, purple and yellow and the purplish sunset light was over everything.

The order came to march. They marched down a rutted road where the puddles were so deep they had continually to break ranks to avoid them. In a little pine-wood on one side were rows of heavy motor trucks and ammunition caissons; supper was cooking in a field kitchen about which clustered the truck drivers in their wide visored caps. Beyond the wood the column turned off into a field behind a little group of stone and stucco houses that had lost their roofs. In the field they halted. The grass was brilliant emerald and the wood and the distant hills were shades of clear deep blue. Wisps of pale-blue mist lay across the field. In the turf here and there were small clean bites, that might have been made by some strange animal. The men looked at them curiously.

"No lights, remember we're in sight of the enemy. A match might annihilate the detachment," announced the lieutenant dramatically after having given the orders for the pup tents to be set up.

When the tents were ready, the men stood about in the chilly white mist that kept growing denser, eating their cold rations. Everywhere were grumbling snorting voices.

"God, let's turn in, Chris, before our bones are frozen," said Andrews.

Guards had been posted and walked up and down with a business-like stride, peering now and then suspiciously into the little wood where the truck-drivers were.

Chrisfield and Andrews crawled into their little tent and rolled up together in their blankets, getting as close to each other as they could. At first it was very cold and hard, and they squirmed about restlessly, but gradually the warmth from their bodies filled their thin blankets and their muscles began to relax. Andrews went to sleep first and Chrisfield lay listening to his deep breathing. There was a frown on his face. He was thinking of the man who had walked past the train at Dijon. The last time he had seen that man Anderson was at training camp. He had only been a corporal then. He remembered the day the man had been made corporal. It had not been long before that that Chrisfield had drawn his knife on him, one night in the barracks. A fellow had caught his hand just in time. Anderson had looked a bit pale that time and had walked away. But he'd never spoken a word to Chrisfield since. As he lay with his eyes closed, pressed close against Andrew's limp sleeping body, Chrisfield could see the man's face, the eyebrows that joined across the nose and the jaw, always blackish from the heavy beard, that looked blue when he had just shaved. At last the tenseness of his mind slackened; he thought of women for a moment, of a fair-haired girl he'd seen from the train, and then suddenly crushing sleepiness closed down on him and everything went softly warmly black, as he drifted off to sleep with no sense but the coldness of one side and the warmth of his bunkie's body on the other.

In the middle of the night he awoke and crawled out of the tent. Andrews followed him. Their teeth chattered a little, and they stretched their legs stiffly. It was cold, but the mist had vanished. The stars shone brilliantly. They walked out a little way into the field away from the bunch of tents to make water.

A faint rustling and breathing noise, as of animals herded together, came from the sleeping regiment. Somewhere a brook made a shrill gurgling. They strained their ears, but they could hear no guns. They stood side by side looking up at the multitudes of stars.

"That's Orion," said Andrews.

"What?"

"That bunch of stars there is called Orion. D'you see 'em. It's supposed to look like a man with a bow, but he always looks to me like a fellow striding across the sky."

"Some stars tonight, ain't there? Gee, what's that?"

Behind the dark hills a glow rose and fell like the glow in a forge.

"The front must be that way," said Andrews, shivering.

"I guess we'll know tomorrow."

"Yes; tomorrow night we'll know more about it," said Andrews.

They stood silent a moment listening to the noise the brook made.

"God, it's quiet, ain't it? This can't be the front. Smell that?"

"What is it?"

"Smells like an apple tree in bloom somewhere. . . . Hell, let's git in, before our blankets git cold."

Andrews was still staring at the group of stars he had said was Orion.

Chrisfield pulled him by the arm. They crawled into their tent again, rolled up together and immediately were crushed under an exhausted sleep.

As far ahead of him as Chrisfield could see were packs and heads with caps at a variety of angles, all bobbing up and down with the swing of the brisk marching time. A fine warm rain was falling, mingling with the sweat that ran down his face. The column had been marching a long time along a straight road that was worn and scarred with heavy traffic. Fields and hedges where clusters of yellow flowers were in bloom had given place to an avenue of poplars. The light wet trunks and the stiff branches hazy with green filed by, interminable, as interminable as the confused tramp of feet and jingle of equipment that sounded in his ears.

"Say, are we goin' towards the front?"

"Goddamned if I know."

"Ain't no front within miles."

Men's sentences came shortly through their heavy breathing. The column shifted over to the side of the road to avoid a train of motor trucks going the other way. Chrisfield felt the heavy mud spurt up over him as truck after truck rumbled by. With the wet back of one hand he tried to wipe it off his face, but the grit, when he rubbed it, hurt his skin, made tender by the rain. He swore long and whiningly, half aloud. His rifle felt as heavy as an iron girder.

They entered a village of plaster-and-timber houses. Through open doors they could see into comfortable kitchens where copper pots gleamed and where the floors were of clean red tiles. In front of some of the houses were little gardens full of crocuses and hyacinths where box-bushes shone a very dark green in the rain. They marched through the square with its pavement of little yellow rounded cobbles, its grey church with a pointed arch in the door, its cafés with names painted over them. Men and women looked out of doors and windows. The column perceptibly slackened its speed, but kept on, and as the houses dwindled and became farther apart along the road the men's hope of stopping vanished. Ears were deafened by the confused tramp of feet on the macadam road. Men's feet seemed as lead, as if all the weight of the pack hung on them. Shoulders, worn callous, began to grow tender and sore under the constant sweating. Heads drooped. Each man's eyes were on the heels of the man ahead of him that rose and fell, rose and fell endlessly. Marching became for each man a personal struggle with his pack, that seemed to have come alive, that seemed something malicious and overpowering, wrestling to throw him.

The rain stopped and the sky brightened a little, taking on pale yellowish lights as if the clouds that hid the sun were growing thin.

The column halted at the edge of a group of farms and barns that scattered along the road. The men sprawled in all directions along the roadside hiding the bright green grass with the mud-color of their uniforms.

Chrisfield lay in the field beside the road, pressing his hot face into the wet sprouting clover. The blood throbbed through his ears. His arms and legs seemed to cleave to the ground, as if he would never be able to move them again. He closed his eyes. Gradually a cold chill began stealing through his body. He sat up and slipped his arms out of the harness of his pack. Someone was handing him a cigarette, and he sniffed a little acrid sweet smoke.

Andrews was lying beside him, his head propped against his pack, smoking, and poking a cigarette towards his friend with a muddy hand. His blue eyes looked strangely from out the flaming red of his mud-splotched face.

Chrisfield took the cigarette, and fumbled in his pocket for a match.

"That nearly did it for me," said Andrews.

Chrisfield grunted. He pulled greedily on the cigarette.

A whistle blew.

Slowly the men dragged themselves off the ground and fell into line, drooping under the weight of their equipment.

The companies marched off separately.

Chrisfield overheard the lieutenant saying to a sergeant:

"Damn fool business that. Why the hell couldn't they have sent us here in the first place?"

"So we ain't goin' to the front after all?" said the sergeant.

"Front, hell!" said the lieutenant. The lieutenant was a small man who looked like a jockey with a coarse red face, which, now that he was angry, was almost purple.

"I guess they're going to quarter us here," said somebody.

Immediately everybody began saying: "We're going to be quartered here."

They stood waiting in formation a long while, the packs cutting into their backs and shoulders.

At last the sergeant shouted out:

"All right, take yer stuff upstairs." Stumbling on each others' heels they climbed up into a dark loft, where the air was heavy with the smell of hay and with an acridity of cow manure from the stables below. There was a little straw in the corners, on which those who got there first spread their blankets.

Chrisfield and Andrews tucked themselves in a corner from which through a hole where the tiles had fallen off the roof, they could see down into the barnyard, where white and speckled chickens pecked about with jerky movements. A middle-aged woman stood in the doorway of the house looking suspiciously at the files of khaki-clad soldiers that shuffled slowly into the barns by every door.

An officer went up to her, a little red book in his hand. A

conversation about some matter proceeded painfully. The officer grew very red. Andrews threw back his head and laughed, luxuriously rolling from side to side in the straw. Chrisfield laughed too, he hardly knew why. Over their heads they could hear the feet of pigeons on the roof, and a constant drowsy rou-cou-cou-cou.

Through the barnyard smells began to drift the greasiness of food cooking in the field kitchen.

"Ah hope they give us somethin' good to eat," said Chrisfield. "Ah'm hongry as a thrasher."

"So am I," said Andrews.

"Say, Andy, you kin talk their language a li'l', can't ye?"

Andrews nodded his head vaguely.

"Well, maybe we kin git some aigs or somethin' out of the lady down there. Will ye try after mess?"

"All right."

They both lay back in the straw and closed their eyes. Their cheeks still burned from the rain. Everything seemed very peaceful; the men sprawled about talking in low drowsy voices. Outside, another shower had come up and beat softly on the tiles of the roof. Chrisfield thought he had never been so comfortable in his life, although his soaked shoes pinched his cold feet and his knees were wet and cold. But in the drowsiness of the rain and of voices talking quietly about him, he fell asleep.

He dreamed he was home in Indiana, but instead of his mother cooking at the stove in the kitchen, there was the Frenchwoman who had stood in the farmhouse door, and near her stood a lieutenant with a little red book in his hand. He was eating cornbread and syrup off a broken plate. It was fine cornbread with a great deal of crust on it, crisp and hot, on which the butter was cold and sweet to his tongue. Suddenly he stopped eating and started swearing, shouting at the top of his lungs: "You goddam . . ." he started, but he couldn't seem to think of anything more to say. "You goddam . . ." he started again. The lieutenant looked towards him, wrinkling his black eyebrows that met across his nose. He was Sergeant Anderson. Chris drew his knife and ran at him, but it was Andy his bunkie he had run his knife into. He threw his arms round Andy's body, crying hot tears. . . . He woke up. Mess kits were clinking all about the dark crowded loft. The men had already started piling down the stairs.

The larks filled the wine-tinged air with a constant chiming of little bells. Chrisfield and Andrews were strolling across a field of white clover that covered the brow of a hill. Below in the valley they could see a cluster of red roofs of farms and the white ribbon of the road where long trains of motor trucks crawled like beetles. The sun had just set behind the blue hills the other side of the shallow valley. The air was full of the smell of clover and of hawthorn from the hedgerows. They took deep breaths as they crossed the field.

"It's great to get away from that crowd," Andrews was saying.

Chrisfield walked on silently, dragging his feet through the matted clover. A leaden dullness weighed like some sort of warm choking coverlet on his limbs, so that it seemed an effort to walk, an effort to speak. Yet under it his muscles were taut and trembling as he had known them to be before when he was about to get into a fight or to make love to a girl.

"Why the hell don't they let us git into it?" he said suddenly.

"Yes, anything'ld be better than this . . . wait, wait, wait."

They walked on, hearing the constant chirrup of the larks, the brush of their feet through the clover, the faint jingle of some coins in Chrisfield's pocket, and in the distance the irregular snoring of an aëroplane motor. As they walked Andrews leaned over from time to time and picked a couple of the white clover flowers.

The aëroplane came suddenly nearer and swooped in a wide curve above the field, drowning every sound in the roar of its exhaust. They made out the figures of the pilot and the observer before the plane rose again and vanished against the ragged purple clouds of the sky. The observer had waved a hand at them as he passed. They stood still in the darkening field, staring up at the sky, where a few larks still hung chirruping.

"Ah'd lahk to be one o' them guys," said Chrisfield.

"You would?"

"God damn it, Ah'd do anything to git out o' this hellish infantry. This ain't no sort o' life for a man to be treated lahk he was a nigger."

"No, it's no sort of life for a man."

"If they'd let us git to the front an' do some fightin' an' be done with it. . . . But all we do is drill and have grenade practice an' drill again and then have bayonet practice an' drill again. 'Nough to drive a feller crazy."

"What the hell's the use of talking about it, Chris? We can't be any lower than we are, can we?" Andrews laughed.

"There's that plane again."

"Where?"

"There, just goin' down behind the piece o' woods."

"That's where their field is."

"Ah bet them guys has a good time. Ah put in an application back in trainin' camp for Aviation. Ain't never heard nothing from it though. If Ah had, Ah wouldn't be lower than dirt in this hawg-pen."

"It's wonderful up here on the hill this evening," said Andrews, looking dreamily at the pale orange band of light where the sun had set. "Let's go down and get a bottle of wine."

"Now yo're talkin'. Ah wonder if that girl's down there tonight."

"Antoinette?"

"Um-hum. . . . Boy, Ah'd lahk to have her all by maself some night."

Their steps grew brisker as they strode along a grass-grown road that led through high hedgerows to a village under the brow of the hill. It was almost dark under the shadow of the bushes on either side. Overhead the purple clouds were washed over by a pale yellow light that gradually faded to grey. Birds chirped and rustled among the young leaves.

Andrews put his hand on Chrisfield's shoulder.

"Let's walk slow," he said, "we don't want to get out of here too soon." He grabbed carelessly at little clusters of hawthorn flowers as he passed them, and seemed reluctant to untangle the thorny branches that caught in his coat and on his loosely wound puttees.

"Hell, man," said Chrisfield, "we won't have time to get a bellyful. It must be gettin' late already."

They hastened their steps again and came in a moment to the first tightly shuttered houses of the village.

In the middle of the road was an M.P., who stood with his legs wide apart, waving his "billy" languidly. He had a red face, his eyes were fixed on the shuttered upper window of a house, through the chinks of which came a few streaks of yellow light. His lips were puckered up as if to whistle, but no sound came. He swayed back and forth indecisively. An officer came suddenly out of the little green door of the house in front of the M.P., who brought his heels together with a jump and saluted, holding his hand a long while to his cap. The officer flicked a hand up hastily to his hat, snatching his cigar out of his mouth for an instant. As the officer's steps grew fainter down the road, the M.P. gradually returned to his former position.

Chrisfield and Andrews had slipped by on the other side and gone in at the door of a small ramshackle house of which the windows were closed by heavy wooden shutters.

"I bet there ain't many of them bastards at the front," said Chris.

"Not many of either kind of bastards," said Andrews laughing, as he closed the door behind them. They were in a room that had once been the parlor of a farmhouse. The chandelier with its bits of crystal and the orange-blossoms on a piece of dusty red velvet under a bell glass on the mantelpiece denoted that. The furniture had been taken out, and four square oak tables crowded in. At one of the tables sat three Americans and at another a very young olive-skinned French soldier, who sat hunched over his table looking moodily down into his glass of wine.

A girl in a faded frock of some purplish material that showed the strong curves of her shoulders and breasts slouched into the room, her hands in the pocket of a dark blue apron against which her rounded forearms showed golden brown. Her face had the same golden tan under a mass of dark blonde hair. She smiled when she saw the two soldiers, drawing her thin lips away from her ugly yellow teeth.

"Ça va bien, Antoinette?" asked Andrews.

"Oui," she said, looking beyond their heads at the French soldier who sat at the other side of the little room.

"A bottle of vin rouge, vite," said Chrisfield.

"Ye needn't be so damn vite about it tonight, Chris," said one of the men at the other table.

"Why?"

"Ain't a-goin' to be no roll call. Corporal tole me hisself. Sarge's gone out to git stewed, an' the Loot's away."

"Sure," said another man, "we kin stay out as late's we goddam please tonight."

"There's a new M.P. in town," said Chrisfield. . . . "Ah saw him maself. . . . You did, too, didn't you, Andy?"

Andrews nodded. He was looking at the Frenchman, who sat with his face in shadow and his black lashes covering his eyes. A purplish flash had suffused the olive skin at his cheekbones.

"Oh, boy," said Chrisfield. "That ole wine sure do go down fast. . . . Say, Antoinette, got any cognac?"

"I'm going to have some more wine," said Andrews.

"Go ahead, Andy; have all ye want. Ah want somethin' to warm ma guts."

Antoinette brought a bottle of cognac and two small glasses and sat down in an empty chair with her red hands crossed on her apron. Her eyes moved from Chrisfield to the Frenchman and back again.

Chrisfield turned a little round in his chair and looked at the Frenchman, feeling in his eyes for a moment a glance of the man's yellowish-brown eyes.

Andrews leaned back against the wall sipping his dark-colored wine, his eyes contracted dreamily, fixed on the shadow of the chandelier, which the cheap oil-lamp with its tin reflector cast on the peeling plaster of the wall opposite.

Chrisfield punched him.

"Wake up, Andy, are you asleep?"

"No," said Andy smiling.

"Have a li'l mo' cognac."

Chrisfield poured out two more glasses unsteadily. His eyes were on Antoinette again. The faded purple frock was hooked at the neck. The first three hooks were undone revealing a V-shape of golden brown skin and a bit of whitish underwear.

"Say, Andy," he said, putting his arm round his friend's neck and talking into his ear, "talk up to her for me, will yer, Andy? . . . Ah won't let that goddam frog get her, no, I won't, by Gawd. Talk up to her for me, Andy."

Andrews laughed.

"I'll try," he said. "But there's always the Queen of Sheba, Chris."

"Antoinette, j'ai un ami," started Andrews, making a gesture with a long dirty hand towards Chris.

Antoinette showed her bad teeth in a smile.

"Joli garçon," said Andrews.

Antoinette's face became impassive and beautiful again. Chrisfield leaned back in his chair with an empty glass in his hand and watched his friend admiringly.

"Antoinette, mon ami vous . . . vous admire," said Andrews in a courtly voice.

A woman put her head in the door. It was the same face and hair as Antoinette's, ten years older, only the skin, instead of being golden brown, was sallow and wrinkled.

"Viens," said the woman in a shrill voice.

Antoinette got up, brushed heavily against Chrisfield's leg as she passed him and disappeared. The Frenchman walked across the room from his corner, saluted gravely and went out.

Chrisfield jumped to his feet. The room was like a white box reeling about him.

"That frog's gone after her," he shouted.

"No, he ain't, Chris," cried someone from the next table. "Sit tight, ole boy. We're bettin' on yer."

"Yes, sit down and have a drink, Chris," said Andy. "I've got to have somethin' more to drink. I haven't had a thing to drink all the evening." He pulled him back into his chair. Chrisfield tried to get up again. Andrews hung on him so that the chair upset. Then both sprawled on the red tiles of the floor.

"The house is pinched!" said a voice.

Chrisfield saw Judkins standing over him, a grin on his large red face. He got to his feet and sat sulkily in his chair again. Andrews was already sitting opposite him, looking impassive as ever.

The tables were full now. Someone was singing in a droning voice.

"O the oak and the ash and the weeping willow tree,
O green grows the grass in God's countree!"

"Ole Indiana," shouted Chris. "That's the only God's country I know." He suddenly felt that he could tell Andy all about his home and the wide corn-fields shimmering and rustling under the July sun, and the creek with red clay banks where he used to go in swimming. He seemed to see it all before him, to smell the winey smell of the silo, to see the cattle, with their chewing mouths always stained a little with green, waiting to get through the gate to the water trough, and the yellow dust and roar of wheat-thrashing, and the quiet evening breeze cooling his throat and neck when he lay out on a shack of hay that he had been tossing all day long under the tingling sun. But all he managed to say was:

"Indiana's God's country, ain't it, Andy?"

"Oh, he has so many," muttered Andrews.

"Ah've seen a hailstone measured nine inches around out home, honest to Gawd, Ah have."

"Must be as good as a barrage."

"Ah'd like to see any goddam barrage do the damage one of our thunder an' lightnin' storms'll do," shouted Chris.

"I guess all the barrage we're going to see's grenade practice."

"Don't you worry, buddy," said somebody across the room. "You'll see enough of it. This war's going to last damn long . . ."

"Ah'd lak to get in some licks at those Huns tonight, honest to Gawd Ah would, Andy," muttered Chris in a low voice. He felt his muscles contract with a furious irritation. He looked through half-closed eyes at the men in the room, seeing them in distorted white lights and reddish shadows. He thought of himself throwing a grenade among a crowd of men. Then he saw the face of Anderson, a ponderous white face with eyebrows that met across his nose and a bluish, shaved chin.

"Where does he stay at, Andy? I'm going to git him."

Andrews guessed what he meant.

"Sit down and have a drink, Chris," he said, "Remember you're going to sleep with the Queen of Sheba tonight."

"Not if I can't git them goddam . . ." his voice trailed off into an inaudible muttering of oaths.

"O the oak and the ash and the weeping willow tree,
O green grows the grass in God's countree!"

somebody sang again.

Chrisfield saw a woman standing beside the table with her back to him, collecting the bottles. Andy was paying her.

"Antoinette," he said. He got to his feet and put his arms round her shoulders. With a quick movement of the elbows she pushed him back into his chair. She turned round. He saw the sallow face and thin breasts of the older sister. She looked in his eyes with surprise. He was grinning drunkenly. As she left the room she made a sign to him with her head to follow her. He got up and staggered out the door, pulling Andrews after him.

In the inner room was a big bed with curtains where the women slept, and the fireplace where they did their cooking. It was dark except for the corner where he and Andrews stood blinking in the glare of a candle on the table. Beyond they could only see ruddy shadows and the huge curtained bed with its red coverlet.

The Frenchman, somewhere in the dark of the room, said something several times.

"Avions boches . . . ss-t!"

They were quiet.

Above them they heard the snoring of aëroplane motors, rising and falling like the buzzing of a fly against a window pane.

They all looked at each other curiously. Antoinette was leaning against the bed, her face expressionless. Her heavy hair had come undone and fell in smoky gold waves about her shoulders. The older woman was giggling.

"Come on, let's see what's doing, Chris," said Andrews.

They went out into the dark village street.

"To hell with women, Chris, this is the war!" cried Andrews in a loud drunken voice as they reeled arm in arm up the street.

"You bet it's the war. . . . Ah'm a-goin' to beat up . . ." Chrisfield felt his friend's hand clapped over his mouth. He let himself go limply, feeling himself pushed to the side of the road.

Somewhere in the dark he heard an officer's voice say:

"Bring those men to me."

"Yes, sir," came another voice.

Slow heavy footsteps came up the road in their direction. Andrews kept pushing him back along the side of a house, until suddenly they both fell sprawling in a manure pit.

"Lie still for God's sake," muttered Andrews, throwing an arm over Chrisfield's chest. A thick odor of dry manure filled their nostrils.

They heard the steps come nearer, wander about irresolutely and then go off in the direction from which they had come. Meanwhile the throb of motors overhead grew louder and louder.

"Well?" came the officer's voice.

"Couldn't find them, sir," mumbled the other voice.

"Nonsense. Those men were drunk," came the officer's voice.

"Yes, sir," came the other voice humbly.

Chrisfield started to giggle. He felt he must yell aloud with laughter.

The nearest motor stopped its singsong roar, making the night seem deathly silent.

Andrews jumped to his feet.

The air was split by a shriek followed by a racking snorting explosion. They saw the wall above their pit light up with a red momentary glare.

Chrisfield got to his feet, expecting to see flaming ruins. The village street was the same as ever. There was a little light from the glow the moon, still under the horizon, gave to the sky. A window in the house opposite showed yellow. In it was a blue silhouette of an officer's cap and uniform.

A little group stood in the street below.

"What was that?" the form in the window was shouting in a peremptory voice.

"German aëroplane just dropped a bomb, Major," came a breathless voice in reply.

"Why the devil don't he close that window?" a voice was muttering all the while. "Juss a target for 'em to aim at . . . a target to aim at."

"Any damage done?" asked the major.

Through the silence the snoring of the motors singsonged
ominously overhead, like giant mosquitoes.

"I seem to hear more," said the major, in his drawling voice.

"O yes sir, yes sir, lots," answered an eager voice.

"For God's sake tell him to close the window, Lieutenant,"
muttered another voice.

"How the hell can I tell him? You tell him."

"We'll all be killed, that's all there is about it."

"There are no shelters or dugouts," drawled the major
from the window. "That's Headquarters' fault."

"There's the cellar!" cried the eager voice, again.

"Oh," said the major.

Three snorting explosions in quick succession drowned
everything in a red glare. The street was suddenly filled with
a scuttle of villagers running to shelter.

"Say, Andy, they may have a roll call," said Chrisfield.

"We'd better cut for home across country," said Andrews.

They climbed cautiously out of their manure pit. Chrisfield
was surprised to find that he was trembling. His hands were
cold. It was with difficulty he kept his teeth from chattering.

"God, we'll stink for a week."

"Let's git out," muttered Chrisfield, "o' this goddam village."

They ran out through an orchard, broke through a hedge
and climbed up the hill across the open fields.

Down the main road an anti-aircraft gun had started barking and the sky sparkled with exploding shrapnel. The "put,
put, put" of a machine gun had begun somewhere.

Chrisfield strode up the hill in step with his friend. Behind
them bomb followed bomb, and above them the air seemed
full of exploding shrapnel and droning planes. The cognac
still throbbed a little in their blood. They stumbled against
each other now and then as they walked. From the top of the
hill they turned and looked back. Chrisfield felt a tremendous
elation thumping stronger than the cognac through his veins.
Unconsciously he put his arm round his friend's shoulders.
They seemed the only live things in a reeling world.

Below in the valley a house was burning brightly. From all
directions came the yelp of anti-aircraft guns, and overhead
unperturbed continued the leisurely singsong of the motors.

Suddenly Chrisfield burst out laughing.

"By God, Ah always have fun when Ah'm out with you, Andy," he said.

They turned and hurried down the other slope of the hill towards the farms where they were quartered.

II

As far as he could see in every direction were the grey trunks of beeches bright green with moss on one side. The ground was thick with last year's leaves that rustled maddeningly with every step. In front of him his eyes followed other patches of olive-drab moving among the tree trunks. Overhead, through the mottled light and dark green of the leaves he could see now and then a patch of heavy grey sky, greyer than the silvery trunks that moved about him in every direction as he walked. He strained his eyes down each alley until they were dazzled by the reiteration of mottled grey and green. Now and then the rustling stopped ahead of him, and the olive-drab patches were still. Then, above the clamour of the blood in his ears, he could hear batteries "pong, pong, pong" in the distance, and the woods ringing with a sound like hail as a heavy shell hurtled above the tree tops to end in a dull rumble miles away.

Chrisfield was soaked with sweat, but he could not feel his arms or legs. Every sense was concentrated in eyes and ears, and in the consciousness of his gun. Time and again he pictured himself taking sight at something grey that moved, and firing. His forefinger itched to press the trigger. He would take aim very carefully, he told himself; he pictured a dab of grey starting up from behind a grey tree trunk, and the sharp detonation of his rifle, and the dab of grey rolling among the last year's leaves.

A branch carried his helmet off his head so that it rolled at his feet and bounced with a faint metallic sound against the root of a tree.

He was blinded by the sudden terror that seized him. His heart seemed to roll from side to side in his chest. He stood stiff, as if paralyzed for a moment before he could stoop and pick the helmet up. There was a curious taste of blood in his mouth.

"Ah'll pay 'em fer that," he muttered between clenched teeth.

His fingers were still trembling when he stooped to pick up

the helmet, which he put on again very carefully, fastening it with the strap under his chin.

Furious anger had taken hold of him.

The olive-drab patches ahead had moved forward again. He followed, looking eagerly to the right and the left, praying he might see something. In every direction were the silvery trunks of the beeches, each with a vivid green streak on one side. With every step the last year's russet leaves rustled underfoot, maddeningly loud.

Almost out of sight among the moving tree trunks was a log. It was not a log; it was a bunch of grey-green cloth. Without thinking Chrisfield strode towards it. The silver trunks of the beeches circled about him, waving jagged arms. It was a German lying full length among the leaves.

Chrisfield was furiously happy in the angry pumping of blood through his veins.

He could see the buttons on the back of the long coat of the German, and the red band on his cap.

He kicked the German. He could feel the ribs against his toes through the leather of his boot. He kicked again and again with all his might. The German rolled over heavily. He had no face. Chrisfield felt the hatred suddenly ebb out of him. Where the face had been was a spongy mass of purple and yellow and red, half of which stuck to the russet leaves when the body rolled over. Large flies with bright shiny green bodies circled about it. In a brown clay-grimed hand was a revolver.

Chrisfield felt his spine go cold; the German had shot himself.

He ran off suddenly, breathlessly, to join the rest of the reconnoitering squad. The silent beeches whirled about him, waving gnarled boughs above his head. The German had shot himself. That was why he had no face.

Chrisfield fell into line behind the other men. The corporal waited for him.

"See anything?" he asked.

"Not a goddam thing," muttered Chrisfield almost inaudibly.

The corporal went off to the head of the line.

Chrisfield was alone again. The leaves rustled maddeningly loud underfoot.

III

CHRISFIELD'S EYES were fixed on the leaves at the tops of the walnut trees, etched like metal against the bright colorless sky, edged with flicks and fringes of gold where the sunlight struck them. He stood stiff and motionless at attention, although there was a sharp pain in his left ankle that seemed swollen enough to burst the worn boot. He could feel the presence of men on both sides of him, and of men again beyond them. It seemed as if the stiff line of men in olive-drab, standing at attention, waiting endlessly for someone to release them from their erect paralysis, must stretch unbroken round the world. He let his glance fall to the trampled grass of the field where the regiment was drawn up. Somewhere behind him he could hear the clinking of spurs at some officer's heels. Then there was the sound of a motor on the road suddenly shut off, and there were steps coming down the line of men, and a group of officers passed hurriedly, with a business-like stride, as if they did nothing else all their lives. Chrisfield made out eagles on tight khaki shoulders, then a single star and a double star, above which was a red ear and some grey hair; the general passed too soon for him to make out his face. Chrisfield swore to himself a little because his ankle hurt so. His eyes travelled back to the fringe of the trees against the bright sky. So this was what he got for those weeks in dugouts, for all the times he had thrown himself on his belly in the mud, for the bullets he had shot into the unknown at grey specks that moved among the grey mud. Something was crawling up the middle of his back. He wasn't sure if it were a louse or if he were imagining it. An order had been shouted. Automatically he had changed his position to parade rest. Somewhere far away a little man was walking towards the long drab lines. A wind had come up, rustling the stiff leaves of the grove of walnut trees. The voice squeaked above it, but Chrisfield could not make out what it said. The wind in the trees made a vast rhythmic sound like the churning of water astern of the transport he had come over on. Gold flicks and olive shadows danced among the indented clusters of leaves as they swayed, as if sweeping something away, against the bright sky. An idea came into Chrisfield's head. Suppose the leaves should sweep in broader and broader curves until they should reach the ground and sweep and sweep until all this was swept away, all these pains and lice and uniforms and officers with maple leaves or eagles or single stars or double stars or triple stars on their shoulders. He had a sudden picture of himself in his old comfortable overalls, with his shirt open so that the wind caressed his neck like a girl blowing down it playfully, lying on a shuck of hay under the hot Indiana sun. Funny he'd thought all that, he said to himself. Before he'd known Andy he'd never have thought of that. What had come over him these days?

The regiment was marching away in columns of fours. Chrisfield's ankle gave him sharp hot pain with every step. His tunic was too tight and the sweat tingled on his back. All about him were sweating irritated faces; the woollen tunics with their high collars were like straight-jackets that hot afternoon. Chrisfield marched with his fists clenched; he wanted to fight somebody, to run his bayonet into a man as he ran it into the dummy in that everlasting bayonet drill, he wanted to strip himself naked, to squeeze the wrists of a girl until she screamed.

His company was marching past another company that was lined up to be dismissed in front of a ruined barn which had a roof that sagged in the middle like an old cow's back. The sergeant stood in front of them with his arms crossed, looking critically at the company that marched past. He had a white heavy face and black eyebrows that met over his nose. Chrisfield stared hard at him as he passed, but Sergeant Anderson did not seem to recognize him. It gave him a dull angry feeling as if he'd been cut by a friend.

The company melted suddenly into a group of men unbuttoning their shirts and tunics in front of the little board shanty where they were quartered, which had been put up by the French at the time of the Marne, years before, so a man had told Andy.

"What are you dreamin' about, Indiana?" said Judkins punching Chrisfield jovially in the ribs.

Chrisfield doubled his fists and gave him a smashing blow in the jaw that Judkins warded off just in time.

Judkins's face flamed red. He swung with a long bent arm.

"What the hell d'you think this is?" shouted somebody.

"What's he want to hit me for?" spluttered Judkins, breathless.

Men had edged in between them.

"Lemme git at him."

"Shut up, you fool," said Andy, drawing Chrisfield away. The company scattered sullenly. Some of the men lay down in the long uncut grass in the shade of the ruins of the house, one of the walls of which made a wall of the shanty where they lived.

Andrews and Chrisfield strolled in silence down the road, kicking their feet into the deep dust. Chrisfield was limping. On both sides of the road were fields of ripe wheat, golden under the sun. In the distance were low green hills fading to blue, pale yellow in patches with the ripe grain. Here and there a thick clump of trees or a screen of poplars broke the flatness of the long smooth hills. In the hedgerows were blue cornflowers and poppies in all colors from carmine to orange that danced in the wind on their wiry stalks. At the turn in the road they lost the noise of the division and could hear the bees droning in the big dull purple cloverheads and in the gold hearts of the daisies.

"You're a wild man, Chris. What the hell came over you to try an' smash poor old Judkie's jaw? He could lick you anyway. He's twice as heavy as you are."

Chrisfield walked on in silence.

"God, I should think you'ld have had enough of that sort of thing. . . . I should think you'ld be sick of wanting to hurt people. You don't like pain yourself, do you?" Andrews spoke in spurts, bitterly, his eyes on the ground.

"Ah think Ah sprained ma goddam ankle when Ah tumbled off the back o' the truck yesterday."

"Better go on sick call. . . . Say, Chris, I'm sick of this business. . . . Almost like you'd rather shoot yourself than keep on."

"Ah guess you're gettin' the dolefuls, Andy. Look . . . let's go in swimmin'. There's a lake down the road."

"I've got my soap in my pocket. We can wash a few cooties off."

"Don't walk so goddam fast . . . Andy, you got more learnin' than I have. You ought to be able to tell what it is makes a feller go crazy like that. . . . Ah guess Ah got a bit o' the devil in me."

Andrews was brushing the soft silk of a poppy petal against his face.

"I wonder if it'ld have any effect if I ate some of these," he said.

"Why?"

"They say you go to sleep if you lie down in a poppy-field. Wouldn't you like to do that, Chris, an' not wake up till the war was over and you could be a human being again."

Andrews bit into the green seed capsule he held in his hand. A milky juice came out.

"It's bitter. . . . I guess it's the opium," he said.

"What's that?"

"A stuff that makes you go to sleep and have wonderful dreams. In China . . ."

"Dreams," interrupted Chrisfield. "Ah had one of them last night. Dreamed Ah saw a feller that had shot hisself that I saw one time reconnoitrin' out in the Bringy Wood."

"What was that?"

"Nawthin', juss a Fritzie had shot hisself."

"Better than opium," said Andrews, his voice trembling with sudden excitement.

"Ah dreamed the flies buzzin' round him was aëro-planes. . . . Remember the last rest village?"

"And the major who wouldn't close the window? You bet I do!"

They lay down on the grassy bank that sloped from the road to the pond. The road was hidden from them by the tall reeds through which the wind lisped softly. Overhead huge white cumulus clouds, piled tier on tier like fantastic galleons in full sail, floated, changing slowly in a greenish sky. The reflection of clouds in the silvery glisten of the pond's surface was broken by clumps of grasses and bits of floating weeds. They lay on their backs for some time before they started taking their clothes off, looking up at the sky, that seemed vast and free, like the ocean, vaster and freer than the ocean.

"Sarge says a delousin' machine's comin' through this way soon."

"We need it, Chris."

Andrews pulled his clothes off slowly.

"It's great to feel the sun and the wind on your body, isn't it, Chris?"

Andrews walked towards the pond and lay flat on his belly on the fine soft grass near the edge.

"It's great to have your body there, isn't it?" he said in a dreamy voice. "Your skin's so soft and supple, and nothing in the world has the feel a muscle has. . . . Gee, I don't know what I'd do without my body."

Chrisfield laughed.

"Look how ma ole ankle's raised. . . . Found any cooties yet?" he said.

"I'll try and drown 'em," said Andrews. "Chris, come away from those stinking uniforms and you'll feel like a human being with the sun on your flesh instead of like a lousy soldier."

"Hello, boys," came a high-pitched voice unexpectedly. A "Y" man with sharp nose and chin had come up behind them.

"Hello," said Chrisfield sullenly, limping towards the water.

"Want the soap?" said Andrews.

"Going to take a swim, boys?" asked the "Y" man. Then he added in a tone of conviction, "That's great."

"Better come in, too," said Andrews.

"Thanks, thanks. . . . Say, if you don't mind my suggestion, why don't you fellers get under the water. . . . You see there's two French girls looking at you from the road." The "Y" man giggled faintly.

"They don't mind," said Andrews soaping himself vigorously.

"Ah reckon they lahk it," said Chrisfield.

"I know they haven't any morals. . . . But still."

"And why should they not look at us? Maybe there won't be many people who get a chance."

"What do you mean?"

"Have you ever seen what a little splinter of a shell does to a feller's body?" asked Andrews savagely. He splashed into the shallow water and swam towards the middle of the pond.

"Ye might ask 'em to come down and help us pick the cooties off," said Chrisfield and followed in Andrews's wake. In the middle he lay on a sand bank in the warm shallow water and looked back at the "Y" man, who still stood on the bank. Behind him were other men undressing, and soon the grassy slope was filled with naked men and yellowish grey underclothes, and many dark heads and gleaming backs were bobbing up and down in the water. When he came out, he found Andrews sitting cross-legged near his clothes. He reached for his shirt and drew it on him.

"God, I can't make up my mind to put the damn thing on again," said Andrews in a low voice, almost as if he were talking to himself; "I feel so clean and free. It's like voluntarily taking up filth and slavery again. . . . I think I'll just walk off naked across the fields."

"D'you call serving your country slavery, my friend?" The "Y" man, who had been roaming among the bathers, his neat uniform and well-polished boots and puttees contrasting strangely with the mud-clotted, sweat-soaked clothing of the men about him, sat down on the grass beside Andrews.

"You're goddam right I do."

"You'll get into trouble, my boy, if you talk that way," said the "Y" man in a cautious voice.

"Well, what is your definition of slavery?"

"You must remember that you are a voluntary worker in the cause of democracy. . . . You're doing this so that your children will be able to live peaceful. . . ."

"Ever shot a man?"

"No. . . . No, of course not, but I'd have enlisted, really I would. Only my eyes are weak."

"I guess so," said Andrews under his breath.

"Remember that your women folks, your sisters and sweethearts and mothers, are praying for you at this instant."

"I wish somebody'd pray me into a clean shirt," said Andrews, starting to get into his clothes. "How long have you been over here?"

"Just three months." The man's sallow face, with its pinched nose and chin lit up. "But, boys, those three months have been worth all the other years of my min—" he caught himself—"life. . . . I've heard the great heart of America beat. O boys, never forget that you are in a great Christian undertaking."

"Come on, Chris, let's beat it." They left the "Y" man wandering among the men along the bank of the pond, to which the reflection of the greenish silvery sky and the great piled white clouds gave all the free immensity of space. From the road they could still hear his high pitched voice.

"And that's what'll survive you and me," said Andrews.

"Say, Andy, you sure can talk to them guys," said Chris admiringly.

"What's the use of talking? God, there's a bit of honeysuckle still in bloom. Doesn't that smell like home to you, Chris?"

"Say, how much do they pay those 'Y' men, Andy?"

"Damned if I know."

They were just in time to fall into line for mess. In the line everyone was talking and laughing, enlivened by the smell of food and the tinkle of mess-kits. Near the field kitchen Chrisfield saw Sergeant Anderson talking with Higgins, his own sergeant. They were laughing together, and he heard Anderson's big voice saying jovially, "We've pulled through this time, Higgins. . . . I guess we will again." The two sergeants looked at each other and cast a paternal, condescending glance over their men and laughed aloud.

Chrisfield felt powerless as an ox under the yoke. All he could do was work and strain and stand at attention, while that white-faced Anderson could lounge about as if he owned the earth and laugh importantly like that. He held out his plate. The K.P. splashed the meat and gravy into it. He leaned against the tar-papered wall of the shack, eating his food and looking sullenly over at the two sergeants, who laughed and talked with an air of leisure while the men of their two companies ate hurriedly as dogs all round them.

Chrisfield glanced suddenly at Anderson, who sat in the grass at the back of the house, looking out over the wheat fields, while the smoke of a cigarette rose in spirals about his face and his fair hair. He looked peaceful, almost happy. Chrisfield clenched his fists and felt the hatred of that other man rising stingingly within him.

"Guess Ah got a bit of the devil in me," he thought.

*

The windows were so near the grass that the faint light had a greenish color in the shack where the company was quartered. It gave men's faces, tanned as they were, the sickly look of people who work in offices, when they lay on their blankets in the bunks made of chicken wire, stretched across mouldy scantlings. Swallows had made their nests in the peak of the roof, and their droppings made white dobs and blotches on the floorboards in the alley between the bunks, where a few patches of yellow grass had not yet been completely crushed away by footsteps. Now that the shack was empty, Chrisfield could hear plainly the peep-peep of the little swallows in their mud nests. He sat quiet on the end of one of the bunks, looking out of the open door at the blue shadows that were beginning to lengthen on the grass of the meadow behind. His hands, that had got to be the color of terra cotta, hung idly between his legs. He was whistling faintly. His eyes, in their long black eyelashes, were fixed on the distance, though he was not thinking. He felt a comfortable unexpressed well-being all over him. It was pleasant to be alone in the barracks like this, when the other men were out at grenade practice. There was no chance of anyone shouting orders at him.

A warm drowsiness came over him. From the field kitchen alongside came the voice of a man singing:

"O my girl's a lulu, every inch a lulu,
Is Lulu, that pretty lil' girl o' mi-ine."

In their mud nests the young swallows twittered faintly overhead. Now and then there was a beat of wings and a big swallow skimmed into the shack. Chrisfield's cheeks began to feel very softly flushed. His head drooped over on his chest. Outside the cook was singing over and over again in a low voice, amid a faint clatter of pans:

"O my girl's a lulu, every inch a lulu,
Is Lulu, that pretty lil' girl o' mi-ine."

Chrisfield fell asleep.

He woke up with a start. The shack was almost dark. A tall man stood out black against the bright oblong of the door.

"What are you doing here?" said a deep snarling voice.

Chrisfield's eyes blinked. Automatically he got to his feet; it might be an officer. His eyes focussed suddenly. It was Anderson's face that was between him and the light. In the greenish obscurity the skin looked chalk-white in contrast to the heavy eyebrows that met over the nose and the dark stubble on the chin.

"How is it you ain't out with the company?"

"Ah'm barracks guard," muttered Chrisfield. He could feel the blood beating in his wrists and temples, stinging his eyes like fire. He was staring at the floor in front of Anderson's feet.

"Orders was all the companies was to go out an' not leave any guard."

"Ah!"

"We'll see about that when Sergeant Higgins comes in. Is this place tidy?"

"You say Ah'm a goddamed liar, do ye?" Chrisfield felt suddenly cool and joyous. He felt anger taking possession of him. He seemed to be standing somewhere away from himself watching himself get angry.

"This place has got to be cleaned up. . . . That damn General may come back to look over quarters," went on Anderson coolly.

"You call me a goddam liar," said Chrisfield again, putting as much insolence as he could summon into his voice. "Ah guess you doan' remember me."

"Yes, I know, you're the guy tried to run a knife into me once," said Anderson coolly, squaring his shoulders. "I guess you've learned a little discipline by this time. Anyhow you've got to clean this place up. God, they haven't even brushed the birds' nests down! Must be some company!" said Anderson with a half laugh.

"Ah ain't agoin' to neither, fur you."

"Look here, you do it or it'll be the worse for you," shouted the sergeant in his deep rasping voice.

"If ever Ah gits out o' the army Ah'm goin' to shoot you. You've picked on me enough." Chrisfield spoke slowly, as coolly as Anderson.

"Well, we'll see what a court-martial has to say to that."

"Ah doan give a hoot in hell what ye do."

Sergeant Anderson turned on his heel and went out, twisting the corner button of his tunic in his big fingers. Already the sound of tramping feet was heard and the shouted order, "Dis-missed." Then men crowded into the shack, laughing and talking. Chrisfield sat still on the end of the bunk, looking at the bright oblong of the door. Outside he saw Anderson talking to Sergeant Higgins. They shook hands, and Anderson disappeared. Chrisfield heard Sergeant Higgins call after him:

"I guess the next time I see you I'll have to put my heels together an' salute."

Anderson's booming laugh faded as he walked away.

Sergeant Higgins came into the shack and walked straight up to Chrisfield, saying in a hard official voice:

"You're under arrest. . . . Small, guard this man; get your gun and cartridge belt. I'll relieve you so you can get mess."

He went out. Everyone's eyes were turned curiously on Chrisfield. Small, a red-faced man with a long nose that hung down over his upper lip, shuffled sheepishly over to his place beside Chrisfield's cot and let the butt of his rifle come down with a bang on the floor. Somebody laughed. Andrews walked up to them, a look of trouble in his blue eyes and in the lines of his lean tanned cheeks.

"What's the matter, Chris?" he asked in a low voice.

"Tol' that bastard Ah didn't give a hoot in hell what he did," said Chrisfield in a broken voice.

"Say, Andy, I don't think I ought ter let anybody talk to him," said Small in an apologetic tone. "I don't see why Sarge always gives me all his dirty work."

Andrews walked off without replying.

"Never mind, Chris; they won't do nothin' to ye," said Jenkins, grinning at him good-naturedly from the door.

"Ah doan give a hoot in hell what they do," said Chrisfield again.

He lay back in his bunk and looked at the ceiling. The barracks was full of a bustle of cleaning up. Judkins was sweeping the floor with a broom made of dry sticks. Another man was knocking down the swallows' nests with a bayonet. The mud nests crumbled and fell on the floor and the bunks, filling the air with a flutter of feathers and a smell of birdlime.

The little naked bodies, with their orange bills too big for them, gave a soft plump when they hit the boards of the floor, where they lay giving faint gasping squeaks. Meanwhile, with shrill little cries, the big swallows flew back and forth in the shanty, now and then striking the low roof.

"Say, pick 'em up, can't yer?" said Small. Judkins was sweeping the little gasping bodies out among the dust and dirt.

A stoutish man stooped and picked the little birds up one by one, puckering his lips into an expression of tenderness. He made his two hands into a nest-shaped hollow, out of which stretched the long necks and the gaping orange mouths. Andrews ran into him at the door.

"Hello, Dad," he said. "What the hell?"

"I just picked these up."

"So they couldn't let the poor little devils stay there? God! it looks to me as if they went out of their way to give pain to everything, bird, beast or man."

"War ain't no picnic," said Judkins.

"Well, God damn it, isn't that a reason for not going out of your way to raise more hell with people's feelings than you have to?"

A face with peaked chin and nose on which was stretched a parchment-colored skin appeared in the door.

"Hello, boys," said the "Y" man. "I just thought I'd tell you I'm going to open the canteen tomorrow, in the last shack on the Beaucourt road. There'll be chocolate, ciggies, soap, and everything."

Everybody cheered. The "Y" man beamed.

His eye lit on the little birds in Dad's hands.

"How could you?" he said. "An American soldier being deliberately cruel. I would never have believed it."

"Ye've got somethin' to learn," muttered Dad, waddling out into the twilight on his bandy legs.

Chrisfield had been watching the scene at the door with unseeing eyes. A terrified nervousness that he tried to beat off had come over him. It was useless to repeat to himself again and again that he didn't give a damn; the prospect of being brought up alone before all those officers, of being cross-questioned by those curt voices, frightened him. He would rather have been lashed. Whatever was he to say, he kept asking himself; he would get mixed up or say things he didn't mean to, or else he wouldn't be able to get a word out at all. If only Andy could go up with him, Andy was educated, like the officers were; he had more learning than the whole shooting-match put together. He'd be able to defend himself, and defend his friends, too, if only they'd let him.

"I felt just like those little birds that time they got the bead on our trench at Boticourt," said Jenkins, laughing.

Chrisfield listened to the talk about him as if from another world. Already he was cut off from his outfit. He'd disappear and they'd never know or care what became of him.

The mess-call blew and the men filed out. He could hear their talk outside, and the sound of their mess-kits as they opened them. He lay on his bunk staring up into the dark. A faint blue light still came from outside, giving a curious purple color to Small's red face and long drooping nose at the end of which hung a glistening drop of moisture.

Chrisfield found Andrews washing a shirt in the brook that flowed through the ruins of the village the other side of the road from the buildings where the division was quartered. The blue sky flicked with pinkish-white clouds gave a shimmer of blue and lavender and white to the bright water. At the bottom could be seen battered helmets and bits of equipment and tin cans that had once held meat. Andrews turned his head; he had a smudge of mud down his nose and soapsuds on his chin.

"Hello, Chris," he said, looking him in the eyes with his sparkling blue eyes, "how's things?" There was a faint anxious frown on his forehead.

"Two-thirds of one month's pay an' confined to quarters," said Chrisfield cheerfully.

"Gee, they were easy."

"Um-hum, said Ah was a good shot an' all that, so they'd let me off this time."

Andrews started scrubbing at his shirt again.

"I've got this shirt so full of mud I don't think I ever will get it clean," he said.

"Move ye ole hide away, Andy. Ah'll wash it. You ain't no good for nothin'."

"Hell no, I'll do it."

"Move ye hide out of there."

"Thanks awfully."

Andrews got to his feet and wiped the mud off his nose with his bare forearm.

"Ah'm goin' to shoot that bastard," said Chrisfield, scrubbing at the shirt.

"Don't be an ass, Chris."

"Ah swear to God Ah am."

"What's the use of getting all wrought up. The thing's over. You'll probably never see him again."

"Ah ain't all het up. . . . Ah'm goin' to do it though." He wrung the shirt out carefully and flipped Andrews in the face with it. "There ye are," he said.

"You're a good fellow, Chris, even if you are an ass."

"Tell me we're going into the line in a day or two."

"There's been a devil of a lot of artillery going up the road; French, British, every old kind."

"Tell me they's raisin' hell in the Oregon forest."

They walked slowly across the road. A motorcycle despatch-rider whizzed past them.

"It's them guys has the fun," said Chrisfield.

"I don't believe anybody has much."

"What about the officers?"

"They're too busy feeling important to have a real hell of a time."

The hard cold rain beat like a lash in his face. There was no light anywhere and no sound but the hiss of the rain in the grass. His eyes strained to see through the dark until red and yellow blotches danced before them. He walked very slowly and carefully, holding something very gently in his hand under his raincoat. He felt himself full of a strange subdued fury; he seemed to be walking behind himself spying on his own actions, and what he saw made him feel joyously happy, made him want to sing.

He turned so that the rain beat against his cheek. Under his helmet he felt his hair full of sweat that ran with the rain down his glowing face. His fingers clutched very carefully the smooth stick he had in his hand.

He stopped and shut his eyes for a moment; through the

hiss of the rain he had heard a sound of men talking in one of the shanties. When he shut his eyes he saw the white face of Anderson before him, with its unshaven chin and the eyebrows that met across the nose.

Suddenly he felt the wall of a house in front of him. He put out his hand. His hand jerked back from the rough wet feel of the tar paper, as if it had touched something dead. He groped along the wall, stepping very cautiously. He felt as he had felt reconnoitering in the Bringy Wood. Phrases came to his mind as they had then. Without thinking what they meant, the words *Make the world safe for Democracy* formed themselves in his head. They were very comforting. They occupied his thoughts. He said them to himself again and again. Meanwhile his free hand was fumbling very carefully with the fastening that held the wooden shutter over a window. The shutter opened a very little, creaking loudly, louder than the patter of rain on the roof of the shack. A stream of water from the roof was pouring into his face.

Suddenly a beam of light transformed everything, cutting the darkness in two. The rain glittered like a bead curtain. Chrisfield was looking into a little room where a lamp was burning. At a table covered with printed blanks of different size sat a corporal; behind him was a bunk and a pile of equipment. The corporal was reading a magazine. Chrisfield looked at him a long time; his fingers were tight about the smooth stick. There was no one else in the room.

A sort of panic seized Chrisfield; he strode away noisily from the window and pushed open the door of the shack.

"Where's Sergeant Anderson?" he asked in a breathless voice of the first man he saw.

"Corp's there if it's anything important," said the man. "Anderson's gone to an O.T.C. Left day before yesterday."

Chrisfield was out in the rain again. It was beating straight in his face, so that his eyes were full of water. He was trembling. He had suddenly become terrified. The smooth stick he held seemed to burn him. He was straining his ears for an explosion. Walking straight before him down the road, he went faster and faster as if trying to escape from it. He stumbled on a pile of stones. Automatically he pulled the string out of the grenade and threw it far from him.

There was a minute's pause.

Red flame spurted in the middle of the wheatfield. He felt the sharp crash in his eardrums.

He walked fast through the rain. Behind him, at the door of the shack, he could hear excited voices. He walked recklessly on, the rain blinding him. When he finally stepped into the light he was so dazzled he could not see who was in the wine shop.

"Well, I'll be damned, Chris," said Andrews's voice. Chrisfield blinked the rain out of his lashes. Andrews sat writing with a pile of papers before him and a bottle of champagne. It seemed to Chrisfield to soothe his nerves to hear Andy's voice. He wished he would go on talking a long time without a pause.

"If you aren't the crowning idiot of the ages," Andrews went on in a low voice. He took Chrisfield by the arm and led him into the little back room, where there was a high bed with a brown coverlet and a big kitchen table on which were the remnants of a meal.

"What's the matter? Your arm's trembling like the devil. But why. . . . O pardon, Crimpette. C'est un ami. . . . You know Crimpette, don't you?" He pointed to a youngish woman who had just appeared from behind the bed. She had a flabby rosy face and violet circles under her eyes, dark as if they'd been made by blows, and untidy hair. A dirty grey muslin dress with half the hooks off held in badly her large breasts and flabby figure. Chrisfield looked at her greedily, feeling his furious irritation flame into one desire.

"What's the matter with you, Chris? You're crazy to break out of quarters this way."

"Say, Andy, git out o' here. Ah ain't your sort anyway. . . . Git out o' here."

"You're a wild man. I'll grant you that. . . . But I'd just as soon be your sort as anyone else's. . . . Have a drink."

"Not now."

Andrews sat down with his bottle and his papers, pushing away the broken plates full of stale food to make a place on the greasy table. He took a gulp out of the bottle, that made him cough, then put the end of his pencil in his mouth and stared gravely at the paper.

"No, I'm your sort, Chris," he said over his shoulder, "only they've tamed me. O God, how tame I am."

Chrisfield did not listen to what he was saying. He stood in front of the woman, staring in her face. She looked at him in a stupid frightened way. He felt in his pockets for some money. As he had just been paid he had a fifty-franc note. He spread it out carefully before her. Her eyes glistened. The pupils seemed to grow smaller as they fastened on the bit of daintily colored paper. He crumpled it up suddenly in his fist and shoved it down between her breasts.

Some time later Chrisfield sat down in front of Andrews. He still had his wet slicker on.

"Ah guess you think Ah'm a swine," he said in his normal voice. "Ah guess you're about right."

"No, I don't," said Andrews. Something made him put his hand on Chrisfield's hand that lay on the table. It had a feeling of cool health.

"Say, why were you trembling so when you came in here? You seem all right now."

"Oh, Ah dunno," said Chrisfield in a soft resonant voice.

They were silent for a long while. They could hear the woman's footsteps going and coming behind them.

"Let's go home," said Chrisfield.

"All right. . . . Bonsoir, Crimpette."

Outside the rain had stopped. A stormy wind had torn the clouds to rags. Here and there clusters of stars showed through.

They splashed merrily through the puddles. But here and there reflected a patch of stars when the wind was not ruffling them.

"Christ, Ah wish Ah was like you, Andy," said Chrisfield.

"You don't want to be like me, Chris. I'm no sort of a person at all. I'm tame. O you don't know how damn tame I am."

"Learnin' sure do help a feller to git along in the world."

"Yes, but what's the use of getting along if you haven't any world to get along in? Chris, I belong to a crowd that just fakes learning. I guess the best thing that can happen to us is to get killed in this butchery. We're a tame generation. . . . It's you that it matters to kill."

"Ah ain't no good for anythin'. . . . Ah doan give a damn. . . . Lawsee, Ah feel sleepy."

As they slipped in the door of their quarters, the sergeant looked at Chrisfield searchingly. Andrews spoke up at once.

"There's some rumors going on at the latrine, Sarge. The fellows from the Thirty-second say we're going to march into hell's half-acre about Thursday."

"A lot they know about it."

"That's the latest edition of the latrine news."

"The hell it is! Well, d'you want to know something, Andrews. . . . It'll be before Thursday, or I'm a Dutchman." Sergeant Higgins put on a great air of mystery.

Chrisfield went to his bunk, undressed quietly and climbed into his blankets. He stretched his arms languidly a couple of times, and while Andrews was still talking to the sergeant, fell asleep.

IV

THE MOON lay among clouds on the horizon, like a big red pumpkin among its leaves.

Chrisfield squinted at it through the boughs of the apple trees laden with apples that gave a winey fragrance to the crisp air. He was sitting on the ground, his legs stretched limply before him, leaning against the rough trunk of an apple tree. Opposite him, leaning against another tree, was the square form, surmounted by a large long-jawed face, of Judkins. Between them lay two empty cognac bottles. All about them was the rustling orchard, with its crooked twigs that made a crackling sound rubbing together in the gusts of the autumn wind, that came heavy with a smell of damp woods and of rotting fruits and of all the ferment of the over-ripe fields. Chrisfield felt it stirring the moist hair on his forehead and through the buzzing haze of the cognac heard the plunk, plunk, plunk of apples dropping that followed each gust, and the twanging of night insects, and, far in the distance, the endless rumble of guns, like tomtoms beaten for a dance.

"Ye heard what the Colonel said, didn't ye?" said Judkins in a voice hoarse from too much drink.

Chrisfield belched and nodded his head vaguely. He remembered Andrews's white fury after the men had been dismissed,—how he had sat down on the end of a log by the field kitchen, staring at the patch of earth he beat into mud with the toe of his boot.

"Then," went on Judkins, trying to imitate the Colonel's solemn efficient voice, "'On the subject of prisoners'"—he hiccoughed and made a limp gesture with his hand—"'On the subject of prisoners, well, I'll leave that to you, but juss remember . . . juss remember what the Huns did to Belgium, an' I might add that we have barely enough emergency rations as it is, and the more prisoners you have the less you fellers'll git to eat.'"

"That's what he said, Judkie; that's what he said."

"'An the more prisoners ye have, the less youse'll git to eat,'" chanted Judkins, making a triumphal flourish with his hand.

Chrisfield groped for the cognac bottle; it was empty; he waved it in the air a minute and then threw it into the tree opposite him. A shower of little apples fell about Judkins's head. He got unsteadily to his feet.

"I tell you, fellers," he said, "war ain't no picnic."

Chrisfield stood up and grabbed at an apple. His teeth crunched into it.

"Sweet," he said.

"Sweet, nauthin'," mumbled Judkins, "war ain't no picnic. . . . I tell you, buddy, if you take any prisoners"—he hiccoughed—"after what the Colonel said, I'll lick the spots out of you, by God I will. . . . Rip up their guts that's all, like they was dummies. Rip up their guts." His voice suddenly changed to one of childish dismay. "Gee, Chris, I'm going to be sick," he whispered.

"Look out," said Chrisfield, pushing him away. Judkins leaned against a tree and vomited.

The full moon had risen above the clouds and filled the apple orchard with chilly golden light that cast a fantastic shadow pattern of interlaced twigs and branches upon the bare ground littered with apples. The sound of the guns had grown nearer. There were loud eager rumbles as of bowls being rolled very hard on a bowling alley, combined with a continuous roar like sheets of iron being shaken.

"Ah bet it's hell out there," said Chrisfield.

"I feel better," said Judkins. "Let's go get some more cognac."

"Ah'm hungry," said Chrisfield. "Let's go an' get that ole woman to cook us some aigs."

"Too damn late," growled Judkins.

"How the hell late is it?"

"Dunno, I sold my watch."

They were walking at random through the orchard. They came to a field full of big pumpkins that gleamed in the moonlight and cast shadows black as holes. In the distance they could see wooded hills.

Chrisfield picked up a medium-sized pumpkin and threw it

as hard as he could into the air. It split into three when it landed with a thud on the ground, and the moist yellow seeds spilled out.

"Some strong man, you are," said Judkins, tossing up a bigger one.

"Say, there's a farmhouse, maybe we could get some aigs from the hen-roost."

"Hell of a lot of hens. . . ."

At that moment the crowing of a rooster came across the silent fields. They ran towards the dark farm buildings.

"Look out, there may be officers quartered there."

They walked cautiously round the square, silent group of buildings. There were no lights. The big wooden door of the court pushed open easily, without creaking. On the roof of the barn the pigeon-cote was etched dark against the disc of the moon. A warm smell of stables blew in their faces as the two men tiptoed into the manure-littered farmyard. Under one of the sheds they found a table on which a great many pears were set to ripen. Chrisfield put his teeth into one. The rich sweet juice ran down his chin. He ate the pear quickly and greedily, and then bit into another.

"Fill yer pockets with 'em," whispered Judkins.

"They might ketch us."

"Ketch us, hell. We'll be goin' into the offensive in a day or two."

"Ah sure would like to git some aigs."

Chrisfield pushed open the door of one of the barns. A smell of creamy milk and cheeses filled his nostrils.

"Come here," he whispered. "Want some cheese?"

A lot of cheeses ranged on a board shone silver in the moonlight that came in through the open door.

"Hell, no, ain't fit te eat," said Judkins, pushing his heavy fist into one of the new soft cheeses.

"Doan do that."

"Well, ain't we saved 'em from the Huns?"

"But, hell."

"War ain't no picnic, that's all," said Judkins.

In the next door they found chickens roosting in a small room with straw on the floor. The chickens ruffled their feathers and made a muffled squeaking as they slept.

Suddenly there was a loud squawking and all the chickens were cackling with terror.

"Beat it," muttered Judkins, running for the gate of the farmyard.

There were shrill cries of women in the house. A voice shrieking, "C'est les Boches, C'est les Boches," rose above the cackling of chickens and the clamor of guinea-hens. As they ran, they heard the rasping cries of a woman in hysterics, rending the rustling autumn night.

"God damn," said Judkins breathless, "they ain't got no right, those frogs ain't, to carry on like that."

They ducked into the orchard again. Above the squawking of the chicken Judkins still held, swinging it by its legs, Chrisfield could hear the woman's voice shrieking. Judkins dexterously wrung the chicken's neck. Crushing the apples underfoot they strode fast through the orchard. The voice faded into the distance until it could not be heard above the sound of the guns.

"Gee, Ah'm kind o' cut up 'bout that lady," said Chrisfield.

"Well, ain't we saved her from the Huns?"

"Andy don't think so."

"Well, if you want to know what I think about that guy Andy. . . . I don't think much of him. I think he's yaller, that's all," said Judkins.

"No, he ain't."

"I heard the lootenant say so. He's a goddam yeller dawg."

Chrisfield swore sullenly.

"Well, you juss wait 'n see. I tell you, buddy, war ain't no picnic."

"What the hell are we goin' to do with that chicken?" said Judkins.

"You remember what happened to Eddie White?"

"Hell, we'd better leave it here."

Judkins swung the chicken by its neck round his head and threw it as hard as he could into the bushes.

They were walking along the road between chestnut trees that led to their village. It was dark except for irregular patches of bright moonlight in the centre that lay white as milk among the indentated shadows of the leaves. All about them rose a cool scent of woods, of ripe fruits and of decaying leaves, of the ferment of the autumn countryside.

The lieutenant sat at a table in the sun, in the village street outside the company office. In front of him sparkled piles of money and daintily tinted banknotes. Beside him stood Sergeant Higgins with an air of solemnity and the second sergeant and the corporal. The men stood in line and as each came before the table he saluted with deference, received his money and walked away with a self-conscious air. A few villagers looked on from the small windows with grey frames of their rambling whitewashed houses. In the ruddy sunshine the line of men cast an irregular blue-violet shadow, like a gigantic centipede, on the yellow gravel road.

From the table by the window of the café of "Nos Braves Poilus" where Small and Judkins and Chrisfield had established themselves with their pay crisp in their pockets, they could see the little front garden of the house across the road, where, behind a hedge of orange marigolds, Andrews sat on the doorstep talking to an old woman hunched on a low chair in the sun just inside the door, who leant her small white head over towards his yellow one.

"There ye are," said Judkins in a solemn tone. "He don't even go after his pay. That guy thinks he's the whole show, he does."

Chrisfield flushed, but said nothing.

"He don't do nothing all day long but talk to that ole lady," said Small with a grin. "Guess she reminds him of his mother, or somethin'."

"He always does go round with the frogs all he can. Looks to me like he'd rather have a drink with a frog than with an American."

"Reckon he wants to learn their language," said Small.

"He won't never come to much in this army, that's what I'm telling yer," said Judkins.

The little houses across the way had flushed red with the sunset. Andrews got to his feet slowly and languidly and held out his hand to the old woman. She stood up, a small tottering figure in a black silk shawl. He leaned over towards her and she kissed both his cheeks vigorously several times. He walked down the road towards the billets, with his fatigue cap in his hand, looking at the ground.

"He's got a flower behind his ear, like a cigarette," said Judkins, with a disgusted snort.

"Well, I guess we'd better go," said Small. "We got to be in quarters at six."

They were silent a moment. In the distance the guns kept up a continual tomtom sound.

"Guess we'll be in that soon," said Small.

Chrisfield felt a chill go down his spine. He moistened his lips with his tongue.

"Guess it's hell out there," said Judkins. "War ain't no picnic."

"Ah doan give a hoot in hell," said Chrisfield.

The men were lined up in the village street with their packs on, waiting for the order to move. Thin wreaths of white mist still lingered in the trees and over the little garden plots. The sun had not yet risen, but ranks of clouds in the pale blue sky overhead were brilliant with crimson and gold. The men stood in an irregular line, bent over a little by the weight of their equipment, moving back and forth, stamping their feet and beating their arms together, their noses and ears red from the chill of the morning. The haze of their breath rose above their heads.

Down the misty road a drab-colored limousine appeared, running slowly. It stopped in front of the line of men. The lieutenant came hurriedly out of the house opposite, drawing on a pair of gloves. The men standing in line looked curiously at the limousine. They could see that two of the tires were flat and that the glass was broken. There were scratches on the drab paint and in the door three long jagged holes that obliterated the number. A little murmur went down the line of men. The door opened with difficulty, and a major in a light buff-colored coat stumbled out. One arm, wrapped in bloody bandages, was held in a sling made of a handkerchief. His face was white and drawn into a stiff mask with pain. The lieutenant saluted.

"For God's sake where's a repair station?" he asked in a loud shaky voice.

"There's none in this village, Major."

"Where the hell is there one?"

"I don't know," said the lieutenant in a humble tone.

"Why the hell don't you know? This organization's rotten, no good. . . . Major Stanley's just been killed. What the hell's the name of this village?"

"Thiocourt."

"Where the hell's that?"

The chauffeur had leaned out. He had no cap and his hair was full of dust.

"You see, Lootenant, we wants to get to Châlons——"

"Yes, that's it. Châlons sur . . . Châlons-sur-Marne," said the Major.

"The billeting officer has a map," said the lieutenant, "last house to the left."

"O let's go there quick," said the major. He fumbled with the fastening of the door.

The lieutenant opened it for him.

As he opened the door, the men nearest had a glimpse of the interior of the car. On the far side was a long object huddled in blankets, propped up on the seat.

Before he got in the major leaned over and pulled a woolen rug out, holding it away from him with his one good arm. The car moved off slowly, and all down the village street the men, lined up waiting for orders, stared curiously at the three jagged holes in the door.

The lieutenant looked at the rug that lay in the middle of the road. He touched it with his foot. It was soaked with blood that in places had dried into clots.

The lieutenant and the men of his company looked at it in silence. The sun had risen and shone on the roofs of the little whitewashed houses behind them. Far down the road a regiment had begun to move.

V

AT THE BROW of the hill they rested. Chrisfield sat on the red clay bank and looked about him, his rifle between his knees. In front of him on the side of the road was a French burying ground, where the little wooden crosses, tilting in every direction, stood up against the sky, and the bead wreaths glistened in the warm sunlight. All down the road as far as he could see was a long drab worm, broken in places by strings of motor trucks, a drab worm that wriggled down the slope, through the roofless shell of the village and up into the shattered woods on the crest of the next hills. Chrisfield strained his eyes to see the hills beyond. They lay blue and very peaceful in the moon mist. The river glittered about the piers of the wrecked stone bridge, and disappeared between rows of yellow poplars. Somewhere in the valley a big gun fired. The shell shrieked into the distance, towards the blue, peaceful hills.

Chrisfield's regiment was moving again. The men, their feet slipping in the clayey mud, went downhill with long strides, the straps of their packs tugging at their shoulders.

"Isn't this great country?" said Andrews, who marched beside him.

"Ah'd liever be at an O.T.C. like that bastard Anderson."

"Oh, to hell with that," said Andrews. He still had a big faded orange marigold in one of the buttonholes of his soiled tunic. He walked with his nose in the air and his nostrils dilated, enjoying the tang of the autumnal sunlight.

Chrisfield took the cigarette, that had gone out half-smoked, from his mouth and spat savagely at the heels of the man in front of him.

"This ain't no life for a white man," he said.

"I'd rather be this than . . . than that," said Andrews bitterly. He tossed his head in the direction of a staff car full of officers that was stalled at the side of the road. They were drinking something out of a thermos bottle that they passed round with the air of Sunday excursionists. They waved, with a conscious relaxation of discipline, at the men as they passed.

One, a little lieutenant with a black mustache with pointed ends, kept crying: "They're running like rabbits, fellers; they're running like rabbits." A wavering half-cheer would come from the column now and then where it was passing the staff car.

The big gun fired again. Chrisfield was near it this time and felt the concussion like a blow in the head.

"Some baby," said the man behind him.

Someone was singing:

> "Good morning, mister Zip Zip Zip,
>   With your hair cut just as short as,
>   With your hair cut just as short as,
>   With your hair cut just as short as mi-ine."

Everybody took it up. Their steps rang in rhythm in the paved street that zigzagged among the smashed houses of the village. Ambulances passed them, big trucks full of huddled men with grey faces, from which came a smell of sweat and blood and carbolic.

Somebody went on:

> "O ashes to ashes
>   An' dust to dust . . ."

"Can that," cried Judkins, "it ain't lucky."

But everybody had taken up the song. Chrisfield noticed that Andrews's eyes were sparkling. "If he ain't the damnedest," he thought to himself. But he shouted at the top of his lungs with the rest:

> "O ashes to ashes
>   An' dust to dust;
>   If the gasbombs don't get yer
>   The eighty-eights must."

They were climbing the hill again. The road was worn into deep ruts and there were many shell holes, full of muddy water, into which their feet slipped. The woods began, a shattered skeleton of woods, full of old artillery emplacements and dugouts, where torn camouflage fluttered from splintered trees. The ground and the road were littered with tin cans and brass shell-cases. Along both sides of the road the trees were festooned, as with creepers, with strand upon strand of telephone wire.

When next they stopped Chrisfield was on the crest of the hill beside a battery of French seventy-fives. He looked curiously at the Frenchmen, who sat about on logs in their pink and blue shirt-sleeves playing cards and smoking. Their gestures irritated him.

"Say, tell 'em we're advancin'," he said to Andrews.

"Are we?" said Andrews. "All right. . . . Dites-donc, les Boches courent-ils comme des lapins?" he shouted.

One of the men turned his head and laughed.

"He says they've been running that way for four years," said Andrews. He slipped his pack off, sat down on it, and fished for a cigarette. Chrisfield took off his helmet and rubbed a muddy hand through his hair. He took a bite of chewing tobacco and sat with his hands clasped over his knees.

"How the hell long are we going to wait this time?" he muttered. The shadows of the tangled and splintered trees crept slowly across the road. The French artillerymen were eating their supper. A long train of motor trucks growled past, splashing mud over the men crowded along the sides of the road. The sun set, and a lot of batteries down in the valley began firing, making it impossible to talk. The air was full of a shrieking and droning of shells overhead. The Frenchmen stretched and yawned and went down into their dugout. Chrisfield watched them enviously. The stars were beginning to come out in the green sky behind the tall lacerated trees. Chrisfield's legs ached with cold. He began to get crazily anxious for something to happen, for something to happen, but the column waited, without moving, through the gathering darkness. Chrisfield chewed steadily, trying to think of nothing but the taste of the tobacco in his mouth.

The column was moving again; as they reached the brow of another hill Chrisfield felt a curious sweetish smell that made his nostrils smart. "Gas," he thought, full of panic, and put his hand to the mask that hung round his neck. But he did not want to be the first to put it on. No order came. He marched on, cursing the sergeant and the lieutenant. But maybe they'd been killed by it. He had a vision of the whole regiment sinking down in the road suddenly, overcome by the gas.

"Smell anythin', Andy?" he whispered cautiously.

"I can smell a combination of dead horses and tuberoses and banana oil and the ice cream we used to have at college and dead rats in the garret, but what the hell do we care now?" said Andrews, giggling. "This is the damnedest fool business ever. . . ."

"He's crazy," muttered Chrisfield to himself. He looked at the stars in the black sky that seemed to be going along with the column on its march. Or was it that they and the stars were standing still while the trees moved away from them, waving their skinny shattered arms? He could hardly hear the tramp of feet on the road, so loud was the pandemonium of the guns ahead and behind. Every now and then a rocket would burst in front of them and its red and green lights would mingle for a moment with the stars. But it was only overhead he could see the stars. Everywhere else white and red glows rose and fell as if the horizon were on fire.

As they started down the slope, the trees suddenly broke away and they saw the valley between them full of the glare of guns and the white light of star shells. It was like looking into a stove full of glowing embers. The hillside that sloped away from them was full of crashing detonations and yellow tongues of flame. In a battery near the road, that seemed to crush their skulls each time a gun fired, they could see the dark forms of the artillerymen silhouetted in fantastic attitudes against the intermittent red glare. Stunned and blinded, they kept on marching down the road. It seemed to Chrisfield that they were going to step any minute into the flaring muzzle of a gun.

At the foot of the hill, beside a little grove of uninjured trees, they stopped again. A new train of trucks was crawling past them, huge blots in the darkness. There were no batteries near, so they could hear the grinding roar of the gears as the trucks went along the uneven road, plunging in and out of shellholes.

Chrisfield lay down in the dry ditch, full of bracken, and dozed with his head on his pack. All about him were stretched other men. Someone was resting his head on Chrisfield's thigh. The noise had subsided a little. Through his doze he could hear men's voices talking in low crushed tones, as if they were afraid of speaking aloud. On the road the truck-drivers kept calling out to each other shrilly, raspingly. The motors stopped running one after another, making almost a silence, during which Chrisfield fell asleep.

Something woke him. He was stiff with cold and terrified. For a moment he thought he had been left alone, that the company had gone on, for there was no one touching him.

Overhead was a droning as of gigantic mosquitoes, growing fast to a loud throbbing. He heard the lieutenant's voice calling shrilly:

"Sergeant Higgins, Sergeant Higgins!"

The lieutenant stood out suddenly black against a sheet of flame. Chrisfield could see his fatigue cap a little on one side and his trench coat, drawn in tight at the waist and sticking out stiffly at the knees. He was shaken by the explosion. Everything was black again. Chrisfield got to his feet, his ears ringing. The column was moving on. He heard moaning near him in the darkness. The tramp of feet and jingle of equipment drowned all other sound. He could feel his shoulders becoming raw under the tugging of the pack. Now and then the flare from aëroplane bombs behind him showed up wrecked trucks on the side of the road. Somewhere a machine gun spluttered. But the column tramped on, weighed down by the packs, by the deadening exhaustion.

The turbulent flaring darkness was calming to the grey of dawn when Chrisfield stopped marching. His eyelids stung as if his eyeballs were flaming hot. He could not feel his feet and legs. The guns continued incessantly like a hammer beating on his head. He was walking very slowly in a single file, now and then stumbling against the man ahead of him. There was earth on both sides of him, clay walls that dripped moisture. All at once he stumbled down some steps into a dugout, where it was pitch-black. An unfamiliar smell struck him, made him uneasy; but his thoughts seemed to reach him from out of a great distance. He groped to the wall. His knees struck against a bunk with blankets in it. In another second he was sunk fathoms deep in sleep.

When he woke up his mind was very clear. The roof of the dugout was of logs. A bright spot far away was the door. He hoped desperately that he wasn't on duty. He wondered where Andy was; then he remembered that Andy was crazy,—"a yeller dawg," Judkins had called him. Sitting up with difficulty he undid his shoes and puttees, wrapped himself in his blanket. All round him were snores and the deep breathing of exhausted sleep. He closed his eyes.

He was being court-martialled. He stood with his hands at his sides before three officers at a table. All three had the same white faces with heavy blue jaws and eyebrows that met above the nose. They were reading things out of papers aloud, but, although he strained his ears, he couldn't make out what they were saying. All he could hear was a faint moaning. Something had a curious unfamiliar smell that troubled him. He could not stand still at attention, although the angry eyes of officers stared at him from all round. "Anderson, Sergeant Anderson, what's that smell?" he kept asking in a small whining voice. "Please tell a feller what that smell is." But the three officers at the table kept reading from their papers, and the moaning grew louder and louder in his ears until he shrieked aloud. There was a grenade in his hand. He pulled the string out and threw it, and he saw the lieutenant's trench coat stand out against a sheet of flame. Someone sprang at him. He was wrestling for his life with Anderson, who turned into a woman with huge flabby breasts. He crushed her to him and turned to defend himself against three officers who came at him, their trench coats drawn in tightly at the waist until they looked like wasps. Everything faded, he woke up.

His nostrils were still full of the strange troubling smell. He sat on the edge of the bunk, wriggling in his clothes, for his body crawled with lice.

"Gee, it's funny to be in where the Fritzies were not long ago," he heard a voice say.

"Kiddo! we're advancin'," came another voice.

"But, hell, this ain't no kind of an advance. I ain't seen a German yet."

"Ah kin smell 'em though," said Chrisfield, getting suddenly to his feet.

Sergeant Higgins' head appeared in the door. "Fall in," he shouted. Then he added in his normal voice, "It's up and at 'em, fellers."

*

Chrisfield caught his puttee on a clump of briars at the edge of the clearing and stood kicking his leg back and forth to get it free. At last he broke away, the torn puttee dragging behind him. Out in the sunlight in the middle of the clearing he saw a man in olive-drab kneeling beside something on the ground. A German lay face down with a red hole in his back. The man was going through his pockets. He looked up into Chrisfield's face.

"Souvenirs," he said.

"What outfit are you in, buddy?"

"143rd," said the man, getting to his feet slowly.

"Where the hell are we?"

"Damned if I know."

The clearing was empty, except for the two Americans and the German with the hole in his back. In the distance they heard a sound of artillery and nearer the "put, put, put" of isolated machine guns. The leaves of the trees about them, all shades of brown and crimson and yellow, danced in the sunlight.

"Say, that damn money ain't no good, is it?" asked Chrisfield.

"German money? Hell, no. . . . I got a watch that's a peach though." The man held out a gold watch, looking suspiciously at Chrisfield all the while through half-closed eyes.

"Ah saw a feller had a gold-handled sword," said Chrisfield.

"Where's that?"

"Back there in the wood"; he waved his hand vaguely. "Ah've got to find ma outfit; comin' along?" Chrisfield started towards the other edge of the clearing.

"Looks to me all right here," said the other man, lying down on the grass in the sun.

The leaves rustled underfoot as Chrisfield strode through the wood. He was frightened by being alone. He walked ahead as fast as he could, his puttee still dragging behind him. He came to a barbed-wire entanglement half embedded in fallen beech leaves. It had been partly cut in one place, but in crossing he tore his thigh on a barb. Taking off the torn puttee, he wrapped it round the outside of his trousers and kept on walking, feeling a little blood trickle down his leg.

Later he came to a lane that cut straight through the wood where there were many ruts through the putty-coloured mud puddles. Down the lane in a patch of sunlight he saw a figure, towards which he hurried. It was a young man with red hair and a pink-and-white face. By a gold bar on the collar of his shirt Chrisfield saw that he was a lieutenant. He had no coat or hat and there was greenish slime all over the front of his clothes as if he had lain on his belly in a mud puddle.

"Where you going?"

"Dunno, sir."

"All right, come along." The lieutenant started walking as fast as he could up the lane, swinging his arms wildly.

"Seen any machine-gun nests?"

"Not a one."

"Hum."

He followed the lieutenant, who walked so fast he had difficulty keeping up, splashing recklessly through the puddles.

"Where's the artillery? That's what I want to know," cried the lieutenant, suddenly stopping in his tracks and running a hand through his red hair. "Where the hell's the artillery?" He looked at Chrisfield savagely out of green eyes. "No use advancing without artillery." He started walking faster than ever.

All at once they saw sunlight ahead of them and olive-drab uniforms. Machine guns started firing all around them in a sudden gust. Chrisfield found himself running forward across a field full of stubble and sprouting clover among a group of men he did not know. The whip-like sound of rifles had chimed in with the stuttering of the machine guns. Little white clouds sailed above him in a blue sky, and in front of him was a group of houses that had the same color, white with lavender-grey shadows, as the clouds.

He was in a house, with a grenade like a tin pineapple in each hand. The sudden loneliness frightened him again. Outside the house was a sound of machine-gun firing, broken by the occasional bursting of a shell. He looked at the red-tiled roof and at a chromo of a woman nursing a child that hung on the whitewashed wall opposite him. He was in a small kitchen. There was a fire in the hearth where something boiled in a black pot. Chrisfield tiptoed over and looked in.

At the bottom of the bubbling water he saw five potatoes. At the other end of the kitchen, beyond two broken chairs, was a door. Chrisfield crept over to it, the tiles seeming to sway under foot. He put his finger to the latch and took it off again suddenly. Holding in his breath he stood a long time looking at the door. Then he pulled it open recklessly. A young man with fair hair was sitting at a table, his head resting on his hands. Chrisfield felt a spurt of joy when he saw that the man's uniform was green. Very coolly he pressed the spring, held the grenade a second and then threw it, throwing himself backwards into the middle of the kitchen. The light-haired man had not moved; his blue eyes still stared straight before him.

In the street Chrisfield ran into a tall man who was running. The man clutched him by the arm and said:

"The barrage is moving up."

"What barrage?"

"Our barrage; we've got to run, we're ahead of it." His voice came in wheezy pants. There were red splotches on his face. They ran together down the empty village street. As they ran they passed the little red-haired lieutenant, who leaned against a whitewashed wall, his legs a mass of blood and torn cloth. He was shouting in a shrill delirious voice that followed them out along the open road.

"Where's the artillery? That's what I want to know; where's the artillery?"

The woods were grey and dripping with dawn. Chrisfield got stiffly to his feet from the pile of leaves where he had slept. He felt numb with cold and hunger, lonely and lost away from his outfit. All about him were men of another division. A captain with a sandy mustache was striding up and down with a blanket about him, on the road just behind a clump of beech trees. Chrisfield had watched him passing back and forth, back and forth, behind the wet clustered trunks of the trees, ever since it had been light. Stamping his feet among the damp leaves, Chrisfield strolled away from the group of men. No one seemed to notice him. The trees closed about him. He could see nothing but moist trees, grey-green and black, and the yellow leaves of saplings that

cut off the view in every direction. He was wondering dully
why he was walking off that way. Somewhere in the back of
his mind there was a vague idea of finding his outfit. Sergeant
Higgins and Andy and Judkins and Small—he wondered what
had become of them. He thought of the company lined up
for mess, and the smell of greasy food that came from the
field-kitchen. He was desperately hungry. He stopped and
leaned against the moss-covered trunk of a tree. The deep
scratch in his leg was throbbing as if all the blood in his body
beat through it. Now that his rustling footsteps had ceased,
the woods were absolutely silent, except for the dripping of
dew from the leaves and branches. He strained his ears to hear
some other sound. Then he noticed that he was staring at a
tree full of small red crab apples. He picked a handful greedily, but they were hard and sour and seemed to make him
hungrier. The sour flavour in his mouth made him furiously
angry. He kicked at the thin trunk of the tree while tears
smarted in his eyes. Swearing aloud in a whining singsong
voice, he strode off through the woods with his eyes on the
ground. Twigs snapped viciously in his face, crooked branches
caught at him, but he plunged on. All at once he stumbled
against something hard that bounced among the leaves.

He stopped still, looking about him, terrified. Two
grenades lay just under his foot, a little further on a man was
propped against a tree with his mouth open. Chrisfield
thought at first he was asleep, as his eyes were closed. He
looked at the grenades carefully. The fuses had not been
sprung. He put one in each pocket, gave a glance at the man
who seemed to be asleep, and strode off again, striking another alley in the woods, at the end of which he could see
sunlight. The sky overhead was full of heavy purple clouds,
tinged here and there with yellow. As he walked towards the
patch of sunlight, the thought came to him that he ought to
have looked in the pockets of the man he had just passed to
see if he had any hard bread. He stood still a moment in hesitation, but started walking again doggedly towards the patch
of sunlight.

Something glittered in the irregular fringe of sun and
shadow. A man was sitting hunched up on the ground with
his fatigue cap pulled over his eyes so that the little gold bar

just caught the horizontal sunlight. Chrisfield's first thought was that he might have food on him.

"Say, Lootenant," he shouted, "d'you know where a fellow can get somethin' to eat."

The man lifted his head slowly. Chrisfield turned cold all over when he saw the white heavy face of Anderson; an unshaven beard was very black on his square chin; there was a long scratch clotted with dried blood from the heavy eyebrow across the left cheek to the corner of the mouth.

"Give me some water, buddy," said Anderson in a weak voice.

Chrisfield handed him his canteen roughly in silence. He noticed that Anderson's arm was in a sling, and that he drank greedily, spilling the water over his chin and his wounded arm.

"Where's Colonel Evans?" asked Anderson in a thin petulant voice.

Chrisfield did not reply but stared at him sullenly. The canteen had dropped from his hand and lay on the ground in front of him. The water gleamed in the sunlight as it ran out among the russet leaves. A wind had come up, making the woods resound. A shower of yellow leaves dropped about them.

"First you was a corporal, then you was a sergeant, and now you're a lootenant," said Chrisfield slowly.

"You'ld better tell me where Colonel Evans is. . . . You must know. . . . He's up that road somewhere," said Anderson, struggling to get to his feet.

Chrisfield walked away without answering. A cold hand was round the grenade in his pocket. He walked away slowly, looking at his feet.

Suddenly he found he had pressed the spring of the grenade. He struggled to pull it out of his pocket. It stuck in the narrow pocket. His arm and his cold fingers that clutched the grenade seemed paralyzed. Then a warm joy went through him. He had thrown it.

Anderson was standing up, swaying backwards and forwards. The explosion made the woods quake. A thick rain of yellow leaves came down. Anderson was flat on the ground. He was so flat he seemed to have sunk into the ground.

Chrisfield pressed the spring of the other grenade and

threw it with his eyes closed. It burst among the thick new-fallen leaves.

A few drops of rain were falling. Chrisfield kept on along the lane, walking fast, feeling full of warmth and strength. The rain beat hard and cold against his back.

He walked with his eyes to the ground. A voice in a strange language stopped him. A ragged man in green with a beard that was clotted with mud stood in front of him with his hands up. Chrisfield burst out laughing.

"Come along," he said, "quick!"

The man shambled in front of him; he was trembling so hard he nearly fell with each step.

Chrisfield kicked him.

The man shambled on without turning round. Chrisfield kicked him again, feeling the point of the man's spine and the soft flesh of his rump against his toes with each kick, laughing so hard all the while that he could hardly see where he was going.

"Halt!" came a voice.

"Ah've got a prisoner," shouted Chrisfield still laughing.

"He ain't much of a prisoner," said the man, pointing his bayonet at the German. "He's gone crazy, I guess. I'll take keer o' him . . . ain't no use sendin' him back."

"All right," said Chrisfield still laughing. "Say, buddy, where can Ah' git something to eat? Ah ain't had nothin' fur a day an a half."

"There's a reconnoitrin' squad up the line; they'll give you somethin'. . . . How's things goin' up that way?" The man pointed up the road.

"Gawd, Ah doan know. Ah ain't had nothin' to eat fur a day and a half."

The warm smell of a stew rose to his nostrils from the mess-kit. Chrisfield stood, feeling warm and important, filling his mouth with soft greasy potatoes and gravy, while men about him asked him questions. Gradually he began to feel full and content, and a desire to sleep came over him. But he was given a gun, and had to start advancing again with the reconnoitering squad. The squad went cautiously up the same lane through the woods.

"Here's an officer done for," said the captain, who walked ahead. He made a little clucking noise of distress with his tongue. "Two of you fellows go back and git a blanket and take him back to the cross-roads. Poor fellow." The captain walked on again, still making little clucking noises with his tongue.

Chrisfield looked straight ahead of him. He did not feel lonely any more now that he was marching in ranks again. His feet beat the ground in time with the other feet. He would not have to think whether to go to the right or to the left. He would do as the others did.

PART FOUR
RUST

I

THERE WERE tiny green frogs in one of the putty-colored puddles by the roadside. John Andrews fell out of the slowly advancing column a moment to look at them. The frogs' triangular heads stuck out of the water in the middle of the puddle. He leaned over, his hands on his knees, easing the weight of the equipment on his back. That way he could see their tiny jewelled eyes, topaz-colored. His eyes felt as if tears were coming to them with tenderness towards the minute lithe bodies of the frogs. Something was telling him that he must run forward and fall into line again, that he must shamble on through the mud, but he remained staring at the puddle, watching the frogs. Then he noticed his reflection in the puddle. He looked at it curiously. He could barely see the outlines of a stained grimacing mask, and the silhouette of the gun barrel slanting behind it. So this was what they had made of him. He fixed his eyes again on the frogs that swam with elastic, leisurely leg strokes in the putty-colored water.

Absently, as if he had no connection with all that went on about him, he heard the twang of bursting shrapnel down the road. He had straightened himself wearily and taken a step forward, when he found himself sinking into the puddle. A feeling of relief came over him. His legs sunk in the puddle; he lay without moving against the muddy bank. The frogs had gone, but from somewhere a little stream of red was creeping out slowly into the putty-colored water. He watched the irregular files of men in olive-drab shambling by. Their footsteps drummed in his ears. He felt triumphantly separated from them, as if he were in a window somewhere watching soldiers pass, or in a box of a theater watching some dreary monotonous play. He drew farther and farther away from

them until they had become very small, like toy soldiers forgotten among the dust in a garret. The light was so dim he
couldn't see, he could only hear their feet tramping interminably through the mud.

John Andrews was on a ladder that shook horribly. A gritty
sponge in his hand, he was washing the windows of a barracks. He began in the left hand corner and soaped the small
oblong panes one after the other. His arms were like lead
and he felt that he would fall from the shaking ladder, but
each time he turned to look towards the ground before
climbing down he saw the top of the general's cap and the
general's chin protruding from under the visor, and a voice
snarled: "Attention," terrifying him so that the ladder shook
more than ever; and he went on smearing soap over the oblong panes with the gritty sponge through interminable
hours, though every joint in his body was racked by the
shaking of the ladder. Bright light flared from inside the windows which he soaped, pane after pane, methodically. The
windows were mirrors. In each pane he saw his thin face, in
shadow, with the shadow of a gun barrel slanting beside it.
The jolting stopped suddenly. He sank into a deep pit of
blackness.

A shrill broken voice was singing in his ear:

> "There's a girl in the heart of Maryland
> With a heart that belo-ongs to mee."

John Andrews opened his eyes. It was pitch black, except
for a series of bright yellow oblongs that seemed to go up in
the sky, where he could see the stars. His mind became suddenly acutely conscious. He began taking account of himself
in a hurried frightened way. He craned his neck a little. In the
darkness he could make out the form of a man stretched out
flat beside him who kept moving his head strangely from side
to side, singing at the top of his lungs in a shrill broken voice.
At that moment Andrews noticed that the smell of carbolic
was overpoweringly strong, that it dominated all the familiar
smells of blood and sweaty clothes. He wriggled his shoulders
so that he could feel the two poles of the stretcher. Then he
fixed his eyes again in the three bright yellow oblongs, one

above the other, that rose into the darkness. Of course, they were windows; he was near a house.

He moved his arms a little. They felt like lead, but unhurt. Then he realized that his legs were on fire. He tried to move them; everything went black again in a sudden agony of pain. The voice was still shrieking in his ears:

> "There's a girl in the heart of Maryland
> With a heart that belongs to mee."

But another voice could be heard, softer, talking endlessly in tender clear tones:

"An' he said they were goin' to take me way down south where there was a little house on the beach, all so warm an' quiet. . . ."

The song of the man beside him rose to a tuneless shriek, like a phonograph running down:

> "An' Mary-land was fairy-land
> When she said that mine she'd be . . ."

Another voice broke in suddenly in short spurts of whining groans that formed themselves into fragments of drawn-out intricate swearing. And all the while the soft voice went on. Andrews strained his ears to hear it. It soothed his pain as if some cool fragrant oil were being poured over his body.

"An' there'll be a garden full of flowers, roses an' hollyhocks, way down there in the south, an' it'll be so warm an' quiet, an' the sun'll shine all day, and the sky'll be so blue . . ."

Andrews felt his lips repeating the words like lips following a prayer.

"—An' it'll be so warm an' quiet, without any noise at all. An' the garden'll be full of roses an' . . ."

But the other voices kept breaking in, drowning out the soft voice with groans, and strings of whining oaths.

"An' he said I could sit on the porch, an' the sun'll be so warm an' quiet, an' the garden'll smell so good, an' the beach'll be all white, an' the sea . . ."

Andrews felt his head suddenly rise in the air and then his feet. He swung out of the darkness into a brilliant white corridor. His legs throbbed with flaming agony. The face of a man with a cigarette in his mouth peered close to his. A hand fumbled at his throat, where the tag was, and someone read:

"Andrews, 1.432.286."

But he was listening to the voice out in the dark, behind him, that shrieked in rasping tones of delirium:

> "There's a girl in the heart of Mary-land
> With a heart that belongs to mee."

Then he discovered that he was groaning. His mind became entirely taken up in the curious rhythm of his groans. The only parts of his body that existed were his legs and something in his throat that groaned and groaned. It was absorbing. White figures hovered about him, he saw the hairy forearms of a man in shirt sleeves, lights glared and went out, strange smells entered at his nose and circulated through his whole body, but nothing could distract his attention from the singsong of his groans.

Rain fell in his face. He moved his head from side to side, suddenly feeling conscious of himself. His mouth was dry, like leather; he put out his tongue to try to catch raindrops in it. He was swung roughly about in the stretcher. He lifted his head cautiously, feeling a great throb of delight that he still could lift his head.

"Keep yer head down, can't yer?" snarled a voice beside him.

He had seen the back of a man in a gleaming wet slicker at the end of the stretcher.

"Be careful of my leg, can't yer?" he found himself whining over and over again. Then suddenly there was a lurch that rapped his head against the crosspiece of the stretcher, and he found himself looking up at a wooden ceiling from which the white paint had peeled in places. He smelt gasoline and could hear the throb of an engine. He began to think back; how long was it since he had looked at the little frogs in the puddle? A vivid picture came to his mind of the puddle with its putty-colored water and the little triangular heads of the frogs. But it seemed as long ago as a memory of childhood; all of his life before that was not so long as the time that had gone by since the car had started. And he was jolting and swinging about in the stretcher, clutching hard with his hands at the poles of the stretcher. The pain in his legs grew worse; the rest

of his body seemed to shrivel under it. From below him came
a rasping voice that cried out at every lurch of the ambulance.
He fought against the desire to groan, but at last he gave in
and lay lost in the monotonous singsong of his groans.

The rain was in his face again for a moment, then his body
was tilted. A row of houses and russet trees and chimney pots
against a leaden sky swung suddenly up into sight and were
instantly replaced by a ceiling and the coffred vault of a staircase. Andrews was still groaning softly, but his eyes fastened
with sudden interest on the sculptured rosettes of the coffres
and the coats of arms that made the center of each section of
ceiling. Then he found himself staring in the face of the man
who was carrying the lower end of the stretcher. It was a white
face with pimples round the mouth and good-natured, watery
blue eyes. Andrews looked at the eyes and tried to smile, but
the man carrying the stretcher was not looking at him.

Then after more endless hours of tossing about on the
stretcher, lost in a groaning agony of pain, hands laid hold of
him roughly and pulled his clothes off and lifted him on a cot
where he lay gasping, breathing in the cool smell of disinfectant that hung about the bedclothes. He heard voices over his
head.

"Isn't bad at all, this leg wound. . . . I thought you said
we'd have to amputate?"

"Well, what's the matter with him, then?"

"Maybe shell-shock. . . ."

A cold sweat of terror took hold of Andrews. He lay perfectly still with his eyes closed. Spasm after spasm of revolt
went through him. No, they hadn't broken him yet; he still
had hold of his nerves, he kept saying to himself. Still, he felt
that his hands, clasped across his belly, were trembling. The
pain in his legs disappeared in the fright in which he lay, trying desperately to concentrate his mind on something outside
himself. He tried to think of a tune to hum to himself, but he
only heard again shrieking in his ears the voice which, it
seemed to him months and years ago, had sung:

> "There's a girl in the heart of Maryland
> With a heart that belo-ongs to mee."

The voice shrieking the blurred tune and the pain in his

legs mingled themselves strangely, until they seemed one and
the pain seemed merely a throbbing of the maddening tune.

He opened his eyes. Darkness fading into a faint yellow
glow. Hastily he took stock of himself, moved his head and his
arms. He felt cool and very weak and quiet; he must have slept
a long time. He passed his rough dirty hand over his face. The
skin felt soft and cool. He pressed his cheek on the pillow and
felt himself smiling contentedly, he did not know why.

The Queen of Sheba carried a parasol with little vermilion
bells all round it that gave out a cool tinkle as she walked towards him. She wore her hair in a high headdress thickly powdered with blue iris powder, and on her long train, that a
monkey held up at the end, were embroidered in gaudy colors the signs of the zodiac. She was not the Queen of Sheba,
she was a nurse whose face he could not see in the obscurity,
and, sticking an arm behind his head in a deft professional
manner, she gave him something to drink from a glass without looking at him. He said "Thank you," in his natural
voice, which surprised him in the silence; but she went off
without replying and he saw that it was a trayful of glasses
that had tinkled as she had come towards him.

Dark as it was he noticed the self-conscious tilt of the
nurse's body as she walked silently to the next cot, holding
the tray of glasses in front of her. He twisted his head round
on the pillow to watch how gingerly she put her arm under
the next man's head to give him a drink.

"A virgin," he said to himself, "very much a virgin," and he
found himself giggling softly, notwithstanding the twinges of
pain from his legs. He felt suddenly as if his spirit had awak-
ened from a long torpor. The spell of dejection that had dead-
ened him for months had slipped off. He was free. The
thought came to him gleefully, that as long as he stayed in
that cot in the hospital no one would shout orders at him. No
one would tell him to clean his rifle. There would be no one
to salute. He would not have to worry about making himself
pleasant to the sergeant. He would lie there all day long,
thinking his own thoughts.

Perhaps he was badly enough wounded to be discharged
from the army. The thought set his heart beating like mad.
That meant that he, who had given himself up for lost, who

had let himself be trampled down unresistingly into the mud of slavery, who had looked for no escape from the treadmill but death, would live. He, John Andrews, would live.

And it seemed inconceivable that he had ever given himself up, that he had ever let the grinding discipline have its way with him. He saw himself vividly once more as he had seen himself before his life had suddenly blotted itself out, before he had become a slave among slaves. He remembered the garden where, in his boyhood, he had sat dreaming through the droning summer afternoons under the crêpe myrtle bushes, while the cornfields beyond rustled and shimmered in the heat. He remembered the day he had stood naked in the middle of a base room while the recruiting sergeant prodded him and measured him. He wondered suddenly what the date was. Could it be that it was only a year ago? Yet in that year all the other years of his life had been blotted out. But now he would begin living again. He would give up this cowardly cringing before external things. He would be recklessly himself.

The pain in his legs was gradually localizing itself into the wounds. For a while he struggled against it to go on thinking, but its constant throb kept impinging in his mind until, although he wanted desperately to comb through his pale memories to remember, if ever so faintly, all that had been vivid and lusty in his life, to build himself a new foundation of resistance against the world from which he could start afresh to live, he became again the querulous piece of hurt flesh, the slave broken on the treadmill; he began to groan.

Cold steel-gray light filtered into the ward, drowning the yellow glow which first turned ruddy and then disappeared. Andrews began to make out the row of cots opposite him, and the dark beams of the ceiling above his head. "This house must be very old," he said to himself, and the thought vaguely excited him. Funny that the Queen of Sheba had come to his head, it was ages since he'd thought of all that. *From the girl at the cross-roads singing under her street-lamp to the patrician pulling roses to pieces from the height of her litter, all the aspects half-guessed, all the imaginings of your desire . . .* that was the Queen of Sheba. He whispered the words aloud, "la reine de Saba, la reine de Saba"; and, with a tremor of anticipation of the sort he used to feel when he was a small boy the night before Christmas, with a sense of new things in store for him, he pillowed his head on his arm and went quietly to sleep.

"Ain't it juss like them frawgs te make a place like this into a hauspital?" said the orderly, standing with his feet wide apart and his hands on his hips, facing a row of cots and talking to anyone who felt well enough to listen. "Honest, I doan see why you fellers doan all cash in yer checks in this hole. . . . There warn't even electric light till we put it in. . . . What d'you think o' that? That shows how much the goddam frawgs care. . . ." The orderly was a short man with a sallow, lined face and large yellow teeth. When he smiled the horizontal lines in his forehead and the lines that ran from the sides of his nose to the ends of his mouth deepened so that his face looked as if it were made up to play a comic part in the movies.

"It's kind of artistic, though, ain't it?" said Applebaum, whose cot was next Andrews's,—a skinny man with large, frightened eyes and an inordinately red face that looked as if the skin had been peeled off. "Look at the work there is on that ceiling. Must have cost some dough when it was noo."

"Wouldn't be bad as a dance hall with a little fixin' up, but a hauspital; hell!"

Andrews lay, comfortable in his cot, looking into the ward out of another world. He felt no connection with the talk about him, with the men who lay silent or tossed about groaning in the rows of narrow cots that filled the Renaissance hall. In the yellow glow of the electric lights, looking beyond the orderly's twisted face and narrow head, he could see very faintly, where the beams of the ceiling sprung from the wall, a row of half-obliterated shields supported by figures carved out of the grey stone of the wall, handed satyrs with horns and goats' beards and deep-set eyes, little squat figures of warriors and townsmen in square hats with swords between their bent knees, naked limbs twined in scrolls of spiked acanthus leaves, all seen very faintly, so that when the electric lights swung back and forth in the wind made by the orderly's hurried passing, they all seemed to wink and wriggle in shadowy mockery of the rows of prostrate bodies in the room beneath them. Yet they were familiar, friendly to Andrews. He kept feeling a half-formulated desire to be up there too, crowded under a beam, grimacing through heavy wreaths of pomegranates and acanthus leaves, the incarnation of old rich lusts, of clear fires that had sunk to dust ages since. He felt at home in that spacious hall, built for wide gestures and stately steps, in which all the little routine of the army seemed unreal, and the wounded men discarded automatons, broken toys laid away in rows.

Andrews was snatched out of his thoughts. Applebaum was speaking to him; he turned his head.

"How d'you loike it bein' wounded, buddy?"

"Fine."

"Foine, I should think it was. . . . Better than doin' squads right all day."

"Where did you get yours?"

"Ain't got only one arm now. . . . I don't give a damn. . . . I've driven my last fare, that's all."

"How d'you mean?"

"I used to drive a taxi."

"That's a pretty good job, isn't it?"

"You bet, big money in it, if yer in right."

"So you used to be a taxi-driver, did you?" broke in the orderly. "That's a fine job. . . . When I was in the Providence Hospital half the fractures was caused by taxis. We had a little girl of six in the children's ward had her feet cut clean off at the ankles by a taxi. Pretty yellow hair she had, too. Gangrene. . . . Only lasted a day. . . . Well, I'm going off. I guess you guys wish you was going to be where I'm goin' to be tonight. . . . That's one thing you guys are lucky in, don't have to worry about propho." The orderly wrinkled his face up and winked elaborately.

"Say, will you do something for me?" asked Andrews.

"Sure, if it ain't no trouble."

"Will you buy me a book?"

"Ain't ye got enough with all the books at the 'Y'?"

"No. . . . This is a special book," said Andrews smiling, "a French book."

"A French book, is it? Well, I'll see what I can do. What's it called?"

"By Flaubert. . . . Look, if you've got a piece of paper and a pencil, I'll write it down."

Andrews scrawled the title on the back of an order slip. "There."

"What the hell? Who's Antoine? Gee whiz, I bet that's hot stuff. I wish I could read French. We'll have you breakin' loose out o' here an' going down to number four, roo Villiay, if you read that kind o' book."

"Has it got pictures?" asked Applebaum.

"One feller did break out o' here a month ago. . . . Couldn't stand it any longer, I guess. Well, his wound opened an' he had a hemorrhage, an' now he's planted out in the back lot. . . . But I'm goin'. Goodnight." The orderly bustled to the end of the ward and disappeared.

The lights went out, except for the bulb over the nurse's desk at the end, beside the ornate doorway, with its wreathed pinnacles carved out of the grey stone, which could be seen above the white canvas screen that hid the door.

"What's that book about, buddy?" asked Applebaum, twisting his head at the end of his lean neck so as to look Andrews full in the face.

"Oh, it's about a man who wants everything so badly that he decides there's nothing worth wanting."

"I guess youse had a college edication," said Applebaum sarcastically.

Andrews laughed.

"Well, I was goin' to tell youse about when I used to drive a taxi. I was makin' big money when I enlisted. Was you drafted?"

"Yes."

"Well, so was I. I doan think nauthin o' them guys that are so stuck up 'cause they enlisted, d'you?"

"Not a hell of a lot."

"Don't yer?" came a voice from the other side of Andrews, —a thin voice that stuttered. "W-w-well, all I can say is, it'ld have sss-spoiled my business if I hadn't enlisted. No, sir, nobody can say I didn't enlist."

"Well, that's your look-out," said Applebaum.

"You're goddam right, it was."

"Well, ain't your business spoiled anyway?"

"No, sir. I can pick it right up where I left off. I've got an established reputation."

"What at?"

"I'm an undertaker by profession; my dad was before me."

"Gee, you were right at home!" said Andrews.

"You haven't any right to say that, young feller," said the undertaker angrily. "I'm a humane man. I won't never be at home in this dirty butchery."

The nurse was walking by their cots.

"How can you say such dreadful things?" she said. "But lights are out. You boys have got to keep quiet. . . . And you," she plucked at the undertaker's bedclothes, "just remember what the Huns did in Belgium. . . . Poor Miss Cavell, a nurse just like I am."

Andrews closed his eyes. The ward was quiet except for the rasping sound of the snores and heavy breathing of the shattered men all about him. "And I thought she was the Queen of Sheba," he said to himself, making a grimace in the dark. Then he began to think of the music he had intended to write about the Queen of Sheba before he had stripped his life off in the bare room where they had measured him and made a soldier of him. Standing in the dark in the desert of his despair, he would hear the sound of a caravan in the distance, tinkle of bridles, rasping of horns, braying of donkeys, and the throaty voices of men singing the songs of desolate roads. He would look up, and before him he would see, astride their foaming wild asses, the three green horsemen motionless, pointing at him with their long forefingers. Then the music would burst in a sudden hot whirlwind about him, full of flutes and kettledrums and braying horns and whining bagpipes, and torches would flare red and yellow, making a tent of light about him, on the edges of which would crowd the sumpter mules and the brown mule drivers, and the gaudily caparisoned camels, and the elephants glistening with jewelled harness. Naked slaves would bend their gleaming backs before him as they laid out a carpet at his feet; and, through the flare of torchlight, the Queen of Sheba would advance towards him, covered with emeralds and dull-gold ornaments, with a monkey hopping behind holding up the end of her long train. She would put her hand with its slim fantastic nails on his shoulder; and, looking into her eyes, he would suddenly feel within reach all the fiery imaginings of his desire.

Oh, if he could only be free to work. All the months he had wasted in his life seemed to be marching like a procession of ghosts before his eyes. And he lay in his cot, staring with wide open eyes at the ceiling, hoping desperately that his wounds would be long in healing.

Applebaum sat on the edge of his cot, dressed in a clean new uniform, of which the left sleeve hung empty, still showing the creases in which it had been folded.

"So you really are going," said Andrews, rolling his head over on his pillow to look at him.

"You bet your pants I am, Andy. . . . An' so could you, poifectly well, if you'ld talk it up to 'em a little."

"Oh, I wish to God I could. Not that I want to go home, now, but . . . if I could get out of uniform."

"I don't blame ye a bit, kid; well, next time, we'll know better. . . . Local Board Chairman's going to be my job."

Andrews laughed.

"If I wasn't a sucker . . ."

"You weren't the only wewe-one," came the undertaker's stuttering voice from behind Andrews.

"Hell, I thought you enlisted, undertaker."

"Well, I did, by God, but I didn't think it was going to be like this. . . ."

"What did ye think it was goin' to be, a picnic?"

"Hell, I doan care about that, or gettin' gassed, and smashed up, or anythin', but I thought we was goin' to put things to rights by comin' over here. . . . Look here, I had a lively business in the undertaking way, like my father had had before me. . . . We did all the swellest work in Tilletsville. . . ."

"Where?" interrupted Applebaum, laughing.

"Tilletsville; don't you know any geography?"

"Go ahead, tell us about Tilletsville," said Andrews soothingly.

"Why, when Senator Wallace d-d-deceased there, who d'you think had charge of embalming the body and taking it to the station an' seeing everything was done fitting? We did. . . . And I was going to be married to a dandy girl, and I knowed I had enough pull to get fixed up, somehow, or to get a commission even, but there I went like a sucker an' enlisted in the infantry, too. . . . But, hell, everybody was saying that we was going to fight to make the world safe for democracy, and that, if a feller didn't go, no one'ld trade with him any more."

He started coughing suddenly and seemed unable to stop. At last he said weakly, in a thin little voice between coughs:

"Well, here I am. There ain't nothing to do about it."

"Democracy. . . . That's democracy, ain't it: we eat stinkin' goolash an' that there fat 'Y' woman goes out with Colonels eatin' chawklate soufflay. . . . Poifect democracy! . . . But I tell you what: it don't do to be the goat."

"But there's so damn many more goats than anything else," said Andrews.

"There's a sucker born every minute, as Barnum said. You learn that drivin' a taxicab, if ye don't larn nothin' else. . . . No, sir, I'm goin' into politics. I've got good connections up Hundred and Twenty-fif' street way. . . . You see, I've got an aunt, Mrs. Sallie Schultz, owns a hotel on a Hundred and Tirty-tird street. Heard of Jim O'Ryan, ain't yer? Well, he's a good friend o' hers; see? Bein' as they're both Catholics . . . But I'm goin' out this afternoon, see what the town's like . . . an ole Ford says the skirts are just peaches an' cream."

"He juss s-s-says that to torment a feller," stuttered the undertaker.

"I wish I were going with you," said Andrews.

"You'll get well plenty soon enough, Andy, and get yourself marked Class A, and get given a gun, an—'Over the top, boys!' . . . to see if the Fritzies won't make a better shot next time. . . . Talk about suckers! You're the most poifect sucker I ever met. . . . What did you want to tell the loot your legs didn't hurt bad for? They'll have you out o' here before you know it. . . . Well, I'm goin' out to see what the mamzelles look like."

Applebaum, the uniform hanging in folds about his skinny body, swaggered to the door, followed by the envious glances of the whole ward.

"Gee, guess he thinks he's goin' to get to be president," said the undertaker bitterly.

"He probably will," said Andrews.

He settled himself in his bed again, sinking back into the dull contemplation of the teasing, smarting pain where the torn ligaments of his thighs were slowly knitting themselves together. He tried desperately to forget the pain; there was so much he wanted to think out. If he could only lie perfectly quiet, and piece together the frayed ends of thoughts that kept flickering to the surface of his mind. He counted up the days he had been in the hospital; fifteen! Could it be that long? And he had not thought of anything yet. Soon, as Applebaum said, they'd be putting him in Class A and sending him back to the treadmill, and he would not have reconquered his courage, his dominion over himself. What a coward he had been anyway, to submit. The man beside him kept coughing. Andrews stared for a moment at the silhouette of the yellow face on the pillow, with its pointed nose and small greedy eyes. He thought of the swell undertaking establishment, of the black gloves and long faces and soft tactful voices. That man and his father before him lived by pretending things they didn't feel, by swathing reality with all manner of crêpe and trumpery. For those people, no one ever died, they passed away, they deceased. Still, there had to be undertakers. There was no more stain about that than about any other trade. And it was so as not to spoil his trade that the undertaker had enlisted, and to make the world safe for democracy, too. The phrase came to Andrews's mind amid an avalanche of popular tunes, of visions of patriotic numbers on the vaudeville stage. He remembered the great flags waving triumphantly over Fifth Avenue, and the crowds dutifully cheering. But those were valid reasons for the undertaker; but for him, John Andrews, were they valid reasons? No. He had no trade, he had not been driven into the army by the force of public opinion, he had not been carried away by any wave of blind confidence in the phrases of bought propagandists. He had not had the strength to live. The thought came to him of all those who, down the long tragedy of history, had given themselves smilingly for the integrity of their thoughts. He had not had the courage to move a muscle for his freedom, but he had been fairly cheerful about risking his life as a soldier, in a cause he believed useless. What right had a man

to exist who was too cowardly to stand up for what he
thought and felt, for his whole makeup, for everything that
made him an individual apart from his fellows, and not a slave
to stand cap in hand waiting for someone of stronger will to
tell him to act?

Like a sudden nausea, disgust surged up in him. His mind
ceased formulating phrases and thoughts. He gave himself
over to disgust as a man who has drunk a great deal, holding
on tight to the reins of his will, suddenly gives himself over
pellmell to drunkenness.

He lay very still, with his eyes closed, listening to the stir
of the ward, the voices of men talking and the fits of coughing that shook the man next him. The smarting pain
throbbed monotonously. He felt hungry and wondered
vaguely if it were supper time. How little they gave you to eat
in the hospital!

He called over to the man in the opposite cot:

"Hay, Stalky, what time is it?"

"It's after messtime now. Got a good appetite for the steak
and onions and French fried potatoes?"

"Shut up."

A rattling of tin dishes at the other end of the ward made
Andrews wriggle up further on his pillow. Verses from the
"Shropshire Lad" jingled mockingly through his head:

> "The world, it was the old world yet,
> I was I, my things were wet,
> And nothing now remained to do
> But begin the game anew."

After he had eaten, he picked up the "*Tentation de Saint
Antoine*," that lay on the cot beside his immovable legs, and
buried himself in it, reading the gorgeously modulated sentences voraciously, as if the book were a drug in which he
could drink deep forgetfulness of himself.

He put the book down and closed his eyes. His mind was
full of intangible floating glow, like the ocean on a warm
night, when every wave breaks into pale flame, and mysterious milky lights keep rising to the surface out of the dark waters and gleaming and vanishing. He became absorbed in the

strange fluid harmonies that permeated his whole body, as a grey sky at nightfall suddenly becomes filled with endlessly changing patterns of light and color and shadow.

When he tried to seize hold of his thoughts, to give them definite musical expression in his mind, he found himself suddenly empty, the way a sandy inlet on the beach that has been full of shoals of silver fishes, becomes suddenly empty when a shadow crosses the water, and the man who is watching sees wanly his own reflection instead of the flickering of thousands of tiny silver bodies.

John Andrews awoke to feel a cold hand on his head.

"Feeling all right?" said a voice in his ear.

He found himself looking in a puffy, middle-aged face, with a lean nose and grey eyes, with dark rings under them. Andrews felt the eyes looking him over inquisitively. He saw the red triangle on the man's khaki sleeve.

"Yes," he said.

"If you don't mind, I'd like to talk to you a little while, buddy."

"Not a bit; have you got a chair?" said Andrews smiling.

"I don't suppose it was just right of me to wake you up, but you see it was this way. . . . You were the next in line, an' I was afraid I'd forget you, if I skipped you."

"I understand," said Andrews, with a sudden determination to take the initiative away from the "Y" man. "How long have you been in France? D'you like the war?" he asked hurriedly.

The "Y" man smiled sadly.

"You seem pretty spry," he said. "I guess you're in a hurry to get back at the front and get some more Huns." He smiled again, with an air of indulgence.

Andrews did not answer.

"No, sonny, I don't like it here," the "Y" man said, after a pause. "I wish I was home—but it's great to feel you're doing your duty."

"It must be," said Andrews.

"Have you heard about the great air raids our boys have pulled off? They've bombarded Frankfort; now if they could only wipe Berlin off the map."

"Say, d'you hate 'em awful hard?" said Andrews in a low voice. "Because, if you do, I can tell you something will tickle you most to death. . . . Lean over."

The "Y" man leant over curiously.

"Some German prisoners come to this hospital at six every night to get the garbage; now all you need to do if you really hate 'em so bad is borrow a revolver from one of your officer friends, and just shoot up the convoy. . . ."

"Say . . . where were you raised, boy?" The "Y" man sat up suddenly with a look of alarm on his face. "Don't you know that prisoners are sacred?"

"D'you know what our colonel told us before going into the Argonne offensive? The more prisoners we took, the less grub there'ld be; and do you know what happened to the prisoners that were taken? Why do you hate the Huns?"

"Because they are barbarians, enemies of civilization. You must have enough education to know that," said the "Y" man, raising his voice angrily. "What church do you belong to?"

"None."

"But you must have been connected with some church, boy. You can't have been raised a heathen in America. Every Christian belongs or has belonged to some church or other from baptism."

"I make no pretensions to Christianity."

Andrews closed his eyes and turned his head away. He could feel the "Y" man hovering over him irresolutely. After a while he opened his eyes. The "Y" man was leaning over the next bed.

Through the window at the opposite side of the ward he could see a bit of blue sky among white scroll-like clouds, with mauve shadows. He stared at it until the clouds, beginning to grow golden into evening, covered it. Furious, hopeless irritation consumed him. How these people enjoyed hating! At that rate it was better to be at the front. Men were more humane when they were killing each other than when they were talking about it. So was civilization nothing but a vast edifice of sham, and the war, instead of its crumbling, was its fullest and most ultimate expression. Oh, but there must be something more in the world than greed and hatred and cruelty. Were they all shams, too, these gigantic phrases that floated like gaudy kites high above mankind? Kites, that was it, contraptions of tissue paper held at the end of a string, ornaments not to be taken seriously. He thought of all the long procession of men who had been touched by the unutterable futility of the lives of men, who had tried by phrases to make things otherwise, who had taught unworldliness. Dim enigmatic figures they were—Democritus, Socrates, Epicurus, Christ; so many of them, and so vague in the silvery mist of history that he hardly knew that they were not his own imagining; Lucretius, St. Francis, Voltaire, Rousseau, and how many others, known and unknown, through the tragic centuries; they had wept, some of them, and some of them had laughed, and their phrases had risen glittering, soap bubbles to dazzle men for a moment, and had shattered. And he felt a crazy desire to join the forlorn ones, to throw himself into inevitable defeat, to live his life as he saw it in spite of everything, to proclaim once more the falseness of the gospels under the cover of which greed and fear filled with more and yet more pain the already unbearable agony of human life.

As soon as he got out of the hospital he would desert; the determination formed suddenly in his mind, making the excited blood surge gloriously through his body. There was nothing else to do; he would desert. He pictured himself hobbling away in the dark on his lame legs, stripping his uniform off, losing himself in some out of the way corner of France, or slipping by the sentries to Spain and freedom. He was ready to endure anything, to face any sort of death, for the sake of a few months of liberty in which to forget the degradation of this last year. This was his last run with the pack.

An enormous exhilaration took hold of him. It seemed the first time in his life he had ever determined to act. All the rest had been aimless drifting. The blood sang in his ears. He fixed his eyes on the half-obliterated figures that supported the shields under the beams in the wall opposite. They seemed to be wriggling out of their contorted positions and smiling encouragement to him. He imagined them, warriors out of old tales, on their way to slay dragons in enchanted woods, clever-fingered guildsmen and artisans, cupids and satyrs and fauns, jumping from their niches and carrying him off with them in a headlong rout, to a sound of flutes, on a last forlorn assault on the citadels of pain.

The lights went out, and an orderly came round with chocolate that poured with a pleasant soothing sound into the tin cups. With a greasiness of chocolate in his mouth and the warmth of it in his stomach, John Andrews went to sleep.

There was a stir in the ward when he woke up. Reddish sunlight filtered in through the window opposite, and from outside came a confused noise, a sound of bells ringing and whistles blowing.

Andrews looked past his feet towards Stalky's cot opposite. Stalky was sitting bolt upright in bed, with his eyes round as quarters.

"Fellers, the war's over!"

"Put him out."

"Cut that."

"Pull the chain."

"Tie that bull outside," came from every side of the ward.

"Fellers," shouted Stalky louder than ever, "it's straight dope, the war's over. I just dreamt the Kaiser came up to me on Fourteenth Street and bummed a nickel for a glass of beer. The war's over. Don't you hear the whistles?"

"All right; let's go home."

"Shut up, can't you let a feller sleep?"

The ward quieted down again, but all eyes were wide open, men lay strangely still in their cots, waiting, wondering.

"All I can say," shouted Stalky again, "is that she was some war while she lasted. . . . What did I tell yer?"

As he spoke the canvas screen in front of the door collapsed and the major appeared with his cap askew over his red face and a brass bell in his hand, which he rang frantically as he advanced into the ward.

"Men," he shouted in the deep roar of one announcing baseball scores, "the war ended at 4:03 A.M. this morning. . . . The Armistice is signed. To hell with the Kaiser!" Then he rang the dinner bell madly and danced along the aisle between the rows of cots, holding the head nurse by one hand, who held a little yellow-headed lieutenant by the other hand, who, in turn, held another nurse, and so on. The line advanced jerkily into the ward; the front part was singing "The Star Spangled Banner," and the rear the "Yanks are Coming," and through it all the major rang his brass bell. The men who were well enough sat up in bed and yelled. The others rolled restlessly about, sickened by the din.

They made the circuit of the ward and filed out, leaving confusion behind them. The dinner bell could be heard faintly in the other parts of the building.

"Well, what d'you think of it, undertaker?" said Andrews.

"Nothing."

"Why?"

The undertaker turned his small black eyes on Andrews and looked him straight in the face.

"You know what's the matter with me, don't yer, outside o' this wound?"

"No."

"Coughing like I am, I'd think you'd be more observant. I got t.b., young feller."

"How do you know that?"

"They're going to move me out o' here to a t.b. ward to-morrow."

"The hell they are!" Andrews's words were lost in the paroxysm of coughing that seized the man next to him.

"Home, boys, home; it's home we want to be,"

Those well enough were singing, Stalky conducting, standing on the end of his cot in his pink Red Cross pyjamas, that were too short and showed a long expanse of skinny leg, fuzzy with red hairs. He banged together two bed pans to beat time.

"Home. . . . I won't never go home," said the undertaker when the noise had subsided a little. "D'you know what I wish? I wish the war'd gone on and on until everyone of them bastards had been killed in it."

"Which bastards?"

"The men who got us fellers over here." He began coughing again weakly.

"But they'll be safe if every other human being . . ." began Andrews. He was interrupted by a thundering voice from the end of the ward.

"Attention!"

"Home, boys, home; it's home we want to be,"

went on the song. Stalky glanced towards the end of the ward, and seeing it was the major, dropped the bed pans that smashed at the foot of his cot, and got as far as possible under his blankets.

"Attention!" thundered the major again. A sudden uncomfortable silence fell upon the ward, broken only by the coughing of the man next to Andrews.

"If I hear any more noise from this ward, I'll chuck every one of you men out of this hospital; if you can't walk you'll have to crawl. . . . The war may be over, but you men are in the Army, and don't you forget it."

The major glared up and down the lines of cots. He turned on his heel and went out of the door, glancing angrily as he went at the overturned screen. The ward was still. Outside whistles blew and churchbells rang madly, and now and then there was a sound of singing.

II

THE SNOW beat against the windows and pattered on the tin roof of the lean-to, built against the side of the hospital, that went by the name of sun parlor. It was a dingy place, decorated by strings of dusty little paper flags that one of the "Y" men had festooned about the slanting beams of the ceiling to celebrate Christmas. There were tables with torn magazines piled on them, and a counter where cracked white cups were ranged waiting for one of the rare occasions when cocoa could be bought. In the middle of the room, against the wall of the main building, a stove was burning, about which sat several men in hospital denims talking in drowsy voices. Andrews watched them from his seat by the window, looking at their broad backs bent over towards the stove and at the hands that hung over their knees, limp from boredom. The air was heavy with a smell of coal gas mixed with carbolic from men's clothes, and stale cigarette smoke. Behind the cups at the counter a "Y" man, a short, red-haired man with freckles, read the Paris edition of the *New York Herald*. Andrews, in his seat by the window, felt permeated by the stagnation about him. He had a sheaf of pencilled music-papers on his knees, that he rolled and unrolled nervously, staring at the stove and the motionless backs of the men about it. The stove roared a little, the "Y" man's paper rustled, men's voices came now and then in a drowsy whisper, and outside the snow beat evenly and monotonously against the window panes. Andrews pictured himself vaguely walking fast through the streets, with the snow stinging his face and the life of a city swirling about him, faces flushed by the cold, bright eyes under hatbrims, looking for a second into his and passing on; slim forms of women bundled in shawls that showed vaguely the outline of their breasts and hips. He wondered if he would ever be free again to walk at random through city streets. He stretched his legs out across the floor in front of him; strange, stiff, tremulous legs they were, but it was not the wounds that gave them their leaden weight. It was the stagnation of the life about him that he felt sinking into every crevice of his spirit, so that he could never shake it off, the stagnation of dusty ruined automatons that had lost all life of their own, whose limbs had practised the drill manual so long that they had no movements of their own left, who sat limply, sunk in boredom, waiting for orders.

Andrews was roused suddenly from his thoughts; he had been watching the snowflakes in their glittering dance just outside the window pane, when the sound of someone rubbing his hands very close to him made him look up. A little man with chubby cheeks and steel-grey hair very neatly flattened against his skull, stood at the window rubbing his fat little white hands together and making a faint unctuous puffing with each breath. Andrews noticed that a white clerical collar enclosed the little man's pink neck, that starched cuffs peeped from under the well-tailored sleeves of his officer's uniform. Sam Browne belt and puttees, too, were highly polished. On his shoulder was a demure little silver cross. Andrews' glance had reached the pink cheeks again, when he suddenly found a pair of steely eyes looking sharply into his.

"You look quite restored, my friend," said a chanting clerical voice.

"I suppose I am."

"Splendid, splendid. . . . But do you mind moving into the end of the room? That's it." He followed Andrews, saying in a deprecatory tone: "We're going to have just a little bit of a prayer and then I have some interesting things to tell you boys."

The red-headed "Y" man had left his seat and stood in the center of the room, his paper still dangling from his hand, saying in a bored voice: "Please fellows, move down to the end. . . . Quiet, please. . . . Quiet, please."

The soldiers shambled meekly to the folding chairs at the end of the room and after some chattering were quiet. A couple of men left, and several tiptoed in and sat in the front row. Andrews sank into a chair with a despairing sort of resignation, and burying his face in his hands stared at the floor between his feet.

"Fellers," went on the bored voice of the "Y" man, "let me introduce the Reverend Dr. Skinner, who—" the "Y" man's voice suddenly took on deep patriotic emotion—"who has just come back from the Army of Occupation in Germany."

At the words "Army of Occupation," as if a spring had been touched, everybody clapped and cheered.

The Reverend Dr. Skinner looked about his audience with smiling confidence and raised his hands for silence, so that the men could see the chubby pink palms.

"First, boys, my dear friends, let us indulge in a few moments of silent prayer to our Great Creator," his voice rose and fell in the suave chant of one accustomed to going through the episcopal liturgy for the edification of well-dressed and well-fed congregations. "Inasmuch as He has vouchsafed us safety and a mitigation of our afflictions, and let us pray that in His good time He may see fit to return us whole in limb and pure in heart to our families, to the wives, mothers, and to those whom we will some day honor with the name of wife, who eagerly await our return; and that we may spend the remainder of our lives in useful service of the great country for whose safety and glory we have offered up our youth a willing sacrifice. . . . Let us pray!"

Silence fell dully on the room. Andrews could hear the self-conscious breathing of the men about him, and the rustling of the snow against the tin roof. A few feet scraped. The voice began again after a long pause, chanting:

"*Our Father which art in Heaven . . .*"

At the "Amen" everyone lifted his head cheerfully. Throats were cleared, chairs scraped. Men settled themselves to listen.

"Now, my friends, I am going to give you in a few brief words a little glimpse into Germany, so that you may be able to picture to yourselves the way your comrades of the Army of Occupation manage to make themselves comfortable among the Huns. . . . I ate my Christmas dinner in Coblenz. What do you think of that? Never had I thought that a Christmas would find me away from my home and loved ones. But what unexpected things happen to us in this world! Christmas in Coblenz under the American flag!"

He paused a moment to allow a little scattered clapping to subside.

"The turkey was fine, too, I can tell you. . . . Yes, our boys in Germany are very, very comfortable, and just waiting for the word, if necessary, to continue their glorious advance to Berlin. For I am sorry to say, boys, that the Germans have not undergone the change of heart for which we had hoped. They have, indeed, changed the name of their institutions, but their spirit they have not changed. . . . How grave a disappointment it must be to our great President, who has exerted himself so to bring the German people to reason, to make them understand the horror that they alone have brought deliberately upon the world! Alas! Far from it. Indeed, they have attempted with insidious propaganda to undermine the morale of our troops. . . ." A little storm of muttered epithets went through the room. The Reverend Dr. Skinner elevated his chubby pink palms and smiled benignantly . . . "to undermine the morale of our troops; so that the most stringent regulations have had to be made by the commanding general to prevent it. Indeed, my friends, I very much fear that we stopped too soon in our victorious advance; that Germany should have been utterly crushed. But all we can do is watch and wait, and abide by the decision of those great men who in a short time will be gathered together at the Conference at Paris. . . . Let me, boys, my dear friends, express the hope that you may speedily be cured of your wounds, ready again to do willing service in the ranks of the glorious army that must be vigilant for some time yet, I fear, to defend, as Americans and Christians, the civilization you have so nobly saved from a ruthless foe. . . . Let us all join together in singing the hymn, '*Stand up, stand up for Jesus*,' which I am sure you all know."

The men got to their feet, except for a few who had lost their legs, and sang the first verse of the hymn unsteadily. The second verse petered out altogether, leaving only the "Y" man and the Reverend Dr. Skinner singing away at the top of their lungs.

The Reverend Dr. Skinner pulled out his gold watch and looked at it frowning.

"Oh, my, I shall miss the train," he muttered. The "Y" man helped him into his voluminous trench coat and they both hurried out of the door.

"Those are some puttees he had on, I'll tell you," said the legless man who was propped in a chair near the stove.

Andrews sat down beside him, laughing. He was a man with high cheekbones and powerful jaws to whose face the pale brown eyes and delicately pencilled lips gave a look of great gentleness. Andrews did not look at his body.

"Somebody said he was a Red Cross man giving out cigarettes. . . . Fooled us that time," said Andrews.

"Have a butt? I've got one," said the legless man. With a large shrunken hand that was the transparent color of alabaster he held out a box of cigarettes.

"Thanks." When Andrews struck a match he had to lean over the legless man to light his cigarette for him. He could not help glancing down the man's tunic at the drab trousers that hung limply from the chair. A cold shudder went through him; he was thinking of the zigzag scars on his own thighs.

"Did you get it in the legs, too, Buddy?" asked the legless man, quietly.

"Yes, but I had luck. . . . How long have you been here?"

"Since Christ was a corporal. Oh, I doan know. I've been here since two weeks after my outfit first went into the lines. . . . That was on November 16th, 1917. . . . Didn't see much of the war, did I? . . . Still, I guess I didn't miss much."

"No. . . . But you've seen enough of the army."

"That's true. . . . I guess I wouldn't mind the war if it wasn't for the army."

"They'll be sending you home soon, won't they?"

"Guess so. . . . Where are you from?"

"New York," said Andrews.

"I'm from Cranston, Wisconsin. D'you know that country? It's a great country for lakes. You can canoe for days an' days without a portage. We have a camp on Big Loon Lake. We used to have some wonderful times there . . . lived like wild men. I went for a trip for three weeks once without seeing a house. Ever done much canoeing?"

"Not so much as I'd like to."

"That's the thing to make you feel fit. First thing you do when you shake out of your blankets is jump in an' have a swim. Gee, it's great to swim when the morning mist is still on the water an' the sun just strikes the tops of the birch

trees. Ever smelt bacon cooking? I mean out in the woods, in
a frying pan over some sticks of pine and beech wood. . . .
Some great old smell, isn't it? . . . And after you've paddled
all day, an' feel tired and sunburned right to the palms of your
feet, to sit around the fire with some trout roastin' in the
ashes and hear the sizzlin' the bacon makes in the pan. . . .
O boy!" He stretched his arms wide.

"God, I'd like to have wrung that damn little parson's
neck," said Andrews suddenly.

"Would you?" The legless man turned brown eyes on Andrews with a smile. "I guess he's about as much to blame as
anybody is . . . guys like him. . . . I guess they have that
kind in Germany, too."

"You don't think we've made the world quite as safe for
Democracy as it might be?" said Andrews in a low voice.

"Hell, how should I know? I bet you never drove an ice
wagon. . . . I did, all one summer down home. . . . It was
some life. Get up at three o'clock in the morning an' carry a
hundred or two hundred pounds of ice into everybody's ice
box. That was the life to make a feller feel fit. I was goin'
around with a big Norwegian named Olaf, who was the
strongest man I ever knew. An' drink! He was the boy could
drink. I once saw him put away twenty-five dry Martini cocktails an' swim across the lake on top of it. . . . I used to
weigh a hundred and eighty pounds, and he could pick me up
with one hand and put me across his shoulder. . . . That was
the life to make a feller feel fit. Why, after bein' out late the
night before, we'd jump up out of bed at three o'clock feeling springy as a cat."

"What's he doing now?" asked Andrews.

"He died on the transport coming 'cross here. Died o' the
flu. . . . I met a feller came over in his regiment. They
dropped him overboard when they were in sight of the
Azores. . . . Well, I didn't die of the flu. Have another
butt?"

"No, thanks," said Andrews.

They were silent. The fire roared in the stove. No one was
talking. The men lolled in chairs somnolently. Now and then
someone spat. Outside of the window Andrews could see the
soft white dancing of the snowflakes. His limbs felt very

heavy; his mind was permeated with dusty stagnation like the stagnation of old garrets and lumber rooms, where, among superannuated bits of machinery and cracked grimy crockery, lie heaps of broken toys.

John Andrews sat on a bench in a square full of linden trees, with the pale winter sunshine full on his face and hands. He had been looking up through his eyelashes at the sun, that was the color of honey, and he let his dazzled glance sink slowly through the black lacework of twigs, down the green trunks of the trees to the bench opposite where sat two nursemaids and, between them, a tiny girl with a face daintily colored and lifeless like a doll's face, and a frilled dress under which showed small ivory knees and legs encased in white socks and yellow sandals. Above the yellow halo of her hair floated, with the sun shining through it, as through a glass of claret, a bright carmine balloon which the child held by a string. Andrews looked at her for a long time, enraptured by the absurd daintiness of the figure between the big bundles of flesh of the nursemaids. The thought came to him suddenly that months had gone by,—was it only months?—since his hands had touched anything soft, since he had seen any flowers. The last was a flower an old woman had given him in a village in the Argonne, an orange marigold, and he remembered how soft the old woman's withered lips had been against his cheek when she had leaned over and kissed him. His mind suddenly lit up, as with a strain of music, with a sense of the sweetness of quiet lives worn away monotonously in the fields, in the grey streets of little provincial towns, in old kitchens full of fragrance of herbs and tang of smoke from the hearth, where there are pots on the window-sill full of basil in flower.

Something made him go up to the little girl and take her hand. The child, looking up suddenly and seeing a lanky soldier with pale lean face and light, straw-colored hair escaping from under a cap too small for him, shrieked and let go the string of the balloon, which soared slowly into the air trembling a little in the faint cool wind that blew. The child wailed dismally, and Andrews, quailing under the furious glances of the nursemaids, stood before her, flushed crimson, stammering apologies, not knowing what to do. The white caps of the nursemaids bent over and ribbons fluttered about the child's head as they tried to console her. Andrews walked away dejectedly, now and then looking up at the balloon, which soared, a black speck against the grey and topaz-colored clouds.

"Sale Américain!" he heard one nursemaid exclaim to the other.

But this was the first hour in months he had had free, the first moment of solitude; he must live; soon he would be sent back to his division. A wave of desire for furious fleshly enjoyments went through him, making him want steaming dishes of food drenched in rich, spice-flavored sauces; making him want to get drunk on strong wine; to roll on thick carpets in the arms of naked, libidinous women. He was walking down the quiet grey street of the provincial town, with its low houses with red chimney pots, and blue slate roofs and its irregular yellowish cobbles. A clock somewhere was striking four with deep booming strokes. Andrews laughed. He had to be in hospital at six.

Already he was tired; his legs ached.

The window of a pastry shop appeared invitingly before him, denuded as it was by wartime. A sign in English said: "Tea." Walking in, he sat down in a fussy little parlor where the tables had red cloths, and a print, in pinkish and greenish colors, hung in the middle of the imitation brocade paper of each wall. Under a print of a poster bed with curtains in front of which eighteen to twenty people bowed, with the title of "Secret d'Amour," sat three young officers, who cast cold, irritated glances at this private with a hospital badge on who invaded their tea shop. Andrews stared back at them, flaming with dull anger.

Sipping the hot, fragrant tea, he sat with a blank sheet of music paper before him, listening in spite of himself to what the officers were saying. They were talking about Ronsard. It was with irritated surprise that Andrews heard the name. What right had they to be talking about Ronsard? He knew more about Ronsard than they did. Furious, conceited phrases kept surging up in his mind. He was as sensitive, as humane, as intelligent, as well-read as they were; what right had they to the cold suspicious glance with which they had

put him in his place when he had come into the room? Yet
that had probably been as unconscious, as unavoidable as was
his own biting envy. The thought that if one of those men
should come over to him, he would have to stand up and
salute and answer humbly, not from civility, but from the fear
of being punished, was bitter as wormwood, filled him with a
childish desire to prove his worth to them, as when older
boys had ill-treated him at school and he had prayed to have
the house burn down so that he might heroically save them
all. There was a piano in an inner room, where in the dark the
chairs, upside down, perched dismally on the table tops. He
almost obeyed an impulse to go in there and start playing, by
the brilliance of his playing to force these men, who thought
of him as a coarse automaton, something between a man and
a dog, to recognize him as an equal, a superior.

"But the war's over. I want to start living. *Red wine, the
nightingale cries to the rose*," said one of the officers.

"What do you say we go A.W.O.L. to Paris?"

"Dangerous."

"Well, what can they do? We are not enlisted men; they can
only send us home. That's just what I want."

"I'll tell you what; we'll go to the Cochon Bleu and have a
cocktail and think about it."

"*The lion and the lizard keep their courts where* . . . what
the devil was his name? Anyway, we'll glory and drink deep,
while Major Peabody keeps his court in Dijon to his heart's
content."

Spurs jingled as the three officers went out. A fierce disgust
took possession of John Andrews. He was ashamed of his
spiteful irritation. If, when he had been playing the piano to
a roomful of friends in New York, a man dressed as a laborer
had shambled in, wouldn't he have felt a moment of involun-
tary scorn? It was inevitable that the fortunate should hate the
unfortunate because they feared them. But he was so tired of
all those thoughts. Drinking down the last of his tea at a gulp,
he went into the shop to ask the old woman, with little black
whiskers over her bloodless lips, who sat behind the white
desk at the end of the counter, if she minded his playing the
piano.

In the deserted tea room, among the dismal upturned

chairs, his crassened fingers moved stiffly over the keys. He forgot everything else. Locked doors in his mind were swinging wide, revealing forgotten sumptuous halls of his imagination. The Queen of Sheba, grotesque as a satyr, white and flaming with worlds of desire, as the great implacable Aphrodite, stood with her hand on his shoulder sending shivers of warm sweetness rippling through his body, while her voice intoned in his ears all the inexhaustible voluptuousness of life.

An asthmatic clock struck somewhere in the obscurity of the room. "Seven!" John Andrews paid, said good-bye to the old woman with the mustache, and hurried out into the street. "Like Cinderella at the ball," he thought. As he went towards the hospital, down faintly lighted streets, his steps got slower and slower. "Why go back?" a voice kept saying inside him. "Anything is better than that." Better throw himself in the river, even, than go back. He could see the olive-drab clothes in a heap among the dry bullrushes on the river bank. . . . He thought of himself crashing naked through the film of ice into water black as Chinese lacquer. And when he climbed out numb and panting on the other side, wouldn't he be able to take up life again as if he had just been born? How strong he would be if he could begin life a second time! How madly, how joyously he would live now that there was no more war. . . . He had reached the door of the hospital. Furious shudders of disgust went through him.

He was standing dumbly humble while a sergeant bawled him out for being late.

Andrews stared for a long while at the line of shields that supported the dark ceiling beams on the wall opposite his cot. The emblems had been erased and the grey stone figures that crowded under the shields,—the satyr with his shaggy goat's legs, the townsman with his square hat, the warrior with the sword between his legs,—had been clipped and scratched long ago in other wars. In the strong afternoon light they were so dilapidated he could hardly make them out. He wondered how they had seemed so vivid to him when he had lain in his cot, comforted by their comradeship, while his healing wounds itched and tingled. Still he glanced tenderly at the grey stone figures as he left the ward.

Downstairs in the office where the atmosphere was stuffy with a smell of varnish and dusty papers and cigarette smoke, he waited a long time, shifting his weight restlessly from one foot to the other.

"What do you want?" said a red-haired sergeant, without looking up from the pile of papers on his desk.

"Waiting for travel orders."

"Aren't you the guy I told to come back at three?"

"It is three."

"H'm!" The sergeant kept his eyes fixed on the papers, which rustled as he moved them from one pile to another. In the end of the room a typewriter clicked slowly and jerkily. Andrews could see the dark back of a head between bored shoulders in a woolen shirt leaning over the machine. Beside the cylindrical black stove against the wall a man with large mustaches and the complicated stripes of a hospital sergeant was reading a novel in a red cover. After a long silence the red-headed sergeant looked up from his papers and said suddenly:

"Ted."

The man at the typewriter turned slowly round, showing a large red face and blue eyes.

"We-ell," he drawled.

"Go in an' see if the loot has signed them papers yet."

The man got up, stretched himself deliberately, and slouched out through a door beside the stove. The red-haired sergeant leaned back in his swivel chair and lit a cigarette.

"Hell," he said, yawning.

The man with the mustache beside the stove let the book slip from his knees to the floor, and yawned too.

"This goddam armistice sure does take the ambition out of a feller," he said.

"Hell of a note," said the red-haired sergeant. "D'you know that they had my name in for an O.T.C.? Hell of a note goin' home without a Sam Browne."

The other man came back and sank down into his chair in front of the typewriter again. The slow, jerky clicking recommenced.

Andrews made a scraping noise with his foot on the ground.

"Well, what about that travel order?" said the red-haired sergeant.

"Loot's out," said the other man, still typewriting.

"Well, didn't he leave it on his desk?" shouted the red-haired sergeant angrily.

"Couldn't find it."

"I suppose I've got to go look for it. . . . God!" The red-haired sergeant stamped out of the room. A moment later he came back with a bunch of papers in his hand.

"Your name Jones?" he snapped to Andrews.

"No."

"Snivisky?"

"No. . . . Andrews, John."

"Why the hell couldn't you say so?"

The man with the mustaches beside the stove got to his feet suddenly. An alert, smiling expression came over his face.

"Good afternoon, Captain Higginsworth," he said cheerfully.

An oval man with a cigar slanting out of his broad mouth came into the room. When he talked the cigar wobbled in his mouth. He wore greenish kid gloves, very tight for his large hands, and his puttees shone with a dark lustre like mahogany.

The red-haired sergeant turned round and half-saluted.

"Goin' to another swell party, Captain?" he asked.

The Captain grinned.

"Say, have you boys got any Red Cross cigarettes? I ain't only got cigars, an' you can't hand a cigar to a lady, can you?" The Captain grinned again. An appreciative giggle went round.

"Will a couple of packages do you? Because I've got some here," said the red-haired sergeant reaching in the drawer of his desk.

"Fine." The captain slipped them into his pocket and swaggered out doing up the buttons of his buff-colored coat.

The sergeant settled himself at his desk again with an important smile.

"Did you find the travel order?" asked Andrews timidly. "I'm supposed to take the train at four-two."

"Can't make it. . . . Did you say your name was Anderson?"

"Andrews. . . . John Andrews."

"Here it is. . . . Why didn't you come earlier?"

*

The sharp air of the ruddy winter evening, sparkling in John Andrews's nostrils, vastly refreshing after the stale odors of the hospital, gave him a sense of liberation. Walking with rapid steps through the grey streets of the town, where in windows lamps already glowed orange, he kept telling himself that another epoch was closed. It was with relief that he felt that he would never see the hospital again or any of the people in it. He thought of Chrisfield. It was weeks and weeks since Chrisfield had come to his mind at all. Now it was with a sudden clench of affection that the Indiana boy's face rose up before him. An oval, heavily-tanned face with a little of childish roundness about it yet, with black eyebrows and long black eyelashes. But he did not even know if Chrisfield were still alive. Furious joy took possession of him. He, John Andrews, was alive; what did it matter if everyone he knew died? There were jollier companions than ever he had known, to be found in the world, cleverer people to talk to, more vigorous people to learn from. The cold air circulated through his nose and lungs; his arms felt strong and supple; he could feel the muscles of his legs stretch and contract as he walked, while his feet beat jauntily on the irregular cobble stones of the street. The waiting room at the station was cold and stuffy, full of a smell of breathed air and unclean uniforms. French soldiers wrapped in their long blue coats, slept on the benches or stood about in groups, eating bread and drinking from their canteens. A gas lamp in the center gave dingy light. Andrews settled himself in a corner with despairing resignation. He had five hours to wait for a train, and already his legs ached and he had a side feeling of exhaustion. The exhilaration of leaving the hospital and walking free through wine-tinted streets in the sparkling evening air gave way gradually to despair. His life would continue to be this slavery of unclean bodies packed together in places where the air had been breathed over and over, cogs in the great slow-moving Juggernaut of armies. What did it matter if the fighting had stopped? The armies would go on grinding out lives with lives, crushing flesh with flesh. Would he ever again stand free and solitary to live out joyous hours which would make up for all the boredom of the treadmill? He had no hope. His life would continue like this dingy, ill-smelling waiting room where men in uniform slept in the fetid air until they should be ordered out to march or to stand in motionless rows, endlessly, futilely, like toy soldiers a child has forgotten in an attic.

Andrews got up suddenly and went out on the empty platform. A cold wind blew. Somewhere out in the freight yards an engine puffed loudly, and clouds of white steam drifted through the faintly lighted station. He was walking up and down with his chin sunk into his coat and his hands in his pockets, when somebody ran into him.

"Damn," said a voice, and the figure darted through a grimy glass door that bore the sign: "Buvette." Andrews followed absent-mindedly.

"I'm sorry I ran into you. . . . I thought you were an M.P., that's why I beat it." When he spoke, the man, an American private, turned and looked searchingly in Andrews's face. He had very red cheeks and an impudent little brown mustache. He spoke slowly with a faint Bostonian drawl.

"That's nothing," said Andrews.

"Let's have a drink," said the other man. "I'm A.W.O.L. Where are you going?"

"To some place near Bar-le-Duc, back to my Division. Been in hospital."

"Long?"

"Since October."

"Gee. . . . Have some Curaçoa. It'll do you good. You look pale. . . . My name's Henslowe. Ambulance with the French Army."

They sat down at an unwashed marble table where the soot from the trains made a pattern sticking to the rings left by wine and liqueur glasses.

"I'm going to Paris," said Henslowe. "My leave expired three days ago. I'm going to Paris and get taken ill with peritonitis or double pneumonia, or maybe I'll have a cardiac lesion. . . . The army's a bore."

"Hospital isn't any better," said Andrews with a sigh. "Though I shall never forget the delight with which I realized I was wounded and out of it. I thought I was bad enough to be sent home."

"Why, I wouldn't have missed a minute of the war. . . . But now that it's over . . . Hell! Travel is the password now.

I've just had two weeks in the Pyrenees. Nîmes, Arles, Les
Baux, Carcassonne, Perpignan, Lourdes, Gavarnie, Toulouse!
What do you think of that for a trip? . . . What were you in?"

"Infantry."

"Must have been hell."

"Been! It is."

"Why don't you come to Paris with me?"

"I don't want to be picked up," stammered Andrews.

"Not a chance. . . . I know the ropes. . . . All you have
to do is keep away from the Olympia and the railway stations,
walk fast and keep your shoes shined . . . and you've got
wits, haven't you?"

"Not many. . . . Let's drink a bottle of wine. Isn't there
anything to eat to be got here?"

"Not a damn thing, and I daren't go out of the station on
account of the M.P. at the gate. . . . There'll be a diner on
the Marseilles express."

"But I can't go to Paris."

"Sure. . . . Look, how do you call yourself?"

"John Andrews."

"Well, John Andrews, all I can say is that you've let 'em get
your goat. Don't give in. Have a good time, in spite of 'em.
To hell with 'em." He brought the bottle down so hard on
the table that it broke and the purple wine flowed over the
dirty marble and dripped gleaming on the floor.

Some French soldiers who stood in a group round the bar
turned round.

"V'là un gars qui gaspille le bon vin," said a tall red-faced
man, with long sloping whiskers.

"Pour vingt sous j'mangerai la bouteille," cried a little man
lurching forward and leaning drunkenly over the table.

"Done," said Henslowe. "Say, Andrews, he says he'll eat
the bottle for a franc."

He placed a shining silver franc on the table beside the
remnants of the broken bottle. The man seized the neck of
the bottle in a black, claw-like hand and gave it a preparatory
flourish. He was a cadaverous little man, incredibly dirty, with
mustaches and beard of a moth-eaten tow-color, and a purple
flush on his cheeks. His uniform was clotted with mud. When
the others crowded round him and tried to dissuade him, he

said: "M'en fous, c'est mon métier," and rolled his eyes so that the whites flashed in the dim light like the eyes of dead codfish.

"Why, he's really going to do it," cried Henslowe.

The man's teeth flashed and crunched down on the jagged edge of the glass. There was a terrific crackling noise. He flourished the bottle-end again.

"My God, he's eating it," cried Henslowe, roaring with laughter, "and you're afraid to go to Paris."

An engine rumbled into the station, with a great hiss of escaping steam.

"Gee, that's the Paris train! Tiens!" He pressed the franc into the man's dirt-crusted hand.

"Come along, Andrews."

As they left the buvette they heard again the crunching crackling noise as the man bit another piece off the bottle.

Andrews followed Henslowe across the steam-filled platform to the door of a first-class carriage. They climbed in. Henslowe immediately pulled down the black cloth over the half globe of the light. The compartment was empty. He threw himself down with a sigh of comfort on the soft buff-colored cushions of the seat.

"But what on earth?" stammered Andrews.

"M'en fous, c'est mon métier," interrupted Henslowe.

The train pulled out of the station.

III

Henslowe poured wine from a brown earthen crock into the glasses, where it shimmered a bright thin red, the color of currants. Andrews leaned back in his chair and looked through half-closed eyes at the table with its white cloth and little burnt umber loaves of bread, and out of the window at the square dimly lit by lemon-yellow gas lamps and at the dark gables of the little houses that huddled round it.

At a table against the wall opposite a lame boy, with white beardless face and gentle violet-colored eyes, sat very close to the bareheaded girl who was with him and who never took her eyes off his face, leaning on his crutch all the while. A stove hummed faintly in the middle of the room, and from the half-open kitchen door came ruddy light and the sound of something frying. On the wall, in brownish colors that seemed to have taken warmth from all the rich scents of food they had absorbed since the day of their painting, were scenes of the Butte as it was fancied to have once been, with windmills and wide fields.

"I want to travel," Henslowe was saying, dragging out his words drowsily. "Abyssinia, Patagonia, Turkestan, the Caucasus, anywhere and everywhere. What do you say you and I go out to New Zealand and raise sheep?"

"But why not stay here? There can't be anywhere as wonderful as this."

"Then I'll put off starting for New Guinea for a week. But hell, I'd go crazy staying anywhere after this. It's got into my blood . . . all this murder. It's made a wanderer of me, that's what it's done. I'm an adventurer."

"God, I wish it had made me into anything so interesting."

"Tie a rock on to your scruples and throw 'em off the Pont Neuf and set out. . . . O boy, this is the golden age for living by your wits."

"You're not out of the army yet."

"I should worry. . . . I'll join the Red Cross."

"How?"

"I've got a tip about it."

A girl with oval face and faint black down on her upper lip brought them soup, a thick greenish colored soup, that steamed richly into their faces.

"If you tell me how I can get out of the army you'll probably save my life," said Andrews seriously.

"There are two ways . . . Oh, but let me tell you later. Let's talk about something worth while . . . So you write music do you?"

Andrews nodded.

An omelet lay between them, pale golden-yellow with flecks of green; a few amber bubbles of burnt butter still clustered round the edges.

"Talk about tone-poems," said Henslowe.

"But, if you are an adventurer and have no scruples, how is it you are still a private?"

Henslowe took a gulp of wine and laughed uproariously.

"That's the joke."

They ate in silence for a little while. They could hear the couple opposite them talking in low soft voices. The stove purred, and from the kitchen came a sound of something being beaten in a bowl. Andrews leaned back in his chair.

"This is so wonderfully quiet and mellow," he said. . . . "It is so easy to forget that there's any joy at all in life."

"Rot . . . It's a circus parade."

"Have you ever seen anything drearier than a circus parade? One of those jokes that aren't funny."

"Justine, encore du vin," called Henslowe.

"So you know her name?"

"I live here. . . . The Butte is the boss on the middle of the shield. It's the axle of the wheel. That's why it's so quiet, like the centre of a cyclone, of a vast whirling rotary circus parade!"

Justine, with her red hands that had washed so many dishes off which other people had dined well, put down between them a scarlet langouste, of which claws and feelers sprawled over the table-cloth that already had a few purplish stains of wine. The sauce was yellow and fluffy like the breast of a canary bird.

"D'you know," said Andrews suddenly talking fast and excitedly while he brushed the straggling yellow hair off his forehead, "I'd almost be willing to be shot at the end of a year if I could live up here all that time with a piano and a million sheets of music paper . . . It would be worth it."

"But this is a place to come back to. Imagine coming back here after the highlands of Thibet, where you'd nearly got drowned and scalped and had made love to the daughter of an Afghan chief . . . who had red lips smeared with loukoumi so that the sweet taste stayed in your mouth." Henslowe stroked softly his little brown mustache.

"But what's the use of just seeing and feeling things if you can't express them?"

"What's the use of living at all? For the fun of it, man; damn ends."

"But the only profound fun I ever have is that . . ." Andrews's voice broke. "O God, I would give up every joy in the world if I could turn out one page that I felt was adequate. . . . D'you know it's years since I've talked to anybody?"

They both stared silently out of the window at the fog that was packed tightly against it like cotton wool, only softer, and a greenish-gold color.

"The M.P.'s sure won't get us tonight," said Henslowe, banging his fist jauntily on the table. "I've a great mind to go to Rue St. Anne and leave my card on the Provost Marshal. . . . God damn! D'you remember that man who took the bite out of our wine-bottle . . . He didn't give a hoot in hell, did he? Talk about expression. Why don't you express that? I think that's the turning point of your career. That's what made you come to Paris; you can't deny it."

They both laughed loudly rolling about on their chairs. Andrews caught glints of contagion in the pale violet eyes of the lame boy and in the dark eyes of the girl.

"Let's tell them about it," he said still laughing, with his face, bloodless after the months in hospital, suddenly flushed.

"Salut," said Henslowe turning round and elevating his glass. "Nous rions parceque nous sommes gris de vin gris." Then he told them about the man who ate glass. He got to his feet and recounted slowly in his drawling voice, with gestures. Justine stood by with a dish full of stuffed tomatoes of which the red skins showed vaguely through a mantle of dark brown sauce. When she smiled her cheeks puffed out and gave her face a little of the look of a white cat's.

"And you live here?" asked Andrews after they had all laughed.

"Always. It is not often that I go down to town. . . . It's so difficult. . . . I have a withered leg." He smiled brilliantly like a child telling about a new toy.

"And you?"

"How could I be anywhere else?" answered the girl. "It's a misfortune, but there it is." She tapped with the crutch on the floor, making a sound like someone walking with it. The boy laughed and tightened his arm round her shoulder.

"I should like to live here," said Andrews simply.

"Why don't you?"

"But don't you see he's a soldier," whispered the girl hurriedly.

A frown wrinkled the boy's forehead.

"Well, it wasn't by choice, I suppose," he said.

Andrews was silent. Unaccountable shame took possession of him before these people who had never been soldiers, who would never be soldiers.

"The Greeks used to say," he said bitterly, using a phrase that had been a long time on his mind, "that when a man became a slave, on the first day he lost one-half of his virtue."

"When a man becomes a slave," repeated the lame boy softly, "on the first day he loses one-half of his virtue."

"What's the use of virtue? It is love you need," said the girl.

"I've eaten your tomato, friend Andrews," said Henslowe. "Justine will get us some more." He poured out the last of the wine that half filled each of the glasses with its thin sparkle, the color of red currants.

Outside the fog had blotted everything out in even darkness which grew vaguely yellow and red near the sparsely scattered street lamps. Andrews and Henslowe felt their way blindly down the long gleaming flights of steps that led from the quiet darkness of the Butte towards the confused lights and noises of more crowded streets. The fog caught in their throats and tingled in their noses and brushed against their cheeks like moist hands.

"Why did we go away from that restaurant? I'd like to have talked to those people some more," said Andrews.

"We haven't had any coffee either. . . . But, man, we're in Paris. We're not going to be here long. We can't afford to stay all the time in one place. . . . It's nearly closing time already. . . ."

"The boy was a painter. He said he lived by making toys; he whittles out wooden elephants and camels for Noah's Arks. . . . Did you hear that?"

They were walking fast down a straight, sloping street. Below them already appeared the golden glare of a boulevard.

Andrews went on talking, almost to himself.

"What a wonderful life that would be to live up here in a small room that would overlook the great rosy grey expanse of the city, to have some absurd work like that to live on, and to spend all your spare time working and going to concerts. . . . A quiet mellow existence. . . . Think of my life beside it. Slaving in that iron, metallic, brazen New York to write ineptitudes about music in the Sunday paper. God! And this."

They were sitting down at a table in a noisy café, full of yellow light flashing in eyes and on glasses and bottles, of red lips crushed against the thin hard rims of glasses.

"Wouldn't you like to just rip it off?" Andrews jerked at his tunic with both hands where it bulged out over his chest. "Oh, I'd like to make the buttons fly all over the café, smashing the liqueur glasses, snapping in the faces of all those dandified French officers who look so proud of themselves that they survived long enough to be victorious."

"The coffee's famous here," said Henslowe. "The only place I ever had it better was at a bistro in Nice on this last permission."

"Somewhere else again!"

"That's it. . . . For ever and ever, somewhere else! Let's have some prunelle. Before the war prunelle."

The waiter was a solemn man, with a beard cut like a prime minister's. He came with the bottle held out before him, religiously lifted. His lips pursed with an air of intense application, while he poured the white glinting liquid into the glasses. When he had finished he held the bottle upside down with a tragic gesture; not a drop came out.

"It is the end of the good old times," he said.

"Damnation to the good old times," said Henslowe. "Here's to the good old new roughhousy circus parades."

"I wonder how many people they are good for, those circus parades of yours," said Andrews.

"Where are you going to spend the night?" said Henslowe.

"I don't know. . . . I suppose I can find a hotel or something."

"Why don't you come with me and see Berthe; she probably has friends."

"I want to wander about alone, not that I scorn Berthe's friends," said Andrews. . . . "But I am so greedy for solitude."

John Andrews was walking alone down streets full of drifting fog. Now and then a taxi dashed past him and clattered off into the obscurity. Scattered groups of people, their footsteps hollow in the muffling fog, floated about him. He did not care which way he walked, but went on and on, crossing large crowded avenues where the lights embroidered patterns of gold and orange on the fog, rolling in wide deserted squares, diving into narrow streets where other steps sounded sharply for a second now and then and faded leaving nothing in his ears when he stopped still to listen but the city's distant muffled breathing. At last he came out along the river, where the fog was densest and coldest and where he could hear faintly the sound of water gurgling past the piers of bridges. The glow of the lights glared and dimmed, glared and dimmed, as he walked along, and sometimes he could make out the bare branches of trees blurred across the halos of the lamps. The fog caressed him soothingly and shadows kept flicking past him, giving him glimpses of smooth curves of cheeks and glints of eyes bright from the mist and darkness. Friendly, familiar people seemed to fill the fog just out of his sight. The muffled murmur of the city stirred him like the sound of the voices of friends.

From the girl at the cross-roads singing under her street-lamp to the patrician pulling roses to pieces from the height of her litter . . . all the imagining of your desire. . . .

The murmur of life about him kept forming itself into long modulated sentences in his ears,—sentences that gave him by their form a sense of quiet well-being as if he were looking at a low relief of people dancing, carved out of Parian in some workshop in Attica.

Once he stopped and leaned for a long while against the moisture-beaded stern of a street-lamp. Two shadows defined, as they strolled towards him, into the forms of a pale boy and a bareheaded girl, walking tightly laced in each other's arms. The boy limped a little and his violet eyes were contracted to wistfulness. John Andrews was suddenly filled with throbbing expectation, as if those two would come up to him and put their hands on his arms and make some revelation of vast import to his life. But when they reached the full glow of the lamp, Andrews saw that he was mistaken. They were not the boy and girl he had talked to on the Butte.

He walked off hurriedly and plunged again into tortuous streets, where he strode over the cobblestone pavements, stopping now and then to peer through the window of a shop at the light in the rear where a group of people sat quietly about a table under a light, or into a bar where a tired little boy with heavy eyelids and sleeves rolled up from thin grey arms was washing glasses, or an old woman, a shapeless bundle of black clothes, was swabbing the floor. From doorways he heard talking and soft laughs. Upper windows sent yellow rays of light across the fog.

In one doorway the vague light from a lamp bracketed in the wall showed two figures, pressed into one by their close embrace. As Andrews walked past, his heavy army boots clattering loud on the wet pavement, they lifted their heads slowly. The boy had violet eyes and pale beardless cheeks; the girl was bareheaded and kept her brown eyes fixed on the boy's face. Andrews's heart thumped within him. At last he had found them. He made a step towards them, and then strode on losing himself fast in the cool effacing fog. Again he had been mistaken. The fog swirled about him, hiding wistful friendly faces, hands ready to meet his hands, eyes ready to take fire with his glance, lips cold with the mist, to be crushed under his lips. *From the girl at the cross-roads singing under her street-lamp . . .*

And he walked on alone through the drifting fog.

IV

ANDREWS left the station reluctantly, shivering in the raw grey mist under which the houses of the village street and the rows of motor trucks and the few figures of French soldiers swathed in long formless coats, showed as vague dark blurs in the confused dawnlight. His body felt flushed and sticky from a night spent huddled in the warm fetid air of an overcrowded compartment. He yawned and stretched himself and stood irresolutely in the middle of the street with his pack biting into his shoulders. Out of sight, behind the dark mass, in which a few ruddy lights glowed, of the station buildings, the engine whistled and the train clanked off into the distance. Andrews listened to its faint reverberation through the mist with a sick feeling of despair. It was the train that had brought him from Paris back to his division.

As he stood shivering in the grey mist he remembered the curious despairing reluctance he used to suffer when he went back to boarding school after a holiday. How he used to go from the station to the school by the longest road possible, taking frantic account of every moment of liberty left him. Today his feet had the same leaden reluctance as when they used to all but refuse to take him up the long sandy hill to the school.

He wandered aimlessly for a while about the silent village hoping to find a café where he could sit for a few minutes to take a last look at himself before plunging again into the grovelling promiscuity of the army. Not a light showed. All the shutters of the shabby little brick and plaster houses were closed. With dull springless steps he walked down the road they had pointed out to him from the R.T.O.

Overhead the sky was brightening giving the mist that clung to the earth in every direction ruddy billowing outlines. The frozen road gave out a faint hard resonance under his footsteps. Occasionally the silhouette of a tree by the roadside loomed up in the mist ahead, its uppermost branches clear and ruddy with sunlight.

Andrews was telling himself that the war was over, and that

in a few months he would be free in any case. What did a few
months more or less matter? But the same thoughts were
swept recklessly away in the blind panic that was like a stampede of wild steers within him. There was no arguing. His
spirit was contorted with revolt so that his flesh twitched and
dark splotches danced before his eyes. He wondered vaguely
whether he had gone mad. Enormous plans kept rising up
out of the tumult of his mind and dissolving suddenly like
smoke in a high wind. He would run away and if they caught
him, kill himself. He would start a mutiny in his company, he
would lash all these men to frenzy by his words, so that they
too should refuse to form into Guns, so that they should
laugh when the officers got red in the face shouting orders at
them, so that the whole division should march off over the
frosty hills, without arms, without flags, calling all the men of
all the armies to join them, to march on singing, to laugh the
nightmare out of their blood. Would not some lightning
flash of vision sear people's consciousness into life again?
What was the good of stopping the war if the armies continued?

But that was just rhetoric. His mind was flooding itself with
rhetoric that it might keep its sanity. His mind was squeezing
out rhetoric like a sponge that he might not see dry madness
face to face.

And all the while his hard footsteps along the frozen road
beat in his ears bringing him nearer to the village where the
division was quartered. He was climbing a long hill. The mist
thinned about him and became brilliant with sunlight. Then
he was walking in the full sun over the crest of a hill with pale
blue sky above his head. Behind him and before him were
mist-filled valleys and beyond other ranges of long hills, with
reddish-violet patches of woodland, glowing faintly in the
sunlight. In the valley at his feet he could see, in the shadow
of the hill he stood on, a church tower and a few roofs rising
out of the mist, as out of water.

Among the houses bugles were blowing mess-call.

The jauntiness of the brassy notes ringing up through the
silence was agony to him. How long the day would be. He
looked at his watch. It was seven thirty. How did they come
to be having mess so late?

The mist seemed doubly cold and dark when he was buried in it again after his moment of sunlight. The sweat was chilled on his face and streaks of cold went through his clothes, soaked from the effort of carrying the pack. In the village street Andrews met a man he did not know and asked him where the office was. The man, who was chewing something, pointed silently to a house with green shutters on the opposite side of the street.

At a desk sat Chrisfield smoking a cigarette. When he jumped up Andrews noticed that he had a corporal's two stripes on his arm.

"Hello, Andy."

They shook hands warmly.

"A' you all right now, ole boy?"

"Sure, I'm fine," said Andrews. A sudden constraint fell upon them.

"That's good," said Chrisfield.

"You're a corporal now. Congratulations."

"Um hum. Made me more'n a month ago."

They were silent. Chrisfield sat down in his chair again.

"What sort of a town is this?"

"It's a hell-hole, this dump is, a hell-hole."

"That's nice."

"Goin' to move soon, tell me. . . . Army o' Occupation. But Ah hadn't ought to have told you that. . . . Don't tell any of the fellers."

"Where's the outfit quartered?"

"Ye won't know it; we've got fifteen new men. No account all of 'em. Second draft men."

"Civilians in the town?"

"You bet. . . . Come with me, Andy, an Ah'll tell 'em to give you some grub at the cookshack. No . . . wait a minute an' you'll miss the hike. . . . Hikes every day since the goddam armistice. They sent out a general order telling 'em to double up on the drill."

They heard a voice shouting orders outside and the narrow street filled up suddenly with a sound of boots beating the ground in unison. Andrews kept his back to the window. Something in his legs seemed to be tramping in time with the other legs.

"There they go," said Chrisfield. "Loot's with 'em to-day. . . . Want some grub? If it ain't been punk since the armistice."

The "Y" hut was empty and dark; through the grimy windowpanes could be seen fields and a leaden sky full of heavy ocherous light, in which the leafless trees and the fields full of stubble were different shades of dead, greyish brown. Andrews sat at the piano without playing. He was thinking how once he had thought to express all the cramped boredom of this life; the thwarted limbs regimented together, lashed into straight lines, the monotony of servitude. Unconsciously as he thought of it, the fingers of one hand sought a chord, which jangled in the badly tuned piano. "God, how silly!" he muttered aloud, pulling his hands away. Suddenly he began to play snatches of things he knew, distorting them, willfully mutilating the rhythm, mixing into them snatches of ragtime. The piano jangled under his hands, filling the empty hut with clamor. He stopped suddenly, letting his fingers slide from bass to treble, and began to play in earnest.

There was a cough behind him that had an artificial, discreet ring to it. He went on playing without turning round. Then a voice said:

"Beautiful, beautiful."

Andrews turned to find himself staring into a face of vaguely triangular shape with a wide forehead and prominent eyelids over protruding brown eyes. The man wore a Y.M.C.A. uniform which was very tight for him, so that there were creases running from each button across the front of his tunic.

"Oh, do go on playing. It's years since I heard any Debussy."

"It wasn't Debussy."

"Oh, wasn't it? Anyway it was just lovely. Do go on. I'll just stand here and listen."

Andrews went on playing for a moment, made a mistake, started over, made the same mistake, banged on the keys with his fist and turned round again.

"I can't play," he said peevishly.

"Oh, you can, my boy, you can. . . . Where did you learn? I would give a million dollars to play like that, if I had it."

Andrews glared at him silently.

"You are one of the men just back from hospital, I presume."

"Yes, worse luck."

"Oh, I don't blame you. These French towns are the dullest places; though I just love France, don't you?" The "Y" man had a faintly whining voice.

"Anywhere's dull in the army."

"Look, we must get to know each other real well. My name's Spencer Sheffield . . . Spencer B. Sheffield. . . . And between you and me there's not a soul in the division you can talk to. It's dreadful not to have intellectual people about one. I suppose you're from New York."

Andrews nodded.

"Um hum, so am I. You're probably read some of my things in *Vain Endeavor*. . . . What, you've never read *Vain Endeavor*? I guess you didn't go round with the intellectual set. . . . Musical people often don't. . . . Of course I don't mean the Village. All anarchists and society women there. . . ."

"I've never gone round with any set, and I never . . ."

"Never mind, we'll fix that when we all get back to New York. And now you just sit down at that piano and play me Debussy's 'Arabesque.' . . . I know you love it just as much as I do. But first what's your name?"

"Andrews."

"Folks come from Virginia?"

"Yes." Andrews got to his feet.

"Then you're related to the Penneltons."

"I may be related to the Kaiser for all I know."

"The Penneltons . . . that's it. You see my mother was a Miss Spencer from Spencer Falls, Virginia, and her mother was a Miss Pennelton, so you and I are cousins. Now isn't that a coincidence?"

"Distant cousins. But I must go back to the barracks."

"Come in and see me any time," Spencer B. Sheffield shouted after him. "You know where; back of the shack. And knock twice so I'll know it's you."

Outside the house where he was quartered Andrews met the new top sergeant, a lean man with spectacles and a little mustache of the color and texture of a scrubbing brush.

"Here's a letter for you," the top sergeant said. "Better look at the new K.P. list I've just posted."

The letter was from Henslowe. Andrews read it with a smile of pleasure in the faint afternoon light, remembering Henslowe's constant drawling talk about distant places he had never been to, and the man who had eaten glass, and the day and a half in Paris.

"Andy," the letter began, "I've got the dope at last. Courses begin in Paris February fifteenth. Apply at once to your C.O. to study somethin' at University of Paris. Any amount of lies will go. Apply all pull possible via sergeants, lieutenants and their mistresses and laundresses. Yours, Henslowe."

His heart thumping, Andrews ran after the sergeant, passing, in his excitement, a lieutenant without saluting him.

"Look here," snarled the lieutenant.

Andrews saluted, and stood stiffly at attention.

"Why didn't you salute me?"

"I was in a hurry, sir, and didn't see you. I was going on very urgent company business, sir."

"Remember that just because the armistice is signed you needn't think you're out of the army; at ease."

Andrews saluted. The lieutenant saluted, turned swiftly on his heel and walked away.

Andrews caught up to the sergeant.

"Sergeant Coffin. Can I speak to you a minute?"

"I'm in a hell of a hurry."

"Have you heard anything about this army students' corps to send men to universities here in France? Something the Y.M.C.A.'s getting up."

"Can't be for enlisted men. No I ain't heard a word about it. D'you want to go to school again?"

"If I get a chance. To finish my course."

"College man, are ye? So am I. Well, I'll let you know if I get any general order about it. Can't do anything without getting a general order about it. Looks to me like it's all bushwa."

"I guess you're right."

The street was grey dark. Stung by a sense of impotence, surging with despairing rebelliousness, Andrews hurried back towards the buildings where the company was quartered. He would be late for mess. The grey street was deserted. From a window here and there ruddy light streamed out to make a glowing oblong on the wall of a house opposite.

"Goddam it, if ye don't believe me, you go ask the loo-tenant. . . . Look here, Toby, didn't our outfit see hotter work than any goddam engineers?"

Toby had just stepped into the café, a tall man with a brown bulldog face and a scar on his left cheek. He spoke rarely and solemnly with a Maine coast Yankee twang.

"I reckon so," was all he said. He sat down on the bench beside the other man who went on bitterly:

"I guess you would reckon so. . . . Hell, man, you ditch diggers ain't in it."

"Ditch diggers!" The engineer banged his fist down on the table. His lean pickled face was a furious red. "I guess we don't dig half so many ditches as the infantry does . . . an' when we've dug 'em we don't crawl into 'em an' stay there like goddam cottontailed jackrabbits."

"You guys don't git near enough to the front . . ."

"Like goddam cottontailed jackrabbits," shouted the pickle-faced engineer again, roaring with laughter. "Ain't that so?" He looked round the room for approval. The benches at the two long tables were filled with infantry men who looked at him angrily. Noticing suddenly that he had no support, he moderated his voice.

"The infantry's damn necessary, I'll admit that; but where'd you fellers be without us guys to string the barbed wire for you?"

"There warn't no barbed wire strung in the Oregon forest where we was, boy. What d'ye want barbed wire when you're advancin' for?"

"Look here . . . I'll bet you a bottle of cognac my company had more losses than yourn did."

"Tek him up, Joe," said Toby, suddenly showing an interest in the conversation.

"All right, it's a go."

"We had fifteen killed and twenty wounded," announced the engineer triumphantly.

"How badly wounded?"

"What's that to you? Hand over the cognac?"

"Like hell. We had fifteen killed and twenty wounded too, didn't we, Toby?"

"I reckon you're right," said Toby.

"Ain't I right?" asked the other man, addressing the company generally.

"Sure, goddam right," muttered voices.

"Well, I guess it's all off, then," said the engineer.

"No, it ain't," said Toby, "reckon up yer wounded. The feller who's got the worst wounded gets the cognac. Ain't that fair?"

"Sure."

"We've had seven fellers sent home already," said the engineer.

"We've had eight. Ain't we?"

"Sure," growled everybody in the room.

"How bad was they?"

"Two of 'em was blind," said Toby.

"Hell," said the engineer, jumping to his feet as if taking a trick at poker. "We had a guy who was sent home without arms nor legs, and three fellers got t.b. from bein' gassed."

John Andrews had been sitting in a corner of the room. He got up. Something had made him think of the man he had known in the hospital who had said that was the life to make a feller feel fit. Getting up at three o'clock in the morning, you jumped out of bed just like a cat. . . . He remembered how the olive-drab trousers had dangled empty from the man's chair.

"That's nothing; one of our sergeants had to have a new nose grafted on. . . ."

The village street was dark and deeply rutted with mud. Andrews wandered up and down aimlessly. There was only one other café. That would be just like this one. He couldn't go back to the desolate barn where he slept. It would be too early to go to sleep. A cold wind blew down the street and the sky was full of vague movement of dark clouds. The partly-frozen mud clotted about his feet as he walked along; he could feel the water penetrating his shoes. Opposite the Y.M.C.A. hut at the end of the street he stopped. After a

moment's indecision he gave a little laugh, and walked round
to the back where the door of the "Y" man's room was.

He knocked twice, half hoping there would be no reply.
Sheffield's whining high-pitched voice said: "Who is it?"

"Andrews."

"Come right in. . . . You're just the man I wanted to see."
Andrews stood with his hand on the knob.

"Do sit down and make yourself right at home."

Spencer Sheffield was sitting at a little desk in a room with
walls of unplaned boards and one small window. Behind the
desk were piles of cracker boxes and cardboard cases of cigarettes and in the midst of them a little opening, like that of a
railway ticket office, in the wall through which the "Y" man
sold his commodities to the long lines of men who would
stand for hours waiting meekly in the room beyond.

Andrews was looking round for a chair.

"Oh, I just forgot. I'm sitting in the only chair," said Spencer
Sheffield, laughing, twisting his small mouth into a shape like a
camel's mouth and rolling about his large protruding eyes.

"Oh, that's all right. What I wanted to ask you was: do you
know anything about . . . ?"

"Look, do come with me to my room," interrupted
Sheffield. "I've got such a nice sitting-room with an open fire,
just next to Lieutenant Bleezer. . . . An' there we'll talk . . .
about everything. I'm just dying to talk to somebody about
the things of the spirit."

"Do you know anything about a scheme for sending enlisted men to French universities? Men who have not finished
their courses."

"Oh, wouldn't that be just fine. I tell you, boy, there's
nothing like the U.S. government to think of things like
that."

"But have you heard anything about it?"

"No; but I surely shall. . . . D'you mind switching the
light off? . . . That's it. Now just follow me. Oh, I do need
a rest. I've been working dreadfully hard since that Knights of
Columbus man came down here. Isn't it hateful the way they
try to run down the 'Y'? . . . Now we can have a nice long
talk. You must tell me all about yourself."

"But don't you really know anything about that university

scheme? They say it begins February fifteenth," Andrews said in a low voice.

"I'll ask Lieutenant Bleezer if he knows anything about it," said Sheffield soothingly, throwing an arm around Andrews's shoulder and pushing him in the door ahead of him.

They went through a dark hall to a little room where a fire burned brilliantly in the hearth, lighting up with tongues of red and yellow a square black walnut table and two heavy armchairs with leather backs and bottoms that shone like lacquer.

"This is wonderful," said Andrews involuntarily.

"Romantic I call it. Makes you think of Dickens, doesn't it, and Locksley Hall."

"Yes," said Andrews vaguely.

"Have you been in France long?" asked Andrews settling himself in one of the chairs and looking into the dancing flames of the log fire. "Will you smoke?" He handed Sheffield a crumpled cigarette.

"No, thanks, I only smoke special kinds. I have a weak heart. That's why I was rejected from the army. . . . Oh, but I think it was superb of you to join as a private. It was my dream to do that, to be one of the nameless marching throng."

"I think it was damn foolish, not to say criminal," said Andrews sullenly, still staring into the fire.

"You can't mean that. Or do you mean that you think you had abilities which would have been worth more to your country in another position? . . . I have many friends who felt that."

"No. . . . I don't think it's right of a man to go back on himself. . . . I don't think butchering people ever does any good . . . I have acted as if I did think it did good . . . out of carelessness or cowardice, one or the other; that I think bad."

"You mustn't talk that way," said Sheffield hurriedly. "So you are a musician, are you?" He asked the question with a jaunty confidential air.

"I used to play the piano a little, if that's what you mean," said Andrews.

"Music has never been the art I had most interest in. But many things have moved me intensely. . . . Debussy and those beautiful little things of Nevin's. You must know them. . . . Poetry has been more my field. When I was young, younger than you are, quite a lad . . . Oh, if we could only stay young; I am thirty-two."

"I don't see that youth by itself is worth much. It's the most superb medium there is, though, for other things," said Andrews. "Well, I must go," he said. "If you do hear anything about that university scheme, you will let me know, won't you?"

"Indeed I shall, dear boy, indeed I shall."

They shook hands in jerky dramatic fashion and Andrews stumbled down the dark hall to the door. When he stood out in the raw night air again he drew a deep breath. By the light that streamed out from a window he looked at his watch. There was time to go to the regimental sergeant-major's office before tattoo.

At the opposite end of the village street from the Y.M.C.A. hut was a cube-shaped house set a little apart from the rest in the middle of a broad lawn which the constant crossing and re-crossing of a staff of cars and trains of motor trucks had turned into a muddy morass in which the wheel tracks crisscrossed in every direction. A narrow board walk led from the main road to the door. In the middle of this walk Andrews met a captain and automatically got off into the mud and saluted.

The regimental office was a large room that had once been decorated by wan and ill-drawn mural paintings in the manner of Puvis de Chavannes, but the walls had been so chipped and soiled by five years of military occupation that they were barely recognisable. Only a few bits of bare flesh and floating drapery showed here and there above the maps and notices that were tacked on the walls. At the end of the room a group of nymphs in Nile green and pastel blue could be seen emerging from under a French War Loan poster. The ceiling was adorned with an oval of flowers and little plaster cupids in low relief which had also suffered and in places showed the laths. The office was nearly empty. The littered desks and silent type-writers gave a strange air of desolation to the gutted drawing-room. Andrews walked boldly to the furthest desk, where a little red card leaning against the typewriter said "Regimental Sergeant-Major."

Behind the desk, crouched over a heap of typewritten reports, sat a little man with scanty sandy hair, who screwed up his eyes and smiled when Andrews approached the desk.

"Well, did you fix it up for me?" he asked.

"Fix what?" said Andrews.

"Oh, I thought you were someone else." The smile left the regimental sergeant-major's thin lips. "What do you want?"

"Why, Regimental Sergeant-Major, can you tell me anything about a scheme to send enlisted men to colleges over here? Can you tell me who to apply to?"

"According to what general orders? And who told you to come and see me about it, anyway?"

"Have you heard anything about it?"

"No, nothing definite. I'm busy now anyway. Ask one of your own non-coms to find out about it." He crouched once more over the papers.

Andrews was walking towards the door, flushing with annoyance, when he saw that the man at the desk by the window was jerking his head in a peculiar manner, just in the direction of the regimental sergeant-major and then towards the door. Andrews smiled at him and nodded. Outside the door, where an orderly sat on a short bench reading a torn *Saturday Evening Post*, Andrews waited. The hall was part of what must have been a ballroom, for it had a much-scarred hardwood floor and big spaces of bare plaster framed by gilt- and lavender-colored mouldings, which had probably held tapestries. The partition of unplaned boards that formed other offices cut off the major part of a highly decorated ceiling where cupids with crimson-daubed bottoms swam in all attitudes in a sea of pink- and blue- and lavender-colored clouds, wreathing themselves coyly in heavy garlands of waxy hothouse flowers, while cornucopias spilling out squashy fruits gave Andrews a feeling of distinct insecurity as he looked up from below.

"Say are you a Kappa Mu?"

Andrews looked down suddenly and saw in front of him the man who had signalled to him in the regimental sergeant-major's office.

"Are you a Kappa Mu?" he asked again.

"No, not that I know of," stammered Andrews puzzled.

"What school did you go to?"

"Harvard."

"Harvard. . . . Guess we haven't got a chapter there. . . . I'm from North Western. Anyway you want to go to school in France here if you can. So do I."

"Don't you want to come and have a drink?"

The man frowned, pulled his overseas cap down over his forehead, where the hair grew very low, and looked about him mysteriously.

"Yes," he said.

They splashed together down the muddy village street.

"We've got thirteen minutes before tattoo. . . . My name's Walters, what's yours?" He spoke in a low voice in short staccato phrases.

"Andrews."

"Andrews, you've got to keep this dark. If everybody finds out about it we're through. It's a shame you're not a Kappa Mu, but college men have got to stick together, that's the way I look at it."

"Oh, I'll keep it dark enough," said Andrews.

"It's too good to be true. The general order isn't out yet, but I've seen a preliminary circular. What school d'you want to go to?"

"Sorbonne, Paris."

"That's the stuff. D'you know the back room at Baboon's?"

Walters turned suddenly to the left up an alley, and broke through a hole in a hawthorn hedge.

"A guy's got to keep his eyes and ears open if he wants to get anywhere in this army," he said.

As they ducked in the back door of a cottage, Andrews caught a glimpse of the billowy line of a tile roof against the lighter darkness of the sky. They sat down on a bench built into a chimney where a few sticks made a splutter of flames.

"Monsieur désire?" A red-faced girl with a baby in her arms came up to them.

"That's Babette; Baboon I call her," said Walters with a laugh.

"Chocolat," said Walters.

"That'll suit me all right. It's my treat, remember."

"I'm not forgetting it. Now let's get to business. What you do is this. You write an application. I'll make that out for you on the typewriter tomorrow and you meet me here at eight tomorrow night and I'll give it to you. . . . You sign it at once and hand it in to your sergeant. See?"

"This'll just be a preliminary application; when the order's out you'll have to make another."

The woman, this time without the baby, appeared out of the darkness of the room with a candle and two cracked bowls from which steam rose, faint primrose-color in the candle light.

Walters drank his bowl down at a gulp, grunted and went on talking.

"Give me a cigarette, will you? . . . You'll have to make it out darn soon too, because once the order's out every son of a gun in the division'll be making out to be a college man. How did you get your tip?"

"From a fellow in Paris."

"You've been to Paris, have you?" said Walters admiringly. "Is it the way they say it is? Gee, these French are immoral. Look at this woman here. She'll sleep with a feller soon as not. Got a baby too!"

"But who do the applications go in to?"

"To the colonel, or whoever he appoints to handle it. You a Catholic?"

"No."

"Neither am I. That's the hell of it. The regimental sergeant-major is."

"Well?"

"I guess you haven't noticed the way things run up at divisional headquarters. It's a regular cathedral. Isn't a mason in it. . . . But I must beat it. . . . Better pretend you don't know me if you meet me on the street; see?"

"All right."

Walters hurried out of the door. Andrews sat alone looking at the flutter of little flames about the pile of sticks on the hearth, while he sipped chocolate from the warm bowl held between the palms of both hands.

He remembered a speech out of some very bad romantic play he had heard when he was very small.

"About your head I fling . . . the curse of Ro-me."

He started to laugh, sliding back and forth on the smooth
bench which had been polished by the breeches of generations warming their feet at the fire. The red-faced woman
stood with her hands on her hips looking at him in astonish-
ment, while he laughed and laughed.

"Mais quelle gaité, quelle gaité," she kept saying.

The straw under him rustled faintly with every sleepy
movement Andrews made in his blankets. In a minute the bugle was going to blow and he was going to jump out of his
blankets, throw on his clothes and fall into line for roll call in
the black mud of the village street. It couldn't be that only a
month had gone by since he had got back from hospital. No,
he had spent a lifetime in this village being dragged out of his
warm blankets every morning by the bugle, shivering as he
stood in line for roll call, shuffling in a line that moved slowly
past the cookshack, shuffling along in another line to throw
what was left of his food into garbage cans, to wash his mess
kit in the greasy water a hundred other men had washed their
mess kits in; lining up to drill, to march on along muddy
roads, splattered by the endless trains of motor trucks; lining
up twice more for mess, and at last being forced by another
bugle into his blankets again to sleep heavily while a smell
hung in his nostrils of sweating woolen clothing and
breathed-out air and dusty blankets. In a minute the bugle
was going to blow, to snatch him out of even these miserable
thoughts, and throw him into an automaton under other
men's orders. Childish spiteful desires surged into his mind. If
the bugler would only die. He could picture him, a little man
with a broad face and putty-colored cheeks, a small rusty
mustache and bow-legs lying like a calf on a marble slab in a
butcher's shop on top of his blankets. What nonsense! There
were other buglers. He wondered how many buglers there
were in the army. He could picture them all, in dirty little villages, in stone barracks, in towns, in great camps that served
the country for miles with rows of black warehouses and narrow barrack buildings standing with their feet a little apart;
giving their little brass bugles a preliminary tap before putting
out their cheeks and blowing in them and stealing a million

and a half (or was it two million or three million) lives, and throwing the warm sentient bodies into coarse automatons who must be kept busy, lest they grow restive, till killing time began again.

The bugle blew. With the last jaunty notes, a stir went through the barn.

Corporal Chrisfield stood on the ladder that led up from the yard, his head on a level with the floor shouting:

"Shake it up, fellers! If a guy's late to roll call, it's K.P. for a week."

As Andrews, while buttoning his tunic, passed him on the ladder, he whispered:

"Tell me we're going to see service again, Andy . . . Army o' Occupation."

While he stood stiffly at attention waiting to answer when the sergeant called his name, Andrews's mind was whirling in crazy circles of anxiety. What if they should leave before the General Order came on the University plan? The application would certainly be lost in the confusion of moving the Division, and he would be condemned to keep up this life for more dreary weeks and months. Would any years of work and happiness in some future existence make up for the humiliating agony of this servitude?

"Dismissed!"

He ran up the ladder to fetch his mess kit and in a few minutes was in line again in the rutted village street where the grey houses were just forming outlines as light crept slowly into the leaden sky, while a faint odor of bacon and coffee came to him, making him eager for food, eager to drown his thoughts in the heaviness of swiftly-eaten greasy food and in the warmth of watery coffee gulped down out of a tin-curved cup. He was telling himself desperately that he must do something—that he must make an effort to save himself, that he must fight against the deadening routine that numbed him.

Later, while he was sweeping the rough board floor of the company's quarters, the theme came to him which had come to him long ago, in a former incarnation it seemed, when he was smearing windows with soap from a gritty sponge along the endless side of the barracks in the training camp. Time and time again in the past year he had thought of it, and dreamed of weaving it into a fabric of sound which would express the trudging monotony of days bowed under the yoke. "Under the Yoke"; that would be a title for it. He imagined the sharp tap of the conductor's baton, the silence of a crowded hall, the first notes rasping bitterly upon the tense ears of men and women. But as he tried to concentrate his mind on the music, other things intruded upon it, blurred it. He kept feeling the rhythm of the Queen of Sheba slipping from the shoulders of her gaudily caparisoned elephant, advancing towards him through the torchlight, putting her hand, fantastic with rings and long gilded fingernails, upon his shoulders so that ripples of delight, at all the voluptuous images of his desire, went through his whole body, making it quiver like a flame with yearning for unimaginable things. It all muddled into fantastic gibberish—into sounds of horns and trombones and double basses blown off key while a piccolo shrilled the first bars of "The Star Spangled Banner."

He had stopped sweeping and looked about him dazedly. He was alone. Outside, he heard a sharp voice call "Attenshun!" He ran down the ladder and fell in at the end of the line under the angry glare of the lieutenant's small eyes, which were placed very close together on either side of a lean nose, black and hard, like the eyes of a crab.

The company marched off through the mud to the drill field.

After retreat Andrews knocked at the door at the back of the Y.M.C.A., but as there was no reply, he strode off with a long, determined stride to Sheffield's room.

In the moment that elapsed between his knock and an answer, he could feel his heart thumping. A little sweat broke out on his temples.

"Why, what's the matter, boy? You look all wrought up," said Sheffield, holding the door half open, and blocking, with his lean form, entrance to the room.

"May I come in? I want to talk to you," said Andrews.

"Oh, I suppose it'll be all right. . . . You see I have an officer with me . . ." then there was a flutter in Sheffield's voice. "Oh, do come in"; he went on, with sudden enthusiasm. "Lieutenant Bleezer is fond of music too. . . . Lieutenant, this is the boy I was telling you about. We must get him to play for us. If he had the opportunities, I am sure he'd be a famous musician."

Lieutenant Bleezer was a dark youth with a hooked nose and pince-nez. His tunic was unbuttoned and he held a cigar in his hand. He smiled in an evident attempt to put this enlisted man at his ease.

"Yes, I am very fond of music, modern music," he said, leaning against the mantelpiece. "Are you a musician by profession?"

"Not exactly . . . nearly." Andrews thrust his hands into the bottoms of his trouser pockets and looked from one to the other with a certain defiance.

"I suppose you've played in some orchestra? How is it you are not in the regimental band?"

"No, except the Pierian."

"The Pierian? Were you at Harvard?"

Andrews nodded.

"So was I."

"Isn't that a coincidence?" said Sheffield. "I'm so glad I just insisted on your coming in."

"What year were you?" asked Lieutenant Bleezer, with a faint change of tone, drawing a finger along his scant black moustache.

"Fifteen."

"I haven't graduated yet," said the lieutenant with a laugh. "What I wanted to ask you, Mr. Sheffield . . ."

"Oh, my boy; my boy, you know you've known me long enough to call me Spence," broke in Sheffield.

"I want to know," went on Andrews speaking slowly, "can you help me to get put on the list to be sent to the University of Paris? . . . I know that a list has been made out, although the General Order has not come yet. I am disliked by most of the non-coms and I don't see how I can get on without somebody's help . . . I simply can't go this life any longer." Andrews closed his lips firmly and looked at the ground, his face flushing.

"Well, a man of your attainments certainly ought to go," said Lieutenant Bleezer, with a faint tremor of hesitation in his voice. "I'm going to Oxford myself."

"Trust me, my boy," said Sheffield. "I'll fix it up for you, I promise. Let's shake hands on it." He seized Andrews's hand and pressed it warmly in a moist palm. "If it's within human power, within human power," he added.

"Well, I must go," said Lieutenant Bleezer, suddenly striding to the door. "I promised the Marquise I'd drop in. Goodbye. . . . Take a cigar, won't you?" He held out three cigars in the direction of Andrews.

"No, thank you."

"Oh, don't you think the old aristocracy of France is just too wonderful? Lieutenant Bleezer goes almost every evening to call on the Marquise de Rompemouville. He says she is just too spirituelle for words. . . . He often meets the Commanding Officer there."

Andrews had dropped into a chair and sat with his face buried in his hands, looking through his fingers at the fire, where a few white fingers of flame were clutching intermittently at a grey beech log. His mind was searching desperately for expedients.

He got to his feet and shouted shrilly:

"I can't go this life any more, do you hear that? No possible future is worth all this. If I can get to Paris, all right. If not, I'll desert and damn the consequences."

"But I've already promised I'll do all I can. . . ."

"Well, do it now," interrupted Andrews brutally.

"All right, I'll go and see the colonel and tell him what a great musician you are."

"Let's go together, now."

"But that'll look queer, dear boy."

"I don't give a damn, come along. . . . You can talk to him. You seem to be thick with all the officers."

"You must wait till I tidy up," said Sheffield.

"All right."

Andrews strode up and down in the mud in front of the house, snapping his fingers with impatience, until Sheffield came out, then they walked off in silence.

"Now wait outside a minute," whispered Sheffield when they came to the white house with bare grapevines over the front, where the colonel lived.

After a wait, Andrews found himself at the door of a brilliantly-lighted drawing room. There was a dense smell of cigar smoke. The colonel, an elderly man with a benevolent beard, stood before him with a coffee cup in his hand. Andrews saluted punctiliously.

"They tell me you are quite a pianist. . . . Sorry I didn't know it before," said the colonel in a kindly tone. "You want to go to Paris to study under this new scheme?"

"Yes, sir."

"What a shame I didn't know before. The list of the men going is all made out. . . . Of course perhaps at the last minute . . . if somebody else doesn't go . . . your name can go in."

The colonel smiled graciously and turned back into the room.

"Thank you, Colonel," said Andrews, saluting.

Without a word to Sheffield, he strode off down the dark village street towards his quarters.

Andrews stood on the broad village street, where the mud was nearly dry, and a wind streaked with warmth ruffled the few puddles; he was looking into the window of the café to see if there was anyone he knew inside from whom he could borrow money for a drink. It was two months since he had had any pay, and his pockets were empty. The sun had just set on a premature spring afternoon, flooding the sky and the grey houses and the tumultuous tiled roofs with warm violet light. The faint premonition of the stirring of life in the cold earth, that came to Andrews with every breath he drew of the sparkling wind, stung his dull boredom to fury. It was the first of March, he was telling himself over and over again. The fifteenth of February, he had expected to be in Paris, free, or half-free; at least able to work. It was the first of March and here he was still helpless, still tied to the monotonous wheel of routine, incapable of any real effort, spending his spare time wandering like a lost dog up and down this muddy street, from the Y.M.C.A. hut at one end of the village to the church and the fountain in the middle, and to the Divisional Headquarters at the other end, then back again, looking listlessly into windows, staring in people's faces without seeing them. He had given up all hope of being sent to Paris. He had given up thinking about it or about anything; the same

dull irritation of despair droned constantly in his head, grinding round and round like a broken phonograph record.

After looking a long while in the window of the café of the
Braves Alliés, he walked a little down the street and stood in
the same position staring into the Repos du Poilu, where a
large sign "American spoken" blocked up half the window.
Two officers passed. His hand snapped up to the salute automatically, like a mechanical signal. It was nearly dark. After a
while he began to feel serious coolness in the wind, shivered
and started to wander aimlessly down the street.

He recognised Walters coming towards him and was going
to pass him without speaking when Walters bumped into him,
muttered in his ear "Come to Baboon's," and hurried off
with his swift business-like stride. Andrews stood irresolutely
for a while with his head bent, then went with unresilient
steps up the alley, through the hole in the hedge and into Babette's kitchen. There was no fire. He stared morosely at the
grey ashes until he heard Walter's voice beside him:

"I've got you all fixed up."

"What do you mean?"

"Mean . . . are you asleep, Andrews? They've cut a name
off the school list, that's all. Now if you shake a leg and somebody doesn't get in ahead of you, you'll be in Paris before
you know it."

"That's damn decent of you to come and tell me."

"Here's your application," said Walters, drawing a paper
out of his pocket. "Take it to the colonel; get him to O.K. it
and then rush it up to the sergeant-major's office yourself.
They are making out travel orders now. So long."

Walters had vanished. Andrews was alone again, staring at
the grey ashes. Suddenly he jumped to his feet and hurried off
towards headquarters. In the anteroom to the colonel's office
he waited a long while, looking at his boots that were thickly
coated with mud. "Those boots will make a bad impression;
those boots will make a bad impression," a voice was saying
over and over again inside of him. A lieutenant was also waiting to see the colonel, a young man with pink cheeks and a
milky-white forehead, who held his hat in one hand with a
pair of khaki-colored kid gloves, and kept passing a hand over
his light well-brushed hair. Andrews felt dirty and ill-smelling

in his badly-fitting uniform. The sight of this perfect young man in his whipcord breeches, with his manicured nails and immaculately polished puttees exasperated him. He would have liked to fight him, to prove that he was the better man, to outwit him, to make him forget his rank and his important air. . . . The lieutenant had gone in to see the colonel. Andrews found himself reading a chart of some sort tacked up on the wall. There were names and dates and figures, but he could not make out what it was about.

"All right! Go ahead," whispered the orderly to him; and he was standing with his cap in his hand before the colonel who was looking at him severely, fingering the papers he had on the desk with a heavily veined hand.

Andrews saluted. The colonel made an impatient gesture.

"May I speak to you, Colonel, about the school scheme?"

"I suppose you've got permission from somebody to come to me."

"No, sir." Andrews's mind was struggling to find something to say.

"Well, you'd better go and get it."

"But, Colonel, there isn't time; the travel orders are being made out at this minute. I've heard that there's been a name crossed out on the list."

"Too late."

"But, Colonel, you don't know how important it is. I am a musician by trade; if I can't get into practice again before being demobilized, I shan't be able to get a job. . . . I have a mother and an old aunt dependent on me. My family has seen better days, you see, sir. It's only by being high up in my profession that I can earn enough to give them what they are accustomed to. And a man in your position in the world, Colonel, must know what even a few months of study in Paris mean to a pianist."

The colonel smiled.

"Let's see your application," he said.

Andrews handed it to him with a trembling hand. The colonel made a few marks on one corner with a pencil.

"Now if you can get that to the sergeant-major in time to have your name included in the orders, well and good."

Andrews saluted, and hurried out. A sudden feeling of nausea had come over him. He was hardly able to control a mad desire to tear the paper up. "The sons of bitches . . . the sons of bitches," he muttered to himself. Still he ran all the way to the square, isolated building where the regimental office was.

He stopped panting in front of the desk that bore the little red card, Regimental Sergeant-Major. The regimental sergeant-major looked up at him enquiringly.

"Here's an application for School at the Sorbonne, Sergeant. Colonel Wilkins told me to run up to you with it, said he was very anxious to have it go in at once."

"Too late," said the regimental sergeant-major.

"But the colonel said it had to go in."

"Can't help it. . . . Too late," said the regimental sergeant-major.

Andrews felt the room and the men in their olive-drab shirt sleeves at the typewriters and the three nymphs creeping from behind the French War Loan poster whirl round his head. Suddenly he heard a voice behind him:

"Is the name Andrews, John, Sarge?"

"How the hell should I know?" said the regimental sergeant-major.

"Because I've got it in the orders already. . . . I don't know how it got in." The voice was Walters's voice, staccatto and business-like.

"Well, then, why d'you want to bother me about it? Give me that paper." The regimental sergeant-major jerked the paper out of Andrews's hand and looked at it savagely.

"All right, you leave tomorrow. A copy of the orders'll go to your company in the morning," growled the regimental sergeant-major.

Andrews looked hard at Walters as he went out, but got no glance in return. When he stood in the air again, disgust surged up within him, bitterer than before. The fury of his humiliation made tears start in his eyes. He walked away from the village down the main road, splashing carelessly through the puddles, slipping in the wet clay of the ditches. Something within him, like the voice of a wounded man swearing, was whining in his head long strings of filthy names. After walking a long while he stopped suddenly with his fists clenched. It was completely dark, the sky was faintly marbled by a moon behind the clouds. On both sides of the road rose the tall grey skeletons of poplars. When the sound of his footsteps stopped, he heard a faint lisp of running water. Standing still in the middle of the road, he felt his feelings gradually relax. He said aloud in a low voice several times: "You are a damn fool, John Andrews," and started walking slowly and thoughtfully back to the village.

V

ANDREWS felt an arm put around his shoulder.

"Ah've been to hell an' gone lookin' for you, Andy," said Chrisfield's voice in his ear, jerking him out of the reverie he walked in. He could feel in his face Chrisfield's breath, heavy with cognac.

"I'm going to Paris tomorrow, Chris," said Andrews.

"Ah know it, boy. Ah know it. That's why I was that right smart to talk to you. . . . You doan want to go to Paris. . . . Why doan ye come up to Germany with us? Tell me they live like kings up there."

"All right," said Andrews, "let's go to the back room at Babette's."

Chrisfield hung on his shoulder, walking unsteadily beside him. At the hole in the hedge Chrisfield stumbled and nearly pulled them both down. They laughed, and still laughing staggered into the dark kitchen, where they found the red-faced woman with her baby sitting beside the fire with no other light than the flicker of the rare flames that shot up from a little mass of wood embers. The baby started crying shrilly when the two soldiers stamped in. The woman got up and, talking automatically to the baby all the while, went off to get a light and wine.

Andrews looked at Chrisfield's face by the firelight. His cheeks had lost the faint childish roundness they had had when Andrews had first talked to him, sweeping up cigarette butts off the walk in front of the barracks at the training camp.

"Ah tell you, boy, you ought to come with us to Germany . . . nauthin' but whores in Paris."

"The trouble is, Chris, that I don't want to live like a king, or a sergeant or a major-general. . . . I want to live like John Andrews."

"What yer goin' to do in Paris, Andy?"

"Study music."

"Ah guess some day Ah'll go into a movie show an' when they turn on the lights, who'll Ah see but ma ole frien' Andy raggin' the scales on the pyaner."

"Something like that. . . . How d'you like being a corporal, Chris?"

"O, Ah doan know." Chrisfield spat on the floor between his feet. "It's funny, ain't it? You an' me was right smart friends onct. . . . Guess it's bein' a non-com."

Andrews did not answer.

Chrisfield sat silent with his eyes on the fire.

"Well, Ah got him. . . . Gawd, it was easy," he said suddenly.

"What do you mean?"

"Ah got him, that's all."

"You mean . . . ?"

Chrisfield nodded.

"Um-hum, in the Oregon forest," he said.

Andrews said nothing. He felt suddenly very tired. He thought of men he had seen in attitudes of death.

"Ah wouldn't ha' thought it had been so easy," said Chrisfield.

The woman came through the door at the end of the kitchen with a candle in her hand. Chrisfield stopped speaking suddenly.

"Tomorrow I'm going to Paris," cried Andrews boisterously. "It's the end of soldiering for me."

"Ah bet it'll be some sport in Germany, Andy. . . . Sarge says we'll be goin' up to Coab . . . what's its name?"

"Coblenz."

Chrisfield poured a glass of wine out and drank it off, smacking his lips after it and wiping his mouth on the back of his hand.

"D'ye remember, Andy, we was both of us brushin' cigarette butts at that bloody trainin' camp when we first met up with each other?"

"Considerable water has run under the bridge since then."

"Ah reckon we won't meet up again, mos' likely."

"Hell, why not?"

They were silent again, staring at the fading embers of the fire. In the dim edge of the candlelight the woman stood with her hands on her hips, looking at them fixedly.

"Reckon a feller wouldn't know what to do with himself if he did get out of the army, . . . now, would he, Andy?"

"So long, Chris. I'm beating it," said Andrews in a harsh voice, jumping to his feet.

"So long, Andy, ole man. . . . Ah'll pay for the drinks." Chrisfield was beckoning with his hand to the red-faced woman, who advanced slowly through the candlelight.

"Thanks, Chris."

Andrews strode away from the door. A cold, needle-like rain was falling. He pulled up his coat collar and ran down the muddy village street towards his quarters.

VI

IN THE opposite corner of the compartment Andrews could see Walters hunched up in an attitude of sleep, with his cap pulled down far over his eyes. His mouth was open, and his head wagged with the jolting of the train. The shade over the light plunged the compartment in dark-blue obscurity, which made the night sky outside the window and the shapes of trees and houses, evolving and pirouetting as they glided by, seem very near. Andrews felt no desire to sleep; he had sat a long time leaning his head against the frame of the window, looking out at the fleeing shadows and the occasional little red-green lights that darted by and the glow of the stations that flared for a moment and were lost in dark silhouettes of unlighted houses and skeleton trees and black hillsides. He was thinking how all the epochs in his life seemed to have been marked out by railway rides at night. The jolting rumble of the wheels made the blood go faster through his veins; made him feel acutely the clattering of the train along the gleaming rails, spurning fields and trees and houses, piling up miles and miles between the past and future. The gusts of cold night air when he opened the window and the faint whiffs of steam and coal gas that tingled in his nostrils excited him like a smile on a strange face seen for a moment in a crowded street. He did not think of what he had left behind. He was straining his eyes eagerly through the darkness towards the vivid life he was going to live. Boredom and abasement were over. He was free to work and hear music and make friends. He drew deep breaths; warm waves of vigor seemed flowing constantly from his lungs and throat to his finger tips and down through his body and the muscles of his legs. He looked at his watch: "One." In six hours he would be in Paris. For six hours he would sit there looking out at the fleeting shadows of the countryside, feeling in his blood the eager throb of the train, rejoicing in every mile the train carried him away from things past.

Walters still slept, half slipping off the seat, with his mouth open and his overcoat bundled round his head. Andrews looked out of the window, feeling in his nostrils the tingle of steam and coal gas. A phrase out of some translation of the Iliad came to his head: "Ambrosial night, Night ambrosial unending." But better than sitting round a camp fire drinking wine and water and listening to the boastful yarns of long-haired Achæans, was this hustling through the countryside away from the monotonous whine of past unhappiness, towards joyousness and life.

Andrews began to think of the men he had left behind. They were asleep at this time of night, in barns and barracks, or else standing on guard with cold damp feet, and cold hands which the icy rifle barrel burned when they tended it. He might go far away out of sound of the tramp of marching, away from the smell of overcrowded barracks where men slept in rows like cattle, but he would still be one of them. He would not see an officer pass him without an unconscious movement of servility, he would not hear a bugle without feeling sick with hatred. If he could only express these thwarted lives, the miserable dullness of industrialized slaughter, it might have been almost worth while—for him; for the others, it would never be worth while. "But you're talking as if you were out of the woods; you're a soldier still, John Andrews." The words formed themselves in his mind as vividly as if he had spoken them. He smiled bitterly and settled himself again to watch silhouettes of trees and hedges and houses and hillsides fleeing against the dark sky.

When he awoke the sky was grey. The train was moving slowly, clattering loudly over switches, through a town of wet slate roofs that rose in fantastic patterns of shadow above the blue mist. Walters was smoking a cigarette.

"God! These French trains are rotten," he said when he noticed that Andrews was awake. "The most inefficient country I ever was in anyway."

"Inefficiency be damned," broke in Andrews, jumping up and stretching himself. He opened the window. "The heating's too damned efficient. . . . I think we're near Paris."

The cold air, with a flavor of mist in it, poured into the stuffy compartment. Every breath was joy. Andrews felt a crazy buoyancy bubbling up in him. The rumbling clatter of the train wheels sang in his ears. He threw himself on his back on the dusty blue seat and kicked his heels in the air like a colt.

"Liven up, for God's sake, man," he shouted. "We're getting near Paris."

"We are lucky bastards," said Walters, grinning, with the cigarette hanging out of the corner of his mouth. "I'm going to see if I can find the rest of the gang."

Andrews, alone in the compartment, found himself singing at the top of his lungs.

As the day brightened the mist lifted off the flat linden-green fields intersected by rows of leafless poplars. Salmon-colored houses with blue roofs wore already a faintly citified air. They passed brick-kilns and clay-quarries, with reddish puddles of water in the bottom of them; crossed a jade-green river where a long file of canal boats with bright paint on their prows moved slowly. The engine whistled shrilly. They clattered through a small freight yard, and rows of suburban houses began to form, at first chaotically in broad patches of garden-land, and then in orderly ranks with streets between and shops at the corners. A dark-grey dripping wall rose up suddenly and blotted out the view. The train slowed down and went through several stations crowded with people on their way to work,—ordinary people in varied clothes with only here and there a blue or khaki uniform. Then there was more dark-grey wall, and the obscurity of wide bridges under which dusty oil lamps burned orange and red, making a gleam on the wet wall above them, and where the wheels clanged loudly. More freight yards and the train pulled slowly past other trains full of faces and silhouettes of people, to stop with a jerk in a station. And Andrews was standing on the grey cement platform, sniffing smells of lumber and merchandise and steam. His ungainly pack and blanket-roll he carried on his shoulder like a cross. He had left his rifle and cartridge belt carefully tucked out of sight under the seat.

Walters and five other men straggled along the platform towards him, carrying or dragging their packs.

There was a look of apprehension on Walters's face.

"Well, what do we do now?" he said.

"Do!" cried Andrews, and he burst out laughing.

*

Prostrate bodies in olive drab hid the patch of tender green grass by the roadside. The company was resting. Chrisfield sat on a stump morosely whittling at a stick with a pocket knife. Judkins was stretched out beside him.

"What the hell do they make us do this damn hikin' for, Corp?"

"Guess they're askeered we'll forgit how to walk."

"Well, ain't it better than loafin' around yer billets all day, thinkin' an' cursin' an' wishin' ye was home?" spoke up the man who sat the other side, pounding down the tobacco in his pipe with a thick forefinger.

"It makes me sick, trampin' round this way in ranks all day with the goddam frawgs starin' at us an' . . ."

"They're laughin' at us, I bet," broke in another voice.

"We'll be movin' soon to the Army o' Occupation," said Chrisfield cheerfully. "In Germany it'll be a reglar picnic."

"An' d'you know what that means?" burst out Judkins, sitting bolt upright. "D'you know how long the troops is goin' to stay in Germany? Fifteen years."

"Gawd, they couldn't keep us there that long, man."

"They can do anythin' they goddam please with us. We're the guys as is gettin' the raw end of this deal. It ain't the same with an' edicated guy like Andrews or Sergeant Coffin or them. They can suck around after 'Y' men, an' officers an' get on the inside track, an' all we can do is stand up an' salute an' say 'Yes, lootenant' an' 'No, lootenant' an' let 'em ride us all they goddam please. Ain't that gospel truth, corporal?"

"Ah guess you're right, Judkie; we gits the raw end of the stick."

"That damn yellar dawg Andrews goes to Paris an' gets schoolin' free an' all that."

"Hell, Andy waren't yellar, Judkins."

"Well, why did he go bellyachin' around all the time like he knew more'n the lootenant did?"

"Ah reckon he did," said Chrisfield.

"Anyway, you can't say that those guys who went to Paris did a goddam thing more'n any the rest of us did. . . . Gawd, I ain't even had a leave yet."

"Well, it ain't no use crabbin'."

"No, onct we git home an' folks know the way we've been

treated, there'll be a great ole investigation. I can tell you that," said one of the new men.

"It makes you mad, though, to have something like that put over on ye. . . . Think of them guys in Paris, havin' a hell of a time with wine an' women, an' we stay out here an' clean our guns an' drill. . . . God, I'd like to get even with some of them guys."

The whistle blew. The patch of grass became unbroken green again as the men lined up along the side of the road.

"Fall in!" called the Sergeant.

"Atten-shun!"

"Right dress!"

"Front! God, you guys haven't got no snap in yer. . . . Stick yer belly in, you. You know better than to stand like that."

"Squads, right! March! Hep, hep, hep!"

The Company tramped off along the muddy road. Their steps were all the same length. Their arms swung in the same rhythm. Their faces were cowed into the same expression, their thoughts were the same. The tramp, tramp of their steps died away along the road.

Birds were singing among the budding trees. The young grass by the roadside kept the marks of the soldiers' bodies.

PART FIVE
THE WORLD OUTSIDE

I

A NDREWS, and six other men from his division, sat at a table outside the café opposite the Gare de l'Est. He leaned back in his chair with a cup of coffee lifted, looking across it at the stone houses with many balconies. Steam, scented of milk and coffee, rose from the cup as he sipped from it. His ears were full of a rumble of traffic and a clacking of heels as people walked briskly by along the damp pavements. For a while he did not hear what the men he was sitting with were saying. They talked and laughed, but he looked beyond their khaki uniforms and their boat-shaped caps unconsciously. He was taken up with the smell of the coffee and of the mist. A little rusty sunshine shone on the table of the café and on the thin varnish of wet mud that covered the asphalt pavement. Looking down the Avenue, away from the station, the houses, dark grey tending to greenish in the shadow and to violet in the sun, faded into a soft haze of distance. Dull gilt lettering glittered along black balconies. In the foreground were men and women walking briskly, their cheeks whipped a little into color by the rawness of the morning. The sky was a faintly roseate grey.

Walters was speaking:

"The first thing I want to see is the Eiffel Tower."

"Why d'you want to see that?" said the small sergeant with a black mustache and rings round his eyes like a monkey.

"Why, man, don't you know that everything begins from the Eiffel Tower? If it weren't for the Eiffel Tower, there wouldn't be any sky-scrapers. . . ."

"How about the Flatiron Building and Brooklyn Bridge? They were built before the Eiffel Tower, weren't they?" interrupted the man from New York.

"The Eiffel Tower's the first piece of complete girder construction in the whole world," reiterated Walters dogmatically.

"First thing I'm going to do's go to the Folies Berdjairs; me for the w.w.'s."

"Better lay off the wild women, Bill," said Walters.

"I ain't goin' to look at a woman," said the sergeant with the black mustache. "I guess I seen enough women in my time, anyway. . . . The war's over, anyway."

"You just wait, kid, till you fasten your lamps on a real Parizianne," said a burly, unshaven man with a corporal's stripes on his arm, roaring with laughter.

Andrews lost track of the talk again, staring dreamily through half-closed eyes down the long straight street, where greens and violets and browns merged into a bluish grey monochrome at a little distance. He wanted to be alone, to wander at random through the city, to stare dreamily at people and things, to talk by chance to men and women, to sink his life into the misty sparkling life of the streets. The smell of the mist brought a memory to his mind. For a long while he groped for it, until suddenly he remembered his dinner with Henslowe and the faces of the boy and girl he had talked to on the Butte. He must find Henslowe at once. A second's fierce resentment went through him against all these people about him. Christ! He must get away from them all; his freedom had been hard enough won; he must enjoy it to the uttermost.

"Say, I'm going to stick to you, Andy." Walters's voice broke into his reverie. "I'm going to appoint you the corps of interpreters."

Andrews laughed.

"D'you know the way to the School Headquarters?"

"The R.T.O. said take the subway."

"I'm going to walk," said Andrews.

"You'll get lost, won't you?"

"No danger, worse luck," said Andrews, getting to his feet. "I'll see you fellows at the School Headquarters, whatever those are. . . . So long."

"Say, Andy, I'll wait for you there," Walters called after him.

Andrews darted down a side street. He could hardly keep from shouting aloud when he found himself alone, free, with days and days ahead of him to work and think, gradually to rid his limbs of the stiff attitudes of the automaton. The smell of the streets, and the mist, indefinably poignant, rose like incense smoke in fantastic spirals through his brain, making him hungry and dazzled, making his arms and legs feel lithe and as ready for delight as a crouching cat for a spring. His heavy shoes beat out a dance as they clattered on the wet pavements under his springy steps. He was walking very fast, stopping suddenly now and then to look at the greens and oranges and crimsons of vegetables in a push cart, to catch a vista down intricate streets, to look into the rich brown obscurity of a small wine shop where workmen stood at the counter sipping white wine. Oval, delicate faces, bearded faces of men, slightly gaunt faces of young women, red cheeks of boys, wrinkled faces of old women, whose ugliness seemed to have hidden in it, stirringly, all the beauty of youth and the tragedy of lives that had been lived; the faces of the people he passed moved him like rhythms of an orchestra. After much walking, turning always down the street which looked pleasantest, he came to an oval with a statue of a pompous personage on a ramping horse. "Place des Victoires," he read the name, which gave him a faint tinge of amusement. He looked quizzically at the heroic features of the sun king and walked off laughing. "I suppose they did it better in those days, the grand manner," he muttered. And his delight redoubled in rubbing shoulders with the people whose effigies would never appear astride ramping-eared horses in squares built to commemorate victories. He came out on a broad straight avenue, where there were many American officers he had to salute, and M.P.'s and shops with wide plate-glass windows, full of objects that had a shiny, expensive look. "Another case of victories," he thought, as he went off into a side street, taking with him a glimpse of the bluish-grey pile of the Opera, with its pompous windows and its naked bronze ladies holding lamps.

He was in a narrow street full of hotels and fashionable barber shops, from which came an odor of cosmopolitan perfumery, of casinos and ballrooms and diplomatic receptions, when he noticed an American officer coming towards him, reeling a little,—a tall, elderly man with a red face and a bottle nose. He saluted.

The officer stopped still, swaying from side to side, and said in a whining voice:

"Shonny, d'you know where Henry'sh Bar is?"

"No, I don't, Major," said Andrews, who felt himself enveloped in an odor of cocktails.

"You'll help me to find it, shonny, won't you? . . . It's dreadful not to be able to find it. . . . I've got to meet Lootenant Trevors in Henry'sh Bar." The major steadied himself by putting a hand on Andrews' shoulder. A civilian passed them.

"Dee-donc," shouted the major after him, "Dee-donc, Monshier, ou ay Henry'sh Bar?"

The man walked on without answering.

"Now isn't that like a frog, not to understand his own language?" said the major.

"But there's Henry's Bar, right across the street," said Andrews suddenly.

"Bon, bon," said the major.

They crossed the street and went in. At the bar the major, still clinging to Andrews' shoulder, whispered in his ear: "I'm A.W.O.L., shee? . . . Shee? . . . Whole damn Air Service is A.W.O.L. Have a drink with me. . . . You enlisted man? Nobody cares here. . . . Warsh over, Sonny. . . . Democracy is shafe for the world."

Andrews was just raising a champagne cocktail to his lips, looking with amusement at the crowd of American officers and civilians who crowded into the small mahogany barroom, when a voice behind him drawled out:

"I'll be damned!"

Andrews turned and saw Henslowe's brown face and small silky mustache. He abandoned his major to his fate.

"God, I'm glad to see you. . . . I was afraid you hadn't been able to work it." . . . said Henslowe slowly, stuttering a little.

"I'm about crazy, Henny, with delight. I just got in a couple of hours ago. . . ." Laughing, interrupting each other, they chattered in broken sentences.

"But how in the name of everything did you get here?"

"With the major," said Andrews, laughing.

"What the devil?"

"Yes; that major," whispered Andrews in his friend's ear, "rather the worse for wear, asked me to lead him to Henry's Bar and just fed me a cocktail in the memory of Democracy, late defunct. . . . But what are you doing here? It's not exactly . . . exotic."

"I came to see a man who was going to tell me how I could get to Rumania with the Red Cross. . . . But that can wait. . . . Let's get out of here. God, I was afraid you hadn't made it."

"I had to crawl on my belly and lick people's boots to do it. . . . God, it was low! . . . But here I am."

They were out in the street again, walking and gesticulating.

"But 'Libertad, Libertad, allons, ma femme!' as Walt Whitman would have said," shouted Andrews.

"It's one grand and glorious feeling. . . . I've been here three days. My section's gone home; God bless them."

"But what do you have to do?"

"Do? Nothing," cried Henslowe. "Not a blooming bloody goddam thing! In fact, it's no use trying . . . the whole thing is such a mess you couldn't do anything if you wanted to."

"I want to go and talk to people at the Schola Cantorum."

"There'll be time for that. You'll never make anything out of music if you get serious-minded about it."

"Then, last but not least, I've got to get some money from somewhere."

"Now you're talking!" Henslowe pulled a burnt leather pocket book out of the inside of his tunic. "Monaco," he said, tapping the pocket book, which was engraved with a pattern of dull red flowers. He pursed up his lips and pulled out some hundred franc notes, which he pushed into Andrews's hand.

"Give me one of them," said Andrews.

"All or none. . . . They last about five minutes each."

"But it's so damn much to pay back."

"Pay it back—heavens! . . . Here take it and stop your talking. I probably won't have it again, so you'd better make hay this time. I warn you it'll be spent by the end of the week."

"All right. I'm dead with hunger."

"Let's sit down on the Boulevard and think about where we'll have lunch to celebrate Miss Libertad. . . . But let's not call her that, sounds like Liverpool, Andy, a horrid place."

"How about Freiheit?" said Andrews, as they sat down in basket chairs in the reddish yellow sunlight.

"Treasonable . . . off with your head."

"But think of it, man," said Andrews, "the butchery's over, and you and I and everybody else will soon be human beings again. Human; all too human!"

"No more than eighteen wars going," muttered Henslowe.

"I haven't seen any papers for an age. . . . How do you mean?"

"People are fighting to beat the cats everywhere except on the western front," said Henslowe. "But that's where I come in. The Red Cross sends supply trains to keep them at it. . . . I'm going to Russia if I can work it."

"But what about the Sorbonne?"

"The Sorbonne can go to Ballyhack."

"But, Henny, I'm going to croak on your hands if you don't take me somewhere to get some food."

"Do you want a solemn place with red plush or with salmon pink brocade?"

"Why have a solemn place at all?"

"Because solemnity and good food go together. It's only a religious restaurant that has a proper devotion to the belly. O, I know, we'll go over to Brooklyn."

"Where?"

"To the Rive Gauche. I know a man who insists on calling it Brooklyn. Awfully funny man . . . never been sober in his life. You must meet him."

"Oh, I want to. . . . It's a dog's age since I met anyone new, except you. I can't live without having a variegated crowd about, can you?"

"You've got that right on this boulevard. Serbs, French, English, Americans, Australians, Rumanians, Tcheco-Slovaks; God, is there any uniform that isn't here? . . . I tell you, Andy, the war's been a great thing for the people who knew how to take advantage of it. Just look at their puttees."

"I guess they'll know how to make a good thing of the Peace too."

"Oh, that's going to be the best yet. . . . Come along. Let's be little devils and take a taxi."

"This certainly is the main street of Cosmopolis."

They threaded their way through the crowd, full of uniforms and glitter and bright colors, that moved in two streams up and down the wide sidewalk between the cafés and the boles of the bare trees. They climbed into a taxi, and lurched fast through streets where, in the misty sunlight, grey-green and grey-violet mingled with blues and pale lights as the colors mingle in a pigeon's breast feathers. They passed the leafless gardens of the Tuileries on one side, and the great inner Courts of the Louvre, with their purple mansard roofs and their high chimneys on the other, and saw for a second the river, dull jade green, and the plane trees splotched with brown and cream color along the quais, before they were lost in the narrow brownish-grey streets of the old quarters.

"This is Paris; that was Cosmopolis," said Henslowe.

"I'm not particular, just at present," cried Andrews gaily.

The square in front of the Odéon was a splash of white and the collonade a blur of darkness as the cab swerved round the corner and along the edge of the Luxembourg, where, through the black iron fence, many brown and reddish colors in the intricate patterns of leafless twigs opened here and there on statues and balustrades and vistas of misty distances. The cab stopped with a jerk.

"This is the Place des Médicis," said Henslowe.

At the end of a slanting street looking very flat, through the haze, was the dome of the Panthéon. In the middle of the square between the yellow trams and the green low busses, was a quiet pool, where the shadow of horizontals of the house fronts was reflected.

They sat beside the window looking out at the square.

Henslowe ordered.

"Remember how sentimental history books used to talk about prisoners who were let out after years in dungeons, not being able to stand it, and going back to their cells?"

"D'you like sole meunière?"

"Anything, or rather everything! But take it from me, that's all rubbish. Honestly I don't think I've ever been happier in

my life. . . . D'you know, Henslowe, there's something in
you that is afraid to be happy."

"Don't be morbid. . . . There's only one real evil in the
world: being somewhere without being able to get away. . . .
I ordered beer. This is the only place in Paris where it's fit to
drink."

"And I'm going to every blooming concert . . . Colonne
—Lamoureux on Sunday, I know that. . . . The only evil in
the world is not to be able to hear music or to make it. . . .
These oysters are fit for Lucullus."

"Why not say fit for John Andrews and Bob Henslowe,
damn it? . . . Why the ghosts of poor old dead Romans
should be dragged in every time a man eats an oyster, I don't
see. We're as fine specimens as they were. I swear I shan't let
any old turned-to-clay Lucullus outlive me, even if I've never
eaten a lamprey."

"And why should you eat a lamp-chimney, Bob?" came a
hoarse voice beside them.

Andrews looked up into a round, white face with large grey
eyes hidden behind thick steel-rimmed spectacles. Except for
the eyes, the face had a vaguely Chinese air.

"Hello, Heinz! Mr. Andrews, Mr. Heineman," said
Henslowe.

"Glad to meet you," said Heineman in a jovially hoarse
voice. "You guys seem to be overeating, to reckon by the way
things are piled up on the table." Through the hoarseness Andrews could detect a faint Yankee tang in Heineman's voice.

"You'd better sit down and help us," said Henslowe.

"Sure. . . . D'you know my name for this guy?" He
turned to Andrews. . . ."Sinbad!"

> "Sinbad was in bad in Tokio and Rome,
>   In bad in Trinidad
>   And twice as bad at home."

He sang the words loudly, waving a bread stick to keep time.

"Shut up, Heinz, or you'll get us run out of here the way
you got us run out of the Olympia that night."

They both laughed.

"An' d'you remember Monsieur Le Guy with his coat?"

"Do I? God!" They laughed till the tears ran down their

cheeks. Heineman took off his glasses and wiped them. He turned to Andrews.

"Oh, Paris is the best yet. First absurdity: the Peace Conference and its nine hundred and ninety-nine branches. Second absurdity: spies. Third: American officers A.W.O.L. Fourth: The seven sisters sworn to slay." He broke out laughing again, his chunky body rolling about on the chair.

"What are they?"

"Three of them have sworn to slay Sinbad, and four of them have sworn to slay me. . . . But that's too complicated to tell at lunch time. . . . Eight: there are the lady relievers, Sinbad's specialty. Ninth: there's Sinbad. . . ."

"Shut up, Heinz, you're getting me maudlin," spluttered Henslowe.

"O Sinbad was in bad all around,"

chanted Heineman. "But no one's given me anything to drink," he said suddenly in a petulant voice. "Garçon, une bouteille de Macon, pour un Cadet de Gascogne. . . . What's the next? It ends with vergogne. You've seen the play, haven't you? Greatest play going. . . . Seen it twice sober and seven other times."

"Cyrano de Bergerac?"

"That's it. Nous sommes les Cadets de Gascogne, rhymes with ivrogne and sans vergogne. . . . You see I work in the Red Cross. . . . You know Sinbad, old Peterson's a brick. . . . I'm supposed to be taking photographs of tubercular children at this minute. . . . The noblest of my professions is that of artistic photographer. . . . Borrowed the photographs from the rickets man. So I have nothing to do for three months and five hundred francs travelling expenses. Oh, children, my only prayer is 'give us this day our red worker's permit' and the Red Cross does the rest." Heineman laughed till the glasses rang on the table. He took off his glasses and wiped them with a rueful air.

"So now I call the Red Cross the Cadets!" cried Heineman, his voice a thin shriek from laughter.

Andrews was drinking his coffee in little sips, looking out of the window at the people that passed. An old woman with a stand of flowers sat on a small cane chair at the corner. The

pink and yellow and blue-violet shades of the flowers seemed
to intensify the misty straw color and azured grey of the wintry sun and shadow of the streets. A girl in a tight-fitting
black dress and black hat stopped at the stand to buy a bunch
of pale yellow daisies, and then walked slowly past the window of the restaurant in the direction of the gardens. Her
ivory face and slender body and her very dark eyes sent a sudden flush through Andrews's whole frame as he looked at her.
The black erect figure disappeared in the gate of the gardens.

Andrews got to his feet suddenly.

"I've got to go," he said in a strange voice. . . . "I just remember a man was waiting for me at the School Headquarters."

"Let him wait."

"Why, you haven't had a liqueur yet," cried Heineman.

"No . . . but where can I meet you people later?"

"Café de Rohan at five . . . opposite the Palais Royal."

"You'll never find it."

"Yes I will," said Andrews.

"Palais Royal metro station," they shouted after him as he
dashed out of the door.

He hurried into the gardens. Many people sat on benches
in the frail sunlight. Children in bright-colored clothes ran
about chasing hoops. A woman paraded a bunch of toy balloons in carmine and green and purple, like a huge bunch of
parti-colored grapes inverted above her head. Andrews walked
up and down the alleys, scanning faces. The girl had disappeared. He leaned against a grey balustrade and looked down
into the empty pond where traces of the explosion of a Bertha
still subsisted. He was telling himself that he was a fool. That
even if he had found her he could not have spoken to her; just
because he was free for a day or two from the army he needn't
think the age of gold had come back to earth. Smiling at the
thought, he walked across the gardens, wandered through
some streets of old houses in grey and white stucco with slate
mansard roofs and fantastic complications of chimney-pots till
he came out in front of a church with a new classic façade of
huge columns that seemed toppling by their own weight.

He asked a woman selling newspapers what the church's
name was.

"Mais, Monsieur, c'est Saint Sulpice," said the woman in a surprised tone.

Saint Sulpice. Manon's songs came to his head, and the sentimental melancholy of eighteenth century Paris with its gambling houses in the Palais Royal where people dishonored themselves in the presence of their stern Catonian fathers, and its billets doux written at little gilt tables, and its coaches lumbering in covered with mud from the provinces through the Porte d'Orleans and the Porte de Versailles; the Paris of Diderot and Voltaire and Jean-Jacques, with its muddy streets and its ordinaries where one ate bisques and larded pullets and soufflés; a Paris full of mouldy gilt magnificence, full of pompous ennui of the past and insane hope of the future.

He walked down a narrow, smoky street full of antique shops and old bookshops and came out unexpectedly on the river opposite the statue of Voltaire. The name on the corner was quai Malaquais. Andrews crossed and looked down for a long time at the river. Opposite, behind a lacework of leafless trees, were the purplish roofs of the Louvre with their high peaks and their ranks and ranks of chimneys; behind him the old houses of the quai and the wing, topped by a balustrade with great grey stone urns of a domed building of which he did not know the name. Barges were coming upstream, the dense green water spuming under their blunt bows, towed by a little black tugboat with its chimney bent back to pass under the bridges. The tug gave a thin shrill whistle. Andrews started walking downstream. He crossed by the bridge at the corner of the Louvre, turned his back on the arch Napoleon built to receive the famous horses from St. Marc's,—a pinkish pastry-like affair—and walked through the Tuileries which were full of people strolling about or sitting in the sun, of doll-like children and nursemaids with elaborate white caps, of fluffy little dogs straining at the ends of leashes. Suddenly a peaceful sleepiness came over him. He sat down in the sun on a bench, watching, hardly seeing them, the people who passed to and fro casting long shadows. Voices and laughter came very softly to his ears above the distant stridency of traffic. From far away he heard for a few moments notes of a military band playing a march. The shadows of the trees were faint blue-grey in the ruddy yellow gravel. Shadows of people kept passing and repassing across them. He felt very languid and happy.

Suddenly he started up; he had been dozing. He asked an old man with a beautifully pointed white beard the way to rue du Faubourg St. Honoré.

After losing his way a couple of times, he walked listlessly up some marble steps where a great many men in khaki were talking. Leaning against the doorpost was Walters. As he drew near Andrews heard him saying to the man next to him:

"Why, the Eiffel tower was the first piece of complete girder construction ever built. . . . That's the first thing a feller who's wide awake ought to see."

"Tell me the Opery's the grandest thing to look at," said the man next it.

"If there's wine an' women there, me for it."

"An' don't forget the song."

"But that isn't interesting like the Eiffel tower is," persisted Walters.

"Say, Walters, I hope you haven't been waiting for me," stammered Andrews.

"No, I've been waiting in line to see the guy about courses. . . . I want to start this thing right."

"I guess I'll see them tomorrow," said Andrews.

"Say have you done anything about a room, Andy? Let's you and me be bunkies."

"All right. . . . But maybe you won't want to room where I do, Walters."

"Where's that? In the Latin Quarter? . . . You bet. I want to see some French life while I am about it."

"Well, it's too late to get a room to-day."

"I'm going to the 'Y' tonight anyway."

"I'll get a fellow I know to put me up. . . . Then tomorrow, we'll see. Well, so long," said Andrews, moving away.

"Wait. I'm coming with you. . . . We'll walk around town together."

"All right," said Andrews.

The rabbit was rather formless, very fluffy and had a glance of madness in its pink eye with a black center. It hopped like a sparrow along the pavement, emitting a rubber tube from its back, which went up to a bulb in a man's hand which the man pressed to make the rabbit hop. Yet the rabbit had an air of organic completeness. Andrews laughed inordinately when he first saw it. The vendor, who had a basket full of other such rabbits on his arm, saw Andrews laughing and drew timidly near to the table; he had a pink face with little, sensitive lips rather like a real rabbit's, and large frightened eyes of a wan brown.

"Do you make them yourself?" asked Andrews, smiling.

The man dropped his rabbit on the table with a negligent air.

"Oh, oui, Monsieur, d'après la nature."

He made the rabbit turn a summersault by suddenly pressing the bulb hard. Andrews laughed and the rabbit man laughed.

"Think of a big strong man making his living that way," said Walters, disgusted.

"I do it all . . . de matière première au profit de l'accapareur," said the rabbit man.

"Hello, Andy . . . late as hell. . . . I'm sorry," said Henslowe, dropping down into a chair beside them. Andrews introduced Walters, the rabbit man took off his hat, bowed to the company and went off, making the rabbit hop before him along the edge of the curbstone.

"What's happened to Heineman?"

"Here he comes now," said Henslowe.

An open cab had driven up to the curb in front of the café. In it sat Heineman with a broad grin on his face and beside him a woman in a salmon-colored dress, ermine furs and an emerald-green hat. The cab drove off and Heineman, still grinning, walked up to the table.

"Where's the lion cub?" asked Henslowe.

"They say it's got pneumonia."

"Mr. Heineman. Mr. Walters."

The grin left Heineman's face; he said: "How do you do?" curtly, cast a furious glance at Andrews and settled himself in a chair.

The sun had set. The sky was full of lilac and bright purple and carmine. Among the deep blue shadows lights were coming on, primrose-colored street lamps, violet arc lights, ruddy sheets of light poured out of shop windows.

"Let's go inside. I'm cold as hell," said Heineman crossly,

and they filed in through the revolving door, followed by a waiter with their drinks.

"I've been in the Red Cross all afternoon, Andy. . . . I think I am going to work that Roumania business. . . . Want to come?" said Henslowe in Andrews' ear.

"If I can get hold of a piano and some lessons and the concerts keep up you won't be able to get me away from Paris with wild horses. No, sir, I want to see what Paris is like. . . . It's going to my head so it'll be weeks before I know what I think about it."

"Don't think about it. . . . Drink," growled Heineman, scowling savagely.

"That's two things I'm going to keep away from in Paris; drink and women. . . . And you can't have one without the other," said Walters.

"True enough. . . . You sure do need them both," said Heineman.

Andrews was not listening to their talk; twirling the stem of his glass of vermouth in his fingers, he was thinking of the Queen of Sheba slipping down from off the shoulders of her elephant, glistening fantastically with jewels in the light of crackling, resinous torches. Music was seeping up through his mind as the water seeps into a hole dug in the sand of the seashore. He could feel all through his body the tension of rhythms and phrases taking form, not quite to be seized as yet, still hovering on the borderland of consciousness. *From the girl at the cross-roads singing under her street-lamp to the patrician pulling roses to pieces from the height of her litter. . . . All the imaginings of your desire. . . .* He thought of the girl with skin like old ivory he had seen in the Place de Medicis. The Queen of Sheba's face was like that now in his imaginings, quiet and inscrutable. A sudden cymbal-clanging of joy made his heart thump hard. He was free now of the imaginings of his desire, to loll all day at café tables watching the tables move in changing patterns before him, to fill his mind and body with a reverberation of all the rhythms of men and women moving in the frieze of life before his eyes; no more like wooden automatons knowing only the motions of the drill manual, but supple and varied, full of force and tragedy.

"For Heaven's sake let's beat it from here. . . . Gives me a pain this place does." Heineman beat his fist on the table.

"All right," said Andrews, getting up with a yawn.

Henslowe and Andrews walked off, leaving Walters to follow them with Heineman.

"We're going to dine at Le Rat qui Danse," said Henslowe, "an awfully funny place. . . . We just have time to walk there comfortably with an appetite."

They followed the long dimly-lighted Rue de Richelieu to the Boulevards, where they drifted a little while with the crowd. The glaring lights seemed to powder the air with gold. Cafés and the tables outside were crowded. There was an odor of vermouth and coffee and perfume and cigarette smoke mixed with the fumes of burnt gasoline from taxicabs.

"Isn't this mad?" said Andrews.

"It's always carnival at seven on the Grands Boulevards."

They started climbing the steep streets to Montmartre. At a corner they passed a hard-faced girl with rouge-smeared lips and over-powdered cheeks, laughing on the arm of an American soldier, who had a sallow face and dull-green eyes that glittered in the slanting light of a street-lamp.

"Hello, Stein," said Andrews.

"Who's that?"

"A fellow from our division, got here with me this morning."

"He's got curious lips for a Jew," said Henslowe.

At the fork of two slanting streets, they went into a restaurant that had small windows pasted over with red paper, through which the light came dimly. Inside were crowded oak tables and oak wainscoting with a shelf round the top, on which were shell-cans, a couple of skulls, several cracked majolica plates and a number of stuffed rats. The only people there were a fat woman and a man with long grey hair and beard who sat talking earnestly over two small glasses in the center of the room. A husky-looking waitress with a Dutch cap and apron hovered near the inner door from which came a great smell of fish frying in olive oil.

"The cook here's from Marseilles," said Henslowe, as they settled themselves at a table for four.

"I wonder if the rest of them lost the way," said Andrews.

"More likely old Heinz stopped to have a drink," said Henslowe. "Let's have some hors d'œuvre while we are waiting."

The waitress brought a collection of boat-shaped plates of red salads and yellow salads and green salads and two little wooden tubs with herrings and anchovies.

Henslowe stopped her as she was going, saying:

"Rien de plus?"

The waitress contemplated the array with a tragic air, her arms folded over her ample bosom.

"Que voulez-vous, Monsieur, c'est l'armistice."

"The greatest fake about all this war business is the peace. I tell you, not till the hors d'œuvre has been restored to its proper abundance and variety will I admit that the war's over."

The waitress tittered.

"Things aren't what they used to be," she said, going back to the kitchen.

Heineman burst into the restaurant at that moment, slamming the door behind him so that the glass rang, and the fat woman and the hairy man started violently in their chairs. He tumbled into a place, grinning broadly.

"And what have you done to Walters?"

Heineman wiped his glasses meticulously.

"Oh, he died of drinking raspberry shrub," he said. . . . "Dee-dong peteet du ving de Bourgogne," he shouted towards the waitress in his nasal French. Then he added: "Le Guy is coming in a minute, I just met him."

The restaurant was gradually filling up with men and women of very various costumes, with a good sprinkling of Americans in uniform and out.

"God I hate people who don't drink," cried Heineman, pouring out wine. "A man who don't drink just cumbers the earth."

"How are you going to take it in America when they have prohibition?"

"Don't talk about it; here's le Guy. I wouldn't have him know I belong to a nation that prohibits good liquor. . . . Monsieur le Guy, Monsieur Henslowe at Monsieur Andrews," he continued getting up ceremoniously. A little man with twirled mustaches and a small vandyke beard sat down at the fourth place. He had a faintly red nose and little twinkling eyes.

"How glad I am," he said, exposing his starched cuffs with a curious gesture, "to have some one to dine with! When one begins to get old loneliness is impossible. It is only youth that dares think. . . . Afterwards one has only one thing to think about: old age."

"There's always work," said Andrews.

"Slavery. Any work is slavery. What is the use of freeing your intellect if you sell yourself again to the first bidder?"

"Rot!" said Heineman, pouring out from a new bottle.

Andrews had begun to notice the girl who sat at the next table, in front of a pale young soldier in French-blue who resembled her extraordinarily. She had high cheek bones and a forehead in which the modelling of the skull showed through the transparent, faintly-olive skin. Her heavy chestnut hair was coiled carelessly at the back of her head. She spoke very quietly, and pressed her lips together when she smiled. She ate quickly and neatly, like a cat.

The restaurant had gradually filled up with people. The waitress and the patron, a fat man with a wide red sash coiled tightly round his waist, moved with difficulty among the crowded tables. A woman at a table in the corner, with dead white skin and drugged staring eyes, kept laughing hoarsely, leaning her head, in a hat with bedraggled white plumes, against the wall. There was a constant jingle of plates and glasses, and an oily fume of food and women's clothes and wine.

"D'you want to know what I really did with your friend?" said Heineman, leaning towards Andrews.

"I hope you didn't push him into the Seine."

"It was damn impolite. . . . But hell, it was damn impolite of him not to drink. . . . No use wasting time with a man who don't drink. I took him into a café and asked him to wait while I telephoned. I guess he's still waiting. One of the whoreiest cafés on the whole Boulevard Clichy." Heineman laughed uproariously and started explaining it in nasal French to M. le Guy.

Andrews flushed with annoyance for a moment, but soon started laughing. Heineman had started singing again.

> "O, Sinbad was in bad in Tokio and Rome,
>   In bad in Trinidad
>   And twice as bad at home,
>   O, Sinbad was in bad all around!"

Everybody clapped. The white-faced woman in the corner cried "Bravo, Bravo," in a shrill nightmare voice.

Heineman bowed, his big grinning face bobbing up and down like the face of a Chinese figure in porcelain.

"Lui est Sinbad," he cried, pointing with a wide gesture towards Henslowe.

"Give 'em some more, Heinz. Give them some more," said Henslowe, laughing.

> "Big brunettes with long stelets
>   On the shores of Italee,
>   Dutch girls with golden curls
>   Beside the Zuyder Zee . . ."

Everybody cheered again; Andrews kept looking at the girl at the next table, whose face was red from laughter. She had a handkerchief pressed to her mouth, and kept saying in a low voice:

"O, qu'il est drôle, celui-là. . . . O qu'il est drôle."

Heineman picked up a glass and waved it in the air before drinking it off. Several people got up and filled it up from their bottles with white wine and red. The French soldier at the next table pulled an army canteen from under his chair and hung it round Heineman's neck.

Heineman, his face crimson, bowed to all sides, more like a Chinese porcelain figure than ever, and started singing in all solemnity this time.

> "Hulas and hulas would pucker up their lips,
>   He fell for their ball-bearing hips
>   For they were pips . . ."

His chunky body swayed to the ragtime. The woman in the corner kept time with long white arms raised above her head.

"Bet she's a snake charmer," said Henslowe.

"O, wild woman loved that child
He would drive ten women wild!
O, Sinbad was in bad all around!"

Heineman waved his arms, pointed again to Henslowe, and sank into his chair saying in the tones of a Shakespearean actor: "C'est lui Sinbad."

The girl hid her face on the tablecloth, shaken with laughter. Andrews could hear a convulsed little voice saying:

"O qu'il est rigolo. . . ."

Heineman took off the canteen and handed it back to the French soldier.

"Merci, Camarade," he said solemnly.

"Eh bien, Jeanne, c'est temps de ficher le camp," said the French soldier to the girl. They got up. He shook hands with the Americans. Andrews caught the girl's eye and they both started laughing convulsively again. Andrews noticed how erect and supple she walked as his eyes followed her to the door.

Andrews's party followed soon after.

"We've got to hurry if we want to get to the Lapin Agile before closing . . . and I've got to have a drink," said Heineman, still talking in his stagey Shakespearean voice.

"Have you ever been on the stage?" asked Andrews.

"What stage, sir? I'm in the last stages now, sir. . . . I am an artistic photographer and none other. . . . Moki and I are going into the movies together when they decide to have peace."

"Who's Moki?"

"Moki Hadj is the lady in the salmon-colored dress," said Henslowe, in a loud stage whisper in Andrews's ear. "They have a lion cub named Bubu."

"Our first born," said Heineman with a wave of the hand.

The streets were deserted. A thin ray of moonlight, bursting now and then through the heavy clouds, lit up low houses and roughly-cobbled streets and the flights of steps with rare dim lamps bracketed in house walls that led up to the Butte.

There was a gendarme in front of the door of the Lapin Agile. The street was still full of groups that had just come out, American officers and Y.M.C.A. women with a sprinkling of the inhabitants of the region.

"Now look, we're late," groaned Heineman in a tearful voice.

"Never mind, Heinz," said Henslowe, "le Guy'll take us to see de Clocheville like he did last time, n'est pas, le Guy?" Then Andrews heard him add, talking to a man he had not seen before, "Come along Aubrey, I'll introduce you later."

They climbed further up the hill. There was a scent of wet gardens in the air, entirely silent except for the clatter of their feet on the cobbles. Heineman was dancing a sort of a jig at the head of the procession. They stopped before a tall cadaverous house and started climbing a rickety wooden stairway.

"Talk about inside dope. . . . I got this from a man who's actually in the room when the Peace Conference meets." Andrews heard Aubrey's voice with a Chicago burr in the r's behind him in the stairs.

"Fine, let's hear it," said Henslowe.

"Did you say the Peace Conference took dope?" shouted Heineman, whose puffing could be heard as he climbed the dark stairs ahead of them.

"Shut up, Heinz."

They stumbled over a raised doorstep into a large garret room with a tile floor, where a tall lean man in a monastic-looking dressing gown of some brown material received them. The only candle made all their shadows dance fantastically on the slanting white walls as they moved about. One side of the room had three big windows, with an occasional cracked pane mended with newspaper, stretching from floor to ceiling. In front of them were two couches with rugs piled on them. On the opposite wall was a confused mass of canvases piled one against the other, leaning helter skelter against the slanting wall of the room.

> "C'est le bon vin, le bon vin,
> C'est la chanson du vin,"

chanted Heineman. Everybody settled themselves on couches. The lanky man in the brown dressing gown brought a table out of the shadow, put some black bottles and heavy glasses on it, and drew up a camp stool for himself.

"He lives that way. . . . They say he never goes out. Stays here and paints, and when friends come in, he feeds them wine and charges them double," said Henslowe. "That's how he lives."

The lanky man began taking bits of candle out of a drawer of the table and lighting them. Andrews saw that his feet and legs were bare below the frayed edge of the dressing gown. The candle light lit up the men's flushed faces and the crude banana yellows and arsenic greens of the canvases along the walls, against which jars full of paint brushes cast blurred shadows.

"I was going to tell you, Henny," said Aubrey, "the dope is that the President's going to leave the conference, going to call them all damn blackguards to their faces and walk out, with the band playing the 'Internationale.'"

"God, that's news," cried Andrews.

"If he does that he'll recognize the Soviets," said Henslowe. "Me for the first Red Cross Mission that goes to save starving Russia. . . . Gee, that's great.—I'll write you a postal from Moscow, Andy, if they haven't been abolished as delusions of the bourgeoisie."

"Hell, no. . . . I've got five hundred dollars' worth of Russian bonds that girl Vera gave me. . . . But worth five million, ten million, fifty million if the Czar gets back. . . . I'm backing the little white father," cried Heineman. "Anyway Moki says he's alive; that Savaroff's got him locked up in a suite in the Ritz. . . . And Moki knows."

"Moki knows a damn lot, I'll admit that," said Henslowe.

"But just think of it," said Aubrey, "that means world revolution with the United States at the head of it. What do you think of that?"

"Moki doesn't think so," said Heineman. "And Moki knows."

"She just knows what a lot of reactionary warlords tell her," said Aubrey. "This man I was talking with at the Crillon—I wish I could tell you his name—heard it directly from . . . Well, you know who." He turned to Henslowe, who smiled knowingly. "There's a mission in Russia at this minute making peace with Lenin."

"A goddam outrage!" cried Heineman, knocking a bottle

off the table. The lanky man picked up the pieces patiently, without comment.

"The new era is opening, men, I swear it is . . ." began Aubrey. "The old order is dissolving. It is going down under a weight of misery and crime. . . . This will be the first great gesture towards a newer and better world. There is no alternative. The chance will never come back. It is either for us to step courageously forward, or sink into unbelievable horrors of anarchy and civil war. . . . Peace or the dark ages again."

Andrews had felt for some time an uncontrollable sleepiness coming over him. He rolled himself in a rug and stretched out on the empty couch. The voices arguing, wrangling, enunciating emphatic phrases, dinned for a minute in his ears. He went to sleep.

When Andrews woke up he found himself staring at the cracked plaster of an unfamiliar ceiling. For some moments he could not guess where he was. Henslowe was sleeping, wrapped in another rug, on the couch beside him. Except for Henslowe's breathing, there was complete silence. Floods of silvery-grey light poured in through the wide windows, behind which Andrews could see a sky full of bright dove-colored clouds. He sat up carefully. Some time in the night he must have taken off his tunic and boots and puttees, which were on the floor beside the couch. The tables with the bottles had gone and the lanky man was nowhere to be seen.

Andrews went to the window in his stockinged feet. Paris was a slate-grey and dove-color lay spread out like a Turkish carpet, with a silvery band of mist where the river was, out of which the Eiffel Tower stood up like a man wading. Here and there blue smoke and brown spiralled up to lose itself in the faint canopy of brown fog that hung high above the houses. Andrews stood a long while leaning against the window frame, until he heard Henslowe's voice behind him:

"*Depuis le jour où je me suis donnée.*"

"You look like 'Louise.'"

Andrews turned round.

Henslowe was sitting on the edge of the bed with his hair in disorder, combing his little silky mustache with a pocket comb.

"Gee, I have a head," he said. "My tongue feels like a nutmeg grater. . . . Doesn't yours?"

"No. I feel like a fighting cock."

"What do you say we go down to the Seine and have a bath in Benny Franklin's bathtub?"

"Where's that? It sounds grand."

"Then we'll have the biggest breakfast ever."

"That's the right spirit. . . . Where's everybody gone to?"

"Old Heinz has gone to his Moki, I guess, and Aubrey's gone to collect more dope at the Crillon. He says four in the morning when the drunks come home is the prime time for a newspaper man."

"And the Monkish man?"

"Search me."

The streets were full of men and girls hurrying to work. Everything sparkled, had an air of being just scrubbed. They passed bakeries from which came a rich smell of fresh-baked bread. From cafés came whiffs of roasting coffee. They crossed through the markets that were full of heavy carts lumbering to and fro, and women with net bags full of vegetables. There was a pungent scent of crushed cabbage leaves and carrots and wet clay. The mist was raw and biting along the quais, and made the blood come into their cheeks and their hands stiff with cold.

The bathhouse was a huge barge with a house built on it in a lozenge shape. They crossed to it by a little gangplank on which were a few geraniums in pots. The attendant gave them two rooms side by side on the lower deck, painted grey, with steamed over windows, through which Andrews caught glimpses of hurrying green water. He stripped his clothes off quickly. The tub was of copper varnished with some white metal inside. The water flowed in through two copper swans' necks. When Andrews stepped into the hot green water, a little window in the partition flew open and Henslowe shouted in to him:

"Talk about modern conveniences. You can converse while you bathe!"

Andrews scrubbed himself jauntily with a square piece of pink soap, splashing the water about like a small boy. He stood up and lathered himself all over and then let himself slide into the water, which splashed out over the floor.

"Do you think you're a performing seal?" shouted Henslowe.

"It's all so preposterous," cried Andrews, going off into convulsions of laughter. "She has a lion cub named Bubu and Nicolas Romanoff lives in the Ritz, and the Revolution is scheduled for day after tomorrow at twelve noon."

"I'd put it about the first of May," answered Henslowe, amid a sound of splashing. "Gee, it'd be great to be a people's Commissary. . . . You could go and revolute the grand Llama of Thibet."

"O, it's too deliciously preposterous," cried Andrews, letting himself slide a second time into the bathtub.

II

Two M.P.'s passed outside the window. Andrews watched the yellow pigskin revolver cases until they were out of sight. He felt joyfully secure from them. The waiter, standing by the door with a napkin on his arm, gave him a sense of security so intense it made him laugh. On the marble table before him were a small glass of beer, a notebook full of ruled sheets of paper and a couple of yellow pencils. The beer, the color of topaz in the clear grey light that streamed in through the window, threw a pale yellow glow with a bright center on the table. Outside was the boulevard with a few people walking hurriedly. An empty market wagon passed now and then, rumbling loud. On a bench a woman in a black knitted shawl, with a bundle of newspapers in her knees, was counting sous with loving concentration.

Andrews looked at his watch. He had an hour before going to the Schola Cantorum.

He got to his feet, paid the waiter and strolled down the center of the boulevard, thinking smilingly of pages he had written, of pages he was going to write, filled with a sense of leisurely well-being. It was a grey morning with a little yellowish fog in the air. The pavements were damp, reflected women's dresses and men's legs and the angular outlines of taxicabs. From a flower stand with violets and red and pink carnations irregular blotches of color ran down into the brownish grey of the pavement. Andrews caught a faint smell of violets in the smell of the fog as he passed the flower stand and remembered suddenly that spring was coming. He would not miss a moment of this spring, he told himself; he would follow it step by step, from the first violets. Oh, how fully he must live now to make up for all the years he had wasted in his life.

He kept on walking along the boulevard. He was remembering how he and the girl the soldier had called Jeanne had both kindled with uncontrollable laughter when their eyes had met that night in the restaurant. He wished he could go down the boulevard with a girl like that, laughing through the foggy morning.

353

He wondered vaguely what part of Paris he was getting to, but was too happy to care. How beautifully long the hours were in the early morning!

At a concert at the Salle Gaveau the day before he had heard Debussy's Nocturnes and Les Sirènes. Rhythms from them were the warp of all his thoughts. Against the background of the grey street and the brownish fog that hung a veil at the end of every vista he began to imagine rhythms of his own, modulations and phrases that grew brilliant and faded, that flapped for a while like gaudy banners above his head through the clatter of the street.

He noticed that he was passing a long building with blank rows of windows, at the central door of which stood groups of American soldiers smoking. Unconsciously he hastened his steps, for fear of meeting an officer he would have to salute. He passed the men without looking at them.

A voice detained him.

"Say, Andrews."

When he turned he saw that a short man with curly hair, whose face, though familiar, he could not place, had left the group at the door and was coming towards him.

"Hello, Andrews. . . . Your name's Andrews, ain't it?"

"Yes." Andrews shook his hand, trying to remember.

"I'm Fuselli. . . . Remember? Last time I saw you you was goin' up to the lines on a train with Chrisfield. . . . Chris we used to call him. . . . At Cosne, don't you remember?"

"Of course I do."

"Well, what's happened to Chris?"

"He's a corporal now," said Andrews.

"Gee he is. . . . I'll be goddamned. . . . They was goin' to make me a corporal once."

Fuselli wore stained olive-drab breeches and badly rolled puttees; his shirt was open at the neck. From his blue denim jacket came a smell of stale grease that Andrews recognised; the smell of army kitchens. He had a momentary recollection of standing in line cold dark mornings and of the sound the food made slopping into mess kits.

"Why didn't they make you a corporal, Fuselli?" Andrews said, after a pause, in a constrained voice.

"Hell, I got in wrong, I suppose."

They were leaning against the dusty house wall. Andrews looked at his feet. The mud of the pavement, splashing up on the wall, made an even dado along the bottom, on which Andrews scraped the toe of his shoe up and down.

"Well, how's everything?" Andrews asked looking up suddenly.

"I've been in a labor battalion. That's how everything is."

"God, that's tough luck!"

Andrews wanted to go on. He had a sudden fear that he would be late. But he did not know how to break away.

"I got sick," said Fuselli grinning. "I guess I am yet. G.O. 42. It's a hell of a note the way they treat a feller . . . like he was lower than the dirt."

"Were you at Cosne all the time? That's damned rough luck, Fuselli."

"Cosne sure is a hell of a hole. . . . I guess you saw a lot of fighting. God! you must have been glad not to be in the goddam medics."

"I don't know that I'm glad I saw fighting. . . . Oh, yes, I suppose I am."

"You see, I had it a hell of a time before they found out. Court-martial was damn stiff . . . after the armistice too. . . . Oh, God! why can't they let a feller go home?"

A woman in a bright blue hat passed them. Andrews caught a glimpse of a white over-powdered face; her hips trembled like jelly under the blue skirt with each hard clack of her high heels on the pavement.

"Gee, that looks like Jenny. . . . I'm glad she didn't see me. . . ." Fuselli laughed. "Ought to 'a seen her one night last week. We were so dead drunk we just couldn't move."

"Isn't that bad for what's the matter with you?"

"I don't give a damn now; what's the use?"

"But God, man!" Andrews stopped himself suddenly. Then he said in a different voice, "What outfit are you in now?"

"I'm on the permanent K.P. here." Fuselli jerked his thumb towards the door of the building. "Not a bad job, off two days a week; no drill, good eats. . . . At least you get all you want. . . . But it surely has been hell emptying ash cans and shovelling coal an' now all they've done is dry me up."

"But you'll be goin' home soon now, won't you? They can't discharge you till they cure you."

"Damned if I know. . . . Some guys say a guy never can be cured. . . ."

"Don't you find K.P. work pretty damn dull?"

"No worse than anything else. What are you doin' in Paris?"

"School detachment."

"What's that?"

"Men who wanted to study in the university, who managed to work it."

"Gee, I'm glad I ain't goin' to school again."

"Well, so long, Fuselli."

"So long, Andrews."

Fuselli turned and slouched back to the group of men at the door. Andrews hurried away. As he turned the corner he had a glimpse of Fuselli with his hands in his pockets and his legs crossed leaning against the wall behind the door of the barracks.

III

THE DARKNESS, where the rain fell through the vague halos of light round the street lamps, glittered with streaks of pale gold. Andrews's ears were full of the sound of racing gutters and spattering waterspouts, and of the hard unceasing beat of the rain on the pavements. It was after closing time. The corrugated shutters were drawn down, in front of café windows. Andrews's cap was wet; water trickled down his forehead and the sides of his nose, running into his eyes. His feet were soaked and he could feel the wet patches growing on his knees where they received the water running off his overcoat. The street stretched wide and dark ahead of him, with an occasional glimmer of greenish reflection from a lamp. As he walked, splashing with long strides through the rain, he noticed that he was keeping pace with a woman under an umbrella, a slender person who was hurrying with small resolute steps up the boulevard. When he saw her, a mad hope flamed suddenly through him. He remembered a vulgar little theatre and the crude light of a spot light. Through the paint and powder a girl's golden-brown skin had shone with a firm brilliance that made him think of wide sun-scorched uplands, and dancing figures on Greek vases. Since he had seen her two nights ago, he had thought of nothing else. He had feverishly found out her name. "Naya Selikoff!" A mad hope flared through him that this girl he was walking beside was the girl whose slender limbs moved in an endless frieze through his thoughts. He peered at her with eyes blurred with rain. What an ass he was! Of course it couldn't be; it was too early. She was on the stage at this minute. Other hungry eyes were staring at her slenderness, other hands were twitching to stroke her golden-brown skin. Walking under the steady downpour that stung his face and ears and sent a tiny cold trickle down his back, he felt a sudden dizziness of desire come over him. His hands, thrust to the bottom of his coat pockets, clutched convulsively. He felt that he would die, that his pounding blood vessels would burst. The bead curtains of rain rustled and tinkled about him, awakening his nerves, making his skin flash and tingle. In the gurgle of water in gutters and water spouts he could imagine he heard orchestras droning libidinous music. The feverish excitement of his senses began to create frenzied rhythms in his ears:

"O ce pauvre poilu! Qu'il doit etre mouillé," said a small tremulous voice beside him.

He turned.

The girl was offering him part of her umbrella.

"O c'est un Americain!" she said again, still speaking as if to herself.

"Mais ça ne vaut pas la peine."

"Mais oui, mais oui."

He stepped under the umbrella beside her.

"But you must let me hold it."

"Bien."

As he took the umbrella he caught her eye. He stopped still in his tracks.

"But you're the girl at the Rat qui Danse."

"And you were at the next table with the man who sang?"

"How amusing!"

"Et celui-la! O il était rigolo. . . ." She burst out laughing; her head, encased in a little round black hat, bobbed up and down under the umbrella. Andrews laughed too. Crossing the Boulevard St. Germain, a taxi nearly ran them down and splashed a great wave of mud over them. She clutched his arm and then stood roaring with laughter.

"O quelle horreur! Quelle horreur!" she kept exclaiming.

Andrews laughed and laughed.

"But hold the umbrella over us. . . . You're letting the rain in on my best hat," she said again.

"Your name is Jeanne," said Andrews.

"Impertinent! You heard my brother call me that. . . . He went back to the front that night, poor little chap. . . . He's only nineteen . . . he's very clever. . . . O, how happy I am now that the war's over."

"You are older than he?"

"Two years. . . . I am the head of the family. . . . It is a dignified position."

"Have you always lived in Paris?"

"No, we are from Laon. . . . It's the war."

"Refugees?"

"Don't call us that. . . . We work."

Andrews laughed.

"Are you going far?" she asked peering in his face.

"No, I live up here. . . . My name is the same as yours."

"Jean? How funny!"

"Where are you going?"

"Rue Descartes. . . . Behind St. Etienne."

"I live near you."

"But you mustn't come. The concierge is a tigress. . . .
Etienne calls her Mme. Clemenceau."

"Who? The saint?"

"No, you silly—my brother. He is a socialist. He's a type-
setter at *l'Humanité*."

"Really? I often read *l'Humanité*."

"Poor boy, he used to swear he'd never go in the army. He
thought of going to America."

"That wouldn't do him any good now," said Andrews bitterly. "What do you do?"

"I?" a gruff bitterness came into her voice. "Why should I
tell you? I work at a dressmaker's."

"Like Louise?"

"You've heard Louise? Oh, how I cried."

"Why did it make you sad?"

"Oh, I don't know. . . . But I'm learning stenography.
. . . But here we are!"

The great bulk of the Pantheon stood up dimly through
the rain beside them. In front the tower of St. Etienne-du-
Mont was just visible. The rain roared about them.

"Oh, how wet I am!" said Jeanne.

"Look, they are giving Louise day after tomorrow at the
Opera Comique. . . . Won't you come with me?"

"No, I should cry too much."

"I'll cry too."

"But it's not . . ."

"C'est l'armistice," interrupted Andrews.

They both laughed!

"All right! Meet me at the café at the end of the Boul'
Mich' at a quarter past seven. . . . But you probably won't
come."

"I swear I will," cried Andrews eagerly.

"We'll see!" She darted away down the street beside St. Etienne-du-Mont. Andrews was left alone amid the seethe of the rain and the tumultuous gurgle of waterspouts. He felt calm and tired.

When he got to his room, he found he had no matches in his pocket. No light came from the window through which he could hear the hissing clamor of the rain in the court. He stumbled over a chair.

"Are you drunk?" came Walters's voice swathed in bed-clothes. "There are matches on the table."

"But where the hell's the table?"

At last his hand, groping over the table, closed on the matchbox.

The match's red and white flicker dazzled him. He blinked his eyes; the lashes were still full of raindrops. When he had lit a candle and set it amongst the music papers upon the table, he tore off his dripping clothes.

"I just met the most charming girl, Walters." Andrews stood naked beside the pile of his clothes, rubbing himself with a towel. "Gee! I was wet. . . . But she was the most charming person I've met since I've been in Paris."

"I thought you said you let the girls alone."

"Whores, I must have said."

"Well! Any girl you could pick up on the street. . . ."

"Nonsense!"

"I guess they are all that way in this damned country. . . . God, it will do me good to see a nice sweet wholesome American girl."

Andrews did not answer. He blew out the light and got into bed.

"But I've got a new job," Walters went on. "I'm working in the school detachment office."

"Why the hell do that? You came here to take courses in the Sorbonne, didn't you?"

"Sure. I go to most of them now. But in this army I like to be in the middle of things, see? Just so they can't put anything over on me."

"There's something in that."

"There's a damn lot in it, boy. The only way is to keep in

right and not let the man higher up forget you. . . . Why, we may start fighting again. These damn Germans ain't showin' the right spirit at all . . . after all the President's done for them. I expect to get my sergeantcy out of it anyway."

"Well, I'm going to sleep," said Andrews sulkily.

John Andrews sat at a table outside the café de Rohan. The sun had just set on a ruddy afternoon, flooding everything with violet-blue light and cold greenish shadow. The sky was bright lilac color, streaked with a few amber clouds. The lights were on in all the windows of the Magazin du Louvre opposite, so that the windows seemed bits of polished glass in the afterglow. In the colonnade of the Palais Royal the shadows were deepening and growing colder. A steady stream of people poured in and out of the Metro. Green buses stuffed with people kept passing. The roar of the traffic and the clatter of footsteps and the grumble of voices swirled like dance music about Andrews's head. He noticed all at once that the rabbit man stood in front of him, a rabbit dangling forgotten at the end of its rubber tube.

"Et ça va bien? le commerce," said Andrews.

"Quietly, quietly," said the rabbit man, distractedly making the rabbit turn a somersault at his feet. Andrews watched the people going into the Metro.

"The gentleman amuses himself in Paris?" asked the rabbit man timidly.

"Oh, yes; and you?"

"Quietly," the rabbit man smiled. "Women are very beautiful at this hour of the evening," he said again in his very timid tone.

"There is nothing more beautiful than this moment of the evening . . . in Paris."

"Or Parisian women." The eyes of the rabbit man glittered. "Excuse me, sir," he went on. "I must try and sell some rabbits."

"Au revoir," said Andrews holding out his hand.

The rabbit man shook it with sudden vigor and went off, making a rabbit hop before him along the curbstone. He was hidden by the swiftly moving crowds.

In the square, flaring violet arclights were flickering on,

lighting up their net-covered globes that hung like harsh moons above the pavement.

Henslowe sat down on a chair beside Andrews.

"How's Sinbad?"

"Sinbad, old boy, is functioning. . . . Aren't you frozen?"

"How do you mean, Henslowe?"

"Overheated, you chump, sitting out here in polar weather."

"No, but I mean. . . . How are you functioning?" said Andrews laughing.

"I'm going to Poland tomorrow."

"How?"

"As guard on a Red Cross supply train. I think you might make it if you want to come, if we beat it right over to the Red Cross before Major Smithers goes. Or we might take him out to dinner."

"But, Henny, I'm staying."

"Why the hell stay in this hole?"

"I like it. I'm getting a better course in orchestration than I imagined existed, and I met a girl the other day, and I'm crazy over Paris."

"If you go and get entangled, I swear I'll beat your head in with a Polish shillaughly. . . . Of course you've met a girl— so have I—lots. We can meet some more in Poland and dance polonaises with them."

"No, but this girl's charming. . . . You've seen her. She's the girl who was with the poilu at the Rat qui Danse the first night I was in Paris. We went to Louise together."

"Must have been a grand sentimental party. . . . I swear. . . . I may run after a Jane now and again but I never let them interfere with the business of existence," muttered Henslowe crossly.

They were both silent.

"You'll be as bad as Heinz with his Moki and the lion cub named Bubu. . . . By the way, it's dead. . . . Well, where shall we have dinner?"

"I'm dining with Jeanne. . . . I'm going to meet her in half an hour. . . . I'm awfully sorry, Henny. We might all dine together."

"A fat chance! No, I'll have to go and find that ass Aubrey,

and hear all about the Peace Conference. . . . Heinz can't
leave Moki because she's having hysterics on account of Bubu.
I'll probably be driven to going to see Berthe in the end.
. . . You're a nice one."

"We'll have a grand seeing-off party for you tomorrow,
Henny."

"Look! I forgot! You're to meet Aubrey at the Crillon at
five tomorrow, and he's going to take you to see Geneviève
Rod."

"Who the hell's Geneviève Rod?"

"Darned if I know. But Aubrey said you'd got to come. She
is an intellectual, so Aubrey says."

"That's the last thing I want to meet."

"Well, you can't help yourself. So long!"

Andrews sat a while more at the table outside the café. A
cold wind was blowing. The sky was blue-black and the ashen
white arc lamps cast a mortuary light over everything. In the
Colonnade of the Palais Royal the shadows were harsh and
inky. In the square the people were gradually thinning. The
lights in the Magazin du Louvre had gone out. From the café
behind him, a faint smell of fresh-cooked food began to saturate the cold air of the street.

Then he saw Jeanne advancing across the ash-grey pavement of the square, slim and black under the arc lights. He
ran to meet her.

The cylindrical stove in the middle of the floor roared
softly. In front of it the white cat was rolled into a fluffy ball
in which ears and nose made tiny splashes of pink like those
at the tips of the petals of certain white roses. One side of the
stove at the table against the window, sat an old brown man
with a bright red stain on each cheek bone, who wore formless corduroy clothes, the color of his skin. Holding the small
spoon in a knotted hand he was stirring slowly and continuously a liquid that was yellow and steamed in a glass. Behind
him was the window with sleet beating against it in the leaden
light of a wintry afternoon. The other side of the stove was a
zinc bar with yellow bottles and green bottles and a water
spigot with a neck like a giraffe's that rose out of the bar beside a varnished wood pillar that made the decoration of the

corner, with a terra cotta pot of ferns on top of it. From where Andrews sat on the padded bench at the back of the room the fern fronds made a black lacework against the left-hand side of the window, while against the other was the brown silhouette of the old man's head, and the slant of his cap. The stove hid the door and the white cat, round and symmetrical, formed the center of the visible universe.

On the marble table beside Andrews were some pieces of crisp bread with butter on them, a saucer of damson jam and a bowl with coffee and hot milk from which the steam rose in a faint spiral. His tunic was unbuttoned and he rested his head on his two hands, staring through his fingers at a thick pile of ruled paper full of hastily drawn signs, some in ink and some in pencil, where now and then he made a mark with a pencil. At the other edge of the pile of papers were two books, one yellow and one white with coffee stains on it.

The fire roared and the cat slept and the old brown man stirred and stirred, rarely stopping for a moment to lift the glass to his lips. Occasionally the scratching of sleet upon the windows became audible, or there was a distant sound of dish pans through the door in the back.

The sallow-faced clock that hung above the mirror that backed the bar, jerked out one jingly strike, a half hour. Andrews did not look up. The cat still slept in front of the stove which roared with a gentle singsong. The old brown man still stirred the yellow liquid in his glass. The clock was ticking up-hill towards the hour.

Andrews's hands were cold. There was a nervous flutter in his wrists and in his chest. Inside of him was a great rift of light, infinitely vast and infinitely distant. Through it sounds poured from somewhere, so that he trembled with them to his finger tips, sounds modulated into rhythms that washed back and forth and crossed each other like sea waves in a cove, sounds clotted into harmonies.

Behind everything the Queen of Sheba, out of Flaubert, held her fantastic hand with its long, gilded finger nails on his shoulder; and he was leaning forward over the brink of life. But the image was vague, like a shadow cast on the brilliance of his mind.

The clock struck four.

The white fluffy ball of the cat unrolled very slowly. Its eyes were very round and yellow. It put first one leg and then the other out before it on the tiled floor, spreading wide the pinkey-grey claws. Its tail rose up behind it straight as the mast of a ship. With slow processional steps the cat walked towards the door.

The old brown man drank down the yellow liquid and smacked his lips twice, loudly, meditatively.

Andrews raised his head, his blue eyes looking straight before him without seeing anything. Dropping the pencil, he leaned back against the wall and stretched his arms out. Taking the coffee bowl between his two hands, he drank a little. It was cold. He piled some jam on a piece of bread and ate it, licking a little off his fingers afterwards. Then he looked towards the old brown man and said:

"On est bien ici, n'est ce pas, Monsieur Morue?"

"Oui, on est bien ici," said the old brown man in a voice so gruff it seemed to rattle. Very slowly he got to his feet.

"Good. I am going to the barge," he said. Then he called, "Chipette!"

"Oui, m'sieu."

A little girl in a black apron with her hair in two tight pigtails that stood out behind her tiny bullet head as she ran, came through the door from the back part of the house.

"There, give that to your mother," said the old brown man, putting some coppers in her hand.

"Oui, m'sieu."

"You'd better stay here where it's warm," said Andrews yawning.

"I have to work. It's only soldiers don't have to work," rattled the old brown man.

When the door opened a gust of raw air circled about the wine shop, and a roar of wind and hiss of sleet came from the slush-covered quai outside. The cat took refuge beside the stove, with its back up and its tail waving. The door closed and the old brown man's silhouette, slanted against the wind, crossed the grey oblong of the window.

Andrews settled down to work again.

"But you work a lot a lot, don't you; M'sieu Jean?" said
Chipette, putting her chin on the table beside the books and
looking up into his eyes with little eyes like black beads.

"I wonder if I do."

"When I'm grown up I shan't work a bit. I'll drive round
in a carriage."

Andrews laughed. Chipette looked at him for a minute and
then went into the other room carrying away the empty coffee bowl.

In front of the stove the cat sat on its haunches, licking a
paw rhythmically with a pink curling tongue like a rose
petal.

Andrews whistled a few bars, staring at the cat.

"What d'you think of that, Minet? That's la reine de
Saba . . . la reine de Saba."

The cat curled into a ball again with great deliberation and
went to sleep.

Andrews began thinking of Jeanne and the thought gave
him a sense of quiet well-being. Strolling with her in the
evening through the streets full of men and women walking
significantly together sent a languid calm through his jangling
nerves which he had never known in his life before. It excited
him to be with her, but very suavely, so that he forgot that his
limbs were swathed stiffly in an uncomfortable uniform, so
that his feverish desire seemed to fly out of him until with her
body beside him, he seemed to drift effortlessly in the stream
of the lives of all the people he passed, so languid from the
quiet loves that streamed up about him that the hard walls of
his personality seemed to have melted entirely into the mistiness of twilight streets. And for a moment as he thought of it
a scent of flowers, heavy with pollen, and sprouting grass and
damp moss and swelling sap, seemed to tingle in his nostrils.
Sometimes, swimming in the ocean on a rough day, he had
felt that same reckless exhilaration when, towards the shore, a
huge seething wave had caught him up and sped him forward
on its crest. Sitting quietly in the empty wine shop that grey
afternoon, he felt his blood grumble and swell in his veins as
the new life was grumbling and swelling in the sticky buds of
the trees, in the tender green quick under their rough bark, in
the little furry animals of the woods and in the sweet-smelling

cattle that tramped into mud the lush meadows. In the premonition of spring was a resistless wave of force that carried
him and all of them with it tumultuously.

The clock struck five.

Andrews jumped to his feet and still struggling into his
overcoat darted out of the door.

A raw wind blew on the square. The river was a muddy
grey-green, swollen and rapid. A hoarse triumphant roaring
came from it. The sleet had stopped; but the pavements were
covered with slush and in the gutters were large puddles
which the wind ruffled. Everything,—houses, bridges, river
and sky,—was in shades of cold grey-green, broken by one
jagged ochre-colored rift across the sky against which the
bulk of Notre Dame and the slender spire of the crossing rose
dark and purplish. Andrews walked with long strides, splashing through the puddles, until, opposite the low building of
the Morgue, he caught a crowded green bus.

Outside the Hotel Crillon were many limousines, painted
olive-drab, with numbers in white letters on the doors; the
drivers, men with their olive-drab coat collars turned up
round their red faces, stood in groups under the portico. Andrews passed the sentry and went through the revolving
doors into the lobby, which was vividly familiar. It had the
smell he remembered having smelt in the lobbies of New
York hotels,—a smell of cigar smoke and furniture polish. On
one side a door led to a big dining room where many men
and women were having tea, from which came a smell of pastry and rich food. On the expanse of red carpet in front of
him officers and civilians stood in groups talking in low
voices. There was a sound of jingling spurs and jingling dishes
from the restaurant, and near where Andrews stood, shifting
his weight from one foot to the other, sprawled in a leather
chair a fat man with a black felt hat over his eyes and a large
watch chain dangling limply over his bulbous paunch. He
cleared his throat occasionally with a rasping noise and spat
loudly into the spittoon beside him.

At last Andrews caught sight of Aubrey, who was dapper
with white cheeks and tortoise shell glasses.

"Come along," he said, seizing Andrews by the arm.

"You are late." Then, he went on, whispering in Andrews's

ear as they went out through the revolving doors: "Great things happened in the Conference today. . . . I can tell you that, old man."

They crossed the bridge towards the portico of the Chamber of Deputies with its high pediment and its grey columns. Down the river they could see faintly the Eiffel Tower with a drift of mist athwart it, like a section of spider web spun between the city and the clouds.

"Do we have to go to see these people, Aubrey?"

"Yes, you can't back out now. Geneviève Rod wants to know about American music."

"But what on earth can I tell her about American music?"

"Wasn't there a man named MacDowell who went mad or something?"

Andrews laughed.

"But you know I haven't any social graces. . . . I suppose I'll have to say I think Foch is a little tin god."

"You needn't say anything if you don't want to. . . . They're very advanced, anyway."

"Oh, rats!"

They were going up a brown-carpeted stair that had engravings on the landings, where there was a faint smell of stale food and dustpans. At the top landing Aubrey rang the bell at a varnished door. In a moment a girl opened it. She had a cigarette in her hand, her face was pale under a mass of reddish-chestnut hair, her eyes very large, a pale brown, as large as the eyes of women in those paintings of Artemisias and Berenikes found in tombs in the Fayum. She wore a plain black dress.

"Enfin!" she said, and held out her hand to Aubrey.

"There's my friend Andrews." She held out her hand to him absently, still looking at Aubrey.

"Does he speak French? . . . Good. . . . This way."

They went into a large room with a piano where an elderly woman, with grey hair and yellow teeth and the same large eyes as her daughter, stood before the fireplace.

"Maman . . . enfin ils arrivent, ces messieurs."

"Geneviève was afraid you weren't coming," Mme. Rod said to Andrews, smiling. "Monsieur Aubrey gave us such a picture of your playing that we have been excited all day. . . . We adore music."

"I wish I could do something more to the point with it than adore it," said Geneviève Rod hastily, then she went on with a laugh: "But I forget. . . . Monsieur Andreffs. . . . Monsieur Ronsard." She made a gesture with her hand from Andrews to a young Frenchman in a cut-away coat, with small mustaches and a very tight vest, who bowed towards Andrews.

"Now we'll have tea," said Geneviève Rod. "Everybody talks sense until they've had tea. . . . It's only after tea that anyone is ever amusing." She pulled open some curtains that covered the door into the adjoining room.

"I understand why Sarah Bernhardt is so fond of curtains," she said. "They give an air of drama to existence. . . . There is nothing more heroic than curtains."

She sat at the head of an oak table where were china platters with vari-colored pastries, an old pewter kettle under which an alcohol lamp burned, a Dresden china teapot in pale yellows and greens, and cups and saucers and plates with a double-headed eagle design in dull vermilion.

"Tout ça," said Geneviève, waving her hand across the table, "c'est Boche. . . . But we haven't any others, so they'll have to do."

The older woman, who sat beside her, whispered something in her ear and laughed.

Geneviève put on a pair of tortoise-shell spectacles and starting pouring out tea.

"Debussy once drank out of that cup. . . . It's cracked," she said, handing a cup to John Andrews. "Do you know anything of Moussorgski's you can play to us after tea?"

"I can't play anything any more. . . . Ask me three months from now."

"Oh, yes, but nobody expects you to do any tricks with it. You can certainly make it intelligible. That's all I want."

"I have my doubts."

Andrews sipped his tea slowly, looking now and then at Geneviève Rod who had suddenly begun talking very fast to Ronsard. She held a cigarette between the fingers of a long thin hand. Her large pale-brown eyes kept their startled look of having just opened on the world; a little smile appeared and disappeared maliciously in the curve of her cheek away from her small firm lips. The older woman beside her kept looking round the table with a jolly air of hospitality, and showing her yellow teeth in a smile.

Afterwards they went back to the sitting room and Andrews sat down at the piano. The girl sat very straight on a little chair beside the piano. Andrews ran his fingers up and down the keys.

"Did you say you knew Debussy?" he said suddenly.

"I? No; but he used to come to see my father when I was a little girl. . . . I have been brought up in the middle of music. . . . That shows how silly it is to be a woman. There is no music in my head. Of course I am sensitive to it, but so are the tables and chairs in this apartment, after all they've heard."

Andrews started playing Schumann. He stopped suddenly.

"Can you sing?" he said.

"No."

"I'd like to do the *Proses Lyriques*. . . . I've never heard them."

"I once tried to sing *Le Soir*," she said.

"Wonderful. Do bring it out."

"But, good Lord, it's too difficult."

"What is the use of being fond of music if you aren't willing to mangle it for the sake of producing it? . . . I swear I'd rather hear a man picking out *Auprès de ma Blonde* on a trombone than Kreisler playing Paganini impeccably enough to make you ill."

"But there is a middle ground."

He interrupted her by starting to play again. As he played without looking at her, he felt that her eyes were fixed on him, that she was standing tensely behind him. Her hand touched his shoulder. He stopped playing.

"Oh, I am dreadfully sorry," she said.

"Nothing. I am finished."

"You were playing something of your own?"

"Have you ever read *La Tentation de Saint Antoine*?" he asked in a low voice.

"Flaubert's?"

"Yes."

"It's not his best work. A very interesting failure though," she said.

Andrews got up from the piano with difficulty, controlling a sudden growing irritation.

"They seem to teach everybody to say that," he muttered.

Suddenly he realized that other people were in the room. He went up to Mme. Rod.

"You must excuse me," he said, "I have an engagement. . . . Aubrey, don't let me drag you away. I am late, I've got to run."

"You must come to see us again."

"Thank you," mumbled Andrews.

Geneviève Rod went with him to the door.

"We must know each other better," she said. "I like you for going off in a huff."

Andrews flushed.

"I was badly brought up," he said, pressing her thin cold hand. "And you French must always remember that we are barbarians. . . . Some are repentant barbarians. . . . I am not."

She laughed, and John Andrews ran down the stairs and out into the grey-blue streets, where the lamps were blooming into primrose color. He had a confused feeling that he had made a fool of himself, which made him writhe with helpless anger. He walked with long strides through the streets of the Rive Gauche full of people going home from work, towards the little wine shop on the Quai de la Tournelle.

It was a Paris Sunday morning. Old women in black shawls were going into the church of St. Etienne-du-Mont. Each time the leather doors opened it let a little whiff of incense out into the smoky morning air. Three pigeons walked about the cobblestones, putting their coral feet one before the other with an air of importance. The pointed façade of the church and its slender tower and cupola cast a bluish shadow on the square in front of it, into which the shadows the old women trailed behind them vanished as they hobbled towards the church. The opposite side of the square and the railing of the Panthéon and its tall brownish-gray flank were flooded with dull orange-colored sunlight.

Andrews walked back and forth in front of the church, looking at the sky and the pigeons and the façade of the Library of Ste. Geneviève, and at the rare people who passed across the end of the square, noting forms and colors and small comical aspects of things with calm delight, savoring everything almost with complacency. His music, he felt, was progressing now that, undisturbed, he lived all day long in the rhythm of it; his mind and his fingers were growing supple. The hard moulds that had grown up about his spirit were softening. As he walked back and forth in front of the church waiting for Jeanne, he took an inventory of his state of mind; he was very happy.

"Eh bien?"

Jeanne had come up behind him. They ran like children hand in hand across the sunny square.

"I have not had any coffee yet," said Andrews.

"How late you must get up! . . . But you can't have any till we get to the Porte Maillot, Jean."

"Why not?"

"Because I say you can't."

"But that's cruelty."

"It won't be long."

"But I am dying with hunger. I will die in your hands."

"Can't you understand? Once we get to the Porte Maillot we'll be far from your life and my life. The day will be ours. One must not tempt fate."

"You funny girl."

The Métro was not crowded. Andrews and Jeanne sat opposite each other without talking. Andrews was looking at the girl's hands, limp on her lap, small overworked hands with places at the tips of the fingers where the skin was broken and scarred, with chipped uneven nails. Suddenly she caught his glance. He flushed, and she said jauntily:

"Well, we'll all be rich some day, like princes and princesses in fairy tales."

They both laughed.

As they were leaving the train at the terminus, he put his arm timidly round her waist. She wore no corsets. His fingers trembled at the litheness of the flesh under her clothes. Feeling a sort of terror go through him he took away his arm.

"Now," she said quietly as they emerged into the sunlight and the bare trees of the broad avenue, "you can have all the café-au-lait you want."

"You'll have some too."

"Why be extravagant? I've had my petit déjeuner."

"But I'm going to be extravagant all day. . . . We might as well start now. I don't know exactly why, but I am very happy. We'll eat brioches."

"But, my dear, it's only profiteers who can eat brioches now-a-days."

"You just watch us."

They went into a pâtisserie. An elderly woman with a lean yellow face and thin hair waited on them, casting envious glances up through her eyelashes as she piled the rich brown brioches on a piece of tissue paper.

"You'll pass the day in the country?" she asked in a little wistful voice as she handed Andrews the change.

"Yes," he said, "how well you guessed."

As they went out of the door they heard her muttering, "O la jeunesse, la jeunesse."

They found a table in the sun at a café opposite the gate from which they could watch people and automobiles and carriages coming in and out. Beyond, a grass-grown bit of fortifications gave an 1870 look to things.

"How jolly it is at the Porte Maillot!" cried Andrews.

She looked at him and laughed.

"But how gay he is to-day."

"No. I always like it here. It's the spot in Paris where you always feel well. . . . When you go out you have all the fun of leaving town, when you go in you have all the fun of coming back to town. . . . But you aren't eating any brioches?"

"I've eaten one. You eat them. You are hungry."

"Jeanne, I don't think I have ever been so happy in my life. . . . It's almost worth having been in the army for the joy your freedom gives you. That frightful life. . . . How is Etienne?"

"He is in Mayence. He's bored."

"Jeanne, we must live very much, we who are free to make up for all the people who are still . . . bored."

"A lot of good it'll do them," she cried laughing.

"It's funny, Jeanne, I threw myself into the army. I was so sick of being free and not getting anywhere. Now I have learnt that life is to be used, not just held in the hand like a box of bonbons that nobody eats."

She looked at him blankly.

"I mean, I don't think I get enough out of life," he said. "Let's go."

They got to their feet.

"What do you mean?" she said slowly. "One takes what life gives, that is all, there's no choice. . . . But look, there's the Malmaison train. . . . We must run."

Giggling and breathless they climbed on the trailer, squeezing themselves on the back platform where everyone was pushing and exclaiming. The car began to joggle its way through Neuilly. Their bodies were pressed together by the men and women about them. Andrews put his arm firmly round Jeanne's waist and looked down at her pale cheek that was pressed against his chest. Her little round black straw hat with a bit of a red flower on it was just under his chin.

"I can't see a thing," she gasped, still giggling.

"I'll describe the landscape," said Andrews. "Why, we are crossing the Seine already."

"Oh, how pretty it must be!"

An old gentleman with a pointed white beard who stood beside them laughed benevolently.

"But don't you think the Seine's pretty?" Jeanne looked up at him impudently.

"Without a doubt, without a doubt. . . . It was the way you said it," said the old gentleman. . . . "You are going to St. Germain?" he asked Andrews.

"No, to Malmaison."

"Oh, you should go to St. Germain. M. Reinach's prehistoric museum is there. It is very beautiful. You should not go home to your country without seeing it."

"Are there monkeys in it?" asked Jeanne.

"No," said the old gentleman turning away.

"I adore monkeys," said Jeanne.

The car was going along a broad empty boulevard with trees and grass plots and rows of low store-houses and little dilapidated rooming houses along either side. Many people had got out and there was plenty of room, but Andrews kept his arm round the girl's waist. The constant contact with her body made him feel very languid.

"How good it smells!" said Jeanne.

"It's the spring."

"I want to lie on the grass and eat violets. . . . Oh, how good you were to bring me out like this, Jean. You must know lots of fine ladies you could have brought out, because you are so well educated. How is it you are only an ordinary soldier?"

"Good God! I wouldn't be an officer."

"Why? It must be rather nice to be an officer."

"Does Etienne want to be an officer?"

"But he's a socialist, that's different."

"Well, I suppose I must be a socialist too, but let's talk of something else."

Andrews moved over to the other side of the platform. They were passing little villas with gardens on the road where yellow and pale-purple crocuses bloomed. Now and then there was a scent of violets in the moist air. The sun had disappeared under soft purplish-grey clouds. There was occasionally a rainy chill in the wind.

Andrews suddenly thought of Geneviève Rod. Curious how vividly he remembered her face, her wide, open eyes and her way of smiling without moving her firm lips. A feeling of annoyance went through him. How silly of him to go off rudely like that! And he became very anxious to talk to her again; things he wanted to say to her came to his mind.

"Well, are you asleep?" said Jeanne tugging at his arm. "Here we are."

Andrews flushed furiously.

"Oh, how nice it is here, how nice it is here!" Jeanne was saying.

"Why, it is eleven o'clock," said Andrews.

"We must see the palace before lunch," cried Jeanne, and she started running up a lane of linden trees, where the fat buds were just bursting into little crinkling fans of green. New grass was sprouting in the wet ditches on either side. Andrews ran after her, his feet pounding hard in the moist gravel road. When he caught up to her he threw his arms round her recklessly and kissed her panting mouth. She broke away from him and strode demurely arranging her hat.

"Monster," she said, "I trimmed this hat specially to come out with you and you do your best to wreck it."

"Poor little hat," said Andrews, "but it is so beautiful to-day, and you are very lovely, Jeanne."

"The great Napoleon must have said that to the Empress Josephine and you know what he did to her," said Jeanne almost solemnly.

"But she must have been awfully bored with him long before."

"No," said Jeanne, "that's how women are."

They went through big iron gates into the palace grounds.

Later they sat at a table in the garden of a little restaurant. The sun, very pale, had just showed itself, making the knives and forks and the white wine in their glasses gleam faintly. Lunch had not come yet. They sat looking at each other silently. Andrews felt weary and melancholy. He could think of nothing to say. Jeanne was playing with some tiny white daisies with pink tips to their petals, arranging them in circles and crosses on the table-cloth.

"Aren't they slow?" said Andrews.

"But it's nice here, isn't it?" Jeanne smiled brilliantly. "But how glum he looks now." She threw some daisies at him. Then, after a pause, she added mockingly: "It's hunger, my dear. Good Lord, how dependent men are on food!"

Andrews drank down his wine at a gulp. He felt that if he could only make an effort he could lift off the stifling melancholy that was settling down on him like a weight that kept growing heavier.

A man in khaki, with his face and neck scarlet, staggered into the garden dragging beside him a mud-encrusted bicycle. He sank into an iron chair, letting the bicycle fall with a clatter at his feet.

"Hi, hi," he called in a hoarse voice.

A waiter appeared and contemplated him suspiciously. The man in khaki had hair as red as his face, which was glistening with sweat. His shirt was torn, and he had no coat. His breeches and puttees were invisible for mud.

"Gimme a beer," croaked the man in khaki.

The waiter shrugged his shoulders and walked away.

"Il demande une bière," said Andrews.

"Mais Monsieur. . . ."

"I'll pay. Get it for him."

The waiter disappeared.

"Thankee, Yank," roared the man in khaki.

The waiter brought a tall narrow yellow glass. The man in khaki took it from his hand, drank it down at a draught and handed back the empty glass. Then he spat, wiped his mouth on the back of his hand, got with difficulty to his feet and shambled towards Andrews's table.

"Oi presoom the loidy and you don't mind, Yank, if Oi parley wi' yez a bit. Do yez?"

"No, come along; where did you come from?"

The man in khaki dragged an iron chair behind him to a spot near the table. Before sitting down he bobbed his head in the direction of Jeanne with an air of solemnity tugging at the same time at a lock of his red hair. After some fumbling he got a red-bordered handkerchief out of his pocket and wiped his face with it, leaving a long black smudge of machine oil on his forehead.

"Oi'm a bearer of important secret messages, Yank," he said, leaning back in the little iron chair. "Oi'm a despatch-rider."

"You look all in."

"Not a bit of it. Oi just had a little hold up, that's all, in a woodland lane. Some buggers tried to do me in."

"What d'you mean?"

"Oi guess they had a little information . . . that's all. Oi'm carryin' important messages from our headquarters in Rouen to your president. Oi was goin' through a bloody thicket past this side. Oi don't know how you pronounce the bloody town. . . . Oi was on my bike making about thoity for the road was all a-murk when Oi saw four buggers standing acrost the road . . . lookter me suspicious-like, so Oi jus' jammed the juice into the boike and made for the middle 'un. He dodged all right. Then they started shootin' and a bloody bullet buggered the boike. . . . It was bein' born with a caul that saved me. . . . Oi picked myself up outer the ditch an lost 'em in the woods. Then Oi got to another bloody town and commandeered this old sweatin' machine. . . . How many kills is there to Paris, Yank?"

"Fifteen or sixteen, I think."

"What's he saying, Jean?"

"Some men tried to stop him on the road. He's a despatch rider."

"Isn't he ugly? Is he English?"

"Irish."

"You bet you, miss; Hirlanday; that's me. . . . You picked a good looker this toime, Yank. But wait till Oi git to Paree. Oi clane up a good hundre' pound on this job in bonuses. What part d'ye come from, Yank?"

"Virginia. I live in New York."

"Oi been in Detroit; goin' back there to git in the auto-moebile business soon as Oi clane up a few more bonuses. Europe's dead an stinkin', Yank. Ain't no place for a young fellow. It's dead an stinkin', that's what it is."

"It's pleasanter to live here than in America. . . . Say, d'you often get held up that way?"

"Ain't happened to me before, but it has to pals o' moine."

"Who d'you think it was?"

"Oi dunno; 'Unns or some of these bloody secret agents round the Peace Conference. . . . But Oi got to go; that despatch won't keep."

"All right. The beer's on me."

"Thank ye, Yank." The man got to his feet, shook hands with Andrews and Jeanne, jumped on the bicycle and rode out of the garden to the road, threading his way through the iron chairs and tables.

"Wasn't he a funny customer?" cried Andrews, laughing. "What a wonderful joke things are!"

The waiter arrived with the omelette that began their lunch.

"Gives you an idea of how the old lava's bubbling in the volcano. There's nowhere on earth a man can dance so well as on a volcano."

"But don't talk that way," said Jeanne laying down her knife and fork. "It's terrible. We will waste our youth to no purpose. Our fathers enjoyed themselves when they were young. . . . And if there had been no war we should have been so happy, Etienne and I. My father was a small manu-facturer of soap and perfumery. Etienne would have had a splendid situation. I should never have had to work. We had a nice house. I should have been married. . . ."

"But this way, Jeanne, haven't you more freedom?"

She shrugged her shoulders. Later she burst out:

"But what's the good of freedom? What can you do with it? What one wants is to live well and have a beautiful house and be respected by people. Oh, life was so sweet in France before the war."

"In that case it's not worth living," said Andrews in a savage voice, holding himself in.

They went on eating silently. The sky became overcast. A few drops splashed on the table-cloth.

"We'll have to take coffee inside," said Andrews.

"And you think it is funny that people shoot at a man on a motorcycle going through a wood. All that seems to me terrible, terrible," said Jeanne.

"Look out. Here comes the rain!"

They ran into the restaurant through the first hissing sheet of the shower and sat at a table near a window watching the rain drops dance and flicker on the green iron tables. A scent of wet earth and the mushroom-like odor of sodden leaves came in borne on damp gusts through the open door. A waiter closed the glass doors and bolted them.

"He wants to keep out the spring. He can't," said Andrews.

They smiled at each other over their coffee cups. They were in sympathy again.

When the rain stopped they walked across wet fields by a footpath full of little clear puddles that reflected the blue sky and the white- and amber-tinged clouds where the shadows were light purplish-grey. They walked slowly arm in arm, pressing their bodies together. They were very tired, they did not know why and stopped often to rest, leaning against the damp boles of trees. Beside a pond pale blue and amber and silver from the reflected sky, they found under a big beech tree a patch of wild violets, which Jeanne picked greedily, mixing them with a little crimson-tipped daisies in the tight bouquet. At the suburban railway station, they sat silent, side by side on a bench, sniffing the flowers now and then, so sunk in languid weariness that they could hardly summon strength to climb into a seat on top of a third class coach, which was crowded with people coming home from a day in the country. Everybody had violets and crocuses and twigs with buds on them. In people's stiff, citified clothes lingered a smell of wet fields and sprouting woods. All the girls shrieked and threw their arms round the men when the train went through a tunnel or under a bridge. Whatever happened, everybody laughed. When the train arrived in the station, it was almost with reluctance that they left it, as if they felt that from that moment their work-a-day lives began again. Andrews and Jeanne walked down the platform without touching each other. Their fingers were stained and sticky from touching buds and crushing young sappy leaves and grass stalks. The air of the city seemed dense and unbreathable after the scented moisture of the fields.

They dined at a little restaurant on the Quai Voltaire and afterwards walked slowly towards the Place St. Michel, feeling the wine and the warmth of the food sending new vigor into their tired bodies. Andrews had his arm round her shoulder and they talked in low intimate voices, hardly moving their lips, looking long at the men and women they saw sitting twined in each other's arms on benches, at the couples of boys and girls that kept passing them, talking slowly and quietly, as they were, bodies pressed together as theirs were.

"How many lovers there are," said Andrews.

"Are we lovers?" asked Jeanne with a curious little laugh.

"I wonder. . . . Have you ever been crazily in love, Jeanne?"

"I don't know. There was a boy in Laon named Marcelin. But I was a little fool then. The last news of him was from Verdun."

"Have you had many . . . like I am?"

"How sentimental we are," she cried laughing.

"No. I wanted to know. I know so little of life," said Andrews.

"I have amused myself, as best I could," said Jeanne in a serious tone. "But I am not frivolous. . . . There have been very few men I have liked. . . . So I have had few friends . . . do you want to call them lovers? But lovers are what married women have on the stage. . . . All that sort of thing is very silly."

"Not so very long ago," said Andrews, "I used to dream of being romantically in love, with people climbing up the ivy on castle walls, and fiery kisses on balconies in the moonlight."

"Like at the Opéra Comique," cried Jeanne laughing.

"That was all very silly. But even now, I want so much more of life than life can give."

They leaned over the parapet and listened to the hurrying swish of the river, now soft and now loud, where the reflections of the lights on the opposite bank writhed like golden snakes.

Andrews noticed that there was someone beside them. The faint, greenish glow from the lamp on the quai enabled him to recognize the lame boy he had talked to months ago on the Butte.

"I wonder if you'll remember me," he said.

"You are the American who was in the restaurant, Place du Tertre, I don't remember when, but it was long ago."

They shook hands.

"But you are alone," said Andrews.

"Yes, I am always alone," said the lame boy firmly. He held out his hand again.

"Au revoir," said Andrews.

"Good luck!" said the lame boy. Andrews heard his crutch tapping on the pavement as he went away along the quai.

"Jeanne," said Andrews, suddenly, "you'll come home with me, won't you?"

"But you have a friend living with you."

"He's gone to Brussels. He won't be back till tomorrow."

"I suppose one must pay for one's dinner," said Jeanne maliciously.

"Good God, no." Andrews buried his face in his hands. The singsong of the river pouring through the bridges filled his ears. He wanted desperately to cry. Bitter desire that was like hatred made his flesh tingle, made his hands ache to crush her hands in them.

"Come along," he said gruffly.

"I didn't mean to say that," she said in a gentle, tired voice. "You know, I'm not a very nice person." The greenish glow of the lamp lit up the contour of one of her cheeks as she tilted her head up, and glimmered in her eyes. A soft sentimental sadness suddenly took hold of Andrews; he felt as he used to feel when, as a very small child, his mother used to tell him Br' Rabbit stories, and he would feel himself drifting helplessly on the stream of her soft voice, narrating, drifting towards something unknown and very sad, which he could not help.

They started walking again, past the Pont Neuf, towards the glare of the Place St. Michel. Three names had come into Andrews's head, "Arsinoë, Berenike, Artemisia." For a little while he puzzled over them, and then he remembered that Geneviève Rod had the large eyes and the wide, smooth forehead and the firm little lips the women had in the portraits that were sewn on the mummy cases in the Fayum. But those patrician women of Alexandria had not had chestnut hair with a glimpse of burnished copper in it; they might have dyed it, though!

"Why are you laughing?" asked Jeanne.

"Because things are so silly."

"Perhaps you mean people are silly," she said, looking up at him out of the corners of her eyes.

"You're right."

They walked in silence till they reached Andrews's door.

"You go up first and see that there's no one there," said Jeanne in a business-like tone.

Andrews's hands were cold. He felt his heart thumping while he climbed the stairs.

The room was empty. A fire was ready to light in the small fireplace. Andrews hastily tidied up the table and kicked under the bed some soiled clothes that lay in a heap in a corner. A thought came to him: how like his performances in his room at college when he had heard that a relative was coming to see him.

He tiptoed downstairs.

"Bien. Tu peux venir, Jeanne," he said.

She sat down rather stiffly in the straight-backed armchair beside the fire.

"How pretty the fire is," she said.

"Jeanne, I think I'm crazily in love with you," said Andrews in an excited voice.

"Like at the Opéra Comique." She shrugged her shoulders. "The room's nice," she said. "Oh, but, what a big bed!"

"You're the first woman who's been up here in my time, Jeanne. . . . Oh, but this uniform is frightful."

Andrews thought suddenly of all the tingling bodies constrained into the rigid attitudes of automatons in uniforms
like this one; of all the hideous farce of making men into machines. Oh, if some gesture of his could only free them all for
life and freedom and joy. The thought drowned everything
else for the moment.

"But you pulled a button off," cried Jeanne laughing hysterically. "I'll just have to sew it on again."

"Never mind. If you knew how I hated them."

"What white skin you have, like a woman's. I suppose
that's because you are blond," said Jeanne.

The sound of the door being shaken vigorously woke Andrews. He got up and stood in the middle of the floor for a
moment without being able to collect his wits. The shaking of
the door continued, and he heard Walters's voice crying
"Andy, Andy." Andrews felt shame creeping up through him
like nausea. He felt a passionate disgust towards himself and
Jeanne and Walters. He had an impulse to move furtively as if
he had stolen something. He went to the door and opened it
a little.

"Say, Walters, old man," he said, "I can't let you in. . . .
I've got a girl with me. I'm sorry. . . . I thought you
wouldn't get back till tomorrow."

"You're kidding, aren't you?" came Walters's voice out of
the dark hall.

"No." Andrews shut the door decisively and bolted it
again.

Jeanne was still asleep. Her black hair had come undone
and spread over the pillow. Andrews pulled the covers up
about her carefully.

Then he got into the other bed, where he lay awake a long
time, staring at the ceiling

IV

People walking along the boulevard looked curiously through the railing at the line of men in olive-drab that straggled round the edge of the courtyard. The line moved slowly, past a table where an officer and two enlisted men sat poring over big lists of names and piles of palely tinted banknotes and silver francs that glittered white. Above the men's heads a thin haze of cigarette smoke rose into the sunlight. There was a sound of voices and of feet shuffling on the gravel. The men who had been paid went off jauntily, the money jingling in their pockets.

The men at the table had red faces and tense, serious expressions. They pushed the money into the soldiers' hands with a rough jerk and pronounced the names as if they were machines clicking.

Andrews saw that one of the men at the table was Walters; he smiled and whispered "Hello" as he came up to him. Walters kept his eyes fixed on the list.

While Andrews was waiting for the man ahead of him to be paid, he heard two men in the line talking.

"Wasn't that a hell of a place? D'you remember the lad that died in the barracks one day?"

"Sure, I was in the medicks there too. There was a hell of a sergeant in that company tried to make the kid get up, and the loot came and said he'd court-martial him, an' then they found out that he'd cashed in his checks."

"What'd 'ee die of?"

"Heart failure, I guess. I dunno, though, he never did take to the life."

"No. That place Cosne was enough to make any guy cash in his checks."

Andrews got his money. As he was walking away, he strolled up to the two men he had heard talking.

"Were you fellows in Cosne?"

"Sure."

"Did you know a fellow named Fuselli?"

"I dunno. . . ."

"Sure, you do," said the other man. "You remember Dan Fuselli, the little wop thought he was goin' to be corporal."

"He had another think comin'." They both laughed.

Andrews walked off, vaguely angry. There were many soldiers on the Boulevard Montparnasse. He turned into a side street, feeling suddenly furtive and humble, as if he would hear any minute the harsh voice of a sergeant shouting orders at him.

The silver in his breeches pocket jingled with every step.

Andrews leaned on the balustrade of the balcony, looking down into the square in front of the Opéra Comique. He was dizzy with the beauty of the music he had been hearing. He had a sense somewhere in the distances of his mind of the great rhythm of the sea. People chattered all about him on the wide, crowded balcony, but he was only conscious of the blue-grey mistiness of the night where the lights made patterns in green-gold and red-gold. And compelling his attention from everything else, the rhythm swept through him like sea waves.

"I thought you'd be here," said Geneviève Rod in a quiet voice beside him.

Andrews felt strangely tongue-tied.

"It's nice to see you," he blurted out, after looking at her silently for a moment.

"Of course you love Pelléas."

"It is the first time I've heard it."

"Why haven't you been to see us? It's two weeks. . . . We've been expecting you."

"I didn't know . . . Oh, I'll certainly come. I don't know anyone at present I can talk music to."

"You know me."

"Anyone else, I should have said."

"Are you working?"

"Yes. . . . But this hinders frightfully." Andrews yanked at the front of his tunic. "Still, I expect to be free very soon. I'm putting in an application for discharge."

"I suppose you will feel you can do so much better. . . . You will be much stronger now that you have done your duty."

"No . . . by no means."

"Tell me, what was that you played at our house?"

"'The Three Green Riders on Wild Asses,'" said Andrews smiling.

"What do you mean?"

"It's a prelude to the 'Queen of Sheba,'" said Andrews. "If you didn't think the same as M. Emile Faguet and everyone else about St. Antoine, I'd tell you what I mean."

"That was very silly of me. . . . But if you pick up all the silly things people say accidentally . . . well, you must be angry most of the time."

In the dim light he could not see her eyes. There was a little glow on the curve of her cheek coming from under the dark of her hat to her rather pointed chin. Behind it he could see other faces of men and women crowded on the balcony talking, lit up crudely by the gold glare that came out through the French windows from the lobby.

"I have always been tremendously fascinated by the place in La Tentation where the Queen of Sheba visited Antoine, that's all," said Andrews gruffly.

"Is that the first thing you've done? It made me think a little of Borodine."

"The first that's at all pretentious. It's probably just a steal from everything I've ever heard."

"No, it's good. I suppose you had it in your head all through those dreadful and glorious days at the front. . . . Is it for piano or orchestra?"

"All that's finished is for piano. I hope to orchestrate it eventually. . . . Oh, but it's really silly to talk this way. I don't know enough. . . . I need years of hard work before I can do anything. . . . And I have wasted so much time. . . . That is the most frightful thing. One has so few years of youth!"

"There's the bell, we must scuttle back to our seats. Till the next intermission." She slipped through the glass doors and disappeared. Andrews went back to his seat very excited, full of unquiet exultation. The first strains of the orchestra were pain, he felt them so acutely.

After the last act they walked in silence down a dark street, hurrying to get away from the crowds of the Boulevards.

When they reached the Avenue de l'Opéra, she said:

"Did you say you were going to stay in France?"

"Yes, indeed, if I can. I am going tomorrow to put in an application for discharge in France."

"What will you do then?"

"I shall have to find a job of some sort that will let me study at the Schola Cantorum. But I have enough money to last a little while."

"You are courageous."

"I forgot to ask you if you would rather take the Métro."

"No; let's walk."

They went under the arch of the Louvre. The air was full of a fine wet mist, so that every street lamp was surrounded by a blur of light.

"My blood is full of the music of Debussy," said Geneviève Rod, spreading out her arms.

"It's no use trying to say what one feels about it. Words aren't much good, anyway, are they?"

"That depends."

They walked silently along the quais. The mist was so thick they could not see the Seine, but whenever they came near a bridge they could hear the water rustling through the arches.

"France is stifling," said Andrews, all of a sudden. "It stifles you very slowly, with beautiful silk bands. . . . America beats your brains out with a policeman's billy."

"What do you mean?" she asked, letting pique chill her voice.

"You know so much in France. You have made the world so neat. . . ."

"But you seem to want to stay here," she said with a laugh.

"It's that there's nowhere else. There is nowhere except Paris where one can find out things about music, particularly. . . . But I am one of those people who was not made to be contented."

"Only sheep are contented."

"I think I have been happier this month in Paris than ever before in my life. It seems six, so much has happened in it."

"Poissac is where I am happiest."

"Where is that?"

"We have a country house there, very old and very tumbledown. They say that Rabelais used to come to the village. But our house is from later, from the time of Henri Quatre.

Poissac is not far from Tours. An ugly name, isn't it? But to me it is very beautiful. The house has orchards all round it, and yellow roses with flushed centers poke themselves in my window, and there is a little tower like Montaigne's."

"When I get out of the army, I shall go somewhere in the country and work and work."

"Music should be made in the country, when the sap is rising in the trees."

"'D'après nature,' as the rabbit man said."

"Who's the rabbit man?"

"A very pleasant person," said Andrews, bubbling with laughter. "You shall meet him some day. He sells little stuffed rabbits that jump, outside the Café de Rohan."

"Here we are. . . . Thank you for coming home with me."

"But how soon. Are you sure it is the house? We can't have got there as soon as this."

"Yes, it's my house," said Geneviève Rod laughing. She held out her hand to him and he shook it eagerly. The latchkey clicked in the door.

"Why don't you have a cup of tea with us here tomorrow?" she said.

"With pleasure."

The big varnished door with its knocker in the shape of a ring closed behind her. Andrews walked away with a light step, feeling jolly and exhilarated.

As he walked down the mist-filled quai towards the Place St. Michel, his ears were filled with the lisping gurgle of the river past the piers of the bridges.

Walters was asleep. On the table in his room was a card from Jeanne. Andrews read the card holding it close to the candle.

"How long it is since I saw you!" it read. "I shall pass the Café de Rohan Wednesday at seven, along the pavement opposite the Magazin du Louvre."

It was a card of Malmaison.

Andrews flushed. Bitter melancholy throbbed through him. He walked languidly to the window and looked out into the dark court. A window below his spilled a warm golden haze into the misty night, through which he could make out vaguely some pots of ferns standing on the wet flagstones. From somewhere came a dense smell of hyacinths. Fragments of thought slipped one after another through his mind. He thought of himself washing windows long ago at training camp, and remembered the way the gritty sponge scraped his hands. He could not help feeling shame when he thought of those days. "Well, that's all over now," he told himself. He wondered, in a half-irritated way, about Geneviève Rod. What sort of a person was she? Her face, with its wide eyes and pointed chin and the reddish-chestnut hair, unpretentiously coiled above the white forehead, was very vivid in his mind, though when he tried to remember what it was like in profile, he could not. She had thin hands, with long fingers that ought to play the piano well. When she grew old would she be yellow-toothed and jolly, like her mother? He could not think of her old; she was too vigorous; there was too much malice in her passionately-restrained gestures. The memory of her faded, and there came to his mind Jeanne's overworked little hands, with callous places, and the tips of the fingers grimy and scarred from needlework. But the smell of hyacinths that came up from the mist-filled courtyard was like a sponge wiping all impressions from his brain. The dense sweet smell in the damp air made him feel languid and melancholy.

He took off his clothes slowly and got into bed. The smell of the hyacinths came to him very faintly, so that he did not know whether or not he was imagining it.

The major's office was a large white-painted room, with elaborate mouldings and mirrors in all four walls, so that while Andrews waited, cap in hand, to go up to the desk, he could see the small round major with his pink face and bald head repeated to infinity in two directions in the grey brilliance of the mirrors.

"What do you want?" said the major, looking up from some papers he was signing.

Andrews stepped up to the desk. On both sides of the room a skinny figure in olive-drab, repeated endlessly, stepped up to endless mahogany desks, which faded into each other in an endless dusty perspective.

"Would you mind O.K.-ing this application for discharge, Major?"

"How many dependents?" muttered the major through his teeth, poring over the application.

"None. It's for discharge in France to study music."

"Won't do. You need an affidavit that you can support yourself, that you have enough money to continue your studies. You want to study music, eh? D'you think you've got talent? Needs a very great deal of talent to study music."

"Yes, sir. . . . But is there anything else I need except the affidavit?"

"No. . . . It'll go through in short order. We're glad to release men. . . . We're glad to release any man with a good military record. . . . Williams!"

"Yes, sir."

A sergeant came over from a small table by the door.

"Show this man what he needs to do to get discharged in France."

Andrews saluted. Out of the corner of his eye he saw the figures in the mirror, saluting down an endless corridor.

When he got out on the street in front of the great white building where the major's office was, a morose feeling of helplessness came over him. There were many automobiles of different sizes and shapes, limousines, runabouts, touring cars, lined up along the curb, all painted olive-drab and neatly stenciled with numbers in white. Now and then a personage came out of the white marble building, puttees and Sam Browne belt gleaming, and darted into an automobile, or a noisy motorcycle stopped with a jerk in front of the wide door to let out an officer in goggles and mud-splattered trench coat, who disappeared immediately through revolving doors. Andrews could imagine him striding along halls, where from every door came an imperious clicking of typewriters, where papers were piled high on yellow varnished desks, where sallow-faced clerks in uniform loafed in rooms, where the four walls were covered from floor to ceiling with card catalogues. And every day they were adding to the paper, piling up more little drawers with index cards. It seemed to Andrews that the shiny white marble building would have to burst with all the paper stored up within it, and would flood the broad avenue with avalanches of index cards.

"Button yer coat," snarled a voice in his ear.

Andrews looked up suddenly. An M.P. with a raw-looking face in which was a long sharp nose, had come up to him.

Andrews buttoned up his overcoat and said nothing.

"Ye can't hang around here this way," the M.P. called after him.

Andrews flushed and walked away without turning his head. He was stinging with humiliation; an angry voice inside him kept telling him that he was a coward, that he should make some futile gesture of protest. Grotesque pictures of revolt flamed through his mind, until he remembered that when he was very small, the same tumultuous pride had seethed and ached in him whenever he had been reproved by an older person. Helpless despair fluttered about within him like a bird beating against the wires of a cage. Was there no outlet, no gesture of expression, would he have to go on this way day after day, swallowing the bitter gall of indignation, that every new symbol of his slavery brought to his lips?

He was walking in an agitated way across the Jardin des Tuileries, full of little children and women with dogs on leashes and nursemaids with starched white caps, when he met Geneviève Rod and her mother. Geneviève was dressed in pearl grey, with an elegance a little too fashionable to please Andrews. Mme. Rod wore black. In front of them a black and tan terrier ran from one side to the other, on nervous little legs that trembled like steel springs.

"Isn't it lovely this morning?" cried Geneviève.

"I didn't know you had a dog."

"Oh, we never go out without Santo, a protection to two lone women, you know," said Mme. Rod, laughing. "Viens, Santo, dis bonjour au Monsieur."

"He usually lives at Poissac," said Geneviève.

The little dog barked furiously at Andrews, a shrill bark like a child squalling.

"He knows he ought to be suspicious of soldiers. . . . I imagine most soldiers would change with him if they had a chance. . . . Viens Santo, viens Santo. . . . Will you change lives with me, Santo?"

"You look as if you'd been quarrelling with somebody," said Geneviève Rod lightly.

"I have, with myself. . . . I'm going to write a book on slave psychology. It would be very amusing," said Andrews in a gruff, breathless voice.

"But we must hurry, dear, or we'll be late to the tailor's," said Mme. Rod. She held out her black-gloved hand to Andrews.

"We'll be in at tea time this afternoon. You might play me some more of the 'Queen of Sheba,'" said Geneviève.

"I'm afraid I shan't be able to, but you never can tell. . . . Thank you."

He was relieved to have left them. He had been afraid he would burst out into some childish tirade. What a shame old Henslowe hadn't come back yet. He could have poured out all his despair to him; he had often enough before; and Henslowe was out of the army now. Wearily Andrews decided that he would have to start scheming and intriguing again as he had schemed and intrigued to come to Paris in the first place. He thought of the white marble building and the officers with shiny puttees going in and out, and the typewriters clicking in every room, and the understanding of his helplessness before all that complication made him shiver.

An idea came to him. He ran down the steps of a métro station. Aubrey would know someone at the Crillon who could help him.

But when the train reached the Concorde station, he could not summon the will power to get out. He felt a harsh repugnance to any effort. What was the use of humiliating himself and begging favors of people? It was hopeless anyway. In a fierce burst of pride a voice inside of him was shouting that he, John Andrews, should have no shame, that he should force people to do things for him, that he, who lived more acutely than the rest, suffering more pain and more joy, who had the power to express his pain and his joy so that it would impose itself on others, should force his will on those around him. "More of the psychology of slavery," said Andrews to himself, suddenly smashing the soap-bubble of his egoism.

The train had reached the Porte Maillot.

Andrews stood in the sunny boulevard in front of the métro station, where the plane trees were showing tiny gold-brown leaves, sniffing the smell of a flower-stall in front of which a woman stood, with a deft abstracted gesture tying up bunch after bunch of violets. He felt a desire to be out in the country, to be away from houses and people. There was a line of men and women buying tickets for St. Germain; still indecisive, he joined it, and at last, almost without intending it, found himself jolting through Neuilly in the green trailer of the electric car, that waggled like a duck's tail when the car went fast.

He remembered his last trip on that same car with Jeanne, and wished mournfully that he might have fallen in love with her, that he might have forgotten himself and the army and everything in crazy, romantic love.

When he got off the car at St. Germain, he had stopped formulating his thoughts; soggy despair throbbed in him like an infected wound.

He sat for a while at the café opposite the Château looking at the light red walls and the strong stone-bordered windows and the jaunty turrets and chimneys that rose above the classic balustrade with its big urns on the edge of the roof. The park, through the tall iron railings, was full of russet and pale lines, all mist of new leaves. Had they really lived more vividly, the people of the Renaissance? Andrews could almost see men with plumed hats and short cloaks and elaborate brocaded tunics swaggering with a hand at the sword hilt, about the quiet square in front of the gate of the Château. And he thought of the great, sudden wind of freedom that had blown out of Italy, before which dogmas and slaveries had crumbled to dust. In contrast, the world today seemed pitifully arid. Men seemed to have shrunk in stature before the vastness of the mechanical contrivances they had invented. Michael Angelo, da Vinci, Aretino, Cellini; would the strong figures of men ever so dominate the world again? Today everything was congestion, the scurrying of crowds; men had become antlike. Perhaps it was inevitable that the crowds should sink deeper and deeper in slavery. Whichever won, tyranny from above, or spontaneous organization from below, there could be no individuals.

He went through the gates into the park, laid out with a few flower beds where pansies bloomed; through the dark ranks of elm trunks, was brilliant sky, with here and there a moss-green statue standing out against it. At the head of an alley he came out on a terrace. Beyond the strong curves of the pattern of the iron balustrade was an expanse of country, pale green, falling to blue towards the horizon, patched with pink and slate-colored houses and carved with railway tracks. At his feet the Seine shone like a curved sword blade.

He walked with long strides along the terrace, and followed a road that turned into the forest, forgetting the monotonous tread mill of his thoughts, in the flush that the fast walking sent through his whole body, in the rustling silence of the woods, where the moss on the north side of the boles of the trees was emerald, and where the sky was soft grey through a lavender lacework of branches. The green gnarled woods made him think of the first act of Pelléas. With his tunic unbuttoned and his shirt open at the neck and his hands stuck deep in his pockets, he went along whistling like a school boy.

After an hour he came out of the woods on a highroad, where he found himself walking beside a two-wheeled cart, that kept pace with him exactly, try as he would to get ahead of it. After a while, a boy leaned out:

"Hey, l'Américain, vous voulez monter?"

"Where are you going?"

"Conflans-Ste.-Honorine."

"Where's that?"

The boy flourished his whip vaguely towards the horse's head.

"All right," said Andrews.

"These are potatoes," said the boy, "make yourself comfortable."

Andrews offered him a cigarette, which he took with muddy fingers. He had a broad face, red cheeks and chunky features. Reddish-brown hair escaped spikily from under a mud-spattered beret.

"Where did you say you were going?"

"Conflans-Ste.-Honorine. Silly all these saints, aren't they?"

Andrews laughed.

"Where are you going?" the boy asked.

"I don't know. I was taking a walk."

The boy leaned over to Andrews and whispered in his ear: "Deserter?"

"No. . . . I had a day off and wanted to see the country."

"I just thought, if you were a deserter, I might be able to help you. Must be silly to be a soldier. Dirty life. . . . But

you like the country. So do I. You can't call this country. I'm
not from this part; I'm from Brittany. There we have real
country. It's stifling near Paris here, so many people, so many
houses."

"It seems mighty fine to me."

"That's because you're a soldier. Better than barracks, hein?
Dirty life that. I'll never be a soldier. I'm going into the navy.
Merchant marine, and then if I have to do service I'll do it on
the sea."

"I suppose it is pleasanter."

"There's more freedom. And the sea. . . . We Bretons,
you know, we all die of the sea or of liquor."

They laughed.

"Have you been long in this part of the country?" asked
Andrews.

"Six months. It's very dull, this farming work. I'm head of
a gang in a fruit orchard, but not for long. I have a brother
shipped on a sailing vessel. When he comes back to Bordeaux,
I'll ship on the same boat."

"Where to?"

"South America, Peru; how should I know?"

"I'd like to ship on a sailing vessel," said Andrews.

"You would? It seems very fine to me to travel, and see new
countries. And perhaps I shall stay over there."

"Where?"

"How should I know? If I like it, that is. . . . Life is very
bad in Europe."

"It is stifling, I suppose," said Andrews slowly, "all these
nations, all these hatreds, but still . . . it is very beautiful. Life
is very ugly in America."

"Let's have something to drink. There's a bistro!"

The boy jumped down from the cart and tied the horse to
a tree. They went into a small wine shop with a counter and
one square oak table.

"But won't you be late?" said Andrews.

"I don't care. I like talking, don't you?"

"Yes, indeed."

They ordered wine of an old woman in a green apron, who
had three yellow teeth that protruded from her mouth when
she spoke.

"I haven't had anything to eat," said Andrews.

"Wait a minute." The boy ran out to the cart and came back with a canvas bag, from which he took half a loaf of bread and some cheese.

"My name's Marcel," the boy said when they had sat for a while sipping wine.

"Mine is Jean . . . Jean André."

"I have a brother named Jean, and my father's name is André. That's pleasant, isn't it?"

"But it must be a splendid job, working in a fruit orchard," said Andrews, munching bread and cheese.

"It's well paid; but you get tired of being in one place all the time. It's not as it is in Brittany. . . ." Marcel paused. He sat, rocking a little on the stool, holding on to the seat between his legs. A curious brilliance came into his grey eyes. "There," he went on in a soft voice, "it is so quiet in the fields, and from every hill you look at the sea. . . . I like that, don't you?" he turned to Andrews, with a smile.

"You are lucky to be free," said Andrews bitterly. He felt as if he would burst into tears.

"But you will be demobilized soon; the butchery is over. You will go home to your family. That will be good, hein?"

"I wonder. It's not far enough away. Restless!"

"What do you expect?"

A fine rain was falling. They climbed in on the potato sacks and the horse started a jog trot; its lanky brown shanks glistened a little from the rain.

"Do you come out this way often?" asked Marcel.

"I shall. It's the nicest place near Paris."

"Some Sunday you must come and I'll take you round. The Castle is very fine. And then there is Malmaison, where the great Emperor lived with the Empress Joséphine."

Andrews suddenly remembered Jeanne's card. This was Wednesday. He pictured her dark figure among the crowd of the pavement in front of the Café de Rohan. Of course it had to be that way. Despair, so helpless as to be almost sweet, came over him.

"And girls," he said suddenly to Marcel, "are they pretty round here?"

Marcel shrugged his shoulders.

"It's not women that we lack, if a fellow has money," he said.

Andrews felt a sense of shame, he did not exactly know why.

"My brother writes that in South America the women are very brown and very passionate," added Marcel with a wistful smile. "But travelling and reading books, that's what I like. . . . But look, if you want to take the train back to Paris. . . ." Marcel pulled up the horse to a standstill. "If you want to take the train, cross that field by the foot path and keep right along the road to the left till you come to the river. There's a ferryman. The town's Herblay, and there's a station. . . . And any Sunday before noon I'll be at 3 rue des Evèques, Reuil. You must come and we'll take a walk together."

They shook hands, and Andrews strode off across the wet fields. Something strangely sweet and wistful that he could not analyse lingered in his mind from Marcel's talk. Somewhere, beyond everything, he was conscious of the great free rhythm of the sea.

Then he thought of the Major's office that morning, and of his own skinny figure in the mirrors, repeated endlessly, standing helpless and humble before the shining mahogany desk. Even out here in these fields where the wet earth seemed to heave with the sprouting of new growth, he was not free. In those office buildings, with white marble halls full of the clank of officers' heels, in index cards and piles of typewritten papers, his real self, which they had power to kill if they wanted to, was in his name and his number, on lists with millions of other names and other numbers. This sentient body of his, full of possibilities and hopes and desires, was only a pale ghost that depended on the other self, that suffered for it and cringed for it. He could not drive out of his head the picture of himself, skinny, in an ill-fitting uniform, repeated endlessly in the two mirrors of the Major's white-painted office.

All of a sudden, through bare poplar trees, he saw the Seine.

He hurried along the road, splashing now and then in a shining puddle, until he came to a landing place. The river was very wide, silvery, streaked with pale-green and violet, and straw-color from the evening sky. Opposite were bare poplars and behind them clusters of buff-colored houses climbing up a green hill to a church, all repeated upside down in the color-streaked river. The river was very full, and welled up above its banks, the way the water stands up above the rim of a glass filled too full. From the water came an indefinable rustling, flowing sound that rose and fell with quiet rhythm in Andrews's ears.

Andrews forgot everything in the great wave of music that rose impetuously through him, poured with the hot blood through his veins, with the streaked colors of the river and the sky through his eyes, with the rhythm of the flowing river through his ears.

V

"So I came without," said Andrews, laughing.

"What fun!" cried Geneviève. "But anyway they couldn't do anything to you. Chartres is so near. It's at the gates of Paris."

They were alone in the compartment. The train had pulled out of the station and was going through suburbs where the trees were in leaf in the gardens, and fruit trees foamed above the red brick walls, among the box-like villas.

"Anyway," said Andrews, "it was an opportunity not to be missed."

"That must be one of the most amusing things about being a soldier, avoiding regulations. I wonder whether Damocles didn't really enjoy his sword, don't you think so?"

They laughed.

"But mother was very doubtful about my coming with you this way. She's such a dear, she wants to be very modern and liberal, but she always gets frightened at the last minute. And my aunt will think the world's end has come when we appear."

They went through some tunnels, and when the train stopped at Sèvres, had a glimpse of the Seine valley, where the blue mist made a patina over the soft pea-green of new leaves. Then the train came out on wide plains, full of the glaucous shimmer of young oats and the golden-green of fresh-sprinkled wheat fields, where the mist on the horizon was purplish. The train's shadow, blue, sped along beside them over the grass and fences.

"How beautiful it is to go out of the city this way in the early morning! . . . Has your aunt a piano?"

"Yes, a very old and tinkly one."

"It would be amusing to play you all I have done at the 'Queen of Sheba.' You say the most helpful things."

"It is that I am interested. I think you will do something some day."

Andrews shrugged his shoulders.

They sat silent, their ears filled up by the jerking rhythm of wheels over rails, now and then looking at each other, almost furtively. Outside, fields and hedges and patches of blossom, and poplar trees faintly powdered with green, unrolled, like a scroll before them, behind the flicker of telegraph poles and the festooned wires on which the sun gave glints of red copper. Andrews discovered all at once that the coppery glint on the telegraph wires was the same as the glint in Geneviève's hair. "Berenike, Artemisia, Arsinoë," the names lingered in his mind. So that as he looked out of the window at the long curves of the telegraph wires that seemed to rise and fall as they glided past, he could imagine her face, with its large, pale brown eyes and its small mouth and broad smooth forehead, suddenly stilled into the encaustic painting on the mummy case of some Alexandrian girl.

"Tell me," she said, "when did you begin to write music?"

Andrews brushed the light, disordered hair off his forehead.

"Why, I think I forgot to brush my hair this morning," he said. "You see, I was so excited by the idea of coming to Chartres with you."

They laughed.

"But my mother taught me to play the piano when I was very small," he went on seriously. "She and I lived alone in an old house belonging to her family in Virginia. How different all that was from anything you have ever lived. It would not be possible in Europe to be as isolated as we were in Virginia. . . . Mother was very unhappy. She had led a dreadfully thwarted life . . . that unrelieved hopeless misery that only a woman can suffer. She used to tell me stories, and I used to make up little tunes about them, and about anything. The great success," he laughed, "was, I remember, to a dandelion. . . . I can remember so well the way Mother pursed up her lips as she leaned over the writing desk. . . . She was very tall, and as it was dark in our old sitting room, had to lean far over to see. . . . She used to spend hours making beautiful copies of tunes I made up. My mother is the only person who has ever really had any importance in my life. . . . But I lack technical training terribly."

"Do you think it is so important?" said Geneviève, leaning towards him to make herself heard above the clatter of the train.

"Perhaps it isn't. I don't know."

"I think it always comes sooner or later, if you feel intensely enough."

"But it is so frightful to feel all you want to express getting away beyond you. An idea comes into your head, and you feel it grow stronger and stronger and you can't grasp it; you have no means to express it. It's like standing on a street corner and seeing a gorgeous procession go by without being able to join it, or like opening a bottle of beer and having it foam all over you without having a glass to pour it into."

Geneviève burst out laughing.

"But you can drink from the bottle, can't you?" she said, her eyes sparkling.

"I'm trying to," said Andrews.

"Here we are. There's the cathedral. No, it's hidden," cried Geneviève.

They got to their feet. As they left the station, Andrews said:

"But after all, it's only freedom that matters. When I'm out of the army! . . ."

"Yes, I suppose you are right . . . for you that is. The artist should be free from any sort of entanglement."

"I don't see what difference there is between an artist and any other sort of workman," said Andrews savagely.

"No, but look."

From the square where they stood, above the green blur of a little park, they could see the cathedral, creamy yellow and rust color, with the sober tower and the gaudy tower, and the great rose window between, the whole pile standing nonchalantly, knee deep in the packed roofs of the town.

They stood shoulder to shoulder, looking at it without speaking.

In the afternoon they walked down the hill towards the river, that flowed through a quarter of tottering, peak-gabled houses and mills, from which came a sound of grinding wheels. Above them, towering over gardens full of pear trees in bloom, the apse of the cathedral bulged against the pale sky. On a narrow and very ancient bridge they stopped and looked at the water, full of a shimmer of blue and green and grey from the sky and from the vivid new leaves of the willow trees along the bank.

Their senses glutted with the beauty of the day and the intricate magnificence of the cathedral, languid with all they had seen and said, they were talking of the future with quiet voices.

"It's all in forming a habit of work," Andrews was saying. "You have to be a slave to get anything done. It's all a question of choosing your master, don't you think so?"

"Yes. I suppose all the men who have left their imprint on people's lives have been slaves in a sense," said Geneviève slowly. "Everyone has to give up a great deal of life to live anything deeply. But it's worth it." She looked Andrews full in the eyes.

"Yes, I think it's worth it," said Andrews. "But you must help me. Now I am like a man who has come up out of a dark cellar. I'm almost too dazzled by the gorgeousness of everything. But at least I am out of the cellar."

"Look, a fish jumped," cried Geneviève.

"I wonder if we could hire a boat anywhere. . . . Don't you think it'd be fun to go out in a boat?"

A voice broke in on Geneviève's answer:

"Let's see your pass, will you?"

Andrews turned round. A soldier with a round brown face and red cheeks stood beside him on the bridge. Andrews looked at him fixedly. A little zigzag scar above his left eye showed white on his heavily tanned skin.

"Let's see your pass," the man said again; he had a high pitched, squeaky voice.

Andrews felt the blood thumping in his ears.

"Are you an M.P.?"

"Yes."

"Well I'm in the Sorbonne Detachment."

"What the hell's that?" said the M.P., laughing thinly.

"What does he say?" asked Geneviève, smiling.

"Nothing. I'll have to go see the officer and explain," said Andrews in a breathless voice. "You go back to your Aunt's and I'll come as soon as I've arranged it."

"No, I'll come with you."

"Please go back. It may be serious. I'll come as soon as I can," said Andrews harshly.

She walked up the hill with swift decisive steps, without turning round.

"Tough luck, buddy," said the M.P. "She's a good-looker. I'd like to have a half-hour with her myself."

"Look here. I'm in the Sorbonne School Detachment in Paris, and I came down here without a pass. Is there anything I can do about it?"

"They'll fix you up, don't worry," cried the M.P. shrilly. "You ain't a member of the General Staff in disguise, are ye? School Detachment! Gee, won't Bill Huggis laugh when he hears that? You pulled the best one yet, buddy. . . . But come along," he added in a confidential tone. "If you come quiet I won't put the handcuffs on ye."

"How do I know you're an M.P.?"

"You'll know soon enough."

They turned down a narrow street between grey stucco walls leprous with moss and water stains.

At a chair inside the window of a small wine shop a man with a red M.P. badge sat smoking. He got up when he saw them pass and opened the door with one hand on his pistol holster.

"I got one bird, Bill," said the man, shoving Andrews roughly in the door.

"Good for you, Handsome; is he quiet?"

"Um." Handsome grunted.

"Sit down there. If you move you'll git a bullet in your guts." The M.P. stuck out a square jaw; he had a sallow skin, puffy under the eyes that were grey and lustreless.

"He says he's in some goddam School Detachment. First time that's been pulled, ain't it?"

"School Detachment. D'you mean an O.T.C.?" Bill sank laughing into his chair by the window, spreading his legs out over the floor.

"Ain't that rich?" said Handsome, laughing shrilly again.

"Got any papers on ye? Ye must have some sort of papers."

Andrews searched his pockets. He flushed.

"I ought to have a school pass."

"You sure ought. Gee, this guy's simple," said Bill, leaning far back in the chair and blowing smoke through his nose.

"Look at his dawg-tag, Handsome."

The man strode over to Andrews and jerked open the top of his tunic. Andrews pulled his body away.

"I haven't got any on. I forgot to put any on this morning."

"No tag, no insignia."

"Yes, I have, infantry."

"No papers. . . . I bet he's been out a hell of a time," said Handsome meditatively.

"Better put the cuffs on him," said Bill in the middle of a yawn.

"Let's wait a while. When's the loot coming?"

"Not till night."

"Sure?"

"Yes. Ain't no train."

"How about a side car?"

"No, I know he ain't comin'," snarled Bill.

"What d'you say we have a little liquor, Bill? Bet this bloke's got money. You'll set us up to a glass o' cognac, won't you, School Detachment?"

Andrews sat very stiff in his chair, staring at them.

"Yes," he said, "order up what you like."

"Keep an eye on him, Handsome. You never can tell what this quiet kind's likely to pull off on you."

Bill Huggis strode out of the room with heavy steps. In a moment he came back swinging a bottle of cognac in his hand.

"Tole the Madame you'd pay, Skinny," said the man as he passed Andrews's chair. Andrews nodded.

The two M.P.'s drew up to the table beside which Andrews sat. Andrews could not keep his eyes off them. Bill Huggis hummed as he pulled the cork out of the bottle.

> "It's the smile that makes you happy,
> It's the smile that makes you sad."

Handsome watched him, grinning.

Suddenly they both burst out laughing.

"An' the damn fool thinks he's in a school battalion," said Handsome in his shrill voice.

"It'll be another kind of a battalion you'll be in, Skinny," cried Bill Huggis. He stifled his laughter with a long drink from the bottle.

He smacked his lips.

"Not so goddam bad," he said. Then he started humming again:

> "It's the smile that makes you happy,
> It's the smile that makes you sad."

"Have some, Skinny?" said Handsome, pushing the bottle towards Andrews.

"No, thanks," said Andrews.

"Ye won't be gettin' good cognac where yer goin', Skinny, not by a damn sight," growled Bill Huggis in the middle of a laugh.

"All right, I'll take a swig." An idea had suddenly come into Andrews's head.

"Gee, the bastard kin drink cognac," cried Handsome.

"Got enough money to buy us another bottle?"

Andrews nodded. He wiped his mouth absently with his handkerchief; he had drunk the raw cognac without tasting it.

"Get another bottle, Handsome," said Bill Huggis carelessly. A purplish flush had appeared in the lower part of his cheeks. When the other man came back, he burst out laughing.

"The last cognac this Skinny guy from the school detachment'll get for many a day. Better drink up strong, Skinny. . . . They don't have that stuff down on the farm. . . . School Detachment; I'll be goddamned!" He leaned back in his chair, shaking with laughter.

Handsome's face was crimson. Only the zigzag scar over his eye remained white. He was swearing in a low voice as he worked the cork out of the bottle.

Andrews could not keep his eyes off the men's faces. They went from one to the other, in spite of him. Now and then, for an instant, he caught a glimpse of the yellow and brown squares of the wall paper and the bar with a few empty bottles behind it.

He tried to count the bottles; "one, two, three . . ." but he was staring in the lustreless grey eyes of Bill Huggis, who lay back in his chair, blowing smoke out of his nose, now and then reaching for the cognac bottle, all the while humming faintly, under his breath:

> "It's the smile that makes you happy,
> It's the smile that makes you sad."

Handsome sat with his elbows on the table, and his chin in his beefy hands. His face was flushed crimson, but the skin was softly moulded, like a woman's.

The light in the room was beginning to grow grey.

Handsome and Bill Huggis stood up. A young officer, with clearly-marked features and a campaign hat worn a little on one side, came in, stood with his feet wide apart in the middle of the floor.

Andrews went up to him.

"I'm in the Sorbonne Detachment, Lieutenant, stationed in Paris."

"Don't you know enough to salute?" said the officer, looking him up and down. "One of you men teach him to salute," he said slowly.

Handsome made a step towards Andrews and hit him with his fist between the eyes. There was a flash of light and the room swung round, and there was a splitting crash as his head struck the floor. He got to his feet. The fist hit him in the same place, blinding him, the three figures and the bright oblong of the window swung round. A chair crashed down with him, and a hard rap in the back of his skull brought momentary blackness.

"That's enough, let him be," he heard a voice far away at the end of a black tunnel.

A great weight seemed to be holding him down as he struggled to get up, blinded by tears and blood. Rending pains darted like arrows through his head. There were handcuffs on his wrists.

"Git up," snarled a voice.

He got to his feet, faint light came through the streaming tears in his eyes. His forehead flamed as if hot coals were being pressed against it.

"Prisoner, attention!" shouted the officer's voice. "March!"

Automatically, Andrews lifted one foot and then the other. He felt in his face the cool air of the street. On either side of him were the hard steps of the M.P.'s. Within him a nightmare voice was shrieking, shrieking.

I

THE UNCOVERED garbage cans clattered as they were thrown one by one into the truck. Dust, and a smell of putrid things, hung in the air about the men as they worked. A guard stood by with his legs wide apart, and his rifle-butt on the pavement between them. The early mist hung low, hiding the upper windows of the hospital. From the door beside which the garbage cans were ranged came a thick odor of carbolic. The last garbage can rattled into place on the truck, the four prisoners and the guard clambered on, finding room as best they could among the cans, from which dripped bloody bandages, ashes, and bits of decaying food, and the truck rumbled off towards the incinerator, through the streets of Paris that sparkled with the gaiety of early morning.

The prisoners wore no tunics; their shirts and breeches had dark stains of grease and dirt; on their hands were torn canvas gloves. The guard was a sheepish, pink-faced youth, who kept grinning apologetically, and had trouble keeping his balance when the truck went round corners.

"How many days do they keep a guy on this job, Happy?" asked a boy with mild blue eyes and a creamy complexion, and reddish curly hair.

"Damned if I know, kid; as long as they please, I guess," said the bull-necked man next him, who had a lined prize fighter's face, with a heavy protruding jaw. Then, after looking at the boy for a minute, with his face twisted into an astonished sort of grin, he went on: "Say, kid, how in hell did you git here? Robbin' the cradle, Oi call it, to send you here, kid."

"I stole a Ford," the boy answered cheerfully.

"Like hell you did!"

"Sold it for five hundred francs."

Happy laughed, and caught hold of an ash can to keep from being thrown out of the jolting truck.

"Kin ye beat that, guard?" he cried. "Ain't that somethin'?"

The guard sniggered.

"Didn't send me to Leavenworth 'cause I was so young," went on the kid placidly.

"How old are you, kid?" asked Andrews, who was leaning against the driver's seat.

"Seventeen," said the boy, blushing and casting his eyes down.

"He must have lied like hell to git in this goddam army," boomed the deep voice of the truck driver, who had leaned over to spit a long squirt of tobacco juice.

The truck driver jammed the brakes on. The garbage cans banged against each other.

The Kid cried out in pain: "Hold your horses, can't you? You nearly broke my leg."

The truck driver was swearing in a long string of words.

"Goddam these dreamin', skygazin' sons of French bastards. Why don't they get out of your way? Git out an' crank her up, Happy."

"Guess a feller'd be lucky if he'd break his leg or somethin'; don't you think so, Skinny?" said the fourth prisoner in a low voice.

"It'll take mor'n a broken leg to git you out o' this labor battalion, Hoggenback. Won't it, guard?" said Happy, as he climbed on again.

The truck jolted away, trailing a haze of cinder dust and a sour stench of garbage behind it. Andrews noticed all at once that they were going down the quais along the river. Notre Dame was rosy in the misty sunlight, the color of lilacs in full bloom. He looked at it fixedly a moment, and then looked away. He felt very far from it, like a man looking at the stars from the bottom of a pit.

"My mate, he's gone to Leavenworth for five years," said the Kid when they had been silent some time listening to the rattle of the garbage cans as the trucks jolted over the cobbles.

"Helped yer steal the Ford, did he?" asked Happy.

"Ford nothin'! He sold an ammunition train. He was a railroad man. He was a mason, that's why he only got five years."

"I guess five years in Leavenworth's enough for anybody," muttered Hoggenback, scowling. He was a square shouldered dark man, who always hung his head when he worked.

"We didn't meet up till we got to Paris; we was on a hell of a party together at the Olympia. That's where they picked us up. Took us to the Bastille. Ever been in the Bastille?"

"I have," said Hoggenback.

"Ain't no joke, is it?"

"Christ!" said Hoggenback. His face flushed a furious red. He turned away and looked at the civilians walking briskly along the early morning streets, at the waiters in shirt sleeves swabbing off the café tables, at the women pushing handcarts full of bright-colored vegetables over the cobblestones.

"I guess they ain't nobody gone through what we guys go through with," said Happy. "It'd be better if the ole war was still a' goin', to my way o' thinkin'. They'd chuck us into the trenches then. Ain't so low as this."

"Look lively," shouted the truck driver, as the truck stopped in a dirty yard full of cinder piles. "Ain't got all day. Five more loads to get yet."

The guard stood by with angry face and stiff limbs; for he feared there were officers about, and the prisoners started unloading the garbage cans; their nostrils were full of the stench of putrescence; between their lips was a gritty taste of cinders.

The air in the dark mess shack was thick with steam from the kitchen at one end. The men filed past the counter, holding out their mess kits, into which the K.P.'s splashed the food. Occasionally someone stopped to ask for a larger helping in an ingratiating voice. They ate packed together at long tables of roughly planed boards, stained from the constant spilling of grease and coffee and still wet from a perfunctory scrubbing. Andrews sat at the end of a bench, near the door through which came the glimmer of twilight, eating slowly, surprised at the relish with which he ate the greasy food, and at the exhausted contentment that had come over him almost in spite of himself. Hoggenback sat opposite him.

"Funny," he said to Hoggenback, "it's not really as bad as I thought it would be."

"What d'you mean, this labor battalion? Hell, a feller can put up with anything; that's one thing you learn in the army."

"I guess people would rather put up with things than make an effort to change them."

"You're goddam right. Got a butt?"

Andrews handed him a cigarette. They got to their feet and walked out into the twilight, holding their mess kits in front of them. As they were washing their mess kits in a tub of greasy water, where bits of food floated in a thick scum, Hoggenback suddenly said in a low voice:

"But it all piles up, Buddy; some day there'll be an accountin'. D'you believe in religion?"

"No."

"Neither do I. I come of folks as done their own accountin'. My father an' my gran'father before him. A feller can't eat his bile day after day, day after day."

"I'm afraid he can, Hoggenback," broke in Andrews. They walked towards the barracks.

"Goddam it, no," cried Hoggenback aloud. "There comes a point where you can't eat yer bile any more, where it don't do no good to cuss. Then you runs amuck."

Hanging his head he went slowly into the barracks.

Andrews leaned against the outside of the building, staring up at the sky. He was trying desperately to think, to pull together a few threads of his life in this moment of respite from the nightmare. In five minutes the bugle would din in his ears, and he would be driven into the barracks. A tune came to his head that he played with eagerly for a moment, and then, as memory came to him, tried to efface with a shudder of disgust.

> "There's the smile that makes you happy,
> There's the smile that makes you sad."

It was almost dark. Two men walked slowly by in front of him.

"Sarge, may I speak to you?" came a voice in a whisper.

The sergeant grunted.

"I think there's two guys trying to break loose out of here."

"Who? If you're wrong it'll be the worse for you, remember that."

"Surley an' Watson. I heard 'em talkin' about it behind the latrine."

"Damn fools."

"They was sayin' they'd rather be dead than keep up this life."

"They did, did they?"

"Don't talk so loud, Sarge. It wouldn't do for any of the fellers to know I was talkin' to yer. Say, Sarge . . ." the voice became whining, "don't you think I've nearly served my time down here?"

"What do I know about that? 'Tain't my job."

"But, Sarge, I used to be company clerk with my old outfit. Don't ye need a guy round the office?"

Andrews strode past them into the barracks. Dull fury possessed him. He took off his clothes and got silently into his blankets.

Hoggenback and Happy were talking beside his bunk.

"Never you mind," said Hoggenback, "somebody'll get that guy sooner or later."

"Git him, nauthin'! The fellers in that camp was so damn skeered they jumped if you snapped yer fingers at 'em. It's the discipline. I'm tellin' yer, it gits a feller in the end," said Happy.

Andrews lay without speaking, listening to their talk, aching in every muscle from the crushing work of the day.

"They court-martialled that guy, a feller told me," went on Hoggenback. "An' what d'ye think they did to him? Retired on half pay. He was a major."

"Gawd, if I iver git out o' this army, I'll be so goddam glad," began Happy. Hoggenback interrupted:

"That you'll forgit all about the raw deal they gave you, an' tell everybody how fine ye liked it."

Andrews felt the mocking notes of the bugle outside stabbing his ears. A non-com's voice roared: "Quiet," from the end of the building, and the lights went out. Already Andrews could hear the deep breathing of men asleep. He lay awake, staring into the darkness, his body throbbing with the monotonous rhythms of the work of the day. He seemed still to hear the sickening whine in the man's voice as he talked to the sergeant outside in the twilight. "And shall I be reduced to that?" he was asking himself.

*

Andrews was leaving the latrine when he heard a voice call softly, "Skinny."

"Yes," he said.

"Come here, I want to talk to you." It was the Kid's voice. There was no light in the ill-smelling shack that served for a latrine. Outside they could hear the guard humming softly to himself as he went back and forth before the barracks door.

"Let's you and me be buddies, Skinny."

"Sure," said Andrews.

"Say, what d'you think the chance is o' cuttin' loose?"

"Pretty damn poor," said Andrews.

"Couldn't you just make a noise like a hoop an' roll away?" They giggled softly.

Andrews put his hand on the boy's arm.

"But, Kid, it's too risky. I got in this fix by taking a risk. I don't feel like beginning over again, and if they catch you, it's desertion. Leavenworth for twenty years, or life. That'd be the end of everything."

"Well, what the hell's this?"

"Oh, I don't know; they've got to let us out some day."

"Sh . . . sh. . . ."

Kid put his hand suddenly over Andrews's mouth. They stood rigid, so that they could hear their hearts pounding.

Outside there was a brisk step on the gravel. The sentry halted and saluted. The steps faded into the distance, and the sentry's humming began again.

"They put two fellers in the jug for a month for talking like we are. . . . In solitary," whispered Kid.

"But, Kid, I haven't got the guts to try anything now."

"Sure you have, Skinny. You an' me's got more guts than all the rest of 'em put together. God, if people had guts, you couldn't treat 'em like they were curs. Look, if I can ever get out o' this, I've got a hunch I can make a good thing writing movie scenarios. I want to get on in the world, Skinny."

"But, Kid, you won't be able to go back to the States."

"I don't care. New Rochelle's not the whole world. They got the movies in Italy, ain't they?"

"Sure. Let's go to bed."

"All right. Look, you an' me are buddies from now on, Skinny."

Andrews felt the Kid's hand press his arm.

In his dark, airless bunk, in the lowest of three tiers, Andrews lay awake a long time, listening to the snores and the heavy breathing about him. Thoughts fluttered restlessly in his head, but in his blank hopelessness he could only frown and bite his lips, and roll his head from side to side on the rolled-up tunic he used for a pillow, listening with desperate attention to the heavy breathing of the men who slept above him and beside him.

When he fell asleep he dreamed that he was alone with Geneviève Rod in the concert hall of the Schola Cantorum, and that he was trying desperately hard to play some tune for her on the violin, a tune he kept forgetting, and in the agony of trying to remember, the tears streamed down his cheeks. Then he had his arms round Geneviève's shoulders and was kissing her, kissing her, until he found that it was a wooden board he was kissing, a wooden board on which was painted a face with broad forehead and great pale brown eyes, and small tight lips, and all the while a boy who seemed to be both Chrisfield and the Kid kept telling him to run or the M.P.'s would get him. Then he sat frozen in icy terror with a bottle in his hand, while a frightful voice behind him sang very loud:

"There's the smile that makes you happy,
There's the smile that makes you sad."

The bugle woke him, and he sat up with such a start that he hit his head hard against the bunk above him. He lay back cringing from the pain like a child. But he had to hurry desperately to get his clothes on in time for roll call. It was with a feeling of relief that he found that mess was not ready, and that men were waiting in line outside the kitchen shack, stamping their feet and clattering their mess kits as they moved about through the chilly twilight of the spring morning. Andrews found he was standing behind Hoggenback.

"How's she comin', Skinny?" whispered Hoggenback, in his low mysterious voice.

"Oh, we're all in the same boat," said Andrews with a laugh.

"Wish it'd sink," muttered the other man. "D'ye know," he went on after a pause, "I kinder thought an edicated guy like you'd be able to keep out of a mess like this. I wasn't brought up without edication, but I guess I didn't have enough."

"I guess most of 'em can; I don't see that it's much to the point. A man suffers as much if he doesn't know how to read and write as if he had a college education."

"I dunno, Skinny. A feller who's led a rough life can put up with an awful lot. The thing is, Skinny, I might have had a commission if I hadn't been so damned impatient. . . . I'm a lumberman by trade, and my dad's cleaned up a pretty thing in war contracts jus' a short time ago. He could have got me in the engineers if I hadn't gone off an' enlisted."

"Why did you?"

"I was restless-like. I guess I wanted to see the world. I didn't care about the goddam war, but I wanted to see what things was like over here."

"Well, you've seen," said Andrews, smiling.

"In the neck," said Hoggenback, as he pushed out his cup for coffee.

In the truck that was taking them to work, Andrews and the Kid sat side by side on the jouncing backboard and tried to talk above the rumble of the exhaust.

"Like Paris?" asked the Kid.

"Not this way," said Andrews.

"Say, one of the guys said you could parlay French real well. I want you to teach me. A guy's got to know languages to get along in this country."

"But you must know some."

"Bedroom French," said the Kid, laughing.

"Well?"

"But if I want to write a movie scenario for an Eytalian firm, I can't just write 'voulay-vous couchezavecmoa' over and over again."

"But you'll have to learn Italian, Kid."

"I'm goin' to. Say, ain't they taking us a hell of a ways to-day, Skinny?"

"We're goin' to Passy Wharf to unload rock," said somebody in a grumbling voice.

"No, it's a cement . . . cement for the stadium we're presentin' the French Nation. Ain't you read in the '*Stars and Stripes*' about it?"

"I'd present 'em with a swift kick, and a hell of a lot of other people, too."

"So we have to sweat unloadin' ce-ment all day," muttered Hoggenback, "to give these goddam frawgs a stadium."

"If it weren't that it'd be somethin' else."

"But, ain't we got folks at home to work for?" cried Hoggenback. "Mightn't all this sweat be doin' some good for us? Building a stadium! My gawd!"

"Pile out there. . . . Quick!" rasped a voice from the driver's seat.

Through the haze of choking white dust, Andrews got now and then a glimpse of the grey-green river, with its tugboats sporting their white cockades of steam and their long trailing plumes of smoke, and its blunt-nosed barges and its bridges, where people walked jauntily back and forth, going about their business, going where they wanted to go. The bags of cement were very heavy, and the unaccustomed work sent racking pains through his back. The biting dust stung under his finger nails, and in his mouth and eyes. All the morning a sort of refrain went through his head: "People have spent their lives . . . doing only this. People have spent their lives doing only this." As he crossed and recrossed the narrow plank from the barge to the shore, he looked at the black water speeding seawards and took extraordinary care not to let his foot slip. He did not know why, for one-half of him was thinking how wonderful it would be to drown, to forget in eternal black silence the hopeless struggle. Once he saw the Kid standing before the sergeant in charge in an attitude of complete exhaustion, and caught a glint of his blue eyes as he looked up appealingly, looking like a child begging out of a spanking. The sight amused him, and he said to himself: "If I had pink cheeks and cupid's bow lips, I might be able to go through life on my blue eyes"; and he pictured the Kid, a fat, cherubic old man, stepping out of a white limousine, the way people do in the movies, and looking about him with those same mild blue eyes. But soon he forgot everything in the agony of the heavy cement bags bearing down on his back and hips.

In the truck on the way back to the mess the Kid, looking fresh and smiling among the sweating men, like ghosts from the white dust, talking hoarsely above the clatter of the truck, sidled up very close to Andrews.

"D'you like swimmin', Skinny?"

"Yes. I'd give a lot to get some of this cement dust off me," said Andrews, without interest.

"I once won a boy's swimmin' race at Coney," said the Kid. Andrews did not answer.

"Were you in the swimmin' team or anything like that, Skinny, when you went to school?"

"No. . . . It would be wonderful to be in the water, though. I used to swim way out in Chesapeake Bay at night when the water was phosphorescent."

Andrews suddenly found the Kid's blue eyes, bright as flames from excitement, staring into his.

"God, I'm an ass," he muttered.

He felt the Kid's fist punch him softly in the back. "Sergeant said they was goin' to work us late as hell tonight," the Kid was saying aloud to the men round him.

"I'll be dead if they do," muttered Hoggenback.

"An' you a lumberjack!"

"It ain't that. I could carry their bloody bags two at a time if I wanted ter. A feller gets so goddam mad, that's all; so goddam mad. Don't he, Skinny?" Hoggenback turned to Andrews and smiled.

Andrews nodded his head.

After the first two or three bags Andrews carried in the afternoon, it seemed as if every one would be the last he could possibly lift. His back and thighs throbbed with exhaustion; his face and the tips of his fingers felt raw from the biting cement dust.

When the river began to grow purple with evening, he noticed that the two civilians, young men with buff-colored coats and canes, were watching the gang at work.

"They says they's newspaper reporters, writing up how fast the army's being demobilized," said one man in an awed voice.

"They come to the right place."

"Tell 'em we're leavin' for home now. Loadin' our barracks bags on the steamer."

The newspaper men were giving out cigarettes. Several men grouped round them. One shouted out:

"We're the guys does the light work. Blackjack Pershing's own pet labor battalion."

"They like us so well they just can't let us go."

"Damn jackasses," muttered Hoggenback, as, with his eyes to the ground, he passed Andrews. "I could tell 'em some things'd make their goddam ears buzz."

"Why don't you?"

"What the hell's the use? I ain't got the edication to talk up to guys like that."

The sergeant, a short, red-faced man with a mustache clipped very short, went up to the group round the newspaper men.

"Come on, fellers, we've got a hell of a lot of this cement to get in before it rains," he said in a kindly voice; "the sooner we get it in, the sooner we get off."

"Listen to that bastard, ain't he juss too sweet for pie when there's company?" muttered Hoggenback on his way from the barge with a bag of cement.

The Kid brushed past Andrews without looking at him.

"Do what I do, Skinny," he said.

Andrews did not turn round, but his heart started thumping very fast. A dull sort of terror took possession of him. He tried desperately to summon his will power, to keep from cringing, but he kept remembering the way the room had swung round when the M.P. had hit him, and heard again the cold voice of the lieutenant saying: "One of you men teach him how to salute."

Time dragged out interminably.

At last, coming back to the edge of the wharf, Andrews saw that there were no more bags in the barge. He sat down on the plank, too exhausted to think. Blue-grey dusk was closing down on everything. The Passy bridge stood out, purple against a great crimson afterglow.

The Kid sat down beside him, and threw an arm trembling with excitement round his shoulders.

"The guard's lookin' the other way. They won't miss us till they get to the truck. . . . Come on, Skinny," he said in a low, quiet voice.

Holding on to the plank, he let himself down into the speeding water. Andrews slipped after him, hardly knowing what he was doing. The icy water closing about his body made him suddenly feel awake and vigorous. As he was swept by the big rudder of the barge, he caught hold of the Kid, who was holding on to a rope. They worked their way without speaking round to the outer side of the rudder. The swift river tugging savagely at them made it hard to hold on.

"Now they can't see us," said the Kid between clenched teeth. "Can you work your shoes an' pants off?"

Andrews started struggling with one boot, the Kid helping to hold him up with his free hand.

"Mine are off," he said. "I was all fixed." He laughed, though his teeth were chattering.

"All right. I've broken the laces," said Andrews.

"Can you swim under water?"

Andrews nodded.

"We want to make for that bunch of barges the other side of the bridge. The barge people'll hide us."

"How d'ye know they will?"

The Kid had disappeared.

Andrews hesitated a moment, then let go his hold and started swimming with the current for all his might.

At first he felt strong and exultant, but very soon he began to feel the icy grip of the water bearing him down; his arms and legs seemed to stiffen. More than against the water, he was struggling against paralysis within him, so that he thought that every moment his limbs would go rigid. He came to the surface and gasped for air. He had a second's glimpse of figures, tiny like toy soldiers, gesticulating wildly on the deck of the barge. The report of a rifle snapped through the air. He dove again, without thinking, as if his body were working independently of his mind.

The next time he came up, his eyes were blurred from the cold. There was a taste of blood in his mouth. The shadow of the bridge was just above him. He turned on his back for a second. There were lights on the bridge.

A current swept him past one barge and then another. Certainty possessed him that he was going to be drowned. A voice seemed to sob in his ears grotesquely: "And so John Andrews was drowned in the Seine, drowned in the Seine, in the Seine."

Then he was kicking and fighting in a furious rage against the coils about him that wanted to drag him down and away.

The black side of a barge was slipping up stream beside him with lightning speed. How fast those barges go, he thought. Then suddenly he found that he had hold of a rope, that his shoulders were banging against the bow of a small boat, while in front of him, against the dull purple sky, towered the rudder of the barge. A strong warm hand grasped his shoulder from behind, and he was being drawn up and up, over the bow of the boat that hurt his numbed body like blows, out of the clutching coils of the water.

"Hide me, I'm a deserter," he said over and over again in French. A brown and red face with a bristly white beard, a bulbous, mullioned sort of face, hovered over him in the middle of a pinkish mist.

II

"OH, QU'IL EST PROPRE! Oh, qu'il a la peau blanche!" Women's voices were shrilling behind the mist. A coverlet that felt soft and fuzzy against his skin was being put about him. He was very warm and torpid. But somewhere in his thoughts a black crawling thing like a spider was trying to reach him, trying to work its way through the pinkish veils of torpor. After a long while he managed to roll over, and looked about him.

"Mais reste tranquille," came the woman's shrill voice again.

"And the other one? Did you see the other one?" he asked in a choked whisper.

"Yes, it's all right. I'm drying it by the stove," came another woman's voice, deep and growling, almost like a man's.

"Maman's drying your money by the stove. It's all safe. How rich they are, these Americans!"

"And to think that I nearly threw it overboard with the trousers," said the other woman again.

John Andrews began to look about him. He was in a dark low cabin. Behind him, in the direction of the voices, a yellow light flickered. Great dishevelled shadows of heads moved about on the ceiling. Through the close smell of the cabin came a warmth of food cooking. He could hear the soothing hiss of frying grease.

"But didn't you see the Kid?" he asked in English, dazedly trying to pull himself together, to think coherently. Then he went on in French in a more natural voice:

"There was another one with me."

"We saw no one. Rosaline, ask the old man," said the older woman.

"No, he didn't see anyone," came the girl's shrill voice. She walked over to the bed and pulled the coverlet round Andrews with an awkward gesture. Looking up at her, he had a glimpse of the bulge of her breasts and her large teeth that glinted in the lamplight, and very vague in the shadow, a mop of snaky, disordered hair.

"Qu'il parle bien français," she said, beaming at him.

Heavy steps shuffled across the cabin as the older woman came up to the bed and peered in his face.

"Il va mieux," she said, with a knowing air.

She was a broad woman with a broad flat face and a swollen body swathed in shawls. Her eyebrows were very bushy, and she had thick grey whiskers that came down to a point on either side of her mouth, as well as a few bristling hairs on her chin. Her voice was deep and growling, and seemed to come from far down inside her huge body.

Steps creaked somewhere, and the old man looked at him through spectacles placed on the end of his nose. Andrews recognized the irregular face full of red knobs and protrusions.

"Thanks very much," he said.

All three looked at him silently for some time. Then the old man pulled a newspaper out of his pocket, unfolded it carefully, and fluttered it above Andrews's eyes. In the scant light Andrews made out the name: "Libertaire."

"That's why," said the old man, looking at Andrews fixedly, through his spectacles.

"I'm a sort of a socialist," said Andrews.

"Socialists are good-for-nothings," snarled the old man, every red protrusion on his face seeming to get redder.

"But I have great sympathy for anarchist comrades," went on Andrews, feeling a certain liveliness of amusement go through him and fade again.

"Lucky you caught hold of my rope, instead of getting on to the next barge. He'd have given you up for sure. Sont des royalistes, ces salauds-là."

"We must give him something to eat; hurry, Maman. . . . Don't worry, he'll pay, won't you, my little American?"

Andrews nodded his head.

"All you want," he said.

"No, if he says he's a comrade, he shan't pay, not a sou," growled the old man.

"We'll see about that," cried the old woman, drawing her breath in with an angry whistling sound.

"It's only that living's so dear nowadays," came the girl's voice.

"Oh, I'll pay anything I've got," said Andrews peevishly, closing his eyes again.

He lay a long while on his back without moving.

A hand shoved in between his back and the pillow roused him. He sat up. Rosaline was holding a bowl of broth in front of him that steamed in his face.

"Mange ça," she said.

He looked into her eyes, smiling. Her rusty hair was neatly combed. A bright green parrot with a scarlet splash in its wings, balanced itself unsteadily on her shoulder, looking at Andrews out of angry eyes, hard as gems.

"Il est jaloux, Coco," said Rosaline, with a shrill little giggle.

Andrews took the bowl in his two hands and drank some of the scalding broth.

"It's too hot," he said, leaning back against the girl's arm.

The parrot squawked out a sentence that Andrews did not understand.

Andrews heard the old man's voice answer from somewhere behind him:

"Nom de Dieu!"

The parrot squawked again.

Rosaline laughed.

"It's the old man who taught him that," she said. "Poor Coco, he doesn't know what he's saying."

"What does he say?" asked Andrews.

"'Les bourgeois à la lanterne, nom de dieu!' It's from a song," said Rosaline. "Oh, qu'il est malin, ce Coco!"

Rosaline was standing with her arms folded beside the bunk. The parrot stretched out his neck and rubbed it against her cheek, closing and unclosing his gem-like eyes. The girl formed her lips into a kiss, and murmured in a drowsy voice:

"Tu m'aimes, Coco, n'est-ce pas, Coco? Bon Coco."

"Could I have something more, I'm awfully hungry," said Andrews.

"Oh, I was forgetting," cried Rosaline, running off with the empty bowl.

In a moment she came back without the parrot, with the bowl in her hand full of a brown stew of potatoes and meat.

Andrews ate it mechanically, and handed back the bowl.

"Thank you," he said, "I am going to sleep."

He settled himself into the bunk. Rosaline drew the covers up about him and tucked them in round his shoulders. Her hand seemed to linger a moment as it brushed past his cheek. But Andrews had already sunk into a torpor again, feeling nothing but the warmth of the food within him and a great stiffness in his legs and arms.

When he woke up the light was grey instead of yellow, and a swishing sound puzzled him. He lay listening to it for a long time, wondering what it was. At last the thought came with a sudden warm spurt of joy that the barge must be moving.

He lay very quietly on his back, looking up at the faint silvery light on the ceiling of the bunk, thinking of nothing, with only a vague dread in the back of his head that someone would come to speak to him, to question him.

After a long time he began to think of Geneviève Rod. He was having a long conversation with her about his music, and in his imagination she kept telling him that he must finish the "Queen of Sheba," and that she would show it to Monsieur Gibier, who was a great friend of a certain concert director, who might get it played. How long ago it must be since they had talked about that. A picture floated through his mind of himself and Geneviève standing shoulder to shoulder looking at the Cathedral at Chartres, which stood up nonchalantly, above the tumultuous roofs of the town, with its sober tower and its gaudy towers and the great rose windows between. Inexorably his memory carried him forward, moment by moment, over that day, until he writhed with shame and revolt. Good god! Would he have to go on all his life remembering that? "Teach him how to salute," the officer had said, and Handsome had stepped up to him and hit him. Would he have to go on all his life remembering that?

"We tied up the uniform with some stones, and threw it overboard," said Rosaline, jabbing him in the shoulder to draw his attention.

"That was a good idea."

"Are you going to get up? It's nearly time to eat. How you have slept."

"But I haven't anything to put on," said Andrews, laughing, and waved a bare arm above the bedclothes.

"Wait, I'll find something of the old man's. Say, do all Americans have skin so white as that? Look."

She put her brown hand, with its grimed and broken nails,

on Andrews's arm, that was white with a few silky yellow hairs.

"It's because I'm blond," said Andrews. "There are plenty of blond Frenchmen, aren't there?"

Rosaline ran off giggling, and came back in a moment with a pair of corduroy trousers and a torn flannel shirt that smelt of pipe tobacco.

"That'll do for now," she said. "It's warm today for April. Tonight we'll buy you some clothes and shoes. Where are you going?"

"By God, I don't know."

"We're going to Havre for cargo." She put both hands to her head and began rearranging her straggling rusty-colored hair. "Oh, my hair," she said, "it's the water, you know. You can't keep respectable-looking on these filthy barges. Say, American, why don't you stay with us a while? You can help the old man run the boat."

He found suddenly that her eyes were looking into his with trembling eagerness.

"I don't know what to do," he said carelessly. "I wonder if it's safe to go on deck."

She turned away from him petulantly and led the way up the ladder.

"Oh, v'là le camarade," cried the old man who was leaning with all his might against the long tiller of the barge. "Come and help me."

The barge was the last of a string of four that were describing a wide curve in the midst of a reach of silvery river full of glittering patches of pale, pea-green lavender, hemmed in on either side by frail blue roots of poplars. The sky was a mottled luminous grey with occasional patches, the color of robins' eggs. Andrews breathed in the dank smell of the river and leaned against the tiller when he was told to, answering the old man's curt questions.

He stayed with the tiller when the rest of them went down to the cabin to eat. The pale colors and the swishing sound of the water and the blue-green banks slipping by and unfolding on either hand, were as soothing as his deep sleep had been. Yet they seemed only a veil covering other realities, where men stood interminably in line and marched with legs made all the same length on the drill field, and wore the same clothes and cringed before the same hierarchy of polished belts and polished puttees and stiff-visored caps, that had its homes in vast offices crammed with index cards and card catalogues; a world full of the tramp of marching, where cold voices kept saying: —"Teach him how to salute." Like a bird in a net, Andrews's mind struggled to free itself from the obsession.

Then he thought of his table in his room in Paris, with its piled sheets of ruled paper, and he felt he wanted nothing in the world except to work. It would not matter what happened to him if he could only have time to weave into designs the tangled skein of music that seethed through him as the blood seethed through his veins.

There he stood, leaning against the long tiller, watching the blue-green poplars glide by, here and there reflected in the etched silver mirror of the river, feeling the moist river wind flutter his ragged shirt, thinking of nothing.

After a while the old man came up out of the cabin, his face purplish, puffing clouds of smoke out of his pipe.

"All right, young fellow, go down and eat," he said.

Andrews lay flat on his belly on the deck, with his chin resting on the back of his two hands. The barge was tied up along the river bank among many other barges. Beside him, a small fuzzy dog barked furiously at a yellow mongrel on the shore. It was nearly dark, and through the pearly mist of the river came red oblongs of light from the taverns along the bank. A slip of a new moon, shrouded in haze, was setting behind the poplar trees. Amid the round of despairing thoughts, the memory of the Kid intruded itself. He had sold a Ford for five hundred francs, and gone on a party with a man who'd stolen an ammunition train, and he wanted to write for the Italian movies. No war could down people like that. Andrews smiled, looking into the black water. Funny, the Kid was dead, probably, and he, John Andrews, was alive and free. And he lay there moping, still whimpering over old wrongs. "For God's sake be a man!" he said to himself. He got to his feet.

At the cabin door, Rosaline was playing with the parrot.

"Give me a kiss, Coco," she was saying in a drowsy voice,

"just a little kiss. Just a little kiss for Rosaline, poor little Rosaline."

The parrot, which Andrews could hardly see in the dusk, leaned towards her, fluttering his feathers, making little clucking noises.

Rosaline caught sight of Andrews.

"Oh, I thought you'd gone to have a drink with the old man," she cried.

"No. I stayed here."

"D'you like it, this life?"

Rosaline put the parrot back on his perch, where he swayed from side to side, squawking in protest: "Les bourgeois à la lanterne, nom de dieu!"

They both laughed.

"Oh, it must be a wonderful life. This barge seems like heaven after the army."

"But they pay you well, you Americans."

"Seven francs a day."

"That's luxury, that."

"And be ordered around all day long!"

"But you have no expenses. . . . It's clear gain. . . . You men are funny. The old man's like that too. . . . It's nice here all by ourselves, isn't it, Jean?"

Andrews did not answer. He was wondering what Geneviève Rod would say when she found out he was a deserter.

"I hate it. . . . It's dirty and cold and miserable in winter," went on Rosaline. "I'd like to see them at the bottom of the river, all these barges. . . . And Paris women, did you have a good time with them?"

"I only knew one. I go very little with women."

"All the same, love's nice, isn't it?"

They were sitting on the rail at the bow of the barge. Rosaline had sidled up so that her leg touched Andrews's leg along its whole length.

The memory of Geneviève Rod became more and more vivid in his mind. He kept thinking of things she had said, of the intonations of her voice, of the blundering way she poured tea, and of her pale-brown eyes wide open on the world, like the eyes of a woman in an encaustic painting from a tomb in the Fayoum.

"Mother's talking to the old woman at the Creamery. They're great friends. She won't be home for two hours yet," said Rosaline.

"She's bringing my clothes, isn't she?"

"But you're all right as you are."

"But they're your father's."

"What does that matter?"

"I must go back to Paris soon. There is somebody I must see in Paris."

"A woman?"

Andrews nodded.

"But it's not so bad, this life on the barge. I'm just lonesome and sick of the old people. That's why I talk nastily about it. . . . We could have good times together if you stayed with us a little."

She leaned her head on his shoulder and put a hand awkwardly on his bare forearm.

"How cold these Americans are!" she muttered, giggling drowsily.

Andrews felt her hair tickle his cheek.

"No, it's not a bad life on the barge, honestly. The only thing is, there's nothing but old people on the river. It isn't life to be always with old people. . . . I want to have a good time."

She pressed her cheek against his. He could feel her breath heavy in his face.

"After all, it's lovely in summer to drowse on the deck that's all warm with the sun, and see the trees and the fields and the little houses slipping by on either side . . . If there weren't so many old people. . . . All the boys go away to the cities. . . . I hate old people; they're so dirty and slow. We mustn't waste our youth, must we?"

Andrews got to his feet.

"What's the matter?" she cried sharply.

"Rosaline," Andrews said in a low, soft voice, "I can only think of going to Paris."

"Oh, the Paris woman," said Rosaline scornfully. "But what does that matter? She isn't here now."

"I don't know . . . Perhaps I shall never see her again anyway," said Andrews.

"You're a fool. You must amuse yourself when you can in this life. And you a deserter . . . Why, they may catch you and shoot you any time."

"Oh, I know, you're right. You're right. But I'm not made like that, that's all."

"She must be very good to you, your little Paris girl."

"I've never touched her."

Rosaline threw her head back and laughed raspingly.

"But you aren't sick, are you?" she cried.

"Probably I remember too vividly, that's all. . . . Anyway, I'm a fool, Rosaline, because you're a nice girl."

There were steps on the plank that led to the shore. A shawl over her head and a big bundle under her arm, the old woman came up to them, panting wheezily. She looked from one to the other, trying to make out their faces in the dark.

"It's a danger . . . like that . . . youth," she muttered between hard short breaths.

"Did you find the clothes?" asked Andrews in a casual voice.

"Yes. That leaves you forty-five francs out of your money, when I've taken out for your food and all that. Does that suit you?"

"Thank you very much for your trouble."

"You paid for it. Don't worry about that," said the old woman. She gave him the bundle. "Here are your clothes and the forty-five francs. If you want, I'll tell you exactly what each thing cost."

"I'll put them on first," he said, with a laugh.

He climbed down the ladder into the cabin.

Putting on new, unfamiliar-shaped clothes made him suddenly feel strong and joyous. The old woman had bought him corduroy trousers, cheap cloth shoes, a blue cotton shirt, woollen socks, and a second-hand black serge jacket. When he came on deck she held up a lantern to look at him.

"Doesn't he look fine, altogether French?" she said.

Rosaline turned away without answering. A little later she picked up the perch and carried the parrot, that swayed sleepily on the crosspiece, down the ladder.

"Les bourgeois à la lanterne, nom de dieu!" came the old man's voice singing on the shore.

"He's drunk as a pig," muttered the old woman. "If only he doesn't fall off the gang plank."

A swaying shadow appeared at the end of the plank, standing out against the haze of light from the houses behind the poplar trees.

Andrews put out a hand to catch him, as he reached the side of the barge. The old man sprawled against the cabin.

"Don't bawl me out, dearie," he said, dangling an arm round Andrews's neck, and a hand beckoning vaguely towards his wife. "I've found a comrade for the little American."

"What's that?" said Andrews sharply. His mouth suddenly went dry with terror. He felt his nails pressing into the palms of his cold hands.

"I've found another American for you," said the old man in an important voice. "Here he comes." Another shadow appeared at the end of the gangplank.

"Les bourgeois à la lanterne, nom de dieu!" shouted the old man.

Andrews backed away cautiously towards the other side of the barge. All the little muscles of his thighs were trembling. A hard voice was saying in his head: "Drown yourself, drown yourself. Then they won't get you."

The man was standing on the end of the plank. Andrews could see the contour of the uniform against the haze of light behind the poplar trees.

"God, if I only had a pistol," he thought.

"Say, Buddy, where are you?" came an American voice.

The man advanced towards him across the deck.

Andrews stood with every muscle taut.

"Gee! You've taken off your uniform. . . . Say, I'm not an M.P. I'm A.W.O.L. too. Shake." He held out his hand.

Andrews took the hand doubtfully, without moving from the edge of the barge.

"Say, Buddy, it's a damn fool thing to take off your uniform. Ain't you got any? If they pick you up like that it's life, kid."

"I can't help it. It's done now."

"Gawd, you still think I'm an M.P., don't yer? . . . I swear I ain't. Maybe you are. Gawd, it's hell, this life. A feller can't put his trust in nobody."

"What division are you from?"

"Hell, I came to warn you this bastard frawg's got soused an' has been blabbin' in the gin mill there how he was an anarchist an' all that, an' how he had an American deserter who was an anarchist an' all that, an' I said to myself: 'That guy'll git nabbed if he ain't careful,' so I cottoned up to the old frawg an' said I'd go with him to see the camarade, an' I think we'd better both of us make tracks out o' this burg."

"It's damn decent. I'm sorry I was so suspicious. I was scared green when I first saw you."

"You were goddam right to be. But why did yous take yer uniform off?"

"Come along, let's beat it. I'll tell you about that."

Andrews shook hands with the old man and the old woman. Rosaline had disappeared.

"Goodnight. . . . Thank you," he said, and followed the other man across the gangplank.

As they walked away along the road they heard the old man's voice roaring:

"Les bourgeois à la lanterne, nom de dieu!"

"My name's Eddy Chambers," said the American.

"Mine's John Andrews."

"How long 've you been out?"

"Two days."

Eddy let the air out through his teeth in a whistle.

"I got away from a labor battalion in Paris. They'd picked me up in Chartres without a pass."

"Gee, I've been out a month an' more. Was you infantry too?"

"Yes. I was in the School Detachment in Paris when I was picked up. But I never could get word to them. They just put me to work without a trial. Ever been in a labor battalion?"

"No, thank Gawd, they ain't got my number yet."

They were walking fast along a straight road across a plain under a clear star-powdered sky.

"I been out eight weeks yesterday. What'd you think o' that?" said Eddy.

"Must have had plenty of money to go on."

"I've been flat fifteen days."

"How d'you work it?"

"I dunno. I juss work it through. . . . Ye see, it was this way. The gang I was with went home when I was in hauspital, and the damn skunks put me in class A and was goin' to send me to the Army of Occupation. Gawd, it made me sick, goin' out to a new outfit where I didn't know anybody, an' all the rest of my bunch home walkin' down Water Street with brass bands an' reception committees an' girls throwing kisses at 'em an' all that. Where are yous goin'?"

"Paris."

"Gee, I wouldn't. Risky."

"But I've got friends there. I can get hold of some money."

"Looks like I hadn't got a friend in the world. I wish I'd gone to that goddam outfit now. . . . I ought to have been in the engineers all the time, anyway."

"What did you do at home?"

"Carpenter."

"But gosh, man, with a trade like that you can always make a living anywhere."

"You're goddam right, I could, but a guy has to live underground, like a rabbit, at this game. If I could git to a country where I could walk around like a man, I wouldn't give a damn what happened. If the army ever moves out of here an' the goddam M.P.'s, I'll set up in business in one of these here little towns. I can parlee pretty well. I'd juss as soon marry a French girl an' git to be a regular frawg myself. After the raw deal they've given me in the army, I don't want to have nothin' more to do with their damn country. Democracy!"

He cleared his throat and spat angrily on the road before him.

They walked on silently. Andrews was looking at the sky, picking out constellations he knew among the glittering masses of stars.

"Why don't you try Spain or Italy?" he said after a while.

"Don't know the lingo. No, I'm going to Scotland."

"But how can you get there?"

"Crossing on the car ferries to England from Havre. I've talked to guys has done it."

"But what'll you do when you do get there?"

"How should I know? Live around best I can. What can a feller do when he don't dare show his face in the street?"

"Anyway, it makes you feel as if you had some guts in you to be out on your own this way," cried Andrews boisterously.

"Wait till you've been at it two months, boy, and you'll think what I'm tellin' yer. . . . The army's hell when you're in it; but it's a hell of a lot worse when you're out of it, at the wrong end."

"It's a great night, anyway," said Andrews.

"Looks like we ought to be findin' a haystack to sleep in."

"It'd be different," burst out Andrews, suddenly, "if I didn't have friends here."

"O, you've met up with a girl, have you?" asked Eddy ironically.

"Yes. The thing is we really get along together, besides all the rest."

Eddy snorted.

"I bet you ain't ever even kissed her," he said. "Gee, I've had buddies has met up with that friendly kind. I know a guy married one, an' found out after two weeks."

"It's silly to talk about it. I can't explain it. . . . It gives you confidence in anything to feel there's someone who'll always understand anything you do."

"I s'pose you're goin' to git married."

"I don't see why. That would spoil everything."

Eddy whistled softly.

They walked along briskly without speaking for a long time, their steps ringing on the hard road, while the dome of the sky shimmered above their heads. And from the ditches came the singsong shrilling of toads. For the first time in months Andrews felt himself bubbling with a spirit of joyous adventure. The rhythm of the three green horsemen that was to have been the prelude to the Queen of Sheba began rollicking through his head.

"But, Eddy, this is wonderful. It's us against the universe," he said in a boisterous voice.

"You wait," said Eddy.

When Andrews walked by the M.P. at the Gare St. Lazare, his hands were cold with fear. The M.P. did not look at him.

He stopped on the crowded pavement a little way from the station and stared into a mirror in a shop window. Unshaven, with a check cap on the side of his head and his corduroy trousers, he looked like a young workman who had been out of work for a month.

"Gee, clothes do make a difference," he said to himself.

He smiled when he thought how shocked Walters would be when he turned up in that rig, and started walking with leisurely stride across Paris, where everything bustled and jingled with early morning, where from every café came a hot smell of coffee, and fresh bread steamed in the windows of the bakeries. He still had three francs in his pocket. On a side street the fumes of coffee roasting attracted him into a small bar. Several men were arguing boisterously at the end of the bar. One of them turned a ruddy, tow-whiskered face to Andrews, and said:

"Et toi, tu vas chômer le premier mai?"

"I'm on strike already," answered Andrews laughing.

The man noticed his accent, looked at him sharply a second, and turned back to the conversation, lowering his voice as he did so. Andrews drank down his coffee and left the bar, his heart pounding. He could not help glancing back over his shoulder now and then to see if he was being followed. At a corner he stopped with his fists clenched and leaned a second against a house wall.

"Where's your nerve. Where's your nerve?" he was saying to himself.

He strode off suddenly, full of bitter determination not to turn round again. He tried to occupy his mind with plans. Let's see, what should he do? First he'd go to his room and look up old Henslowe and Walters. Then he would go to see Geneviève. Then he'd work, work, forget everything in his work, until the army should go back to America and there should be no more uniforms on the streets. And as for the future, what did he care about the future?

When he turned the corner into the familiar street where his room was, a thought came to him. Suppose he should find M.P.'s waiting for him there? He brushed it aside angrily and strode fast up the sidewalk, catching up to a soldier who was slouching along in the same direction, with his hands in his pockets and eyes on the ground. Andrews stopped suddenly as he was about to pass the soldier and turned. The man looked up. It was Chrisfield.

Andrews held out his hand.

Chrisfield seized it eagerly and shook it for a long time.

"Jesus Christ! Ah thought you was a Frenchman, Andy. . . . Ah guess you got yer dis-charge then. God, Ah'm glad."

"I'm glad I look like a Frenchman, anyway. . . . Been on leave long, Chris?"

Two buttons were off the front of Chrisfield's uniform; there were streaks of dirt on his face, and his puttees were clothed with mud. He looked Andrews seriously in the eyes, and shook his head.

"No. Ah done flew the coop, Andy," he said in a low voice.

"Since when?"

"Ah been out a couple o' weeks. Ah'll tell you about it, Andy. Ah was comin' to see you now. Ah'm broke."

"Well look, I'll be able to get hold of some money tomorrow. . . . I'm out too."

"What d'ye mean?"

"I haven't got a discharge. I'm through with it all. I've deserted."

"God damn! That's funny that you an' me should both do it, Andy. But why the hell did you do it?"

"Oh, it's too long to tell here. Come up to my room."

"There may be fellers there. Ever been at the Chink's?"

"No."

"I'm stayin' there. There're other fellers who's A.W.O.L. too. The Chink's got a gin mill."

"Where is it?"

"Eight, rew day Petee Jardings."

"Where's that?"

"Way back of that garden where the animals are."

"Look, I can find you there tomorrow morning, and I'll bring some money."

"Ah'll wait for ye, Andy, at nine. It's a bar. Ye won't be able to git in without me, the kids is pretty scared of plainclothes men."

"I think it'll be perfectly safe to come up to my place now."

"Now, Ah'm goin' to git the hell out of here."

"But Chris, why did you go A.W.O.L.?"

"Oh, Ah doan know. . . . A guy who's in the Paris detachment got yer address for me."

"But, Chris, did they say anything to him about me?"

"No, nauthin'."

"That's funny. . . . Well, Chris, I'll be there tomorrow, if I can find the place."

"Man, you've got to be there."

"Oh, I'll turn up," said Andrews with a smile.

They shook hands nervously.

"Say, Andy," said Chrisfield, still holding on to Andrews's hand, "Ah went A.W.O.L. 'cause a sergeant . . . God damn it; it's weighin' on ma mind awful these days. . . . There's a sergeant that knows."

"What you mean?"

"Ah told ye about Anderson . . . Ah know you ain't tole anybody, Andy." Chrisfield dropped Andrews's hand and looked at him in the face with an unexpected sideways glance. Then he went on through clenched teeth: "Ah swear to Gawd Ah ain't tole another livin' soul. . . . An' the sergeant in Company D knows."

"For God's sake, Chris, don't lose your nerve like that."

"Ah ain't lost ma nerve. Ah tell you that guy knows." Chrisfield's voice rose, suddenly shrill.

"Look, Chris, we can't stand talking out here in the street like this. It isn't safe."

"But mebbe you'll be able to tell me what to do. You think, Andy. Mebbe, tomorrow, you'll have thought up somethin' we can do . . . So long."

Chrisfield walked away hurriedly. Andrews looked after him a moment, and then went in through the court to the house where his room was.

At the foot of the stairs an old woman's voice startled him.

"Mais, Monsieur André, que vous avez l'air étrange; how funny you look dressed like that."

The concierge was smiling at him from her cubbyhole beside the stairs. She sat knitting with a black shawl round her head, a tiny old woman with a hooked bird-like nose and eyes sunk in depressions full of little wrinkles, like a monkey's eyes.

"Yes, at the town where I was demobilized, I couldn't get anything else," stammered Andrews.

"Oh, you're demobilized, are you? That's why you've been away so long. Monsieur Valters said he didn't know where you were. . . . It's better that way, isn't it?"

"Yes," said Andrews, starting up the stairs.

"Monsieur Valters is in now," went on the old woman, talking after him. "And you've got in just in time for the first of May."

"Oh, yes, the strike," said Andrews, stopping half-way up the flight.

"It'll be dreadful," said the old woman. "I hope you won't go out. Young folks are so likely to get into trouble . . . Oh, but all your friends have been worried about your being away so long."

"Have they?" said Andrews. He continued up the stairs.

"Au revoir, Monsieur."

"Au revoir, Madame."

III

N O, NOTHING can make me go back now. It's no use talking about it."

"But you're crazy, man. You're crazy. One man alone can't buck the system like that, can he, Henslowe?"

Walters was talking earnestly, leaning across the table beside the lamp. Henslowe, who sat very stiff on the edge of a chair, nodded with compressed lips. Andrews lay at full length on the bed, out of the circle of light.

"Honestly, Andy," said Henslowe with tears in his voice, "I think you'd better do what Walters says. It's no use being heroic about it."

"I'm not being heroic, Henny," cried Andrews, sitting up on the bed. He drew his feet under him, tailor fashion, and went on talking very quietly. "Look . . . It's a purely personal matter. I've got to a point where I don't give a damn what happens to me. I don't care if I'm shot, or if I live to be eighty . . . I'm sick of being ordered round. One more order shouted at my head is not worth living to be eighty . . . to me. That's all. For God's sake let's talk about something else."

"But how many orders have you had shouted at your head since you got in this School Detachment? Not one. You can put through your discharge application probably . . ." Walters got to his feet, letting the chair crash to the floor behind him. He stopped to pick it up. "Look here; here's my proposition," he went on. "I don't think you are marked A.W.O.L. in the School office. Things are so damn badly run there. You can turn up and say you've been sick and draw your back pay. And nobody'll say a thing. Or else I'll put it right up to the guy who's top sergeant. He's a good friend of mine. We can fix it up on the records some way. But for God's sake don't ruin your whole life on account of a little stubbornness, and some damn fool anarchistic ideas or other a feller like you ought to have had more sense than to pick up. . . ."

"He's right, Andy," said Henslowe in a low voice.

"Please don't talk any more about it. You've told me all

that before," said Andrews sharply. He threw himself back on the bed and rolled over towards the wall.

They were silent a long time. A sound of voices and footsteps drifted up from the courtyard.

"But, look here, Andy," said Henslowe nervously stroking his moustache. "You care much more about your work than any abstract idea of asserting your right of individual liberty. Even if you don't get caught. . . . I think the chances of getting caught are mighty slim if you use your head. . . . But even if you don't, you haven't enough money to live for long over here, you haven't. . . ."

"Don't you think I've thought of all that? I'm not crazy, you know. I've figured up the balance perfectly sanely. The only thing is, you fellows can't understand. Have you ever been in a labor battalion? Have you ever had a man you'd been chatting with five minutes before deliberately knock you down? Good God, you don't know what you are talking about, you two. . . . I've got to be free, now. I don't care at what cost. Being free's the only thing that matters."

Andrews lay on his back talking towards the ceiling.

Henslowe was on his feet, striding nervously about the room.

"As if anyone was ever free," he muttered.

"All right, quibble, quibble. You can argue anything away if you want to. Of course, cowardice is the best policy, necessary for survival. The man who's got most will to live is the most cowardly . . . go on." Andrews's voice was shrill and excited, breaking occasionally like a half-grown boy's voice.

"Andy, what on earth's got hold of you? . . . God, I hate to go away this way," added Henslowe after a pause.

"I'll pull through all right, Henny. I'll probably come to see you in Syria, disguised as an Arab sheik." Andrews laughed excitedly.

"If I thought I'd do any good, I'd stay. . . . But there's nothing I can do. Everybody's got to settle their own affairs, in their own damn fool way. So long, Walters."

Walters and Henslowe shook hands absently.

Henslowe came over to the bed and held out his hand to Andrews.

"Look, old man, you will be as careful as you can, won't

you? And write me care American Red Cross, Jerusalem. I'll
be damned anxious, honestly."

"Don't you worry, we'll go travelling together yet," said
Andrews, sitting up and taking Henslowe's hand.

They heard Henslowe's steps fade down the stairs and then
ring for a moment on the pavings of the courtyard.

Walters moved his chair over beside Andrews's bed.

"Now, look, let's have a man-to-man talk, Andrews. Even
if you want to ruin your life, you haven't a right to. There's
your family, and haven't you any patriotism? . . . Remember,
there is such a thing as duty in the world."

Andrews sat up and said in a low, furious voice, pausing between each word:

"I can't explain it. . . . But I shall never put a uniform on
again. . . . So for Christ's sake shut up."

"All right, do what you goddam please; I'm through with
you." Walters suddenly flashed into a rage. He began undressing silently. Andrews lay a long while flat on his back in
the bed, staring at the ceiling, then he too undressed, put the
light out, and got into bed.

The rue des Petits-Jardins was a short street in a district of
warehouses. A grey, windowless wall shut out the light along
all of one side. Opposite was a cluster of three old houses
leaning together as if the outer ones were trying to support
the beetling mansard roof of the center house. Behind them
rose a huge building with rows and rows of black windows.
When Andrews stopped to look about him, he found the
street completely deserted. The ominous stillness that had
brooded over the city during all the walk from his room near
the Pantheon seemed here to culminate in sheer desolation.
In the silence he could hear the light padding noise made by
the feet of a dog that trotted across the end of the street. The
house with the mansard roof was number eight. The front of
the lower storey had once been painted in chocolate-color,
across the top of which was still decipherable the sign: "Char-
bon, Bois. Lhomond." On the grimed window beside the
door was painted in white: "Débit de Boissons."

Andrews pushed on the door, which opened easily. Somewhere in the interior a bell jangled, startlingly loud after the

silence of the street. On the wall opposite the door was a speckled mirror with a crack in it, the shape of a star, and under it a bench with three marble-top tables. The zinc bar filled up the third wall. In the fourth was a glass door pasted up with newspapers. Andrews walked over to the bar. The jangling of the bell faded to silence. He waited, a curious uneasiness gradually taking possession of him. Anyways, he thought, he was wasting his time; he ought to be doing something to arrange his future. He walked over to the street door. The bell jangled again when he opened it. At the same moment a man came out through the door the newspapers were pasted over. He was a stout man in a dirty white shirt stained to a brownish color round the armpits and caught in very tightly at the waist by the broad elastic belt that held up his yellow corduroy trousers. His face was flabby, of a greenish color; black eyes looked at Andrews fixedly through barely open lids, so that they seemed long slits above the cheekbones. "That's the Chink," thought Andrews.

"Well," said the man, taking his place behind the bar with his legs far apart.

"A beer, please," said Andrews.

"There isn't any."

"A glass of wine then."

The man nodded his head, and keeping his eyes fastened on Andrews all the while, strode out of the door again.

A moment later, Chrisfield came out, with rumpled hair, yawning, rubbing an eye with the knuckles of one fist.

"Lawsie, Ah juss woke up, Andy. Come along in back."

Andrews followed him through a small room with tables and benches, down a corridor where the reek of ammonia bit into his eyes, and up a staircase littered with dirt and garbage. Chrisfield opened a door directly on the stairs, and they stumbled into a large room with a window that gave on the court. Chrisfield closed the door carefully, and turned to Andrews with a smile.

"Ah was right smart 'askeered ye wouldn't find it, Andy."

"So this is where you live?"

"Um hum, a bunch of us lives here."

A wide bed without coverings, where a man in olive-drab slept rolled in a blanket, was the only furniture of the room.

"Three of us sleeps in that bed," said Chrisfield.

"Who's that?" cried the man in the bed, sitting up suddenly.

"All right, Al, he's a buddy o' mine," said Chrisfield. "He's taken off his uniform."

"Jesus, you got guts," said the man in the bed.

Andrews looked at him sharply. A piece of towelling, splotched here and there with dried blood, was wrapped round his head, and a hand, swathed in bandages, was drawn up to his body. The man's mouth took on a twisted expression of pain as he let his head gradually down to the bed again.

"Gosh, what did you do to yourself?" cried Andrews.

"I tried to hop a freight at Marseilles."

"Needs practice to do that sort o' thing," said Chrisfield, who sat on the bed, pulling his shoes off. "Ah'm goin' to git back to bed, Andy. Ah'm juss dead tired. Ah chucked cabbages all night at the market. They give ye a job there without askin' no questions."

"Have a cigarette." Andrews sat down on the foot of the bed and threw a cigarette towards Chrisfield. "Have one?" he asked Al.

"No. I couldn't smoke. I'm almost crazy with this hand. One of the wheels went over it. . . . I cut what was left of the little finger off with a razor." Andrews could see the sweat rolling down his cheek as he spoke.

"Christ, that poor beggar's been havin' a time, Andy. We was 'askeert to get a doctor, and we all didn't know what to do.".

"I got some pure alcohol an' washed it in that. It's not infected. I guess it'll be all right."

"Where are you from, Al?" asked Andrews.

"'Frisco. Oh, I'm goin' to try to sleep. I haven't slept a wink for four nights."

"Why don't you get some dope?"

"Oh, we all ain't had a cent to spare for anythin', Andy."

"Oh, if we had kale we could live like kings—not," said Al in the middle of a nervous little giggle.

"Look, Chris," said Andrews, "I'll halve with you. I've got five hundred francs."

"Jesus Gawd, man, don't kid about anything like that."

"Here's two hundred and fifty. . . . It's not so much as it sounds."

Andrews handed him five fifty-franc notes.

"Say, how did you come to bust loose?" said Al, turning his head towards Andrews.

"I got away from a labor battalion one night. That's all."

"Tell me about it, buddy. I don't feel my hand so much when I'm talking to somebody. . . . I'd be home now if it wasn't for a gin mill in Alsace. Say, don't ye think that big headgear they sport up there is awful good looking? Got my goat every time I saw one. . . . I was comin' back from leave at Grenoble, an' I went through Strasburg. Some town. My outfit was in Coblenz. That's where I met up with Chris here. Anyway, we was raisin' hell round Strasburg, an' I went into a gin mill down a flight of steps. Gee, everything in that town's plumb picturesque, just like a kid I used to know at home whose folks were Eytalian used to talk about when he said how he wanted to come overseas. Well, I met up with a girl down there, who said she'd just come down to a place like that to look for her brother who was in the foreign legion."

Andrews and Chrisfield laughed.

"What you laughin' at?" went on Al in an eager taut voice. "Honest to Gawd. I'm goin' to marry her if I ever get out of this. She's the best little girl I ever met up with. She was waitress in a restaurant, an' when she was off duty she used to wear that there Alsatian costume. . . . Hell, I just stayed on. Every day, I thought I'd go away the next day. . . . Anyway, the war was over. I warn't a damn bit of use. . . . Hasn't a fellow got any rights at all? Then the M.P.'s started cleanin' up Strasburg after A.W.O.L.'s, an' I beat it out of there, an' Christ, it don't look as if I'd ever be able to get back."

"Say, Andy," said Chrisfield, suddenly, "let's go down after some booze."

"All right."

"Say, Al, do you want me to get you anything at the drug store?"

"No. I won't do anythin' but lay low and bathe it with alcohol now and then, against infection. Anyways, it's the first of May. You'll be crazy to go out. You might get pulled. They say there's riots going on."

"Gosh, I forgot it was the first of May," cried Andrews. "They're running a general strike to protest against the war with Russia and . . ."

"A guy told me," interrupted Al, in a shrill voice, "there might be a revolution."

"Come along, Andy," said Chris from the door.

On the stairs Andrews felt Chrisfield's hand squeezing his arm hard.

"Say, Andy," Chris put his lips close to Andrews's ear and spoke in a rasping whisper. "You're the only one that knows . . . you know what. You an' that sergeant. Doan you say anythin' so that the guys here kin ketch on, d'ye hear?"

"All right, Chris, I won't, but man alive, you oughtn't to lose your nerve about it. You aren't the only one who ever shot an . . ."

"Shut yer face, d'ye hear?" muttered Chrisfield savagely.

They went down the stairs in silence. In the room next to the bar they found the Chink reading a newspaper.

"Is he French?" whispered Andrews.

"Ah doan know what he is. He ain't a white man, Ah'll wager that," said Chris, "but he's square."

"D'you know anything about what's going on?" asked Andrews in French, going up to the Chink.

"Where?" The Chink got up, flashing a glance at Andrews out of the corners of his slit-like eyes.

"Outside, in the streets, in Paris, anywhere where people are out in the open and can do things. What do you think about the revolution?"

The Chink shrugged his shoulders.

"Anything's possible," he said.

"D'you think they really can overthrow the army and the government in one day, like that?"

"Who?" broke in Chrisfield.

"Why, the people, Chris, the ordinary people like you and me, who are tired of being ordered round, who are tired of being trampled down by other people just like them, who've had the luck to get in right with the system."

"D'you know what I'll do when the revolution comes?" broke in the Chink with sudden intensity, slapping himself on the chest with one hand. "I'll go straight to one of those jewelry stores, rue Royale, and fill my pockets and come home with my hands full of diamonds."

"What good'll that do you?"

"What good? I'll bury them back there in the court and wait. I'll need them in the end. D'you know what it'll mean, your revolution? Another system! When there's a system there are always men to be bought with diamonds. That's what the world's like."

"But they won't be worth anything. It'll only be work that is worth anything."

"We'll see," said the Chink.

"D'you think it could happen, Andy, that there'd be a revolution, an' there wouldn't be any more armies, an' we'd be able to go round like we are civilians? Ah doan think so. Fellers like us ain't got it in 'em to buck the system, Andy."

"Many a system's gone down before; it will happen again."

"They're fighting the Garde Républicaine now before the Gare de l'Est," said the Chink in an expressionless voice. "What do you want down here? You'd better stay in the back. You never know what the police may put over on us."

"Give us two bottles of vin blank, Chink," said Chrisfield.

"When'll you pay?"

"Right now. This guy's given me fifty francs."

"Rich, are you?" said the Chink with hatred in his voice, turning to Andrews. "Won't last long at that rate. Wait here."

He strode into the bar, closing the door carefully after him. A sudden jangling of the bell was followed by a sound of loud voices and stamping feet. Andrews and Chrisfield tiptoed into the dark corridor, where they stood a long time, waiting, breathing the foul air that stung their nostrils with the stench of plaster-damp and rotting wine. At last the Chink came back with three bottles of wine.

"Well, you're right," he said to Andrews. "They are putting up barricades on the Avenue Magenta."

On the stairs they met a girl sweeping. She had untidy hair that straggled out from under a blue handkerchief tied under her chin, and a pretty-colored fleshy face. Chrisfield caught her up to him and kissed her, as he passed.

"We all calls her the dawg-faced girl," he said to Andrews in explanation. "She does our work. Ah like to had a fight with Slippery over her yisterday. . . . Didn't Ah, Slippery?"

When he followed Chrisfield into the room, Andrews saw a man sitting on the window ledge smoking. He was dressed as a second lieutenant, his puttees were brilliantly polished, and he smoked through a long, amber cigarette-holder. His pink nails were carefully manicured.

"This is Slippery, Andy," said Chrisfield. "This guy's an ole buddy o' mine. We was bunkies together a hell of a time, wasn't we, Andy?"

"You bet we were."

"So you've taken your uniform off, have you? Mighty foolish," said Slippery. "Suppose they nab you?"

"It's all up now anyway. I don't intend to get nabbed," said Andrews.

"We got booze," said Chrisfield.

Slippery had taken dice from his pocket and was throwing them meditatively on the floor between his feet, snapping his fingers with each throw.

"I'll shoot you one of them bottles, Chris," he said.

Andrews walked over to the bed. Al was stirring uneasily, his face flushed and his mouth twitching.

"Hello," he said. "What's the news?"

"They say they're putting up barricades near the Gare de l'Est. It may be something."

"God, I hope so. God, I wish they'd do everything here like they did in Russia; then we'd be free. We couldn't go back to the States for a while, but there wouldn't be no M.P.'s to hunt us like we were criminals. . . . I'm going to sit up a while and talk." Al giggled hysterically for a moment.

"Have a swig of wine?" asked Andrews.

"Sure, it may set me up a bit; thanks." He drank greedily from the bottle, spilling a little over his chin.

"Say, is your face badly cut up, Al?"

"No, it's just scotched, skin's off; looks like beefsteak, I reckon. . . . Ever been to Strasburg?"

"No."

"Man, that's the town. And the girls in that costume. . . . Whee!"

"Say, you're from San Francisco, aren't you?"

"Sure."

"Well, I wonder if you knew a fellow I knew at training camp, a kid named Fuselli from 'Frisco?"

"Knew him! Jesus, man, he's the best friend I've got. . . . Ye don't know where he is now, do you?"

"I saw him here in Paris two months ago."

"Well, I'll be damned. . . . God, that's great!" Al's voice was staccato from excitement. "So you knew Dan at training camp? The last letter from him was 'bout a year ago. Dan'd just got to be corporal. He's a damn clever kid, Dan is, an' ambitious too, one of the guys always makes good. . . . Gawd, I'd hate to see him this way. D'you know, we used to see a hell of a lot of each other in 'Frisco, an' he always used to tell me how he'd make good before I did. He was goddam right, too. Said I was too soft about girls. . . . Did ye know him real well?"

"Yes. I even remember that he used to tell me about a fellow he knew who was called Al. . . . He used to tell me about how you two used to go down to the harbor and watch the big liners come in at night, all aflare with lights through the Golden Gate. And he used to tell you he'd go over to Europe in one, when he'd made his pile."

"That's why Strasburg made me think of him," broke in Al, tremendously excited. "'Cause it was so picturesque like. . . . But honest, I've tried hard to make good in this army. I've done everything a feller could. An' all I did was to get into a cushy job in the regimental office. . . . But Dan, Gawd, he may even be an officer by this time."

"No, he's not that," said Andrews. "Look here, you ought to keep quiet with that hand of yours."

"Damn my hand. Oh, it'll heal all right if I forget about it. You see, my foot slipped when they shunted a car I was just climbing into, an' . . . I guess I ought to be glad I wasn't killed. But, gee, when I think that if I hadn't been a fool about that girl I might have been home by now. . . ."

"The Chink says they're putting up barricades on the Avenue Magenta."

"That means business, kid!"

"Business nothin'," shouted Slippery from where he and

Chrisfield leaned over the dice on the tile floor in front of the window. "One tank an' a few husky Senegalese'll make your goddam socialists run so fast they won't stop till they get to Dijon. . . . You guys ought to have more sense." Slippery got to his feet and came over to the bed, jingling the dice in his hand. "It'll take more'n a handful o' socialists paid by the Boches to break the army. If it could be broke, don't ye think people would have done it long ago?"

"Shut up a minute. Ah thought Ah heard somethin'," said Chrisfield suddenly, going to the window.

They held their breath. The bed creaked as Al stirred uneasily in it.

"No, warn't anythin'; Ah'd thought Ah'd heard people singin'."

"The Internationale," cried Al.

"Shut up," said Chrisfield in a low gruff voice.

Through the silence of the room they heard steps on the stairs.

"All right, it's only Smiddy," said Slippery, and he threw the dice down on the tiles again.

The door opened slowly to let in a tall, stoop-shouldered man with a long face and long teeth.

"Who's the frawg?" he asked in a startled way, with one hand on the door knob.

"All right, Smiddy; it ain't a frawg; it's a guy Chris knows. He's taken his uniform off."

"'Lo, buddy," said Smiddy, shaking Andrews's hand. "Gawd, you look like a frawg."

"That's good," said Andrews.

"There's hell to pay," broke out Smiddy breathlessly. "You know Gus Evans and the little black-haired guy goes 'round with him? They been picked up. I seen 'em myself with some M.P.'s at Place de la Bastille. An' a guy I talked to under the bridge where I slep' last night said a guy'd tole him they were goin' to clean the A.W.O.L.'s out o' Paris if they had to search through every house in the place."

"If they come here they'll git somethin' they ain't lookin' for," muttered Chrisfield.

"I'm goin' down to Nice; getting too hot around here," said Slippery. "I've got travel orders in my pocket now."

"How did you get 'em?"

"Easy as pie," said Slippery, lighting a cigarette and puffing affectedly towards the ceiling. "I met up with a guy, a second loot, in the Knickerbocker Bar. We gets drunk together, an' goes on a party with two girls I know. In the morning I get up bright an' early, and now I've got five thousand francs, a leave slip and a silver cigarette case, an' Lootenant J. B. Franklin's runnin' around sayin' how he was robbed by a Paris whore, or more likely keepin' damn quiet about it. That's my system."

"But, gosh darn it, I don't see how you can go around with a guy an' drink with him, an' then rob him," cried Al from the bed.

"No different from cleaning a guy up at craps."

"Well?"

"An' suppose that feller knew that I was only a bloody private. Don't you think he'd have turned me over to the M.P.'s like winkin'?"

"No, I don't think so," said Al. "They're juss like you an me, skeered to death they'll get in wrong, but they won't light on a feller unless they have to."

"That's a goddam lie," cried Chrisfield. "They like ridin' yer. A doughboy's less'n a dawg to 'em. Ah'd shoot anyone of 'em lake Ah'd shoot a nigger."

Andrews was watching Chrisfield's face; it suddenly flushed red. He was silent abruptly. His eyes met Andrews's eyes with a flash of fear.

"They're all sorts of officers, like they're all sorts of us," Al was insisting.

"But you damn fools, quit arguing," cried Smiddy. "What the hell are we goin' to do? It ain't safe here no more, that's how I look at it."

They were silent.

At last Chrisfield said:

"What you goin' to do, Andy?"

"I hardly know. I think I'll go out to St. Germain to see a boy I know there who works on a farm to see if it's safe to take a job there. I won't stay in Paris. Then there's a girl here I want to look up. I must see her." Andrews broke off suddenly, and started walking back and forth across the end of the room.

"You'd better be damn careful; they'll probably shoot you if they catch you," said Slippery.

Andrews shrugged his shoulders.

"Well, I'd rather be shot than go to Leavenworth for twenty years, Gawd! I would," cried Al.

"How do you fellers eat here?" asked Slippery.

"We buy stuff an' the dawg-faced girl cooks it for us."

"Got anything for this noon?"

"I'll go see if I can buy some stuff," said Andrews. "It's safer for me to go out than for you."

"All right, here's twenty francs," said Slippery, handing Andrews a bill with an offhand gesture.

Chrisfield followed Andrews down the stairs. When they reached the passage at the foot of the stairs, he put his hand on Andrews's shoulder and whispered:

"Say, Andy, d'you think there's anything in that revolution business? Ah hadn't never thought they could buck the system thataway."

"They did in Russia."

"Then we'd be free, civilians, like we all was before the draft. But that ain't possible, Andy; that ain't possible, Andy."

"We'll see," said Andrews, as he opened the door to the bar.

He went up excitedly to the Chink, who sat behind the row of bottles along the bar.

"Well, what's happening?"

"Where?"

"By the Gare de l'Est, where they were putting up barricades?"

"Barricades!" shouted a young man in a red sash who was drinking at a table. "Why, they tore down some of the iron guards round the trees, if you call that barricades. But they're cowards. Whenever the cops charge they run. They're dirty cowards."

"D'you think anything's going to happen?"

"What can happen when you've got nothing but a bunch of dirty cowards?"

"What d'you think about it?" said Andrews, turning to the Chink.

The Chink shook his head without answering. Andrews went out.

When he came back he found Al and Chrisfield alone in their room. Chrisfield was walking up and down, biting his finger nails. On the wall opposite the window was a square of sunshine reflected from the opposite wall of the Court.

"For God's sake beat it, Chris. I'm all right," Al was saying in a weak, whining voice, his face twisted up by pain.

"What's the matter?" cried Andrews, putting down a large bundle.

"Slippery's seen a M.P. nosin' around in front of the gin mill."

"Good God!"

"They've beat it. . . . The trouble is Al's too sick. . . . Honest to gawd, Ah'll stay with you, Al."

"No. If you know somewhere to go, beat it, Chris. I'll stay here with Al and talk French to the M.P.'s if they come. We'll fool 'em somehow." Andrews felt suddenly amused and joyous.

"Honest to gawd, Andy, Ah'd stay if it warn't that that sergeant knows," said Chrisfield in a jerky voice.

"Beat it, Chris. There may be no time to waste."

"So long, Andy." Chrisfield slipped out of the door.

"It's funny, Al," said Andrews, sitting on the edge of the bed and unwrapping the package of food, "I'm not a damn bit scared any more. I think I'm free of the army, Al. . . . How's your hand?"

"I dunno. Oh, how I wish I was in my old bunk at Coblenz. I warn't made for buckin' against the world this way. . . . If we had old Dan with us. . . . Funny that you know Dan. . . . He'd have a million ideas for gettin' out of this fix. But I'm glad he's not here. He'd bawl me out so, for not havin' made good. He's a powerful ambitious kid, is Dan."

"But it's not the sort of thing a man can make good in, Al," said Andrews slowly. They were silent. There was no sound in the courtyard, only very far away the clatter of a patrol of cavalry over cobblestones. The sky had become overcast and the room was very dark. The mouldy plaster peeling off the walls had streaks of green in it. The light from the courtyard had a greenish tinge that made their faces look pale and dead, like the faces of men that have long been shut up between damp prison walls.

"And Fuselli had a girl named Mabe," said Andrews.

"Oh, she married a guy in the Naval Reserve. They had a grand wedding," said Al.

IV

A T LAST I've got to you!"

John Andrews had caught sight of Geneviève on a bench at the end of the garden under an arbor of vines. Her hair flamed bright in a splotch of sun as she got to her feet. She held out both hands to him.

"How good-looking you are like that," she cried.

He was conscious only of her hands in his hands and of her pale-brown eyes and of the bright sun-splotches and the green shadows fluttering all about them.

"So you are out of prison," she said, "and demobilized. How wonderful! Why didn't you write? I have been very uneasy about you. How did you find me here?"

"Your mother said you were here."

"And how do you like it, my Poissac?"

She made a wide gesture with her hand. They stood silent a moment, side by side, looking about them. In front of the arbor was a parterre of rounded box-bushes edging beds where disorderly roses hung in clusters of pink and purple and apricot-color. And beyond it a brilliant emerald lawn full of daisies sloped down to an old grey house with, at one end, a squat round tower that had an extinguisher-shaped roof. Beyond the house were tall, lush-green poplars, through which glittered patches of silver-grey river and of yellow sand banks. From somewhere came a drowsy scent of mown grass.

"How brown you are!" she said again. "I thought I had lost you. . . . You might kiss me, Jean."

The muscles of his arms tightened about her shoulders. Her hair flamed in his eyes. The wind that rustled through broad grape-leaves made a flutter of dancing light and shadow about them.

"How hot you are with the sun!" she said. "I love the smell of the sweat of your body. You must have run very hard, coming here."

"Do you remember one night in the spring we walked home from *Pelléas and Mélisande*? How I should have liked to have kissed you then, like this!" Andrews's voice was strange, hoarse, as if he spoke with difficulty.

"There is the château très froid et très profond," she said with a little laugh.

"And your hair. '*Je les tiens dans les doigts, je les tiens dans la bouche. . . . Toute ta chevelure, toute ta chevelure, Mélisande, est tombée de la tour. . . .*' D'you remember?"

"How wonderful you are."

They sat side by side on the stone bench without touching each other.

"It's silly," burst out Andrews excitedly. "We should have faith in our own selves. We can't live a little rag of romance without dragging in literature. We are drugged with literature so that we can never live at all, of ourselves."

"Jean, how did you come down here? Have you been de-mobilized long?"

"I walked almost all the way from Paris. You see, I am very dirty."

"How wonderful! But I'll be quiet. You must tell me every-thing from the moment you left me in Chartres."

"I'll tell you about Chartres later," said Andrews gruffly. "It has been superb, one of the biggest weeks in my life, walk-ing all day under the sun, with the road like a white ribbon in the sun over the hills and along river banks, where there were yellow irises blooming, and through woods full of blackbirds, and with the dust in a little white cloud round my feet, and all the time walking towards you, walking towards you."

"And *la Reine de Saba*, how is it coming?"

"I don't know. It's a long time since I thought of it. . . . You have been here long?"

"Hardly a week. But what are you going to do?"

"I have a room overlooking the river in a house owned by a very fat woman with a very red face and a tuft of hair on her chin. . . ."

"Madame Boncour."

"Of course. You must know everybody. . . . It's so small."

"And you're going to stay here a long time?"

"Almost forever, and work, and talk to you; may I use your piano now and then?"

"How wonderful!"

Geneviève Rod jumped to her feet. Then she stood looking at him, leaning against one of the twisted stems of the vines, so that the broad leaves fluttered about her face. A white cloud, bright as silver, covered the sun, so that the hairy young leaves and the wind-blown grass of the lawn took on a silvery sheen. Two white butterflies fluttered for a second about the arbor.

"You must always dress like that," she said after a while.

Andrews laughed.

"A little cleaner, I hope," he said. "But there can't be much change. I have no other clothes and ridiculously little money."

"Who cares for money?" cried Geneviève. Andrews fancied he detected a slight affectation in her tone, but he drove the idea from his mind immediately.

"I wonder if there is a farm round here where I could get work."

"But you couldn't do the work of a farm labourer," cried Geneviève, laughing.

"You just watch me."

"It'll spoil your hands for the piano."

"I don't care about that; but all that's later, much later. Before anything else I must finish a thing I am working on. There is a theme that came to me when I was first in the army, when I was washing windows at the training camp."

"How funny you are, Jean! Oh, it's lovely to have you about again. But you're awfully solemn today. Perhaps it's because I made you kiss me."

"But, Geneviève, it's not in one day that you can unbend a slave's back. But with you, in this wonderful place . . . Oh, I've never seen such sappy richness of vegetation! And think of it, a week's walking first across those grey rolling uplands, and then at Blois down into the haze of richness of the Loire. . . . D'you know Vendôme? I came by a funny little town from Vendôme to Blois. You see, my feet. . . . And what wonderful cold baths I've had on the sand banks of the Loire. . . . No, after a while the rhythm of legs all being made the same length on drill fields, the hopeless caged dullness will be buried deep in me by the gorgeousness of this world of yours!"

He got to his feet and crushed a leaf softly between his fingers.

"You see, the little grapes are already forming. . . . Look up there," she said as she brushed the leaves aside just above his head. "These grapes here are the earliest; but I must show you my domain, and my cousins and the hen yard and everything."

She took his hand and pulled him out of the arbor. They ran like children, hand in hand, round the box-bordered paths.

"What I mean is this," he stammered, following her across the lawn. "If I could once manage to express all that misery in music, I could shove it far down into my memory. I should be free to live my own existence, in the midst of this carnival of summer."

At the house she turned to him. "You see the very battered ladies over the door," she said. "They are said to be by a pupil of Jean Goujon."

"They fit wonderfully in the landscape, don't they? Did I ever tell you about the sculptures in the hospital where I was when I was wounded?"

"No, but I want you to look at the house now. See, that's the tower; all that's left of the old building. I live there, and right under the roof there's a haunted room I used to be terribly afraid of. I'm still afraid of it. . . . You see this Henri Quatre part of the house was just a fourth of the house as planned. This lawn would have been the court. We dug up foundations where the roses are. There are all sorts of traditions as to why the house was never finished."

"You must tell me them."

"I shall later; but now you must come and meet my aunt and my cousins."

"Please, not just now, Geneviève. . . . I don't feel like talking to anyone except you. I have so much to talk to you about."

"But it's nearly lunch time, Jean. We can have all that after lunch."

"No, I can't talk to anyone else now. I must go and clean myself up a little anyway."

"Just as you like. . . . But you must come this afternoon and play to us. Two or three people are coming to tea. . . . It would be very sweet of you, if you'd play to us, Jean."

"But can't you understand? I can't see you with other people now."

"Just as you like," said Geneviève, flushing, her hand on
the iron latch of the door.

"Can't I come to see you tomorrow morning? Then I shall
feel more like meeting people, after talking to you a long
while. You see, I . . ." He paused with his eyes on the
ground. Then he burst out in a low, passionate voice: "Oh, if
I could only get it out of my mind . . . those tramping feet,
those voices shouting orders."

His hand trembled when he put it in Geneviève's hand. She
looked in his eyes calmly with her wide brown eyes.

"How strange you are today, Jean! Anyway, come back
early tomorrow."

She went in the door. He walked round the house, through
the carriage gate, and went off with long strides down the
road along the river that led under linden trees to the village.

Thoughts swarmed teasingly through his head, like wasps
about a rotting fruit. So at last he had seen Geneviève, and
had held her in his arms and kissed her. And that was all. His
plans for the future had never gone beyond that point. He
hardly knew what he had expected, but in all the sunny days
of walking, in all the furtive days in Paris, he had thought of
nothing else. He would see Geneviève and tell her all about
himself; he would unroll his life like a scroll before her eyes.
Together they would piece together the future. A sudden terror took possession of him. She had failed him. Floods of denial seethed through his mind. It was that he had expected so
much; he had expected her to understand him without explanation, instinctively. He had told her nothing. He had not
even told her he was a deserter. What was it that had kept him
from telling her? Puzzle as he would, he could not formulate
it. Only, far within him, the certainty lay like an icy weight:
she had failed him. He was alone. What a fool he had been to
build his whole life on a chance of sympathy? No. It was
rather this morbid playing at phrases that was at fault. He was
like a touchy old maid, thinking imaginary results. "Take life
at its face value," he kept telling himself. They loved each
other anyway, somehow; it did not matter how. And he was
free to work. Wasn't that enough?

But how could he wait until tomorrow to see her, to tell her everything, to break down all the silly little barriers between them, so that they might look directly into each other's lives?

The road turned inland from the river between garden walls at the entrance to the village. Through half-open doors Andrews got glimpses of neatly-cultivated kitchen-gardens and orchards where silver-leaved boughs swayed against the sky. Then the road swerved again into the village, crowded into a narrow paved street by the white and cream-colored houses with green or grey shutters and pale, red-tiled roofs. At the end, stained golden with lichen, the mauve-grey tower of the church held up its bells against the sky in a belfry of broad pointed arches. In front of the church Andrews turned down a little lane towards the river again, to come out in a moment on a quay shaded by skinny acacia trees. On the corner house, a ramshackle house with roofs and gables projecting in all directions, was a sign: "Rendezvous de la Marine." The room he stepped into was so low, Andrews had to stoop under the heavy brown beams as he crossed it. Stairs went up from a door behind a worn billiard table in the corner. Mme. Boncour stood between Andrews and the stairs. She was a flabby, elderly woman with round eyes and a round, very red face and a curious smirk about the lips.

"Monsieur payera un petit peu d'advance, n'est-ce pas, Monsieur?"

"All right," said Andrews, reaching for his pocketbook. "Shall I pay you a week in advance?"

The woman smiled broadly.

"Si Monsieur désire. . . . It's that life is so dear nowadays. Poor people like us can barely·get along."

"I know that only too well," said Andrews.

"Monsieur est étranger . . ." began the woman in a wheedling tone, when she had received the money.

"Yes. I was only demobilized a short time ago."

"Aha! Monsieur est démobilisé. Monsieur remplira la petite feuille pour la police, n'est-ce pas?"

The woman brought from behind her back a hand that held a narrow printed slip.

"All right. I'll fill it out now," said Andrews, his heart thumping.

Without thinking what he was doing, he put the paper on the edge of the billiard table and wrote: "John Brown, aged 23. Chicago, Ill., Etats-Unis. Musician. Holder of passport No. 1,432,286."

"Merci, Monsieur. A bientôt, Monsieur. Au revoir, Monsieur."

The woman's singing voice followed him up the rickety stairs to his room. It was only when he had closed the door that he remembered that he had put down for a passport number his army number. "And why did I write John Brown as a name?" he asked himself.

> "John Brown's body lies a-mouldering in the grave,
> But his soul goes marching on.
> Glory, glory, hallelujah!
> But his soul goes marching on."

He heard the song so vividly that he thought for an instant someone must be standing beside him singing it. He went to the window and ran his hand through his hair. Outside the Loire rambled in great loops towards the blue distance, silvery reach upon silvery reach, with here and there the broad gleam of a sand bank. Opposite were poplars and fields patched in various greens rising to hills tufted with dense shadowy groves. On the bare summit of the highest hill a windmill waved lazy arms against the marbled sky.

Gradually John Andrews felt the silvery quiet settle about him. He pulled a sausage and a piece of bread out of the pocket of his coat, took a long swig of water from the pitcher on his washstand, and settled himself at the table before the window in front of a pile of ruled sheets of music paper. He nibbled the bread and the sausage meditatively for a long while, then wrote "Arbeit und Rhythmus" in a large careful hand at the top of the paper. After that he looked out of the window without moving, watching the plumed clouds sail like huge slow ships against the slate-blue sky. Suddenly he scratched out what he had written and scrawled above it: "*The Body and Soul of John Brown.*" He got to his feet and walked about the room with clenched hands.

"How curious that I should have written that name. How curious that I should have written that name!" he said aloud.

He sat down at the table again and forgot everything in the music that possessed him.

The next morning he walked out early along the river, trying to occupy himself until it should be time to go to see Geneviève. The memory of his first days in the army, spent washing windows at the training camp, was very vivid in his mind. He saw himself again standing naked in the middle of a wide, bare room, while the recruiting sergeant measured and prodded him. And now he was a deserter. Was there any sense to it all? Had his life led in any particular direction, since he had been caught haphazard in the treadmill, or was it all chance? A toad hopping across a road in front of a steam roller.

He stood still, and looked about him. Beyond a clover field was the river with its sand banks and its broad silver reaches. A boy was wading far out in the river catching minnows with a net. Andrews watched his quick movements as he jerked the net through the water. And that boy, too, would be a soldier; the lithe body would be thrown into a mould to be made the same as other bodies, the quick movements would be standardized into the manual at arms, the inquisitive, petulant mind would be battered into servility. The stockade was built; not one of the sheep would escape. And those that were not sheep? They were deserters; every rifle muzzle held death for them; they would not live long. And yet other nightmares had been thrown off the shoulders of men. Every man who stood up courageously to die loosened the grip of the nightmare.

Andrews walked slowly along the road, kicking his feet into the dust like a schoolboy. At a turning he threw himself down on the grass under some locust trees. The heavy fragrance of their flowers and the grumbling of the bees that hung drunkenly on the white racemes made him feel very drowsy. A cart passed, pulled by heavy white horses; an old man with his back curbed like the top of a sunflower stalk hobbled after, using the whip as a walking stick. Andrews saw the old man's eyes turned on him suspiciously. A faint pang of fright went through him; did the old man know he was a deserter? The cart and the old man had already disappeared round the bend in the road. Andrews lay a long while listening to the jingle of the harness thin into the distance, leaving him again to the sound of the drowsy bees among the locust blossoms.

When he sat up, he noticed that through a break in the hedge beyond the slender black trunks of the locusts, he could see rising above the trees the extinguisher-shaped roof of the tower of Geneviève Rod's house. He remembered the day he had first seen Geneviève, and the boyish awkwardness with which she poured tea. Would he and Geneviève ever find a moment of real contact? All at once a bitter thought came to him. "Or is it that she wants a tame pianist as an ornament to a clever young woman's drawing room?" He jumped to his feet and started walking fast towards the town again. He would go to see her at once and settle all that forever. The village clock had begun to strike; the clear notes vibrated crisply across the fields: ten.

Walking back to the village he began to think of money. His room was twenty francs a week. He had in his purse a hundred and twenty-four francs. After fishing in all his pockets for silver, he found three francs and a half more. A hundred and twenty-seven francs fifty. If he could live on forty francs a week, he would have three weeks in which to work on the "Body and Soul of John Brown." Only three weeks; and then he must find work. In any case he would write Henslowe to send him money if he had any; this was no time for delicacy; everything depended on his having money. And he swore to himself that he would work for three weeks, that he would throw the idea that flamed within him into shape on paper, whatever happened. He racked his brains to think of someone in America he could write to for money. A ghastly sense of solitude possessed him. And would Geneviève fail him too?

Geneviève was coming out by the front door of the house when he reached the carriage gate beside the road.

She ran to meet him.

"Good morning. I was on my way to fetch you."

She seized his hand and pressed it hard.

"How sweet of you!"

"But, Jean, you're not coming from the village."

"I've been walking."

"How early you must get up!"

"You see, the sun rises just opposite my window, and shines in on my bed. That makes me get up early."

She pushed him in the door ahead of her. They went through the hall to a long high room that had a grand piano and many old high-backed chairs, and in front of the French windows that opened on the garden, a round table of black mahogany littered with books. Two tall girls in muslin dresses stood beside the piano.

"These are my cousins. . . . Here he is at last. Monsieur Andrews, ma cousine Berthe et ma cousine Jeanne. Now you've got to play to us; we are bored to death with everything we know."

"All right. . . . But I have a great deal to talk to you about later," said Andrews in a low voice.

Geneviève nodded understandingly.

"Why don't you play us *La Reine de Saba*, Jean?"

"Oh, do play that," twittered the cousins.

"If you don't mind, I'd rather play some Bach."

"There's a lot of Bach in that chest in the corner," cried Geneviève. "It's ridiculous; everything in the house is jammed with music."

They leaned over the chest together, so that Andrews felt her hair brush against his cheek, and the smell of her hair in his nostrils. The cousins remained by the piano.

"I must talk to you alone soon," whispered Andrews.

"All right," she said, her face reddening as she leaned over the chest.

On top of the music was a revolver.

"Look out, it's loaded," she said, when he picked it up.

He looked at her inquiringly. "I have another in my room. You see Mother and I are often alone here, and then, I like firearms. Don't you?"

"I hate them," muttered Andrews.

"Here's tons of Bach."

"Fine. . . . Look, Geneviève," he said suddenly, "lend me that revolver for a few days. I'll tell you why I want it later."

"Certainly. Be careful, because it's loaded," she said in an offhand manner, walking over to the piano with two volumes under each arm. Andrews closed the chest and followed her, suddenly bubbling with gaiety. He opened a volume haphazard.

"To a friend to dissuade him from starting on a journey," he read. "Oh, I used to know that."

He began to play, putting boisterous vigor into the tunes. In a pianissimo passage he heard one cousin whisper to the other:

"Qu'il a l'air intéressant."

"Farouche, n'est-ce pas? Genre révolutionnaire," answered the other cousin, tittering. Then he noticed that Mme. Rod was smiling at him. He got to his feet.

"Mais ne vous dérangez pas," she said.

A man with white flannel trousers and tennis shoes and a man in black with a pointed grey beard and amused grey eyes had come into the room, followed by a stout woman in hat and veil, with long white cotton gloves on her arms. Introductions were made. Andrews's spirits began to ebb. All these people were making strong the barrier between him and Geneviève. Whenever he looked at her, some well-dressed person stepped in front of her with a gesture of politeness. He felt caught in a ring of well-dressed conventions that danced about him with grotesque gestures of politeness. All through lunch he had a crazy desire to jump to his feet and shout: "Look at me; I'm a deserter. I'm under the wheels of your system. If your system doesn't succeed in killing me, it will be that much weaker, it will have less strength to kill others." There was talk about his demobilization, and his music, and the Schola Cantorum. He felt was being exhibited. "But they don't know what they're exhibiting," he said to himself with a certain bitter joy.

After lunch they went out into the grape arbor, where coffee was brought. Andrews sat silent, not listening to the talk, which was about Empire furniture and the new taxes, staring up into the broad sun-splotched leaves of the grape vines, remembering how the sun and shade had danced about Geneviève's hair when they had been in the arbor alone the day before, turning it all to red flame. Today she sat in shadow, and her hair was rusty and dull. Time dragged by very slowly.

At last Geneviève got to her feet.

"You haven't seen my boat," she said to Andrews. "Let's go for a row. I'll row you about."

Andrews jumped up eagerly.

"Make her be careful, Monsieur Andrews, she's dreadfully imprudent," said Madame Rod.

"You were bored to death," said Geneviève, as they walked out on the road.

"No, but those people all seemed to be building new walls between you and me. God knows there are enough already."

She looked him sharply in the eyes a second, but said nothing.

They walked slowly through the sand of the river edge, till they came to an old flat-bottomed boat painted green with an orange stripe, drawn up among the reeds.

"It will probably sink; can you swim?" she asked, laughing.

Andrews smiled, and said in a stiff voice:

"I can swim. It was by swimming that I got out of the army."

"What do you mean?"

"When I deserted."

"When you deserted?"

Geneviève leaned over to pull on the boat. Their heads almost touching, they pulled the boat down to the water's edge, then pushed it half out on to the river.

"And if you are caught?"

"They might shoot me; I don't know. Still, as the war is over, it would probably be life imprisonment, or at least twenty years."

"You can speak of it as coolly as that?"

"It is no new idea to my mind."

"What induced you to do such a thing?"

"I was not willing to submit any longer to the treadmill."

"Come, let's go out on the river."

Geneviève stepped into the boat and caught up the oars.

"Now push her off, and don't fall in," she cried.

The boat glided out into the water. Geneviève began pulling on the oars slowly and regularly. Andrews looked at her without speaking.

"When you're tired, I'll row," he said after a while.

Behind them the village, patched white and buff-color and russet and pale red with stucco walls and steep, tiled roofs, rose in an irregular pyramid to the church. Through the wide pointed arches of the belfry they could see the bells hanging against the sky. Below in the river the town was reflected complete, with a great rift of steely blue across it where the wind ruffled the water.

The oars creaked rhythmically as Geneviève pulled on them.

"Remember, when you are tired," said Andrews again after a long pause.

Geneviève spoke through clenched teeth:

"Of course, you have no patriotism."

"As you mean it, none."

They rounded the edge of a sand bank where the current ran hard. Andrews put his hands beside her hands on the oars and pushed with her. The bow of the boat grounded in some reeds under willows.

"We'll stay here," she said, pulling in the oars that flashed in the sun as she jerked them, dripping silver, out of the water.

She clasped her hands round her knees and leaned over towards him.

"So that is why you want my revolver. . . . Tell me all about it, from Chartres," she said, in a choked voice.

"You see, I was arrested at Chartres and sent to a labor battalion, the equivalent for your army prison, without being able to get word to my commanding officer in the School Detachment. . . ." He paused.

A bird was singing in the willow tree. The sun was under a cloud; beyond the long pale green leaves that fluttered ever so slightly in the wind, the sky was full of silvery and cream-colored clouds, with here and there a patch the color of a robin's egg. Andrews began laughing softly.

"But, Geneviève, how silly those words are, those pompous, efficient words: detachment, battalion, commanding officer. It would have all happened anyway. Things reached the breaking point; that was all. I could not submit any longer to the discipline. . . . Oh, those long Roman words, what millstones they are about men's necks! That was silly, too; I was quite willing to help in the killing of Germans I had no quarrel with, out of curiosity or cowardice. . . . You see, it has taken me so long to find out how the world is. There was no one to show me the way."

He paused as if expecting her to speak. The bird in the willow tree was still singing.

Suddenly a dangling twig blew aside a little so that Andrews could see him—a small grey bird, his throat all puffed out with song.

"It seems to me," he said very softly, "that human society has been always that, and perhaps will be always that: organizations growing and stifling individuals, and individuals revolting hopelessly against them, and at last forming new societies to crush the old societies and becoming slaves again in their turn. . . ."

"I thought you were a socialist," broke in Geneviève sharply, in a voice that hurt him to the quick, he did not know why.

"A man told me at the labor battalion," began Andrews again, "that they'd tortured a friend of his there once by making him swallow lighted cigarettes; well, every order shouted at me, every new humiliation before the authorities, was as great an agony to me. Can't you understand?" His voice rose suddenly to a tone of entreaty.

She nodded her head. They were silent. The willow leaves shivered in a little wind. The bird had gone.

"But tell me about the swimming part of it. That sounds exciting."

"We were working unloading cement at Passy—cement to build the stadium the army is presenting to the French, built by slave labor, like the pyramids."

"Passy's where Balzac lived. Have you ever seen his house there?"

"There was a boy working with me, the Kid, 'le gosse,' it'd be in French. Without him, I should never have done it. I was completely crushed. . . . I suppose that he was drowned. . . . Anyway, we swam under water as far as we could, and, as it was nearly dark, I managed to get on a barge, where a funny anarchist family took care of me. I've never heard of the Kid since. Then I bought these clothes that amuse you so, Geneviève, and came back to Paris to find you, mainly."

"I mean as much to you as that?" whispered Geneviève.

"In Paris, too. I tried to find a boy named Marcel, who

worked on a farm near St. Germain. I met him out there one day. I found he'd gone to sea. . . . If it had not been that I had to see you, I should have gone straight to Bordeaux or Marseilles. They aren't too particular who they take as a sea-man now."

"But in the army didn't you have enough of that dread-ful life, always thrown among uneducated people, always in dirty, foul-smelling surroundings, you, a sensitive person, an artist? No wonder you are almost crazy after years of that." Geneviève spoke passionately, with her eyes fixed on his face.

"Oh, it wasn't that," said Andrews with despair in his voice. "I rather like the people you call low. Anyway, the differences between people are so slight. . . ." His sentence trailed away. He stopped speaking, sat stirring uneasily on the seat, afraid he would cry out. He noticed the hard shape of the revolver against his leg.

"But isn't there something you can do about it? You must have friends," burst out Geneviève. "You were treated with horrible injustice. You can get yourself reinstated and properly demobilised. They'll see you are a person of intelligence. They can't treat you as they would anybody."

"I must be, as you say, a little mad, Geneviève," said An-drews. "But now that I, by pure accident, have made a ges-ture, feeble as it is, towards human freedom, I can't feel that . . . Oh, I suppose I'm a fool. . . . But there you have me, just as I am, Geneviève."

He sat with his head drooping over his chest, his two hands clasping the gunwales of the boat. After a long while Geneviève said in a dry little voice:

"Well, we must go back now; it's time for tea."

Andrews looked up. There was a dragon fly poised on the top of a reed, with silver wings and a long crimson body.

"Look just behind you, Geneviève."

"Oh, a dragon fly! What people was it that made them the symbol of life? It wasn't the Egyptians. O, I've forgotten."

"I'll row," said Andrews.

The boat was hurried along by the current. In a very few minutes they had pulled it up on the bank in front of the Rods' house.

"Come and have some tea," said Geneviève.

"No, I must work."

"You are doing something new, aren't you?"

Andrews nodded.

"What's its name?"

"The Soul and Body of John Brown."

"Who's John Brown?"

"He was a madman who wanted to free people. There's a song about him."

"It is based on popular themes?"

"Not that I know of. . . . I only thought of the name yesterday. It came to me by a very curious accident."

"You'll come tomorrow?"

"If you're not too busy."

"Let's see, the Boileaus are coming to lunch. There won't be anybody at tea time. We can have tea together alone."

He took her hand and held it, awkward as a child with a new playmate.

"All right, at about four. If there's nobody there, we'll play music," he said.

She pulled her hand from him hurriedly, made a curious formal gesture of farewell, and crossed the road to the gate without looking back. There was one idea in his head, to get to his room and lock the door and throw himself face down on the bed. The idea amused some distant part of his mind. That had been what he had always done when, as a child, the world had seemed too much for him. He would run upstairs and lock the door and throw himself face downward on the bed. "I wonder if I shall cry?" he thought.

Madame Boncour was coming down the stairs as he went up. He backed down and waited. When she got to the bottom, pouting a little, she said:

"So you are a friend of Mme. Rod, Monsieur?"

"How did you know that?"

A dimple appeared near her mouth in either cheek.

"You know, in the country, one knows everything," she said.

"Au revoir," he said, starting up the stairs.

"Mais, Monsieur. You should have told me. If I had known I should not have asked you to pay in advance. Oh, never. You must pardon me, Monsieur."

"All right."

"Monsieur est Américain? You see I know a lot." Her puffy cheeks shook when she giggled. "And Monsieur has known Mme. Rod et Mlle. Rod a long time. An old friend. Monsieur is a musician."

"Yes. Bon soir." Andrews ran up the stairs.

"Au revoir, Monsieur." Her chanting voice followed him up the stairs.

He slammed the door behind him and threw himself on the bed.

When Andrews awoke next morning, his first thought was how long he had to wait that day to see Geneviève. Then he remembered their talk of the day before. Was it worth while going to see her at all, he asked himself. And very gradually he felt cold despair taking hold of him. He felt for a moment that he was the only living thing in a world of dead machines; the toad hopping across the road in front of a steam roller. Suddenly he thought of Jeanne. He remembered her grimy, overworked fingers lying in her lap. He pictured her walking up and down in front of the Café de Rohan one Wednesday night, waiting for him. In the place of Geneviève, what would Jeanne have done? Yet people were always alone, really; how-ever much they loved each other, there could be no real union. Those who rode in the great car could never feel as the others felt; the toads hopping across the road. He felt no ran-cour against Geneviève.

These thoughts slipped from him while he was drinking the coffee and eating the dry bread that made his breakfast; and afterwards, walking back and forth along the river bank, he felt his mind and body becoming as if fluid, and supple, trem-bling, bent in the rush of his music like a poplar tree bent in a wind. He sharpened a pencil and went up to his room again.

The sky was cloudless that day. As he sat at his table the square of blue through the window and the hills topped by their windmill and the silver-blue of the river, were constantly in his eyes. Sometimes he wrote notes down fast, thinking nothing, feeling nothing, seeing nothing; other times he sat for long periods staring at the sky and at the windmill, vaguely happy, playing with unexpected thoughts that came and vanished, as now and then a moth fluttered in the window to blunder about the ceiling beams, and, at last, to disappear without his knowing how.

When the clock struck twelve, he found he was very hungry. For two days he had eaten nothing but bread, sausage and cheese. Finding Madame Boncour behind the bar downstairs, polishing glasses, he ordered dinner of her. She brought him a stew and a bottle of wine at once, and stood over him watching him eat it, her arms akimbo and the dimples showing in her huge red cheeks.

"Monsieur eats less than any young man I ever saw," she said.

"I'm working hard," said Andrews, flushing.

"But when you work you have to eat a great deal, a great deal."

"And if the money is short?" asked Andrews with a smile. Something in the steely searching look that passed over her eyes for a minute startled him.

"There are not many people here now, Monsieur, but you should see it on a market day. . . . Monsieur will take some dessert?"

"Cheese and coffee."

"Nothing more? It's the season of strawberries."

"Nothing more, thank you."

When Madame Boncour came back with the cheese, she said:

"I had Americans here once, Monsieur. A pretty time I had with them, too. They were deserters. They went away without paying, with the gendarmes after them. I hope they were caught and sent to the front, those good-for-nothings."

"There are all sorts of Americans," said Andrews in a low voice. He was angry with himself because his heart beat so.

"Well, I'm going for a little walk. Au revoir, Madame."

"Monsieur is going for a little walk. Amusez-vous bien, Monsieur. Au revoir, Monsieur," Madame Boncour's singsong tones followed him out.

A little before four Andrews knocked at the front door of the Rods' house. He could hear Santo, the little black and tan, barking inside. Madame Rod opened the door for him herself.

"Oh, here you are," she said. "Come and have some tea. Did the work go well to-day?"

"And Geneviève?" stammered Andrews.

"She went out motoring with some friends. She left a note for you. It's on the tea-table."

He found himself talking, making questions and answers, drinking tea, putting cakes into his mouth, all through a white dead mist.

Geneviève's note said:

"Jean:—I'm thinking of ways and means. You must get away to a neutral country. Why couldn't you have talked it over with me first, before cutting off every chance of going back. I'll be in tomorrow at the same time.

"Bien à vous.   G.R."

"Would it disturb you if I played the piano a few minutes, Madame Rod?" Andrews found himself asking all at once.

"No, go ahead. We'll come in later and listen to you."

It was only as he left the room that he realized he had been talking to the two cousins as well as to Madame Rod.

At the piano he forgot everything and regained his mood of vague joyousness. He found paper and a pencil in his pocket, and played the theme that had come to him while he had been washing windows at the top of a stepladder at training camp arranging it, modelling it, forgetting everything, absorbed in his rhythms and cadences. When he stopped work it was nearly dark. Geneviève Rod, a veil round her head, stood in the French window that led to the garden.

"I heard you," she said. "Go on."

"I'm through. How was your motor ride?"

"I loved it. It's not often I get a chance to go motoring."

"Nor is it often I get a chance to talk to you alone," cried Andrews bitterly.

"You seem to feel you have rights of ownership over me. I resent it. No one has rights over me." She spoke as if it were not the first time she had thought of the phrase.

He walked over and leaned against the window beside her.

"Has it made such a difference to you, Geneviève, finding out that I am a deserter?"

"No, of course not," she said hastily.

"I think it has, Geneviève. . . . What do you want me to

do? Do you think I should give myself up? A man I knew in Paris has given himself up, but he hadn't taken his uniform off. It seems that makes a difference. He was a nice fellow. His name was Al, he was from San Francisco. He had nerve, for he amputated his own little finger when his hand was crushed by a freight car."

"Oh, no, no. Oh, this is so frightful. And you would have been a great composer. I feel sure of it."

"Why, would have been? The stuff I'm doing now's better than any of the dribbling things I've done before, I know that."

"Oh, yes, but you'll need to study, to get yourself known."

"If I can pull through six months, I'm safe. The army will have gone. I don't believe they extradite deserters."

"Yes, but the shame of it, the danger of being found out all the time."

"I am ashamed of many things in my life, Geneviève. I'm rather proud of this."

"But can't you understand that other people haven't your notions of individual liberty?"

"I must go, Geneviève."

"You must come in again soon."

"One of these days."

And he was out in the road in the windy twilight, with his music papers crumpled in his hand. The sky was full of tempestuous purple clouds; between them were spaces of clear claret-colored light, and here and there a gleam of opal. There were a few drops of rain in the wind that rustled the broad leaves of the lindens and filled the wheat fields with waves like the sea, and made the river very dark between rosy sand banks. It began to rain. Andrews hurried home so as not to drench his only suit. Once in his room he lit four candles and placed them at the corners of his table. A little cold crimson light still filtered in through the rain from the afterglow, giving the candles a ghostly glimmer. Then he lay on his bed, and staring up at the flickering light on the ceiling, tried to think.

"Well, you're alone now, John Andrews," he said aloud, after a half-hour, and jumped jauntily to his feet. He stretched himself and yawned. Outside the rain pattered loudly and steadily. "Let's have a general accounting," he said to himself. "It'll be easily a month before I hear from old Howe in America, and longer before I hear from Henslowe, and already I've spent twenty francs on food. Can't make it this way. Then, in real possessions, I have one volume of Villon, a green book on counterpoint, a map of France torn in two, and a moderately well-stocked mind."

He put the two books on the middle of the table before him, on top of his disorderly bundle of music papers and notebooks. Then he went on, piling his possessions there as he thought of them. Three pencils, a fountain pen. Automatically he reached for his watch, but he remembered he'd given it to Al to pawn in case he didn't decide to give himself up, and needed money. A toothbrush. A shaving set. A piece of soap. A hairbrush and a broken comb. Anything else? He groped in the musette that hung on the foot of the bed. A box of matches. A knife with one blade missing, and a mashed cigarette. Amusement growing on him every minute, he contemplated the pile. Then, in the drawer, he remembered, was a clean shirt and two pairs of soiled socks. And that was all, absolutely all. Nothing saleable there. Except Geneviève's revolver. He pulled it out of his pocket. The candlelight flashed on the bright nickel. No, he might need that; it was too valuable to sell. He pointed it towards himself. Under the chin was said to be the best place. He wondered if he would pull the trigger when the barrel was pressed against his chin. No, when his money gave out he'd sell the revolver. An expensive death for a starving man. He sat on the edge of the bed and laughed.

Then he discovered he was very hungry. Two meals in one day; shocking! he said to himself. Whistling joyfully, like a schoolboy, he strode down the rickety stairs to order a meal of Madame Boncour.

It was with a strange start that he noticed that the tune he was whistling was:

> "John Brown's body lies a-mouldering in the grave,
> But his soul goes marching on."

The lindens were in bloom. From a tree beside the house great gusts of fragrance, heavy as incense, came in through the open window. Andrews lay across the table with his eyes closed and his cheek in a mass of ruled papers. He was very tired. The first movement of the "Soul and Body of John Brown" was down on paper. The village clock struck two. He got to his feet and stood a moment looking absently out of the window. It was a sultry afternoon of swollen clouds that hung low over the river. The windmill on the hilltop opposite was motionless. He seemed to hear Geneviève's voice the last time he had seen her, so long ago. "You would have been a great composer." He walked over to the table and turned over some sheets without looking at them. "Would have been." He shrugged his shoulders. So you couldn't be a great composer and a deserter too in the year 1919. Probably Geneviève was right. But he must have something to eat.

"But how late it is," expostulated Madame Boncour, when he asked for lunch.

"I know it's very late. I have just finished a third of the work I'm doing."

"And do you get paid a great deal, when that is finished?" asked Madame Boncour, the dimples appearing in her broad cheeks.

"Some day, perhaps."

"You will be lonely now that the Rods have left."

"Have they left?"

"Didn't you know? Didn't you go to say goodby? They've gone to the seashore. . . . But I'll make you a little omelette."

"Thank you."

When Madame Boncour came back with the omelette and fried potatoes, she said to him in a mysterious voice:

"You didn't go to see the Rods as often these last weeks."

"No."

Madame Boncour stood staring at him, with her red arms folded round her breasts, shaking her head.

When he got up to go upstairs again, she suddenly shouted:

"And when are you going to pay me? It's two weeks since you have paid me."

"But, Madame Boncour, I told you I had no money. If you wait a day or two, I'm sure to get some in the mail. It can't be more than a day or two."

"I've heard that story before."

"I've even tried to get work at several farms round here."

Madame Boncour threw back her head and laughed, showing the blackened teeth of her lower jaw.

"Look here," she said at length, "after this week, it's finished. You either pay me, or . . . And I sleep very lightly, Monsieur." Her voice took on suddenly its usual sleek singsong tone.

Andrews broke away and ran upstairs to his room.

"I must fly the coop tonight," he said to himself. But suppose then letters came with money the next day. He writhed in indecision all the afternoon.

That evening he took a long walk. In passing the Rods' house he saw that the shutters were closed. It gave him a sort of relief to know that Geneviève no longer lived near him. His solitude was complete, now.

And why, instead of writing music that would have been worth while if he hadn't been a deserter, he kept asking himself, hadn't he tried long ago to act, to make a gesture, however feeble, however forlorn, for other people's freedom? Half by accident he had managed to free himself from the treadmill. Couldn't he have helped others? If he only had his life to live over again. No; he had not lived up to the name of John Brown.

It was dark when he got back to the village. He had decided to wait one more day.

The next morning he started working on the second movement. The lack of a piano made it very difficult to get ahead, yet he said to himself that he should put down what he could, as it would be long before he found leisure again.

One night he had blown out his candle and stood at the window watching the glint of the moon on the river. He heard a soft heavy step on the landing outside his room. A floorboard creaked, and the key turned in the lock. The step was heard again on the stairs. John Andrews laughed aloud. The window was only twenty feet from the ground, and there was a trellis. He got into bed contentedly. He must sleep well, for tomorrow night he would slip out of the window and make for Bordeaux.

Another morning. A brisk wind blew, fluttering Andrews's papers as he worked. Outside the river was streaked blue and silver and slate-colored. The windmill's arms waved fast against the piled clouds. The scent of the lindens came only intermittently on the sharp wind. In spite of himself, the tune of "John Brown's Body" had crept in among his ideas. Andrews sat with a pencil at his lips, whistling softly, while in the back of his mind a vast chorus seemed singing:

> "John Brown's body lies a-mouldering in the grave,
> But his soul goes marching on.
> Glory, glory, hallelujah!
> But his soul goes marching on."

If one could only find freedom by marching for it, came the thought.

All at once he became rigid, his hands clutched the table edge.

There was an American voice under his window:

"D'you think she's kiddin' us, Charley?"

Andrews was blinded, falling from a dizzy height. God, could things repeat themselves like that? Would everything be repeated? And he seemed to hear voices whisper in his ears: "One of you men teach him how to salute."

He jumped to his feet and pulled open the drawer. It was empty. The woman had taken the revolver. "It's all planned, then. She knew," he said aloud in a low voice.

He became suddenly calm.

A man in a boat was passing down the river. The boat was painted bright green; the man wore a curious jacket of a burnt-brown color, and held a fishing pole.

Andrews sat in his chair again. The boat was out of sight now, but there was the windmill turning, turning against the piled white clouds.

There were steps on the stairs.

Two swallows, twittering, curved past the window, very near, so that Andrews could make out the marking on their wings and the way they folded their legs against their pale-grey bellies.

There was a knock.

"Come in," said Andrews firmly.

"I beg yer pardon," said a soldier with his hat, that had a band, in his hand. "Are you the American?"

"Yes."

"Well, the woman down there said she thought your papers wasn't in very good order." The man stammered with embarrassment.

Their eyes met.

"No, I'm a deserter," said Andrews.

The M.P. snatched for his whistle and blew it hard. There was an answering whistle from outside the window.

"Get your stuff together."

"I have nothing."

"All right, walk downstairs slowly in front of me."

Outside the windmill was turning, turning, against the piled white clouds of the sky.

Andrews turned his eyes towards the door. The M.P. closed the door after them, and followed on his heels down the steps.

On John Andrews's writing table the brisk wind rustled among the broad sheets of paper. First one sheet, then another, blew off the table, until the floor was littered with them.

MANHATTAN TRANSFER

CONTENTS

I. Ferryslip

Three gulls wheel above the broken boxes, orangerinds, spoiled cabbage heads that heave between the splintered plank walls, the green waves spume under the round bow as the ferry, skidding on the tide, crashes, gulps the broken water, slides, settles slowly into the slip. Handwinches whirl with jingle of chains. Gates fold upwards, feet step out across the crack, men and women press through the manuresmelling wooden tunnel of the ferryhouse, crushed and jostling like apples fed down a chute into a press.

The nurse, holding the basket at arm's length as if it were a bedpan, opened the door to a big dry hot room with greenish distempered walls where in the air tinctured with smells of alcohol and iodoform hung writhing a faint sourish squalling from other baskets along the wall. As she set her basket down she glanced into it with pursedup lips. The newborn baby squirmed in the cottonwool feebly like a knot of earthworms.

On the ferry there was an old man playing the violin. He had a monkey's face puckered up in one corner and kept time with the toe of a cracked patent-leather shoe. Bud Korpenning sat on the rail watching him, his back to the river. The breeze made the hair stir round the tight line of his cap and dried the sweat on his temples. His feet were blistered, he was leadentired, but when the ferry moved out of the slip, bucking the little slapping scalloped waves of the river he felt something warm and tingling shoot suddenly through all his veins. "Say, friend, how fur is it into the city from where this ferry lands?" he asked a young man in a straw hat wearing a blue and white striped necktie who stood beside him.

The young man's glance moved up from Bud's roadswelled shoes to the red wrist that stuck out from the frayed sleeves of his coat, past the skinny turkey's throat and slid up cockily into the intent eyes under the broken visored cap.

"That depends where you want to get to."

"How do I get to Broadway? . . . I want to get to the center of things."

"Walk east a block and turn down Broadway and you'll find the center of things if you walk far enough."

"Thank you sir. I'll do that."

The violinist was going through the crowd with his hat held out, the wind ruffling the wisps of gray hair on his shabby bald head. Bud found the face tilted up at him, the crushed eyes like two black pins looking into his. "Nothin," he said gruffly and turned away to look at the expanse of river bright as knifeblades. The plank walls of the slip closed in, cracked as the ferry lurched against them; there was rattling of chains, and Bud was pushed forward among the crowd through the ferryhouse. He walked between two coal wagons and out over a dusty expanse of street towards yellow streetcars. A trembling took hold of his knees. He thrust his hands deep in his pockets.

EAT on a lunchwagon halfway down the block. He slid stiffly onto a revolving stool and looked for a long while at the pricelist.

"Fried eggs and a cup o coffee."

"Want 'em turned over?" asked the redhaired man behind the counter who was wiping off his beefy freckled forearms with his apron. Bud Korpenning sat up with a start.

"What?"

"The eggs? Want em turned over or sunny side up?"

"Oh sure, turn 'em over." Bud slouched over the counter again with his head between his hands.

"You look all in, feller," the man said as he broke the eggs into the sizzling grease of the frying pan.

"Came down from upstate. I walked fifteen miles this mornin."

The man made a whistling sound through his eyeteeth. "Comin to the big city to look for a job, eh?"

Bud nodded. The man flopped the eggs sizzling and netted with brown out onto the plate and pushed it towards Bud with some bread and butter on the edge of it. "I'm goin to slip you a bit of advice, feller, and it won't cost you nutten. You go an git a shave and a haircut and brush the hayseeds out o yer suit a bit before you start lookin. You'll be more likely to git somethin. It's looks that count in this city."

"I kin work all right. I'm a good worker," growled Bud with his mouth full.

"I'm tellin yez, that's all," said the redhaired man and turned back to his stove.

When Ed Thatcher climbed the marble steps of the wide hospital entry he was trembling. The smell of drugs caught at his throat. A woman with a starched face was looking at him over the top of a desk. He tried to steady his voice.

"Can you tell me how Mrs. Thatcher is?"

"Yes, you can go up."

"But please, miss, is everything all right?"

"The nurse on the floor will know anything about the case. Stairs to the left, third floor, maternity ward."

Ed Thatcher held a bunch of flowers wrapped in green waxed paper. The broad stairs swayed as he stumbled up, his toes kicking against the brass rods that held the fiber matting down. The closing of a door cut off a strangled shriek. He stopped a nurse.

"I want to see Mrs. Thatcher, please."

"Go right ahead if you know where she is."

"But they've moved her."

"You'll have to ask at the end of the hall."

He gnawed his cold lips. At the end of the hall a redfaced woman looked at him, smiling.

"Everything's fine. You're the happy father of a bouncing baby girl."

"You see it's our first and Susie's so delicate, " he stammered with blinking eyes.

"Oh yes, I understand, naturally you worried. . . . You can go in and talk to her when she wakes up. The baby was born two hours ago. Be sure not to tire her."

Ed Thatcher was a little man with two blond wisps of mustache and washedout gray eyes. He seized the nurse's hand and shook it showing all his uneven yellow teeth in a smile.

"You see it's our first."

"Congratulations," said the nurse.

Rows of beds under bilious gaslight, a sick smell of restlessly stirring bedclothes, faces fat, lean, yellow, white; that's her. Susie's yellow hair lay in a loose coil round her little white face that looked shriveled and twisted. He unwrapped the roses and put them on the night table. Looking out the window was like looking down into water. The trees in the square were tangled in blue cobwebs. Down the avenue lamps were coming on marking off with green shimmer brickpurple blocks of houses; chimney pots and water tanks cut sharp into a sky flushed like flesh. The blue lids slipped back off her eyes.

"That you Ed?. . . . Why Ed they are Jacks. How extravagant of you."

"I couldn't help it dearest. I knew you liked them."

A nurse was hovering near the end of the bed.

"Couldn't you let us see the baby, miss?"

The nurse nodded. She was a lanternjawed grayfaced woman with tight lips.

"I hate her," whispered Susie. "She gives me the fidgets that woman does; she's nothing but a mean old maid."

"Never mind dear, it's just for a day or two." Susie closed her eyes.

"Do you still want to call her Ellen?"

The nurse brought back a basket and set it on the bed beside Susie.

"Oh isn't she wonderful!" said Ed. "Look she's breathing. . . . And they've oiled her." He helped his wife to raise herself on her elbow; the yellow coil of her hair unrolled, fell over his hand and arm. "How can you tell them apart nurse?"

"Sometimes we cant," said the nurse, stretching her mouth in a smile. Susie was looking querulously into the minute purple face. "You're sure this is mine."

"Of course."

"But it hasnt any label on it."

"I'll label it right away."

"But mine was dark." Susie lay back on the pillow, gasping for breath.

"She has lovely little light fuzz just the color of your hair."

Susie stretched her arms out above her head and shrieked: "It's not mine. It's not mine. Take it away. . . . That woman's stolen my baby."

"Dear, for Heaven's sake! Dear, for Heaven's sake!" He tried to tuck the covers about her.

"Too bad," said the nurse, calmly, picking up the basket. "I'll have to give her a sedative."

Susie sat up stiff in bed. "Take it away," she yelled and fell back in hysterics, letting out continuous frail moaning shrieks.

"O my God!" cried Ed Thatcher, clasping his hands.

"You'd better go away for this evening, Mr. Thatcher. . . . She'll quiet down, once you've gone. . . . I'll put the roses in water."

On the last flight he caught up with a chubby man who was strolling down slowly, rubbing his hands as he went. Their eyes met.

"Everything all right, sir?" asked the chubby man.

"Oh yes, I guess so," said Thatcher faintly.

The chubby man turned on him, delight bubbling through his thick voice. "Congradulade me, congradulade me; mein vife has giben birth to a poy."

Thatcher shook a fat little hand. "Mine's a girl," he admitted, sheepishly.

"It is fif years yet and every year a girl, and now dink of it, a poy."

"Yes," said Ed Thatcher as they stepped out on the pavement, "it's a great moment."

"Vill yous allow me sir to invite you to drink a congradulation drink mit me?"

"Why with pleasure."

The latticed halfdoors were swinging in the saloon at the corner of Third Avenue. Shuffling their feet politely they went through into the back room.

"Ach," said the German as they sat down at a scarred brown table, "family life is full of vorries."

"That it is sir; this is my first."

"Vill you haf beer?"

"All right anything suits me."

"Two pottles Culmbacher imported to drink to our little folk." The bottles popped and the sepia-tinged foam rose in the glasses. "Here's success. . . . Prosit," said the German, and raised his glass. He rubbed the foam out of his mustache and pounded on the table with a pink fist. "Vould it be indiscreet meester . . . ?"

"Thatcher's my name."

"Vould it be indiscreet, Mr. Thatcher, to inquvire vat might your profession be?"

"Accountant. I hope before long to be a certified accountant."

"I am a printer and my name is Zucher—Marcus Antonius Zucher."

"Pleased to meet you Mr. Zucher."

They shook hands across the table between the bottles.

"A certified accountant makes big money," said Mr. Zucher.

"Big money's what I'll have to have, for my little girl."

"Kids, they eat money," continued Mr. Zucher, in a deep voice.

"Wont you let me set you up to a bottle?" said Thatcher, figuring up how much he had in his pocket. Poor Susie wouldn't like me to be drinking in a saloon like this. But just this once, and I'm learning, learning about fatherhood.

"The more the merrier," said Mr. Zucher. ". . . But kids, they eat money. . . . Dont do nutten but eat and vear out clothes. Vonce I get my business on its feet. . . . Ach! Now vot mit hypothecations and the difficult borrowing of money and vot mit vages going up und these here crazy tradeunion socialists and bomsters . . ."

"Well here's how, Mr. Zucher." Mr. Zucher squeezed the foam out of his mustache with the thumb and forefinger of each hand. "It aint every day ve pring into the voirld a papy poy, Mr. Thatcher."

"Or a baby girl, Mr. Zucher."

The barkeep wiped the spillings off the table when he brought the new bottles, and stood near listening, the rag dangling from his red hands.

"And I have the hope in mein heart that ven my poy drinks to his poy, it vill be in champagne vine. Ach, that is how things go in this great city."

"I'd like my girl to be a quiet homey girl, not like these young women nowadays, all frills and furbelows and tight lacings. And I'll have retired by that time and have a little place up the Hudson, work in the garden evenings. . . . I know fellers downtown who have retired with three thousand a year. It's saving that does it."

"Aint no good in savin," said the barkeep. "I saved for ten years and the savings bank went broke and left me nutten but a bankbook for my trouble. Get a close tip and take a chance, that's the only system."

"That's nothing but gambling," snapped Thatcher.

"Well sir it's a gamblin game," said the barkeep as he walked back to the bar swinging the two empty bottles.

"A gamblin game. He aint so far out," said Mr. Zucher, looking down into his beer with a glassy meditative eye. "A man vat is ambeetious must take chances. Ambeetions is vat I came here from Frankfort mit at the age of tvelf years, und now that I haf a son to vork for . . . Ach, his name shall be Vilhelm after the mighty Kaiser."

"My little girl's name will be Ellen after my mother." Ed Thatcher's eyes filled with tears.

Mr. Zucher got to his feet. "Vell goodpy Mr. Thatcher. Happy to have met you. I must go home to my little girls."

Thatcher shook the chubby hand again, and thinking warm soft thoughts of motherhood and fatherhood and birthday cakes and Christmas watched through a sepia-tinged foamy haze Mr. Zucher waddle out through the swinging doors. After a while he stretched out his arms. Well poor little Susie wouldn't like me to be here. . . . Everything for her and the bonny wee bairn.

"Hey there yous how about settlin?" bawled the barkeep after him when he reached the door.

"Didnt the other feller pay?"

"Like hell he did."

"But he was t-t-treating me. . . ."

The barkeep laughed as he covered the money with a red lipper. "I guess that bloat believes in savin."

A small bearded bandylegged man in a derby walked up Allen Street, up the sunstriped tunnel hung with skyblue and smokedsalmon and mustardyellow quilts, littered with second hand gingerbread-colored furniture. He walked with his cold hands clasped over the tails of his frockcoat, picking his way among packing boxes and scuttling children. He kept gnawing his lips and clasping and unclasping his hands. He walked without hearing the yells of the children or the annihilating clatter of the L trains overhead or smelling the rancid sweet huddled smell of packed tenements.

At a yellowpainted drugstore at the corner of Canal, he stopped and stared abstractedly at a face on a green advertising card. It was a highbrowed cleanshaven distinguished face with arched eyebrows and a bushy neatly trimmed mustache, the face of a man who had money in the bank, poised prosperously above a crisp wing collar and an ample dark cravat. Under it in copybook writing was the signature King C. Gillette. Above his head hovered the motto NO STROPPING NO HONING. The little bearded man pushed his derby back off his sweating brow and looked for a long time into the dollarproud eyes of King C. Gillette. Then he clenched his fists, threw back his shoulders and walked into the drugstore.

His wife and daughters were out. He heated up a pitcher of water on the gasburner. Then with the scissors he found on the mantel he clipped the long brown locks of his beard. Then he started shaving very carefully with the new nickelbright safety razor. He stood trembling running his fingers down his smooth white cheeks in front of the stained mirror. He was trimming his mustache when he heard a noise behind him. He turned towards them a face smooth as the face of King C. Gillette, a face with a dollarbland smile. The two little girls' eyes were popping out of their heads. "Mommer . . . it's popper," the biggest one yelled. His wife dropped like a laundrybag into the rocker and threw the apron over her head.

"Oyoy! Oyoy!" she moaned rocking back and forth.

"Vat's a matter? Dontye like it?" He walked back and forth with the safety razor shining in his hand now and then gently fingering his smooth chin.

II. Metropolis

There were Babylon and Nineveh; they were built of brick. Athens was gold marble columns. Rome was held up on broad arches of rubble. In Constantinople the minarets flame like great candles round the Golden Horn . . . Steel, glass, tile, concrete will be the materials of the skyscrapers. Crammed on the narrow island the millionwindowed buildings will jut glittering, pyramid on pyramid like the white cloudhead above a thunderstorm.

When the door of the room closed behind him, Ed Thatcher felt very lonely, full of prickly restlessness. If Susie were only here he'd tell her about the big money he was going to make and how he'd deposit ten dollars a week in the savings bank just for little Ellen; that would make five hundred and twenty dollars a year. . . . Why in ten years without the interest that'd come to more than five thousand dollars. I must compute the compound interest on five hundred and twenty dollars at four per cent. He walked excitedly about the narrow room. The gas jet purred comfortably like a cat. His eyes fell on the headline on a *Journal* that lay on the floor by the coalscuttle where he had dropped it to run for the hack to take Susie to the hospital.

MORTON SIGNS THE GREATER NEW YORK BILL
Completes the Act Making New York
World's Second Metropolis

Breathing deep he folded the paper and laid it on the table. The world's second metropolis. . . . And dad wanted me to stay in his ole fool store in Onteora. Might have if it hadn't been for Susie. . . . Gentlemen tonight that you do me the signal honor of offering me the junior partnership in your firm I want to present to you my little girl, my wife. I owe everything to her.

In the bow he made towards the grate his coat-tails flicked a piece of china off the console beside the bookcase. He made a little clicking noise with his tongue against his teeth as he stooped to pick it up. The head of the blue porcelain Dutch girl had broken off from her body. "And poor Susie's so fond of her knicknacks. I'd better go to bed."

He pushed up the window and leaned out. An L train was rumbling past the end of the street. A whiff of coal smoke stung his nostrils. He hung out of the window a long while looking up and down the street. The world's second metropolis. In the brick houses and the dingy lamplight and the voices of a group of boys kidding and quarreling on the steps of a house opposite, in the regular firm tread of a policeman, he felt a marching like soldiers, like a sidewheeler going up the Hudson under the Palisades, like an election parade, through long streets towards something tall white full of colonnades and stately. Metropolis.

The street was suddenly full of running. Somebody out of breath let out the word Fire.

"Where at?"

The group of boys melted off the stoop across the way. Thatcher turned back into the room. It was stifling hot. He was all tingling to be out. I ought to go to bed. Down the street he heard the splattering hoofbeats and the frenzied bell of a fire engine. Just take a look. He ran down the stairs with his hat in his hand.

"Which way is it?"

"Down on the next block."

"It's a tenement house."

It was a narrowwindowed sixstory tenement. The hookand-ladder had just drawn up. Brown smoke, with here and there a little trail of sparks was pouring fast out of the lower windows. Three policemen were swinging their clubs as they packed the crowd back against the steps and railings of the houses opposite. In the empty space in the middle of the street the fire engine and the red hosewagon shone with bright brass. People watched silent staring at the upper windows where shadows moved and occasional light flickered. A thin pillar of flame began to flare above the house like a romancandle.

"The airshaft," whispered a man in Thatcher's ear. A gust of wind filled the street with smoke and a smell of burning rags. Thatcher felt suddenly sick. When the smoke cleared he saw people hanging in a kicking cluster, hanging by their hands from a windowledge. The other side firemen were helping women down a ladder. The flame in the center of the house flared brighter. Something black had dropped from a window and lay on the pavement shrieking. The policemen were shoving the crowd back to the ends of the block. New fire engines were arriving.

"Theyve got five alarms in," a man said. "What do you think of that? Everyone of 'em on the two top floors was trapped. It's an incendiary done it. Some goddam firebug."

A young man sat huddled on the curb beside the gas lamp. Thatcher found himself standing over him pushed by the crowd from behind.

"He's an Italian."

"His wife's in that buildin."

"Cops wont let him get by." "His wife's in a family way. He cant talk English to ask the cops."

The man wore blue suspenders tied up with a piece of string in back. His back was heaving and now and then he left out a string of groaning words nobody understood.

Thatcher was working his way out of the crowd. At the corner a man was looking into the fire alarm box. As Thatcher brushed past him he caught a smell of coaloil from the man's clothes. The man looked up into his face with a smile. He had tallowy sagging cheeks and bright popeyes. Thatcher's hands and feet went suddenly cold. The firebug. The papers say they hang round like that to watch it. He walked home fast, ran up the stairs, and locked the room door behind him. The room was quiet and empty. He'd forgotten that Susie wouldnt be there waiting for him. He began to undress. He couldnt forget the smell of coaloil on the man's clothes.

Mr. Perry flicked at the burdock leaves with his cane. The real-estate agent was pleading in a singsong voice:

"I dont mind telling you, Mr. Perry, it's an opportunity not to be missed. You know the old saying sir . . . opportunity knocks but once on a young man's door. In six months I can virtually guarantee that these lots will have doubled in value. Now that we are a part of New York, the second city in the world, sir, dont forget that. . . . Why the time will come, and I firmly believe that you and I will see it, when bridge after bridge spanning the East River have made Long Island and Manhattan one, when the Borough of Queens will be as much the heart and throbbing center of the great metropolis as is Astor Place today."

"I know, I know, but I'm looking for something dead safe. And besides I want to build. My wife hasnt been very well these last few years. . . ."

"But what could be safer than my proposition? Do you realize Mr. Perry, that at considerable personal loss I'm letting you in on the ground floor of one of the greatest real-estate certainties of modern times. I'm putting at your disposal not only security, but ease, comfort, luxury. We are caught up Mr. Perry on a great wave whether we will or no, a great wave of expansion and progress. A great deal is going to happen in the next few years. All these mechanical inventions— telephones, electricity, steel bridges, horseless vehicles—they are all leading somewhere. It's up to us to be on the inside, in the forefront of progress. . . . My God! I cant begin to tell you what it will mean. . . ." Poking amid the dry grass and the burdock leaves Mr. Perry had moved something with his stick. He stooped and picked up a triangular skull with a pair of spiralfluted horns. "By gad!" he said. "That must have been a fine ram."

Drowsy from the smell of lather and bayrum and singed hair that weighed down the close air of the barbershop, Bud sat nodding, his hands dangling big and red between his knees. In his eardrums he could still feel through the snipping of scissors the pounding of his feet on the hungry road down from Nyack.

"Next!"

"Whassat? . . . All right I just want a shave an a haircut."

The barber's pudgy hands moved through his hair, the scissors whirred like a hornet behind his ears. His eyes kept closing; he jerked them open fighting sleep. He could see beyond the striped sheet littered with sandy hair the bobbing hammerhead of the colored boy shining his shoes.

"Yessir" a deepvoiced man droned from the next chair, "it's time the Democratic party nominated a strong . . ."

"Want a neckshave as well?" The barber's greasyskinned moonface poked into his.

He nodded.

"Shampoo?"

"No."

When the barber threw back the chair to shave him he wanted to crane his neck like a mudturtle turned over on its back. The lather spread drowsily on his face, prickling his nose, filling up his ears. Drowning in featherbeds of lather, blue lather, black, slit by the faraway glint of the razor, glint of the grubbing hoe through blueblack lather clouds. The old man on his back in the potatofield, his beard sticking up lathery white full of blood. Full of blood his socks from those blisters on his heels. His hands gripped each other cold and horny like a dead man's hands under the sheet. Lemme git up. . . . He opened his eyes. Padded fingertips were stroking his chin. He stared up at the ceiling where four flies made figure eights round a red crêpe-paper bell. His tongue was dry leather in his mouth. The barber righted the chair again. Bud looked about blinking. "Four bits, and a nickel for the shine."

ADMITS KILLING CRIPPLED MOTHER . . .

"D'yous mind if I set here a minute an read that paper?" he hears his voice drawling in his pounding ears.

"Go right ahead."

PARKER'S FRIENDS PROTECT . . .

The black print squirms before his eyes. Russians . . . MOB STONES . . . (Special Dispatch to the *Herald*) Trenton, N. J.

Nathan Sibbetts, fourteen years old, broke down today after two weeks of steady denial of guilt and confessed to the police that he was responsible for the death of his aged and crippled mother, Hannah Sibbetts, after a quarrel in their home at Jacob's Creek, six miles above this city. Tonight he was committed to await the action of the Grand Jury.

RELIEVE PORT ARTHUR IN FACE OF ENEMY . . .
Mrs. Rix Loses Husband's Ashes.

On Tuesday May 24 at about half past eight o'clock I came home after sleeping on the steam roller all night, he said, and went upstairs to sleep some more. I had only gotten to sleep when my mother came upstairs and told me to get up and if I didn't get up she would throw me downstairs. My mother grabbed hold of me to throw me downstairs. I threw her first and she fell to the bottom. I went downstairs and found that her head was twisted to one side. I then saw that she was dead and then I straightened her neck and covered her up with the cover from my bed.

Bud folds the paper carefully, lays it on the chair and leaves the barbershop. Outside the air smells of crowds, is full of noise and sunlight. No more'n a needle in a haystack . . . "An I'm twentyfive years old," he muttered aloud. Think of a kid fourteen. . . . He walks faster along roaring pavements where the sun shines through the Elevated striping the blue street with warm seething yellow stripes. No more'n a needle in a haystack.

Ed Thatcher sat hunched over the pianokeys picking out the Mosquito Parade. Sunday afternoon sunlight streamed dustily through the heavy lace curtains of the window, squirmed in the red roses of the carpet, filled the cluttered parlor with specks and splinters of light. Susie Thatcher sat limp by the window watching him out of eyes too blue for her sallow face. Between them, stepping carefully among the roses on the sunny field of the carpet, little Ellen danced. Two small hands held up the pinkfrilled dress and now and then an emphatic little voice said, "Mummy watch my expression."

"Just look at the child," said Thatcher, still playing. "She's a regular little balletdancer."

Sheets of the Sunday paper lay where they had fallen from the table; Ellen started dancing on them, tearing the sheets under her nimble tiny feet.

"Dont do that Ellen dear," whined Susie from the pink plush chair.

"But mummy I can do it while I dance."

"Dont do that mother said." Ed Thatcher had slid into the Barcarole. Ellen was dancing to it, her arms swaying to it, her feet nimbly tearing the paper.

"Ed for Heaven's sake pick the child up; she's tearing the paper."

He brought his fingers down in a lingering chord. "Deary you mustnt do that. Daddy's not finished reading it."

Ellen went right on. Thatcher swooped down on her from the pianostool and set her squirming and laughing on his knee. "Ellen you should always mind when mummy speaks to you, and dear you shouldnt be destructive. It costs money to make that paper and people worked on it and daddy went out to buy it and he hasnt finished reading it yet. Ellie understands dont she now? We need con-struction and not de-struction in this world." Then he went on with the Barcarole and Ellen went on dancing, stepping carefully among the roses on the sunny field of the carpet.

There were six men at the table in the lunch room eating fast with their hats on the backs of their heads.

"Jiminy crickets!" cried the young man at the end of the table who was holding a newspaper in one hand and a cup of coffee in the other. "Kin you beat it?"

"Beat what?" growled a longfaced man with a toothpick in the corner of his mouth.

"Big snake appears on Fifth Avenue. . . . Ladies screamed and ran in all directions this morning at eleven thirty when a big snake crawled out of a crack in the masonry of the retaining wall of the reservoir at Fifth Avenue and Fortysecond Street and started to cross the sidewalk. . . ."

"Some fish story. . . ."

"That aint nothin," said an old man. "When I was a boy we used to go snipeshootin on Brooklyn Flats. . . ."

"Holy Moses! it's quarter of nine," muttered the young man folding his paper and hurrying out into Hudson Street that was full of men and girls walking briskly through the ruddy morning. The scrape of the shoes of hairyhoofed drayhorses and the grind of the wheels of producewagons made a deafening clatter and filled the air with sharp dust. A girl in a flowered bonnet with a big lavender bow under her pert tilted chin was waiting for him in the door of M. Sullivan & Co., Storage and Warehousing. The young man felt all fizzy inside, like a freshly uncorked bottle of pop.

"Hello Emily! . . . Say Emily I've got a raise."

"You're pretty near late, d'you know that?"

"But honest injun I've got a two-dollar raise."

She tilted her chin first to oneside and then to the other.

"I dont give a rap."

"You know what you said if I got a raise." She looked in his eyes giggling.

"An this is just the beginnin . . ."

"But what good's fifteen dollars a week?"

"Why it's sixty dollars a month, an I'm learning the import business."

"Silly boy you'll be late." She suddenly turned and ran up the littered stairs, her pleated bellshaped skirt swishing from side to side.

"God! I hate her. I hate her." Sniffing up the tears that were hot in his eyes, he walked fast down Hudson Street to the office of Winkle & Gulick, West India Importers.

The deck beside the forward winch was warm and briny damp. They were sprawled side by side in greasy denims talking drowsily in whispers, their ears full of the seethe of broken water as the bow shoved bluntly through the long grassgray swells of the Gulf Stream.

"J'te dis mon vieux, moi j'fou l'camp à New York. . . . The minute we tie up I go ashore and I stay ashore. I'm through with this dog's life." The cabinboy had fair hair and an oval pink-and-cream face; a dead cigarette butt fell from between his lips as he spoke. "Merde!" He reached for it as it rolled down the deck. It escaped his hand and bounced into the scuppers.

"Let it go. I've got plenty," said the other boy who lay on his belly kicking a pair of dirty feet up into the hazy sunlight. "The consul will just have you shipped back."

"He wont catch me."

"And your military service?"

"To hell with it. And with France too for that matter."

"You want to make yourself an American citizen?"

"Why not? A man has a right to choose his country."

The other rubbed his nose meditatively with his fist and then let his breath out in a long whistle. "Emile you're a wise guy," he said.

"But Congo, why dont you come too? You dont want to shovel crap in a stinking ship's galley all your life."

Congo rolled himself round and sat up crosslegged, scratching his head that was thick with kinky black hair.

"Say how much does a woman cost in New York?"

"I dunno, expensive I guess. . . . I'm not going ashore to raise hell; I'm going to get a good job and work. Cant you think of nothing but women?"

"What's the use? Why not?" said Congo and settled himself flat on the deck again, burying his dark sootsmudged face in his crossed arms.

"I want to get somewhere in the world, that's what I mean. Europe's rotten and stinking. In America a fellow can get ahead. Birth dont matter, education dont matter. It's all getting ahead."

"And if there was a nice passionate little woman right here now where the deck's warm, you wouldn't like to love her up?"

"After we're rich, we'll have plenty of everything."

"And they dont have any military service?"

"Why should they? It's the coin they're after. They dont want to fight people; they want to do business with them."

Congo did not answer.

The cabin boy lay on his back looking at the clouds. They floated from the west, great piled edifices with the sunlight crashing through between, bright and white like tinfoil. He was walking through tall white highpiled streets, stalking in a frock coat with a tall white collar up tinfoil stairs, broad, cleanswept, through blue portals into streaky marble halls where money rustled and clinked on long tinfoil tables, banknotes, silver, gold.

"Merde v'là l'heure." The paired strokes of the bell in the crowsnest came faintly to their ears. "But dont forget, Congo, the first night we get ashore . . ." He made a popping noise with his lips. "We're gone."

"I was asleep. I dreamed of a little blonde girl. I'd have had her if you hadnt waked me." The cabinboy got to his feet with a grunt and stood a moment looking west to where the swells ended in a sharp wavy line against a sky hard and abrupt as nickel. Then he pushed Congo's face down against the deck and ran aft, the wooden clogs clattering on his bare feet as he went.

Outside, the hot June Saturday was dragging its frazzled ends down 110th Street. Susie Thatcher lay uneasily in bed, her hands spread blue and bony on the coverlet before her. Voices came through the thin partition. A young girl was crying through her nose:

"I tell yer mommer I aint agoin back to him."

Then came expostulating an old staid Jewish woman's voice: "But Rosie, married life aint all beer and skittles. A vife must submit and vork for her husband."

"I wont. I cant help it. I wont go back to the dirty brute."

Susie sat up in bed, but she couldn't hear the next thing the old woman said.

"But I aint a Jew no more," suddenly screeched the young girl. "This aint Russia; it's little old New York. A girl's got some rights here." Then a door slammed and everything was quiet.

Susie Thatcher stirred in bed moaning fretfully. Those awful people never give me a moment's peace. From below came the jingle of a pianola playing the Merry Widow Waltz. O Lord! why dont Ed come home? It's cruel of them to leave a sick woman alone like this. Selfish. She twisted up her mouth and began to cry. Then she lay quiet again, staring at the ceiling watching the flies buzz teasingly round the electriclight fixture. A wagon clattered by down the street. She could hear children's voices screeching. A boy passed yelling an extra. Suppose there'd been a fire. That terrible Chicago theater fire. Oh I'll go mad! She tossed about in the bed, her pointed nails digging into the palms of her hands. I'll take another tablet. Maybe I can get some sleep. She raised herself on her elbow and took the last tablet out of a little tin box. The gulp of water that washed the tablet down was soothing to her throat. She closed her eyes and lay quiet.

She woke with a start. Ellen was jumping round the room, her green tam falling off the back of her head, her coppery curls wild.

"Oh mummy I want to be a little boy."

"Quieter dear. Mother's not feeling a bit well."

"I want to be a little boy."

"Why Ed what have you done to the child? She's all wrought up."

"We're just excited, Susie. We've been to the most wonderful play. You'd have loved it, it's so poetic and all that sort of thing. And Maude Adams was fine. Ellie loved every minute of it."

"It seems silly, as I said before, to take such a young child . . ."

"Oh daddy I want to be a boy."

"I like my little girl the way she is. We'll have to go again Susie and take you."

"Ed you know very well I wont be well enough." She sat bolt upright, her hair hanging a straight faded yellow down her back. "Oh, I wish I'd die . . . I wish I'd die, and not be a burden to you any more. . . . You hate me both of you. If you didnt hate me you wouldnt leave me alone like this." She choked and put her face in her hands. "Oh I wish I'd die," she sobbed through her fingers.

"Now Susie for Heaven's sakes, it's wicked to talk like that." He put his arm round her and sat on the bed beside her.

Crying quietly she dropped her head on his shoulder. Ellen stood staring at them out of round gray eyes. Then she started jumping up and down, chanting to herself, "Ellie's goin to be a boy, Ellie's goin to be a boy."

With a long slow stride, limping a little from his blistered feet, Bud walked down Broadway, past empty lots where tin cans glittered among grass and sumach bushes and ragweed, between ranks of billboards and Bull Durham signs, past shanties and abandoned squatters' shacks, past gulches heaped with wheelscarred rubbishpiles where dumpcarts were dumping ashes and clinkers, past knobs of gray outcrop where steamdrills continually tapped and nibbled, past excavations out of which wagons full of rock and clay toiled up plank roads to the street, until he was walking on new sidewalks along a row of yellow brick apartment houses, looking in the windows of grocery stores, Chinese laundries, lunchrooms, flower and vegetable shops, tailors', delicatessens. Passing under a scaffolding in front of a new building, he caught the eye of an old man who sat on the edge of the sidewalk trimming oil lamps. Bud stood beside him, hitching up his pants; cleared his throat:

"Say mister you couldnt tell a feller where a good place was to look for a job?"

"Aint no good place to look for a job, young feller. . . . There's jobs all right. . . . I'll be sixty-five years old in a month and four days an I've worked sence I was five I reckon, an I aint found a good job yet."

"Anything that's a job'll do me."

"Got a union card?"

"I aint got nothin."

"Cant git no job in the buildin trades without a union card," said the old man. He rubbed the gray bristles of his chin with the back of his hand and leaned over the lamps again. Bud stood staring into the dustreeking girder forest of the new building until he found the eyes of a man in a derby hat fixed on him through the window of the watchman's shelter. He shuffled his feet uneasily and walked on. If I could git more into the center of things. . . .

At the next corner a crowd was collecting round a high-slung white automobile. Clouds of steam poured out of its rear end. A policeman was holding up a small boy by the armpits. From the car a redfaced man with white walrus whiskers was talking angrily.

"I tell you officer he threw a stone. . . . This sort of thing has got to stop. For an officer to countenance hoodlums and rowdies. . . ."

A woman with her hair done up in a tight bunch on top of her head was screaming, shaking her fist at the man in the car, "Officer he near run me down he did, he near run me down."

Bud edged up next to a young man in a butcher's apron who had a baseball cap on backwards.

"Wassa matter?"

"Hell I dunno. . . . One o them automoebile riots I guess. Aint you read the paper? I dont blame em do you? What right have those golblamed automoebiles got racin round the city knockin down wimen an children?"

"Gosh do they do that?"

"Sure they do."

"Say . . . er . . . kin you tell me about where's a good place to find out about gettin a job?" The butcherboy threw back head and laughed.

"Kerist I thought you was goin to ask for a handout. . . . I guess you aint a Newyorker. . . . I'll tell you what to do.

You keep right on down Broadway till you get to City Hall. . . ."

"Is that kinder the center of things?"

"Sure it is. . . . An then you go upstairs and ask the Mayor. . . . Tell me there are some seats on the board of aldermen . . ."

"Like hell they are," growled Bud and walked away fast.

"Roll ye babies . . . roll ye lobsided sons o bitches."

"That's it talk to em Slats."

"Come seven!" Slats shot the bones out of his hand, brought the thumb along his sweaty fingers with a snap. "Aw hell."

"You're some great crapshooter I'll say, Slats."

Dirty hands added each a nickel to the pile in the center of the circle of patched knees stuck forward. The five boys were sitting on their heels under a lamp on South Street.

"Come on girlies we're waitin for it. . . . Roll ye little bastards, goddam ye, roll."

"Cheeze it fellers! There's Big Leonard an his gang acomin down the block."

"I'd knock his block off for a . . ."

Four of them were already slouching off along the wharf, gradually scattering without looking back. The smallest boy with a chinless face shaped like a beak stayed behind quietly picking up the coins. Then he ran along the wall and vanished into the dark passageway between two houses. He flattened himself behind a chimney and waited. The confused voices of the gang broke into the passageway; then they had gone on down the street. The boy was counting the nickels in his hand. Ten. "Jez, that's fifty cents. . . . I'll tell 'em Big Leonard scooped up the dough." His pockets had no bottoms, so he tied the nickels into one of his shirt tails.

A goblet for Rhine wine hobnobbed with a champagne glass at each place along the glittering white oval table. On eight glossy white plates eight canapés of caviar were like rounds of black beads on the lettuceleaves, flanked by sections of lemon, sprinkled with a sparse chopping of onion and white of egg. "Beaucoup de soing and dont you forget it," said the old waiter puckering up his knobbly forehead. He was a short waddling man with a few black strands of hair plastered tight across a domed skull.

"Awright." Emile nodded his head gravely. His collar was too tight for him. He was shaking a last bottle of champagne into the nickelbound bucket of ice on the servingtable.

"Beaucoup de soing, sporca madonna. . . . Thisa guy trows money about lika confetti, see. . . . Gives tips, see. He's a verra rich gentleman. He dont care how much he spend." Emile patted the crease of the tablecloth to flatten it. "Fais pas, como, ça. . . . Your hand's dirty, maybe leava mark."

Resting first on one foot then on the other they stood waiting, their napkins under their arms. From the restaurant below among the buttery smells of food and the tinkle of knives and forks and plates, came the softly gyrating sound of a waltz.

When he saw the headwaiter bow outside the door Emile compressed his lips into a deferential smile. There was a longtoothed blond woman in a salmon operacloak swishing on the arm of a moonfaced man who carried his top hat ahead of him like a bumper; there was a little curlyhaired girl in blue who was showing her teeth and laughing, a stout woman in a tiara with a black velvet ribbon round her neck, a bottlenose, a long cigarcolored face . . . shirtfronts, hands straightening white ties, black gleams on top hats and patent leather shoes; there was a weazlish man with gold teeth who kept waving his arms spitting out greetings in a voice like a crow's and wore a diamond the size of a nickel in his shirtfront. The redhaired cloakroom girl was collecting the wraps. The old waiter nudged Emile. "He's de big boss," he said out of the corner of his mouth as he bowed. Emile flattened himself against the wall as they shuffled rustled into the room. A whiff of patchouli when he drew his breath made him go suddenly hot to the roots of his hair.

"But where's Fifi Waters?" shouted the man with the diamond stud.

"She said she couldnt get here for a half an hour. I guess the Johnnies wont let her get by the stage door."

"Well we cant wait for her even if it is her birthday; never waited for anyone in my life." He stood a second running a roving eye over the women round the table, then shot his cuffs out a little further from the sleeves of his swallowtail coat, and abruptly sat down. The caviar vanished in a twinkling. "And waiter what about that Rhine wine coupe?" he croaked huskily. "De suite monsieur. . . ." Emile holding his breath and sucking in his cheeks, was taking away the plates. A frost came on the goblets as the old waiter poured out the coupe from a cut glass pitcher where floated mint and ice and lemon rind and long slivers of cucumber.

"Aha, this'll do the trick." The man with the diamond stud raised his glass to his lips, smacked them and set it down with a slanting look at the woman next him. She was putting dabs of butter on bits of bread and popping them into her mouth, muttering all the while:

"I can only eat the merest snack, only the merest snack."

"That dont keep you from drinkin Mary does it?"

She let out a cackling laugh and tapped him on the shoulder with her closed fan. "O Lord, you're a card, you are."

"Allume moi ça, sporca madonna," hissed the old waiter in Emile's ear.

When he lit the lamps under the two chafing dishes on the serving table a smell of hot sherry and cream and lobster began to seep into the room. The air was hot, full of tinkle and perfume and smoke. After he had helped serve the lobster Newburg and refilled the glasses Emile leaned against the wall and ran his hand over his wet hair. His eyes slid along the plump shoulders of the woman in front of him and down the powdered back to where a tiny silver hook had come undone under the lace rushing. The baldheaded man next to her had his leg locked with hers. She was young, Emile's age, and kept looking up into the man's face with moist parted lips. It made Emile dizzy, but he couldn't stop looking.

"But what's happened to the fair Fifi?" creaked the man with the diamond stud through a mouthful of lobster. "I suppose that she made such a hit again this evening that our simple little party dont appeal to her."

"It's enough to turn any girl's head."

"Well she'll get the surprise of her young life if she expected us to wait. Haw, haw, haw," laughed the man with the diamond stud. "I never waited for anybody in my life and I'm not going to begin now."

Down the table the moonfaced man had pushed back his plate and was playing with the bracelet on the wrist of the woman beside him. "You're the perfect Gibson girl tonight, Olga."

"I'm sitting for my portrait now," she said holding up her goblet against the light.

"To Gibson?"

"No to a real painter."

"By Gad I'll buy it."

"Maybe you wont have a chance."

She nodded her blond pompadour at him.

"You're a wicked little tease, Olga."

She laughed keeping her lips tight over her long teeth.

A man was leaning towards the man with the diamond stud, tapping with a stubby finger on the table.

"No sir as a real estate proposition, Twentythird Street has crashed. . . . That's generally admitted. . . . But what I want to talk to you about privately sometime Mr. Godalming, is this. . . . How's all the big money in New York been made? Astor, Vanderbilt, Fish. . . . In real estate of course. Now it's up to us to get in on the next great cleanup. . . . It's almost here. . . . Buy Forty. . . ."

The man with the diamond stud raised one eyebrow and shook his head. "For one night on Beauty's lap, O put gross care away . . . or something of the sort. . . . Waiter why in holy hell are you so long with the champagne?" He got to his feet, coughed in his hand and began to sing in his croaking voice:

> O would the Atlantic were all champagne
> Bright billows of champagne.

Everybody clapped. The old waiter had just divided a baked Alaska and, his face like a beet, was prying out a stiff champagnecork. When the cork popped the lady in the tiara let out a yell. They toasted the man in the diamond stud.

> For he's a jolly good fellow . . .

"Now what kind of a dish d'ye call this?" the man with the bottlenose leaned over and asked the girl next to him. Her black hair parted in the middle; she wore a palegreen dress with puffy sleeves. He winked slowly and then stared hard into her black eyes.

"This here's the fanciest cookin I ever put in my mouth. . . . D'ye know young leddy, I dont come to this town often. . . ." He gulped down the rest of his glass. "An when I do I usually go away kinder disgusted. . . ." His look bright and feverish from the champagne explored the contours of her neck and shoulders and roamed down a bare arm. "But this time I kinder think. . . ."

"It must be a great life prospecting," she interrupted flushing.

"It was a great life in the old days, a rough life but a man's life. . . . I'm glad I made my pile in the old days. . . . Wouldnt have the same luck now."

She looked up at him. "How modest you are to call it luck."

Emile was standing outside the door of the private room. There was nothing more to serve. The redhaired girl from the cloakroom walked by with a big flounced cape on her arm. He smiled, tried to catch her eye. She sniffed and tossed her nose in the air. Wont look at me because I'm a waiter. When I make some money I'll show 'em.

"Dis; tella Charlie two more bottle Moet and Chandon, Gout Americain," came the old waiter's hissing voice in his ear.

The moonfaced man was on his feet. "Ladies and Gentlemen. . . ."

"Silence in the pigsty . . ." piped up a voice.

"The big sow wants to talk," said Olga under her breath.

"Ladies and gentlemen owing to the unfortunate absence of our star of Bethlehem and fulltime act. . . ."

"Gilly dont blaspheme," said the lady with the tiara.

"Ladies and gentlemen, unaccustomed as I am. . . ."

"Gilly you're drunk."

" . . . Whether the tide . . . I mean whether the waters be with us or against us . . ."

Somebody yanked at his coat-tails and the moonfaced man sat down suddenly in his chair.

"It's terrible," said the lady in the tiara addressing herself to a man with a long face the color of tobacco who sat at the end of the table . . . "It's terrible, Colonel, the way Gilly gets blasphemous when he's been drinking . . ."

The Colonel was meticulously rolling the tinfoil off a cigar. "Dear me, you dont say?" he drawled. Above the bristly gray mustache his face was expressionless. "There's a most dreadful story about poor old Atkins, Elliott Atkins who used to be with Mansfield . . ."

"Indeed?" said the Colonel icily as he slit the end of the cigar with a small pearlhandled penknife.

"Say Chester did you hear that Mabie Evans was making a hit?"

"Honestly Olga I dont see how she does it. She has no figure . . ."

"Well he made a speech, drunk as a lord you understand, one night when they were barnstorming in Kansas . . ."

"She cant sing . . ."

"The poor fellow never did go very strong in the bright lights . . ."

"She hasnt the slightest particle of figure . . ."

"And made a sort of Bob Ingersoll speech . . ."

"The dear old feller. . . . Ah I knew him well out in Chicago in the old days . . ."

"You dont say." The Colonel held a lighted match carefully to the end of his cigar . . .

"And there was a terrible flash of lightning and a ball of fire came in one window and went out the other."

"Was he . . . er . . . killed?" The Colonel sent a blue puff of smoke towards the ceiling.

"What, did you say Bob Ingersoll had been struck by lightning?" cried Olga shrilly. "Serve him right the horrid atheist."

"No not exactly, but it scared him into a realization of the important things of life and now he's joined the Methodist church."

"Funny how many actors get to be ministers."

"Cant get an audience any other way," creaked the man with the diamond stud.

The two waiters hovered outside the door listening to the racket inside. "Tas de sacrés cochons . . . sporca madonna!" hissed the old waiter. Emile shrugged his shoulders. "That brunette girl make eyes at you all night . . ." He brought his face near Emile's and winked. "Sure, maybe you pick up somethin good."

"I dont want any of them or their dirty diseases either."

The old waiter slapped his thigh. "No young men nowadays. . . . When I was young man I take heap o chances."

"They dont even look at you . . ." said Emile through clenched teeth. "An animated dress suit that's all."

"Wait a minute, you learn by and by."

The door opened. They bowed respectfully towards the diamond stud. Somebody had drawn a pair of woman's legs on his shirtfront. There was a bright flush on each of his cheeks. The lower lid of one eye sagged, giving his weasle face a quizzical lobsided look.

"Wazzahell, Marco wazzahell?" he was muttering. "We aint got a thing to drink. . . . Bring the Atlantic Ozz-shen and two quarts."

"De suite monsieur. . . ." The old waiter bowed. "Emile tell Auguste, immediatement et bien frappé."

As Emile went down the corridor he could hear singing.

O would the Atlantic were all champagne
Bright bi-i-i. . . .

The moonface and the bottlenose were coming back from the lavatory reeling arm in arm among the palms in the hall.

"These damn fools make me sick."

"Yessir these aint the champagne suppers we used to have in Frisco in the ole days."

"Ah those were great days those."

"By the way," the moonfaced man steadied himself against the wall, "Holyoke ole fella, did you shee that very nobby little article on the rubber trade I got into the morning papers. . . . That'll make the investors nibble . . . like lil mishe."

"Whash you know about rubber? . . . The stuff aint no good."

"You wait an shee, Holyoke ole fella or you looshing opportunity of your life. . . . Drunk or sober I can smell money . . . on the wind."

"Why aint you got any then?" The bottlenosed man's beefred face went purple; he doubled up letting out great hoots of laughter.

"Because I always let my friends in on my tips," said the other man soberly. "Hay boy where's zis here private dinin room?"

"Par ici monsieur."

A red accordionpleated dress swirled past them, a little oval face framed by brown flat curls, pearly teeth in an open-mouthed laugh.

"Fifi Waters," everyone shouted. "Why my darlin lil Fifi, come to my arms."

She was lifted onto a chair where she stood jiggling from one foot to the other, champagne dripping out of a tipped glass.

"Merry Christmas."

"Happy New Year."

"Many returns of the day. . . ."

A fair young man who had followed her in was reeling intricately round the table singing:

> O we went to the animals' fair
> And the birds and the beasts were there
> And the big baboon
> By the light of the moon
> Was combing his auburn hair.

"Hoopla," cried Fifi Waters and mussed the gray hair of the man with the diamond stud. "Hoopla." She jumped down with a kick, pranced round the room, kicking high with her skirts fluffed up round her knees.

"Oh la la ze French high kicker!"

"Look out for the Pony Ballet."

Her slender legs, shiny black silk stockings tapering to red rosetted slippers flashed in the men's faces.

"She's a mad thing," cried the lady in the tiara.

Hoopla. Holyoke was swaying in the doorway with his top hat tilted over the glowing bulb of his nose. She let out a whoop and kicked it off.

"It's a goal," everyone cried.

"For crissake you kicked me in the eye."

She stared at him a second with round eyes and then burst into tears on the broad shirtfront of the diamond stud. "I wont be insulted like that," she sobbed.

"Rub the other eye."

"Get a bandage someone."

"Goddam it she may have put his eye out."

"Call a cab there waiter."

"Where's a doctor?"

"That's hell to pay ole fella."

A handkerchief full of tears and blood pressed to his eye the bottlenosed man stumbled out. The men and women crowded through the door after him; last went the blond young man, reeling and singing:

> An the big baboon by the light of the moon
> Was combing his auburn hair.

Fifi Waters was sobbing with her head on the table.

"Don't cry Fifi," said the Colonel who was still sitting where he had sat all the evening. "Here's something I rather fancy might do you good." He pushed a glass of champagne towards her down the table.

She sniffled and began drinking it in little sips. "Hullo Roger, how's the boy?"

"The boy's quite well thank you. . . . Rather bored, dont you know? An evening with such infernal bounders. . . ."

"I'm hungry."

"There doesnt seem to be anything left to eat."

"I didnt know you'd be here or I'd have come earlier, honest."

"Would you indeed? . . . Now that's very nice."

The long ash dropped from the Colonel's cigar; he got to his feet. "Now Fifi, I'll call a cab and we'll go for a ride in the Park. . . ."

She drank down her champagne and nodded brightly. "Dear me it's four o'clock. . . ." "You have the proper wraps haven't you?"

She nodded again.

"Splendid Fifi . . . I say you are in form." The Colonel's cigarcolored face was unraveling in smiles. "Well, come along."

She looked about her in a dazed way. "Didnt I come with somebody?"

"Quite unnecessary!"

In the hall they came upon the fair young man quietly vomiting into a firebucket under an artificial palm.

"Oh let's leave him," she said wrinkling up her nose.

"Quite unnecessary," said the Colonel.

Emile brought their wraps. The redhaired girl had gone home.

"Look here, boy." The Colonel waved his cane. "Call me a cab please. . . . Be sure the horse is decent and the driver is sober."

"De suite monsieur."

The sky beyond roofs and chimneys was the blue of a sapphire. The Colonel took three or four deep sniffs of the dawnsmelling air and threw his cigar into the gutter. "Suppose we have a bit of breakfast at Cleremont. I haven't had anything fit to eat all night. That beastly sweet champagne, ugh!"

Fifi giggled. After the Colonel had examined the horse's fetlocks and patted his head, they climbed into the cab. The Colonel fitted in Fifi carefully under his arm and they drove off. Emile stood a second in the door of the restaurant uncrumpling a five dollar bill. He was tired and his insteps ached.

When Emile came out of the back door of the restaurant he found Congo waiting for him sitting on the doorstep. Congo's skin had a green chilly look under the frayed turned up coatcollar.

"This is my friend," Emile said to Marco. "Came over on the same boat."

"You havent a bottle of fine under your coat have you? Sapristi I've seen some chickens not half bad come out of this place."

"But what's the matter?"

"Lost my job that's all. . . . I wont have to take any more off that guy. Come over and drink a coffee."

They ordered coffee and doughnuts in a lunchwagon on a vacant lot.

"Eh bien you like it this sacred pig of a country?" asked Marco.

"Why not? I like it anywhere. It's all the same, in France you are paid badly and live well; here you are paid well and live badly."

"Questo paese e completamente soto sopra."

"I think I'll go to sea again. . . ."

"Say why de hell doan yous guys loin English?" said the man with a cauliflower face who slapped the three mugs of coffee down on the counter.

"If we talk Engleesh," snapped Marco, "maybe you no lika what we say."

"Why did they fire you?"

"Merde. I don't know. I had an argument with the old camel who runs the place. . . . He lived next door to the stables; as well as washing the carriages he made me scrub the floors in his house. . . . His wife, she had a face like this." Congo sucked in his lips and tried to look crosseyed.

Marco laughed. "Santissima Maria putana!"

"How did you talk to them?"

"They pointed to things; then I nodded my head and said Awright. I went there at eight and worked till six and they gave me every day more filthy things to do. . . . Last night they tell me to clean out the toilet in the bathroom. I shook my head. . . . That's woman's work. . . . She got very angry and started screeching. Then I began to learn Angleesh. . . . Go awright to 'ell, I says to her. . . . Then the old man comes and chases me out into a street with a carriage whip and says he wont pay me my week. . . . While we were arguing he got a policeman, and when I try to explain to the policeman that the old man owed me ten dollars for the week, he says Beat it you lousy wop, and cracks me on the coco with his nightstick. . . . Merde alors . . ."

Marco was red in the face. "He call you lousy wop?"

Congo nodded his mouth full of doughnut.

"Notten but shanty Irish himself," muttered Marco in English. "I'm fed up with this rotten town. . . ."

"It's the same all over the world, the police beating us up, rich people cheating us out of their starvation wages, and who's fault? . . . Dio cane! Your fault, my fault, Emile's fault. . . ."

"We didn't make the world. . . . They did or maybe God did."

"God's on their side, like a policeman. . . . When the day comes we'll kill God. . . . I am an anarchist."

Congo hummed "les bourgeois à la lanterne nom de dieu."

"Are you one of us?"

Congo shrugged his shoulders. "I'm not a catholic or a protestant; I haven't any money and I haven't any work. Look at that." Congo pointed with a dirty finger to a long rip on his trouserknee. "That's anarchist. . . . Hell I'm going out to Senegal and get to be a nigger."

"You look like one already," laughed Emile.

"That's why they call me Congo."

"But that's all silly," went on Emile. "People are all the same. It's only that some people get ahead and others dont. . . . That's why I came to New York."

"Dio cane I think that too twentyfive years ago. . . . When you're old like me you know better. Doesnt the shame of it get you sometimes? Here" . . . he tapped with his knuckles on his stiff shirtfront . . . "I feel it hot and like choking me here. . . . Then I say to myself Courage our day is coming, our day of blood."

"I say to myself," said Emile, "When you have some money old kid."

"Listen, before I leave Torino when I go last time to see the mama I go to a meetin of comrades. . . . A fellow from Capua got up to speak . . . a very handsome man, tall and very thin. . . . He said that there would be no more force when after the revolution nobody lived off another man's work. . . . Police, governments, armies, presidents, kings . . . all that is force. Force is not real; it is illusion. The working man makes all that himself because he believes it. The day that we stop believing in money and property it will be like a dream when we wake up. We will not need bombs or barricades. . . . Religion, politics, democracy all that is to keep us asleep. . . . Everybody must go round telling people: Wake up!"

"When you go down into the street I'll be with you," said Congo.

"You know that man I tell about? . . . That man Errico Malatesta, in Italy greatest man after Garibaldi. . . . He give his whole life in jail and exile, in Egypt, in England, in South America, everywhere. . . . If I could be a man like that, I dont care what they do; they can string me up, shoot me . . . I dont care . . . I am very happy."

"But he must be crazy a feller like that," said Emile slowly. "He must be crazy."

Marco gulped down the last of his coffee. "Wait a minute. You are too young. You will understand. . . . One by one they make us understand. . . . And remember what I say. . . . Maybe I'm too old, maybe I'm dead, but it will come when the working people awake from slavery. . . . You will walk out in the street and the police will run away, you will go into a bank and there will be money poured out on the floor and you wont stoop to pick it up, no more good. . . . All over the world we are preparing. There are comrades even in China. . . . Your Commune in France was the beginning. . . . socialism failed. It's for the anarchists to strike the next blow. . . . If we fail there will be others. . . ."

Congo yawned, "I am sleepy as a dog."

Outside the lemoncolored dawn was drenching the empty streets, dripping from cornices, from the rails of fire escapes, from the rims of ashcans, shattering the blocks of shadow between buildings. The streetlights were out. At a corner they looked up Broadway that was narrow and scorched as if a fire had gutted it.

"I never see the dawn," said Marco, his voice rattling in his throat, "that I dont say to myself perhaps . . . perhaps today." He cleared his throat and spat against the base of a lamppost; then he moved away from them with his waddling step, taking hard short sniffs of the cool air.

"Is that true, Congo, about shipping again?"

"Why not? Got to see the world a bit . . ."

"I'll miss you. . . . I'll have to find another room."

"You'll find another friend to bunk with."

"But if you do that you'll stay a sailor all your life."

"What does it matter? When you are rich and married I'll come and visit you."

They were walking down Sixth Avenue. An L train roared above their heads leaving a humming rattle to fade among the girders after it had passed.

"Why dont you get another job and stay on a while?"

Congo produced two bent cigarettes out of the breast pocket of his coat, handed one to Emile, struck a match on the seat of his trousers, and let the smoke out slowly through his nose. "I'm fed up with it here I tell you. . . ." He brought his flat hand up across his Adam's apple, "up to here. . . . Maybe I'll go home an visit the little girls of Bordeaux. . . . At least they are not all made of whalebone. . . . I'll engage myself as a volunteer in the navy and wear a red pompom. . . . The girls like that. That's the only life. . . . Get drunk and raise cain payday and see the extreme orient."

"And die of the syph in a hospital at thirty. . . ."

"What's it matter? . . . Your body renews itself every seven years."

The steps of their rooming house smelled of cabbage and stale beer. They stumbled up yawning.

"Waiting's a rotten tiring job. . . . Makes the soles of your feet ache. . . . Look it's going to be a fine day; I can see the sun on the watertank opposite."

Congo pulled off his shoes and socks and trousers and curled up in bed like a cat.

"Those dirty shades let in all the light," muttered Emile as he stretched himself on the outer edge of the bed. He lay tossing uneasily on the rumpled sheets. Congo's breathing beside him was low and regular. If I was only like that, thought Emile, never worrying about a thing. . . . But it's not that way you get along in the world. My God it's stupid. . . . Marco's gaga the old fool.

And he lay on his back looking up at the rusty stains on the ceiling, shuddering every time an elevated train shook the room. Sacred name of God I must save up my money. When he turned over the knob on the bedstead rattled and he remembered Marco's hissing husky voice: I never see the dawn that I dont say to myself perhaps.

"If you'll excuse me just a moment Mr. Olafson," said the houseagent. "While you and the madam are deciding about the apartment . . ." They stood side by side in the empty room, looking out the window at the slatecolored Hudson and the warships at anchor and a schooner tacking upstream.

Suddenly she turned to him with glistening eyes; "O Billy, just think of it."

He took hold of her shoulders and drew her to him slowly. "You can smell the sea, almost."

"Just think Billy that we are going to live here, on Riverside Drive. I'll have to have a day at home . . . Mrs. William C. Olafson, 218 Riverside Drive. . . . I wonder if it is all right to put the address on our visiting cards." She took his hand and led him through the empty cleanswept rooms that no one had ever lived in. He was a big shambling man with eyes of a washed out blue deepset in a white infantile head.

"It's a lot of money Bertha."

"We can afford it now, of course we can. We must live up to our income. . . . Your position demands it. . . . And think how happy we'll be."

The house agent came back down the hall rubbing his hands. "Well, well, well . . . Ah I see that we've come to a favorable decision. . . . You are very wise too, not a finer location in the city of New York and in a few months you wont be able to get anything out this way for love or money. . . ."

"Yes we'll take it from the first of the month."

"Very good. . . . You wont regret your decision, Mr. Olafson."

"I'll send you a check for the amount in the morning."

"At your own convenience. . . . And what is your present address please. . . ." The houseagent took out a notebook and moistened a stub of pencil with his tongue.

"You had better put Hotel Astor." She stepped in front of her husband.

"Our things are stored just at the moment."

Mr. Olafson turned red.

"And . . . er . . . we'd like the names of two references please in the city of New York."

"I'm with Keating and Bradley, Sanitary Engineers, 43 Park Avenue . . ."

"He's just been made assistant general manager," added Mrs. Olafson.

When they got out on the Drive walking downtown against a tussling wind she cried out: "Darling I'm so happy. . . . It's really going to be worth living now."

"But why did you tell him we lived at the Astor?"

"I couldn't tell him we lived in the Bronx could I? He'd

have thought we were Jews and wouldn't have rented us the apartment."

"But you know I dont like that sort of thing."

"Well we'll just move down to the Astor for the rest of the week, if you're feeling so truthful. . . . I've never in my life stopped in a big downtown hotel."

"Oh Bertha it's the principle of the thing. . . . I don't like you to be like that."

She turned and looked at him with twitching nostrils. "You're so nambypamby, Billy. . . . I wish to heavens I'd married a man for a husband."

He took her by the arm. "Let's go up here," he said gruffly with his face turned away.

They walked up a cross street between buildinglots. At a corner the rickety half of a weatherboarded farmhouse was still standing. There was half a room with blueflowered paper eaten by brown stains on the walls, a smoked fireplace, a shattered builtin cupboard, and an iron bedstead bent double.

Plates slip endlessly through Bud's greasy fingers. Smell of swill and hot soapsuds. Twice round with the little mop, dip, rinse and pile in the rack for the longnosed Jewish boy to wipe. Knees wet from spillings, grease creeping up his forearms, elbows cramped.

"Hell this aint no job for a white man."

"I dont care so long as I eat," said the Jewish boy above the rattle of dishes and the clatter and seething of the range where three sweating cooks fried eggs and ham and hamburger steak and browned potatoes and cornedbeef hash.

"Sure I et all right," said Bud and ran his tongue round his teeth dislodging a sliver of salt meat that he mashed against his palate with his tongue. Twice round with the little mop, dip, rinse and pile in the rack for the longnosed Jewish boy to wipe. There was a lull. The Jewish boy handed Bud a cigarette. They stood leaning against the sink.

"Aint no way to make money dishwashing." The cigarette wabbled on the Jewish boy's heavy lip as he spoke.

"Aint no job for a white man nohow," said Bud. "Waitin's better, they's the tips."

A man in a brown derby came in through the swinging

door from the lunchroom. He was a bigjawed man with pigeyes and a long cigar sticking straight out of the middle of his mouth. Bud caught his eye and felt the cold glint twisting his bowels.

"Whosat?" he whispered.

"Dunno. . . . Customer I guess."

"Dont he look to you like one o them detectives?"

"How de hell should I know? I aint never been in jail." The Jewish boy turned red and stuck out his jaw.

The busboy set down a new pile of dirty dishes. Twice round with the little mop, dip, rinse and pile in the rack. When the man in the brown derby passed back through the kitchen, Bud kept his eyes on his red greasy hands. What the hell even if he is a detective. . . . When Bud had finished the batch, he strolled to the door wiping his hands, took his coat and hat from the hook and slipped out the side door past the garbage cans out into the street. Fool to jump two hours pay. In an optician's window the clock was at twentyfive past two. He walked down Broadway, past Lincoln Square, across Columbus Circle, further downtown towards the center of things where it'd be more crowded.

She lay with her knees doubled up to her chin, the nightgown pulled tight under her toes.

"Now straighten out and go to sleep dear. . . . Promise mother you'll go to sleep."

"Wont daddy come and kiss me good night?"

"He will when he comes in; he's gone back down to the office and mother's going to Mrs. Spingarn's to play euchre."

"When'll daddy be home?"

"Ellie I said go to sleep. . . . I'll leave the light."

"Dont mummy, it makes shadows. . . . When'll daddy be home?"

"When he gets good and ready." She was turning down the gaslight. Shadows out of the corners joined wings and rushed together. "Good night Ellen." The streak of light of the door narrowed behind mummy, slowly narrowed to a thread up and along the top. The knob clicked; the steps went away down the hall; the front door slammed. A clock ticked somewhere in the silent room; outside the apartment, outside the house, wheels and gallumping of hoofs, trailing voices; the roar grew. It was black except for the two strings of light that made an upside down L in the corner of the door.

Ellie wanted to stretch out her feet but she was afraid to. She didnt dare take her eyes from the upside down L in the corner of the door. If she closed her eyes the light would go out. Behind the bed, out of the windowcurtains, out of the closet, from under the table shadows nudged creakily towards her. She held on tight to her ankles, pressed her chin in between her knees. The pillow bulged with shadow, rummaging shadows were slipping into the bed. If she closed her eyes the light would go out.

Black spiraling roar outside was melting through the walls making the cuddled shadows throb. Her tongue clicked against her teeth like the ticking of the clock. Her arms and legs were stiff; her neck was stiff; she was going to yell. Yell above the roaring and the rattat outside, yell to make daddy hear, daddy come home. She drew in her breath and shrieked again. Make daddy come home. The roaring shadows staggered and danced, the shadows lurched round and round. Then she was crying, her eyes were full of safe warm tears, they were running over her cheeks and into her ears. She turned over and lay crying with her face in the pillow.

The gaslamps tremble a while down the purplecold streets and then go out under the lurid dawn. Gus McNiel, the sleep still gumming his eyes, walks beside his wagon swinging a wire basket of milkbottles, stopping at doors, collecting the empties, climbing chilly stairs, remembering grades A and B and pints of cream and buttermilk, while the sky behind cornices, tanks, roofpeaks, chimneys becomes rosy and yellow. Hoarfrost glistens on doorsteps and curbs. The horse with dangling head lurches jerkily from door to door. There begin to be dark footprints on the frosty pavement. A heavy brewers' dray rumbles down the street.

"Howdy Moike, a little chilled are ye?" shouts Gus McNiel at a cop threshing his arms on the corner of Eighth Avenue.

"Howdy Gus. Cows still milkin'?"

It's broad daylight when he finally slaps the reins down on the gelding's threadbare rump and starts back to the dairy, empties bouncing and jiggling in the cart behind him. At Ninth Avenue a train shoots overhead clattering downtown behind a little green engine that emits blobs of smoke white and dense as cottonwool to melt in the raw air between the stiff blackwindowed houses. The first rays of the sun pick out the gilt lettering of DANIEL McGILLYCUDDY'S WINES AND LIQUORS at the corner of Tenth Avenue. Gus McNiel's tongue is dry and the dawn has a salty taste in his mouth. A can o beer'd be the makin of a guy a cold mornin like this. He takes a turn with the reins round the whip and jumps over the wheel. His numb feet sting when they hit the pavement. Stamping to get the blood back into his toes he shoves through the swinging doors.

"Well I'll be damned if it aint the milkman bringin us a pint o cream for our coffee." Gus spits into the newly polished cuspidor beside the bar.

"Boy, I got a thoist on me. . . ."

"Been drinkin too much milk again, Gus, I'll warrant," roars the barkeep out of a square steak face.

The saloon smells of brasspolish and fresh sawdust. Through an open window a streak of ruddy sunlight caresses the rump of a naked lady who reclines calm as a hardboiled egg on a bed of spinach in a giltframed picture behind the bar.

"Well Gus what's yer pleasure a foine cold mornin loike this?"

"I guess beer'll do, Mac."

The foam rises in the glass, trembles up, slops over. The barkeep cuts across the top with a wooden scoop, lets the foam settle a second, then puts the glass under the faintly wheezing spigot again. Gus is settling his heel comfortably against the brass rail.

"Well how's the job?"

Gus gulps the glass of beer and makes a mark on his neck with his flat hand before wiping his mouth with it. "Full up to the neck wid it. . . . I tell yer what I'm goin to do, I'm goin to go out West, take up free land in North Dakota or somewhere an raise wheat. . . . I'm pretty handy round a farm. . . . This here livin in the city's no good."

"How'll Nellie take that?"

"She wont cotton to it much at foist, loikes her comforts of home an all that she's been used to, but I think she'll loike it foine onct she's out there an all. This aint no loife for her nor me neyther."

"You're right there. This town's goin to hell. . . . Me and the misses'll sell out here some day soon I guess. If we could buy a noice genteel restaurant uptown or a roadhouse, that's what'd suit us. Got me eye on a little property out Bronxville way, within easy drivin distance." He lifts a malletshaped fist meditatively to his chin. "I'm sick o bouncin these goddam drunks every night. Whade hell did I get outen the ring for xep to stop fightin? Jus last night two guys starts asluggin an I has to mix it up with both of em to clear the place out. . . . I'm sick o fighten every drunk on Tenth Avenoo. . . . Have somethin on the house?"

"Jez I'm afraid Nellie'll smell it on me."

"Oh, niver moind that. Nellie ought to be used to a bit o drinkin. Her ole man loikes it well enough."

"But honest Mac I aint been slopped once since me weddinday."

"I dont blame ye. She's a real sweet girl Nellie is. Those little spitcurls o hers'd near drive a feller crazy."

The second beer sends a foamy acrid flush to Gus's fingertips. Laughing he slaps his thigh.

"She's a pippin, that's what she is Gus, so ladylike an all."

"Well I reckon I'll be gettin back to her."

"You lucky young divil to be goin home to bed wid your wife when we're all startin to go to work."

Gus's red face gets redder. His ears tingle. "Sometimes she's abed yet. . . . So long Mac." He stamps out into the street again.

The morning has grown bleak. Leaden clouds have settled down over the city. "Git up old skin an bones," shouts Gus jerking at the gelding's head. Eleventh Avenue is full of icy dust, of grinding rattle of wheels and scrape of hoofs on the cobblestones. Down the railroad tracks comes the clang of a locomotive bell and the clatter of shunting freightcars. Gus is in bed with his wife talking gently to her: Look here Nellie, you wouldn't moind movin West would yez? I've filed application for free farmin land in the state o North Dakota, black soil land where we can make a pile o money in wheat; some fellers git rich in foive good crops. . . . Healthier for the kids anyway. . . . "Hello Moike!" There's poor old Moike still on his beat. Cold work bein a cop. Better be a wheatfarmer an have a big farmhouse an barns an pigs an horses an cows an chickens. . . . Pretty curlyheaded Nellie feedin the chickens at the kitchen door. . . .

"Hay dere for crissake. . . ." a man is yelling at Gus from the curb. "Look out for de cars!"

A yelling mouth gaping under a visored cap, a green flag waving. "Godamighty I'm on the tracks." He yanks the horse's head round. A crash rips the wagon behind him. Cars, the gelding, a green flag, red houses whirl and crumble into blackness.

III. Dollars

All along the rails there were faces; in the portholes there were faces. Leeward a stale smell came from the tubby steamer that rode at anchor listed a little to one side with the yellow quarantine flag drooping at the foremast.

"I'd give a million dollars," said the old man resting on his oars, "to know what they come for."

"Just for that pop," said the young man who sat in the stern. "Aint it the land of opportoonity?"

"One thing I do know," said the old man. "When I was a boy it was wild Irish came in the spring with the first run of shad. . . . Now there aint no more shad, an them folks, Lord knows where they come from."

"It's the land of opportoonity."

A leanfaced young man with steel eyes and a thin high-bridged nose sat back in a swivel chair with his feet on his new mahogany-finish desk. His skin was sallow, his lips gently pouting. He wriggled in the swivel chair watching the little scratches his shoes were making on the veneer. Damn it I dont care. Then he sat up suddenly making the swivel shriek and banged on his knee with his clenched fist. "Results," he shouted. Three months I've sat rubbing my tail on this swivel chair. . . . What's the use of going through lawschool and being admitted to the bar if you cant find anybody to practice on? He frowned at the gold lettering through the ground-glass door.

NIWDLAB EGROEG
waL-tA-yenrottA

Niwdlab, Welsh. He jumped to his feet. I've read that damn sign backwards every day for three months. I'm going crazy. I'll go out and eat lunch.

He straightened his vest and brushed some flecks of dust off his shoes with a handkerchief, then, contracting his face into an expression of intense preoccupation, he hurried out of his office, trotted down the stairs and out onto Maiden Lane.

In front of the chophouse he saw the headline on a pink extra; JAPS THROWN BACK FROM MUKDEN. He bought the paper and folded it under his arm as he went in through the swinging door. He took a table and pored over the bill of fare. Mustn't be extravagant now. "Waiter you can bring me a New England boiled dinner, a slice of applepie and coffee." The longnosed waiter wrote the order on his slip looking at it sideways with a careful frown. . . . That's the lunch for a lawyer without any practice. Baldwin cleared his throat and unfolded the paper. . . . Ought to liven up the Russian bonds a bit. Veterans Visit President. . . . ANOTHER ACCIDENT ON ELEVENTH AVENUE TRACKS. Milkman seriously injured. Hello, that'd make a neat little damage suit.

Augustus McNiel, 253 W. 4th Street, who drives a milkwagon for the Excelsior Dairy Co. was severely injured early this morning when a freight train backing down the New York Central tracks . . .

He ought to sue the railroad. By gum I ought to get hold of that man and make him sue the railroad. . . . Not yet recovered consciousness. . . . Maybe he's dead. Then his wife can sue them all the more. . . . I'll go to the hospital this very afternoon. . . . Get in ahead of any of these shysters. He took a determined bite of bread and chewed it vigorously. Of course not; I'll go to the house and see if there isn't a wife or mother or something: Forgive me Mrs. McNiel if I intrude upon your deep affliction, but I am engaged in an investigation at this moment. . . . Yes, retained by prominent interests. . . . He drank up the last of the coffee and paid the bill.

Repeating 253 W. 4th Street over and over he boarded an uptown car on Broadway. Walking west along 4th he skirted Washington Square. The trees spread branches of brittle purple into a dovecolored sky; the largewindowed houses opposite glowed very pink, nonchalant, prosperous. The very place for a lawyer with a large conservative practice to make his residence. We'll just see about that. He crossed Sixth Avenue and followed the street into the dingy West Side, where there was a smell of stables and the sidewalks were littered with scraps of garbage and crawling children. Imagine living down here among low Irish and foreigners, the scum of the universe. At 253 there were several unmarked bells. A woman

with gingham sleeves rolled up on sausageshaped arms stuck
a gray mophead out the window.

"Can you tell me if Augustus McNiel lives here?"

"Him that's up there alayin in horspital. Sure he does."

"That's it. And has he any relatives living here?"

"An what would you be wantin wid 'em?"

"It's a little matter of business."

"Go up to the top floor an you'll foind his wife there but
most likely she cant see yez. . . . The poor thing's powerful
wrought up about her husband, an them only eighteen
months married."

The stairs were tracked with muddy footprints and sprinkled here and there with the spilling of ashcans. At the top he
found a freshpainted darkgreen door and knocked.

"Who's there?" came a girl's voice that sent a little shiver
through him. Must be young.

"Is Mrs. McNiel in?"

"Yes," came the lilting girl's voice again. "What is it?"

"It's a matter of business about Mr. McNiel's accident."

"About the accident is it?" The door opened in little cautious jerks. She had a sharpcut pearlywhite nose and chin and
a pile of wavy redbrown hair that lay in little flat curls round
her high narrow forehead. Gray eyes sharp and suspicious
looked him hard in the face.

"May I speak to you a minute about Mr. McNiel's accident? There are certain legal points involved that I feel it my
duty to make known to you. . . . By the way I hope he's
better."

"Oh yes he's come to."

"May I come in? It's a little long to explain."

"I guess you can." Her pouting lips flattened into a wry
smile. "I guess you wont eat me."

"No honestly I wont." He laughed nervously in his throat.

She led the way into the darkened sitting room. "I'm not
pulling up the shades so's you wont see the pickle everythin's
in."

"Allow me to introduce myself, Mrs. McNiel. . . . George
Baldwin, 88 Maiden Lane. . . . You see I make a specialty of
cases like this. . . . To put the whole matter in a nutshell.
. . . Your husband was run down and nearly killed through

the culpable or possibly criminal negligence of the employees of the New York Central Railroad. There is full and ample cause for a suit against the railroad. Now I have reason to believe that the Excelsior Dairy Company will bring suit for the losses incurred, horse and wagon etcetera. . . ."

"You mean you think Gus is more likely to get damages himself?"

"Exactly."

"How much do you think he could get?"

"Why that depends on how badly hurt he is, on the attitude of the court, and perhaps on the skill of the lawyer. . . . I think ten thousand dollars is a conservative figure."

"And you dont ask no money down?"

"The lawyer's fee is rarely paid until the case is brought to a successful termination."

"An you're a lawyer, honest? You look kinder young to be a lawyer."

The gray eyes flashed in his. They both laughed. He felt a warm inexplicable flush go through him.

"I'm a lawyer all the same. I make a specialty of cases like these. Why only last Tuesday I got six thousand dollars for a client who was kicked by a relay horse riding on the loop. . . . Just at this moment as you may know there is considerable agitation for revoking altogether the franchise of the Eleventh Avenue tracks. . . . I think this is a most favorable moment."

"Say do you always talk like that, or is it just business?"

He threw back his head and laughed.

"Poor old Gus, I always said he had a streak of luck in him."

The wail of a child crept thinly through the partition into the room.

"What's that?"

"It's only the baby. . . . The little wretch dont do nothin but squall."

"So you've got children Mrs. McNiel?" The thought chilled him somehow.

"Juss one . . . what kin ye expect?"

"Is it the Emergency Hospital?"

"Yes I reckon they'll let you see him as it's a matter of business. He's groanin somethin dreadful."

"Now if I could get a few good witnesses."

"Mike Doheny seen it all. . . . He's on the force. He's a good frien of Gus's."

"By gad we've got a case and a half. . . . Why they'll settle out of court. . . . I'll go right up to the hospital."

A fresh volley of wails came from the other room.

"Oh, that brat," she whispered, screwing up her face. "We could use the money all right Mr. Baldwin. . . ."

"Well I must go." He picked up his hat. "And I certainly will do my best in this case. May I come by and report progress to you from time to time?"

"I hope you will."

When they shook hands at the door he couldn't seem to let go her hand. She blushed.

"Well goodby and thank you very much for callin," she said stiffly.

Baldwin staggered dizzily down the stairs. His head was full of blood. The most beautiful girl I've ever seen in my life. Outside it had begun to snow. The snowflakes were cold furtive caresses to his hot cheeks.

The sky over the Park was mottled with little tiptailed clouds like a field of white chickens.

"Look Alice, lets us go down this little path."

"But Ellen, my dad told me to come straight home from school."

"Scarecat!"

"But Ellen those dreadful kidnappers. . . ."

"I told you not to call me Ellen any more."

"Well Elaine then, Elaine the lily maid of Astalot."

Ellen had on her new Black Watch plaid dress. Alice wore glasses and had legs thin as hairpins.

"Scarecat!"

"They're dreadful men sitting on that bench. Come along Elaine the fair, let's go home."

"I'm not scared of them. I could fly like Peter Pan if I wanted to."

"Why dont you do it?"

"I dont want to just now."

Alice began to whimper. "Oh Ellen I think you're mean. . . . Come along home Elaine."

"No I'm going for a walk in the Park."

Ellen started down the steps. Alice stood a minute on the top step balancing first on one foot then on the other.

"Scaredy scaredy scarecat!" yelled Ellen.

Alice ran off blubbering. "I'm goin to tell your mommer."

Ellen walked down the asphalt path among the shrubbery kicking her toes in the air.

Ellen in her new dress of Black Watch plaid mummy'd bought at Hearn's walked down the asphalt path kicking her toes in the air. There was a silver thistle brooch on the shoulder of the new dress of Black Watch plaid mummy'd bought at Hearn's. Elaine of Lammermoor was going to be married. The Betrothed. Wangnaan nainainai, went the bagpipes going through the rye. The man on the bench has a patch over his eye. A watching black patch. A black watching patch. The kidnapper of the Black Watch, among the rustling shrubs kidnappers keep their Black Watch. Ellen's toes dont kick in the air. Ellen is terribly scared of the kidnapper of the Black Watch, big smelly man of the Black Watch with a patch over his eye. She's scared to run. Her heavy feet scrape on the asphalt as she tries to run fast down the path. She's scared to turn her head. The kidnapper of the Black Watch is right behind. When I get to the lamppost I'll run as far as the nurse and the baby, when I get to the nurse and the baby I'll run as far as the big tree, when I get to the big tree. . . . Oh I'm so tired. . . . I'll run out onto Central Park West and down the street home. She was scared to turn round. She ran with a stitch in her side. She ran till her mouth tasted like pennies.

"What are you running for Ellie?" asked Gloria Drayton who was skipping rope outside the Norelands.

"Because I wanted to," panted Ellen.

Winey afterglow stained the muslin curtains and filtered into the blue gloom of the room. They stood on either side of the table. Out of a pot of narcissus still wrapped in tissue paper starshaped flowers gleamed with dim phosphorescence, giving off a damp earthsmell enmeshed in indolent prickly perfume.

"It was nice of you to bring me these Mr. Baldwin. I'll take them up to Gus at the hospital tomorrow."

"For God's sake dont call me that."

"But I dont like the name of George."

"I dont care, I like your name, Nellie."

He stood looking at her; perfumed weights coiled about his arms. His hands dangled like empty gloves. Her eyes were black, dilating, her lips pouting towards him across the flowers. She jerked her hands up to cover her face. His arm was round her little thin shoulders.

"But honest Georgy, we've got to be careful. You mustn't come here so often. I dont want all the old hens in the house to start talkin."

"Dont worry about that. . . . We mustn't worry about anything."

"I've been actin' like I was crazy this last week. . . . I've got to quit."

"You dont think I've been acting naturally, do you? I swear to God Nellie I've never done anything like this before. I'm not that kind of a person."

She showed her even teeth in a laugh. "Oh you kin never tell about men."

"But if it weren't something extraordinary and exceptional you dont think I'd be running after you this way do you? I've never been in love with anybody but you Nellie."

"That's a good one."

"But it's true. . . . I've never gone in for that sort of thing. I've worked too hard getting through lawschool and all that to have time for girls."

"Makin up for lost time I should say."

"Oh Nellie dont talk like that."

"But honestly Georgy I've got to cut this stuff out. What'll we do when Gus comes out of the hospital? An I'm neglectin the kid an everythin."

"Christ I dont care what happens. . . . Oh Nellie." He pulled her face round. They clung to each other swaying, mouths furiously mingling.

"Look out we almost had the lamp over."

"God you're wonderful, Nellie." Her head had dropped on his chest, he could feel the pungence of her tumbled hair all through him. It was dark. Snakes of light from the streetlamp wound greenly about them. Her eyes looked up into his frighteningly solemnly black.

"Look Nellie lets go in the other room," he whispered in a tiny trembling voice.

"Baby's in there."

They stood apart with cold hands looking at each other. "Come here an help me. I'll move the cradle in here. . . . Careful not to wake her or she'll bawl her head off." Her voice crackled huskily.

The baby was asleep, her little rubbery face tight closed, minute pink fists clenched on the coverlet.

"She looks happy," he said with a forced titter.

"Keep quiet cant you. . . . Here take yer shoes off. . . . There's been enough trampin o men's shoes up here. . . . Georgy I wouldn't do this, but I juss cant help. . . ."

He fumbled for her in the dark. "You darling. . . ." Clumsy he brooded over her, breathing crazily deep.

"Flatfoot you're stringin us. . . ."

"I aint, honest I'd swear by me muder's grave it's de trutt. . . . Latitude toityseven soutt by twelve west. . . . You go dere an see. . . . On dat island we made in de second officer's boat when de *Elliot P. Simkins* foundered der was four males and fortyseven females includin women an children. Waren't it me dat tole de reporter guy all about it an it came out in all de Sunday papers?"

"But Flatfoot how the hell did they ever get you away from there?"

"Dey carried me off on a stretcher or I'm a cockeyed lyer. I'll be a sonofabitch if I warnt founderin, goin down by de bows like de ole *Elliot P.*"

Heads tossed back on thick necks let out volleys of laughter, glasses were banged on the round ringmarked table, thighs resounded with slaps, elbows were poked into ribs.

"An how many guys was in de boat?"

"Six includin Mr. Dorkins de second officer."

"Seven and four makes eleven. . . . Jez. . . . Four an three-elevenths broads per capita. . . . Some island."

"When does the next ferry leave?"

"Better have another drink on that. . . . Hay Charlie fill 'em up."

Emile pulled at Congo's elbow. "Come outside a sec. J'ai que'quechose a te dire." Congo's eyes were wet, he staggered a little as he followed Emile into the outer bar. "O le p'tit mysterieux."

"Look here, I've got to go call on a lady friend."

"Oh that's what's eating you is it? I always said you was a wise guy Emile."

"Look, here's my address on a piece of paper in case you forget it: 945 West 22nd. You can come and sleep there if you're not too pickled, and dont you bring any friends or women or anything. I'm in right with the landlady and I dont want to spoil it. . . . Tu comprends."

"But I wanted you to come on a swell party. . . . Faut faire un peu la noce, nom de dieu! . . ."

"I got to work in the morning."

"But I got eight months' pay in my pocket. . . ."

"Anyway come round tomorrow at about six. I'll wait for you."

"Tu m'emmerdes tu sais avec tes manières;" Congo aimed a jet of saliva at the spittoon in the corner of the bar and turned back frowning into the inside room.

"Hay dere sit down Congo; Barney's goin to sing de Bastard King of England."

Emile jumped on a streetcar and rode uptown. At Eighteenth Street he got off and walked west to Eighth Avenue. Two doors from the corner was a small store. Over one window was CONFISERIE, over the other DELICATESSEN. In the middle of the glass door white enamel letters read Emile Rigaud, High Class Table Dainties. Emile went in. The bell jangled on the door. A dark stout woman with black hairs over the corners of her mouth was drowsing behind the counter. Emile took off his hat. "Bonsoir Madame Rigaud." She looked up with a start, then showed two dimples in a profound smile.

"Tieng c'est comma ça qu'ong oublie ses ami-es," she said in a booming Bordelais voice. "Here's a week that I say to myself, Monsieur Loustec is forgetting his friends."

"I never have any time any more."

"Lots of work, lots of money, heing?" When she laughed her shoulders shook and the big breasts under the tight blue bodice.

Emile screwed up one eye. "Might be worse. . . . But I'm sick of waiting. . . . It's so tiring; nobody regards a waiter."

"You are a man of ambition, Monsieur Loustec."

"Que voulez vous?" He blushed, and said timidly "My name's Emile."

Mme. Rigaud rolled her eyes towards the ceiling. "That was my dead husband's name. I'm used to that name." She sighed heavily.

"And how's business?"

"Comma ci comma ça. . . . Ham's gone up again."

"It's the Chicago ring's doing that. . . . A corner in pork, that's the way to make money."

Emile found Mme. Rigaud's bulgy black eyes probing his. "I enjoyed your singing so last time. . . . I've thought of it often. . . . Music does one good dont it?" Mme. Rigaud's dimples stretched and stretched as she smiled. "My poor husband had no ear. . . . That gave me a great deal of pain."

"Couldn't you sing me something this evening?"

"If you want me to, Emile? . . . But there is nobody to wait on customers."

"I'll run in when we hear the bell, if you will permit me."

"Very well. . . . I've learned a new American song . . . C'est chic vous savez."

Mme. Rigaud locked the till with a key from the bunch that hung at her belt and went through the glass door in the back of the shop. Emile followed with his hat in his hand.

"Give me your hat Emile."

"Oh dont trouble yourself."

The room beyond was a little parlor with yellow flowered wallpaper, old salmon pink portières and, under the gasbracket from which hung a bunch of crystals, a piano with photographs on it. The pianostool creaked when Mme. Rigaud sat down. She ran her fingers over the keys. Emile sat carefully on the very edge of the chair beside the piano with his hat on his knees and pushed his face forward so that as she played she could see it out of the corner of her eye tilted up towards hers. Madame Rigaud began to sing:

> Just a birrd in a geelded cage
> A beauteeful sight to see
> You'd tink se vas 'appee
> And free from all care
> Se's not zo se seems to be. . . .

The bell on the door of the shop jangled loud.

"Permettez," cried Emile running out.

"Half a pound o bolony sausage sliced," said a little girl with pigtails. Emile passed the knife across the palm of his hand and sliced the sausage carefully. He tiptoed back into the parlor and put the money on the edge of the piano. Madame Rigaud was still singing:

> Tis sad ven you tink of a vasted life
> For yout cannot mate vit age
> Beautee vas soooold
> For an old man's gooold
> Se's a birrd in a geelded cage.

Bud stood on the corner of West Broadway and Franklin Street eating peanuts out of a bag. It was noon and his money was all gone. The Elevated thundered overhead. Dustmotes danced before his eyes in the girderstriped sunlight. Wondering which way to go he spelled out the names of the streets for the third time. A black shiny cab drawn by two black shinyrumped horses turned the corner sharp in front of him with a rasp on the cobblestones of red shiny wheels suddenly braked. There was a yellow leather trunk on the seat beside the driver. In the cab a man in a brown derby talked loud to a woman with a gray feather boa round her neck and gray ostrich plumes in her hat. The man jerked a revolver up to his mouth. The horses reared and plunged in the middle of a shoving crowd. Policemen elbowing through. They had the man out on the curbstone vomiting blood, head hanging limp over his checked vest. The woman stood tall and white beside him twisting her feather boa in her hands, the gray plumes in her hat nodding in the striped sunlight under the elevated.

"His wife was taking him to Europe. . . . The *Deutschland* sailing at twelve. I'd said goodby to him forever. He was sailing on the *Deutschland* at twelve. He'd said goodby to me forever."

"Git oute de way dere;" a cop jabbed Bud in the stomach with his elbow. His knees trembled. He got to the edge of the crowd and walked away trembling. Mechanically he shelled a peanut and put it in his mouth. Better save the rest till evenin. He twisted the mouth of the bag and dropped it into his pocket.

Under the arclight that spluttered pink and green-edged violet the man in the checked suit passed two girls. The full-lipped oval face of the girl nearest to him; her eyes were like a knifethrust. He walked a few paces then turned and followed them fingering his new satin necktie. He made sure the horseshoe diamond pin was firm in its place. He passed them again. Her face was turned away. Maybe she was. . . . No he couldn't tell. Good luck he had fifty dollars on him. He sat on a bench and let them pass him. Wouldnt do to make a mistake and get arrested. They didnt notice him. He followed them down the path and out of the Park. His heart was pounding. I'd give a million dollars for . . . Pray pardon me, isn't this Miss Anderson? The girls walked fast. In the crowd crossing Columbus Circle he lost sight of them. He hurried down Broadway block after block. The full lips, the eyes like the thrust of a knife. He stared in girls' faces right and left. Where could she have gone? He hurried on down Broadway.

Ellen was sitting beside her father on a bench at the Battery. She was looking at her new brown button shoes. A glint of sunlight caught on the toes and on each of the little round buttons when she swung her feet out from under the shadow of her dress.

"Think how it'd be," Ed Thatcher was saying, "to go abroad on one of those liners. Imagine crossing the great Atlantic in seven days."

"But daddy what do people do all that time on a boat?"

"I dunno . . . I suppose they walk round the deck and play cards and read and all that sort of thing. Then they have dances."

"Dances on a boat! I should think it'd be awful tippy." Ellen giggled.

"On the big modern liners they do."

"Daddy why dont we go?"

"Maybe we will some day if I can save up the money."

"Oh daddy do hurry up an save a lot of money. Alice Vaughan's mother an father go to the White Mountains every summer, but next summer they're going abroad."

Ed Thatcher looked out across the bay that stretched in blue sparkling reaches into the brown haze towards the Narrows. The statue of Liberty stood up vague as a sleepwalker among the curling smoke of tugboats and the masts of schooners and the blunt lumbering masses of brickbarges and sandscows. Here and there the glary sun shone out white on a sail or on the superstructure of a steamer. Red ferryboats shuttled back and forth.

"Daddy why arent we rich?"

"There are lots of people poorer than us Ellie. . . . You wouldn't like your daddy any better if he were rich would you?"

"Oh yes I would daddy."

Thatcher laughed. "Well it might happen someday. . . . How would you like the firm of Edward C. Thatcher and Co., Certified Accountants?"

Ellen jumped to her feet: "Oh look at that big boat. . . . That's the boat I want to go on."

"That there's the *Harabic*," croaked a cockney voice beside them.

"Oh is it really?" said Thatcher.

"Indeed it is, sir; as fahne a ship as syles the sea sir," explained eagerly a frayed creakyvoiced man who sat on the bench beside them. A cap with a broken patentleather visor was pulled down over a little peaked face that exuded a faded smell of whiskey. "Yes sir, the *Harabic* sir."

"Looks like a good big boat that does."

"One of the biggest afloat sir. I syled on er many's the tahme and on the *Majestic* and the *Teutonic* too sir, fahne ships both, though a bit light'eaded in a sea as you might say. I've signed as steward on the Hinman and White Star lahnes these thirty years and now in me old age they've lyed me hoff."

"Oh well, we all have hard luck sometimes."

"And some of us as it hall the tahme sir. . . . I'd be a appy man sir, if I could get back to the old country. This arent any plyce for an old man, it's for the young and strong, this is." He drew a gout-twisted hand across the bay and pointed to the statue. "Look at er, she's alookin towards Hengland she is."

"Daddy let's go away. I dont like this man," whispered Ellen tremulously in her father's ear.

"All right we'll go and take a look at the sealions. . . . Good day."

"You couldn't fahnd me the price of a cup o coffee, could you now sir? I'm fair foundered." Thatcher put a dime in the grimy knobbed hand.

"But daddy, mummy said never to let people speak to you in the street an to call a policeman if they did an to run away as fast as you could on account of those horrible kidnappers."

"No danger of their kidnapping me Ellie. That's just for little girls."

"When I grow up will I be able to talk to people on the street like that?"

"No deary you certainly will not."

"If I'd been a boy could I?"

"I guess you could."

In front of the Aquarium they stopped a minute to look down the bay. The liner with a tug puffing white smoke against either bow was abreast of them towering above the ferryboats and harborcraft. Gulls wheeled and screamed. The sun shone creamily on the upper decks and on the big yellow blackcapped funnel. From the foremast a string of little flags fluttered jauntily against the slate sky.

"And there are lots of people coming over from abroad on that boat arent there daddy?"

"Look you can see . . . the decks are black with people."

Walking across Fiftythird Street from the East River Bud Korpenning found himself standing beside a pile of coal on the sidewalk. On the other side of the pile of coal a grayhaired woman in a flounced lace shirtwaist with a big pink cameo poised on the curve of her high bosom was looking at his stubbly chin and at the wrists that hung raw below the frayed sleeves of his coat. Then he heard himself speak:

"Dont spose I could take that load of coal in back for you ma'am?" Bud shifted his weight from one foot to the other.

"That's just what you could do," the woman said in a cracked voice. "That wretched coal man left it this morning and said he'd be back to bring it in. I suppose he's drunk like the rest of them. I wonder if I can trust you in the house."

"I'm from upstate ma'am," stammered Bud.

"From where?"

"From Cooperstown."

"Hum. . . . I'm from Buffalo. This is certainly the city for everyone being from somewhere else. . . . Well you're probably a burglar's accomplice, but I cant help it I've got to have that coal in. . . . Come in my man, I'll give you a shovel and a basket and if you dont drop any in the passage or on the kitchen floor, because the scrubwoman's just left . . . naturally the coal had to come when the floor was clean. . . . I'll give you a dollar."

When he carried in the first load she was hovering in the kitchen. His caving hungersniff stomach made him totter lightheadedly, but he was happy to be working instead of dragging his feet endlessly along pavements, across streets, dodging drays and carts and streetcars.

"How is it you haven't got a regular job my man," she asked as he came back breathless with the empty basket.

"I reckon it's as I aint caught on to city ways yet. I was born an raised on a farm."

"And what did you want to come to this horrible city for?"

"Couldn't stay on the farm no more."

"It's terrible what's going to become of this country if all the fine strong young men leave the farms and come into the cities."

"Thought I could git a work as a longshoreman, ma'am, but they're layin' men off down on the wharves. Mebbe I kin go to sea as a sailor but nobody wants a green hand. . . . I aint et for two days now."

"How terrible. . . . Why you poor man couldn't you have gone to some mission or something?"

When Bud had brought the last load in he found a plate of cold stew on the corner of the kitchen table, half a loaf of stale bread and a glass of milk that was a little sour. He ate quickly barely chewing and put the last of the stale bread in his pocket.

"Well did you enjoy your little lunch?"

"Thankye ma'am." He nodded with his mouth full.

"Well you can go now and thank you very much." She put a quarter into his hand. Bud blinked at the quarter in the palm of his hand.

"But ma'am you said you'd give me a dollar."

"I never said any such thing. The idea. . . . I'll call my husband if you dont get out of here immediately. In fact I've a great mind to notify the police as it is. . . ."

Without a word Bud pocketed the quarter and shuffled out.

"Such ingratitude," he heard the woman snort as he closed the door behind him.

A cramp was tying knots in his stomach. He turned east again and walked the long blocks to the river with his fists pressed tight in under his ribs. At any moment he expected to throw up. If I lose it it wont do me no good. When he got to the end of the street he lay down on the gray rubbish slide beside the wharf. A smell of hops seeped gruelly and sweet out of the humming brewery behind him. The light of the sunset flamed in the windows of factories on the Long Island side, flashed in the portholes of tugs, lay in swaths of curling yellow and orange over the swift browngreen water, glowed on the curved sails of a schooner that was slowly bucking the tide up into Hell Gate. Inside him the pain was less. Something flamed and glowed like the sunset seeping through his body. He sat up. Thank Gawd I aint agoin to lose it.

On deck it's damp and shivery in the dawn. The ship's rail is wet when you put your hand on it. The brown harborwater smells of washbasins, rustles gently against the steamer's sides. Sailors are taking the hatches off the hold. There's a rattle of chains and a clatter from the donkeyengine where a tall man in blue overalls stands at a lever in the middle of a cloud of steam that wraps round your face like a wet towel.

"Muddy is it really the Fourth of July?"

Mother's hand has grasped his firmly trailing him down the companionway into the dining saloon. Stewards are piling up baggage at the foot of the stairs.

"Muddy is it really the Fourth of July?"

"Yes deary I'm afraid it is. . . . A holiday is a dreadful time to arrive. Still I guess they'll all be down to meet us."

She has her blue serge on and a long trailing brown veil and the little brown animal with red eyes and teeth that are real teeth round her neck. A smell of mothballs comes from it, of unpacking trunks, of wardrobes littered with tissue-paper. It's hot in the dining saloon, the engines sob soothingly behind the bulkhead. His head nods over his cup of hot milk just colored with coffee. Three bells. His head snaps up with a start. The dishes tinkle and the coffee spills with the trembling of the ship. Then a thud and rattle of anchorchains and gradually quiet. Muddy gets up to look through the porthole.

"Why it's going to be a fine day after all. I think the sun will burn through the mist. . . . Think of it dear; home at last. This is where you were born deary."

"And it's the Fourth of July."

"Worst luck. . . . Now Jimmy you must promise me to stay on the promenade deck and be very careful. Mother has to finish packing. Promise me you wont get into any mischief."

"I promise."

He catches his toe on the brass threshold of the smoking-room door and sprawls on deck, gets up rubbing his bare knee just in time to see the sun break through chocolate clouds and swash a red stream of brightness over the putty-colored water. Billy with the freckles on his ears whose people are for Roosevelt instead of for Parker like mother is waving a silk flag the size of a handkerchief at the men on a yellow and white tugboat.

"Didjer see the sun rise?" he asks as if he owned it.

"You bet I saw it from my porthole," says Jimmy walking away after a lingering look at the silk flag. There's land close on the other side; nearest a green bank with trees and wide white grayroofed houses.

"Well young feller, how does it feel to be home?" asks the tweedy gentleman with droopy mustaches.

"Is that way New York?" Jimmy points out over the still water broadening in the sunlight.

"Yessiree-bobby, behind yonder bank of fog lies Manhattan."

"Please sir what's that?"

"That's New York. . . . You see New York is on Manhattan Island."

"Is it really on an island?"

"Well what do you think of a boy who dont know that his own home town is on an island?"

The tweedy gentleman's gold teeth glitter as he laughs with his mouth wide open. Jimmy walks on round the deck, kicking his heels, all foamy inside; New York's on an island.

"You look right glad to get home little boy," says the Southern lady.

"Oh I am, I could fall down and kiss the ground."

"Well that's a fine patriotic sentiment. . . . I'm glad to hear you say it."

Jimmy scalds all over. Kiss the ground, kiss the ground, echoes in his head like a catcall. Round the deck.

"That with the yellow flag's the quarantine boat." A stout man with rings on his fingers—he's a Jew—is talking to the tweedy man. "Ha we're under way again. . . . That was quick, what?"

"We'll be in for breakfast, an American breakfast, a good old home breakfast."

Muddy coming down the deck, her brown veil floating. "Here's your overcoat Jimmy, you've got to carry it."

"Muddy, can I get out that flag?"

"What flag?"

"The silk American flag."

"No dear it's all put away."

"Please I'd so like to have that flag cause it's the Fourth of July an everything."

"Now dont whine Jimmy. When mother says no she means no."

Sting of tears; he swallows a lump and looks up in her eyes.

"Jimmy it's put away in the shawlstrap and mother's so tired of fussing with those wretched bags."

"But Billy Jones has one."

"Look deary you're missing things . . . There's the statue of Liberty." A tall green woman in a dressing gown standing on an island holding up her hand.

"What's that in her hand?"

"That's a light, dear . . . Liberty enlightening the world. . . . And there's Governors Island the other side. There where the trees are . . . and see, that's Brooklyn Bridge. . . . That is a fine sight. And look at all the docks . . . that's the Battery . . . and the masts and the ships . . . and there's the spire of Trinity Church and the Pulitzer building." . . . Mooing of steamboat whistles, ferries red and waddly like ducks churning up white water, a whole train of cars on a barge pushed by a tug chugging beside it that lets out cotton steampuffs all the same size. Jimmy's hands are cold and he's chugging and chugging inside.

"Dear you mustn't get too excited. Come on down and see if mother left anything in the stateroom."

Streak of water crusted with splinters, groceryboxes, orange-peel, cabbageleaves, narrowing, narrowing between the boat and the dock. A brass band shining in the sun, white caps, sweaty red faces, playing Yankee Doodle. "That's for the ambassador, you know the tall man who never left his cabin." Down the slanting gangplank, careful not to trip. *Yankee Doodle went to town.* . . . Shiny black face, white enameled eyes, white enameled teeth. "Yas ma'am, yas ma'am" . . . *Stucka feather in his hat, an called it macaroni.* . . . "We have the freedom of the port." Blue custom officer shows a bald head bowing low . . . *Tumte boomboom* BOOM BOOM BOOM . . . *cakes and sugar candy.* . . .

"Here's Aunt Emily and everybody. . . . Dear how sweet of you to come."

"My dear I've been here since six o'clock!"

"My how he's grown."

Light dresses, sparkle of brooches, faces poked into Jimmy's, smell of roses and uncle's cigar.

"Why he's quite a little man. Come here sir, let me look at you."

"Well goodby Mrs. Herf. If you ever come down our way. . . . Jimmy I didn't see you kiss the ground young man."

"Oh he's killing, he's so oldfashioned . . . such an oldfashioned child."

The cab smells musty, goes rumbling and lurching up a wide avenue swirling with dust, through brick streets soursmelling full of grimy yelling children, and all the while the trunks creak and thump on top.

"Muddy dear, you dont think it'll break through do you?"

"No dear," she laughs tilting her head to one side. She has pink cheeks and her eyes sparkle under the brown veil.

"Oh muddy." He stands up and kisses her on the chin. "What lots of people muddy."

"That's on account of the Fourth of July."

"What's that man doing?"

"He's been drinking dear I'm afraid."

From a little stand draped with flags a man with white whiskers with little red garters on his shirtsleeves is making a speech. "That's a Fourth of July orator. . . . He's reading the Declaration of Independence."

"Why?"

"Because it's the Fourth of July."

Crang! . . . that's a cannon-cracker. "That wretched boy might have frightened the horse. . . . The Fourth of July dear is the day the Declaration of Independence was signed in 1776 in the War of the Revolution. My great grandfather Harland was killed in that war."

A funny little train with a green engine clatters overhead.

"That's the Elevated . . . and look this is Twentythird Street . . . and the Flatiron Building."

The cab turns sharp into a square glowering with sunlight, smelling of asphalt and crowds and draws up before a tall door where colored men in brass buttons run forward.

"And here we are at the Fifth Avenue Hotel."

Icecream at Uncle Jeff's, cold sweet peachy taste thick against the roof of the mouth. Funny after you've left the ship you can still feel the motion. Blue chunks of dusk melting into the squarecut uptown streets. Rockets spurting bright in the blue dusk, colored balls falling, Bengal fire, Uncle Jeff tacking pinwheels on the tree outside the apartmenthouse door, lighting them with his cigar. Roman candles you have to hold. "Be sure and turn your face away, kiddo." Hot thud and splutter in your hands, eggshaped balls soaring, red, yellow, green, smell of powder and singed paper. Down the fizzing glowing street a bell clangs, clangs nearer, clangs faster. Hoofs of lashed horses striking sparks, a fire engine roars by, round the corner red and smoking and brassy. "Must be on Broadway." After it the hookandladder and the firechief's highpacing horses. Then the tinkletinkle of an ambulance. "Somebody got his."

The box is empty, gritty powder and sawdust get under your nails when you feel along it, it's empty, no there are still some little wooden fire engines on wheels. Really truly fire engines. "We must set these off Uncle Jeff. Oh these are the best of all Uncle Jeff." They have squibs in them and go sizzling off fast over the smooth asphalt of the street, pushed by sparkling plumed fiery tails, leaving smoke behind some real fire engines.

Tucked into bed in a tall unfriendly room, with hot eyes and aching legs. "Growing pains darling," muddy said when she tucked him in, leaning over him in a glimmering silk dress with drooping sleeves.

"Muddy what's that little black patch on your face?"

"That," she laughed and her necklace made a tiny tinkling, "is to make mother look prettier."

He lay there hemmed by tall nudging wardrobes and dressers. From outside came the sound of wheels and shouting, and once in a while a band of music in the distance. His legs ached as if they'd fall off, and when he closed his eyes he was speeding through flaring blackness on a red fire engine that shot fire and sparks and colored balls out of its sizzling tail.

The July sun pricked out the holes in the worn shades on the office windows. Gus McNiel sat in the morrischair with his crutches between his knees. His face was white and puffy from months in hospital. Nellie in a straw hat with red poppies rocked herself to and fro in the swivel chair at the desk.

"Better come an set by me Nellie. That lawyer might not like it if he found yez at his desk."

She wrinkled up her nose and got to her feet. "Gus I declare you're scared to death."

"You'd be scared too if you'd had what I'd had wid de

railroad doctor pokin me and alookin at me loike I was a jail-
bird and the Jew doctor the lawyer got tellin me as I was to-
tally in-cap-aciated. Gorry I'm all in. I think he was lyin
though."

"Gus you do as I tell ye. Keep yer mouth shut an let the
other guys do the talkin'."

"Sure I wont let a peep outa me."

Nellie stood behind his chair and began stroking the crisp
hair back from his forehead.

"It'll be great to be home again, Nellie, wid your cookin an
all." He put an arm round her waist and drew her to him.

"Juss think, maybe I wont have to do any."

"I don't think I'd loike that so well. . . . Gosh if we dont
git that money I dunno how we'll make out."

"Oh pop'll help us like he's been doin."

"Hope to the Lord I aint goin to be sick all me loife."

George Baldwin came in slamming the glass door behind
him. He stood looking at the man and his wife a second with
his hands in his pockets. Then he said quietly smiling:

"Well it's done people. As soon as the waiver of any further
claims is signed the railroad's attorneys will hand me a check
for twelve thousand five hundred. That's what we finally com-
promised on."

"Twelve thousand iron men," gasped Gus. "Twelve thousand five hundred. Say wait a second. . . . Hold me crutches
while I go out an git run over again. . . . Wait till I tell
McGillycuddy about it. The ole divil'll be throwin hisself
in front of a market train. . . . Well Mr. Baldwin sir,"
Gus propped himself onto his feet. . . . "you're a great man.
. . . Aint he Nellie?"

"To be sure he is."

Baldwin tried to keep from looking her in the eye. Spurts
of jangling agitation were going through him, making his legs
feel weak and trembly.

"I'll tell yez what let's do," said Gus. "Sposin we all take a
horsecab up to ole McGillycuddy's an have somethin to wet
our whistles in the private bar. . . . My treat. I need a bit of
a drink to cheer me up. Come on Nellie."

"I wish I could," said Baldwin, "but I'm afraid I cant. I'm
pretty busy these days. But just give me your signature before

you go and I'll have the check for you tomorrow. . . . Sign here . . . and here."

McNiel had stumped over to the desk and was leaning over the papers. Baldwin felt that Nellie was trying to make a sign to him. He kept his eyes down. After they had left he noticed her purse, a little leather purse with pansies burned on the back, on the corner of the desk. There was a tap on the glass door. He opened.

"Why wouldn't you look at me?" she said breathlessly low.

"How could I with him here." He held the purse out to her.

She put her arms round his neck and kissed him hard on the mouth. "What are we goin to do? Shall I come in this afternoon? Gus'll be liquorin up to get himself sick again now he's out of the hospital."

"No I cant Nellie. . . . Business . . . business. . . . I'm busy every minute."

"Oh yes you are. . . . All right have it your own way." She slammed the door.

Baldwin sat at his desk biting his knuckles without seeing the pile of papers he was staring at. "I've got to cut it out," he said aloud and got to his feet. He paced back and forth across the narrow office looking at the shelves of lawbooks and the Gibson girl calendar over the telephone and the dusty square of sunlight by the window. He looked at his watch. Lunchtime. He drew the palm of a hand over his forehead and went to the telephone.

"Rector 1237. . . . Mr. Sandbourne there? . . . Say Phil suppose I come by for you for lunch? Do you want to go out right now? . . . Sure. . . . Say Phil I clinched it, I got the milkman his damages. I'm pleased as the dickens. I'll set you up to a regular lunch on the strength of it . . . So long. . . ."

He came away from the telephone smiling, took his hat off its hook, fitted it carefully on his head in front of the little mirror over the hatrack, and hurried down the stairs.

On the last flight he met Mr. Emery of Emery & Emery who had their offices on the first floor.

"Well Mr. Baldwin how's things?" Mr. Emery of Emery & Emery was a flatfaced man with gray hair and eyebrows and a protruding wedgeshaped jaw. "Pretty well sir, pretty well."

"They tell me you are doing mighty well. . . . Something about the New York Central Railroad."

"Oh Simsbury and I settled it out of court."

"Humph,"said Mr. Emery of Emery & Emery.

As they were about to part in the street Mr. Emery said suddenly "Would you care to dine with me and my wife some time?"

"Why . . . er . . . I'd be delighted."

"I like to see something of the younger fellows in the profession you understand. . . . Well I'll drop you a line. . . . Some evening next week. It would give us a chance to have a chat."

Baldwin shook a blueveined hand in a shinystarched cuff and went off down Maiden Lane hustling with a springy step through the noon crowd. On Pearl Street he climbed a steep flight of black stairs that smelt of roasting coffee and knocked on a groundglass door.

"Come in," shouted a bass voice. A swarthy man lanky in his shirtsleeves strode forward to meet him. "Hello George, thought you were never comin'. I'm hongry as hell."

"Phil I'm going to set you up to the best lunch you ever ate in your life."

"Well I'm juss waitin' to be set."

Phil Sandbourne put on his coat, knocked the ashes out of his pipe on the corner of a draftingtable, and shouted into a dark inner office, "Goin out to eat, Mr. Specker."

"All right go ahead," replied a goaty quavering from the inner office.

"How's the old man?" asked Baldwin as they went out the door.

"Ole Specker? Bout on his last legs . . . but he's been thataway for years poa ole soul. Honest George I'd feel mighty mean if anythin happened to poa ole Specker. . . . He's the only honest man in the city of New York, an he's got a head on his shoulders too."

"He's never made anything much by it," said Baldwin.

"He may yet. . . . He may yet. . . . Man you ought to see his plans for allsteel buildins. He's got an idea the skyscraper of the future'll be built of steel and glass. We've been experimenting with vitrous tile recently. . . . cristamighty some of his plans would knock yer eye out. . . . He's got a great sayin about some Roman emperor who found Rome of brick and left it of marble. Well he says he's found New York of brick an that he's goin to leave it of steel . . . steel an glass. I'll have to show you his project for a rebuilt city. It's some pipedream."

They settled on a cushioned bench in the corner of the restaurant that smelled of steak and the grill. Sandbourne stretched his legs out under the table.

"Wow this is luxury," he said.

"Phil let's have a cocktail," said Baldwin from behind the bill of fare. "I tell you Phil, it's the first five years that's the hardest."

"You needn't worry George, you're the hustlin kind. . . . I'm the ole stick in the mud."

"I don't see why, you can always get a job as a draftsman."

"That's a fine future I muss say, to spend ma life with the corner of a draftintable stuck in ma bally. . . . Christamighty man!"

"Well Specker and Sandbourne may be a famous firm yet."

"People'll be goin round in flyin machines by that time an you and me'll be laid out with our toes to the daisies."

"Here's luck anyway."

"Here's lead in yer pencil, George."

They drank down the Martinis and started eating their oysters.

"I wonder if it's true that oysters turn to leather in your stomach when you drink alcohol with em."

"Search me. . . . Say by the way Phil how are you getting on with that little stenographer you were taking out?"

"Man the food an drink an theaters I've wasted on that lil girl. . . . She's got me run to a standstill. . . . Honest she has. You're a sensible feller, George, to keep away from the women."

"Maybe," said Baldwin slowly and spat an olive stone into his clenched fist.

The first thing they heard was the quavering whistle that came from a little wagon at the curb opposite the entrance to the ferry. A small boy broke away from the group of immigrants that lingered in the ferryhouse and ran over to the little wagon.

"Sure it's like a steam engine an its fulla monkeynuts," he yelled running back.

"Padraic you stay here."

"And this here's the L station, South Ferry," went on Tim Halloran who had come down to meet them. "Up thataway's Battery Park an Bowling Green an Wall Street an th' financial district. . . . Come along Padraic your Uncle Timothy's goin to take ye on th' Ninth Avenoo L."

There were only three people left at the ferrylanding, an old woman with a blue handkerchief on her head and a young woman with a magenta shawl, standing at either end of a big corded trunk studded with brass tacks; and an old man with a greenish stub of a beard and a face lined and twisted like the root of a dead oak. The old woman was whimpering with wet eyes: "Dove andiamo Madonna mia, Madonna mia?" The young woman was unfolding a letter blinking at the ornate writing. Suddenly she went over to the old man, "Non posso leggere," holding out the letter to him. He wrung his hands, letting his head roll back and forth, saying over and over again something she couldn't understand. She shrugged her shoulders and smiled and went back to the trunk. A Sicilian with sideburns was talking to the old woman. He grabbed the trunk by its cord and pulled it over to a spring wagon with a white horse that stood across the street. The two women followed the trunk. The Sicilian held out his hand to the young woman. The old woman still muttering and whimpering hoisted herself painfully onto the back of the wagon. When the Sicilian leaned over to read the letter he nudged the young woman with his shoulder. She stiffened. "Awright," he said. Then as he shook the reins on the horse's back he turned back towards the old woman and shouted, "Cinque le due. . . . Awright."

IV. Tracks

*T*he rumpetybump rumpetybump spaced out, slackened; bumpers banged all down the train. The
man dropped off the rods. He couldnt move for stiffness. It was pitchblack. Very slowly he crawled out,
hoisted himself to his knees, to his feet until he leaned
panting against the freightcar. His body was not his
own; his muscles were smashed wood, his bones were
twisted rods. A lantern burst his eyes.

"Get outa here quick yous. Company detectives is
beatin through de yards."

"Say feller, is this New York?"

"You're goddam right it is. Juss foller my lantern;
you kin git out along de waterfront."

His feet could barely stumble through the long
gleaming v's and crisscrossed lines of tracks, he tripped
and fell over a bundle of signal rods. At last he was sitting on the edge of a wharf with his head in his hands.
The water made a soothing noise against the piles like
the lapping of a dog. He took a newspaper out of his
pocket and unwrapped a hunk of bread and a slice of
gristly meat. He ate them dry, chewing and chewing
before he could get any moisture in his mouth. Then he
got unsteadily to his feet, brushed the crumbs off his
knees, and looked about him. Southward beyond the
tracks the murky sky was drenched with orange glow.

"The Gay White Way," he said aloud in a croaking
voice. "The Gay White Way."

Through the rainstriped window Jimmy Herf was watching
the umbrellas bob in the slowly swirling traffic that flowed up
Broadway. There was a knock at the door; "Come in," said
Jimmy and turned back to the window when he saw that the
waiter wasn't Pat. The waiter switched on the light. Jimmy
saw him reflected in the windowpane, a lean spikyhaired man
holding aloft in one hand the dinnertray on which the silver
covers were grouped like domes. Breathing hard the waiter
advanced into the room dragging a folding stand after him

with his free hand. He jerked open the stand, set the tray on it and laid a cloth on the round table. A greasy pantry smell came from him. Jimmy waited till he'd gone to turn round. Then he walked about the table tipping up the silver covers; soup with little green things in it, roast lamb, mashed potatoes, mashed turnips, spinach, no desert either.

"Muddy." "Yes deary," the voice wailed frailly through the folding doors.

"Dinner's ready mother dear."

"You begin darling boy, I'll be right in. . . ."

"But I dont want to begin without you mother."

He walked round the table straightening knives and forks. He put a napkin over his arm. The head waiter at Delmonico's was arranging the table for Graustark and the Blind King of Bohemia and Prince Henry the Navigator and . . .

"Mother who d'you want to be Mary Queen of Scots or Lady Jane Grey?"

"But they both had their heads chopped off honey. . . . I dont want to have my head chopped off." Mother had on her salmoncolored teagown. When she opened the folding doors a wilted smell of cologne and medicines seeped out of the bedroom, trailed after her long lacefringed sleeves. She had put a little too much powder on her face, but her hair, her lovely brown hair was done beautifully. They sat down opposite one another; she set a plate of soup in front of him, lifting it between two long blueveined hands.

He ate the soup that was watery and not hot enough. "Oh I forgot the croûtons, honey."

"Muddy . . . mother why arent you eating your soup?"

"I dont seem to like it much this evening. I couldn't think what to order tonight my head ached so. It doesn't matter."

Would you rather be Cleopatra? She had a wonderful appetite and ate everything that was put before her like a good little girl."

"Even pearls. . . . She put a pearl in a glass of vinegar and drank it down. . . ." Her voice trembled. She stretched out her hand to him across the table; he patted her hand manfully and smiled. "Only you and me Jimmy boy. . . . Honey you'll always love your mother wont you?"

"What's the matter muddy dear?"

"Oh nothing; I feel strange this evening. . . . Oh I'm so tired of never really feeling well."

"But after you've had your operation. . . ."

"Oh yes after I've had my operation. . . . Deary there's a paper of fresh butter on the windowledge in the bathroom. . . . I'll put some on these turnips if you fetch it for me. . . . I'm afraid I'll have to complain about the food again. This lamb's not all it should be; I hope it wont make us sick."

Jimmy ran through the folding doors and his mother's room into the little passage that smelled of mothballs and silky bits of clothing littered on a chair; the red rubber tubing of a douche swung in his face as he opened the bathroom door; the whiff of medicines made his ribs contract with misery. He pushed up the window at the end of the tub. The ledge was gritty and feathery specks of soot covered the plate turned up over the butter. He stood a moment staring down the airshaft, breathing through his mouth to keep from smelling the coalgas that rose from the furnaces. Below him a maid in a white cap leaned out of a window and talked to one of the furnacemen who stood looking up at her with his bare grimy arms crossed over his chest. Jimmy strained his ears to hear what they were saying; to be dirty and handle coal all day and have grease in your hair and up to your armpits.

"Jimmee!"

"Coming mother." Blushing he slammed down the window and walked back to the sittingroom, slowly so that the red would have time to fade out of his face.

"Dreaming again, Jimmy. My little dreamer."

He put the butter beside his mother's plate and sat down.

"Hurry up and eat your lamb while it's hot. Why dont you try a little French mustard on it? It'll make it taste better."

The mustard burnt his tongue, brought tears to his eyes.

"Is it too hot?" mother asked laughing. "You must learn to like hot things. . . . He always liked hot things."

"Who mother?"

"Someone I loved very much."

They were silent. He could hear himself chewing. A few rattling sounds of cabs and trolleycars squirmed in brokenly through the closed windows. The steampipes knocked and hissed. Down the airshaft the furnaceman with grease up to his armpits was spitting words out of his wabbly mouth up at the maid in the starched cap—dirty words. Mustard's the color of . . .

"A penny for your thoughts."

"I wasn't thinking of anything."

"We mustn't have any secrets from each other dear. Remember you're the only comfort your mother has in the world."

"I wonder what it'd be like to be a seal, a little harbor seal."

"Very chilly I should think."

"But you wouldn't feel it. . . . Seals are protected by a layer of blubber so that they're always warm even sitting on an iceberg. But it would be such fun to swim around in the sea whenever you wanted to. They travel thousands of miles without stopping."

"But mother's traveled thousands of miles without stopping and so have you."

"When?"

"Going abroad and coming back." She was laughing at him with bright eyes.

"Oh but that's in a boat."

"And when we used to go cruising on the *Mary Stuart*."

"Oh tell me about that muddy."

There was a knock. "Come." The spikyhaired waiter put his head in the door.

"Can I clear mum?"

"Yes and bring me some fruit salad and see that the fruit is fresh cut. . . . Things are wretched this evening."

Puffing, the waiter was piling dishes on the tray. "I'm sorry mum," he puffed.

"All right, I know it's not your fault waiter. . . . What'll you have Jimmy?"

"May I have a meringue glacé muddy?"

"All right if you'll be very good."

"Yea," Jimmy let out a yell.

"Darling you mustn't shout like that at table."

"But we dont mind when there are just the two of us. . . . Hooray meringue glacé."

"James a gentleman always behaves the same way whether he's in his own home or in the wilds of Africa."

"Gee I wish we were in the wilds of Africa."

"I'd be terrified, dear."

"I'd shout like that and scare away all the lions and tigers. . . . Yes I would."

The waiter came back with two plates on the tray. "I'm sorry mum but meringue glacé's all out. . . . I brought the young gentleman chocolate icecream instead."

"Oh mother."

"Never mind dear. . . . It would have been too rich anyway. . . . You eat that and I'll let you run out after dinner and buy some candy."

"Oh goody."

"But dont eat the icecream too fast or you'll have collywobbles."

"I'm all through."

"You bolted it you little wretch. . . . Put on your rubbers honey."

"But it's not raining at all."

"Do as mother wants you dear. . . . And please dont be long. I put you on your honor to come right back. Mother's not a bit well tonight and she gets so nervous when you're out in the street. There are such terrible dangers. . . ."

He sat down to pull on his rubbers. While he was snapping them tight over his heels she came to him with a dollar bill. She put her arm with its long silky sleeve round his shoulder. "Oh my darling."

She was crying.

"Mother you mustnt." He squeezed her hard; he could feel the ribs of her corset against his arms. "I'll be back in a minute, in the teenciest weenciest minute."

On the stairs where a brass rod held the dull crimson carpet in place on each step, Jimmy pulled off his rubbers and stuffed them into the pockets of his raincoat. With his head in the air he hurried through the web of prying glances of the bellhops on the bench beside the desk. "Goin fer a walk?" the youngest lighthaired bellhop asked him. Jimmy nodded wisely, slipped past the staring buttons of the doorman and out onto Broadway full of clangor and footsteps and faces putting on shadowmasks when they slid out of the splotches of light from stores and arclamps. He walked fast uptown past the Ansonia. In the doorway lounged a blackbrowed man with a cigar in his mouth, maybe a kidnapper. But nice people live in the Ansonia like where we live. Next a telegraph office, drygoods stores, a dyers and cleaners; a Chinese laundry sending out a scorched mysterious steamy smell. He walks faster, the chinks are terrible kidnappers. Footpads. A man with a can of coaloil brushes past him, a greasy sleeve brushes against his shoulder, smells of sweat and coaloil; suppose he's a firebug. The thought of firebug gives him gooseflesh. Fire. Fire.

Huyler's; there's a comfortable fudgy odor mixed with the smell of nickel and wellwiped marble outside the door, and the smell of cooking chocolate curls warmly from the gratings under the windows. Black and orange crêpepaper favors for Hallowe'en. He is just going in when he thinks of the Mirror place two blocks further up, those little silver steamengines and automobiles they give you with your change. I'll hurry; on rollerskates it'd take less time, you could escape from bandits, thugs, holdupmen, on rollerskates, shooting over your shoulder with a long automatic, bing . . . one of em down! that's the worst of em, bing . . . there's another; the rollerskates are magic rollerskates, whee . . . up the brick walls of the houses, over the roofs, vaulting chimneys, up the Flatiron Building, scooting across the cables of Brooklyn Bridge.

Mirror candies; this time he goes in without hesitating. He stands at the counter a while before anyone comes to wait on him. "Please a pound of sixty cents a pound mixed chocolate creams," he rattled off. She is a blond lady, a little crosseyed, and looks at him spitefully without answering. "Please I'm in a hurry if you dont mind."

"All right, everybody in their turn," she snaps. He stands blinking at her with flaming cheeks. She pushes him a box all wrapped up with a check on it "Pay at the desk." I'm not going to cry. The lady at the desk is small and greyhaired. She takes his dollar through a little door like the little doors little animals go in and out of in the Small Mammal House. The cash register makes a cheerful tinkle, glad to get the money. A quarter, a dime, a nickel and a little cup, is that forty cents?

But only a little cup instead of a steamengine or an automobile. He picks up the money and leaves the little cup and hurries out with the box under his arm. Mother'll say I've been too long. He walks home looking straight ahead of him, smarting from the meanness of the blond lady.

"Ha . . . been out abuyin candy," said the lighthaired bellhop. "I'll give you some if you come up later," whispered Jimmy as he passed. The brass rods rang when he kicked them running up the stairs. Outside the chocolatecolored door that had 503 on it in white enameled letters he remembered his rubbers. He set the candy on the floor and pulled them on over his damp shoes. Lucky Muddy wasn't waiting for him with the door open. Maybe she'd seen him coming from the window.

"Mother." She wasn't in the sittingroom. He was terrified. She'd gone out, she'd gone away. "Mother!"

"Come here dear," came her voice weakly from the bedroom.

He pulled off his hat and raincoat and rushed in. "Mother what's the matter?"

"Nothing honey. . . . I've a headache that's all, a terrible headache. . . . Put some cologne on a handkerchief and put it on my head nicely, and dont please dear get it in my eye the way you did last time."

She lay on the bed in a skyblue wadded wrapper. Her face was purplish pale. The silky salmoncolored teagown hung limp over a chair; on the floor lay her corsets in a tangle of pink strings. Jimmy put the wet handkerchief carefully on her forehead. The cologne reeked strong, prickling his nostrils as he leaned over her.

"That's so good," came her voice feebly. "Dear call up Aunt Emily, Riverside 2466, and ask her if she can come round this evening. I want to talk to her. . . . Oh my head's bursting."

His heart thumping terribly and tears blearing his eyes he went to the telephone. Aunt Emily's voice came unexpectedly soon.

"Aunt Emily mother's kinder sick. . . . She wants you to come around. . . . She's coming right away mother dear," he shouted, "isn't that fine? She's coming right around." He tiptoed back into his mother's room, picked up the corset and the teagown and hung them in the wardrobe.

"Deary" came her frail voice "take the hairpins out of my hair, they hurt my head. . . . Oh honeyboy I feel as if my head would burst. . . ." He felt gently through her brown hair that was silkier than the teagown and pulled out the hairpins.

"Ou dont, you are hurting me."

"Mother I didn't mean to."

Aunt Emily, thin in a blue mackintosh thrown over her evening dress, hurried into the room, her thin mouth in a pucker of sympathy. She saw her sister lying twisted with pain on the bed and the skinny whitefaced boy in short pants standing beside her with his hands full of hairpins.

"What is it Lil?" she asked quietly.

"My dear something terrible's the matter with me," came Lily Herf's voice in a gasping hiss.

"James," said Aunt Emily harshly, "you must run off to bed. . . . Mother needs perfect quiet."

"Good night muddy dear," he said.

Aunt Emily patted him on the back. "Dont worry James I'll attend to everything." She went to the telephone and began calling a number in a low precise voice.

The box of candy was on the parlor table; Jimmy felt guilty when he put it under his arm. As he passed the bookcase he snatched out a volume of the American Cyclopædia and tucked it under the other arm. His aunt did not notice when he went out the door. The dungeon gates opened. Outside was an Arab stallion and two trusty retainers waiting to speed him across the border to freedom. Three doors down was his room. It was stuffed with silent chunky darkness. The light switched on obediently lighting up the cabin of the schooner *Mary Stuart*. All right Captain weigh anchor and set your course for the Windward Isles and dont let me be disturbed before dawn; I have important papers to peruse. He tore off his clothes and knelt beside the bed in his pyjamas. Nowilay-medowntosleep Ipraythelordmysoultokeep Ifishoulddiebefore iawake Ipraythelordmysoultotake.

Then he opened the box of candy and set the pillows together at the end of the bed under the light. His teeth

broke through the chocolate into a squashysweet filling.
Let's see . . .

A the first of the vowels, the first letter in all written alphabets except the Amharic Abyssinian, of which it is the thirteenth, and the Runic of which it is the tenth. . . .

Darn it that's a hairy one. . . .

AA, Aachen (see Aix-la-Chapelle).
Aardvark . . .

Gee he's funny looking . . .

(orycteropus capensis), a plantigrade animal of the class mammalia, order edentata, peculiar to Africa.
Abd,
Abd-el-halim, an Egyptian prince, son of Mehmet Ali and a white slave woman. . . .

His cheeks burned as he read:

The Queen of the White Slaves.
Abdomen (lat. of undetermined etymology) . . . the lower part of the body included between the level of the diaphragm and that of the pelvis. . . .
Abelard . . . The relation of master and pupil was not long preserved. A warmer sentiment than esteem filled their hearts and the unlimited opportunities of intercourse which were afforded them by the canon who confided in Abelard's age (he was now almost forty), and in his public character, were fatal to the peace of both. The condition of Heloise was on the point of betraying their intimacy. . . . Fulbert now abandoned himself to a transport of savage vindictiveness . . . burst into Abelard's chamber with a band of ruffians and gratified his revenge by inflicting on him an atrocious mutilation. . . .
Abelites . . . denounced sexual intercourse as service of Satan.
Abimelech I, son of Gideon by a Sheshemite concubine, who made himself king after murdering all his seventy brethren except Jotham, and was killed while besieging the tower of Thebez . . .
Abortion . . .

No; his hands were icy and he felt a little sick from stuffing down so many chocolates.

Abracadabra.
Abydos . . .

He got up to drink a glass of water before Abyssinia with engravings of desert mountains and the burning of Magdala by the British.

His eyes smarted. He was stiff and sleepy. He looked at his Ingersoll. Eleven o'clock. Terror gripped him suddenly. If mother was dead . . . ? He pressed his face into the pillow. She stood over him in her white ballgown that had lace crisply on it and a train sweeping behind on satin rustling ruffles and her hand softly fragrant gently stroked his cheek. A rush of sobs choked him. He tossed on the bed with his face shoved hard into the knotty pillow. For a long time he couldn't stop crying.

He woke up to find the light burning dizzily and the room stuffy and hot. The book was on the floor and the candy squashed under him oozing stickily from its box. The watch had stopped at 1.45. He opened the window, put the chocolates in the bureau drawer and was about to snap off the light when he remembered. Shivering with terror he put on his bathrobe and slippers and tiptoed down the darkened hall. He listened outside the door. People were talking low. He knocked faintly and turned the knob. A hand pulled the door open hard and Jimmy was blinking in the face of a tall clean-shaven man with gold eyeglasses. The folding doors were closed; in front of them stood a starched nurse.

"James dear, go back to bed and dont worry," said Aunt Emily in a tired whisper. "Mother's very ill and must be absolutely quiet, but there's no more danger."

"Not for the present at least, Mrs. Merivale," said the doctor breathing on his eyeglasses.

"The little dear," came the nurse's voice low and purry and reassuring, "he's been sitting up worrying all night and he never bothered us once."

"I'll go back and tuck you into bed," said Aunt Emily. "My James always likes that."

"May I see mother, just a peek so's I'll know she's all right." Jimmy looked up timidly at the big face with the eyeglasses.

The doctor nodded. "Well I must go. . . . I shall drop by at four or five to see how things go. . . . Goodnight Mrs. Merivale. Goodnight Miss Billings. Goodnight son. . . ."

"This way. . . ." The trained nurse put her hand on Jimmy's shoulder. He wriggled out from under and walked behind her.

There was a light on in the corner of mother's room shaded by a towel pinned round it. From the bed came the rasp of breathing he did not recognize. Her crumpled face was towards him, the closed eyelids violet, the mouth screwed to one side. For a half a minute he stared at her. "All right I'll go back to bed now," he whispered to the nurse. His blood pounded deafeningly. Without looking at his aunt or at the nurse he walked stiffly to the outer door. His aunt said something. He ran down the corridor to his own room, slammed the door and bolted it. He stood stiff and cold in the center of the room with his fists clenched. "I hate them. I hate them," he shouted aloud. Then gulping a dry sob he turned out the light and slipped into bed between the shiverycold sheets.

"With all the business you have, madame," Emile was saying in a singsong voice, "I should think you'd need someone to help you with the store."

"I know that . . . I'm killing myself with work; I know that," sighed Madame Rigaud from her stool at the cashdesk. Emile was silent a long time staring at the cross section of a Westphalia ham that lay on a marble slab beside his elbow. Then he said timidly: "A woman like you, a beautiful woman like you, Madame Rigaud, is never without friends."

"Ah ça. . . . I have lived too much in my time. . . . I have no more confidence. . . . Men are a set of brutes, and women, Oh I dont get on with women a bit!"

"History and literature . . ." began Emile.

The bell on the top of the door jangled. A man and a woman stamped into the shop. She had yellow hair and a hat like a flowerbed.

"Now Billy dont be extravagant," she was saying.

"But Norah we got have sumpen te eat. . . . An I'll be all jake by Saturday."

"Nutten'll be jake till you stop playin the ponies."

"Aw go long wud yer. . . . Let's have some liverwurst. . . . My that cold breast of turkey looks good. . . ."

"Piggywiggy," cooed the yellowhaired girl.

"Lay off me will ye, I'm doing this."

"Yes sir ze breast of turkee is veree goud. . . . We ave ole cheekens too, steel 'ot. . . . Emile mong ami cherchez moi uns de ces petits poulets dans la cuisin-e." Madame Rigaud spoke like an oracle without moving from her stool by the cashdesk. The man was fanning himself with a thickbrimmed straw hat that had a checked band.

"Varm tonight," said Madame Rigaud.

"It sure is. . . . Norah we ought to have gone down to the Island instead of bummin round this town."

"Billy you know why we couldn't go perfectly well."

"Don't rub it in. Aint I tellin ye it'll be all jake by Saturday."

"History and literature," continued Emile when the customers had gone off with the chicken, leaving Madame Rigaud a silver half dollar to lock up in the till . . . "history and literature teach us that there are friendships, that there sometimes comes love that is worthy of confidence. . . ."

"History and literature!" Madame Rigaud growled with internal laughter. "A lot of good that'll do us."

"But dont you ever feel lonely in a big foreign city like this . . . ? Everything is so hard. Women look in your pocket not in your heart. . . . I cant stand it any more."

Madame Rigaud's broad shoulders and her big breasts shook with laughter. Her corsets creaked when she lifted herself still laughing off the stool. "Emile, you're a goodlooking fellow and steady and you'll get on in the world. . . . But I'll never put myself in a man's power again. . . . I've suffered too much. . . . Not if you came to me with five thousand dollars."

"You're a very cruel woman."

Madame Rigaud laughed again. "Come along now, you can help me close up."

Sunday weighed silent and sunny over downtown. Baldwin sat at his desk in his shirtsleeves reading a calfbound lawbook. Now and then he wrote down a note on a scratchpad in a wide regular hand. The phone rang loud in the hot stillness. He finished the paragraph he was reading and strode over to answer it.

"Yes I'm here alone, come on over if you want to." He put

down the receiver. "God damn it," he muttered through clenched teeth.

Nellie came in without knocking, found him pacing back and forth in front of the window.

"Hello Nellie," he said without looking up; she stood still staring at him.

"Look here Georgy this cant go on."

"Why cant it?"

"I'm sick of always pretendin an deceivin."

"Nobody's found out anything, have they?"

"Oh of course not."

She went up to him and straightened his necktie. He kissed her gently on the mouth. She wore a frilled muslin dress of a reddish lilac color and had a blue sunshade in her hand.

"How's things Georgy?"

"Wonderful. D'you know, you people have brought me luck? I've got several good cases on hand now and I've made some very valuable connections."

"Little luck it's brought me. I haven't dared go to confession yet. The priest'll be thinkin I've turned heathen."

"How's Gus?"

"Oh full of his plans. . . . Might think he'd earned the money, he's gettin that cocky about it."

"Look Nellie how would it be if you left Gus and came and lived with me? You could get a divorce and we could get married. . . . Everything would be all right then."

"Like fun it would. . . . You dont mean it anyhow."

"But it's been worth it Nellie, honestly it has." He put his arms round her and kissed her hard still lips. She pushed him away.

"Anyways I aint comin here again. . . . Oh I was so happy comin up the stairs thinkin about seein you. . . . You're paid an the business is all finished."

He noticed that the little curls round her forehead were loose. A wisp of hair hung over one eyebrow.

"Nellie we mustn't part bitterly like this."

"Why not will ye tell me?"

"Because we've both loved one another."

"I'm not goin to cry." She patted her nose with a little

rolledup handkerchief. "Georgy I'm goin to hate ye. . . . Goodby." The door snapped sharply to behind her.

Baldwin sat at his desk and chewed the end of a pencil. A faint pungence of her hair lingered in his nostrils. His throat was stiff and lumpy. He coughed. The pencil fell out of his mouth. He wiped the saliva off with his handkerchief and settled himself in his chair. From bleary the crowded paragraphs of the lawbook became clear. He tore the written sheet off the scratchpad and clipped it to the top of a pile of documents. On the new sheet he began: Decision of the Supreme Court of the State of New York. . . . Suddenly he sat up straight in his chair, and started biting the end of his pencil again. From outside came the endless sultry whistle of a peanut wagon. "Oh well, that's that," he said aloud. He went on writing in a wide regular hand: Case of Patterson vs. The State of New York. . . . Decision of the Supreme . . .

Bud sat by a window in the Seamen's Union reading slowly and carefully through a newspaper. Next him two men with freshly shaved rawsteak cheeks cramped into white collars and blue serge storesuits were ponderously playing chess. One of them smoked a pipe that made a little clucking noise when he drew on it. Outside rain beat incessantly on a wide glimmering square.

Banzai, live a thousand years, cried the little gray men of the fourth platoon of Japanese sappers as they advanced to repair the bridge over the Yalu River . . . Special correspondent of the New York Herald . . .

"Checkmate, said the man with the pipe. "Damn it all let's go have a drink. This is no night to be sitting here sober."

"I promised the ole woman . . ."

"None o that crap Jess, I know your kinda promises." A big crimson hand thickly furred with yellow hairs brushed the chessmen into their box. "Tell the ole woman you had to have a nip to keep the weather out."

"That's no lie neither."

Bud watched their shadows hunched into the rain pass the window.

"What you name?"

Bud turned sharp from the window startled by a shrill squeaky voice in his ear. He was looking into the fireblue eyes of a little yellow man who had a face like a toad, large mouth, protruding eyes and thick closecropped black hair.

Bud's jaw set. "My name's Smith, what about it?"

The little man held out a square callouspalmed hand. "Plis to meet yez. Me Matty."

Bud took the hand in spite of himself. It squeezed his until he winced. "Matty what?" he asked. "Me juss Matty . . . Laplander Matty . . . Come have drink."

"I'm flat," said Bud. "Aint got a red cent."

"On me. Me too much money, take some. . . ." Matty shoved a hand into either pocket of his baggy checked suit and punched Bud in the chest with two fistfuls of greenbacks.

"Aw keep yer money . . . I'll take a drink with yous though."

By the time they got to the saloon on the corner of Pearl Street Bud's elbows and knees were soaked and a trickle of cold rain was running down his neck. When they went up to the bar Laplander Matty put down a five dollar bill.

"Me treat everybody; very happy yet tonight."

Bud was tackling the free lunch. "Hadn't et in a dawg's age," he explained when he went back to the bar to take his drink. The whisky burnt his throat all the way down, dried wet clothes and made him feel the way he used to feel when he was a kid and got off to go to a baseball game Saturday afternoon.

"Put it there Lap," he shouted slapping the little man's broad back. "You an me's friends from now on."

"Hey landlubber, tomorrow me an you ship togezzer. What say?"

"Sure we will."

"Now we go up Bowery Street look at broads. Me pay."

"Aint a Bowery broad would go wid yer, ye little Yap," shouted a tall drunken man with drooping black mustaches who had lurched in between them as they swayed in the swinging doors.

"Zey vont, vont zey?" said the Lap hauling off. One of his hammershaped fists shot in a sudden uppercut under the man's jaw. The man rose off his feet and soared obliquely in through the swinging doors that closed on him. A shout went up from inside the saloon.

"I'll be a sonofabitch, Lappy, I'll be a sonofabitch," roared Bud and slapped him on the back again.

Arm in arm they careened up Pearl Street under the drenching rain. Bars yawned bright to them at the corners of rainseething streets. Yellow light off mirrors and brass rails and gilt frames round pictures of pink naked women was looped and slopped into whiskyglasses guzzled fiery with tipped back head, oozed bright through the blood, popped bubbly out of ears and eyes, dripped spluttering off fingertips. The raindark houses heaved on either side, streetlamps swayed like lanterns carried in a parade, until Bud was in a back room full of nudging faces with a woman on his knees. Laplander Matty stood with his arms round two girls' necks, yanked his shirt open to show a naked man and a naked woman tattooed in red and green on his chest, hugging, stiffly coiled in a seaserpent and when he puffed out his chest and wiggled the skin with his fingers the tattooed man and woman wiggled and all the nudging faces laughed.

Phineas P. Blackhead pushed up the wide office window. He stood looking out over the harbor of slate and mica in the uneven roar of traffic, voices, racket of building that soared from the downtown streets bellying and curling like smoke in the stiff wind shoving down the Hudson out of the northwest.

"Hay Schmidt, bring me my field glasses," he called over his shoulder. "Look . . ." He was focusing the glasses on a thickwaisted white steamer with a sooty yellow stack that was abreast of Governors Island. "Isn't that the *Anonda* coming in now?"

Schmidt was a fat man who had shrunk. The skin hung in loose haggard wrinkles on his face. He took one look through the glasses. "Sure it is." He pushed down the window; the roar receded tapering hollowly like the sound of a sea shell.

"Jiminy they were quick about it. . . . They'll be docked in half an hour. . . . You beat it along over and get hold of Inspector Mulligan. He's all fixed. . . . Dont take your eyes off him. Old Matanzas is out on the warpath trying to get an injunction against us. If every spoonful of manganese isnt off by tomorrow night I'll cut your commission in half. . . . Do you get that?"

Schmidt's loose jowls shook when he laughed. "No danger sir. . . . You ought to know me by this time."

"Of course I do. . . . You're a good feller Schmidt. I was just joking."

Phineas P. Blackhead was a lanky man with silver hair and a red hawkface; he slipped back into the mahogany armchair at his desk and rang an electric bell. "All right Charlie, show em in," he growled at the towheaded officeboy who appeared in the door. He rose stiffly from his desk and held out a hand. "How do you do Mr. Storrow . . . How do you do Mr. Gold. . . . Make yourselves comfortable. . . . That's it. . . . Now look here, about this strike. The attitude of the railroad and docking interests that I represent is one of frankness and honesty, you know that. . . . I have confidence, I can say I have the completest confidence, that we can settle this matter amicably and agreeably. . . . Of course you must meet me halfway. . . . We have I know the same interests at heart, the interests of this great city, of this great seaport. . . ." Mr. Gold moved his hat to the back of his head and cleared his throat with a loud barking noise. "Gentlemen, one of two roads lies before us . . ."

In the sunlight on the windowledge a fly sat scrubbing his wings with his hinder legs. He cleaned himself all over, twisting and untwisting his forelegs like a person soaping his hands, stroking the top of his lobed head carefully; brushing his hair. Jimmy's hand hovered over the fly and slapped down. The fly buzzed tinglingly in his palm. He groped for it with two fingers, held it slowly squeezing it into mashed gray jelly between finger and thumb. He wiped it off under the windowledge. A hot sick feeling went through him. Poor old fly, after washing himself so carefully, too. He stood a long time looking down the airshaft through the dusty pane where the sun gave a tiny glitter to the dust. Now and then a man in shirtsleeves crossed the court below with a tray of dishes. Orders shouted and the clatter of dishwashing came up faintly from the kitchens.

He stared through the tiny glitter of the dust on the windowpane. Mother's had a stroke and next week I'll go back to school.

"Say Herfy have you learned to fight yet?"

"Herfy an the Kid are goin to fight for the flyweight championship before lights."

"But I dont want to."

"Kid wants to. . . . Here he comes. Make a ring there you ginks."

"I dont want to, please."

"You've damn well got to, we'll beat hell outa both of ye if you dont."

"Say Freddy that's a nickel fine from you for swearing."

"Jez I forgot."

"There you go again. . . . Paste him in the slats."

"Go it Herfy, I'm bettin on yer."

"That's it sock him."

The Kid's white screwedup face bouncing in front of him like a balloon; his fist gets Jimmy in the mouth; a salty taste of blood from the cut lip. Jimmy strikes out, gets him down on the bed, pokes his knee in his belly. They pull him off and throw him back against the wall.

"Go it Kid."

"Go it Herfy."

There's a smell of blood in his nose and lungs; his breath rasps. A foot shoots out and trips him up.

"That's enough, Herfy's licked."

"Girlboy . . . Girlboy."

"But hell Freddy he had the Kid down."

"Shut up, don't make such a racket. . . . Old Hoppy'll be coming up."

"Just a little friendly bout, wasn't it Herfy?"

"Get outa my room, all of you, all of you," Jimmy screeches, tear-blinded, striking out with both arms.

"Crybaby . . . crybaby."

He slams the door behind them, pushes the desk against it and crawls trembling into bed. He turns over on his face and lies squirming with shame, biting the pillow.

Jimmy stared through the tiny glitter of the dust on the windowpane.

DARLING

Your poor mother was very unhappy when she finally put you on the train and went back to her big empty rooms at the hotel. Dear, I am very lonely without you. Do you know what I did? I got out all your toy soldiers, the ones that used to be in the taking of Port Arthur, and set them all out in battalions on the library shelf. Wasn't that silly? Never mind dear, Christmas'll soon come round and I'll have my boy again. . . .

A crumpled face on a pillow; mother's had a stroke and next week I'll go back to school. Darkgrained skin growing flabby under her eyes, gray creeping up her brown hair. Mother never laughs. The stroke.

He turned back suddenly into the room, threw himself on the bed with a thin leather book in his hand. The surf thundered loud on the barrier reef. He didn't need to read. Jack was swimming fast through the calm blue waters of the lagoon, stood in the sun on the yellow beach shaking the briny drops off him, opened his nostrils wide to the smell of breadfruit roasting beside his solitary campfire. Birds of bright plumage shrieked and tittered from the tall ferny tops of the coconut palms. The room was drowsy hot. Jimmy fell asleep. There was a strawberry lemon smell, a smell of pineapples on the deck and mother was there in a white suit and a dark man in a yachtingcap, and the sunlight rippled on the milkytall sails. Mother's soft laugh rises into a shriek O-o-o-ohee. A fly the size of a ferryboat walks towards them across the water, reaching out jagged crabclaws. "Yump Yimmy, yump; you can do it in two yumps," the dark man yells in his ear. "But please I dont want to . . . I dont want to," Jimmy whines. The dark man's beating him, yump yump yump. . . . "Yes one moment. Who is it?"

Aunt Emily was at the door. "Why do you keep your door locked Jimmy. . . . I never allow James to lock his door."

"I like it better that way, Aunt Emily."

"Imagine a boy asleep this time of the afternoon."

"I was reading *The Coral Island* and I fell asleep." Jimmy was blushing.

"All right. Come along. Miss Billings said not to stop by mother's room. She's asleep."

They were in the narrow elevator that smelled of castor oil; the colored boy grinned at Jimmy.

"What did the doctor say Aunt Emily?"

"Everything's going as well as could be expected. . . . But you mustn't worry about that. This evening you must have a real good time with your little cousins. . . . You dont see enough children of your own age Jimmy."

They were walking towards the river leaning into a gritty wind that swirled up the street cast out of iron under a dark silvershot sky.

"I guess you'll be glad to get back to school, James."

"Yes Aunt Emily."

"A boy's school days are the happiest time in his life. You must be sure to write your mother once a week at least James. . . . You are all she has now. . . . Miss Billings and I will keep you informed."

"Yes Aunt Emily."

"And James I want you to know my James better. He's the same age you are, only perhaps a little more developed and all that, and you ought to be good friends. . . . I wish Lily had sent you to Hotchkiss too."

"Yes Aunt Emily."

There were pillars of pink marble in the lower hall of Aunt Emily's apartmenthouse and the elevatorboy wore a chocolate livery with brass buttons and the elevator was square and decorated with mirrors. Aunt Emily stopped before a wide red mahogany door on the seventh floor and fumbled in her purse for her key. At the end of the hall was a leaded window through which you could see the Hudson and steamboats and tall trees of smoke rising against the yellow sunset from the yards along the river. When Aunt Emily got the door open they heard the piano. "That's Maisie doing her practicing." In the room where the piano was the rug was thick and mossy, the wallpaper was yellow with silveryshiny roses between the cream woodwork and the gold frames of oilpaintings of woods and people in a gondola and a fat cardinal drinking. Maisie tossed the pigtails off her shoulders as she jumped off the pianostool. She had a round creamy face and a slight pugnose. The metronome went on ticking.

"Hello James," she said after she had tilted her mouth up to her mother's to be kissed. "I'm awfully sorry poor Aunt Lily's so sick."

"Arent you going to kiss your cousin, James?" said Aunt Emily.

Jimmy shambled up to Maisie and pushed his face against hers.

"That's a funny kind of a kiss," said Maisie.

"Well you two children can keep each other company till dinner." Aunt Emily rustled through the blue velvet curtains into the next room.

"We wont be able to go on calling you James." After she had stopped the metronome, Maisie stood staring with serious brown eyes at her cousin. "There cant be two Jameses can there?"

"Mother calls me Jimmy."

"Jimmy's a kinder common name, but I guess it'll have to do till we can think of a better one. . . . How many jacks can you pick up?"

"What are jacks?"

"Gracious dont you know what jackstones are? Wait till James comes back, wont he laugh!"

"I know Jack roses. Mother used to like them better'n any other kind."

"American Beauties are the only roses I like," announced Maisie flopping into a Morris chair. Jimmy stood on one leg kicking his heel with the toes of the other foot.

"Where's James?"

"He'll be home soon. . . . He's having his riding lesson."

The twilight became leadensilent between them. From the trainyards came the scream of a locomotivewhistle and the clank of couplings on shunted freight cars. Jimmy ran to the window.

"Say Maisie, do you like engines?" he asked.

"I think they are horrid. Daddy says we're going to move on account of the noise and smoke."

Through the gloom Jimmy could make out the beveled smooth bulk of a big locomotive. The smoke rolled out of the stack in huge bronze and lilac coils. Down the track a red light snapped green. The bell started to ring slowly, lazily.

Forced draft snorting loud the train clankingly moved, gathered speed, slid into dusk swinging a red tail-light.

"Gee I wish we lived here," said Jimmy. "I've got two hundred and seventytwo pictures of locomotives, I'll show em to you sometime if you like. I collect em."

"What a funny thing to collect. . . . Look Jimmy you pull the shade down and I'll light the light."

When Maisie pushed the switch they saw James Merivale standing in the door. He had light wiry hair and a freckled face with a pugnose like Maisie's. He had on riding breeches and black leather gaiters and was flicking a long peeled stick about.

"Hullo Jimmy," he said. "Welcome to our city."

"Say James," cried Maisie, "Jimmy doesn't know what jackstones are."

Aunt Emily appeared through the blue velvet curtains. She wore a highnecked green silk blouse with lace on it. Her white hair rose in a smooth curve from her forehead. "It's time you children were washing up," she said, "dinner's in five minutes. . . . James take your cousin back to your room and hurry up and take off those ridingclothes."

Everybody was already seated when Jimmy followed his cousin into the diningroom. Knives and forks tinkled discreetly in the light of six candles in red and silver shades. At the end of the table sat Aunt Emily, next to her a rednecked man with no back to his head, and at the other end Uncle Jeff with a pearl pin in his checked necktie filled a broad armchair. The colored maid hovered about the fringe of light passing toasted crackers. Jimmy ate his soup stiffly, afraid of making a noise. Uncle Jeff was talking in a booming voice between spoonfuls of soup.

"No I tell you, Wilkinson, New York is no longer what it used to be when Emily and I first moved up here about the time the Ark landed. . . . City's overrun with kikes and low Irish, that's what's the matter with it. . . . In ten years a Christian wont be able to make a living. . . . I tell you the Catholics and the Jews are going to run us out of our own country, that's what they are going to do."

"It's the New Jerusalem," put in Aunt Emily laughing.

"It's no laughing matter; when a man's worked hard all his

life to build up a business and that sort of thing he dont want
to be run out by a lot of damn foreigners, does he Wilkinson?"

"Jeff you are getting all excited. You know it gives you in-
digestion. . . ."

"I'll keep cool, mother."

"The trouble with the people of this country is this, Mr.
Merivale" . . . Mr. Wilkinson frowned ponderously. "The
people of this country are too tolerant. There's no other
country in the world where they'd allow it. . . . After all we
built up this country and then we allow a lot of foreigners,
the scum of Europe, the offscourings of Polish ghettos to
come and run it for us."

"The fact of the matter is that an honest man wont soil his
hands with politics, and he's given no inducement to take
public office."

"That's true, a live man, nowadays, wants more money,
needs more money than he can make honestly in public
life. . . . Naturally the best men turn to other channels."

"And add to that the ignorance of these dirty kikes and
shanty Irish that we make voters before they can even talk
English . . ." began Uncle Jeff.

The maid set a highpiled dish of fried chicken edged by
corn fritters before Aunt Emily. Talk lapsed while everyone
was helped. "Oh I forgot to tell you Jeff," said Aunt Emily,
"we're to go up to Scarsdale Sunday."

"Oh mother I hate going out Sundays."

"He's a perfect baby about staying home."

"But Sunday's the only day I get at home."

"Well it was this way: I was having tea with the Harland
girls at Maillard's and who should sit down at the next table
but Mrs. Burkhart . . ."

"Is that Mrs. John B. Burkhart? Isnt he one of the vicepresidents of the National City Bank?"

"John's a fine feller and a coming man downtown."

"Well as I was saying dear, Mrs. Burkhart said we just had
to come up and spend Sunday with them and I just couldn't
refuse."

"My father," continued Mr. Wilkinson, "used to be old
Johannes Burkhart's physician. The old man was a cranky old
bird, he'd made his pile in the fur trade way back in Colonel

Astor's day. He had the gout and used to swear something terrible. . . . I remember seeing him once, a redfaced old man with long white hair and a silk skullcap over his baldspot. He had a parrot named Tobias and people going along the street never knew whether it was Tobias or Judge Burkhart cussing."

"Ah well, times have changed," said Aunt Emily.

Jimmy sat in his chair with pins and needles in his legs. Mother's had a stroke and next week I'll go back to school. Friday, Saturday, Sunday, Monday. . . . He and Skinny coming back from playing with the hoptoads down by the pond, in their blue suits because it was Sunday afternoon. Smokebushes were in bloom behind the barn. A lot of fellows teasing little Harris, calling him Iky because he was supposed to be a Jew. His voice rose in a singsong whine; "Cut it fellers, cant you fellers. I've got my best suit on fellers."

"Oy Oy Meester Solomon Levy with his best Yiddisher garments all marked down," piped jeering voices. "Did you buy it in a five and ten Iky?"

"I bet he got it at a firesale."

"If he got it at a firesale we ought to turn the hose on him."

"Let's turn the hose on Solomon Levy."

"Oh stop it fellers."

"Shut up; dont yell so loud."

"They're juss kiddin, they wont hurt him," whispered Skinny.

Iky was carried kicking and bawling down towards the pond, his white tearwet face upside down. "He's not a Jew at all," said Skinny. "But I'll tell you who is a Jew, that big bully Fat Swanson."

"Howjer know?"

"His roommate told me."

"Gee whiz they're going to do it."

They ran in all directions. Little Harris with his hair full of mud was crawling up the bank, water running out of his coatsleeves.

There was hot chocolate sauce with the icecream. "An Irishman and a Scotchman were walking down the street and the Irishman said to the Scotchman, Sandy let's have a drink. . . ." A prolonged ringing at the front door bell was making them inattentive to Uncle Jeff's story. The colored maid flurried back into the diningroom and began whispering in Aunt Emily's ear. ". . . And the Scotchman said, Mike . . . Why what's the matter?"

"It's Mr. Joe sir."

"The hell it is."

"Well maybe he's all right," said Aunt Emily hastily.

"A bit whipsey, ma'am."

"Sarah why the dickens did you let him in?"

"I didnt let him, he juss came."

Uncle Jeff pushed his plate away and slapped down his napkin. "Oh hell . . . I'll go talk to him."

"Try and make him go . . ." Aunt Emily had begun; she stopped with her mouth partly open. A head was stuck through the curtains that hung in the wide doorway to the livingroom. It had a birdlike face, with a thin drooping nose, topped by a mass of straight black hair like an Indian's. One of the redrimmed eyes winked quietly.

"Hullo everybody! . . . How's every lil thing? Mind if I butt in?" His voice perked hoarsely as a tall skinny body followed the head through the curtains. Aunt Emily's mouth arranged itself in a frosty smile. "Why Emily you must . . . er . . . excuse me; I felt an evening . . . er . . . round the family hearth . . . er . . . would be . . . er . . . er . . . beneficial. You understand, the refining influence of the home." He stood jiggling his head behind Uncle Jeff's chair. "Well Jefferson ole boy, how's the market?" He brought a hand down on Uncle Jeff's shoulder.

"Oh all right. Want to sit down?" he growled.

"They tell me . . . if you'll take a tip from an old timer . . . er . . . a retired broker . . . broker and broker every day . . . ha-ha. . . . But they tell me that Interborough Rapid Transit's worth trying a snifter of. . . . Doan look at me crosseyed like that Emily. I'm going right away. . . . Why howdedo Mr. Wilkinson. . . . Kids are looking well. Well I'll be if that isn't Lily Herf's lil boy. . . . Jimmy you dont remember your . . . er . . . cousin, Joe Harland do you? Nobody remembers Joe Harland. . . . Except you Emily and you wish you could forget him . . . ha-ha. . . . How's your mother Jimmy?"

"A little better thank you," Jimmy forced the words out through a tight throat.

"Well when you go home you give her my love . . . she'll understand. Lily and I have always been good friends even if I am the family skeleton. . . . They dont like me, they wish I'd go away. . . . I'll tell you what boy, Lily's the best of the lot. Isn't she Emily, isn't she the best of the lot of us?"

Aunt Emily cleared her throat. "Sure she is, the best looking, the cleverest, the realest. . . . Jimmy your mother's an emperess. . . . Aways been too fine for all this. By gorry I'd like to drink her health."

"Joe you might moderate your voice a little;" Aunt Emily clicked out the words like a typewriter.

"Aw you all think I'm drunk. . . . Remember this Jimmy" . . . he leaned across the table, stroked Jimmy's face with his grainy whisky breath . . . "these things aren't always a man's fault . . . circumstances . . . er . . . circumstances." He upset a glass staggering to his feet. "If Emily insists on looking at me crosseyed I'm goin out. . . . But remember give Lily Herf Joe Harland's love even if he has gone to the demnition bowbows." He lurched out through the curtains again.

"Jeff I know he'll upset the Sèvres vase. . . . See that he gets out all right and get him a cab." James and Maisie burst into shrill giggles from behind their napkins. Uncle Jeff was purple.

"I'll be damned to hell if I put him in a cab. He's not my cousin. . . . He ought to be locked up. And next time you see him you can tell him this from me, Emily: if he ever comes here in that disgusting condition again I'll throw him out."

"Jefferson dear, it's no use getting angry. . . . There's no harm done. He's gone."

"No harm done! Think of our children. Suppose there'd been a stranger here instead of Wilkinson. What would he have thought of our home?"

"Dont worry about that," croaked Mr. Wilkinson, "accidents will happen in the best regulated families."

"Poor Joe's such a sweet boy when he's himself," said Aunt Emily. "And think that it looked for a while years ago as if Harland held the whole Curb Market in the palm of his hand. The papers called him the King of the Curb, dont you remember?" "That was before the Lottie Smithers affair. . . ."

"Well suppose you children go and play in the other room

while we have our coffee," chirped Aunt Emily. "Yes, they ought to have gone long ago."

"Can you play Five Hundred, Jimmy?" asked Maisie.

"No I cant."

"What do you think of that James, he cant play jacks and he cant play Five Hundred."

"Well they're both girl's games," said James loftily. "I wouldn't play em either xept on account of you."

"Oh wouldn't you, Mr. Smarty."

"Let's play animal grabs."

"But there aren't enough of us for that. It's no fun without a crowd."

"An last time you got the giggles so bad mother made us stop."

"Mother made us stop because you kicked little Billy Schmutz in the funnybone an made him cry."

"Spose we go down an look at the trains," put in Jimmy.

"We're not allowed to go down stairs after dark," said Maisie severely.

"I'll tell you what lets play stock exchange. . . . I've got a million dollars in bonds to sell and Maisie can be the bulls an Jimmy can be the bears."

"All right, what do we do?"

"Oh juss run round an yell mostly. . . . I'm selling short."

"All right Mr. Broker I'll buy em all at five cents each."

"No you cant say that. . . . You say ninetysix and a half or something like that."

"I'll give you five million for them," cried Maisie waving the blotter of the writing desk.

"But you fool, they're only worth one million," shouted Jimmy.

Maisie stood still in her tracks. "Jimmy what did you say then?" Jimmy felt shame flame up through him; he looked at his stubby shoes. "I said, you fool."

"Haven't you ever been to Sunday school? Don't you know that God says in the Bible that if you call anybody Thou fool you'll be in danger of hellfire?"

Jimmy didn't dare raise his eyes.

"Well I'm not going to play any more," said Maisie drawing herself up. Jimmy somehow found himself out in the hall.

He grabbed his hat and ran out the door and down the six flights of white stone stairs past the brass buttons and chocolate livery of the elevator boy, out through the hall that had pink marble pillars in to Seventysecond Street. It was dark and blowy, full of ponderous advancing shadows and chasing footsteps. At last he was climbing the familiar crimson stairs of the hotel. He hurried past his mother's door. They'd ask him why he had come home so soon. He burst into his own room, shot the bolt, doublelocked the door and stood leaning against it panting.

"Well are you married yet?" was the first thing Congo asked when Emile opened the door to him. Emile was in his undershirt. The shoebox-shaped room was stuffy, lit and heated by a gas crown with a tin cap on it.

"Where are you in from this time?"

"Bizerta and Trondjeb. . . . I'm an able seaman."

"That's a rotten job, going to sea. . . . I've saved two hundred dollars. I'm working at Delmonico's."

They sat down side by side on the unmade bed. Congo produced a package of gold tipped Egyptian Deities. "Four months' pay"; he slapped his thigh. "Seen May Sweitzer?" Emile shook his head. "I'll have to find the little son of a gun. . . . In those goddam Scandinavian ports they come out in boats, big fat blond women in bumboats. . . ."

They were silent. The gas hummed. Congo let his breath out in a whistle. "Whee . . . C'est chic ça, Delmonico . . . Why havent you married her?"

"She likes to have me hang around. . . . I'd run the store better than she does."

"You're too easy; got to use rough stuff with women to get anything outa them. . . . Make her jealous."

"She's got me going."

"Want to see some postalcards?" Congo pulled a package, wrapped in newspaper out of his pocket. "Look these are Naples; everybody there wants to come to New York. . . . That's an Arab dancing girl. Nom d'une vache they got slippery bellybuttons. . . ."

"Say, I know what I'll do," cried Emile suddenly dropping the cards on the bed. "I'll make her jealous. . . ."

"Who?"

"Ernestine . . . Madame Rigaud. . . ."

"Sure walk up an down Eighth Avenue with a girl a couple of times an I bet she'll fall like a ton of bricks."

The alarmclock went off on the chair beside the bed. Emile jumped up to stop it and began splashing water on his face in the washbasin.

"Merde I got to go to work."

"I'll go over to Hell's Kitchen an see if I can find May."

"Don't be a fool an spend all your money," said Emile who stood at the cracked mirror with his face screwed up, fastening the buttons in the front of a clean boiled shirt.

"It's a sure thing I'm tellin yer," said the man again and again, bringing his face close to Ed Thatcher's face and rapping the desk with his flat hand.

"Maybe it is Viler but I seen so many of em go under, honest I dont see how I can risk it."

"Man I've hocked the misses's silver teaset and my diamond ring an the baby's mug. . . . It's a sure sure thing. . . . I wouldn't let you in on it, xept you an me's been pretty good friends an I owe you money an everythin. . . . You'll make twentyfive percent on your money by tomorrow noon. . . . Then if you want to hold you can on a gamble, but if you sell three quarters and hold the rest two or three days on a chance you're safe as . . . as the Rock of Gibraltar."

"I know Viler, it certainly sounds good. . . ."

"Hell man you dont want to be in this damned office all your life, do you? Think of your little girl."

"I am, that's the trouble."

"But Ed, Gibbons and Swandike had started buying already at three cents when the market closed this evening. . . . Klein got wise an'll be right there with bells on first thing in the morning. The market'll go crazy on it. . . ."

"Unless the fellers doin the dirty work change their minds. I know that stuff through and through, Viler. . . . Sounds like a topnotch proposition. . . . But I've examined the books of too many bankrupts."

Viler got to his feet and threw his cigar into the cuspidor. "Well do as you like, damn it all. . . . I guess you must like commuting from Hackensack an working twelve hours a day. . . ."

"I believe in workin my way up, that's all."

"What's the use of a few thousands salted away when you're old and cant get any satisfaction? Man I'm goin in with both feet."

"Go to it Viler. . . . You tellem," muttered Thatcher as the other man stamped out slamming the office door.

The big office with its series of yellow desks and hooded typewriters was dark except for the tent of light in which Thatcher sat at a desk piled with ledgers. The three windows at the end were not curtained. Through them he could see the steep bulk of buildings scaled with lights and a plank-shaped bit of inky sky. He was copying memoranda on a long sheet of legal cap.

FanTan Import and Export Company (statement of assets and liabilities up to and including February 29) . . . Branches New York, Shanghai, Hongkong and Straights Settlements. . . .

Balance carried over	$345,789.84
Real Estate	500,087.12
Profit and Loss	399,765.90

"A bunch of goddam crooks," growled Thatcher out loud. "Not an item on the whole thing that aint faked. I dont believe they've got any branches in Hongkong or anywhere. . . ."

He leaned back in his chair and stared out of the window. The buildings were going dark. He could just make out a star in the patch of sky. Ought to go out an eat, bum for the digestion to eat irregularly like I do. Suppose I'd taken a plunge on Viler's red hot tip. Ellen, how do you like these American Beauty roses? They have stems eight feet long, and I want you to look over the itinerary of the trip abroad I've mapped out to finish your education. Yes it will be a shame to leave our fine new apartment looking out over Central Park. . . . And downtown; The Fiduciary Accounting Institute, Edward C. Thatcher, President. . . . Blobs of steam were drifting up across the patch of sky, hiding the star. Take a plunge . . . they're all crooks and gamblers anyway . . . take a plunge and come up with your hands full, pockets full, bankaccount full, vaults full of money. If I only dared take the risk. Fool to waste your time fuming about it. Get back to the FanTan Import. Steam faintly ruddy with light reflected from the streets swarmed swiftly up across the patch of sky, twisting scattering.

Goods on hand in U. S. bonded warehouses . . . $325,666.00

Take a plunge and come up with three hundred and twenty-five thousand, six hundred and sixtysix dollars. Dollars swarming up like steam, twisting scattering against the stars. Millionaire Thatcher leaned out of the window of the bright patchouliscented room to look at the darkjutting city steaming with laughter, voices, tinkling and lights; behind him orchestras played among the azaleas, private wires click click clickclicked dollars from Singapore, Valparaiso, Mukden, Hongkong, Chicago. Susie leaned over him in a dress made of orchids, breathed in his ear.

Ed Thatcher got to his feet with clenched fists sniveling; You poor fool whats the use now she's gone. I'd better go eat or Ellen'll scold me.

V. Steamroller

*D*usk *gently smooths crispangled streets. Dark
*presses tight the steaming asphalt city, crushes the
fretwork of windows and lettered signs and chimneys
and watertanks and ventilators and firescapes and
moldings and patterns and corrugations and eyes and
hands and neckties into blue chunks, into black enormous blocks. Under the rolling heavier heavier pres-
sure windows blurt light. Night crushes bright milk
out of arclights, squeezes the sullen blocks until they
drip red, yellow, green into streets resounding with
feet. All the asphalt oozes light. Light spurts from lettering on roofs, mills dizzily among wheels, stains
rolling tons of sky.*

A steamroller was clattering back and forth over the freshly
tarred metaling of the road at the cemetery gate. A smell of
scorched grease and steam and hot paint came from it.
Jimmy Herf picked his way along the edge of the road; the
stones were sharp against his feet through the worn soles of
his shoes. He brushed past swarthy-necked workmen and
walked on over the new road with a whiff of garlic and sweat
from them in his nostrils. After a hundred yards he stopped
over the gray suburban road, laced tight on both sides with
telegraph poles and wires, over the gray paperbox houses
and the gray jagged lots of monumentmakers, the sky was
the color of a robin's egg. Little worms of May were
writhing in his blood. He yanked off his black necktie and
put it in his pocket. A tune was grinding crazily through his
head:

> I'm so tired of vi-olets
> Take them all away.

There is one glory of the sun and another glory of the
moon and another glory of the stars: for one star differeth
from another star in glory. So also is the resurrection of the
dead. . . . He walked on fast splashing through puddles full
of sky, trying to shake the droning welloiled words out of his

579

ears, to get the feeling of black crêpe off his fingers, to forget the smell of lilies.

> I'm so tired of vi-olets
> Take them all away.

He walked faster. The road climbed a hill. There was a bright runnel of water in the ditch, flowing through patches of grass and dandelions. There were fewer houses; on the sides of barns peeling letters spelled out LYDIA PINKHAM'S VEGETABLE COMPOUND, BUDWEISER, RED HEN, BARKING DOG. . . . And muddy had had a stroke and now she was buried. He couldn't think how she used to look; she was dead that was all. From a fencepost came the moist whistling of a songsparrow. The minute rusty bird flew ahead, perched on a telegraph wire and sang, and flew ahead to the rim of an abandoned boiler and sang, and flew ahead and sang. The sky was getting a darker blue, filling with flaked motherofpearl clouds. For a last moment he felt the rustle of silk beside him, felt a hand in a trailing lacefrilled sleeve close gently over his hand. Lying in his crib with his feet pulled up cold under the menace of the shaggy crouching shadows; and the shadows scuttled melting into corners when she leaned over him with curls round her forehead, in silkpuffed sleeves, with a tiny black patch at the corner of the mouth that kissed his mouth. He walked faster. The blood flowed full and hot in his veins. The flaked clouds were melting into rosecolored foam. He could hear his steps on the worn macadam. At a crossroad the sun glinted on the sticky pointed buds of a beechsapling. Opposite a sign read YONKERS. In the middle of the road teetered a dented tomatocan. Kicking it hard in front of him he walked on. One glory of the sun and another glory of the moon and another glory of the stars. . . . He walked on.

"Hullo Emile!" Emile nodded without turning his head. The girl ran after him and grabbed his coatsleeve. "That's the way you treat your old friends is it? Now that you're keepin company with that delicatessen queen . . ."

Emile yanked his hand away. "I am in a 'urree zat's all."

"How'd ye like it if I went an told her how you an me

framed it up to stand in front of the window on Eighth Avenue huggin an kissin juss to make her fall for yez."

"Zat was Congo's idea."

"Well didn't it woik?"

"Sure."

"Well aint there sumpen due me?"

"May you're a veree nice leetle girl. Next week my night off is ·Wednesday. . . . I'll come by an take you to a show. . . . 'Ow's 'ustlin?"

"Worse'n hell. . . . I'm tryin out for a dancin job up at the Campus. . . . That's where you meet guys wid jack. . . . No more of dese sailor boys and shorefront stiffs. . . . I'm gettin respectable."

"May 'ave you 'eard from Congo?"

"Got a postalcard from some goddam place I couldn't read the name of. . . . Aint it funny when you write for money an all ye git 's a postal ca-ard. . . . That's the kid gits me for the askin any night. . . . An he's the only one, savvy, Frogslegs?"

"Goodby May." He suddenly pushed the straw bonnet trimmed with forgetmenots back on her and kissed her.

"Hey quit dat Frogslegs . . . Eighth Avenue aint no place to kiss a girl," she whined pushing a yellow curl back under her hat. "I could git you run in an I've half a mind to."

Emile walked off.

A fire engine, a hosewagon, and a hookandladder passed him, shattering the street with clattering roar. Three blocks down smoke and an occasional gasp of flame came from the roof of a house. A crowd was jammed up against the policelines. Beyond backs and serried hats Emile caught a glimpse of firemen on the roof of the next house and of three silently glittering streams of water playing into the upper windows. Must be right opposite the delicatessen. He was making his way through the jam on the sidewalk when the crowd suddenly opened. Two policemen were dragging out a negro whose arms snapped back and forth like broken cables. A third cop came behind cracking the negro first on one side of the head, then on the other with his billy.

"It's a shine 'at set the fire."

"They caught the firebug."

"'At's 'e incendiary."

"God he's a meanlookin smoke."

The crowd closed in. Emile was standing beside Madame Rigaud in front of the door of her store.

"Cheri que ça me fait une emotiong. . . . J'ai horriblemong peu du feu."

Emile was standing a little behind her. He let one arm crawl slowly round her waist and patted her arm with his other hand. "Everything awright. Look no more fire, only smoke. . . . But you are insured, aint you?"

"Oh yes for fifteen tousand." He squeezed her hand and then took his arms away. "Viens ma petite on va rentrer."

Once inside the shop he took both her plump hands. "Ernestine when we get married?"

"Next month."

"I no wait zat long, imposseeble. . . . Why not next Wednesday? Then I can help you make inventory of stock. . . . I tink maybe we can sell this place and move uptown, make bigger money."

She patted him on the cheek. "P'tit ambitieux," she said through her hollow inside laugh that made her shoulders and her big bust shake.

They had to change at Manhattan Transfer. The thumb of Ellen's new kid glove had split and she kept rubbing it nervously with her forefinger. John wore a belted raincoat and a pinkishgray felt hat. When he turned to her and smiled she couldn't help pulling her eyes away and staring out at the long rain that shimmered over the tracks.

"Here we are Elaine dear. Oh prince's daughter, you see we get the train that comes from the Penn station. . . . It's funny this waiting in the wilds of New Jersey this way." They got into the parlorcar. John made a little clucking sound in his mouth at the raindrops that made dark dimes on his pale hat. "Well we're off, little girl. . . . Behold thou art fair my love, thou art fair, thou hast dove's eyes within thy locks."

Ellen's new tailored suit was tight at the elbows. She wanted to feel very gay and listen to his purring whisper in her ears, but something had set her face in a tight frown; she could only look out at the brown marshes and the million black windows of factories and the puddly streets of towns and a rusty steamboat in a canal and barns and Bull Durham signs and round-faced Spearmint gnomes all barred and crisscrossed with bright flaws of rain. The jeweled stripes on the window ran straight down when the train stopped and got more and more oblique as it speeded up. The wheels rumbled in her head, saying Man-hattan Tran-sfer. Man-hattan Tran-sfer. Anyway it was a long time before Atlantic City. By the time we get to Atlantic City . . . *Oh it rained forty days* . . . I'll be feeling gay. . . . *And it rained forty nights.* . . . I've got to be feeling gay.

"Elaine Thatcher Oglethorpe, that's a very fine name, isn't it, darling? Oh stay me with flagons, comfort me with apples for I am sick of love. . ."

It was so comfortable in the empty parlorcar in the green velvet chair with John leaning towards her reciting nonsense with the brown marshlands slipping by behind the rainstriped window and a smell like clams seeping into the car. She looked into his face and laughed. A blush ran all over his face to the roots of his redblond hair. He put his hand in its yellow glove over her hand in its white glove. "You're my wife now Elaine."

"You're my husband now John." And laughing they looked at each other in the coziness of the empty parlorcar.

White letters, ATLANTIC CITY, spelled doom over the rainpitted water.

Rain lashed down the glaring boardwalk and crashed in gusts against the window like water thrown out of a bucket. Beyond the rain she could hear the intermittent rumble of the surf along the beach between the illuminated piers. She lay on her back staring at the ceiling. Beside her in the big bed John lay asleep breathing quietly like a child with a pillow doubled up under his head. She was icy cold. She slid out of bed very carefully not to wake him, and stood looking out the window down the very long V of lights of the boardwalk. She pushed up the window. The rain lashed in her face spitefully stinging her flesh, wetting her nightdress. She pushed her forehead against the frame. Oh I want to die. I want to die. All the tight coldness of her body was clenching in her stomach. Oh I'm going to be sick. She went into the bathroom and closed the door. When she had vomited she felt better. Then she climbed into bed again careful not to touch John. If she touched him she would die. She lay on her back with her hands tight against her sides and her feet together. The parlor-car rumbled cozily in her head; she fell asleep.

Wind rattling the windowframes wakened her. John was far away, the other side of the big bed. With the wind and the rain streaming in the window it was as if the room and the big bed and everything were moving, running forward like an airship over the sea. *Oh it rained forty days. . . .* Through a crack in the cold stiffness the little tune trickled warm as blood. . . . *And it rained forty nights.* Gingerly she drew a hand over her husband's hair. He screwed his face up in his sleep and whined "Dont" in a littleboy's voice that made her giggle. She lay giggling on the far edge of the bed, giggling desperately as she used to with girls at school. And the rain lashed through the window and the song grew louder until it was a brass band in her ears:

> Oh it rained forty days
> And it rained forty nights
> And it didn't stop till Christmas
> And the only man that survived the flood
> Was longlegged Jack of the Isthmus.

Jimmy Herf sits opposite Uncle Jeff. Each has before him on a blue plate a chop, a baked potato, a little mound of peas and a sprig of parsley.

"Well look about you Jimmy," says Uncle Jeff. Bright top-story light brims the walnutpaneled diningroom, glints twist-edly on silver knives and forks, gold teeth, watch-chains, scarfpins, is swallowed up in the darkness of broadcloth and tweed, shines roundly on polished plates and bald heads and covers of dishes. "Well what do you think of it?" asks Uncle Jeff burying his thumbs in the pockets of his fuzzy buff vest.

"It's a fine club all right," says Jimmy.

"The wealthiest and the most successful men in the country eat lunch up here. Look at the round table in the corner. That's the Gausenheimers' table. Just to the left." . . . Uncle Jeff leans forward lowering his voice, "the man with the powerful jaw is J. Wilder Laporte." Jimmy cuts into his mutton-chop without answering. "Well Jimmy, you probably know why I brought you down here . . . I want to talk to you. Now that your poor mother has . . . has been taken, Emily and I are your guardians in the eyes of the law and the executors of poor Lily's will. . . . I want to explain to you just how things stand." Jimmy puts down his knife and fork and sits staring at his uncle, clutching the arms of his chair with cold hands, watching the jowl move blue and heavy above the ruby stickpin in the wide satin cravat. "You are sixteen now aren't you Jimmy?"

"Yes sir."

"Well it's this way. . . . When your mother's estate is all settled up you'll find yourself in the possession of approximately fiftyfive hundred dollars. Luckily you are a bright fellow and will be ready for college early. Now, properly husbanded that sum ought to see you through Columbia, since you insist on going to Columbia. . . . I myself, and I'm sure your Aunt Emily feels the same way about it, would much rather see you go to Yale or Princeton. . . . You are a very lucky fellow in my estimation. At your age I was sweeping out an office in Fredericksburg and earning fifteen dollars a month. Now what I wanted to say was this . . . I have not noticed that you felt sufficient responsibility about moneymatters . . . er . . . sufficient enthusiasm about earning your living, making good in a man's world. Look around you. . . . Thrift and enthusiasm has made these men what they are. It's made me, put me in the position to offer you the comfortable home, the cultured surroundings that I do offer you. . . . I realize that your education has been a little peculiar, that poor Lily did not have quite the same ideas that we have on many subjects, but the really formative period of your life is beginning. Now's the time to take a brace and lay the foundations of your future career. . . . What I advise is that you follow James's example and work your way up through the firm. . . . From now on you are both sons of mine. . . . It will mean hard work but it'll eventually offer a very substantial opening. And don't forget this, if a man's a success in New York, he's a success!" Jimmy sits watching his uncle's broad serious mouth forming words, without tasting the juicy mutton of the chop he is eating. "Well what are you going to make of yourself?" Uncle Jeff leaned towards him across the table with bulging gray eyes.

Jimmy chokes on a piece of bread, blushes, at last stammers weakly, "Whatever you say Uncle Jeff."

"Does that mean you'll go to work for a month this summer in my office? Get a taste of how it feels to make a living, like a man in a man's world, get an idea of how the business is run?" Jimmy nods his head. "Well I think you've come to a very sensible decision," booms Uncle Jeff leaning back in his chair so that the light strikes across the wave of his steelgray hair. "By the way what'll you have for dessert? . . . Years from now Jimmy, when you are a successful man with a business of your own we'll remember this talk. It's the beginning of your career."

The hatcheck girl smiles from under the disdainful pile of her billowy blond hair when she hands Jimmy his hat that looks squashed flat and soiled and limp among the bigbellied derbies and the fedoras and the majestic panamas hanging on the pegs. His stomach turns a somersault with the drop of the elevator. He steps out into the crowded marble hall. For a moment not knowing which way to go, he stands back against the wall with his hands in his pockets, watching people elbow their way through the perpetually revolving doors; softcheeked girls chewing gum, hatchetfaced girls with bangs, creamfaced boys his own age, young toughs with their hats on one side, sweatyfaced messengers, crisscross glances, sauntering hips, red jowls masticating cigars, sallow concave faces, flat bodies of young men and women, paunched bodies of elderly men, all elbowing, shoving, shuffling, fed in two endless tapes through the revolving doors out into Broadway, in off Broadway. Jimmy fed in a tape in and out the revolving doors, noon and night and morning, the revolving doors grinding out his years like sausage meat. All of a sudden his muscles stiffen. Uncle Jeff and his office can go plumb to hell. The words are so loud inside him he glances to one side and the other to see if anyone heard him say them.

They can all go plumb to hell. He squares his shoulders and shoves his way to the revolving doors. His heel comes down on a foot. "For crissake look where yer steppin." He's out in the street. A swirling wind down Broadway blows grit in his mouth and eyes. He walks down towards the Battery with the wind in his back. In Trinity Churchyard stenographers and officeboys are eating sandwiches among the tombs. Outlandish people cluster outside steamship lines; towhaired Norwegians, broadfaced Swedes, Polacks, swarthy stumps of men that smell of garlic from the Mediterranean, mountainous Slavs, three Chinamen, a bunch of Lascars. On the little triangle in front of the Customhouse, Jim Herf turns and stares long up the deep gash of Broadway, facing the wind squarely. Uncle Jeff and his office can go plumb to hell.

Bud sat on the edge of his cot and stretched out his arms and yawned. From all round through a smell of sweat and sour breath and wet clothes came snores, the sound of men stirring in their sleep, creaking of bedsprings. Far away through the murk burned a single electric light. Bud closed his eyes and let his head fall over on his shoulder. O God I want to go to sleep. Sweet Jesus I want to go to sleep. He pressed his knees together against his clasped hands to keep them from trembling. Our father which art in Heaven I want to go to sleep.

"Wassa matter pardner cant ye sleep?" came a quiet whisper from the next cot.

"Hell, no." "Me neither."

Bud looked at the big head of curly hair held up on an elbow turned towards him.

"This is a hell of a lousy stinking flop," went on the voice evenly. "I'll tell the world . . . Forty cents too! They can take their Hotel Plaza an . . ."

"Been long in the city?"

"Ten years come August."

"Great snakes!"

A voice rasped down the line of cots, "Cut de comedy yous guys, what do you tink dis is, a Jewish picnic?"

Bud lowered his voice: "Funny, it's years I been thinkin an wantin to come to the city. . . . I was born an raised on a farm upstate."

"Why dont ye go back?"

"I cant go back." Bud was cold; he wanted to stop trembling. He pulled the blanket up to his chin and rolled over facing the man who was talking. "Every spring I says to myself I'll hit the road again, go out an plant myself among the weeds an the grass an the cows comin home milkin time, but I dont; I juss kinder hangs on."

"What d'ye do all this time in the city?"

"I dunno. . . . I used to set in Union Square most of the time, then I set in Madison Square. I been up in Hoboken an Joisey and Flatbush an now I'm a Bowery bum."

"God I swear I'm goin to git outa here tomorrow. I git sceered here. Too many bulls an detectives in this town."

"You could make a livin in handouts. . . . But take it from me kid you go back to the farm an the ole folks while the goin's good."

Bud jumped out of bed and yanked roughly at the man's shoulder. "Come over here to the light, I want to show ye sumpen." Bud's own voice crinkled queerly in his ears. He strode along the snoring lane of cots. The bum, a shambling man with curly weatherbleached hair and beard and eyes as if hammered into his head, climbed fully dressed out from the blankets and followed him. Under the light Bud unbuttoned the front of his unionsuit and pulled it off his knottymuscled gaunt arms and shoulders. "Look at my back."

"Christ Jesus," whispered the man running a grimy hand with long yellow nails over the mass of white and red deep-gouped scars. "I aint never seen nothin like it."

"That's what the ole man done to me. For twelve years he licked me when he had a mind to. Used to strip me and take a piece of light chain to my back. They said he was my dad but I know he aint. I run away when I was thirteen. That was when he ketched me an began to lick me. I'm twentyfive now."

They went back without speaking to their cots and lay down.

Bud lay staring at the ceiling with the blanket up to his eyes. When he looked down towards the door at the end of the room, he saw standing there a man in a derby hat with a cigar in his mouth. He crushed his lower lip between his teeth to keep from crying out. When he looked again the man was gone. "Say are you awake yet?" he whispered.

The bum grunted. "I was goin to tell yer. I mashed his head in with the grubbinhoe, mashed it in like when you kick a rotten punkin. I told him to lay offn me an he wouldn't.

. . . He was a hard godfearin man an he wanted you to be sceered of him. We was grubbin the sumach outa the old pasture to plant pertoters there. . . . I let him lay till night with his head mashed in like a rotten punkin. A bit of scrub along the fence hid him from the road. Then I buried him an went up to the house an made me a pot of coffee. He hadn't never let me drink no coffee. Before light I got up an walked down the road. I was tellin myself in a big city it'd be like lookin for a needle in a haystack to find yer. I knowed where the ole man kep his money; he had a roll as big as your head but I was sceered to take more'en ten dollars. . . . You awake yet?"

The bum grunted. "When I was a kid I kep company with ole man Sackett's girl. Her and me used to keep company in the ole icehouse down in Sackett's woods an we used to talk about how we'd come to New York City an git rich and now I'm here I cant git work an I cant git over bein sceered. There's detectives follow me all round, men in derbyhats with badges under their coats. Last night I wanted to go with a hooker an she saw it in my eyes an throwed me out. . . . She could see it in my eyes." He was sitting on the edge of the cot, leaning over, talking into the other man's face in a hissing whisper. The bum suddenly grabbed him by the wrists.

"Look here kid, you're goin blooy if you keep up like this. . . . Got any mazuma?" Bud nodded. "You better give it to me to keep. I'm an old timer an I'll git yez outa this. You put yer clothes on an take a walk round the block to a hash joint an eat up strong. How much you got?"

"Change from a dollar."

"You give me a quarter an eat all the stuff you kin git offn the rest." Bud pulled on his trousers and handed the man a quarter. "Then you come back here an you'll sleep good an tomorrer me'n you'll go upstate an git that roll of bills. Did ye say it was as big as yer head? Then we'll beat it where they cant ketch us. We'll split fifty fifty. Are you on?"

Bud shook his hand with a wooden jerk, then with the laces flickering round his shoes he shuffled to the door and down the spitmarked stairs.

The rain had stopped, a cool wind that smelled of woods and grass was ruffling the puddles in the cleanwashed streets.

In the lunchroom in Chatham Square three men sat asleep with their hats over their eyes. The man behind the counter was reading a pink sportingsheet. Bud waited long for his order. He felt cool, unthinking, happy. When it came he ate the browned corned beef hash, deliberately enjoying every mouthful, mashing the crisp bits of potato against his teeth with his tongue, between sips of heavily sugared coffee. After polishing the plate with a crust of bread he took a toothpick and went out.

Picking his teeth he walked through the grimydark entrance to Brooklyn Bridge. A man in a derby hat was smoking a cigar in the middle of the broad tunnel. Bud brushed past him walking with a tough swagger. I dont care about him; let him follow me. The arching footwalk was empty except for a single policeman who stood yawning, looking up at the sky. It was like walking among the stars. Below in either direction streets tapered into dotted lines of lights between square blackwindowed buildings. The river glimmered underneath like the Milky Way above. Silently smoothly the bunch of lights of a tug slipped through the moist darkness. A car whirred across the bridge making the girders rattle and the spiderwork of cables thrum like a shaken banjo.

When he got to the tangle of girders of the elevated railroads of the Brooklyn side, he turned back along the southern driveway. Dont matter where I go, cant go nowhere now. An edge of the blue night had started to glow behind him the way iron starts to glow in a forge. Beyond black chimneys and lines of roofs faint rosy contours of the downtown buildings were brightening. All the darkness was growing pearly, warming. They're all of em detectives chasin me, all of em, men in derbies, bums on the Bowery, old women in kitchens, barkeeps, streetcar conductors, bulls, hookers, sailors, longshoremen, stiffs in employment agencies. . . . He thought I'd tell him where the ole man's roll was, the lousy bum. . . . One on him. One on all them goddam detectives. The river was smooth, sleek as a bluesteel gunbarrel. Dont matter where I go; cant go nowhere now. The shadows between the wharves and the buildings were powdery like washingblue. Masts fringed the river; smoke, purple chocolatecolor fleshpink climbed into light. Cant go nowhere now.

In a swallowtail suit with a gold watchchain and a red seal ring riding to his wedding beside Maria Sackett, riding in a carriage to City Hall with four white horses to be made an alderman by the mayor; and the light grows behind them brighter brighter, riding in satins and silks to his wedding, riding in pinkplush in a white carriage with Maria Sackett by his side through rows of men waving cigars, bowing, doffing brown derbies, Alderman Bud riding in a carriage full of diamonds with his milliondollar bride. . . . Bud is sitting on the rail of the bridge. The sun has risen behind Brooklyn. The windows of Manhattan have caught fire. He jerks himself forward, slips, dangles by a hand with the sun in his eyes. The yell strangles in his throat as he drops.

Captain McAvoy of the tugboat *Prudence* stood in the pilothouse with one hand on the wheel. In the other he held a piece of biscuit he had just dipped into a cup of coffee that stood on the shelf beside the binnacle. He was a wellset man with bushy eyebrows and a bushy black mustache waxed at the tips. He was about to put the piece of coffeesoaked biscuit into his mouth when something black dropped and hit the water with a thudding splash a few yards off the bow. At the same moment a man leaning out of the engineroom door shouted, "A guy juss jumped offn de bridge."

"God damn it to hell," said Captain McAvoy dropping his piece of biscuit and spinning the wheel. The strong ebbtide whisked the boat round like a straw. Three bells jangled in the engineroom. A negro ran forward to the bow with a boathook.

"Give a hand there Red," shouted Captain McAvoy.

After a tussle they landed a long black limp thing on the deck. One bell. Two bells, Captain McAvoy frowning and haggard spun the tug's nose into the current again.

"Any life in him Red?" he asked hoarsely. The negro's face was green, his teeth were chattering.

"Naw sir," said the redhaired man slowly. "His neck's broke clear off."

Captain McAvoy sucked a good half of his mustache into his mouth. "God damn it to hell," he groaned. "A pretty thing to happen on a man's wedding day."

I. Great Lady on a White Horse

*M*orning clatters with the first L train down
Allen Street. Daylight rattles through the windows, shaking the old brick houses, splatters the girders
of the L structure with bright confetti.

The cats are leaving the garbage cans, the chinches
are going back into the walls, leaving sweaty limbs,
leaving the grimetender necks of little children asleep.
Men and women stir under blankets and bedquilts on
mattresses in the corners of rooms, clots of kids begin to
untangle to scream and kick.

At the corner of Riverton the old man with the
hempen beard who sleeps where nobody knows is
putting out his picklestand. Tubs of gherkins, pimentos,
melonrind, piccalilli give out twining vines and cold
tendrils of dank pepperyfragrance that grow like a
marshgarden out of the musky bedsmells and the rancid clangor of the cobbled awakening street.

The old man with the hempen beard who sleeps
where nobody knows sits in the midst of it like Jonah
under his gourd.

Jimmy Herf walked up four creaky flights and knocked at a
white door fingermarked above the knob where the name
Sunderland appeared in old English characters on a card
neatly held in place by brass thumbtacks. He waited a long
while beside a milkbottle, two creambottles, and a copy of the
Sunday *Times*. There was a rustle behind the door and the
creak of a step, then no more sound. He pushed a white
button in the doorjamb.

"An he said, Margie I've got a crush on you so bad, an she
said, Come in outa the rain, you're all wet. . . ." Voices
coming down the stairs, a man's feet in button shoes, a girl's
feet in sandals, pink silk legs; the girl in a fluffy dress and a
Spring Maid hat; the young man had white edging on his vest
and a green, blue, and purple striped necktie.

"But you're not that kind of a girl."

"How do you know what kind of a girl I am?"

The voices trailed out down the stairs.

Jimmy Herf gave the bell another jab.

"Who is it?" came a lisping female voice through a crack in the door.

"I want to see Miss Prynne please."

Glimpse of a blue kimono held up to the chin of a fluffy face. "Oh I don't know if she's up yet."

"She said she would be."

"Look will you please wait a second to let me make my getaway," she tittered behind the door. "And then come in. Excuse us but Mrs. Sunderland thought you were the rent collector. They sometimes come on Sunday just to fool you." A smile coyly bridged the crack in the door.

"Shall I bring in the milk?"

"Oh do and sit down in the hall and I'll call Ruth." The hall was very dark; smelled of sleep and toothpaste and massagecream; across one corner a cot still bore the imprint of a body on its rumpled sheets. Straw hats, silk eveningwraps, and a couple of men's dress overcoats hung in a jostling tangle from the staghorns of the hatrack. Jimmy picked a corsetcover off a rockingchair and sat down. Women's voices, a subdued rustling of people dressing, Sunday newspaper noises seeped out through the partitions of the different rooms.

The bathroom door opened; a stream of sunlight reflected out of a pierglass cut the murky hall in half, out of it came a head of hair like copper wire, bluedark eyes in a brittlewhite eggshaped face. Then the hair was brown down the hall above a slim back in a tangerine-colored slip, nonchalant pink heels standing up out of the bathslippers at every step.

"Ou-ou, Jimmee . . ." Ruth was yodling at him from behind her door. "But you mustn't look at me or at my room." A head in curlpapers stuck out like a turtle's.

"Hullo Ruth."

"You can come in if you promise not to look. . . . I'm a sight and my room's a pigeon. . . . I've just got to do my hair. Then I'll be ready." The little gray room was stuffed with clothes and photographs of stage people. Jimmy stood with his back to the door, some sort of silky stuff that dangled from the hook tickling his ears.

"Well how's the cub reporter?"

"I'm on Hell's Kitchen. . . . It's swell. Got a job yet Ruth?"

"Um-um. . . . a couple of things may materialize during the week. But they wont. Oh Jimmy I'm getting desperate." She shook her hair loose of the crimpers and combed out the new mousybrown waves. She had a pale startled face with a big mouth and blue underlids. "This morning I knew I ought to be up and ready, but I just couldn't. It's so discouraging to get up when you haven't got a job. . . . Sometimes I think I'll go to bed and just stay there till the end of the world."

"Poor old Ruth."

She threw a powderpuff at him that covered his necktie and the lapels of his blue serge suit with powder. "Dont you poor old me you little rat."

"That's a nice thing to do after all the trouble I took to make myself look respectable. . . . Darn your hide Ruth. And the smell of the carbona not off me yet."

Ruth threw back her head with a shrieking laugh. "Oh you're so comical Jimmy. Try the whisk-broom."

Blushing he blew down his chin at his tie. "Who's the funny-looking girl opened the halldoor?"

"Shush you can hear everything through the partition. . . . That's Cassie," she whispered giggling. "Cassah-ndrah Wilkins . . . used to be with the Morgan Dancers. But we oughtnt to laugh at her, she's very nice. I'm very fond of her." She let out a whoop of laughter. "You nut Jimmy." She got to her feet and punched him in the muscle of the arm. "You always make me act like I was crazy."

"God did that. . . . No but look, I'm awfully hungry. I walked up."

"What time is it?"

"It's after one."

"Oh Jimmy I dont know what to do about time. . . . Like this hat? . . . Oh I forgot to tell you. I went to see Al Harrison yesterday. It was simply dreadful. . . . If I hadnt got to the phone in time and threatened to call the police. . . ."

"Look at that funny woman opposite. She's got a face exactly like a llama."

"It's on account of her I have to keep my shades drawn all the time . . ."

"Why?"

"Oh you're much too young to know. You'd be shocked Jimmy." Ruth was leaning close to the mirror running a stick of rouge between her lips.

"So many things shock me, I dont see that it matters much. . . . But come along let's get out of here. The sun's shining outside and people are coming out of church and going home to overeat and read at their Sunday papers among the rubberplants . . ."

"Oh Jimmy you're a shriek . . . Just one minute. Look out you're hooked onto my best shimmy."

A girl with short black hair in a yellow jumper was folding the sheets off the cot in the hall. For a second under the ambercolored powder and the rouge Jimmy did not recognize the face he had seen through the crack in the door.

"Hello Cassie, this is . . . Beg pardon, Miss Wilkins this is Mr. Herf. You tell him about the lady across the airshaft, you know Sappo the Monk."

Cassandra Wilkins lisped and pouted. "Isn't she dweadful Mr. Herf. . . . She says the dweadfullest things."

"She merely does it to annoy."

"Oh Mr. Herf I'm so pleased to meet you at last, Ruth does nothing but talk about you. . . . Oh I'm afwaid I was indiscweet to say that. . . . I'm dweadfully indiscweet."

The door across the hall opened and Jimmy found himself looking in the white face of a crookednosed man whose red hair rode in two unequal mounds on either side of a straight part. He wore a green satin bathrobe and red morocco slippers.

"What heow Cassahndrah?" he said in a careful Oxford drawl. "What prophecies today?"

"Nothing except a wire from Mrs. Fitzsimmons Green. She wants me to go to see her at Scarsdale tomorrow to talk about the Gweenery Theater. . . . Excuse me this is Mr. Herf, Mr. Oglethorpe." The redhaired man raised one eyebrow and lowered the other and put a limp hand in Jimmy's.

"Herf, Herf. . . . Let me see, it's not a Georgiah Herf? In Atlahnta there's an old family of Herfs. . . ."

"No I dont think so."

"Too bad. Once upon a time Josiah Herf and I were boon companions. Today he is the president of the First National Bank and leading citizen of Scranton Pennsylvahnia and I . . . a mere mountebank, a thing of rags and patches." When he shrugged his shoulders the bathrobe fell away exposing a flat smooth hairless chest.

"You see Mr. Oglethorpe and I are going to do the Song of Songs. He weads it and I interpwet it in dancing. You must come up and see us wehearse sometime."

"Thy navel is like a round goblet which wanteth not liquor, thy belly is like a heap of wheat set about with lilies . . ."

"Oh dont begin now." She tittered and pressed her legs together.

"Jojo close that door," came a quiet deep girl's voice from inside the room.

"Oh poo-er deah Elaine, she wants to sleep. . . . So glahd to have met you, Mr. Herf."

"Jojo!"

"Yes my deah. . . ."

Through the leaden drowse that cramped him the girl's voice set Jimmy tingling. He stood beside Cassie constrainedly without speaking in the dingydark hall. A smell of coffee and singeing toast seeped in from somewhere. Ruth came up behind them.

"All right Jimmy I'm ready. . . . I wonder if I've forgotten anything."

"I dont care whether you have or not, I'm starving." Jimmy took hold of her shoulders and pushed her gently towards the door. "It's two o'clock."

"Well goodby Cassie dear, I'll call you up at about six."

"All wight Wuthy . . . So pleased to have met you Mr. Herf." The door closed on Cassie's tittering lisp.

"Wow, Ruth that place gives me the infernal jimjams."

"Now Jimmy dont get peevish because you need food."

"But tell me Ruth, what the hell is Mr. Oglethorpe? He beats anything I ever saw."

"Oh did the Ogle come out of his lair?" Ruth let out a whoop of laughter. They came out into grimy sunlight. "Did he tell you he was of the main brawnch, dontcher know, of the Oglethorpes of Georgiah?"

"Is that lovely girl with copper hair his wife?"

"Elaine Oglethorpe has reddish hair. She's not so darn lovely either. . . . She's just a kid and she's upstage as the deuce already. All because she made a kind of a hit in Peach Blossoms. You know one of these tiny exquisite bits everybody makes such a fuss over. She can act all right."

"It's a shame she's got that for a husband."

"Ogle's done everything in the world for her. If it hadnt been for him she'd still be in the chorus . . ."

"Beauty and the beast."

"You'd better look out if he sets his lamps on you Jimmy."

"Why?"

"Strange fish, Jimmy, strange fish."

An Elevated train shattered the barred sunlight overhead. He could see Ruth's mouth forming words.

"Look," he shouted above the diminishing clatter. "Let's go have brunch at the Campus and then go for a walk on the Palisades."

"You nut Jimmy what's brunch?"

"You'll eat breakfast and I'll eat lunch."

"It'll be a scream." Whooping with laughter she put her arm in his. Her silvernet bag knocked against his elbow as they walked.

"And what about Cassie, the mysterious Cassandra?"

"You mustn't laugh at her, she's a peach. . . . If only she wouldn't keep that horrid little white poodle. She keeps it in her room and it never gets any exercise and it smells something terrible. She has that little room next to mine. . . . Then she's got a steady . . ." Ruth giggled. "He's worse than the poodle. They're engaged and he borrows all her money away from her. For Heaven's sake dont tell anybody."

"I dont know anybody to tell."

"Then there's Mrs. Sunderland . . ."

"Oh yes I got a glimpse of her going into the bathroom— an old lady in a wadded dressing gown with a pink boudoir cap on."

"Jimmy you shock me. . . . She keeps losing her false teeth," began Ruth; an L train drowned out the rest. The restaurant door closing behind them choked off the roar of wheels on rails.

An orchestra was playing *When It's Appleblossom Time in Normandee*. The place was full of smokewrithing slants of sunlight, paper festoons, signs announcing LOBSTERS ARRIVE DAILY, EAT CLAMS NOW, TRY OUR DELICIOUS FRENCH STYLE STEAMED MUSSLES (Recommended by the Department of Agriculture). They sat down under a redlettered placard BEEFSTEAK PARTIES UPSTAIRS and Ruth made a pass at him with a breadstick. "Jimmy do you think it'd be immoral to eat scallops for breakfast? But first I've got to have coffee coffee coffee . . ."

"I'm going to eat a small steak and onions."

"Not if you're intending to spend the afternoon with me, Mr. Herf."

"Oh all right. Ruth I lay my onions at your feet."

"That doesn't mean I'm going to let you kiss me."

"What . . . on the Palisades?" Ruth's giggle broke into a whoop of laughter. Jimmy blushed crimson. "I never axed you maam, he say-ed."

Sunlight dripped in her face through the little holes in the brim of her straw hat. She was walking with brisk steps too short on account of her narrow skirt; through the thin china silk the sunlight tingled like a hand stroking her back. In the heavy heat streets, stores, people in Sunday clothes, strawhats, sunshades, surfacecars, taxis, broke and crinkled brightly about her grazing her with sharp cutting glints as if she were walking through piles of metalshavings. She was groping continually through a tangle of gritty saw-edged brittle noise.

At Lincoln Square a girl rode slowly through the traffic on a white horse; chestnut hair hung down in even faky waves over the horse's chalky rump and over the giltedged saddlecloth where in green letters pointed with crimson, read DANDERINE. She had on a green Dolly Varden hat with a crimson plume; one hand in a white gauntlet nonchalantly jiggled at the reins, in the other wabbled a goldknobbed riding crop.

Ellen watched her pass; then she followed a smudge of green through a cross-street to the Park. A smell of trampled sunsinged grass came from boys playing baseball. All the shady benches were full of people. When she crossed the curving automobile road her sharp French heels sank into the asphalt. Two sailors were sprawling on a bench in the sun; one of them popped his lips as she passed, she could feel their seagreedy eyes cling stickily to her neck, her thighs, her ankles. She tried to keep her hips from swaying so much as she walked. The leaves were shriveled on the saplings along the path. South and east sunnyfaced buildings hemmed in the Park, to the west they were violet with shadow. Everything was itching sweaty dusty constrained by policemen and Sunday clothes. Why hadn't she taken the L? She was looking in the black eyes of a young man in a straw hat who was drawing up a red Stutz roadster to the curb. His eyes twinkled in hers, he jerked back his head smiling an upsidedown smile, pursing his lips so that they seemed to brush her cheek. He pulled the lever of the brake and opened the door with the other hand. She snapped her eyes away and walked on with her chin up. Two pigeons with metalgreen necks and feet of coral waddled out of her way. An old man was coaxing a squirrel to fish for peanuts in a paper bag.

All in green on a white stallion rode the Lady of the Lost Battalion. . . . Green, green, danderine . . . Godiva in the haughty mantle of her hair. . . .

General Sherman in gold interrupted her. She stopped a second to look at the Plaza that gleamed white as mother of pearl. . . . Yes this is Elaine Oglethorpe's apartment. . . . She climbed up onto a Washington Square bus. Sunday afternoon Fifth Avenue filed by rosily dustily jerkily. On the shady side there was an occasional man in a top hat and frock coat. Sunshades, summer dresses, straw hats were bright in the sun that glinted in squares on the upper windows of houses, lay in bright slivers on the hard paint of limousines and taxicabs. It smelled of gasoline and asphalt, of spearmint and talcumpowder and perfume from the couples that jiggled closer and closer together on the seats of the bus. In an occasional storewindow, paintings, maroon draperies, varnished antique chairs behind plate glass. The St. Regis. Sherry's. The man beside her wore spats and lemon gloves, a floorwalker probably. As they passed St. Patrick's she caught a whiff of incense through the tall doors open into gloom. Delmonico's. In front of her the young man's arm was stealing round the narrow gray flannel back of the girl beside him.

"Jez ole Joe had rotten luck, he had to marry her. He's only nineteen."

"I suppose you would think it was hard luck."

"Myrtle I didn't mean us."

"I bet you did. An anyways have you ever seen the girl?"

"I bet it aint his."

"What?"

"The kid."

"Billy how dreadfully you do talk."

Fortysecond Street. Union League Club. "It was a most amusing gathering . . . most amusing. . . . Everybody was there. For once the speeches were delightful, made me think of old times," croaked a cultivated voice behind her ear. The Waldorf. "Aint them flags swell Billy. . . . That funny one is cause the Siamese ambassador is staying there. I read about it in the paper this morning."

When thou and I my love shall come to part, Then shall I press an ineffable last kiss Upon your lips and go . . . heart, start, who art . . . Bliss, this, miss . . . When thou . . . When you and I my love . . .

Eighth Street. She got down from the bus and went into the basement of the Brevoort. George sat waiting with his back to the door snapping and unsnapping the lock of his briefcase. "Well Elaine it's about time you turned up. . . . There aren't many people I'd sit waiting three quarters of an hour for."

"George you mustn't scold me; I've been having the time of my life. I haven't had such a good time in years. I've had the whole day all to myself and I walked all the way down from 105th Street to Fiftyninth through the Park. It was full of the most comical people."

"You must be tired." His lean face where the bright eyes were caught in a web of fine wrinkles kept pressing forward into hers like the prow of a steamship.

"I suppose you've been at the office all day George."

"Yes I've been digging out some cases. I cant rely on anyone else to do even routine work thoroughly, so I have to do it myself."

"Do you know I had it all decided you'd say that."

"What?"

"About waiting three quarters of an hour."

"Oh you know altogether too much Elaine. . . . Have some pastries with your tea?"

"Oh but I dont know anything about anything, that's the trouble. . . . I think I'll take lemon please."

Glasses clinked about them; through blue cigarettesmoke faces hats beards wagged, repeated greenish in the mirrors.

"But my de-e-ar it's always the same old complex. It may be true of men but it says nothing in regard to women," droned a woman's voice from the next table. . . . "Your feminism rises into an insuperable barrier," trailed a man's husky meticulous tones. "What if I am an egoist? God knows I've suffered for it." "Fire that purifies, Charley. . . ." George was speaking, trying to catch her eye. "How's the famous Jojo?"

"Oh let's not talk about him."

"The less said about him the better eh?"

"Now George I wont have you sneer at Jojo, for better or worse he is my husband, till divorce do us part. . . . No I wont have you laugh. You're too crude and simple to understand him anyway. Jojo's a very complicated rather tragic person."

"For God's sake don't let's talk about husbands and wives. The important thing, little Elaine, is that you and I are sitting here together without anyone to bother us. . . . Look when are we going to see each other again, really see each other, really. . . ."

"We're not going to be too real about this, are we George?" She laughed softly into her cup.

"Oh but I have so many things to say to you. I want to ask you so many things."

She looked at him laughing, balancing a small cherry tartlet that had one bite out of it between a pink squaretipped finger and thumb. "Is that the way you act when you've got some miserable sinner on the witnessbox? I thought it was more like: Where were you on the night of February thirtyfirst?"

"But I'm dead serious, that's what you cant understand, or wont."

A young man stood at the table, swaying a little, looking down at them. "Hello Stan, where the dickens did you come from?" Baldwin looked up at him without smiling. "Look Mr. Baldwin I know it's awful rude, but may I sit down at your table a second. There's somebody looking for me who I just cant meet. O God that mirror! Still they'd never look for me if they saw you."

"Miss Oglethorpe this is Stanwood Emery, the son of the senior partner in our firm."

"Oh it's so wonderful to meet you Miss Oglethorpe. I saw you last night, but you didn't see me."

"Did you go to the show?"

"I almost jumped over the foots I thought you were so wonderful."

He had a ruddy brown skin, anxious eyes rather near the bridge of a sharp fragillycut nose, a big mouth never still, wavy brown hair that stood straight up. Ellen looked from one to the other inwardly giggling. They were all three stiffening in their chairs.

"I saw the danderine lady this afternoon," she said. "She impressed me enormously. Just my idea of a great lady on a white horse."

"With rings on her finger and bells on her toes, And she shall make mischief wherever she goes." Stan rattled it off quickly under his breath.

"Music, isn't it?" put in Ellen laughing. "I always say mischief."

"Well how's college?" asked Baldwin in a dry uncordial voice.

"I guess it's still there," said Stan blushing. "I wish they'd burn it down before I got back." He got to his feet. "You must excuse me Mr. Baldwin. . . . My intrusion was infernally rude." As he turned leaning towards Ellen she smelled his grainy whiskey breath. "Please forgive it, Miss Oglethorpe."

She found herself holding out her hand; a dry skinny hand squeezed it hard. He strode out with swinging steps bumping into a waiter as he went.

"I cant make out that infernal young puppy," burst out Baldwin. "Poor old Emery's heartbroken about it. He's darn clever and has a lot of personality and all that sort of thing, but all he does is drink and raise Cain. . . . I guess all he needs is to go to work and get a sense of values. Too much money's what's the matter with most of those college-boys. . . . Oh but Elaine thank God we're alone again. I have worked continuously all my life ever since I was fourteen. The time has come when I want to lay aside all that for a while. I want to live and travel and think and be happy. I cant stand the pace of downtown the way I used to. I want to learn to play, to ease off the tension. . . . That's where you come in."

"But I don't want to be the nigger on anybody's safety-valve." She laughed and let the lashes fall over her eyes.

"Let's go out to the country somewhere this evening. I've been stifling in the office all day. I hate Sunday anyway."

"But my rehearsal."

"You could be sick. I'll phone for a car."

"Golly there's Jojo. . . . Hello Jojo"; she waved her gloves above her head.

John Oglethorpe, his face powdered, his mouth arranged in a careful smile above his standup collar, advanced between the crowded tables, holding out his hand tightly squeezed into buff gloves with black stripes. "Heow deo you deo, my deah, this is indeed a surprise and a pleajah."

"You know each other, don't you? This is Mr. Baldwin."

"Forgive me if I intrude . . . er . . . upon a tête à tête."

"Nothing of the sort, sit down and we'll all have a high-ball. . . . I was just dying to see you really Jojo. . . . By the way if you havent anything else to do this evening you might slip in down front for a few minutes. I want to know what you think about my reading of the part. . . ."

"Certainly my deah, nothing could give me more pleajah."

His whole body tense George Baldwin leaned back with his hand clasped behind the back of his chair. "Waiter . . ." He broke his words off sharp like metal breaking. "Three Scotch highballs at once please."

Oglethorpe rested his chin on the silver ball of his cane. "Confidence, Mr. Baldwin," he began, "confidence between husband and wife is a very beautiful thing. Space and time have no effect on it. Were one of us to go to China for a thousand years it would not change our affection one tittle."

"You see George, what's the matter with Jojo is that he read too much Shakespeare in his youth. . . . But I've got to go or Merton will be bawling me out again. . . . Talk about industrial slavery. Jojo tell him about Equity."

Baldwin got to his feet. There was a slight flush on his cheekbones. "Wont you let me take you up to the theater," he said through clenched teeth.

"I never let anyone take me anywhere . . . And Jojo you must stay sober to see me act."

Fifth Avenue was pink and white under pink and white clouds in a fluttering wind that was fresh after the cloying talk and choke of tobaccosmoke and cocktails. She waved the taxistarter off merrily and smiled at him. Then she found a pair of anxious eyes looking into hers seriously out of a high-arched brown face.

"I waited round to see you come out. Cant I take you somewhere? I've got my Ford round the corner. . . . Please."

"But I'm just going up to the theater. I've got a rehearsal."

"All right do let me take you there."

She began putting a glove on thoughtfully. "All right, but it's an awful imposition on you."

"That's fine. It's right round here. . . . It was awfully rude of me to butt in that way, wasn't it? But that's another story. . . . Anyway I've met you. The Ford's name is Dingo, but that's another story too. . . ."

"Still it's nice to meet somebody humanly young. There's nobody humanly young round New York."

His face was scarlet when he leaned to crank the car. "Oh I'm too damn young."

The motor sputtered, started with a roar. He jumped round and cut off the gas with a long hand. "We'll probably get arrested; my muffler's loose and liable to drop off."

At Thirtyfourth Street they passed a girl riding slowly through the traffic on a white horse; chestnut hair hung down in even faky waves over the horse's chalky rump and over the giltedged saddlecloth where in green letters pointed with crimson read DANDERINE.

"Rings on her fingers," chanted Stan pressing his buzzer, "And bells on her toes, And she shall cure dandruff wherever it grows."

II. Longlegged Jack of the Isthmus

*N*oon on Union Square. Selling out. Must vacate.
WE HAVE MADE A TERRIBLE MISTAKE.
*Kneeling on the dusty asphalt little boys shine shoes
lowshoes tans buttonshoes oxfords. The sun shines like a
dandelion on the toe of each new-shined shoe. Right
this way buddy, mister miss maam at the back of the
store our new line of fancy tweeds highest value lowest
price . . . Gents, misses, ladies, cutrate . . . WE
HAVE MADE A TERRIBLE MISTAKE. Must
vacate.*

*Noon sunlight spirals dimly into the chopsuey joint.
Muted music spirals Hindustan. He eats fooyong, she
eats chowmein. They dance with their mouths full, slim
blue jumper squeezed to black slick suit, peroxide curls
against black slick hair.*

*Down Fourteenth Street, Glory Glory comes the
Army, striding lasses, Glory Glory four abreast, the rotund shining, navy blue, Salvation Army band.*

*Highest value, lowest price. Must vacate. WE
HAVE MADE A TERRIBLE MISTAKE. Must
vacate.*

From Liverpool, British steamer Raleigh, Captain Kettlewell; 933
bales, 881 boxes, 10 baskets, 8 packages fabrics: 57 boxes, 89 bales, 18
baskets cotton thread: 156 bales felt: 4 bales asbestos: 100 sacks
spools. . . .

Joe Harland stopped typing and looked up at the ceiling.
The tips of his fingers were sore. The office smelled stalely of
paste and manifests and men in shirtsleeves. Through the open
window he could see a piece of the dun wall of an airshaft and
a man with a green eyeshade staring vacantly out of a window.
The towheaded officeboy set a note on the corner of his desk:
Mr. Pollock will see you at 5:10. A hard lump caught in his
throat; he's going to fire me. His fingers started tapping again:

From Glasgow, Dutch steamer Delft, Captain Tromp; 200 bales,
123 boxes, 14 kegs. . . .

Joe Harland roamed about the Battery till he found an empty seat on a bench, then he let himself flop into it. The sun was drowning in tumultuous saffron steam behind Jersey. Well that's over. He sat a long while staring at the sunset like at a picture in a dentist's waiting room. Great whorls of smoke from a passing tug curled up black and scarlet against it. He sat staring at the sunset, waiting. That's eighteen dollars and fifty cents I had before, less six dollars for the room, one dollar and eighty-four cents for laundry, and four dollars and fifty cents I owe Charley, makes seven dollars and eighty-four cents, eleven dollars and eighty four cents, twelve dollars and thirty-four cents from eighteen dollars and fifty cents leaves me six dollars and sixteen cents, three days to find another job if I go without drinks. O God wont my luck ever turn; used to have good enough luck in the old days. His knees were trembling, there was a sick burning in the pit of his stomach.

A fine mess you've made of your life Joseph Harland. Forty-five and no friends and not a cent to bless yourself with.

The sail of a catboat was a crimson triangle when it luffed a few feet from the concrete walk. A young man and a young girl ducked together as the slender boom swung across. They both were bronzed with the sun and had yellow weather bleached hair. Joe Harland gnawed his lip to keep back the tears as the catboat shrank into the ruddy murk of the bay. By God I need a drink.

"Aint it a croime? Aint it a croime?" The man in the seat to the left of him began to say over and over again. Joe Harland turned his head; the man had a red puckered face and silver hair. He held the dramatic section of the paper taut between two grimy flippers. "Them young actresses all dressed naked like that . . . Why cant they let you alone."

"Dont you like to see their pictures in the papers?"

"Why cant they let you alone I say. . . . If you aint got no work and you aint got no money, what's the good of em I say?"

"Well lots of people like to see their pictures in the paper. Used to myself in the old days."

"Used to be work in the old days. . . . You aint got no job now?" he growled savagely. Joe Harland shook his head.

"Well what the hell? They ought to leave you alone oughtn't they? Wont be no jobs till snow shoveling begins."

"What'll you do till then?"

The old man didnt answer. He bent over the paper again screwing up his eyes and muttering. "All dressed naked, it's a croime I'm tellin yez."

Joe Harland got to his feet and walked away.

It was almost dark; his knees were stiff from sitting still so long. As he walked wearily he could feel his potbelly cramped by his tight belt. Poor old warhorse you need a couple of drinks to think about things. A mottled beery smell came out through swinging doors. Inside the barkeep's face was like a russet apple on a snug mahogany shelf.

"Gimme a shot of rye." The whiskey stung his throat hot and fragrant. Makes a man of me that does. Without drinking the chaser he walked over to the free lunch and ate a ham sandwich and an olive. "Let's have another rye Charley. That's the stuff to make a man of you. I been laying off it too much, that's what's the matter with me. You wouldnt think it to look at me now, would you friend, but they used to call me the Wizard of Wall Street which is only another illustration of the peculiar predominance of luck in human affairs. . . . Yes sir with pleasure. Well, here's health and long life and to hell with the jinx. . . . Hah makes a man of you . . . Well I suppose there's not one of you gentlemen here who hasnt at some time or other taken a plunger, and how many of you hasnt come back sadder and wiser. Another illustration of the peculiar predominance of luck in human affairs. But not so with me; gentlemen for ten years I played the market, for ten years I didn't have a ticker ribbon out of my hand day or night, and in ten years I only took a cropper three times, till the last time. Gentlemen I'm going to tell you a secret. I'm going to tell you a very important secret. . . . Charley give these very good friends of mine another round, my treat, and have a nip yourself. . . . My, that tickles her in the right place. . . . Gentlemen just another illustration of the peculiar predominance of luck in human affairs. Gentlemen the secret of my luck . . . this is exact I assure you; you can verify it yourselves in newspaper articles, magazines, speeches, lectures delivered in those days; a man, and a dirty blackguard he turned out to be eventually, even wrote a detective story about me called the Secret of Success, which you can find in the New York Public Library if you care to look the matter up. . . . The secret of my success was . . . and when you hear it you'll laugh among yourselves and say Joe Harland's drunk, Joe Harland's an old fool. . . . Yes you will. . . . For ten years I'm telling you I traded on margins, I bought outright, I covered on stocks I'd never even heard the name of and every time I cleaned up. I piled up money. I had four banks in the palm of my hand. I began eating my way into sugar and gutta percha, but in that I was before my time. . . . But you're getting nervous to know my secret, you think you could use it. . . . Well you couldnt. . . . It was a blue silk crocheted necktie that my mother made for me when I was a little boy. . . . Dont you laugh, God damn you. . . . No I'm not starting anything. Just another illustration of the peculiar predominance of luck. The day I chipped in with another fellow to spread a thousand dollars over some Louisville and Nashville on margin I wore that necktie. Soared twentyfive points in twentyfive minutes. That was the beginning. Then gradually I began to notice that the times I didnt wear that necktie were the times I lost money. It got so old and ragged I tried carrying it in my pocket. Didnt do any good. I had to wear it, do you understand? . . . The rest is the old old story gentlemen. . . . There was a girl, God damn her and I loved her. I wanted to show her that there was nothing in the world I wouldnt do for her so I gave it to her. I pretended it was a joke and laughed it off, ha ha ha. She said, Why it's no good, it's all worn out, and she threw it in the fire. . . . Only another illustration. . . . Friend you wouldn't set me up to another drink would you? I find myself unexpectedly out of funds this afternoon. . . . I thank you sir. . . . Ah that puts ginger in you again."

In the crammed subway car the messenger boy was pressed up against the back of a tall blond woman who smelled of Mary Garden. Elbows, packages, shoulders, buttocks, jiggled closer with every lurch of the screeching express. His sweaty Western Union cap was knocked onto the side of his head. If I could have a dame like dat, a dame like dat'd be wort havin de train stalled, de lights go out, de train wrecked. I could have her if I had de noive an de jack. As the train slowed up she fell against him, he closed his eyes, didnt breathe, his nose was mashed against her neck. The train stopped. He was carried in a rush of people out the door.

Dizzy he staggered up into the air and the blinking blocks of lights. Upper Broadway was full of people. Sailors lounged in twos and threes at the corner of Ninetysixth. He ate a ham and a leberwurst sandwich in a delicatessen store. The woman behind the counter had buttercolored hair like the girl in the subway but she was fatter and older. Still chewing the crust of the last sandwich he went up in the elevator to the Japanese Garden. He sat thinking a while with the flicker of the screen in his eyes. Jeze dey'll tink it funny to see a messengerboy up here in dis suit. I better get de hell outa here. I'll go deliver my telegrams.

He tightened his belt as he walked down the stairs. Then he slouched up Broadway to 105th Street and east towards Columbus Avenue, noting doors, fire escapes, windows, cornices, carefully as he went. Dis is de joint. The only lights were on the second floor. He rang the second floor bell. The doorcatch clicked. He ran up the stairs. A woman with weedy hair and a face red from leaning over the stove poked her head out.

"Telegram for Santiono."

"No such name here."

"Sorry maam I musta rung de wrong bell."

Door slammed in his nose. His sallow sagging face tightened up all of a sudden. He ran lightly on tiptoe up the stairs to the top landing then up the little ladder to a trapdoor. The bolt ground as he slid it back. He caught in his breath. Once on the cindergritty roof he let the trapdoor back softly into place. Chimneys stood up in alert ranks all about him, black against the glare from the streets. Crouching he stepped gingerly to the rear edge of the house, let himself down from the gutter to the fire escape. His foot grazed a flowerpot as he landed. Everything dark. Crawled through a window into a stuffy womansmelling room, slid a hand under the pillow of an unmade bed, along a bureau, spilled some facepowder, in tiny jerks pulled open the drawer, a watch, ran a pin into his finger, a brooch, something that crinkled in the back corner;

bills, a roll of bills. Getaway, no chances tonight. Down the fire escape to the next floor. No light. Another window open. Takin candy from a baby. Same room, smelling of dogs and incense, some kind of dope. He could see himself faintly, fumbling, in the glass of the bureau, put his hand into a pot of cold cream, wiped it off on his pants. Hell. Something fluffysoft shot with a yell from under his feet. He stood trembling in the middle of the narrow room. The little dog was yapping loud in a corner.

The room swung into light. A girl stood in the open door, pointing a revolver at him. There was a man behind her.

"What are you doing? Why it's a Western Union boy. . . ." The light was a coppery tangle about her hair, picked out her body under the red silk kimono. The young man was wiry and brown in his unbuttoned shirt. "Well what are you doing in that room?"

"Please maam it was hunger brought me to it, hunger an my poor ole muder starvin."

"Isnt that wonderful Stan? He's a burglar." She brandished the revolver. "Come on out in the hall."

"Yes miss anythin you say miss, but dont give me up to de bulls. Tink o de ole muder starvin her heart out."

"All right but if you took anything you must give it back."

"Honest I didn't have a chanct."

Stan flopped into a chair laughing and laughing. "Ellie you take the cake. . . . Wouldnt a thought you could do it."

"Well didnt I play this scene in stock all last summer? . . . Give up your gun."

"No miss I wouldn't carry no gun."

"Well I dont believe you but I guess I'll let you go."

"Gawd bless you miss."

"But you must make some money as a messengerboy."

"I was fired last week miss, it's only hunger made me take to it."

Stan got to his feet. "Let's give him a dollar an tell him to get the hell out of here."

When he was outside the door she held out the dollarbill to him.

"Jez you're white," he said choking. He grabbed the hand with the bill in it and kissed it; leaning over her hand kissing it wetly he caught a glimpse of her body under the arm in the drooping red silk sleeve. As he walked, still trembling, down the stairs, he looked back and saw the man and the girl standing side by side with their arms around each other watching him. His eyes were full of tears. He stuffed the dollarbill into his pocket.

Kid if you keep on bein a softie about women you're goin to find yourself in dat lil summer hotel up de river. . . . Pretty soft though. Whistling under his breath he walked to the L and took an uptown train. Now and then he put his hand over his back pocket to feel the roll of bills. He ran up to the third floor of an apartmenthouse that smelled of fried fish and coal gas, and rang three times at a grimy glass door. After a pause he knocked softly.

"Zat you Moike?" came faintly the whine of a woman's voice.

"No it's Nicky Schatz."

A sharpfaced woman with henna hair opened the door. She had on a fur coat over frilly lace underclothes.

"Howsa boy?"

"Jeze a swell dame caught me when I was tidying up a little job and whatjer tink she done?" He followed the woman, talking excitedly, into a dining room with peeling walls. On the table were used glasses and a bottle of Green River whiskey. "She gave me a dollar an tole me to be a good little boy."

"The hell she did?"

"Here's a watch."

"It's an Ingersoll, I dont call 'at a watch."

"Well set yer lamps on dis." He pulled out the roll of bills. "Aint dat a wad o lettuce? . . . Got in himmel, dey's tousands."

"Lemme see." She grabbed the bills out of his hand, her eyes popping. "Hay ye're cookoo kid." She threw the roll on the floor and wrung her hands with a swaying Jewish gesture. "Oyoy it's stage money. It's stage money ye simple saphead, you goddam . . ."

Giggling they sat side by side on the edge of the bed. Through the stuffy smell of the room full of little silky bits of clothing falling off chairs a fading freshness came from a bunch of yellow roses on the bureau. Their arms tightened round each other's shoulders; suddenly he wrenched himself away and leaned over her to kiss her mouth. "Some burglar," he said breathlessly.

"Stan . . ."

"Ellie."

"I thought it might be Jojo;" she managed to force a whisper through a tight throat. "It'll be just like him to come sneaking around."

"Ellie I don't understand how you can live with him among all these people. You're so lovely. I just dont see you in all this."

"It was easy enough before I met you. . . . And honestly Jojo's all right. He's just a peculiar very unhappy person."

"But you're out of another world old kid. . . . You ought to live on top of the Woolworth Building in an apartment made of cutglass and cherry blossoms."

"Stan your back's brown all the way down."

"That's swimming."

"So soon?"

"I guess most of it's left over from last summer."

"You're the fortunate youth all right. I never learned how to swim properly."

"I'll teach you. . . . Look next Sunday bright and early we'll hop into Dingo and go down to Long Beach. Way down at the end there's never anybody. . . . You dont even have to wear a bathingsuit."

"I like the way you're so lean and hard Stan. . . . Jojo's white and flabby almost like a woman."

"For crissake don't talk about him now."

Stan stood with his legs apart buttoning his shirt. "Look Ellie let's beat it out an have a drink. . . . God I'd hate to run into somebody now an have to talk lies to 'em. . . . I bet I'd crown 'em with a chair."

"We've got time. Nobody ever comes home here before twelve. . . . I'm just here myself because I've got a sick headache."

"Ellie, d'you like your sick headache?"

"I'm crazy about it Stan."

"I guess that Western Union burglar knew that. . . . Gosh. . . . Burglary, adultery, sneaking down fireescapes, cattreading along gutters. Judas it's a great life."

Ellen gripped his hand hard as they came down the stairs stepping together. In front of the letterboxes in the shabby hallway he grabbed her suddenly by the shoulders and pressed her head back and kissed her. Hardly breathing they floated down the street toward Broadway. He had his hand under her arm, she squeezed it tight against her ribs with her elbow. Aloof, as if looking through thick glass into an aquarium, she watched faces, fruit in storewindows, cans of vegetables, jars of olives, redhotpokerplants in a florist's, newspapers, electric signs drifting by. When they passed cross-streets a puff of air came in her face off the river. Sudden jetbright glances of eyes under straw hats, attitudes of chins, thin lips, pouting lips, Cupid's bows, hungry shadow under cheekbones, faces of girls and young men nuzzled fluttering against her like moths as she walked with her stride even to his through the tingling yellow night.

Somewhere they sat down at a table. An orchestra throbbed. "No Stan I cant drink anything. . . . You go ahead."

"But Ellie, arent you feeling swell like I am?"

"Sweller. . . . I just couldnt stand feeling any better. . . . I couldnt keep my mind on a glass long enough to drink it." She winced under the brightness of his eyes.

Stan was bubbling drunk. "I wish earth had thy body as fruit to eat," he kept repeating. Ellen was all the time twisting about bits of rubbery cold Welsh rabbit with her fork. She had started to drop with a lurching drop like a rollercoaster's into shuddering pits of misery. In a square place in the middle of the floor four couples were dancing the tango. She got to her feet.

"Stan I'm going home. I've got to get up early and rehearse all day. Call me up at twelve at the theater."

He nodded and poured himself another highball. She stood behind his chair a second looking down at his long head of close ruffled hair. He was spouting verses softly to himself. "Saw the white implacable Aphrodite, damn fine, Saw the hair unbound and the feet unsandaled, Jiminy. . . . Shine as fire of sunset on western waters. Saw the reluctant . . . goddam fine sapphics."

Once out on Broadway again she felt very merry. She stood in the middle of the street waiting for the uptown car. An occasional taxi whizzed by her. From the river on the warm wind came the long moan of a steamboat whistle. In the pit inside her thousands of gnomes were building tall brittle glittering towers. The car swooped ringing along the rails, stopped. As she climbed in she remembered swooningly the smell of Stan's body sweating in her arms. She let herself drop into a seat, biting her lips to keep from crying out. God it's terrible to be in love. Opposite two men with chinless bluefish faces were talking hilariously, slapping fat knees.

"I'll tell yer Jim it's Irene Castle that makes the hit wid me. . . . To see her dance the onestep juss makes me hear angels hummin."

"Naw she's too skinny."

"But she's made the biggest hit ever been made on Broadway."

Ellen got off the car and walked east along the desolate empty pavements of 105th Street. A fetor of mattresses and sleep seeped out from the blocks of narrow-windowed houses. Along the gutters garbagecans stank sourly. In the shadow of a doorway a man and girl swayed tightly clamped in each other's arms. Saying good night. Ellen smiled happily. Greatest hit on Broadway. The words were an elevator carrying her up dizzily, up into some stately height where electric light signs crackled scarlet and gold and green, where were bright roofgardens that smelled of orchids, and the slow throb of a tango danced in a goldgreen dress with Stan while handclapping of millions beat in gusts like a hailstorm about them. Greatest hit on Broadway.

She was walking up the scaling white stairs. Before the door marked Sunderland a feeling of sick disgust suddenly choked her. She stood a long time her heart pounding with the key poised before the lock. Then with a jerk she pushed the key in the lock and opened the door.

"Strange fish, Jimmy, strange fish." Herf and Ruth Prynne sat giggling over plates of paté in the innermost corner of a clattery lowceilinged restaurant. "All the ham actors in the world seem to eat here."

"All the ham actors in the world live up at Mrs. Sunderland's."

"What's the latest news from the Balkans?"

"Balkans is right . . ."

Beyond Ruth's black straw hat with red poppies round the crown Jimmy looked at the packed tables where faces decomposed into a graygreen blur. Two sallow hawkfaced waiters elbowed their way through the seesawing chatter of talk. Ruth was looking at him with dilated laughing eyes while she bit at a stalk of celery.

"Whee I feel so drunk," she was spluttering. "It went straight to my head. . . . Isnt it terrible?"

"Well what were these shocking goingson at 105th Street?"

"O you missed it. It was a shriek. . . . Everybody was out in the hall, Mrs. Sunderland with her hair in curlpapers, and Cassie was crying and Tony Hunter was standing in his door in pink pyjamas. . . ."

"Who's he?"

"Just a juvenile. . . . But Jimmy I must have told you about Tony Hunter. Peculiar poissons Jimmy, peculiar poissons."

Jimmy felt himself blushing, he bent over his plate. "Oh is that's what's his trouble?" he said stiffly.

"Now you're shocked, Jimmy; admit that you're shocked."

"No I'm not; go ahead, spill the dirt."

"Oh Jimmy you're such a shriek. . . . Well Cassie was sobbing and the little dog was barking, and the invisible Costello was yelling Police and fainting into the arms of an unknown man in a dress suit. And Jojo was brandishing a revolver, a little nickel one, may have been a waterpistol for all I know. . . . The only person who looked in their right senses was Elaine Olgethorpe. . . . You know the titianhaired vision that so impressed your infant mind."

"Honestly Ruth my infant mind wasnt as impressed as all that."

"Well at last the Ogle got tired of his big scene and cried out in ringing tones, Disarm me or I shall kill this woman. And Tony Hunter grabbed the pistol and took it into his room. Then Elaine Oglethorpe made a little bow as if she were taking a curtaincall, said Well goodnight everybody, and ducked into her room cool as a cucumber. . . . Can you picture it?" Ruth suddenly lowered her voice. "But everybody in the restaurant is listening to us. . . . And really I think its very disgusting. But the worst is yet to come. After the Ogle had banged on the door a couple of times and not gotten any answer he went up to Tony and rolling his eyes like Forbes Robertson in Hamlet put his arm round him and said Tony can a broken man crave asylum in your room for the night. . . . Honestly I was just so shocked."

"Is Oglethorpe that way too?"

Ruth nodded several times.

"Then why did she marry him?"

"Why that girl'd marry a trolleycar if she thought she could get anything by it."

"Ruth honestly I think you've got the whole thing sized up wrong."

"Jimmy you're too innocent to live. But let me finish the tragic tale. . . . After those two had disappeared and locked the door behind them the most awful powwow you've ever imagined went on in the hall. Of course Cassie had been having hysterics all along just to add to the excitement. When I came back from getting her some sweet spirits of ammonia in the bathroom I found the court in session. It was a shriek. Miss Costello wanted the Oglethorpes thrown out at dawn and said she'd leave if they didn't and Mrs. Sunderland kept moaning that in thirty years of theatrical experience she'd never seen a scene like that, and the man in the dress suit who was Benjamin Arden . . . you know he played a character part in Honeysuckle Jim . . . said he thought people like Tony Hunter ought to be in jail. When I went to bed it was still going on. Do you wonder that I slept late after all that and kept you waiting, poor child, an hour in the Times Drug Store?"

Joe Harland stood in his hall bedroom with his hands in his pockets staring at the picture of The Stag at Bay that hung crooked in the middle of the verdegris wall that hemmed in the shaky iron bed. His clawcold fingers moved restlessly in the bottoms of his trousers pockets. He was talking aloud in a low even voice: "Oh, it's all luck you know, but that's the last time I try the Merivales. Emily'd have given it to me if it hadn't been for that damned old tightwad. Got a soft spot in her heart Emily has. But none of em seem to realize that these things aren't always a man's own fault. It's luck that's all it is, and Lord knows they used to eat out of my hand in the old days." His rising voice grated on his ears. He pressed his lips together. You're getting batty old man. He stepped back and forth in the narrow space between the bed and the wall. Three steps. Three steps. He went to the washstand and drank out of the pitcher. The water tasted of rank wood and sloppails. He spat the last mouthful back. I need a good tenderloin steak not water. He pounded his clenched fists together. I got to do something.

He put on his overcoat to hide the rip in the seat of his trousers. The frayed sleeves tickled his wrists. The dark stairs creaked. He was so weak he kept grabbing the rail for fear of falling. The old woman pounced out of a door on him in the lower hall. The rat had squirmed sideways on her head as if trying to escape from under the thin gray pompadour.

"Meester Harland how about you pay me tree veeks rent?"

"I'm just on my way out to cash a check now, Mrs. Budkowitz. You've been so kind about this little matter. . . . And perhaps it will interest you to know that I have the promise, no I may say the certainty of a very good position beginning Monday."

"I vait tree veeks . . . I not vait any more."

"But my dear lady I assure you upon my honor as a gentleman . . ."

Mrs. Budkowitz began to jerk her shoulders about. Her voice rose thin and wailing like the sound of a peanut wagon. "You pay me tat fifteen dollar or I rent te room to somebody else."

"I'll pay you this very evening."

"Vat time?"

"Six o'clock."

"Allright. Plis you give me key."

"But I cant do that. Suppose I was late?"

"Tat's vy I vant te key. I'm trough vit vaiting."

"All right take the key. . . . . I hope you understand that after this insulting behavior it will be impossible for me to remain longer under your roof."

Mrs. Budkowitz laughed hoarsely. "Allright ven you pay me fifteen dollar you can take avay your grip." He put the two keys tied together with string into her gray hand and slammed the door and strode down the street.

At the corner of Third Avenue he stopped and stood shivering in the hot afternoon sunlight, sweat running down behind his ears. He was too weak to swear. Jagged oblongs of harsh sound broke one after another over his head as an elevated passed over. Trucks grated by along the avenue raising a dust that smelled of gasoline and trampled horsedung. The dead air stank of stores and lunchrooms. He began walking slowly uptown towards Fourteenth Street. At a corner a crinkly warm smell of cigars stopped him like a hand on his shoulder. He stood a while looking in the little shop watching the slim stained fingers of the cigarroller shuffle the brittle outside leaves of tobacco. Remembering Romeo and Juliet Arguelles Morales he sniffed deeply. The slick tearing of tinfoil, the careful slipping off of the band, the tiny ivory penknife for the end that slit delicately as flesh, the smell of the wax match, the long inhaling of bitter crinkled deep sweet smoke. And now sir about this little matter of the new Northern Pacific bond issue. . . . He clenched his fists in the clammy pockets of his raincoat. Take my key would she the old harridan? I'll show her, damn it. Joe Harland may be down and out but he's got his pride yet.

He walked west along Fourteenth and without stopping to think and lose his nerve went down into a small basement stationery store, strode through unsteadily to the back, and stood swaying in the doorway of a little office where sat at a rolltop desk a blueeyed baldheaded fat man.

"Hello Felsius," croaked Harland.

The fat man got to his feet bewildered. "God it aint Mr. Harland is it?"

"Joe Harland himself Felsius . . . er somewhat the worse for wear." A titter died in his throat.

"Well I'll be . . . Sit right down Mr. Harland."

"Thank you Felsius. . . . Felsius I'm down and out."

"It must be five years since I've seen you Mr. Harland."

"A rotten five years it's been for me. . . . I suppose its all luck. My luck wont ever change on this earth again. Remember when I'd come in from romping with the bulls and raise hell round the office? A pretty good bonus I gave the office force that Christmas."

"Indeed it was Mr. Harland."

"Must be a dull life storekeeping after the Street."

"More to my taste Mr. Harland, nobody to boss me here."

"And how's the wife and kids?"

"Fine, fine; the oldest boy's just out of highschool."

"That the one you named for me?"

Felsius nodded. His fingers fat as sausages were tapping uneasily on the edge of the desk.

"I remember I thought I'd do something for that kid someday. It's a funny world." Harland laughed feebly. He felt a shuddery blackness stealing up behind his head. He clenched his hands round his knee and contracted the muscles of his arms. "You see Felsius, it's this way. . . . I find myself for the moment in a rather embarrassing situation financially. . . . You know how those things are." Felsius was staring straight ahead of him into the desk. Beads of sweat were starting out of his bald head. "We all have our spell of bad luck dont we? I want to float a very small loan for a few days, just a few dollars, say twentyfive until certain combinations . . ."

"Mr. Harland I cant do it." Felsius got to his feet. "I'm sorry but principles is principles. . . . I've never borrowed or lent a cent in my life. I'm sure you understand that. . . ."

"All right, dont say any more." Harland got meekly to his feet. "Let me have a quarter. . . . I'm not so young as I was and I haven't eaten for two days," he mumbled, looking down at his cracked shoes. He put out his hand to steady himself by the desk.

Felsius moved back against the wall as if to ward off a blow. He held out a fiftycent piece on thick trembling fingers. Harland took it, turned without a word and stumbled out through the shop. Felsius pulled a violet bordered handkerchief out of his pocket, mopped his brow and turned to his letters again.

We take the liberty of calling the trade's attention to four new superfine Mullen products that we feel the greatest confidence in recommending to our customers as a fresh and absolutely unparalleled departure in the papermanufacturer's art . . .

They came out of the movie blinking into bright pools of electric glare. Cassie watched him stand with his feet apart and eyes absorbed lighting a cigar. McAvoy was a stocky man with a beefy neck; he wore a single-button coat, a checked vest and a dogshead pin in his brocade necktie.

"That was a rotton show or I'm a Dutchman," he was growling.

"But I loved the twavel pictures, Morris, those Swiss peasants dancing; I felt I was wight there."

"Damn hot in there. . . . I'd like a drink."

"Now Morris you promised," she whined.

"Oh I just meant sodawater, dont get nervous." "Oh that'd be lovely. I'd just love a soda."

"Then we'll go for a walk in the Park."

She let the lashes fall over her eyes. "Allwight Morris," she whispered without looking at him. She put her hand a little tremulously through his arm.

"If only I wasn't so goddam broke."

"I dont care Morris."

"I do by God."

At Columbus Circle they went into a drugstore. Girls in green, violet, pink summer dresses, young men in straw hats were three deep along the sodafountain. She stood back and admiringly watched him shove his way through. A man was leaning across the table behind her talking to a girl; their faces were hidden by their hatbrims.

"You juss tie that bull outside, I said to him, then I resigned."

"You mean you were fired."

"No honest I resigned before he had a chance. . . . He's a stinker d'you know it? I wont take no more of his lip. When I was walkin outa the office he called after me. . . . Young man lemme tell ye sumpen. You wont never make good till you learn who's boss around this town, till you learn that it aint you."

Morris was holding out a vanilla icecream soda to her. "Dreamin' again Cassie; anybody'd think you was a snowbird." Smiling brighteyed, she took the soda; he was drinking coca-cola. "Thank you," she said. She sucked with pouting lips at a spoonful of icecream. "Ou Morris it's delicious."

The path between round splashes of arclights ducked into darkness. Through slant lights and nudging shadows came a smell of dusty leaves and trampled grass and occasionally a rift of cool fragrance from damp earth under shrubberies.

"Oh I love it in the Park," chanted Cassie. She stifled a belch. "D'you know Morris I oughtnt to have eaten that icecweam. It always gives me gas."

Morris said nothing. He put his arm round her and held her tight to him so that his thigh rubbed against hers as they walked. "Well Pierpont Morgan is dead. . . . I wish he'd left me a couple of million."

"Oh Morris wouldn't it be wonderful? Where'd we live? On Central Park South." They stood looking back at the glow of electric signs that came from Columbus Circle. To the left they could see curtained lights in the windows of a whitefaced apartmenthouse. He looked stealthily to the right and left and then kissed her. She twisted her mouth out from under his.

"Dont. . . . Somebody might see us," she whispered breathless. Inside something like a dynamo was whirring, whirring. "Morris I've been saving it up to tell you. I think Goldweiser's going to give me a specialty bit in his next show. He's stagemanager of the second woad company and he's got a lot of pull up at the office. He saw me dance yesterday."

"What did he say?"

"He said he'd fix it up for me to see the big boss Monday. . . . Oh but Morris it's not the sort of thing I want to do, it's so vulgar and howid. . . . I want to do such beautiful things. I feel I've got it in me, something without a name fluttering inside, a bird of beautiful plumage in a howid iron cage."

"That's the trouble with you, you'll never make good, you're too upstage." She looked up at him with streaming eyes that glistened in the white powdery light of an arclamp.

"Oh don't cry for God's sake. I didnt mean anythin."

"I'm not upstage with you Morris, am I?" She sniffed and wiped her eyes.

"You are kinda, that's what makes me sore. I like my little girl to pet me an love me up a little. Hell Cassie life aint all beer an sourkraut." As they walked tightly pressed one to another they felt rock under their feet. They were on a little hill of granite outcrop with shrubbery all round. The lights from the buildings that hemmed in the end of the Park shone in their faces. They stood apart holding each other's hands.

"Take that redhaired girl up at 105th Street. . . . I bet she wouldnt be upstage when she was alone with a feller."

"She's a dweadful woman, she dont care what kind of a wep she has. . . . Oh I think you're howid." She began to cry again.

He pulled her to him roughly, pressed her to him hard with his spread hands on her back. She felt her legs tremble and go weak. She was falling through colored shafts of faintness. His mouth wouldnt let her catch her breath.

"Look out," he whispered pulling himself away from her. They walked on unsteadily down the path through the shrubbery. "I guess it aint."

"What Morris?"

"A cop. God it's hell not havin anywhere to go. Cant we go to your room?"

"But Morris they'll all see us."

"Who cares? They all do it in that house."

"Oh I hate you when you talk that way. . . . Weal love is all pure and lovely. . . . Morris you don't love me."

"Quit pickin on me cant you Cassie for a minute. . . ? Goddam it's hell to be broke."

They sat down on a bench in the light. Behind them automobiles slithered with a constant hissing scuttle in two streams along the roadway. She put her hand on his knee and he covered it with his big stubby hand.

"Morris I feel that we are going to be very happy from now on, I feel it. You're going to get a fine job, I'm sure you are."

"I aint so sure. . . . I'm not so young as I was Cassie. I aint got any time to lose."

"Why you're terribly young, you're only thirtyfive Morris.

. . . And I think that something wonderful is going to happen. I'm going to get a chance to dance."

"Why you ought to make more than that redhaired girl."

"Elaine Oglethorpe. . . . She doesnt make so much. But I'm different from her. I dont care about money; I want to live for my dancing."

"I want money. Once you got money you can do what you like."

"But Morris dont you believe that you can do anything if you just want to hard enough? I believe that." He edged his free arm round her waist. Gradually she let her head fall on his shoulder. "Oh I dont care," she whispered with dry lips. Behind them limousines, roadsters, touringcars, sedans, slithered along the roadway with snaky glint of lights running in two smooth continuous streams.

The brown serge smelled of mothballs as she folded it. She stooped to lay it in the trunk; a layer of tissuepaper below rustled when she smoothed the wrinkles with her hand. The first violet morning light outside the window was making the electriclight bulb grow red like a sleepless eye. Ellen straightened herself suddenly and stood stiff with her arms at her sides, her face flushed pink. "It's just too low," she said. She spread a towel over the dresses and piled brushes, a handmirror, slippers, chemises, boxes of powder in pellmell on top of them. Then she slammed down the lid of the trunk, locked it and put the key in her flat alligatorskin purse. She stood looking dazedly about the room sucking a broken fingernail. Yellow sunlight was obliquely drenching the chimneypots and cornices of the houses across the street. She found herself staring at the white E.T.O. at the end of her trunk. "It's all too terribly disgustingly low," she said again. Then she grabbed a nailfile off the bureau and scratched out the O. "Whee," she whispered and snapped her fingers. After she had put on a little bucketshaped black hat and a veil, so that people wouldn't see she'd been crying, she piled a lot of books, *Youth's Encounter, Thus Spoke Zarathustra, The Golden Ass, Imaginary Conversations, Aphrodite, Chansons de Bilitis* and the *Oxford Book of French Verse* in a silk shawl and tied them together.

There was a faint tapping at the door. "Who's that," she whispered.

"It just me," came a tearful voice.

Ellen unlocked the door. "Why Cassie what's the matter?" Cassie rubbed her wet face in the hollow of Ellen's neck. "Oh Cassie you're gumming my veil. . . . What on earth's the matter?"

"I've been up all night thinking how unhappy you must be."

"But Cassie I've never been happier in my life."

"Aren't men dweadful?"

"No. . . . They are much nicer than women anyway."

"Elaine I've got to tell you something. I know you dont care anything about me but I'm going to tell you all the same."

"Of course I care about you Cassie. . . . Dont be silly. But I'm busy now. . . . Why dont you go back to bed and tell me later?"

"I've got to tell you now." Ellen sat down on her trunk resignedly. "Elaine I've bwoken it off with Morris. . . . Isn't it tewible?" Cassie wiped her eyes on the sleeve of her lavender dressinggown and sat down beside Ellen on the trunk.

"Look dear," said Ellen gently. "Suppose you wait just a second, I'm going to telephone for a taxi. I want to make a getaway before Jojo's up. I'm sick of big scenes." The hall smelled stuffily of sleep and massagecream. Ellen talked very low into the receiver. The gruff man's voice at the garage growled pleasantly in her ears. "Sure right away miss." She tiptoed springily back into the room and closed the door.

"I thought he loved me, honestly I did Elaine. Oh men are so dweadful. Morris was angwy because I wouldn't live with him. I think it would be wicked. I'd work my fingers to the bone for him, he knows that. Havent I been doing it two years? He said he couldnt go on unless he had me weally, you know what he meant, and I said our love was so beautiful it could go on for years and years. I could love him for a lifetime without even kissing him. Dont you think love should be pure? And then he made fun of my dancing and said I was Chalif's mistwess and just kidding him along and we quaweled dweadfully and he called me dweadful names and went away and said he'd never come back."

"Dont worry about that Cassie, he'll come back all right."

"No but you're so material, Elaine. I mean spiwitually our union is bwoken forever. Cant you see there was this beautiful divine spiwitual thing between us and it's bwoken." She began to sob again with her face pressed into Ellen's shoulder.

"But Cassie I dont see what fun you get out of it all?"

"Oh you dont understand. You're too young. I was like you at first except that I wasnt mawied and didnt wun awound with men. But now I want spiwitual beauty. I want to get it through my dancing and my life, I want beauty everywhere and I thought Morris wanted it."

"But Morris evidently did."

"Oh Elaine you're howid, and I love you so much."

Ellen got to her feet. "I'm going to run downstairs so that the taximan wont ring the bell."

"But you cant go like this."

"You just watch me." Ellen gathered up the bundle of books in one hand and in the other carried the black leather dressingcase. "Look Cassie will you be a dear and show him the trunk when he comes up to get it. . . . And one other thing, when Stan Emery calls up tell him to call me at the Brevoort or at the Lafayette. Thank goodness I didnt deposit my money last week. . . . And Cassie if you find any little odds and ends of mine around you just keep em. . . . Goodby." She lifted her veil and kissed Cassie quickly on the cheeks.

"Oh how can you be so bwave as to go away all alone like this. . . . You'll let Wuth and me come down to see you wont you? We're so fond of you. Oh Elaine you're going to have a wonderful career, I know you are."

"And promise not to tell Jojo where I am. . . . He'll find out soon enough anyway. . . . I'll call him up in a week."

She found the taxidriver in the hall looking at the names above the pushbuttons. He went up to fetch her trunk. She settled herself happily on the dusty buff seat of the taxi, taking deep breaths of the riversmelling morning air. The taxidriver smiled roundly at her when he had let the trunk slide off his back onto the dashboard.

"Pretty heavy, miss."

"It's a shame you had to carry it all alone."

"Oh I kin carry heavier'n 'at."

"I want to go to the Hotel Brevoort, Fifth Avenue at about Eighth Street."

When he leaned to crank the car the man pushed his hat back on his head letting ruddy curly hair out over his eyes. "All right I'll take you anywhere you like," he said as he hopped into his seat in the jiggling car. When they turned down into the very empty sunlight of Broadway a feeling of happiness began to sizzle and soar like rockets inside her. The air beat fresh, thrilling in her face. The taxidriver talked back at her through the open window.

"I thought yous was catchin a train to go away somewhere, miss."

"Well I am going away somewhere."

"It'd be a foine day to be goin away somewhere."

"I'm going away from my husband." The words popped out of her mouth before she could stop them.

"Did he trow you out?"

"No I cant say he did that," she said laughing.

"My wife trun me out tree weeks ago."

"How was that?"

"Locked de door when I came home one night an wouldnt let me in. She'd had the lock changed when I was out workin."

"That's a funny thing to do."

"She says I git slopped too often. I aint goin back to her an I aint goin to support her no more. . . . She can put me in jail if she likes. I'm troo. I'm gettin an apartment on Twenty-second Avenoo wid another feller an we're goin to git a pianer an live quiet an lay offen the skoits."

"Matrimony isnt much is it?"

"You said it. What leads up to it's all right, but gettin married is loike de mornin after."

Fifth Avenue was white and empty and swept by a sparkling wind. The trees in Madison Square were unexpectedly bright green like ferns in a dun room. At the Brevoort a sleepy French nightporter carried her baggage. In the low white-painted room the sunlight drowsed on a faded crimson armchair. Ellen ran about the room like a small child kicking her heels and clapping her hands. With pursed lips and tilted head she arranged her toilet things on the bureau. Then she hung her yellow nightgown on a chair and undressed, caught sight of herself in the mirror, stood naked looking at herself with her hands on her tiny firm appleshaped breasts.

She pulled on her nightgown and went to the phone. "Please send up a pot of chocolate and rolls to 108 . . . as soon as you can please." Then she got into bed. She lay laughing with her legs stretched wide in the cool slippery sheets.

Hairpins were sticking into her head. She sat up and pulled them all out and shook the heavy coil of her hair down about her shoulders. She drew her knees up to her chin and sat thinking. From the street she could hear the occasional rumble of a truck. In the kitchens below her room a sound of clattering had begun. From all around came a growing rumble of traffic beginning. She felt hungry and alone. The bed was a raft on which she was marooned alone, always alone, afloat on a growling ocean. A shudder went down her spine. She drew her knees up closer to her chin.

III. Nine Days' Wonder

The sun's moved to Jersey, the sun's behind Hoboken. Covers are clicking on typewriters, rolltop desks are closing; elevators go up empty, come down jammed. It's ebbtide in the downtown district, flood in Flatbush, Woodlawn, Dyckman Street, Sheepshead Bay, New Lots Avenue, Canarsie.

Pink sheets, green sheets, gray sheets, FULL MARKET REPORTS, FINALS ON HAVRE DE GRACE. Print squirms among the shopworn officeworn sagging faces, sore fingertips, aching insteps, strongarm men cram into subway expresses. SENATORS 8, GIANTS 2, DIVA RECOVERS PEARLS, $800,000 ROBBERY.

It's ebbtide on Wall Street, floodtide in the Bronx.
The sun's gone down in Jersey.

"Godamighty," shouted Phil Sandbourne and pounded with his fist on the desk, "I don't think so. . . . A man's morals arent anybody's business. It's his work that counts."

"Well?"

"Well I think Stanford White has done more for the city of New York than any other man living. Nobody knew there was such a thing as architecture before he came. . . . And to have this Thaw shoot him down in cold blood and then get away with it. . . . By gad if the people of this town had the spirit of guineapigs they'd——"

"Phil you're getting all excited over nothing." The other man took his cigar out of his mouth and leaned back in his swivel chair and yawned.

"Oh hell I want a vacation. Golly it'll be good to get out in those old Maine woods again."

"What with Jew lawyers and Irish judges . . ." spluttered Phil.

"Aw pull the chain, old man."

"A fine specimen of a public-spirited citizen you are Hartly."

Hartly laughed and rubbed the palm of his hand over his bald head. "Oh that stuff's all right in winter, but I cant go it

628

in summer. . . . Hell all I live for is three weeks' vacation
anyway. What do I care if all the architects in New York get
bumped off as long as it dont raise the price of commutation
to New Rochelle. . . . Let's go eat." As they went down in
the elevator Phil went on talking: "The only other man I ever
knew who was really a born in the bone architect was ole
Specker, the feller I worked for when I first came north, a fine
old Dane he was too. Poor devil died o cancer two years ago.
Man, he was an architect. I got a set of plans and specifica-
tions home for what he called a communal building. . . .
Seventyfive stories high stepped back in terraces with a sort of
hanging garden on every floor, hotels, theaters, Turkish
baths, swimming pools, department stores, heating plant, re-
frigerating and market space all in the same buildin."

"Did he eat coke?"

"No siree he didnt."

They were walking east along Thirtyfourth Street, sparse of
people in the sultry midday. "Gad," burst out Phil Sandbourne, suddenly. "The girls in this town get prettier every
year." "Like these new fashions, do you?"

"Sure. All I wish is that I was gettin younger every year instead of older."

"Yes about all us old fellers can do is watch em go past."

"That's fortunate for us or we'd have our wives out after us
with bloodhounds. . . . Man when I think of those
mighthavebeens!"

As they crossed Fifth Avenue Phil caught sight of a girl in
a taxicab. From under the black brim of a little hat with a red
cockade in it two gray eyes flash green black into his. He
swallowed his breath. The traffic roars dwindled into distance.
She shant take her eyes away. Two steps and open the door
and sit beside her, beside her slenderness perched like a bird
on the seat. Driver drive to beat hell. Her lips are pouting towards him, her eyes flutter gray caught birds. "Hay look
out. . ." A pouncing iron rumble crashes down on him from
behind. Fifth Avenue spins in red blue purple spirals. O
Kerist. "That's all right, let me be. I'll get up myself in a
minute." "Move along there. Git back there." Braying voices,
blue pillars of policemen. His back, his legs are all warm
gummy with blood. Fifth Avenue throbs with loudening pain.

A little bell jinglejangling nearer. As they lift him into the ambulance Fifth Avenue shrieks to throttling agony and bursts. He cranes his neck to see her, weakly, like a terrapin on its back; didnt my eyes snap steel traps on her? He finds himself whimpering. She might have stayed to see if I was killed. The jinglejangling bell dwindles fainter, fainter into the night.

The burglaralarm across the street had rung on steadily. Jimmy's sleep had been strung on it in hard knobs like beads on a string. Knocking woke him. He sat up in bed with a lurch and found Stan Emery, his face gray with dust, his hands in the pockets of a red leather coat, standing at the foot of the bed. He was laughing swaying back and forth on the balls of his feet.

"Gosh what time is it?" Jimmy sat up in bed digging his knuckles into his eyes. He yawned and looked about with bitter dislike, at the wallpaper the dead green of Poland Water bottles, at the split green shade that let in a long trickle of sunlight, at the marble fireplace blocked up by an enameled tin plate painted with scaly roses, at the frayed blue bathrobe on the foot of the bed, at the mashed cigarettebutts in the mauve glass ashtray.

Stan's face was red and brown and laughing under the chalky mask of dust. "Eleven thirty," he was saying.

"Let's see that's six hours and a half. I guess that'll do. But Stan what the hell are you doing here?"

"You havent got a little nip of liquor anywhere have you Herf? Dingo and I are extraordinarily thirsty. We came all the way from Boston and only stopped once for gas and water. I havent been to bed for two days. I want to see if I can last out the week."

"Kerist I wish I could last out the week in bed."

"What you need's a job on a newspaper to keep you busy Herfy."

"What's going to happen to you Stan . . ." Jimmy twisted himself round so that he was sitting on the edge of the bed ". . . is that you're going to wake up one morning and find yourself on a marble slab at the morgue."

The bathroom smelled of other people's toothpaste and of chloride disinfectant. The bathmat was wet and Jimmy folded it into a small square before he stepped gingerly out of his slippers. The cold water set the blood jolting through him. He ducked his head under and jumped out and stood shaking himself like a dog, the water streaming into his eyes and ears. Then he put on his bathrobe and lathered his face.

> Flow river flow
> Down to the sea,

he hummed off key as he scraped his chin with the safety-razor. Mr. Grover I'm afraid I'm going to have to give up the job after next week. Yes I'm going abroad; I'm going to do foreign correspondent work for the A.P. To Mexico for the U.P. To Jericho more likely, Halifax Correspondent of the Mudturtle Gazette. *It was Christmas in the harem and the eunuchs all were there.*

> . . . from the banks of the Seine
> To the banks of the Saskatchewan.

He doused his face with listerine, bundled his toilet things into his wet towel and smarting ran back up a flight of green-carpeted cabbagy stairs and down the hall to his bedroom. Halfway he passed the landlady dumpy in a mob cap who stopped her carpet sweeper to give an icy look at his skinny bare legs under the blue bathrobe.

"Good morning Mrs. Maginnis."

"It's goin to be powerful hot today, Mr. Herf."

"I guess it is all right."

Stan was lying on the bed reading *La Revolte des Anges.* "Darn it, I wish I knew some languages the way you do Herfy."

"Oh I dont know any French any more. I forget em so much quicker than I learn em."

"By the way I'm fired from college."

"How's that?"

"Dean told me he thought it advisable I shouldnt come back next year . . . felt that there were other fields of activity where my activities could be more actively active. You know the crap."

"That's a darn shame."

"No it isnt; I'm tickled to death. I asked him why he hadnt fired me before if he felt that way. Father'll be sore as a crab

. . . but I've got enough cash on me not to go home for a week. I dont give a damn anyway. Honest havent you got any liquor?"

"Now Stan how's a poor wageslave like myself going to have a cellar on thirty dollars a week?"

"This is a pretty lousy room. . . . You ought to have been born a capitalist like me."

"Room's not so bad. . . . What drives me crazy is that paranoiac alarm across the street that rings all night."

"That's a burglar alarm isn't it?"

"There cant be any burglars because the place is vacant. The wires must get crossed or something. I dont know when it stopped but it certainly drove me wild when I went to bed this morning."

"Now James Herf you dont mean me to infer that you come home sober every night?"

"A man'd have to be deaf not to hear that damn thing, drunk or sober."

"Well in my capacity of bloated bondholder I want you to come out and eat lunch. Do you realize that you've been playing round with your toilet for exactly one hour by the clock?"

They went down the stairs that smelled of shavingsoap and then of brasspolish and then of bacon and then of singed hair and then of garbage and coalgas.

"You're damn lucky Herfy, never to have gone to college."

"Didnt I graduate from Columbia you big cheese, that's more than you could do?"

The sunlight swooped tingling in Jimmy's face when he opened the door.

"That doesnt count."

"God I like sun," cried Jimmy, "I wish it'd been real Co-lombia. . . ."

"Do you mean Hail Columbia?"

"No I mean Bogota and the Orinoco and all that sort of thing."

"I knew a darn good feller went down to Bogota. Had to drink himself to death to escape dying of elephantiasis."

"I'd be willing to risk elephantiasis and bubonic plague and spotted fever to get out of this hole."

"City of orgies walks and joys . . ."

"Orgies nutten, as we say at a hun'an toitytoird street. . . . Do you realize that I've lived all my life in this goddam town except four years when I was little and that I was born here and that I'm likely to die here? . . . I've a great mind to join the navy and see the world."

"How do you like Dingo in her new coat of paint?"

"Pretty nifty, looks like a regular Mercedes under the dust."

"I wanted to paint her red like a fire engine, but the garageman finally persuaded me to paint her blue like a cop. . . . Do you mind going to Mouquin's and having an absinthe cocktail."

"Absinthe for breakfast. . . . Good Lord."

They drove west along Twenty-third Street that shone with sheets of reflected light off windows, oblong glints off delivery wagons, figureeight-shaped flash of nickel fittings.

"How's Ruth, Jimmy?"

"She's all right. She hasnt got a job yet."

"Look there's a Daimlier."

Jimmy grunted vaguely. As they turned up Sixth Avenue a policeman stopped them.

"Your cut out," he yelled.

"I'm on my way to the garage to get it fixed. Muffler's coming off."

"Better had. . . . Get a ticket another time."

"Gee you get away with murder Stan . . . in everything," said Jimmy. "I never can get away with a thing even if I am three years older than you."

"It's a gift."

The restaurant smelled merrily of fried potatoes and cocktails and cigars and cocktails. It was hot and full of talking and sweaty faces.

"But Stan dont roll your eyes romantically when you ask about Ruth and me. . . . We're just very good friends."

"Honestly I didnt mean anything, but I'm sorry to hear it all the same. I think it's terrible."

"Ruth doesn't care about anything but her acting. She's so crazy to succeed, she cuts out everything else."

"Why the hell does everybody want to succeed? I'd like to meet somebody who wanted to fail. That's the only sublime thing."

"It's all right if you have a comfortable income."

"That's all bunk. . . . Golly this is some cocktail. Herfy I think you're the only sensible person in this town. You have no ambitions."

"How do you know I havent?"

"But what can you do with success when you get it? You cant eat it or drink it. Of course I understand that people who havent enough money to feed their faces and all that should scurry round and get it. But success . . ."

"The trouble with me is I cant decide what I want most, so my motion is circular, helpless and confoundedly discouraging."

"Oh but God decided that for you. You know all the time, but you wont admit it to yourself."

"I imagine what I want most is to get out of this town, preferably first setting off a bomb under the Times Building."

"Well why don't you do it? It's just one foot after another."

"But you have to know which direction to step."

"That's the last thing that's of any importance."

"Then there's money."

"Why money's the easiest thing in the world to get."

"For the eldest son of Emery and Emery."

"Now Herf it's not fair to cast my father's iniquities in my face. You know I hate that stuff as much as you do."

"I'm not blaming you Stan; you're a damn lucky kid, that's all. Of course I'm lucky too, a hell of a lot luckier than most. My mother's leftover money supported me until I was twenty-two and I still have a few hundreds stowed away for that famous rainy day, and my uncle, curse his soul, gets me new jobs when I get fired."

"Baa baa black sheep."

"I guess I'm really afraid of my uncles and aunts. . . . You ought to see my cousin James Merivale. Has done everything he was told all his life and flourished like a green bay tree. . . . The perfect wise virgin."

"Ah guess youse one o dem dere foolish virgins."

"Stan you're feeling your liquor, you're beginning to talk niggertalk."

"Baa baa." Stan put down his napkin and leaned back laughing in his throat.

The smell of absinthe sicklytingling grew up like the magician's rosebush out of Jimmy's glass. He sipped it wrinkling his nose. "As a moralist I protest," he said. "Whee it's amazing."

"What I need is a whiskey and soda to settle those cocktails."

"I'll watch you. I'm a working man. I must be able to tell between the news that's fit and the news that's not fit. . . . God I dont want to start talking about that. It's all so criminally silly. . . . I'll say that this cocktail sure does knock you for a loop."

"You neednt think you're going to do anything else but drink this afternoon. There's somebody I want to introduce you to."

"And I was going to sit down righteously and write an article."

"What's that?"

"Oh a dodaddle called Confessions of a Cub Reporter."

"Look is this Thursday?"

"Yare."

"Then I know where she'll be."

"I'm going to light out of it all," said Jimmy somberly, "and go to Mexico and make my fortune. . . . I'm losing all the best part of my life rotting in New York."

"How'll you make your fortune?"

"Oil, gold, highway robbery, anything so long as it's not newspaper work."

"Baa baa black sheep baa baa."

"You quit baaing at me."

"Let's get the hell out of here and take Dingo to have her muffler fastened."

Jimmy stood waiting in the door of the reeking garage. The dusty afternoon sunlight squirmed in bright worms of heat on his face and hands. Brownstone, redbrick, asphalt flickering with red and green letters of signs, with bits of paper in the gutter rotated in a slow haze about him. Two carwashers talking behind him.

"Yep I was making good money until I went after that lousy broad."

"I'll say she's a goodlooker, Charley. I should worry. . . . Dont make no difference after the first week."

Stan came up behind him and ran him along the street by the shoulders. "Car wont be fixed until five o'clock. Let's taxi. . . . Hotel Lafayette," he shouted at the driver and slapped Jimmy on the knee. "Well Herfy old fossil, you know what the Governor of North Carolina said to the Governor of South Carolina."

"No."

"It's a long time between drinks."

"Baa, baa," Stan was bleating under his breath as they stormed into the café. "Ellie here are the black sheep," he shouted laughing. His face froze suddenly stiff. Opposite Ellen at the table sat her husband, one eyebrow lifted very high and the other almost merging with the eyelashes. A teapot sat impudently between them.

"Hello Stan, sit down," she said quietly. Then she continued smiling into Oglethorpe's face. "Isnt that wonderful Jojo?"

"Ellie this is Mr. Herf," said Stan gruffly.

"Oh I'm so glad to meet you. I used to hear about you up at Mrs. Sunderland's."

They were silent. Oglethorpe was tapping on the table with his spoon. "Why heow deo you deo Mr. Herf," he said with sudden unction. "Dont you remember how we met?"

"By the way how's everything up there Jojo?"

"Just topping thanks. Cassahndrah's beau has left her and there's been the most appalling scandal about that Costello creature. It seems that she came home foxed the other night, to the ears my deah, and tried to take the taxi driver into her room with her, and the poor boy protesting all the time that all he wanted was his fare. . . . It was appalling."

Stan got stiffly to his feet and walked out.

The three of them sat without speaking. Jimmy tried to keep from fidgeting in his chair. He was about to get up, when something velvetsoft in her eyes stopped him.

"Has Ruth got a job yet, Mr. Herf?" she asked.

"No she hasnt."

"It's the rottenest luck."

"Oh it's a darn shame. I know she can act. The trouble is she has too much sense of humor to play up to managers and people."

"Oh the stage is a nasty dirty game, isn't it Jojo?"

"The nawstiest, my deah."

Jimmy couldn't keep his eyes off her; her small squarely shaped hands, her neck molded with a gold sheen between the great coil of coppery hair and the bright blue dress.

"Well my deah . . ." Oglethorpe got to his feet.

"Jojo I'm going to sit here a little longer."

Jimmy was staring at the thin triangles of patent leather that stuck out from Oglethorpe's pink buff spats. Cant be feet in them. He stood up suddenly.

"Now Mr. Herf couldnt you keep me company for fifteen minutes? I've got to leave here at six and I forgot to bring a book and I cant walk in these shoes."

Jimmy blushed and sat down again stammering: "Why of course I'd be delighted. . . . Suppose we drink something."

"I'll finish my tea, but why dont you have a gin fizz? I love to see people drink gin fizzes. It makes me feel that I'm in the tropics sitting in a jujube grove waiting for the riverboat to take us up some ridiculous melodramatic river all set about with fevertrees."

"Waiter I want a gin fizz please."

Joe Harland had slumped down in his chair until his head rested on his arms. Between his grimestiff hands his eyes followed uneasily the lines in the marbletop table. The gutted lunchroom was silent under the sparse glower of two bulbs hanging over the counter where remained a few pies under a bellglass, and a man in a white coat nodding on a tall stool. Now and then the eyes in his gray doughy face flicked open and he grunted and looked about. At the last table over were the hunched shoulders of men asleep, faces crumpled like old newspapers pillowed on arms. Joe Harland sat up straight and yawned. A woman blobby under a raincoat with a face red and purplish streaked like rancid meat was asking for a cup of coffee at the counter. Carrying the mug carefully between her two hands she brought it over to the table and sat down opposite him. Joe Harland let his head down onto his arms again.

"Hay yous how about a little soivice?" The woman's voice shrilled in Harland's ears like the screech of chalk on a blackboard.

"Well what d'ye want?" snarled the man behind the counter. The woman started sobbing. "He asts me what I want. . . . I aint used to bein talked to brutal."

"Well if there's anythin you want you kin juss come an git it. . . . Soivice at this toime o night!"

Harland could smell her whisky breath as she sobbed. He raised his head and stared at her. She twisted her flabby mouth into a smile and bobbed her head towards him.

"Mister I aint accustomed to bein treated brutal. If my husband was aloive he wouldn't have the noive. Who's the loikes o him to say what toime o night a lady ought to have soivice, the little shriveled up shrimp." She threw back her head and laughed so that her hat fell off backwards. "That's what he is, a little shriveled up shrimp, insultin a lady with his toime o night."

Some strands of gray hair with traces of henna at the tips had fallen down about her face. The man in the white coat walked over to the table.

"Look here Mother McCree I'll trow ye out o here if you raise any more distoirbance. . . . What do you want?"

"A nickel's woirt o doughnuts," she sniveled with a sidelong leer at Harland.

Joe Harland shoved his face into the hollow of his arm again and tried to go to sleep. He heard the plate set down followed by her toothless nibbling and an occasional sucking noise when she drank the coffee. A new customer had come in and was talking across the counter in a low growling voice.

"Mister, mister aint it terrible to want a drink?" He raised his head again and found her eyes the blurred blue of watered milk looking into his. "What ye goin to do now darlin?"

"God knows."

"Virgin an Saints it'd be noice to have a bed an a pretty lace shimmy and a noice feller loike you darlin. . . mister."

"Is that all?"

"Oh mister if my poor husband was aloive, he wouldn't let em treat me loike they do. I lost my husband on the *General Slocum* might ha been yesterday."

"He's not so unlucky."

"But he doid in his sin without a priest, darlin. It's terrible to die in yer sin. . ."

"Oh hell I want to sleep."

Her voice went on in a faint monotonous screech setting his teeth on edge. "The Saints has been agin me ever since I lost my husband on the *General Slocum*. I aint been an honest woman." . . . She began to sob again. "The Virgin and Saints an Martyrs is agin me, everybody's agin me. . . . Oh wont somebody treat me noice."

"I want to sleep. . . . Cant you shut up?"

She stooped and fumbled for her hat on the floor. She sat sobbing rubbing her swollen redgrimed knuckles into her eyes.

"Oh mister dont ye want to treat me noice?"

Joe Harland got to his feet breathing hard. "Goddam you cant you shut up?" His voice broke into a whine. "Isn't there anywhere you can get a little peace? There's nowhere you can get any peace." He pulled his cap over his eyes, shoved his hands down into his pockets and shambled out of the lunchroom. Over Chatham Square the sky was brightening redviolet through the latticework of elevated tracks. The lights were two rows of bright brass knobs up the empty Bowery.

A policeman passed swinging his nightstick. Joe Harland felt the policeman's eyes on him. He tried to walk fast and briskly as if he were going somewhere on business.

"Well Miss Oglethorpe how do you like it?"

"Like what?"

"Oh you know . . . being a nine days' wonder."

"Why I don't know at all Mr. Goldweiser."

"Women know everything but they wont let on."

Ellen sits in a gown of nilegreen silk in a springy armchair at the end of a long room jingling with talk and twinkle of chandeliers and jewelry, dotted with the bright moving black of evening clothes and silveredged colors of women's dresses. The curve of Harry Goldweiser's nose merges directly into the curve of his bald forehead, his big rump bulges over the edges of a triangular gilt stool, his small brown eyes measure her face like antennae as he talks to her. A woman nearby smells of sandalwood. A woman with orange lips and a chalk face under an orange turban passes talking to a man with a pointed beard. A hawkbeaked woman with crimson hair puts her hand on a man's shoulder from behind. "Why how do you do, Miss Cruikshank; it's surprising isn't it how everybody in the world is always at the same place at the same time." Ellen sits in the armchair drowsily listening, coolness of powder on her face and arms, fatness of rouge on her lips, her body just bathed fresh as a violet under the silk dress, under the silk underclothes; she sits dreamily, drowsily listening. A sudden twinge of men's voices knotting about her. She sits up cold white out of reach like a lighthouse. Men's hands crawl like bugs on the unbreakable glass. Men's looks blunder and flutter against it helpless as moths. But in deep pitblackness inside something clangs like a fire engine.

George Baldwin stood beside the breakfast table with a copy of the New York *Times* folded in his hand. "Now Cecily," he was saying, "we must be sensible about these things."

"Cant you see that I'm trying to be sensible?" she said in a jerking snivelly voice. He stood looking at her without sitting down rolling a corner of the paper between his finger and thumb. Mrs. Baldwin was a tall woman with a mass of carefully curled chestnut hair piled on top of her head. She sat before the silver coffeeservice fingering the sugarbowl with mushroomwhite fingers that had very sharp pink nails.

"George I cant stand it any more that's all." She pressed her quaking lips hard together.

"But my dear you exaggerate. . . ."

"How exaggerate? . . . It means our life has been a pack of lies."

"But Cecily we're fond of each other."

"You married me for my social position, you know it. . . . I was fool enough to fall in love with you. All right, it's over."

"It's not true. I really loved you. Dont you remember how terrible you thought it was you couldnt really love me?"

"You brute to refer to that. . . . Oh it's horrible!"

The maid came in from the pantry with bacon and eggs on a tray. They sat silent looking at each other. The maid swished out of the room and closed the door. Mrs. Baldwin put her forehead down on the edge of the table and began to cry. Baldwin sat staring at the headlines in the paper. ASSASSINATION OF ARCHDUKE WILL HAVE GRAVE CONSEQUENCES.

AUSTRIAN ARMY MOBILIZED. He went over and put his hand on her crisp hair.

"Poor old Cecily," he said.

"Dont touch me."

She ran out of the room with her handkerchief to her face. He sat down, helped himself to bacon and eggs and toast and began to eat; everything tasted like paper. He stopped eating to scribble a note on a scratchpad he kept in his breast pocket behind his handkerchief: See Collins vs. Arbuthnot, N.Y.S.C. Appel. Div.

The sound of a step in the hall outside caught his ear, the click of a latch. The elevator had just gone down. He ran four flights down the steps. Through the glass and wroughtiron doors of the vestibule downstairs he caught sight of her on the curb, standing tall and stiff, pulling on her gloves. He rushed out and took her by the hand just as a taxi drove up. Sweat beaded on his forehead and was prickly under his collar. He could see himself standing there with the napkin ridiculous in his hand and the colored doorman grinning and saying, "Good mornin, Mr. Baldwin, looks like it going to be a fine day." Gripping her hand tight, he said in a low voice through his teeth:

"Cecily there's something I want to talk to you about. Wont you wait a minute and we'll go downtown together? . . . Wait about five minutes please," he said to the taxidriver. "We'll be right down." Squeezing her wrist hard he walked back with her to the elevator. When they stood in the hall of their own apartment, she suddenly looked him straight in the face with dry blazing eyes.

"Come in here Cecily," he said gently. He closed their bedroom door and locked it. "Now lets talk this over quietly. Sit down dear." He put a chair behind her. She sat down suddenly stiffly like a marionette.

"Now look here Cecily you have no right to talk the way you do about my friends. Mrs. Oglethorpe is a friend of mine. We occasionally take tea together in some perfectly public place and that's all. I would invite her up here but I've been afraid you would be rude to her. . . . You cant go on giving away to your insane jealously like this. I allow you complete liberty and trust you absolutely. I think I have the right to expect the same confidence from you. . . . Cecily do be my sensible little girl again. You've been listening to what a lot of old hags fabricate out of whole cloth maliciously to make you miserable."

"She's not the only one."

"Cecily I admit frankly there were times soon after we were married . . . when . . . But that's all over years ago. . . . And who's fault was it? . . . Oh Cecily a woman like you cant understand the physical urgences of a man like me."

"Havent I done my best?"

"My dear these things arent anybody's fault. . . . I dont blame you. . . . If you'd really loved me then . . ."

"What do you think I stay in this hell for except for you? Oh you're such a brute." She sat dryeyed staring at her feet in their gray buckskin slippers, twisting and untwisting in her fingers the wet string of her handkerchief.

"Look here Cecily a divorce would be very harmful to my situation downtown just at the moment, but if you really dont want to go on living with me I'll see what I can arrange. . . . But in any event you must have more confidence in me. You know I'm fond of you. And for God's sake dont go to see anybody about it without consulting me. You dont want a scandal and headlines in the papers, do you?"

"All right . . . leave me alone. . . . I dont care about anything."

"All right. . . . I'm pretty late. I'll go on downtown in that taxi. You don't want to come shopping or anything?"

She shook her head. He kissed her on the forehead, took his straw hat and stick in the hall and hurried out.

"Oh I'm the most miserable woman," she groaned and got to her feet. Her head ached as if it were bound with hot wire. She went to the window and leaned out into the sunlight. Across Park Avenue the flameblue sky was barred with the red girder cage of a new building. Steam riveters rattled incessantly; now and then a donkeyengine whistled and there was a jingle of chains and a fresh girder soared crosswise in the air. Men in blue overalls moved about the scaffolding. Beyond to the northwest a shining head of clouds soared blooming compactly like a cauliflower. Oh if it would only rain. As the thought came to her there was a low growl of thunder above the din of building and of traffic. Oh if it would only rain.

*

Ellen had just hung a chintz curtain in the window to hide with its blotchy pattern of red and purple flowers the vista of desert backyards and brick flanks of downtown houses. In the middle of the bare room was a boxcouch cumbered with teacups, a copper chafingdish and percolator; the yellow hardwood floor was littered with snippings of chintz and curtainpins; books, dresses, bedlinen cascaded from a trunk in the corner; from a new mop in the fireplace exuded a smell of cedar oil. Ellen was leaning against the wall in a daffodilcolored kimono looking happily about the big shoebox-shaped room when the buzzer startled her. She pushed a rope of hair up off her forehead and pressed the button that worked the latch. There was a little knock on the door. A woman was standing in the dark of the hall.

"Why Cassie I couldn't make out who you were. Come in. . . . What's the matter?"

"You are sure I'm not intwuding?"

"Of course not." Ellen leaned to give her a little pecking kiss. Cassandra Wilkins was very pale and there was a nervous quiver about her eyelids. "You can give me some advice. I'm just getting my curtains up. . . . Look do you think that purple goes all right with the gray wall? It looks kind of funny to me."

"I think it's beautiful. What a beautiful woom. How happy you're going to be here."

"Put that chafingdish down on the floor and sit down. I'll make some tea. There's a kind of bathroom kitchenette in the alcove there."

"You're sure it wouldn't be too much twouble?"

"Of course not. . . . But Cassie what's the matter?"

"Oh everything. . . . I came down to tell you but I cant. I cant ever tell anybody."

"I'm so excited about this apartment. Imagine Cassie it's the first place of my own I ever had in my life. Daddy wants me to live with him in Passaic, but I just felt I couldn't."

"And what does Mr. Oglethorpe . . . ? Oh but that's impertinent of me. . . . Do forgive me Elaine. I'm almost cwazy. I don't know what I'm saying."

"Oh Jojo's a dear. He's even going to let me divorce him if

I want to. . . . Would you if you were me?" Without waiting
for an answer she disappeared between the folding doors.
Cassie remained hunched up on the edge of the couch.

Ellen came back with a blue teapot in one hand and a pan
of steaming water in the other. "Do you mind not having
lemon or cream? There's some sugar on the mantelpiece.
These cups are clean because I just washed them. Dont you
think they are pretty? Oh you cant imagine how wonderful
and domestic it makes you feel to have a place all to yourself.
I hate living in a hotel. Honestly this place makes me just so
domestic . . . Of course the ridiculous thing is that I'll probably have to give it up or sublet as soon as I've got it decently
fixed up. Show's going on the road in three weeks. I want to
get out of it but Harry Goldweiser wont let me." Cassie was
taking little sips of tea out of her spoon. She began to cry
softly. "Why Cassie buck up, what's the matter?"

"Oh, you're so lucky in everything Elaine and I'm so miserable."

"Why I always thought it was my jinx that got the beauty-
prize, but what is the matter?"

Cassie put down her cup and pushed her two clenched
hands into her neck. "It's just this," she said in a strangled
voice. . . . "I think I'm going to have a baby." She put her
head down on her knees and sobbed.

"Are you sure? Everybody's always having scares."

"I wanted our love to be always pure and beautiful, but he
said he'd never see me again if I didn't . . . and I hate him."
She shook the words out one by one between tearing sobs.

"Why don't you get married?"

"I cant. I wont. It would interfere."

"How long since you knew?"

"Oh it must have been ten days ago easily. I know it's that
. . . I dont want to have anything but my dancing." She
stopped sobbing and began taking little sips of tea again.

Ellen walked back and forth in front of the fireplace. "Look
here Cassie there's no use getting all wrought up over things,
is there? I know a woman who'll help you. . . . Do pull
yourself together please."

"Oh I couldn't, I couldn't." . . . The saucer slid off her
knees and broke in two on the floor. "Tell me Elaine have you

ever been through this? . . . Oh I'm so sowy. I'll buy you another saucer Elaine." She got totteringly to her feet and put
the cup and spoon on the mantelpiece.

"Oh of course I have. When we were first married I had a
terrible time. . . ."

"Oh Elaine isn't it hideous all this? Life would be so beautiful and free and natural without it. . . . I can feel the howor
of it cweeping up on me, killing me."

"Things are rather like that," said Ellen gruffly.

Cassie was crying again. "Men are so bwutal and selfish."

"Have another cup of tea, Cassie."

"Oh I couldn't. My dear I feel a deadly nausea. . . . Oh I
think I'm going to be sick."

"The bathroom is right through the folding doors and to
the left."

Ellen walked up and down the room with clenched teeth. I
hate women. I hate women.

After a while Cassie came back into the room, her face
greenish white, dabbing her forehead with a washrag.

"Here lie down here you poor kid," said Ellen clearing a
space on the couch. ". . . Now you'll feel much better."

"Oh will you ever forgive me for causing all this twouble?"

"Just lie still a minute and forget everything."

"Oh if I could only relax."

Ellen's hands were cold. She went to the window and
looked out. A little boy in a cowboy suit was running about
the yard waving an end of clothesline. He tripped and fell.
Ellen could see his face puckered with tears as he got to his
feet again. In the yard beyond a stumpy woman with black
hair was hanging out clothes. Sparrows were chirping and
fighting on the fence.

"Elaine dear could you let me have a little powder? I've lost
my vanity case."

She turned back into the room. "I think. . . . Yes there's
some on the mantelpiece. . . . Do you feel better now
Cassie?"

"Oh yes," said Cassie in a trembly voice. "And have you
got a lipstick?"

"I'm awfully sorry. . . . I've never worn any street
makeup. I'll have to soon enough if I keep on acting." She

went into the alcove to take off her kimono, slipped on a plain green dress, coiled up her hair and pushed a small black hat down over it. "Let's run along Cassie. I want to have something to eat at six. . . . I hate bolting my dinner five minutes before a performance."

"Oh I'm so tewified. . . . Pwomise you wont leave me alone."

"Oh she wouldnt do anything today. . . . She'll just look you over and maybe give you something to take. . . . Let's see, have I got my key?"

"We'll have to take a taxi. And my dear I've only got six dollars in the world."

"I'll make daddy give me a hundred dollars to buy furniture. That'll be all right."

"Elaine you're the most angelic cweature in the world. . . . You deserve every bit of your success."

At the corner of Sixth Avenue they got into a taxi.

Cassie's teeth were chattering. "Please let's go another time. I'm too fwightened to go now."

"My dear child it's the only thing to do."

Joe Harland, puffing on his pipe, pulled to and bolted the wide quaking board gates. A last splash of garnetcolored sunlight was fading on the tall housewall across the excavation. Blue arms of cranes stood out dark against it. Harland's pipe had gone out, he stood puffing at it with his back to the gate looking at the files of empty wheelbarrows, the piles of picks and shovels, the little shed for the donkeyengine and the steam drills that sat perched on a split rock like a mountaineer's shack. It seemed to him peaceful in spite of the rasp of traffic from the street that seeped through the hoarding. He went into the leanto by the gate where the telephone was, sat down in the chair, knocked out, filled and lit his pipe and spread the newspaper out on his knees. CONTRACTORS PLAN LOCKOUT TO ANSWER BUILDERS' STRIKE. He yawned and threw back his head. The light was too blue-dim to read. He sat a long time staring at the stub scarred toes of his boots. His mind was a fuzzy comfortable blank. Suddenly he saw himself in a dress-suit wearing a top hat with an orchid in his buttonhole. The Wizard of Wall Street looked at the lined red face and the gray hair under the mangy cap and the big hands with their grimy swollen knuckles and faded with a snicker. He remembered faintly the smell of a Corona-Corona as he reached into the pocket of the peajacket for a can of Prince Albert to refill his pipe. "What dif does it make I'd like to know?" he said aloud. When he lit a match the night went suddenly inky all round. He blew out the match. His pipe was a tiny genial red volcano that made a discreet cluck each time he pulled on it. He smoked very slowly inhaling deep. The tall buildings all round were haloed with ruddy glare from streets and electriclight signs. Looking straight up through glimmering veils of reflected light he could see the blueback sky and stars. The tobacco was sweet. He was very happy.

A glowing cigarend crossed the door of the shack. Harland grabbed his lantern and went out. He held the lantern up in the face of a blond young man with a thick nose and lips and a cigar in the side of his mouth.

"How did you get in here?"

"Side door was open."

"The hell it was? Who are you looking for?"

"You the night watchman round here?" Harland nodded. "Glad to meet yez. . . . Have a cigar. I jus wanted to have a little talk wid ye, see? . . . I'm organizer for Local 47, see? Let's see your card."

"I'm not a union man."

"Well ye're goin to be aint ye. . . . Us guys of the buildin trades have got to stick together. We're tryin to get every bloke from night watchmen to inspectors lined up to make a solid front against this here lockout sitooation."

Harland lit his cigar. "Look here, bo, you're wasting your breath on me. They'll always need a watchman, strike or no strike. . . . I'm an old man and I havent got much fight left in me. This is the first decent job I've had in five years and they'll have to shoot me to get it away from me. . . . All that stuff's for kids like you. I'm out of it. You sure are wasting your breath if you're going round trying to organize night watchmen."

"Say you don't talk like you'd always been in this kind o woik."

"Well maybe I aint."

The young man took off his hat and rubbed his hand over his forehead and up across his dense cropped hair. "Hell it's warm work arguin. . . . Swell night though aint it?"

"Oh the night's all right," said Harland.

"Say my name's O'Keefe, Joe O'Keefe. . . . Gee I bet you could tell a guy a lot o things." He held out his hand.

"My name's Joe too . . . Harland. . . . Twenty years ago that name meant something to people."

"Twenty years from now . . ."

"Say you're a funny fellow for a walking delegate. . . . You take an old man's advice before I run you off the lot, and quit it. . . . It's no game for a likely young feller who wants to make his way in the world."

"Times are changin you know. . . . There's big fellers back o this here strike, see? I was talkin over the sitooation with Assemblyman McNiel jus this afternoon in his office."

"But I'm telling you straight if there's one thing that'll queer you in this town it's this labor stuff. . . . You'll remember someday that an old drunken bum told you that and it'll be too late."

"Oh it was drink was it? That's one thing I'm not afraid of. I don't touch the stuff, except beer to be sociable."

"Look here bo the company detective'll be makin his rounds soon. You'd better be making tracks."

"I ain't ascared of any goddam company detective. . . . Well so long I'll come in to see you again someday."

"Close that door behind you."

Joe Harland drew a little water from a tin container, settled himself in his chair and stretched his arms out and yawned. Eleven o'clock. They would just be getting out of the theaters, men in eveningclothes, girls in lowneck dresses; men were going home to their wives and mistresses; the city was going to bed. Taxis honked and rasped outside the hoarding, the sky shimmered with gold powder from electric signs. He dropped the butt of the cigar and crushed it on the floor with his heel. He shuddered and got to his feet, then paced slowly round the edge of the buildinglot swinging his lantern.

The light from the street yellowed faintly a big sign on which was a picture of a skyscraper, white with black windows against blue sky and white clouds. SEGAL AND HAYNES will erect on this site a modern uptodate TWENTYFOUR STORY OFFICE BUILDING open for occupancy January 1915 renting space still available inquire. . . .

Jimmy Herf sat reading on a green couch under a bulb that lit up a corner of a wide bare room. He had come to the death of Olivier in *Jean Christophe* and read with tightening gullet. In his memory lingered the sound of the Rhine swirling, restlessly gnawing the foot of the garden of the house where Jean Christophe was born. Europe was a green park in his mind full of music and red flags and mobs marching. Occasionally the sound of a steamboat whistle from the river settled breathless snowysoft into the room. From the street came a rattle of taxis and the whining sound of streetcars.

There was a knock at the door. Jimmy got up, his eyes blurred and hot from reading.

"Hello Stan, where the devil did you come from?"

"Herfy I'm tight as a drum."

"That's no novelty."

"I was just giving you the weather report."

"Well perhaps you can tell me why in this country nobody ever does anything. Nobody ever writes any music or starts any revolutions or falls in love. All anybody ever does is to get drunk and tell smutty stories. I think it's disgusting. . . ."

"'Ear, 'ear. . . . But speak for yourself. I'm going to stop drinking. . . . No good drinking, liquor just gets monotonous. . . . Say, got a bathtub?"

"Of course there's a bathtub. Whose apartment do you think this is, mine?"

"Well whose is it Herfy?"

"It belongs to Lester. I'm just caretaker while he's abroad, the lucky dog." Stan started peeling off his clothes letting them drop in a pile about his feet. "Gee I'd like to go swimming. . . . Why the hell do people live in cities?"

"Why do I go on dragging out a miserable existence in this crazy epileptic town . . . that's what I want to know."

"Lead on Horatius, to the baawth slave," bellowed Stan who stood on top of his pile of clothes, brown with tight rounded muscles, swaying a little from his drunkenness.

"It's right through that door." Jimmy pulled a towel out of

the steamertrunk in the corner of the room, threw it after him and went back to reading.

Stan tumbled back into the room, dripping, talking through the towel. "What do you think, I forgot to take my hat off. And look Herfy, there's something I want you to do for me. Do you mind?"

"Of course not. What is it?"

"Will you let me use your back room tonight, this room?"

"Sure you can."

"I mean with somebody."

"Go as far as you like. You can bring the entire Winter Garden Chorus in here and nobody will see them. And there's an emergency exit down the fire escape into the alley. I'll go to bed and close my door so you can have this room and the bath all to yourselves."

"It's a rotten imposition but somebody's husband is on the rampage and we have to be very careful."

"Dont worry about the morning. I'll sneak out early and you can have the place to yourselves."

"Well I'm off so long."

Jimmy gathered up his book and went into his bedroom and undressed. His watch said fifteen past twelve. The night was sultry. When he had turned out the light he sat a long while on the edge of the bed. The faraway sounds of sirens from the river gave him gooseflesh. From the street he heard footsteps, the sound of men and women's voices, low youthful laughs of people going home two by two. A phonograph was playing *Secondhand Rose*. He lay on his back on top of the sheet. There came on the air through the window a sourness of garbage, a smell of burnt gasoline and traffic and dusty pavements, a huddled stuffiness of pigeonhole rooms where men and women's bodies writhed alone tortured by the night and the young summer. He lay with seared eyeballs staring at the ceiling, his body glowed in a brittle shivering agony like redhot metal.

A woman's voice whispering eagerly woke him; someone was pushing open the door. "I wont see him. I wont see him. Jimmy for Heaven's sake you go talk to him. I wont see him." Elaine Oglethorpe draped in a sheet walked into the room.

Jimmy tumbled out of bed. "What on earth?"

"Isn't there a closet or something in here. . . . I will not talk to Jojo when he's in that condition."

Jimmy straightened his pyjamas. "There's a closet at the head of the bed."

"Of course. . . . Now Jimmy do be an angel, talk to him and make him go away."

Jimmy walked dazedly into the outside room. "Slut, slut," was yelling a voice from the window. The lights were on. Stan, draped like an Indian in a gray and pinkstriped blanket was squatting in the middle of the two couches made up together into a vast bed. He was staring impassively at John Oglethorpe who leaned in through the upper part of the window screaming and waving his arms and scolding like a Punch and Judy show. His hair was in a tangle over his eyes, in one hand he waved a stick, in the other a cream and coffee colored felt hat. "Slut come here. . . . Flagrante delictu that's what it is. . . . Flagrante delictu. It was not for nothing that inspiration led me up Lester Jones's fire escape." He stopped and stared a minute at Jimmy with wide drunken eyes. "So here's the cub reporter, the yellow journalist is it, looking as if butter wouldnt melt in his mouth is it? Do you know what my opinion of you is, would you like to know what my opinion of you is? Oh I've heard about you from Ruth and all that. I know you think you're one of the dynamiters and aloof from all that. . . . How do you like being a paid prostitute of the public press? How d'you like your yellow ticket? The brass check, that's the kind of thing. . . . You think that as an actor, an artiste, I dont know about those things. I've heard from Ruth your opinion of actors and all that."

"Why Mr. Oglethorpe I am sure you are mistaken."

"I read and keep silent. I am one of the silent watchers. I know that every sentence, every word, every picayune punctuation that appears in the public press is perused and revised and deleted in the interests of advertisers and bondholders. The fountain of national life is poisoned at the source."

"Yea, you tell em," suddenly shouted Stan from the bed. He got to his feet clapping his hands. "I should prefer to be the meanest stagehand. I should prefer to be the old and feeble charwoman who scrubs off the stage . . . than to sit on velvet in the office of the editor of the greatest daily in the city. Acting is a profession honorable, decent, humble, gentlemanly." The oration ended abruptly.

"Well I dont see what you expect me to do about it," said Jimmy crossing his arms.

"And now it's starting to rain," went on Oglethorpe in a squeaky whining voice.

"You'd better go home," said Jimmy.

"I shall go I shall go where there are no sluts . . . no male and female sluts. . . . I shall go into the great night."

"Do you think he can get home all right Stan?"

Stan had sat down on the edge of the bed shaking with laughter. He shrugged his shoulders.

"My blood will be on your head Elaine forever. . . . Forever, do you hear me? . . . into the night where people dont sit laughing and sneering. Dont you think I dont see you. . . . If the worst happens it will not be my fault."

"Go-od night," shouted Stan. In a last spasm of laughing he fell off the edge of the bed and rolled on the floor. Jimmy went to the window and looked down the fire escape into the alley. Oglethorpe had gone. It was raining hard. A smell of wet bricks rose from the housewalls.

"Well if this isnt the darnedest fool business?" He walked back into his room without looking at Stan. In the door Ellen brushed silkily past him.

"I'm terribly sorry Jimmy . . ." she began.

He closed the door sharply in her face and locked it. "The goddam fools they act like crazy people," he said through his teeth. "What the hell do they think this is?"

His hands were cold and trembling. He pulled a blanket up over him. He lay listening to the steady beat of the rain and the hissing spatter of a gutter. Now and then a puff of wind blew a faint cool spray in his face. There still lingered in the room a frail cedarwood gruff smell of her heavycoiled hair, a silkiness of her body where she had crouched wrapped in the sheet hiding.

Ed Thatcher sat in his bay window among the Sunday papers. His hair was grizzled and there were deep folds in his cheeks. The upper buttons of his pongee trousers were undone to ease his sudden little potbelly. He sat in the open window looking out over the blistering asphalt at the endless stream of automobiles that whirred in either direction past the yellowbrick row of stores and the redbrick station under the eaves of which on a black ground gold letters glinted feebly in the sun: PASSAIC. Apartments round about emitted a querulous Sunday grinding of phonographs playing *It's a Bear.* The Sextette from *Lucia*, selections from *The Quaker Girl.* On his knees lay the theatrical section of the New York *Times.* He looked out with bleared eyes into the quivering heat feeling his ribs tighten with a breathless ache. He had just read a paragraph in a marked copy of *Town Topics.*

Malicious tongues are set wagging by the undeniable fact that young Stanwood Emery's car is seen standing every night outside the Knickerbocker Theatre and never does it leave they say, without a certain charming young actress whose career is fast approaching stellar magnitude. This same young gentleman, whose father is the head of one of the city's most respected lawfirms, who recently left Harvard under slightly unfortunate circumstances, has been astonishing the natives for some time with his exploits which we are sure are merely the result of the ebullience of boyish spirits. A word to the wise.

The bell rang three times. Ed Thatcher dropped his papers and hurried quaking to the door. "Ellie you're so late. I was afraid you weren't coming."

"Daddy dont I always come when I say I will?"

"Of course you do deary."

"How are you getting on? How's everything at the office?"

"Mr. Elbert's on his vacation. . . . I guess I'll go when he comes back. I wish you'd come down to Spring Lake with me for a few days. It'd do you good."

"But daddy I cant." . . . She pulled off her hat and dropped it on the davenport. "Look I brought you some roses, daddy."

"Think of it; they're red roses like your mother used to like. That was very thoughtful of you I must say. . . . But I dont like going all alone on my vacation."

"Oh you'll meet lots of cronies daddy, sure you will."

"Why couldnt you come just for a week?"

"In the first place I've got to look for a job . . . show's going on the road and I'm not going just at present. Harry Goldweiser's awfully sore about it." Thatcher sat down in the bay window again and began piling up the Sunday papers on a chair. "Why daddy what on earth are you doing with that copy of *Town Topics*?"

"Oh nothing, I'd never read it; I just bought it to see what it was like." He flushed and compressed his lips as he shoved it in among the *Times*.

"It's just a blackmail sheet." Ellen was walking about the room. She had put the roses in a vase. A spiced coolness was spreading from them through the dustheavy air. "Daddy, there's something I want to tell you about . . . Jojo and I are going to get divorced." Ed Thatcher sat with his hands on his knees nodding with tight lips, saying nothing. His face was gray and dark, almost the speckled gray of his pongee suit. "It's nothing to take on about. We've just decided we cant get along together. It's all going through quietly in the most approved style . . . George Baldwin, who's a friend of mine, is going to run it through."

"He with Emery and Emery?"

"Yes."

"Hum."

They were silent. Ellen leaned over to breathe deep of the roses. She watched a little green measuring worm cross a bronzed leaf.

"Honestly I'm terribly fond of Jojo, but it drives me wild to live with him. . . . I owe him a whole lot, I know that."

"I wish you'd never set eyes on him."

Thatcher cleared his throat and turned his face away from her to look out the window at the two endless bands of automobiles that passed along the road in front of the station. Dust rose from them and angular glitter of glass enamel and nickel. Tires made a swish on the oily macadam. Ellen dropped onto the davenport and let her eyes wander among the faded red roses of the carpet.

The bell rang. "I'll go daddy. . . . How do you do Mrs. Culveteer?"

A redfaced broad woman in a black and white chiffon dress came into the room puffing. "Oh you must forgive my butting in, I'm just dropping by for a second. . . . How are you Mr. Thatcher? . . . You know my dear your poor father has really been very poorly."

"Nonsense; all I had was a little backache."

"Lumbago my dear."

"Why daddy you ought to have let me know."

"The sermon today was most inspiring, Mr. Thatcher. . . . Mr. Lourton was at his very best."

"I guess I ought to rout out and go to church now and then, but you see I like to lay round the house Sundays."

"Of course Mr. Thatcher it's the only day you have. My husband was just like that. . . . But I think it's different with Mr. Lourton than with most clergymen. He has such an up-todate commonsense view of things. It's really more like attending an intensely interesting lecture than going to church. . . . You understand what I mean."

"I'll tell you what I'll do Mrs. Culveteer, next Sunday if it's not too hot I'll go. . . . I guess I'm getting too set in my ways."

"Oh a little change does us all good. . . . Mrs. Oglethorpe you have no idea how closely we follow your career, in the Sunday papers and all. . . . I think it's simply wonderful. . . . As I was telling Mr. Thatcher only yesterday it must take a lot of strength of character and deep Christian living to withstand the temptations of stage life nowadays. It's inspiring to think of a young girl and wife coming so sweet and unspoiled through all that."

Ellen kept looking at the floor so as not to catch her father's eye. He was tapping with two fingers on the arm of his morrischair. Mrs. Culveteer beamed from the middle of the davenport. She got to her feet. "Well I just must run along. We have a green girl in the kitchen and I'm sure dinner's all ruined. . . . Wont you drop in this afternoon . . . ? quite informally. I made some cookies and we'll have some gingerale out just in case somebody turns up."

"I'm sure we'd be delighted Mrs. Culveteer," said Thatcher getting stiffly to his feet. Mrs. Culveteer in her bunchy dress waddled out the door.

"Well Ellie suppose we go eat. . . . She's a very nice kindhearted woman. She's always bringing me pots of jam and marmalade. She lives upstairs with her sister's family. She's the widow of a traveling man."

"That was quite a line about the temptations of stage life," said Ellen with a little laugh in her throat. "Come along or the place'll be crowded. Avoid the rush is my motto."

Said Thatcher in a peevish crackling voice, "Let's not dawdle around."

Ellen spread out her sunshade as they stepped out of the door flanked on either side by bells and letterboxes. A blast of gray heat beat in their faces. They passed the stationery store, the red A. and P., the corner drugstore from which a stale coolness of sodawater and icecream freezers drifted out under the green awning, crossed the street, where their feet sank into the sticky melting asphalt, and stopped at the Sagamore Cafeteria. It was twelve exactly by the clock in the window that had round its face in old English lettering, TIME TO EAT. Under it was a large rusty fern and a card announcing Chicken Dinner $1.25. Ellen lingered in the doorway looking up the quivering street. "Look daddy we'll probably have a thunderstorm." A cumulus soared in unbelievable snowy contours in the slate sky. "Isnt that a fine cloud? Wouldnt it be fine if we had a riproaring thunderstorm?"

Ed Thatcher looked up, shook his head and went in through the swinging screen door. Ellen followed him. Inside it smelled of varnish and waitresses. They sat down at a table near the door under a droning electric fan.

"How do you do Mr. Thatcher? How you been all the week sir? How do you do miss?" The bonyfaced peroxidehaired waitress hung over them amicably. "What'll it be today sir, roast Long Island duckling or roast Philadelphia milkfed capon?"

IV. Fire Engine

S uch afternoons the buses are crowded into line like elephants in a circusparade. Morningside Heights to Washington Square, Penn Station to Grant's Tomb. Parlorsnakes and flappers joggle hugging downtown uptown, hug joggling gray square, until they see the new moon giggling over Weehawken and feel the gusty wind of a dead Sunday blowing dust in their faces, dust of a typsy twilight.

They are walking up the Mall in Central Park.

"Looks like he had a boil on his neck," says Ellen in front of the statue of Burns.

"Ah," whispers Harry Goldweiser with a fat-throated sigh, "but he was a great poet."

She is walking in her wide hat in her pale loose dress that the wind now and then presses against her legs and arms, silkily, swishily walking in the middle of great rosy and purple and pistachiogreen bubbles of twilight that swell out of the grass and trees and ponds, bulge against the tall houses sharp gray as dead teeth round the southern end of the park, melt into the indigo zenith. When he talks, forming sentences roundly with his thick lips, continually measuring her face with his brown eyes, she feels his words press against her body, nudge in the hollows where her dress clings; she can hardly breathe for fear of listening to him.

"The Zinnia Girl's going to be an absolute knockout, Elaine, I'm telling you and that part's just written for you. I'd enjoy working with you again, honest. . . . You're so different, that's what it is about you. All these girls round New York here are just the same, they're monotonous. Of course you could sing swell if you wanted to. . . . I've been crazy as a loon since I met you, and that's a good six months now. I sit down to eat and the food dont have any taste. . . . You cant understand how lonely a man gets when year after year he's had to crush his feelings down into himself. When I was a young fellow I was different, but what are you to do? I had to make money and make my way in the world. And so I've

657

gone on year after year. For the first time I'm glad I did it, that I shoved ahead and made big money, because now I can offer it all to you. Understand what I mean? . . . All those ideels and beautiful things pushed down into myself when I was making my way in a man's world were like planting seed and you're their flower."

Now and then as they walk the back of his hand brushes against hers; she clenches her fist sullenly drawing it away from the hot determined pudginess of his hand.

The Mall is full of couples, families waiting for the music to begin. It smells of children and dress-shields and talcum powder. A balloonman passes them trailing red and yellow and pink balloons like a great inverted bunch of grapes behind him. "Oh buy me a balloon." The words are out of her mouth before she can stop them.

"Hay you gimme one of each color. . . . And how about one of those gold ones? No keep the change."

Ellen put the strings of the balloons into the dirtsticky hands of three little monkeyfaced girls in red tams. Each balloon caught a crescent of violet glare from the arclight.

"Aw you like children, Elaine, dont you? I like a woman to like children."

Ellen sits numb at a table on the terrace of the Casino. A hot gust of foodsmell and the rhythm of a band playing *He's a Ragpicker* swirls chokingly about her; now and then she butters a scrap of roll and puts it in her mouth. She feels very helpless, caught like a fly in his sticky trickling sentences.

"There's nobody else in New York could have got me to walk that far, I'll tell you that. . . . I walked too much in the old days, do you understand, used to sell papers when I was a kid and run errands for Schwartz's Toystore . . . on my feet all day except when I was in nightschool. I thought I was going to be a lawyer, all us East Side fellers thought we were goin to be lawyers. Then I worked as an usher one summer at the Irving Place and got the theater bug. . . . Not such a bad hunch it turned out to be, but it's too uncertain. Now I dont care any more, only want to cover my losses. That's the trouble with me. I'm thirtyfive an I dont care any more. Ten years ago I was still only a kind of clerk in old man Erlanger's office, and now there's lots of em whose shoes I used to shine

in the old days'd be real glad of the opportunity to sweep my
floors on West Forty-eighth. . . . Tonight I can take you
anywhere in New York, I dont care how expensive or how
chic it is . . . an in the old days us kids used to think it was
paradise if we had five plunks to take a couple of girls down
to the Island. . . . I bet all that was different with you
Elaine. . . . But what I want to do is get that old feelin back,
understand? . . . Where shall we go?"

"Why dont we go down to Coney Island then? I've never
been."

"It's a pretty rough crowd . . . still we can just ride round.
Let's do it. I'll go phone for the car."

Ellen sits alone looking down into her coffeecup. She puts
a lump of sugar on her spoon, dips it in the coffee and pops
it into her mouth where she crunches it slowly, rubbing the
grains of sugar against the roof of her mouth with her tongue.
The orchestra is playing a tango.

The sun streaming into the office under the drawn shades
cut a bright slanting layer like watered silk through the cigarsmoke.

"Mighty easy," George Baldwin was saying dragging out
the words. "Gus we got to go mighty easy on this." Gus Mc-
Niel bullnecked redfaced with a heavy watchchain in his vest
sat in the armchair nodding silently, pulling on his cigar. "As
things are now no court would sustain such an injunction
. . . an injunction that seems to me a pure piece of party
politics on Judge Connor's part, but there are certain
elements. . . ."

"You said it. . . . Look here George I'm goin to leave this
whole blame thing to you. You pulled me through the East
New York dockin space mess and I guess you can pull me
through this."

"But Gus your position in this whole affair has been entirely within the bounds of legality. If it werent I certainly
should not be able to take the case, not even for an old friend
like you."

"You know me George. . . . I never went back on a guy
yet and I dont expect to have anybody go back on me." Gus
got heavily to his feet and began to limp about the office

leaning on a goldknobbed cane. "Connor's a son of a bitch
. . . an honest, you wouldn't believe it but he was a decent
guy before he went up to Albany."

"My position will be that your attitude in this whole matter has been willfully misconstrued. Connor has been using
his position on the bench to further a political end."

"God I wish we could get him. Jez I thought he was one
of the boys; he was until he went up an got mixed up with all
those lousy upstate Republicans. Albany's been the ruination
of many a good man."

Baldwin got up from the flat mahogany table where he sat
between tall sheaves of foolscap and put his hand on Gus's
shoulder. "Dont you lose any sleep over it. . . ."

"I'd feel all right if it wasn't for those Interborough bonds."

"What bonds? Who's seen any bonds? . . . Let's get this
young fellow in here . . . Joe . . . And one more thing Gus,
for heaven's sakes keep your mouth shut. . . . If any reporters or anybody comes round to see you tell 'em about
your trip to Bermuda. . . . We can get publicity enough
when we need it. Just at present we want to keep the papers
out of it or you'll have all the reformers on your heels."

"Well aint they friends of yours? You can fix it up with em."

"Gus I'm a lawyer and not a politician. . . . I dont meddle
in those things at all. They dont interest me."

Baldwin brought the flat of his hand down on a pushbell.
An ivoryskinned young woman with heavy sullen eyes and
jetty hair came into the room.

"How do you do Mr. McNiel."

"My but you're looking well Miss Levitsky."

"Emily tell em to send that young fellow that's waiting for
Mr. McNiel in."

Joe O'Keefe came in dragging his feet a little, with his
straw hat in his hand. "Howde do sir."

"Look here Joe, what does McCarthy say?"

"Contractors and Builders Association's goin to declare a
lockout from Monday on."

"And how's the union?"

"We got a full treasury. We're goin to fight."

Baldwin sat down on the edge of the desk. "I wish I knew
what Mayor Mitchel's attitude was on all this."

"That reform gang's just treadin water like they always do," said Gus savagely biting the end off a cigar. "When's this decision going to be made public?"

"Saturday."

"Well keep in touch with us."

"All right gentlemen. And please dont call me on the phone. It dont look exactly right. You see it aint my office."

"Might be wiretappin goin on too. Those fellers wont stop at nothin. Well see ye later Joey."

Joe nodded and walked out. Baldwin turned frowning to Gus.

"Gus I dont know what I'm goin to do with you if you dont keep out of all this labor stuff. A born politician like you ought to have better sense. You just cant get away with it."

"But we got the whole damn town lined up."

"I know a whole lot of the town that isnt lined up. But thank Heavens that's not my business. This bond stuff is all right, but if you get into a mess with this strike business I couldn't handle your case. The firm wouldnt stand for it," he whispered fiercely. Then he said aloud in his usual voice, "Well how's the wife, Gus?"

Outside in the shiny marble hall, Joe O'Keefe was whistling *Sweet Rosy O'Grady* waiting for the elevator. Imagine a guy havin a knockout like that for a secretary. He stopped whistling and let the breath out silently through pursed lips. In the elevator he greeted a walleyed man in a check suit. "Hullo Buck."

"Been on your vacation yet?"

Joe stood with his feet apart and his hands in his pockets. He shook his head. "I get off Saturday."

"I guess I'll take in a couple o days at Atlantic City myself."

"How do you do it?"

"Oh the kid's clever."

Coming out of the building O'Keefe had to make his way through people crowding into the portal. A slate sky sagging between the tall buildings was spatting the pavements with fiftycent pieces. Men were running to cover with their straw hats under their coats. Two girls had made hoods of newspaper over their summer bonnets. He snatched blue of their eyes, a glint of lips and teeth as he passed. He walked fast to the corner and caught an uptown car on the run. The rain advanced down the street in a solid sheet glimmering, swishing, beating newspapers flat, prancing in silver nipples along the asphalt, striping windows, putting shine on the paint of streetcars and taxicabs. Above Fourteenth there was no rain, the air was sultry.

"A funny thing weather," said an old man next to him. O'Keefe grunted. "When I was a boy onct I saw it rain on one side of the street an a house was struck by lightnin an on our side not a drop fell though the old man wanted it bad for some tomatoplants he'd just set out."

Crossing Twentythird O'Keefe caught sight of the tower of Madison Square Garden. He jumped off the car; the momentum carried him in little running steps to the curb. Turning his coatcollar down again he started across the square. On the end of a bench under a tree drowsed Joe Harland. O'Keefe plunked down in the seat beside him.

"Hello Joe. Have a cigar."

"Hello Joe. I'm glad to see you my boy. Thanks. It's many a day since I've smoked one of these things. . . . What are you up to? Aint this kind of out of your beat?"

"I felt kinder blue so I thought I'd buy me a ticket to the fight Saturday."

"What's the matter?"

"Hell I dunno. . . . Things dont seem to go right. Here I've got myself all in deep in this political game and there dont seem to be no future in it. God I wish I was educated like you."

"A lot of good it's done me."

"I wouldn't say that. . . . If I could ever git on the track you were on I bet ye I wouldn't lose out."

"You cant tell Joe, funny things get into a man."

"There's women and that sort of stuff."

"No I dont mean that. . . . You get kinder disgusted."

"But hell I dont see how a guy with enough jack can git disgusted."

"Then maybe it was booze, I dont know."

They sat silent a minute. The afternoon was flushing with sunset. The cigarsmoke was blue and crinkly about their heads.

"Look at the swell dame. . . . Look at the way she walks.

Aint she a peacherino? That's the way I like 'em, all slick an frilly with their lips made up. . . . Takes jack to go round with dames like that."

"They're no different from anybody else, Joe."

"The hell you say."

"Say Joe you havent got an extra dollar on you?"

"Maybe I have."

"My stomach's a little out of order. . . . I'd like to take a little something to steady it, and I'm flat till I get paid Saturday . . . er . . . you understand . . . you're sure you dont mind? Give me your address and I'll send it to you first thing Monday morning."

"Hell dont worry about it, I'll see yez around somewheres."

"Thank you Joe. And for God's sake dont buy any more Blue Peter Mines on a margin without asking me about it. I may be a back number but I can still tell a goldbrick with my eyes closed."

"Well I got my money back."

"It took the devil's own luck to do it."

"Jez it strikes me funny me loanin a dollar to the guy who owned half the Street."

"Oh I never had as much as they said I did."

"This is a funny place. . . ."

"Where?"

"Oh I dunno, I guess everywhere. . . . Well so long Joe, I guess I'll go along an buy that ticket. . . . Jez it's goin to be a swell fight."

Joe Harland watched the young man's short jerky stride as he went off down the path with his straw hat on the side of his head. Then he got to his feet and walked east along Twenty-third Street. The pavements and housewalls still gave off heat although the sun had set. He stopped outside a corner saloon and examined carefully a group of stuffed ermines, gray with dust, that occupied the center of the window. Through the swinging doors a sound of quiet voices and a malty coolness seeped into the street. He suddenly flushed and bit his upper lip and after a furtive glance up and down the street went in through the swinging doors and shambled up to the brassy bottleglittering bar.

*

After the rain outdoors the plastery backstage smell was pungent in their nostrils. Ellen hung the wet raincoat on the back of the door and put her umbrella in a corner of the dressing room where a little puddle began to spread from it. "And all I could think of," she was saying in a low voice to Stan who followed her staggering, "was a funny song somebody'd told me when I was a little girl about: And the only man who survived the flood was longlegged Jack of the Isthmus."

"God I dont see why people have children. It's an admission of defeat. Procreation is the admission of an incomplete organism. Procreation is an admission of defeat."

"Stan for Heaven's sake dont shout, you'll shock the stagehands. . . . I oughtnt to have let you come. You know the way people gossip round a theater."

"I'll be quiet just like a lil mouse. . . . Just let me wait till Milly comes to dress you. Seeing you dress is my only remaining pleasure . . . I admit that as an organism I'm incomplete."

"You wont be an organism of any kind if you dont sober up."

"I'm going to drink . . . I'm going to drink till when I cut myself whiskey runs out. What's the good of blood when you can have whiskey?"

"Oh Stan."

"The only thing an incomplete organism can do is drink. . . . You complete beautiful organisms dont need to drink. . . . I'm going to lie down and go byby."

"Dont Stan for Heaven's sake. If you go and pass out here I'll never forgive you."

There was a soft doubleknock at the door. "Come in Milly." Milly was a small wrinklefaced woman with black eyes. A touch of negro blood made her purplegray lips thick, gave a lividness to her verywhite skin.

"It's eight fifteen dear," she said as she bustled in. She gave a quick look at Stan and turned to Ellen with a little wry frown.

"Stan you've got to go away. . . . I'll meet you at the Beaux Arts or anywhere you like afterwards."

"I want to go byby."

Sitting in front of the mirror at her dressingtable Ellen was wiping cold cream off her face with quick dabs of a little towel. From her makeup box a smell of greasepaint and cocoabutter melted fatly through the room.

"I dont know what to do with him tonight," she whispered to Milly as she slipped off her dress. "Oh I wish he would stop drinking."

"I'd put him in the shower and turn cold water on him deary."

"How's the house tonight Milly?"

"Pretty thin Miss Elaine."

"I guess it's the bad weather . . . I'm going to be terrible."

"Dont let him get you worked up deary. Men aint worth it."

"I want to go byby." Stan was swaying and frowning in the center of the room. "Miss Elaine I'll put him in the bathroom; nobody'll notice him there."

"That's it, let him go to sleep in the bathtub."

"Ellie I'll go byby in the bathtub."

The two women pushed him into the bathroom. He flopped limply into the tub, and lay there asleep with his feet in the air and his head on the faucets. Milly was making little rapid clucking noises with her tongue.

"He's like a sleepy baby when he's like this," whispered Ellen softly. She stuck the folded bathmat under his head and brushed the sweaty hair off his forehead. He was hardly breathing. She leaned and kissed his eyelids very softly.

"Miss Elaine you must hurry . . . curtain's ringing up."

"Look quick am I all right?"

"Pretty as a picture. . . . Lord love you dear."

Ellen ran down the stairs and round to the wings, stood there, panting with terror as if she had just missed being run over by an automobile grabbed the musicroll she had to go on with from the property man, got her cue and walked on into the glare.

"How do you do it Elaine?" Harry Goldweiser was saying, shaking his calf's head from the chair behind her. She could see him in the mirror as she took her makeup off. A taller man with gray eyes and eyebrows stood beside him. "You remember when they first cast you for the part I said to Mr. Fallik, Sol she cant do it, didnt I Sol?"

"Sure you did Harry."

"I thought that no girl so young and beautiful could put, you know . . . put the passion and terror into it, do you understand? . . . Sol and I were out front for that scene in the last act."

"Wonderful, wonderful," groaned Mr. Fallik. "Tell us how you do it Elaine."

The makeup came off black and pink on the cloth. Milly moved discreetly about the background hanging up dresses.

"Do you know who it was who coached me up on that scene? John Oglethorpe. It's amazing the ideas he has about acting."

"Yes it's a shame he's so lazy. . . . He'd be a very valuable actor."

"It's not exactly laziness . . ." Ellen shook down her hair and twisted it in a coil in her two hands. She saw Harry Goldweiser nudge Mr. Fallik.

"Beautiful isn't it?"

"How's Red Red Rose going?"

"Oh dont ask me Elaine. Played exclusively to the ushers last week, do you understand? I dont see why it dont go, it's catchy. . . . Mae Merrill has a pretty figure. Oh, the show business has all gone to hell."

Ellen put the last bronze pin in the copper coil of her hair. She tossed her chin up. "I'd like to try something like that."

"But one thing at a time my dear young lady; we've just barely got you started as an emotional actress."

"I hate it; it's all false. Sometimes I want to run down to the foots and tell the audience, go home you damn fools. This is a rotten show and a lot of fake acting and you ought to know it. In a musical show you could be sincere."

"Didnt I tell ye she was nuts Sol? Didnt I tell ye she was nuts?"

"I'll use some of that little speech in my publicity next week. . . . I can work it in fine."

"You cant have her crabbin the show."

"No but I can work it in in that column about aspirations of celebrities. . . . You know, this guy is President of the Zozodont Company and would rather have been a fireman and another would rather have been a keeper at the Zoo. . . . Great human interest stuff."

"You can tell them Mr. Fallik that I think the woman's place is in the home . . . for the feebleminded."

"Ha ha ha," laughed Harry Goldweiser showing the gold teeth in the sides of his mouth. "But I know you could dance and sing with the best of em, Elaine."

"Wasnt I in the chorus for two years before I married Oglethorpe?"

"You must have started in the cradle," said Mr. Fallik leering under his gray lashes.

"Well I must ask you gentlemen to get out of here a minute while I change. I'm all wringing wet every night after the last act."

"We got to get along anyway . . . do you understand? . . . Mind if I use your bathroom a sec?"

Milly stood in front of the bathroom door. Ellen caught the jetty glance of her eyes far apart in her blank white face. "I'm afraid you cant Harry, it's out of order."

"I'll go over to Charley's. . . . I'll tell Thompson to have a plumber come and look at it. . . . Well good night kid. Be good."

"Good night Miss Oglethorpe," said Mr. Fallik creakily, "and if you cant be good be careful." Milly closed the door after them.

"Whee, that's a relief," cried Ellen and stretched out her arms.

"I tell you I was scared deary. . . . Dont you ever let any feller like that come to the theater with ye. I've seen many a good trouper ruined by things like that. I'm tellin ye because I'm fond of you Miss Elaine, an I'm old an I know about the showbusiness."

"Of course you are Milly, and you're quite right too . . . Lets see if we can wake him up."

"My God Milly, look at that."

Stan was lying as they had left him in the bathtub full of water. The tail of his coat and one hand were floating on top of the water. "Get up out of there Stan you idiot. . . . He might catch his death. You fool, you fool." Ellen took him by the hair and shook his head from side to side.

"Ooch that hurts," he moaned in a sleepy child's voice.

"Get up out of there Stan. . . . You're soaked."

He threw back his head and his eyes snapped open. "Why so I am." He raised himself with his hands on the sides of the tub and stood swaying, dripping into the water that was yellow from his clothes and shoes, braying his loud laugh. Ellen leaned against the bathroom door laughing with her eyes full of tears.

"You cant get mad at him Milly, that's what makes him so exasperating. Oh what are we going to do?"

"Lucky he wasnt drownded. . . . Give me your papers and pocketbook sir. I'll try and dry em with a towel," said Milly.

"But you cant go past the doorman like that . . . even if we wring you out. . . . Stan you've got to take off all your clothes and put on a dress of mine. Then you can wear my rain cape and we can whisk into a taxicab and take you home. . . . What do you think Milly?"

Milly was rolling her eyes and shaking her head as she wrung out Stan's coat. In the washbasin she had piled the soppy remains of a pocketbook, a pad, pencils, a jacknife, two rolls of film, a flask.

"I wanted a bath anyway," said Stan.

"Oh I could beat you. Well you're sober at least."

"Sober as a penguin."

"Well you've got to dress up in my clothes that's all. . . ."

"I cant wear girl's clothes."

"You've got to. . . . You havent even got a raincoat to cover that mess. If you dont I'll lock you up in the bathroom and leave you."

"All right Ellie. . . . Honest I'm terribly sorry."

Milly was wrapping the clothes in newspaper after wringing them out in the bathtub. Stan looked at himself in the mirror. "Gosh I'm an indecent sight in this dress. . . . Ish gebibble."

"I've never seen anything so disgusting looking. . . . No you look very sweet, a little tough perhaps. . . . Now for God's sake keep your face towards me when you go past old Barney."

"My shoes are all squudgy."

"It cant be helped. . . . Thank Heaven I had this cape here. . . . Milly you're an angel to clear up all this mess."

"Good night deary, and remember what I said. . . . I'm tellin ye that's all. . . ."

"Stan take little steps and if we meet anybody go right on and jump in a taxi. . . . You can get away with anything if you do it quick enough." Ellen's hands were trembling as they came down the steps. She tucked one in under Stan's elbow and began talking in a low chatty voice. . . . "You see dear, daddy came round to see the show two or three nights ago and he was shocked to death. He said he thought a girl demeaned herself showing her feelings like that before a lot of people. . . . Isn't it killing? . . . Still he was impressed by the writeups the *Herald* and *World* gave me Sunday. . . . Goodnight Barney, nasty night. . . . My God. . . . Here's a taxi, get in. Where are you going?" Out of the dark of the taxi, out of his long face muffled in the blue hood, his eyes were so bright black they frightened her like coming suddenly on a deep pit in the dark.

"All right we'll go to my house. Might as well be hanged for a sheep. . . . Driver please go to Bank Street. The taxi started. They were jolting through the crisscross planes of red light, green light, yellow light beaded with lettering of Broadway. Suddenly Stan leaned over her and kissed her hard very quickly on the mouth.

"Stan you've got to stop drinking. It's getting beyond a joke."

"Why shouldn't things get beyond a joke? You're getting beyond a joke and I dont complain."

"But darling you'll kill yourself."

"Well?"

"Oh I dont understand you Stan."

"I dont understand you Ellie, but I love you very . . . exordinately much." There was a broken tremor in his very low voice that stunned her with happiness.

Ellen paid the taxi. Siren throbbing in an upward shriek that burst and trailed in a dull wail down the street, a fire engine went by red and gleaming, then a hookandladder with bell clanging.

"Let's go to the fire Ellie."

"With you in those clothes. . . . We'll do no such thing."

He followed her silent into the house and up the stairs. Her long room was cool and fresh smelling.

"Ellie you're not sore at me?"

"Of course not idiot child."

She undid the sodden bundle of his clothes and took them into the kitchenette to dry beside the gas stove. The sound of the phonograph playing *He's a devil in his own home town* called her back. Stan had taken off the dress. He was dancing round with a chair for a partner, her blue padded dressinggown flying out from his thin hairy legs.

"Oh Stan you precious idiot."

He put down the chair and came towards her brown and male and lean in the silly dressinggown. The phonograph came to the end of the tune and the record went on rasping round and round.

V. Went to the Animals' Fair

*R*ed light. Bell.

  A block deep four ranks of cars wait at the grade crossing, fenders in taillights, mudguards scraping mudguards, motors purring hot, exhausts reeking, cars from Babylon and Jamaica, cars from Montauk, Port Jefferson, Patchogue, limousines from Long Beach, Far Rockaway, roadsters from Great Neck . . . cars full of asters and wet bathingsuits, sunsinged necks, mouths sticky from sodas and hotdawgs. . . . cars dusted with pollen of ragweed and goldenrod.

  Green light. Motors race, gears screech into first. The cars space out, flow in a long ribbon along the ghostly cement road, between blackwindowed blocks of concrete factories, between bright slabbed colors of signboards towards the glow over the city that stands up incredibly into the night sky like the glow of a great lit tent, like the yellow tall bulk of a tentshow.

Sarajevo, the word stuck in her throat when she tried to say it. . . .

"It's terrible to think of, terrible," George Baldwin was groaning. "The Street'll go plumb to hell. . . . They'll close the Stock Exchange, only thing to do."

"And I've never been to Europe either. . . . A war must be an extraordinary thing to see." Ellen in her blue velvet dress with a buff cloak over it leaned back against the cushions of the taxi that whirred smoothly under them. "I always think of history as lithographs in a schoolbook, generals making proclamations, little tiny figures running across fields with their arms spread out, facsimiles of signatures." Cones of light cutting into cones of light along the hot humming roadside, headlights splashing trees, houses, billboards, telegraph poles with broad brushes of whitewash. The taxi made a half turn and stopped in front of a roadhouse that oozed pink light and ragtime through every chink.

"Big crowd tonight," said the taximan to Baldwin when he paid him.

"I wonder why," asked Ellen.

"De Canarsie moider has sumpen to do wid it I guess."

"What's that?"

"Sumpen terrible. I seen it."

"You saw the murder?"

"I didn't see him do it. I seen de bodies laid out stiff before dey took em to de morgue. Us kids used to call de guy Santa Claus cause he had white whiskers. . . . Knowed him since I was a little feller." The cars behind were honking and rasping their klaxons. "I better git a move on. . . . Good night lady."

The red hallway smelt of lobster and steamed clams and cocktails.

"Why hello Gus! . . . Elaine let me introduce Mr. and Mrs. McNiel. . . . This is Miss Oglethorpe." Ellen shook the big hand of a rednecked snubnosed man and the small precisely gloved hand of his wife. "Gus I'll see you before we go. . . ."

Ellen was following the headwaiter's swallowtails along the edge of the dancefloor. They sat at a table beside the wall. The music was playing *Everybody's Doing It.* Baldwin hummed it as he hung over her a second arranging the wrap on the back of her chair.

"Elaine you are the loveliest person . . ." he began as he sat down opposite her. "It seems so horrible. I dont see how it's possible."

"What?"

"This war. I cant think of anything else."

"I can . . ." She kept her eyes on the menu. "Did you notice those two people I introduced to you?"

"Yes. Is that the McNiel whose name is in the paper all the time? Some row about a builders' strike and the Interborough bond issue."

"It's all politics. I bet he's glad of the war, poor old Gus. It'll do one thing, it'll keep that row off the front page. . . . I'll tell you about him in a minute. . . . I dont suppose you like steamed clams do you? They are very good here."

"George I adore steamed clams."

"Then we'll have a regular old fashioned Long Island shore dinner. What do you think of that?" Laying her gloves away on the edge of the table her hand brushed against the vase of rusty red and yellow roses. A shower of faded petals fluttered onto her hand, her gloves, the table. She shook them off her hands.

"And do have him take these wretched roses away George. . . . I hate faded flowers."

Steam from the plated bowl of clams uncoiled in the rosy glow from the lampshade. Baldwin watched her fingers, pink and limber, pulling the clams by their long necks out of their shells, dipping them in melted butter, and popping them dripping in her mouth. She was deep in eating clams. He sighed. "Elaine . . . I'm a very unhappy man. . . . Seeing Gus McNiel's wife. It's the first time in years. Think of it I was crazy in love with her and now I cant remember what her first name was . . . Funny isn't it? Things had been extremely slow ever since I had set up in practice for myself. It was a rash thing to do, as I was only two years out of lawschool and had no money to run on. I was rash in those days. I'd decided that if I didn't get a case that day I'd chuck everything and go back to a clerkship. I went out for a walk to clear my head and saw a freightcar shunting down Eleventh Avenue run into a milkwagon. It was a horrid mess and when we'd picked the fellow up I said to myself I'd get him his rightful damages or bankrupt myself in the attempt. I won his case and that brought me to the notice of various people downtown, and that started him on his career and me on mine."

"So he drove a milkwagon did he? I think milkmen are the nicest people in the world. Mine's the cutest thing."

"Elaine you wont repeat this to anyone. . . . I feel the completest confidence in you."

"That's very nice of you George. Isn't it amazing the way girls are getting to look more like Mrs. Castle every day? Just look round this room."

"She was like a wild rose Elaine, fresh and pink and full of the Irish, and now she's a rather stumpy businesslike looking little woman."

"And you're as fit as you ever were. That's the way it goes."

"I wonder. . . . You dont know how empty and hollow everything was before I met you. All Cecily and I can do is make each other miserable."

"Where is she now?"

"She's up at Bar Harbor. . . . I had luck and all sorts of success when I was still a young man. . . . I'm not forty yet."

"But I should think it would be fascinating. You must enjoy the law or you wouldn't be such a success at it."

"Oh success . . . success . . . what does it mean?"

"I'd like a little of it."

"But my dear girl you have it."

"Oh not what I mean."

"But it isn't any fun any more. All I do is sit in the office and let the young fellows do the work. My future's all cut out for me. I suppose I could get solemn and pompous and practice little private vices . . . but there's more in me than that."

"Why dont you go into politics?"

"Why should I go up to Washington into that greasy backwater when I'm right on the spot where they give the orders? The terrible thing about having New York go stale on you is that there's nowhere else. It's the top of the world. All we can do is go round and round in a squirrel cage."

Ellen was watching the people in light summer clothes dancing on the waxed square of floor in the center; she caught sight of Tony Hunter's oval pink and white face at a table on the far side of the room. Oglethorpe was not with him. Stan's friend Herf sat with his back to her. She watched him laughing, his long rumpled black head poised a little askew on a scraggly neck. The other two men she didn't know.

"Who are you looking at?"

"Just some friends of Jojo's. . . . I wonder how on earth they got way out here. It's not exactly on that gang's beat."

"Always the way when I try to get away with something," said Baldwin with a wry smile.

"I should say you'd done exactly what you wanted to all your life."

"Oh Elaine if you'd only let me do what I want to now. I want you to let me make you happy. You're such a brave little girl making your way all alone the way you do. By gad you are so full of love and mystery and glitter . . ." He faltered, took a deep swallow of wine, went on with flushing face. "I feel like a schoolboy . . . I'm making a fool of myself. Elaine I'd do anything in the world for you."

"Well all I'm going to ask you to do is to send away this lobster. I dont think it's terribly good."

"The devil . . . maybe it isn't. . . . Here waiter! . . . I was so rattled I didn't know I was eating it."

"You can get me some supreme of chicken instead."

"Surely you poor child you must be starved."

". . . And a little corn on the cob. . . . I understand now why you make such a good lawyer, George. Any jury would have burst out sobbing long ago at such an impassioned plea."

"How about you Elaine?"

"George please dont ask me."

At the table where Jimmy Herf sat they were drinking whiskey and soda. A yellowskinned man with light hair and a thin nose standing out crooked between childish blue eyes was talking in a confidential singsong: "Honest I had em lashed to the mast. The police department is cookoo, absolutely cookoo treating it as a rape and suicide case. That old man and his lovely innocent daughter were murdered, foully murdered. And do you know who by . . ." He pointed a chubby cigarettestained finger at Tony Hunter.

"Dont give me the third degree judge I dont know anything about it" he said dropping his long lashes over his eyes.

"By the Black Hand."

"You tell em Bullock," said Jimmy Herf laughing. Bullock brought his fist down on the table so that the plates and glasses jingled. "Canarsie's full of the Black Hand, full of anarchists and kidnappers and undesirable citizens. It's our business to ferret em out and vindicate the honor of this poor old man and his beloved daughter. We are going to vindicate the honor of poor old monkeyface, what's his name?"

"Mackintosh," said Jimmy. "And the people round here used to call him Santa Claus. Of course everybody admits he's been crazy for years."

"We admit nothing but the majesty of American citizenhood. . . . But hell's bells what's the use when this goddam war takes the whole front page? I was going to have a fullpage spread and they've cut me down to half a column. Aint it the life?"

"You might work up something about how he was a lost heir to the Austrian throne and had been murdered for political reasons."

"Not such a bad idear Jimmy."

"But it's such a horrible thing," said Tony Hunter.

"You think we're a lot of callous brutes, dont you Tony?"

"No I just dont see the pleasure people get out of reading about it."

"Oh it's all in the day's work," said Jimmy. "What gives me gooseflesh is the armies mobilizing, Belgrade bombarded, Belgium invaded . . . all that stuff. I just cant imagine it. . . . They've killed Jaures." "Who's he?"

"A French Socialist."

"Those goddam French are so goddam degenerate all they can do is fight duels and sleep with each other's wives. I bet the Germans are in Paris in two weeks."

"It couldn't last long," said Framingham, a tall ceremonious man with a whispy blond moustache who sat beside Hunter.

"Well I'd like to get an assignment as warcorrespondent."

"Say Jimmy do you know this French guy who's barkeep here?"

"Congo Jake? Sure I know him."

"Is he a good guy?"

"He's swell."

"Let's go out and talk to him. He might give us some dope about this here murder. God I'd like it if I could hitch it on to the World Conflict."

"I have the greatest confidence," had begun Framingham, "that the British will patch it up somehow." Jimmy followed Bullock towards the bar.

Crossing the room he caught sight of Ellen. Her hair was very red in the glow from the lamp beside her. Baldwin was leaning towards her across the table with moist lips and bright eyes. Jimmy felt something glittering go off in his chest like a released spring. He turned his head away suddenly for fear she should see him.

Bullock turned and nudged him in the ribs. "Say Jimmy who the hell are those two guys came out with us?"

"They are friends of Ruth's. I dont know them particularly well. Framingham's an interior decorator I think."

At the bar under a picture of the Lusitania stood a dark man in a white coat distended by a deep gorilla chest. He was vibrating a shaker between his very hairy hands. A waiter stood in front of the bar with a tray of cocktail glasses. The cocktail foamed into them greenishwhite.

"Hello Congo," said Jimmy.

"Ah bonsoir monsieur 'Erf, ça biche?"

"Pretty good . . . Say Congo I want you to meet a friend of mine. This is Grant Bullock of the *American*."

"Very please. You an Mr. 'Erf ave someting on the 'ouse sir."

The waiter raised the clinking tray of glasses to shoulder height and carried them out on the flat of his hand.

"I suppose a gin fizz'll ruin all that whiskey but I'd like one. . . . Drink something with us wont you Congo?" Bullock put a foot up on the brass rail and took a sip. "I was wondering," he said slowly, "if there was any dope going round about this murder down the road."

"Everybody ave his teyorie . . ."

Jimmy caught a faint wink from one of Congo's deepset black eyes. "Do you live out here?" he asked to keep from giggling.

"In the middle of the night I hear an automobile go by very fast wid de cutout open. I tink maybe it run into something because it stopped very quick and come back much faster, licketysplit."

"Did you hear a shot?"

Congo shook his head mysteriously. "I ear voices, very angree voices."

"Gosh I'm going to look into this," said Bullock tossing off the end of his drink. "Let's go back to the girls."

Ellen was looking at the face wrinkled like a walnut and the dead codfish eyes of the waiter pouring coffee. Baldwin was leaning back in his chair staring at her through his eyelashes. He was talking in a low monotone:

"Cant you see that I'll go mad if I cant have you. You are the only thing in the world I ever wanted."

"George I dont want to be had by anybody. . . . Cant you understand that a woman wants some freedom? Do be a sport about it. I'll have to go home if you talk like that."

"Why have you kept me dangling then? I'm not the sort of man you can play like a trout. You know that perfectly well."

She looked straight at him with wide gray eyes; the light gave a sheen of gold to the little brown specks in the iris.

"It's not so easy never to be able to have friends." She looked down at her fingers on the edge of the table. His eyes were on the glint of copper along her eyelashes. Suddenly he snapped the silence that was tightening between them.

"Anyway let's dance."

> J'ai fait trois fois le tour du monde
> Dans mes voyages,

hummed Congo Jake as the big shining shaker quivered between his hairy hands. The narrow greenpapered bar was swelled and warped with bubbling voices, spiral exhalations of drinks, sharp clink of ice and glasses, an occasional strain of music from the other room. Jimmy Herf stood alone in the corner sipping a gin fizz. Next him Gus McNiel was slapping Bullock on the back and roaring in his ear:

"Why if they dont close the Stock Exchange . . . god-amighty . . . before the blowup comes there'll be an opportunity. . . . Well begorry dont you forget it. A panic's the time for a man with a cool head to make money."

"There have been some big failures already and this is just the first whiff. . . ."

"Opportunity knocks but once at a young man's door. . . . You listen to me when there's a big failure of one o them brokerage firms honest men can bless themselves. . . . But you're not putting everythin I'm tellin ye in the paper, are you? There's a good guy. . . . Most of you fellers go around puttin words in a man's mouth. Cant trust one of you. I'll tell you one thing though the lockout is a wonderful thing for the contractors. Wont be no house-buildin with a war on anyway." "It wont last more'n two weeks and I dont see what it has to do with us anyway."

"But conditions'll be affected all over the world. . . . Conditions. . . . Hello Joey what the hell do you want?"

"I'd like to talk to you private for a minute sir. There's some big news. . . ."

The bar emptied gradually. Jimmy Herf was still standing at the end against the wall.

"You never get drunk, Mr. 'Erf." Congo Jake sat down back of the bar to drink a cup of coffee.

"I'd rather watch the other fellows."

"Very good. No use spend a lot of money ave a eadache next day."

"That's no way for a barkeep to talk."

"I say what I tink."

"Say I've always wanted to ask you. . . . Do you mind telling me? . . . How did you get the name of Congo Jake?"

Congo laughed deep in his chest. "I dunno. . . . When I very leetle I first go to sea dey call me Congo because I have curly hair an dark like a nigger. Den when I work in America, on American ship an all zat, guy ask me How you feel Congo? and I say Jake . . . so dey call me Congo Jake."

"It's some nickname. . . . I thought you'd followed the sea."

"It's a 'ard life. . . . I tell you Mr. 'Erf, there's something about me unlucky. When I first remember on a peniche, you know what I mean . . . in canal, a big man not my fader beat me up every day. Then I run away and work on sailboats in and out of Bordeaux, you know?"

"I was there when I was a kid I think. . . ."

"Sure. . . . You understand them things Mr. 'Erf. But a feller like you, good education, all 'at, you dont know what life is. When I was seventeen I come to New York . . . no good. I tink of notten but raising Cain. Den I shipped out again and went everywhere to hell an gone. In Shanghai I learned spik American an tend bar. I come back to Frisco an got married. Now I want to be American. But unlucky again see? Before I marry zat girl her and me lived togedder a year sweet as pie, but when we get married no good. She make fun of me and call me Frenchy because I no spik American good and den she kick no out of the house an I tell her go to hell. Funny ting a man's life."

> J'ai fait trois fois le tour du monde
> Dans mes voyages. . . .

he started in his growling baritone.

There was a hand on Jimmy's arm. He turned. "Why Ellie what's the matter?"

"I'm with a crazy man you've got to help me get away."

"Look this is Congo Jake. . . . You ought to know him Ellie, he's a fine man. . . . This is une tres grande artiste, Congo."

"Wont the lady have a leetle anizette?"

"Have a little drink with us. . . . It's awfully cozy in here now that everybody's gone."

"No thanks I'm going home."

"But it's just the neck of the evening."

"Well you'll have to take the consequences of my crazy man. . . . Look Herf, have you seen Stan today?"

"No I haven't."

"He didn't turn up when I expected him."

"I wish you'd keep him from drinking so much, Ellie. I'm getting worried about him."

"I'm not his keeper."

"I know, but you know what I mean."

"What does our friend here think about all this wartalk?"

"I wont go. . . . A workingman has no country. I'm going to be American citizen. . . . I was in the marine once but. . . ." He slapped his jerking bent forearm with one hand, and a deep laugh rattled in his throat. . . . "Twentee tree. Moi je suis anarchiste vous comprennez monsieur."

"But then you cant be an American citizen."

Congo shrugged his shoulders.

"Oh I love him, he's wonderful," whispered Ellen in Jimmy's ear.

"You know why they have this here war. . . . So that workingmen all over wont make big revolution. . . . Too busy fighting. So Guillaume and Viviani and l'Empereur d'Autriche and Krupp and Rothschild and Morgan they say let's have a war. . . . You know the first thing they do? They shoot Jaures, because he socialiste. The socialists are traitors to the International but all de samee. . . ."

"But how can they make people fight if they dont want to?"

"In Europe people are slaves for thousands of years. Not like 'ere. . . . But Ive seen war. Very funny. I tended bar in Port Arthur, nutten but a kid den. It was very funny."

"Gee I wish I could get a job as warcorrespondent."

"I might go as a Red Cross nurse."

"Correspondent very good ting. . . . Always drunk in American bar very far from battlefield."

They laughed.

"But arent we rather far from the battlefield, Herf?"

"All right let's dance. You must forgive me if I dance very badly."

"I'll kick you if you do anything wrong."

His arm was like plaster when he put it round her to dance with her. High ashy walls broke and crackled within him. He was soaring like a fireballoon on the smell of her hair.

"Get up on your toes and walk in time to the music. . . . Move in straight lines that's the whole trick." Her voice cut the quick coldly like a tiny flexible sharp metalsaw. Elbows joggling, faces set, gollywog eyes, fat men and thin women, thin women and fat men rotated densely about them. He was crumbling plaster with something that rattled achingly in his chest, she was an intricate machine of sawtooth steel whitebright bluebright copperbright in his arms. When they stopped her breast and the side of her body and her thigh came against him. He was suddenly full of blood steaming with sweat like a runaway horse. A breeze through an open door hustled the tobaccosmoke and the clotted pink air of the restaurant.

"Herf I want to go down to see the murder cottage; please take me."

"As if I hadn't seen enough of X's marking the spot where the crime was committed."

In the hall George Baldwin stepped in front of them. He was pale as chalk, his black tie was crooked, the nostrils of his thin nose were dilated and marked with little veins of red.

"Hello George."

His voice croaked tartly like a klaxon. "Elaine I've been looking for you. I must speak to you. . . . Maybe you think I'm joking. I never joke."

"Herf excuse me a minute. . . . Now what is the matter George? Come back to the table."

"George I was not joking either. . . . Herf do you mind ordering me a taxi?"

Baldwin grabbed hold of her wrist. "You've been playing with me long enough, do you hear me? Some day some man's going to take a gun and shoot you. You think you can play me like all the other little sniveling fools. . . . You're no better than a common prostitute."

"Herf I told you to go get me a taxi."

Jimmy bit his lip and went out the front door.

"Elaine what are you going to do?"

"George I will not be bullied."

Something nickel flashed in Baldwin's hand. Gus McNiel stepped forward and gripped his wrist with a big red hand.

"Gimme that George. . . . For God's sake man pull yourself together." He shoved the revolver into his pocket. Baldwin tottered to the wall in front of him. The trigger finger of his right hand was bleeding.

"Here's a taxi," said Herf looking from one to another of the taut white faces.

"All right you take the girl home. . . . No harm done, just a little nervous attack, see? No cause for alarm," McNiel was shouting in the voice of a man speaking from a soapbox. The headwaiter and the coatgirl were looking at each other uneasily. "Didn't nutten happen. . . . Gentleman's a little nervous . . . overwork you understand," McNiel brought his voice down to reassuring purr. "You just forget it."

As they were getting into the taxi Ellen suddenly said in a little child's voice: "I forgot we were going down to see the murder cottage. . . . Let's make him wait. I'd like to walk up and down in the air for a minute." There was a smell of saltmarshes. The night was marbled with clouds and moonlight. The toads in the ditches sounded like sleighbells.

"Is it far?" she asked.

"No it's right down at the corner."

Their feet crackled on gravel then ground softly on macadam. A headlight blinded them, they stopped to let the car whir by; the exhaust filled their nostrils, faded into the smell of saltmarshes again.

It was a peaked gray house with a small porch facing the road screened with broken lattice. A big locust shaded it from behind. A policeman walked to and fro in front of it whistling gently to himself. A mildewed scrap of moon came out from behind the clouds for a minute, made tinfoil of a bit of broken glass in a gaping window, picked out the little rounded leaves of the locust and rolled like a lost dime into a crack in the clouds.

Neither of them said anything. They walked back towards the roadhouse.

"Honestly Herf havent you seen Stan?"

"No I havent an idea where he could be hiding himself."

"If you see him tell him I want him to call me up at once. . . . Herf what were those women called who followed the armies in the French Revolution?"

"Let's think. Was it cantonnières?"

"Something like that . . . I'd like to do that."

An electric train whistled far to the right of them, rattled nearer and faded into whining distance.

Dripping with a tango the roadhouse melted pink like a block of icecream. Jimmy was following her into the taxicab.

"No I want to be alone, Herf."

"But I'd like very much to take you home. . . . I dont like the idea of letting you go all alone."

"Please as a friend I ask you."

They didnt shake hands. The taxi kicked dust and a rasp of burnt gasoline in his face. He stood on the steps reluctant to go back into the noise and fume.

Nellie McNiel was alone at the table. In front of her was the chair pushed back with his napkin on the back of it where her husband had sat. She was staring straight ahead of her; the dancers passed like shadows across her eyes. At the other end of the room she saw George Baldwin, pale and lean, walk slowly like a sick man to his table. He stood beside the table examining his check carefully, paid it and stood looking distractedly round the room. He was going to look at her. The waiter brought the change on a plate and bowed low. Baldwin swept the faces of the dancers with a black glance, turned his back square and walked out. Remembering the insupportable sweetness of Chinese lilies, she felt her eyes filling with tears. She took her engagement book out of her silver mesh bag and went through it hurriedly, marking carets with a silver pencil. She looked up after a little while, the tired skin of her face in a pucker of spite, and beckoned to a waiter. "Will you please tell Mr. McNiel that Mrs. McNiel wants to speak to him? He's in the bar."

"Sarajevo, Sarajevo; that's the place that set the wires on fire," Bullock was shouting at the frieze of faces and glasses along the bar.

"Say bo," said Joe O'Keefe confidentially to no one in particular, "a guy works in a telegraph office told me there'd been a big seabattle off St. John's, Newfoundland and the Britishers had sunk the German fleet of forty battleships."

"Jiminy that'd stop the war right there."

"But they aint declared war yet."

"How do you know? The cables are so choked up you cant get any news through."

"Did you see there were four more failures on Wall Street?"

"Tell me Chicago wheat pit's gone crazy."

"They ought to close all the exchanges till this blows over."

"Well maybe when the Germans have licked the pants off her England'll give Ireland her freedom."

"But they are. . . . Stock market wont be open tomorrow."

"If a man's got the capital to cover and could keep his head this here would be the time to clean up."

"Well Bullock old man I'm going home," said Jimmy. "This is my night of rest and I ought to be getting after it."

Bullock winked one eye and waved a drunken hand. The voices in Jimmy's ears were throbbing elastic roar, near, far, near, far. Dies like a dog, march on he said. He'd spent all his money but a quarter. Shot at sunrise. Declaration of war. Commencement of hostilities. And they left him alone in his glory. Leipzig, the Wilderness, Waterloo, where the embattled farmers stood and fired the shot heard round . . . Cant take a taxi, want to walk anyway. Ultimatum. Trooptrains singing to the shambles with flowers on their ears. And shame on the false Etruscan who lingers in his home when . . .

As he was walking down the gravel drive to the road an arm hooked in his.

"Do you mind if I come along? I dont want to stay here."

"Sure come ahead Tony I'm going to walk."

Herf walked with a long stride, looking straight ahead of him. Clouds had darkened the sky where remained the faintest milkiness of moonlight. To the right and left there was outside of the violetgray cones of occasional arclights black pricked by few lights, ahead the glare of streets rose in blurred cliffs yellow and ruddy.

"You dont like me do you?" said Tony Hunter breathlessly after a few minutes.

Herf slowed his pace. "Why I dont know you very well. You seem to me a very pleasant person. . . ."

"Dont lie; there's no reason why you should. . . . I think I'm going to kill myself tonight."

"Heavens! dont do that. . . . What's the matter?"

"You have no right to tell me not to kill myself. You dont know anything about me. If I was a woman you wouldnt be so indifferent."

"What's eating you anyway?"

"I'm going crazy that's all, everything's so horrible. When I first met you with Ruth one evening I thought we were going to be friends, Herf. You seemed so sympathetic and understanding. . . . I thought you were like me, but now you're getting so callous."

"I guess it's the *Times*. . . . I'll get fired soon, don't worry."

"I'm tired of being poor; I want to make a hit."

"Well you're young yet; you must be younger than I am." Tony didnt answer.

They were walking down a broad avenue between two rows of blackened frame houses. A streetcar long and yellow hissed rasping past.

"Why we must be in Flatbush."

"Herf I used to think you were like me, but now I never see you except with some woman."

"What do you mean?"

"I've never told anybody in the world. . . . By God if you tell anybody. . . . When I was a child I was horribly oversexed, when I was about ten or eleven or thirteen." He was sobbing. As they passed under an arclight, Jimmy caught the glisten of the tears on his cheeks. "I wouldn't tell you this if I wasnt drunk."

"But things like that happened to almost everybody when they were kids. . . . You oughtnt to worry about that."

"But I'm that way now, that's what's so horrible. I cant like women. I've tried and tried. . . . You see I was caught. I was so ashamed I wouldn't go to school for weeks. My mother cried and cried. I'm so ashamed. I'm so afraid people will find out about it. I'm always fighting to keep it hidden, to hide my feelings."

"But it all may be an idea. You may be able to get over it. Go to a psychoanalyst."

"I cant talk to anybody. It's just that tonight I'm drunk. I've tried to look it up in the encyclopedia. . . . It's not even in the dictionary." He stopped and leaned against a lamppost with his face in his hands. "It's not even in the dictionary."

Jimmy Herf patted him on the back. "Buck up for Heaven's sake. They're lots of people in the same boat. The stage is full of them."

"I hate them all. . . . It's not people like that I fall in love with. I hate myself. I suppose you'll hate me after tonight."

"What nonsense. It's no business of mine."

"Now you know why I want to kill myself. . . . Oh it's not fair Herf, it's not fair. . . . I've had no luck in my life. I started earning my living as soon as I got out of highschool. I used to be bellhop in summer hotels. My mother lived in Lakewood and I used to send her everything I earned. I've worked so hard to get where I am. If it were known, if there were a scandal and it all came out I'd be ruined."

"But everybody says that of all juveniles and nobody lets it worry them."

"Whenever I fail to get a part I think it's on account of that. I hate and despise all that kind of men. . . . I dont want to be a juvenile. I want to act. Oh it's hell. . . . It's hell."

"But you're rehearsing now aren't you?"

"A fool show that'll never get beyond Stamford. Now when you hear that I've done it you wont be surprised."

"Done what?"

"Killed myself."

They walked without speaking. It had started to rain. Down the street behind the low greenblack shoebox houses there was an occasional mothpink flutter of lightning. A wet dusty smell came up from the asphalt beaten by the big plunking drops.

"There ought to be a subway station near. . . . Isn't that a blue light down there? Let's hurry or we'll get soaked."

"Oh hell Tony I'd just as soon get soaked as not." Jimmy took off his felt hat and swung it in one hand. The raindrops were cool on his forehead, the smell of the rain, of roofs and mud and asphalt, took the biting taste of whiskey and cigarettes out of his mouth.

"Gosh it's horrible," he shouted suddenly.

"What?"

"All the hushdope about sex. I'd never realized it before tonight, the full extent of the agony. God you must have a rotten time. . . . We all of us have a rotten time. In your case it's just luck, hellish bad luck. Martin used to say: Everything would be so much better if suddenly a bell rang and everybody told everybody else honestly what they did about it, how they lived, how they loved. It's hiding things makes them putrefy. By God it's horrible. As if life wasn't difficult enough without that."

"Well I'm going down into this subway station."

"You'll have to wait hours for a train."

"I cant help it I'm tired and I dont want to get wet."

"Well good night."

"Good night Herf."

There was a long rolling thunderclap. It began to rain hard. Jimmy rammed his hat down on his head and yanked his coatcollar up. He wanted to run along yelling sonsobitches at the top of his lungs. Lightning flickered along the staring rows of dead windows. The rain seethed along the pavements, against storewindows, on brownstone steps. His knees were wet, a slow trickle started down his back, there were chilly cascades off his sleeves onto his wrists, his whole body itched and tingled. He walked on through Brooklyn. Obsession of all the beds in all the pigeonhole bedrooms, tangled sleepers twisted and strangled like the roots of potbound plants. Obsession of feet creaking on the stairs of lodginghouses, hands fumbling at doorknobs. Obsession of pounding temples and solitary bodies rigid on their beds.

> J'ai fait trois fois le tour du monde
> Vive le sang, vive le sang. . . .

Moi monsieur je suis anarchiste. . . . *And three times round went our gallant ship, and three times round went . . .*

goddam it between that and money . . . *and she sank to the bottom of the sea* . . . we're in a treadmill for fair.

> J'ai fait trois fois le tour du monde
> Dans mes voy . . . ages.

Declaration of war . . . rumble of drums . . . beefeaters march in red after the flashing baton of a drummajor in a hat like a longhaired muff, silver knob spins flashing grump, grump, grump . . . in the face of revolution mondiale. Commencement of hostilities in a long parade through the empty rainlashed streets. Extra, extra, extra. Santa Claus shoots daughter he has tried to attack. SLAYS SELF WITH SHOTGUN . . . put the gun under his chin and pulled the trigger with his big toe. The stars look down on Fredericktown. Workers of the world, unite. Vive le sang, vive le sang.

"Golly I'm wet," Jimmy Herf said aloud. As far as he could see the street stretched empty in the rain between ranks of dead windows studded here and there with violet knobs of arclights. Desperately he walked on.

VI. Five Statutory Questions

They pair off hurriedly. STANDING UP IN CARS STRICTLY FORBIDDEN. *The climbing chain grates, grips the cogs; jerkily the car climbs the incline out of the whirring lights, out of the smell of crowds and steamed corn and peanuts, up jerkily grating up through the tall night of September meteors.*

Sea, marshsmell, the lights of an Iron Steamboat leaving the dock. Across wide violet indigo a lighthouse blinks. Then the swoop. The sea does a flipflop, the lights soar. Her hair in his mouth, his hand in her ribs, thighs grind together.

The wind of their falling has snatched their yells, they jerk rattling upwards through the tangled girderstructure. Swoop. Soar. Bubbling lights in a sandwich of darkness and sea. Swoop. KEEP YOUR SEATS FOR THE NEXT RIDE.

"Come on in Joe, I'll see if the ole lady kin git us some grub."

"Very kind of you . . . er . . . I'm not . . . er . . . exactly dressed to meet a lady you see."

"Oh she wont care. She's just my mother; sit down, I'll git her."

Harland sat down on a chair beside the door in the dark kitchen and put his hands on his knees. He sat staring at his hands; they were red and dirtgrained and trembling, his tongue was like a nutmeg grater from the cheap whiskey he had been drinking the last week, his whole body felt numb and sodden and sour. He stared at his hands.

Joe O'Keefe came back into the kitchen. "She's loin down. She says there's some soup on the back of the stove. . . . Here ye are. That'll make a man of ye. . . . Joe you ought to been where I was last night. Went out to this here Seaside Inn to take a message to the chief about somebody tippin him off that they was going to close the market. . . . It was the goddamnedest thing you ever saw in your life. This guy who's a wellknown lawyer down town was out in the hall bawlin out his gash about something. Jez he looked hard. And then he had a gun out an was goin to shoot her or some goddam thing when the chief comes up cool as you make em limpin on his stick like he does and took the gun away from him an put it in his pocket before anybody'd half seen what happened. . . . This guy Baldwin's a frien o his see? It was the goddamnedest thing I ever saw. Then he all crumpled up like. . . ."

"I tell you kid," said Joe Harland, "it gets em all sooner or later. . . ."

"Hay there eat up strong. You aint eaten enough."

"I cant eat very well."

"Sure you can. . . . Say Joe what's the dope about this war business?"

"I guess they are in for it this time. . . . I've known it was coming ever since the Agadir incident."

"Jez I like to see somebody wallop the pants off England after the way they wont give home rule to Ireland."

"We'd have to help em. . . . Anyway I dont see how this can last long. The men who control international finance wont allow it. After all it's the banker who holds the purse strings."

"We wouldn't come to the help of England, no sir, not after the way they acted in Ireland and in the Revolution and in the Civil War. . . ."

"Joey you're getting all choked up with that history you're reading up in the public library every night. . . . You follow the stock quotations and keep on your toes and dont let em fool you with all this newspaper talk about strikes and upheavals and socialism. . . . I'd like to see you make good Joey. . . . Well I guess I'd better be going."

"Naw stick around awhile, we'll open a bottle of glue." They heard a heavy stumbling in the passage outside the kitchen.

"Whossat?"

"Zat you Joe?" A big towheaded boy with lumpy shoulders and a square red face and thickset neck lurched into the room.

"What the hell do you think this is? . . . This is my kid brother Mike."

"Well what about it?" Mike stood swaying with his chin on his chest. His shoulders bulged against the low ceiling of the kitchen.

"Aint he a whale? But for crissake Mike aint I told you not to come home when you was drinkin?. . . . He's loible to tear the house down."

"I got to come home sometime aint I? Since you got to be a wardheeler Joey you been pickin on me worsen the old man. I'm glad I aint goin to stay round this goddam town long. It's enough to drive a feller cookoo. If I can get on some kind of a tub that puts to sea before the *Golden Gate* by God I'm going to do it."

"Hell I dont mind you stayin here. It's just that I dont like you raisin hell all the time, see?"

"I'm goin to do what I please, git me?"

"You get outa here, Mike. . . . Come back home when you're sober."

"I'd like to see you put me outa here, git me? I'd like to see you put me outa here."

Harland got to his feet. "Well I'm going," he said. "Got to see if I can get that job."

Mike was advancing across the kitchen with his fists clenched. Joey's jaw set; he picked up a chair.

"I'll crown you with it."

"O saints and martyrs cant a woman have no peace in her own house?" A small grayhaired woman ran screaming between them; she had lustrous black eyes set far apart in a face shrunken like a last year's apple; she beat the air with work-twisted hands. "Shut yer traps both of ye, always cursing an fightin round the house like there warnt no God. . . . Mike you go upstairs an lay down on your bed till yer sober."

"I was jus tellin him that," said Joey.

She turned on Harland, her voice like the screech of chalk on a blackboard. "An you git along outa here. I dont allow no drunken bums in my house. Git along outa here. I dont care who brought you."

Harland looked at Joey with a little sour smile, shrugged his shoulders and went out. "Charwoman," he muttered as he stumbled with stiff aching legs along the dusty street of darkfaced brick houses.

The sultry afternoon sun was like a blow on his back. Voices in his ears of maids, charwomen, cooks, stenographers, secretaries: Yes sir, Mr. Harland, Thank you sir Mr. Harland. Oh sir thank you sir so much sir Mr. Harland sir. . . .

Red buzzing in her eyelids the sunlight wakes her, she sinks back into purpling cottonwool corridors of sleep, wakes again, turns over yawning, pulls her knees up to her chin to pull the drowsysweet cocoon tighter about her. A truck jangles shatteringly along the street, the sun lays hot stripes on her back. She yawns desperately and twists herself over and lies wide awake with her hands under her head staring at the ceiling. From far away through streets and housewalls the long moan of a steamboat whistle penetrates to her like a blunt sprout of crabgrass nudging through gravel. Ellen sits up shaking her head to get rid of a fly blundering about her face. The fly flashes and vanishes in the sunlight, but somewhere in her there lingers a droning pang, unaccountable, something left over from last night's bitter thoughts. But she is happy and wide awake and it's early. She gets up and wanders round the room in her nightgown.

Where the sun hits it the hardwood floor is warm to the soles of her feet. Sparrows chirp on the windowledge. From upstairs comes the sound of a sewingmachine. When she gets out of the bath her body feels smoothwhittled and tense; she rubs herself with a towel, telling off the hours of the long day ahead; take a walk through junky littered downtown streets to that pier on the East River where they pile the great beams of mahogany, breakfast all alone at the Lafayette, coffee and crescent rolls and sweet butter, go shopping at Lord & Taylor's early before everything is stuffy and the salesgirls wilted, have lunch with . . . Then the pain that has been teasing all night wells up and bursts. "Stan, Stan for God's sake," she says aloud. She sits before her mirror staring in the black of her own dilating pupils.

She dresses in a hurry and goes out, walks down Fifth Avenue and east along Eighth Street without looking to the right or left. The sun already hot simmers slatily on the pavements, on plateglass, on dustmarbled enameled signs. Men's and women's faces as they pass her are rumpled and gray like pillows that have been too much slept on. After crossing Lafayette Street roaring with trucks and delivery wagons there is a taste of dust in her mouth, particles of grit crunch between her teeth. Further east she passes pushcarts; men are wiping off the marble counters of softdrink stands, a grindorgan fills the street with shiny jostling coils of the *Blue Danube*, acrid pungence spreads from a picklestand. In Tompkins Square yelling children mill about the soggy asphalt. At her feet a squirming heap of small boys, dirty torn shirts, slobbering mouths, punching, biting, scratching; a squalid smell like moldy bread comes from them. Ellen all of a sudden feels her knees weak under her. She turns and walks back the way she came.

The sun is heavy like his arm across her back, strokes her bare forearm the way his fingers stroke her, it's his breath against her cheek.

"Nothing but the five statutory questions," said Ellen to the rawboned man with big sagging eyes like oysters into whose long shirtfront she was talking.

"And so the decree is granted?" he asked solemnly.

"Surely in an uncontested . . ."

"Well I'm very sorry to hear it as an old family friend of both parties."

"Look here Dick, honestly I'm very fond of Jojo. I owe him a great deal. . . . He's a very fine person in many ways, but it absolutely had to be."

"You mean there is somebody else?"

She looked up at him with bright eyes and half nodded.

"Oh but divorce is a very serious step my dear young lady."

"Oh not so serious as all that."

They saw Harry Goldweiser coming towards them across the big walnut paneled room. She suddenly raised her voice. "They say that this battle of the Marne is going to end the war."

Harry Goldweiser took her hand between his two pudgy-palmed hands and bowed over it. "It's very charming of you Elaine to come and keep a lot of old midsummer bachelors from boring each other to death. Hello Snow old man, how's things?"

"Yes how is it we have the pleasure of still finding you here?"

"Oh various things have held me. . . . Anyway I hate summer resorts." "Nowhere prettier than Long Beach anyway. . . . Why Bar Harbor, I wouldnt go to Bar Harbor if you gave me a million . . . a cool million."

Mr. Snow let out a gruff sniff. "Seems to me I've heard you been going into the realestate game down there, Goldweiser."

"I bought myself a cottage that's all. It's amazing you cant even buy yourself a cottage without every newsboy on Times Square knowing about it. Let's go in and eat; my sister'll be right here." A dumpy woman in a spangled dress came in after they had sat down to table in the big antlerhung diningroom; she was pigeonbreasted and had a sallow skin.

"Oh Miss Oglethorpe I'm so glad to see you," she twittered in a little voice like a parrakeet's. "I've often seen you and thought you were the loveliest thing. . . . I did my best to get Harry to bring you up to see me."

"This is my sister Rachel," said Goldweiser to Ellen without getting up. "She keeps house for me."

"I wish you'd help me, Snow, to induce Miss Oglethorpe to take that part in The Zinnia Girl. . . . Honest it was just written for you."

"But it's such a small part . . ."

"It's not a lead exactly, but from the point of view of your reputation as a versatile and exquisite artist, it's the best thing in the show."

"Will you have a little more fish, Miss Oglethorpe?" piped Miss Goldweiser.

Mr. Snow sniffed. "There's no great acting any more: Booth, Jefferson, Mansfield . . . all gone. Nowadays it's all advertising; actors and actresses are put on the market like patent medicines. Isn't it the truth Elaine? . . . Advertising, advertising."

"But that isn't what makes success. . . . If you could do it with advertising every producer in New York'd be a millionaire," burst in Goldweiser. "It's the mysterious occult force that grips the crowds on the street and makes them turn in at a particular theater that makes the receipts go up at a particular boxoffice, do you understand me? Advertising wont do

it, good criticism wont do it, maybe it's genius maybe it's luck
but if you can give the public what it wants at that time and
at that place you have a hit. Now that's what Elaine gave us
in this last show. . . . She established contact with the audience. It might have been the greatest play in the world acted
by the greatest actors in the world and fallen a flat failure. . . . And I dont know how you do it, nobody dont
know how you do it. . . . You go to bed one night with your
house full of paper and you wake up the next morning with a
howling success. The producer cant control it any more than
the weather man can control the weather. Aint I tellin the
truth?"

"Ah the taste of the New York public has sadly degenerated
since the old days of Wallack's."

"But there have been some beautiful plays," chirped Miss
Goldweiser.

The long day love was crisp in the curls . . . the dark curls
. . . broken in the dark steel light . . . hurls . . . high O
God high into the bright . . . She was cutting with her fork
in the crisp white heart of a lettuce. She was saying words
while quite other words spilled confusedly inside her like a
broken package of beads. She sat looking at a picture of two
women and two men eating at a table in a high paneled room
under a shivering crystal chandelier. She looked up from her
plate to find Miss Goldweiser's little birdeyes kindly querulous fixed hard on her face.

"Oh yes New York is really pleasanter in midsummer than
any other time; there's less hurry and bustle."

"Oh yes that's quite true Miss Goldweiser." Ellen flashed a
sudden smile round the table. . . . All the long day love Was
crisp in the curls of his high thin brow, Flashed in his eyes in
dark steel light. . . .

In the taxi Goldweiser's broad short knees pressed against
hers; his eyes were full of furtive spiderlike industry weaving a
warm sweet choking net about her face and neck. Miss Goldweiser had relapsed pudgily into the seat beside her. Dick
Snow was holding an unlighted cigar in his mouth, rolling it
with his tongue. Ellen tried to remember exactly how Stan
looked, his polevaulter's tight slenderness; she couldn't remember his face entire, she saw his eyes, lips, an ear.

Times Square was full of juggled colored lights, crisscrossed corrugations of glare. They went up in the elevator at the Astor. Ellen followed Miss Goldweiser across the roofgarden among the tables. Men and women in evening dress, in summer muslins and light suits turned and looked after her, like sticky tendrils of vines glances caught at her as she passed. The orchestra was playing *In My Harem*. They arranged themselves at a table.

"Shall we dance?" asked Goldweiser.

She smiled a wry broken smile in his face as she let him put his arm round her back. His big ear with solemn lonely hairs on it was on the level of her eyes.

"Elaine," he was breathing into her ear, "honest I thought I was a wise guy." He caught his breath . . . "but I aint. . . . You've got me goin little girl and I hate to admit it. . . . Why cant you like me a little bit? I'd like . . . us to get married as soon as you get your decree. . . . Wouldn't you be kinder nice to me once in a while . . . ? I'd do anything for you, you know that. . . . There are lots of things in New York I could do for you. . . ." The music stopped. They stood apart under a palm. "Elaine come over to my office and sign that contract. I had Ferrari wait. . . . We can be back in fifteen minutes."

"I've got to think it over . . . I never do anything without sleeping on it."

"Gosh you drive a feller wild."

Suddenly she remembered Stan's face altogether, he was standing in front of her with a bow tie crooked in his soft shirt, his hair rumpled, drinking again.

"Oh Ellie I'm so glad to see you. . . ."

"This is Mr. Emery, Mr. Goldweiser. . . ."

"I've been on the most exordinately spectacular trip, honestly you should have come. . . . We went to Montreal and Quebec and came back through Niagara Falls and we never drew a sober breath from the time we left little old New York till they arrested us for speeding on the Boston Post Road, did we Pearline?" Ellen was staring at a girl who stood groggily behind Stan with a small flowered straw hat pulled down over a pair of eyes the blue of watered milk. "Ellie this is Pearline. . . . Isn't it a fine name? I almost split when she told me what it was. . . . But you dont know the joke. . . . We got so tight in Niagara Falls that when we came to we found we were married. . . . And we have pansies on our marriage license. . . ."

Ellen couldnt see his face. The orchestra, the jangle of voices, the clatter of plates spouted spiraling louder and louder about her . . .

> And the ladies of the harem
> Knew exactly how to wear 'em
> In O-riental Bagdad long ago. . . .

"Good night Stan." Her voice was gritty in her mouth, she heard the words very clearly when she spoke them.

"Oh Ellie I wish you'd come partying with us. . . ."

"Thanks . . . thanks."

She started to dance again with Harry Goldweiser. The roofgarden was spinning fast, then less fast. The noise ebbed sickeningly. "Excuse me a minute Harry," she said. "I'll come back to the table." In the ladies' room she let herself down carefully on the plush sofa. She looked at her face in the round mirror of her vanitycase. From black pinholes her pupils spread blurring till everything was black.

Jimmy Herf's legs were tired; he had been walking all afternoon. He sat down on a bench beside the Aquarium and looked out over the water. The fresh September wind gave a glint of steel to the little crisp waves of the harbor and to the slateblue smutted sky. A big white steamer with a yellow funnel was passing in front of the statue of Liberty. The smoke from the tug at the bow came out sharply scalloped like paper. In spite of the encumbering wharfhouses the end of Manhattan seemed to him like the prow of a barge pushing slowly and evenly down the harbor. Gulls wheeled and cried. He got to his feet with a jerk. "Oh hell I've got to do something."

He stood a second with tense muscles balanced on the balls of his feet. The ragged man looking at the photogravures of a Sunday paper had a face he had seen before. "Hello," he said vaguely. "I knew who you were all along," said the man without holding out his hand. "You're Lily Herf's boy . . . I thought you werent going to speak to me. . . . No reason why you should."

"Oh of course you must be Cousin Joe Harland. . . . I'm awfully glad to see you. . . . I've often wondered about you."

"Wondered what?"

"Oh I dunno . . . funny you never think of your relatives as being people like yourself, do you?" Herf sat down in the seat again. "Will you have a cigarette. . . . It's only a Camel."

"Well I dont mind if I do. . . . What's your business Jimmy? You dont mind if I call you that do you?" Jimmy Herf lit a match; it went out, lit another and held it for Harland. "That's the first tobacco I've had in a week . . . Thank you."

Jimmy glanced at the man beside him. The long hollow of his gray cheek made a caret with the deep crease that came from the end of his mouth. "You think I'm pretty much of a wreck dont you?" spat Harland. "You're sorry you sat down aint you? You're sorry you had a mother who brought you up a gentleman instead of a cad like the rest of 'em. . . ."

"Why I've got a job as a reporter on the *Times* . . . a hellish rotten job and I'm sick of it," said Jimmy, drawling out his words.

"Dont talk like that Jimmy, you're too young. . . . You'll never get anywhere with that attitude."

"Well suppose I dont want to get anywhere."

"Poor dear Lily was so proud of you. . . . She wanted you to be a great man, she was so ambitious for you. . . . You dont want to forget your mother Jimmy. She was the only friend I had in the whole damn family."

Jimmy laughed. "I didnt say I wasnt ambitious."

"For God's sake, for your dear mother's sake be careful what you do. You're just starting out in life . . . everything'll depend on the next couple of years. Look at me."

"Well the Wizard of Wall Street made a pretty good thing of it I'll say. . . . No it's just that I dont like to take all the stuff you have to take from people in this goddam town. I'm sick of playing up to a lot of desk men I dont respect. . . . What are you doing Cousin Joe?"

"Don't ask me. . . ."

"Look, do you see that boat with the red funnels? She's French. Look, they are pulling the canvas off the gun on her stern. . . . I want to go to the war. . . . The only trouble is I'm very poor at wrangling things."

Harland was gnawing his upper lip; after a silence he burst out in a hoarse broken voice. "Jimmy I'm going to ask you to do something for Lily's sake. . . . Er . . . have you any . . . er . . . any change with you? By a rather unfortunate . . . coincidence I have not eaten very well for the last two or three days. . . . I'm a little weak, do you understand?"

"Why yes I was just going to suggest that we go have a cup of coffee or tea or something. . . . I know a fine Syrian restaurant on Washington street."

"Come along then," said Harland, getting up stiffly. "You're sure you don't mind being seen with a scarecrow like this?"

The newspaper fell out of his hand. Jimmy stooped to pick it up. A face made out of modulated brown blurs gave him a twinge as if something had touched a nerve in a tooth. No it wasnt, she doesnt look like that, yes TALENTED YOUNG ACTRESS SCORES HIT IN THE ZINNIA GIRL. . . .

"Thanks, dont bother, I found it there," said Harland. Jimmy dropped the paper; she fell face down.

"Pretty rotten photographs they have dont they?"

"It passes the time to look at them, I like to keep up with what's going on in New York a little bit. . . . A cat may look at a king you know, a cat may look at a king."

"Oh I just meant that they were badly taken."

VII. Rollercoaster

The leaden twilight weighs on the dry limbs of an old man walking towards Broadway. Round the Nedick's stand at the corner something clicks in his eyes. Broken doll in the ranks of varnished articulated dolls he plods up with drooping head into the seethe and throb into the furnace of beaded lettercut light. "I remember when it was all meadows," he grumbles to the little boy.

LOUIS EXPRESSO ASSOCIATION, the red letters on the placard jig before Stan's eye. ANNUAL DANCE. Young men and girls going in. *Two by two the elephant And the kangaroo.* The boom and jangle of an orchestra seeping out through the swinging doors of the hall. Outside it is raining. *One more river, O there's one more river to cross.* He straightens the lapels of his coat, arranges his mouth soberly, pays two dollars and goes into a big resounding hall hung with red white and blue bunting. Reeling, so he leans for a while against the wall. *One more river . . .* The dancefloor full of jogging couples rolls like the deck of a ship. The bar is more stable. "Gus McNiel's here," everybody's saying "Good old Gus." Big hands slap broad backs, mouths roar black in red faces. Glasses rise and tip glinting, rise and tip in a dance. A husky beetfaced man with deepset eyes and curly hair limps through the bar leaning on a stick. "How's a boy Gus?"

"Yay dere's de chief."

"Good for old man McNiel come at last."

"Howde do Mr. McNiel?" The bar quiets down.

Gus McNiel waves his stick in the air. "Attaboy fellers, have a good time. . . . Burke ole man set the company up to a drink on me." "Dere's Father Mulvaney wid him too. Good for Father Mulvaney. . . . He's a prince that feller is."

> For he's a jolly good fellow
> That nobody can deny . . .

Broad backs deferentially hunched follow the slowly pacing group out among the dancers. *O the big baboon by the light of the moon is combing his auburn hair.* "Wont you dance, please?" The girl turns a white shoulder and walks off.

> I am a bachelor and I live all alone
> And I work at the weaver's trade. . . .

Stan finds himself singing at his own face in a mirror. One of his eyebrows is joining his hair, the other's an eyelash. . . . "No I'm not bejases I'm a married man. . . . Fight any man who says I'm not a married man and a citizen of City of New York, County of New York, State of New York. . . ." He's standing on a chair making a speech, banging his fist into his hand. "Friends Roooomans and countrymen, lend me five bucks. . . . We come to muzzle Cæsar not to shaaaave him. . . . According to the Constitution of the City of New York, County of New York, State of New York and duly attested and subscribed before a district attorney according to the provisions of the act of July 13th 1888. . . . To hell with the Pope."

"Hey quit dat." "Fellers lets trow dis guy out. . . . He aint one o de boys. . . . Dunno how he got in here. He's drunk as a pissant." Stan jumps with his eyes closed into a thicket of fists. He's slammed in the eye, in the jaw, shoots like out of a gun out into the drizzling cool silent street. Ha ha ha.

> For I am a bachelor and I live all alone
> And there's one more river to cross
> One more river to Jordan
> One more river to cross . . .

It was blowing cold in his face and he was sitting on the front of a ferryboat when he came to. His teeth were chattering, he was shivering . . . "I'm having DT's. Who am I? Where am I? City of New York, State of New York. . . . Stanwood Emery age twentytwo occupation student. . . . Pearline Anderson twentyone occupation actress. To hell with her. Gosh I've got fortynine dollars and eight cents and where the hell have I been? And nobody rolled me. Why I havent got the DT's at all. I feel fine, only a little delicate. All I need's a little drink, dont you? Hello, I thought there was somebody here. I guess I'd better shut up."

> Fortynine dollars ahanging on the wall
> Fortynine dollars ahanging on the wall

Across the zinc water the tall walls, the birchlike cluster of downtown buildings shimmered up the rosy morning like a sound of horns through a chocolatebrown haze. As the boat drew near the buildings densened to a granite mountain split with knifecut canyons. The ferry passed close to a tubby steamer that rode at anchor listing towards Stan so that he could see all the decks. An Ellis Island tug was alongside. A stale smell came from the decks packed with upturned faces like a load of melons. Three gulls wheeled complaining. A gull soared in a spiral, white wings caught the sun, the gull skimmed motionless in whitegold light. The rim of the sun had risen above the plumcolored band of clouds behind East New York. A million windows flashed with light. A rasp and a humming came from the city.

> The animals went in two by two
> The elephant and the kangaroo
> There's one more river to Jordan
> One more river to cross

In the whitening light tinfoil gulls wheeled above broken boxes, spoiled cabbageheads, orangerinds heaving slowly between the splintered plank walls, the green spumed under the round bow as the ferry skidding on the tide, gulped the broken water, crashed, slid, settled slowly into the slip. Handwinches whirled with jingle of chains, gates folded upward. Stan stepped across the crack, staggered up the manuresmelling wooden tunnel of the ferryhouse out into the sunny glass and benches of the Battery. He sat down on a bench, clasped his hands round his knees to keep them from shaking so. His mind went on jingling like a mechanical piano.

> With bells on her fingers and rings on her toes
> Shall ride a white lady upon a great horse
> And she shall make mischief wherever she goes . . .

There was Babylon and Nineveh, they were built of brick. Athens was goldmarble columns. Rome was held up on broad arches of rubble. In Constantinople the minarets flame like great candles round the Golden Horn. . . . O there's one more river to cross. Steel glass, tile, concrete will be the materials of the skyscrapers. Crammed on the narrow island the millionwindowed buildings will jut, glittering pyramid on pyramid, white cloudsheads piled above a thunderstorm . . .

> And it rained forty days and it rained forty nights
> And it didn't stop till Christmas
> And the only man who survived the flood
> Was longlegged Jack of the Isthmus. . . .

Kerist I wish I was a skyscraper.

The lock spun round in a circle to keep out the key. Dexterously Stan bided his time and caught it. He shot headlong through the open door and down the long hall shouting Pearline into the livingroom. It smelled funny, Pearline's smell, to hell with it. He picked up a chair; the chair wanted to fly, it swung round his head and crashed into the window, the glass shivered and tinkled. He looked out through the window. The street stood up on end. A hookandladder and a fire engine were climbing it licketysplit trailing a droning sirenshriek. *Fire fire, pour on water, Scotland's burning*. A thousand dollar fire, a hundredthousand dollar fire, a million dollar fire. Skyscrapers go up like flames, in flames, flames. He spun back into the room. The table turned a somersault. The chinacloset jumped on the table. Oak chairs climbed on top to the gas jet. *Pour on water, Scotland's burning*. Don't like the smell in this place in the City of New York, County of New York, State of New York. He lay on his back on the floor of the revolving kitchen and laughed and laughed. The only man who survived the flood rode a great lady on a white horse. Up in flames, up, up. Kerosene whispered a greasyfaced can in the corner of the kitchen. *Pour on water*. He stood swaying on the crackling upside down chairs on the upside down table. The kerosene licked him with a white cold tongue. He pitched, grabbed the gasjet, the gasjet gave way, he lay in a puddle on his back striking matches, wet wouldn't light. A match spluttered, lit; he held the flame carefully between his hands.

"Oh yes but my husband's awfully ambitious." Pearline was telling the blue gingham lady in the grocery-store. "Likes to have a good time an all that but he's much more ambitious than anybody I every knew. He's goin to get his old man to send us abroad so he can study architecture. He wants to be an architect."

"My that'll be nice for you wont it? A trip like that . . . Anything else miss?" "No I guess I didn't forget anythin. . . . If it was anybody else I'd be worryin about him. I haven't seen him for two days. Had to go and see his dad I guess."

"And you just newly wed too."

"I wouldnt be tellin ye if I thought there was anythin wrong, would I? No he's playin straight all right. . . . Well goodby Mrs. Robinson." She tucked her packages under one arm and swinging her bead bag in the free hand walked down the street. The sun was still warm although there was a tang of fall in the wind. She gave a penny to a blind man cranking the Merry Widow waltz out of a grindorgan. Still she'd better bawl him out a little when he came home, might get to doing it often. She turned into 200th Street. People were looking out of windows, there was a crowd gathering. It was a fire. She sniffed the singed air. It gave her gooseflesh; she loved seeing fires. She hurried. Why it's outside our building. Outside our apartmenthouse. Smoke dense as gunnysacks rolled out of the fifthstory window. She suddenly found herself all atremble. The colored elevatorboy ran up to her. His face was green. "Oh it's in our apartment" she shrieked, "and the furniture just came a week ago. Let me get by." The packages fell from her, a bottle of cream broke on the sidewalk. A policeman stood in her way, she threw herself at him and pounded on the broad blue chest. She couldnt stop shrieking. "That's all right little lady, that's all right," he kept booming in a deep voice. As she beat her head against it she could feel his voice rumbling in his chest. "They're bringing him down, just overcome by smoke that's all, just overcome by smoke."

"O Stanwood my husband," she shrieked. Everything was blacking out. She grabbed at two bright buttons on the policeman's coat and fainted.

VIII. One More River to Jordan

A man is shouting from a soapbox at Second Avenue and Houston in front of the Cosmopolitan
Café: ". . . these fellers, men . . . wageslaves like I
was . . . are sittin on your chest . . . they're takin the
food outen your mouths. Where's all the pretty girls I
used to see walkin up and down the bullevard? Look
for em in the uptown cabarets. . . . They squeeze us
dry friends . . . feller workers, slaves I'd oughter say
. . . they take our work and our ideers and our
women. . . . They build their Plaza Hotels and their
millionaire's clubs and their million dollar theayters
and their battleships and what do they leave us? . . .
They leave us shopsickness an the rickets and a lot of
dirty streets full of garbage cans. . . . You look pale
you fellers. . . . You need blood. . . . Why dont you
get some blood in your veins? . . . Back in Russia the
poor people . . . not so much poorer'n we are . . . believe in wampires, things come suck your blood at
night. . . . That's what Capitalism is, a wampire
that sucks your blood . . . day . . . and . . . night."*

*It is beginning to snow. The flakes are giltedged
where they pass the streetlamp. Through the plate glass
the Cosmopolitan Café full of blue and green opal rifts
of smoke looks like a muddy aquarium; faces blob
whitely round the tables like illassorted fishes. Umbrellas begin to bob in clusters up the snowmottled street.
The orator turns up his collar and walks briskly east
along Houston, holding the muddy soapbox away from
his trousers.*

Faces, hats, hands, newspapers jiggled in the fetid roaring
subway car like corn in a popper. The downtown express
passed clattering in yellow light, window telescoping window
till they overlapped like scales.

"Look George," said Sandbourne to George Baldwin who
hung on a strap beside him, "you can see Fitzgerald's contraction."

"I'll be seeing the inside of an undertaking parlor if I dont get out of this subway soon."

"It does you plutocrats good now and then to see how the other half travels. . . . Maybe it'll make you induce some of your little playmates down at Tammany Hall to stop squabbling and give us wageslaves a little transportation. . . . cristamighty I could tell em a thing or two. . . . My idea's for a series of endless moving platforms under Fifth Avenue."

"Did you cook that up when you were in hospital Phil?"

"I cooked a whole lot of things up while I was in hospital."

"Look here lets get out at Grand Central and walk. I cant stand this. . . . I'm not used to it."

"Sure . . . I'll phone Elsie I'll be a little late to dinner. . . . Not often I get to see you nowadays George . . . Gee it's like the old days."

In a tangled clot of men and women, arms, legs, hats aslant on perspiring necks, they were pushed out on the platform. They walked up Lexington Avenue quiet in the claretmisted afterglow.

"But Phil how did you come to step out in front of a truck that way?"

"Honestly George I dunno. . . . The last I remember is craning my neck to look at a terribly pretty girl went by in a taxicab and there I was drinking icewater out of a teapot in the hospital."

"Shame on you Phil at your age."

"Cristamighty dont I know it? But I'm not the only one."

"It is funny the way a thing like that comes over you. . . . Why what have you heard about me?"

"Gosh George dont get nervous, it's all right. . . . I've seen her in The Zinnia Girl. . . . She walks away with it. That other girl who's the star dont have a show."

"Look here Phil if you hear any rumors about Miss Oglethorpe for Heaven's sake shut them up. It's so damn silly you cant go out to tea with a woman without everybody starting their dirty gabble all over town. . . . By God I will not have a scandal, I dont care what happens."

"Say hold your horses George."

"I'm in a very delicate position downtown just at the

moment that's all. . . . And then Cecily and I have at last reached a modus vivendi. . . . I wont have it disturbed."

They walked along in silence.

Sandbourne walked with his hat in his hand. His hair was almost white but his eyebrows were still dark and bushy. Every few steps he changed the length of his stride as if it hurt him to walk. He cleared his throat. "George you were asking me if I'd cooked up any schemes when I was in hospital. . . . Do you remember years ago old man Specker used to talk about vitreous and superenameled tile? Well I've been workin on his formula out at Hollis. . . . A friend of mine there has a two thousand degree oven he bakes pottery in. I think it can be put on a commercial basis. . . . Man it would revolutionize the whole industry. Combined with concrete it would enormously increase the flexibility of the materials at the architects' disposal. We could make tile any color, size or finish. . . . Imagine this city when all the buildins instead of bein dirty gray were ornamented with vivid colors. Imagine bands of scarlet round the entablatures of skyscrapers. Colored tile would revolutionize the whole life of the city. . . . Instead of fallin back on the orders or on gothic or romanesque decorations we could evolve new designs, new colors, new forms. If there was a little color in the town all this hardshell inhibited life'd break down. . . . There'd be more love an less divorce. . . ."

Baldwin burst out laughing. "You tell em Phil. . . . I'll talk to you about that sometime. You must come up to dinner when Cecily's there and tell us about it. . . . Why wont Parkhurst do anything?"

"I wouldnt let him in on it. He'd cotton on to the proposition and leave me out in the cold once he had the formula. I wouldn't trust him with a rubber nickel."

"Why doesnt he take you into partnership Phil?"

"He's got me where he wants me anyway. . . . He knows I do all the work in his goddamned office. He knows too that I'm too cranky to make out with most people. He's a slick article."

"Still I should think you could put it up to him."

"He's got me where he wants me and he knows it, so I continue doin the work while he amasses the coin. . . . I guess it's logical. If I had more money I'd just spend it. I'm just shiftless."

"But look here man you're not so much older than I am. . . . You've still got a career ahead of you."

"Sure nine hours a day draftin. . . . Gosh I wish you'd go into this tile business with me."

Baldwin stopped at a corner and slapped his hand on the briefcase he was carrying. "Now Phil you know I'd be very glad to give you a hand in any way I could. . . . But just at the moment my financial situation is terribly involved. I've gotten into some rather rash entanglements and Heaven knows how I'm going to get out of them. . . . That's why I cant have a scandal or a divorce or anything. You dont understand how complicatedly things interact. . . . I couldnt take up anything new, not for a year at least. This war in Europe has made things very unsettled downtown. Anything's liable to happen."

"All right. Good night George."

Sandbourne turned abruptly on his heel and walked down the avenue again. He was tired and his legs ached. It was almost dark. On the way back to the station the grimy brick and brownstone blocks dragged past monotonously like the days of his life.

Under the skin of her temples iron clamps tighten till her head will mash like an egg; she begins to walk with long strides up and down the room that bristles with itching stuffiness; spotty colors of pictures, carpets, chairs wrap about her like a choking hot blanket. Outside the window the backyards are striped with blue and lilac and topaz of a rainy twilight. She opens the window. No time to get tight like the twilight, Stan said. The telephone reached out shivering beady tentacles of sound. She slams the window down. O hell cant they give you any peace?

"Why Harry I didnt know you were back. . . . Oh I wonder if I can. . . . Oh yes I guess I can. Come along by after the theater. . . . Isnt that wonderful? You must tell me all about it." She no sooner puts the receiver down than the bell clutches at her again. "Hello. . . . No I dont. . . . Oh yes maybe I do. . . . When did you get back?" She laughed a

tinkling telephone laugh. "But Howard I'm terribly busy.
. . . Yes I am honestly. . . . Have you been to the show?
Well sometime come round after a performance. . . . I'm
so anxious to hear about your trip . . . you know . . .
Goodby Howard."

A walk'll make me feel better. She sits at her dressingtable
and shakes her hair down about her shoulders. "It's such a
hellish nuisance, I'd like to cut it all off . . . spreads apace.
The shadow of white Death. . . . Oughtnt to stay up so late,
those dark circles under my eyes. . . . And at the door, Invisible Corruption. . . . If I could only cry; there are people
who can cry their eyes out, really cry themselves blind . . .
Anyway the divorce'll go through. . . .

> Far from the shore, far from the trembling throng
> Whose sails were never to the tempest given

Gosh it's six o'clock already. She starts walking up and
down the room again. I am borne darkly fearfully afar. . . .
The phone rings. "Hello. . . . Yes this is Miss Oglethorpe. . . . Why hello Ruth, why I haven't seen you for
ages, since Mrs. Sunderland's. . . . Oh, do I'd love to see
you. Come by and we'll have a bite to eat on the way to the
theater. . . . It's the third floor."

She rings off and gets a raincape out of a closet. The smell
of furs and mothballs and dresses clings in her nostrils. She
throws up the window again and breathes deep of the wet air
full of the cold rot of autumn. She hears the burring boom of
a big steamer from the river. Darkly, fearfully afar from this
nonsensical life, from this fuzzy idiocy and strife; a man can
take a ship for his wife, but a girl. The telephone is shiveringly
beadily ringing, ringing.

The buzzer burrs at the same time. Ellen presses the button to click the latch. "Hello. . . . No, I'm very sorry I'm
afraid you'll have to tell me who it is. Why Larry Hopkins I
thought you were in Tokyo. . . . They havent moved you
again have they? Why of course we must see each other. . . .
My dear it's simply horrible but I'm all dated up for two
weeks. . . . Look I'm sort of crazy tonight. You call up tomorrow at twelve and I'll try to shift things around. . . .
Why of course I've got to see you immediately you funny old

thing." . . . Ruth Prynne and Cassandra Wilkins come in
shaking the water off their umbrellas. "Well goodby
Larry. . . . Why it's so so sweet of both of you. . . . Do take
your things off for a second. . . . Cassie wont you have dinner with us?"

"I felt I just had to see you. . . . It's so wonderful about
your wonderful success," says Cassie in a shaky voice. "And
my dear I felt so terribly when I heard about Mr. Emery. I
cried and cried, didn't I Ruth?"

"Oh what a beautiful apartment you have," Ruth is exclaiming at the same moment. Ellen's ears ring sickeningly.
"We all have to die sometime," gruffly she blurts out.

Ruth's rubberclad foot is tapping the floor; she catches
Cassie's eye and makes her stammer into silence. "Hadnt we
better go along? It's getting rather late," she says.

"Excuse me a minute Ruth." Ellen runs into the bathroom
and slams the door. She sits on the edge of the bathtub
pounding on her knees with her clenched fists. Those wom-
en'll drive me mad. Then the tension in her snaps, she feels
something draining out of her like water out of a washbasin.
She quietly puts a dab of rouge on her lips.

When she goes back she says in her usual voice: "Well let's
get along. . . . Got a part yet Ruth?"

"I had a chance to go out to Detroit with a stock company.
I turned it down. . . . I wont go out of New York whatever
happens."

"What wouldnt I give for a chance to get away from New
York. . . . Honestly if I was offered a job singing in a movie
in Medicine Hat I think I'd take it."

Ellen picks up her umbrella and the three women file down
the stairs and out into the street. "Taxi," calls Ellen.

The passing car grinds to a stop. The red hawk face of the
taxidriver craning into the light of the street lamp. "Go to
Eugenie's on Fortyeighth Street," says Ellen as the others
climb in. Greenish lights and darks flicker past the light-
beaded windows.

She stood with her arm in the arm of Harry Goldweiser's
dinner jacket looking out over the parapet of the roofgarden.
Below them the Park lay twinkling with occasional lights,

streaked with nebular blur like a fallen sky. From behind them came gusts of a tango, inklings of voices, shuffle of feet on a dancefloor. Ellen felt a stiff castiron figure in her metalgreen evening dress.

"Ah but Boirnhardt, Rachel, Dusc, Mrs. Siddons. . . . No Elaine I'm tellin you, d'you understand? There's no art like the stage that soars so high moldin the passions of men. . . . If I could only do what I wanted we'd be the greatest people in the world. You'd be the greatest actress. . . . I'd be the great producer, the unseen builder, d'you understand? But the public dont want art, the people of this country wont let you do anythin for em. All they want's a detective melodrama or a rotten French farce with the kick left out or a lot of pretty girls and music. Well a showman's business is to give the public what they want."

"I think that this city is full of people wanting inconceivable things. . . . Look at it."

"It's all right at night when you cant see it. There's no artistic sense, no beautiful buildins, no old-time air, that's what's the matter with it."

They stood a while without speaking. The orchestra began playing the waltz from The Lilac Domino. Suddenly Ellen turned to Goldweiser and said in a curt tone, "Can you understand a woman who wants to be a harlot, a common tart, sometimes?"

"My dear young lady what a strange thing for a sweet lovely girl to suddenly come out and say."

"I suppose you're shocked." She didnt hear his answer. She felt she was going to cry. She pressed her sharp nails into the palms of her hands, she held her breath until she had counted twenty. Then she said in a choking little girl's voice, "Harry let's go and dance a little."

The sky above the cardboard buildings is a vault of beaten lead. It would be less raw if it would snow. Ellen finds a taxi on the corner of Seventh Avenue and lets herself sink back in the seat rubbing the numb gloved fingers of one hand against the palm of the other. "West Fiftyseventh, please." Out of a sick mask of fatigue she watches fruitstores, signs, buildings being built, trucks, girls, messengerboys, policemen through the jolting window. If I have my child, Stan's child, it will grow up to jolt up Seventh Avenue under a sky of beaten lead that never snows watching fruitstores, signs, buildings being built, trucks, girls, messengerboys, policemen. . . . She presses her knees together, sits up straight on the edge of the seat with her hands clasped over her slender belly. O God the rotten joke they've played on me, taking Stan away, burning him up, leaving me nothing but this growing in me that's going to kill me. She's whimpering into her numb hands. O God why wont it snow?

As she stands on the gray pavement fumbling in her purse for a bill, a dusteddy swirling scraps of paper along the gutter fills her mouth with grit. The elevatorman's face is round ebony with ivory inlay. "Mrs. Staunton Wells?" "Yas ma'am eighth floor."

The elevator hums as it soars. She stands looking at herself in the narrow mirror. Suddenly something recklessly gay goes through her. She rubs the dust off her face with a screwedup handkerchief, smiles at the elevatorman's smile that's wide as the full keyboard of a piano, and briskly rustles to the door of the apartment that a frilled maid opens. Inside it smells of tea and furs and flowers, women's voices chirp to the clinking of cups like birds in an aviary. Glances flicker about her head as she goes into the room.

There was wine spilled on the tablecloth and bits of tomatosauce from the spaghetti. The restaurant was a steamy place with views of the Bay of Naples painted in soupy blues and greens on the walls. Ellen sat back in her chair from the round tableful of young men, watching the smoke from her cigarette crinkle spirally round the fat Chiantibottle in front of her. In her plate a slab of tricolor icecream melted forlornly. "But good God hasnt a man some rights? No, this industrial civilization forces us to seek a complete readjustment of government and social life . . ."

"Doesnt he use long words?" Ellen whispered to Herf who sat beside her.

"He's right all the same," he growled back at her. . . . "The result has been to put more power in the hands of a few men than there has been in the history of the world since the horrible slave civilizations of Egypt and Mesopotamia. . . ."

"Hear hear."

"No but I'm serious. . . . The only way of bucking the interests is for working people, the proletariat, producers and consumers, anything you want to call them, to form unions and finally get so well organized that they can take over the whole government."

"I think you're entirely wrong, Martin, it's the interests as you call em, these horrible capitalists, that have built up this country as we have it today."

"Well look at it for God's sake. . . . That's what I'm saying. I wouldnt kennel a dog in it."

"I dont think so. I admire this country. . . . It's the only fatherland I've got. . . . And I think that all these downtrodden masses really want to be downtrodden, they're not fit for anything else. . . . If they werent they'd be flourishing businessmen . . . Those that are any good are getting to be."

"But I don't think a flourishing businessman is the highest ideal of human endeavor."

"A whole lot higher than a rotten fiddleheaded anarchist agitator. . . . Those that arent crooks are crazy."

"Look here Mead, you've just insulted something that you dont understand, that you know nothing about. . . . I cant allow you to do that. . . . You should try to understand things before you go round insulting them."

"An insult to the intelligence that's what it is all this socialistic drivel."

Ellen tapped Herf on the sleeve. "Jimmy I've got to go home. Do you want to walk a little way with me?"

"Martin, will you settle for us? We've got to go. . . . Ellie you look terribly pale."

"It's just a little hot in here. . . . Whee, what a relief. . . . I hate arguments anyway. I never can think of anything to say."

"That bunch does nothing but chew the rag night after night."

Eighth Avenue was full of fog that caught at their throats. Lights bloomed dimly through it, faces loomed, glinted in silhouette and faded like a fish in a muddy aquarium.

"Feel better Ellie?"

"Lots."

"I'm awfully glad."

"Do you know you're the only person around here who calls me Ellie. I like it. . . . Everybody tries to make me seem so grown up since I've been on the stage."

"Stan used to."

"Maybe that's why I like it," she said in a little trailing voice like a cry heard at night from far away along a beach.

Jimmy felt something clamping his throat. "Oh gosh things are rotten," he said. "God I wish I could blame it all on capitalism the way Martin does."

"It's pleasant walking like this . . . I love a fog."

They walked on without speaking. Wheels rumbled through the muffling fog underlaid with the groping distant lowing of sirens and steamboatwhistles on the river.

"But at least you have a career. . . . You like your work, you're enormously successful," said Herf at the corner of Fourteenth Street, and caught her arm as they crossed.

"Dont say that. . . . You really dont believe it. I dont kid myself as much as you think I do."

"No but it's so."

"It used to be before I met Stan, before I loved him. . . . You see I was a crazy little stagestruck kid who got launched out in a lot of things I didnt understand before I had time to learn anything about life. . . . Married at eighteen and divorced at twentytwo's a pretty good record. . . . But Stan was so wonderful. . . ."

"I know."

"Without ever saying anything he made me feel there were other things . . . unbelievable things. . . ."

"God I resent his craziness though. . . . It's such a waste."

"I cant talk about it."

"Let's not."

"Jimmy you're the only person left I can really talk to."

"Dont want to trust me. I might go berserk on you too some day."

They laughed.

"God I'm glad I'm not dead, arent you Ellie?"

"I dont know. Look here's my place. I dont want you to come up. . . . I'm going right to bed. I feel miserably. . . ." Jimmy stood with his hat off looking at her. She was fumbling in her purse for her key. "Look Jimmy I might as well tell you. . . ." She went up to him and spoke fast with her face turned away pointing at him with the latchkey that caught the light of the streetlamp. The fog was like a tent round about them. "I'm going to have a baby. . . . Stan's baby. I'm going to give up all this silly life and raise it. I dont care what happens."

"O God that's the bravest thing I ever heard of a woman doing. . . . Oh Ellie you're so wonderful. God if I could only tell you what I . . ."

"Oh no." Her voice broke and her eyes filled with tears. "I'm a silly fool, that's all." She screwed up her face like a little child and ran up the steps with the tears streaming down her face.

"Oh Ellie I want to say something to you . . ."

The door closed behind her.

Jimmy Herf stood stockstill at the foot of the brownstone steps. His temples throbbed. He wanted to break the door down after her. He dropped on his knees and kissed the step where she had stood. The fog swirled and flickered with colors in confetti about him. Then the trumpet feeling ebbed and he was falling through a black manhole. He stood stockstill. A policeman's ballbearing eyes searched his face as he passed, a stout blue column waving a nightstick. Then suddenly he clenched his fists and walked off. "O God everything is hellish," he said aloud. He wiped the grit off his lips with his coatsleeve.

She puts her hand in his to jump out of the roadster as the ferry starts, "Thanks Larry," and follows his tall ambling body out on the bow. A faint riverwind blows the dust and gasoline out of their nostrils. Through the pearly night the square frames of houses along the Drive opposite flicker like burned-out fireworks. The waves slap tinily against the shoving bow of the ferry. A hunchback with a violin is scratching Marianela.

"Nothing succeeds like success," Larry is saying in a deep droning voice.

"Oh if you knew how little I cared about anything just now you wouldnt go on teasing me with all these words. . . . You know, marriage, success, love, they're just words."

"But they mean everything in the world to me. . . . I think you'd like it in Lima Elaine. . . . I waited until you were free, didnt I? And now here I am."

"We're none of us that ever. . . . But I'm just numb." The riverwind is brackish. Along the viaduct above 125th Street cars crawl like beetles. As the ferry enters the slip they hear the squudge and rumble of wheels on asphalt.

"Well we'd better get back into the car, you wonderful creature Elaine."

"After all day it's exciting isnt it Larry, getting back into the center of things."

Beside the smudged white door are two pushbuttons marked NIGHT BELL and DAY BELL. She rings with a shaky finger. A short broad man with a face like a rat and sleek black hair brushed straight back opens. Short dollhands the color of the flesh of a mushroom hang at his sides. He hunches his shoulders in a bow.

"Are you the lady? Come in."

"Is this Dr. Abrahms?"

"Yes. . . . You are the lady my friend phoned me about. Sit down my dear lady." The office smells of something like arnica. Her heart joggles desperately between her ribs.

"You understand . . ." She hates the quaver in her voice; she's going to faint. "You understand, Dr. Abrahms that it is absolutely necessary. I am getting a divorce from my husband and have to make my own living."

"Very young, unhappily married . . . I am sorry." The doctor purrs softly as if to himself. He heaves a hissing sigh and suddenly looks in her eyes with black steel eyes like gimlets. "Do not be afraid, dear lady, it is a very simple operation. . . . Are you ready now?"

"Yes. It wont take very long will it? If I can pull myself together I have an engagement for tea at five."

"You are a brave young lady. In an hour it will be forgotten. . . . I am sorry. . . . It is very sad such a thing is necessary. . . . Dear lady you should have a home and many children and a loving husband . . . Will you go in the operating room and prepare yourself. . . . I work without an assistant."

The bright searing bud of light swells in the center of the ceiling, sprays razorsharp nickel, enamel, a dazzling sharp glass case of sharp instruments. She takes off her hat and lets herself sink shuddering sick on a little enamel chair. Then she gets stiffly to her feet and undoes the band of her skirt.

The roar of the streets breaks like surf about a shell of throbbing agony. She watches the tilt of her leather hat, the powder, the rosed cheeks, the crimson lips that are a mask on her face. All the buttons of her gloves are buttoned. She raises her hand. "Taxi!" A fire engine roars past, a hosewagon with sweatyfaced men pulling on rubber coats, a clanging hookandladder. All the feeling in her fades with the dizzy fade of the siren. A wooden Indian, painted, with a hand raised at the streetcorner.

"Taxi!"

"Yes ma'am."

"Drive to the Ritz."

THIRD SECTION

I. Rejoicing City That Dwelt Carelessly

*There are flags on all the flagpoles up Fifth Avenue.
In the shrill wind of history the great flags flap
and tug at their lashings on the creaking goldknobbed
poles up Fifth Avenue. The stars jiggle sedately against
the slate sky, the red and white stripes writhe against
the clouds.*

*In the gale of brassbands and trampling horses and
rumbling clatter of cannon, shadows like the shadows
of claws grasp at the taut flags, the flags are hungry
tongues licking twisting curling.*

Oh it's a long way to Tipperary . . . Over there! Over there!

> *The harbor is packed with zebrastriped skunkstriped
> piebald steamboats, the Narrows are choked with bul-
> lion, they're piling gold sovereigns up to the ceilings in
> the Subtreasury. Dollars whine on the radio, all the
> cables tap out dollars.*

There's a long long trail awinding . . . Over there! Over there!

> *In the subway their eyes pop as they spell out APOCA-
> LYPSE, typhus, cholera, shrapnel, insurrection, death
> in fire, death in water, death in hunger, death in
> mud.*

> *Oh it's a long way to Madymosell from Armenteers,
> over there! The Yanks are coming, the Yanks are com-
> ing. Down Fifth Avenue the bands blare for the Lib-
> erty Loan drive, for the Red Cross drive. Hospital ships
> sneak up the harbor and unload furtively at night in
> old docks in Jersey. Up Fifth Avenue the flags of the
> seventeen nations are flaring curling in the shrill hun-
> gry wind.*

O the oak and the ash and the weeping willow tree
And green grows the grass in God's country.

The great flags flap and tug at their lashings on the creaking goldknobbed poles up Fifth Avenue.

Captain James Merivale D.S.C. lay with his eyes closed while the barber's padded fingers gently stroked his chin. The lather tickled his nostrils; he could smell bay rum, hear the drone of an electric vibrator, the snipping of scissors.

"A little face massage sir, get rid of a few of those blackheads sir," burred the barber in his ear. The barber was bald and had a round blue chin.

"All right," drawled Merivale, "go as far as you like. This is the first decent shave I've had since war was declared."

"Just in from overseas, Captain?"

"Yare . . . been making the world safe for democracy."

The barber smothered his words under a hot towel. "A little lilac water Captain?"

"No dont put any of your damn lotions on me, just a little witchhazel or something antiseptic."

The blond manicure girl had faintly beaded lashes; she looked up at him bewitchingly, her rosebud lips parted. "I guess you've just landed Captain. . . . My you've got a good tan." He gave up his hand to her on the little white table. "It's a long time Captain since anybody took care of these hands."

"How can you tell?"

"Look how the cuticle's grown."

"We were too busy for anything like that. I'm a free man since eight o'clock that's all."

"Oh it must have been terr . . . ible."

"Oh it was a great little war while it lasted."

"I'll say it was . . . And now you're all through Captain?"

"Of course I keep my commission in the reserve corps."

She gave his hand a last playful tap and he got to his feet.

He put tips into the soft palm of the barber and the hard palm of the colored boy who handed him his hat, and walked slowly up the white marble steps. On the landing was a mirror. Captain James Merivale stopped to look at Captain James Merivale. He was a tall straightfeatured young man with a slight heaviness under the chin. He wore a neatfitting whipcord uniform picked out by the insignia of the Rainbow Division, well furnished with ribbons and servicestripes. The light of the mirror was reflected silvery on either calf of his puttees. He cleared his throat as he looked himself up and down. A young man in civilian clothes came up behind him.

"Hello James, all cleaned up?"

"You betcher. . . . Say isnt it a damn fool rule not letting us wear Sam Browne belts? Spoils the whole uniform. . . ."

"They can take all their Sam Browne's belts and hang them on the Commanding General's fanny for all I care. . . . I'm a civilian."

"You're still an officer in the reserve corps, dont forget that."

"They can take their reserve corps and shove it ten thousand miles up the creek. Let's go have a drink."

"I've got to go up and see the folks." They had come out on Fortysecond Street. "Well so long James, I'm going to get so drunk . . . Just imagine being free." "So long Jerry, dont do anything I wouldnt do."

Merivale walked west along Fortysecond. There were still flags out, drooping from windows, waggling lazily from poles in the September breeze. He looked in the shops as he walked along; flowers, women's stockings, candy, shirts and neckties, dresses, colored draperies through glinting plateglass, beyond a stream of faces, men's razorscraped faces, girls' faces with rouged lips and powdered noses. It made him feel flushed and excited. He fidgeted when he got in the subway. "Look at the stripes that one has. . . . He's a D.S.C.," he heard a girl say to another. He got out at Seventysecond and walked with his chest stuck out down the too familiar brownstone street towards the river.

"How do you do, Captain Merivale," said the elevator man.

"Well, are you out James?" cried his mother running into his arms.

He nodded and kissed her. She looked pale and wilted in her black dress. Maisie, also in black, came rustling tall and rosycheeked behind her. "It's wonderful to find you both looking so well."

"Of course we are . . . as well as could be expected. My

dear we've had a terrible time. . . . You're the head of the family now, James."

"Poor daddy . . . to go off like that."

"That was something you missed. . . . Thousands of people died of it in New York alone."

He hugged Maisie with one arm and his mother with the other. Nobody spoke.

"Well," said Merivale walking into the living room, "it was a great war while it lasted." His mother and sister followed on his heels. He sat down in the leather chair and stretched out his polished legs. "You dont know how wonderful it is to get home."

Mrs. Merivale drew up her chair close to his. "Now dear you just tell us all about it."

In the dark of the stoop in front of the tenement door, he reaches for her and drags her to him. "Dont Bouy, dont; dont be rough." His arms tighten like knotted cords round her back; her knees are trembling. His mouth is groping for her mouth along one cheekbone, down the side of her nose. She cant breathe with his lips probing her lips. "Oh I cant stand it." He holds her away from him. She is staggering panting against the wall held up by his big hands.

"Nutten to worry about," he whispers gently.

"I've got to go, it's late. . . . I have to get up at six."

"Well what time do you think I get up?"

"It's mommer who might catch me. . . ."

"Tell her to go to hell."

"I will some day . . . worse'n that . . . if she dont quit pickin on me." She takes hold of his stubbly cheeks and kisses him quickly on the mouth and has broken away from him and run up the four flights of grimy stairs.

The door is still on the latch. She strips off her dancing pumps and walks carefully through the kitchenette on aching feet. From the next room comes the wheezy double-barreled snoring of her uncle and aunt. *Somebody loves me, I wonder who.* . . . The tune is all through her body, in the throb of her feet, in the tingling place on her back where he held her tight dancing with her. Anna you've got to forget it or you wont sleep. Anna you got to forget. Dishes on the table set for breakfast jingle tingle hideously when she bumps against it.

"That you Anna?" comes a sleepy querulous voice from her mother's bed.

"Went to get a drink o water mommer." The old woman lets the breath out in a groan through her teeth, the bedsprings creak as she turns over. Asleep all the time.

Somebody loves me, I wonder who. She slips off her party dress and gets into her nightgown. Then she tiptoes to the closet to hang up the dress and at last slides between the covers little by little so the slats wont creak. *I wonder who.* Shuffle shuffle, bright lights, pink blobbing faces, grabbing arms, tense thighs, bouncing feet. *I wonder who.* Shuffle, droning saxophone tease, shuffle in time to the drum, trombone, clarinet. Feet, thighs, cheek to cheek, *Somebody loves me. . . .* Shuffle shuffle. *I wonder who.*

The baby with tiny shut purplishpink face and fists lay asleep on the berth. Ellen was leaning over a black leather suitcase. Jimmy Herf in his shirtsleeves was looking out the porthole.

"Well there's the statue of Liberty. . . . Ellie we ought to be out on deck."

"It'll be ages before we dock. . . . Go ahead up. I'll come up with Martin in a minute."

"Oh come ahead; we'll put the baby's stuff in the bag while we're warping into the slip."

They came out on deck into a dazzling September afternoon. The water was greenindigo. A steady wind kept sweeping coils of brown smoke and blobs of whitecotton steam off the high enormous blueindigo arch of sky. Against a sootsmudged horizon, tangled with barges, steamers, chimneys of powerplants, covered wharves, bridges, lower New York was a pink and white tapering pyramid cut slenderly out of cardboard.

"Ellie we ought to have Martin out so he can see."

"And start yelling like a tugboat. . . . He's better off where he is."

They ducked under some ropes, slipped past the rattling steamwinch and out to the bow.

"God Ellie it's the greatest sight in the world. . . . I never thought I'd ever come back, did you?"

"I had every intention of coming back."

"Not like this."

"No I dont suppose I did."

"S'il vous plait madame . . ."

A sailor was motioning them back. Ellen turned her face into the wind to get the coppery whisps of hair out of her eyes. "C'est beau, n'est-ce pas?" She smiled into the wind into the sailor's red face.

"J'aime mieux le Havre . . . S'il vous plait madame."

"Well I'll go down and pack Martin up."

The hard chug, chug of the tugboat coming alongside beat Jimmy's answer out of her ears. She slipped away from him and went down to the cabin again.

They were wedged in the jam of people at the end of the gangplank.

"Look we could wait for a porter," said Ellen.

"No dear I've got them." Jimmy was sweating and staggering with a suitcase in each hand and packages under his arms. In Ellen's arms the baby was cooing stretching tiny spread hands towards the faces all round.

"D'you know it?" said Jimmy as they crossed the gangplank, "I kinder wish we were just going on board. . . . I hate getting home."

"I dont hate it. . . . There's H . . . I'll follow right along. . . . I wanted to look for Frances and Bob. Hello. . . ." "Well I'll be . . ." "Helena you've gained, you're looking wonderfully. Where's Jimps?" Jimmy was rubbing his hands together, stiff and chafed from handles of the heavy suitcases.

"Hello Herf. Hello Frances. Isn't this swell?"

"Gosh I'm glad to see you. . . ."

"Jimps the thing for me to do is go right on to the Brevoort with the baby . . ."

"Isn't he sweet."

". . . Have you got five dollars?"

"I've only got a dollar in change. That hundred is in express checks."

"I've got plenty of money. Helena and I'll go to the hotel and you boys can come along with the baggage."

"Inspector is it all right if I go through with the baby? My husband will look after the trunks."

"Why surely madam, go right ahead."

"Isnt he nice? Oh Frances this is lots of fun."

"Go ahead Bob I can finish this up alone quicker. . . . You convoy the ladies to the Brevoort."

"Well we hate to leave you."

"Oh go ahead. . . . I'll be right along."

"Mr. James Herf and wife and infant . . . is that it?"

"Yes that's right."

"I'll be right with you, Mr. Herf. . . . Is all the baggage there?"

"Yes everything's there."

"Isnt he good?" clucked Frances as she and Hildebrand followed Ellen into the cab.

"Who?"

"The baby of course. . . ."

"Oh you ought to see him sometimes. . . . He seems to like traveling."

A plainclothesman opened the door of the cab and looked in as they went out the gate. "Want to smell our breaths?" asked Hildebrand. The man had a face like a block of wood. He closed the door. "Helena doesn't know prohibition yet, does she?"

"He gave me a scare . . . Look. "

"Good gracious!" From under the blanket that was wrapped round the baby she produced a brownpaper package. . . . "Two quarts of our special cognac . . . gout famille 'Erf . . . and I've got another quart in a hotwaterbottle under my waistband. . . . That's why I look as if I was going to have another baby."

The Hildebrands began hooting with laughter.

"Jimp's got a hotwaterbottle round his middle too and chartreuse in a flask on his hip. . . . We'll probably have to go and bail him out of jail."

They were still laughing so that tears were streaming down their faces when they drew up at the hotel. In the elevator the baby began to wail.

As soon as she had closed the door of the big sunny room she fished the hotwaterbottle from under her dress. "Look Bob phone down for some cracked ice and seltzer. . . . We'll all have a cognac a l'eau de selz. . . ."

"Hadn't we better wait for Jimps?"

"Oh he'll be right here. . . . We haven't anything dutiable. . . . Much too broke to have anything. . . . Frances what do you do about milk in New York?"

"How should I know, Helena?" Frances Hildebrand flushed and walked to the window.

"Oh well we'll give him his food again. . . . He's done fairly well on it on the trip." Ellen had laid the baby on the bed. He lay kicking, looking about with dark round goldstone eyes.

"Isnt he fat?"

"He's so healthy I'm sure he must be halfwitted. . . . Oh Heavens and I've got to call up my father. . . . Isnt family life just too desperately complicated?"

Ellen was setting up her little alcohol stove on the washstand. The bellboy came with glasses and a bowl of clinking ice and White Rock on a tray.

"You fix us a drink out of the hotwaterbottle. We've got to use that up or it'll eat the rubber. . . . And we'll drink to the Café d'Harcourt."

"Of course what you kids dont realize," said Hildebrand, "is that the difficulty under prohibition is keeping sober."

Ellen laughed; she stood over the little lamp that gave out a quiet domestic smell of hot nickel and burned alcohol.

George Baldwin was walking up Madison Avenue with his light overcoat on his arm. His fagged spirits were reviving in the sparkling autumn twilight of the streets. From block to block through the taxiwhirring gasoline gloaming two lawyers in black frock coats and stiff wing collars argued in his head. If you go home it will be cozy in the library. The apartment will be gloomy and quiet and you can sit in your slippers under the bust of Scipio Africanus in the leather chair and read and have dinner sent in to you. . . . Nevada would be jolly and coarse and tell you funny stories. . . . She would have all the City Hall gossip . . . good to know. . . . But you're not going to see Nevada any more . . . too dangerous; she gets you all wrought up. . . . And Cecily sitting faded and elegant and slender biting her lips and hating me, hating life. . . . Good God how am I going to get my existence straightened out? He stopped in front of a flowerstore. A moist warm honied expensive smell came from the door, densely out into the keen steelblue street. If I could at least make my financial position impregnable. . . . In the window was a miniature Japanese garden with brokenback bridges and ponds where the goldfish looked big as whales. Proportion, that's it. To lay out your life like a prudent gardener, plowing and sowing. No I wont go to see Nevada tonight. I might send her some flowers though. Yellow roses, those coppery roses . . . it's Elaine who ought to wear those. Imagine her married again and with a baby. He went into the store. "What's that rose?"

"It's Gold of Ophir sir."

"All right I want two dozen sent down to the Brevoort immediately. . . . Miss Elaine . . . No Mr. and Mrs. James Herf. . . . I'll write a card."

He sat down at the desk with a pen in his hand. Incense of roses, incense out of the dark fire of her hair. . . . No nonsense for Heaven's sake . . .

Dear Elaine,

I hope you will allow an old friend to call on you and your husband one of these days. And please remember that I am always sincerely anxious—you know me too well to take this for an empty offer of politeness—to serve you and him in any way that could possibly contribute to your happiness. Forgive me if I subscribe myself your lifelong slave and admirer.

George Baldwin

The letter covered three of the florists' white cards. He read it over with pursed lips, carefully crossing the t's and dotting the i's. Then he paid the florist from the roll of bills he took from his back pocket and went out into the street again. It was already night, going on to seven o'clock. Still hesitating he stood at the corner watching the taxis pass, yellow, red, green, tangerinecolored.

The snubnosed transport sludges slowly through the Narrows in the rain. Sergeant-Major O'Keefe and Private 1st Class Dutch Robertson stand in the lee of the deckhouse looking at the liners at anchor in quarantine and the low wharfcluttered shores.

"Look some of em still got their warpaint—Shippin Board boats. . . . Not worth the powder to blow em up."

"The hell they aint," said Joey O'Keefe vaguely.

"Gosh little old New York's goin to look good to me. . . ."

"Me too Sarge, rain or shine I dont care."

They are passing close to a mass of steamers anchored in a block, some of them listing to one side or the other, lanky ships with short funnels, stumpy ships with tall funnels red with rust, some of them striped and splashed and dotted with puttycolor and blue and green of camouflage paint. A man in a motorboat waved his arms. The men in khaki slickers huddled on the gray dripping deck of the transport begin to sing

> Oh the infantry, the infantry,
> With the dirt behind their ears . . .

Through the brightbeaded mist behind the low buildings of Governors Island they can make out the tall pylons, the curving cables, the airy lace of Brooklyn Bridge. Robertson pulls a package out of his pocket and pitches it overboard.

"What was that?"

"Just my propho kit. . . . Wont need it no more."

"How's that?"

"Oh I'm goin to live clean an get a good job and maybe get married."

"I guess that's not such a bad idear. I'm tired o playin round myself. Jez somebody must a cleaned up good on them Shippin Board boats." "That's where the dollar a year men get theirs I guess."

"I'll tell the world they do."

Up forward they are singing

> Oh she works in a jam factoree
> And that may be all right . . .

"Jez we're goin up the East River Sarge. Where the devil do they think they're goin to land us?"

"God, I'd be willin to swim ashore myself. An just think of all the guys been here all this time cleanin up on us. . . . Ten dollars a day workin in a shipyard mind you . . ."

"Hell Sarge we got the experience."

"Experience . . ."

> Apres la guerre finee
> Back to the States for me. . . .

"I bet the skipper's been drinkin beaucoup highballs an thinks Brooklyn's Hoboken."

"Well there's Wall Street, bo."

They are passing under Brooklyn Bridge. There is a humming whine of electric trains over their heads, an occasional violet flash from the wet rails. Behind them beyond barges tugboats carferries the tall buildings, streaked white with whisps of steam and mist, tower gray into sagged clouds.

Nobody said anything while they ate the soup. Mrs. Merivale sat in black at the head of the oval table looking out through the halfdrawn portieres and the drawingroom window beyond at a column of white smoke that uncoiled in the sunlight above the trainyards, remembering her husband and how they had come years ago to look at the apartment in the unfinished house that smelled of plaster and paint. At last when she had finished her soup she roused herself and said: "Well Jimmy, are you going back to newspaper work?"

"I guess so."

"James has had three jobs offered him already. I think it's remarkable."

"I guess I'll go in with the Major though," said James Merivale to Ellen who sat next to him. "Major Goodyear you know, Cousin Helena. . . . One of the Buffalo Goodyears. He's head of the foreign exchange department of the Banker's Trust. . . . He says he can work me up quickly. We were friends overseas."

"That'll be wonderful," said Maisie in a cooing voice, "wont it Jimmy?" She sat opposite slender and rosy in her black dress.

"He's putting me up for Piping Rock," went on Merivale.

"What's that?"

"Why Jimmy you must know. . . . I'm sure Cousin Helena has been out there to tea many a time."

"You know Jimps," said Ellen with her eyes in her plate. "That's where Stan Emery's father used to go every Sunday."

"Oh did you know that unfortunate young man? That was a horrible thing," said Mrs. Merivale. "So many horrible things have been happening these years. . . . I'd almost forgotten about it."

"Yes I knew him," said Ellen.

The leg of lamb came in accompanied by fried eggplant, late corn, and sweet potatoes. "Do you know I think it is just terrible," said Mrs. Merivale when she had done carving, "the way you fellows wont tell us any of your experiences over there. . . . Lots of them must have been remarkably interesting. Jimmy I should think you'd write a book about your experiences."

"I have tried a few articles."

"When are they coming out?"

"Nobody seems to want to print them. . . . You see I differ radically in certain matters of opinion . . ."

"Mrs. Merivale it's years since I've eaten such delicious sweet potatoes. . . . These taste like yams."

"They are good. . . . It's just the way I have them cooked."

"Well it was a great war while it lasted," said Merivale.

"Where were you Armistice night, Jimmy?"

"I was in Jerusalem with the Red Cross. Isn't that absurd?"

"I was in Paris."

"So was I," said Ellen.

"And so you were over there too Helena? I'm going to call you Helena eventually, so I might as well begin now. . . . Isn't that interesting? Did you and Jimmy meet over there?"

"Oh no we were old friends. . . . But we were thrown together a lot. . . . We were in the same department of the Red Cross—the Publicity Department."

"A real war romance," chanted Mrs. Merivale. "Isn't that interesting?"

"Now fellers it's this way," shouted Joe O'Keefe, the sweat breaking out on his red face. "Are we going to put over this bonus proposition or aint we? . . . We fought for em didnt we, we cleaned up the squareheads, didnt we? And now when we come home we get the dirty end of the stick. No jobs. . . . Our girls have gone and married other fellers. . . . Treat us like a bunch o dirty bums and loafers when we ask for our just and legal and lawful compensation. . . . the bonus. Are we goin to stand for it? . . . No. Are we goin to stand for a bunch of politicians treatin us like we was goin round to the back door to ask for a handout? . . . I ask you fellers. . . ."

Feet stamped on the floor. "No." "To hell wid em," shouted voices. . . . "Now I say to hell wid de politicians. . . . We'll carry our campaign to the country . . . to the great big generous bighearted American people we fought and bled and laid down our lives for."

The long armory room roared with applause. The wounded men in the front row banged the floor with their crutches. "Joey's a good guy," said a man without arms to a man with one eye and an artificial leg who sat beside him. "He is that Buddy." While they were filing out offering each other cigarettes, a man stood in the door calling out, "Committee meeting, Committee on Bonus."

The four of them sat round a table in the room the Colonel had lent them. "Well fellers let's have a cigar." Joe hopped over to the Colonel's desk and brought out four Romeo and Juliets. "He'll never miss em."

"Some little grafter I'll say," said Sid Garnett stretching out his long legs.

"Havent got a case of Scotch in there, have you Joey?" said Bill Dougan.

"Naw I'm not drinkin myself jus for the moment."

"I know where you kin get guaranteed Haig and Haig," put in Segal cockily—"before the war stuff for six dollars a quart."

"An where are we goin to get the six dollars for crissake?"

"Now look here fellers," said Joe, sitting on the edge of the table, "let's get down to brass tacks. . . . What we've got to do is raise a fund from the gang and anywhere else we can. . . . Are we agreed about that?"

"Sure we are, you tell em," said Dougan.

"I know lot of old fellers even, thinks the boys are gettin a raw deal. . . . We'll call it the Brooklyn Bonus Agitation

REJOICING CITY 731

Committee associated with the Sheamus O'Rielly Post of the
A. L. . . . No use doin anythin unless you do it up right.
. . . Now are yous guys wid me or aint yer?"

"Sure we are Joey. . . . You tell em an we'll mark time."

"Well Dougan's got to be president cause he's the best
lookin."

Dougan went crimson and began to stammer.

"Oh you seabeach Apollo," jeered Garnett.

"And I think I can do best as treasurer because I've had
more experience."

"Cause you're the crookedest you mean," said Segal under
his breath.

Joe stuck out his jaw. "Look here Segal are you wid us or
aint yer? You'd better come right out wid it now if you're not."

"Sure, cut de comedy," said Dougan. "Joey's de guy to put
dis ting trough an you know it. . . . Cut de comedy. . . . If
you dont like it you kin git out."

Segal rubbed his thin hooked nose. "I was juss jokin gents,
I didn't mean no harm."

"Look here," went on Joe angrily, "what do you think I'm
givin up my time for? . . . Why I turned down fifty dollars a
week only yesterday, aint that so, Sid? You seen me talkin to
de guy."

"Sure I did Joey."

"Oh pipe down fellers," said Segal. "I was just stringin Joey
along."

"Well I think Segal you ought to be secretary, cause you
know about office work. . . ."

"Office work?"

"Sure," said Joe puffing his chest out. "We're goin to have
desk space in the office of a guy I know. . . . It's all fixed.
He's goin to let us have it free till we get a start. An we're
goin to have office stationery. Cant get nowhere in this world
without presentin things right."

"An where do I come in?" asked Sid Garnett.

"You're the committee, you big stiff."

After the meeting Joe O'Keefe walked whistling down Atlantic Avenue. It was a crisp night; he was walking on springs.
There was a light in Dr. Gordon's office. He rang. A white-
faced man in a white jacket opened the door.

"Hello Doc."

"Is that you O'Keefe? Come on in my boy." Something in the doctor's voice clutched like a cold hand at his spine.

"Well did your test come out all right doc?"

"All right . . . positive all right."

"Christ."

"Dont worry too much about it, my boy, we'll fix you up in a few months."

"Months."

"Why at a conservative estimate fiftyfive percent of the people you meet on the street have a syphilitic taint."

"It's not as if I'd been a damn fool. I was careful over there."

"Inevitable in wartime. . . ."

"Now I wish I'd let loose. . . . Oh the chances I passed up."

The doctor laughed. "You probably wont even have any symptoms. . . . It's just a question of injections. I'll have you sound as a dollar in no time. . . . Do you want to take a shot now? I've got it all ready."

O'Keefe's hands went cold. "Well I guess so," he forced a laugh. "I guess I'll be a goddam thermometer by the time you're through with me." The doctor laughed creakily. "Full up of arsenic and mercury eh. . . . That's it."

The wind was blowing up colder. His teeth were chattering. Through the rasping castiron night he walked home. Fool to pass out that way when he stuck me. He could still feel the sickening lunge of the needle. He gritted his teeth. After this I got to have some luck. . . . I got to have some luck.

Two stout men and a lean man sit at a table by a window. The light of a zinc sky catches brightedged glints off glasses, silverware, oystershells, eyes. George Baldwin has his back to the window. Gus McNiel sits on his right, and Densch on his left. When the waiter leans over to take away the empty oystershells he can see through the window, beyond the graystone parapet, the tops of a few buildings jutting like the last trees at the edge of a cliff and the tinfoil reaches of the harbor littered with ships. "I'm lecturin you this time, George. . . . Lord knows you used to lecture me enough in the old days. Honest it's rank foolishness," Gus McNiel is saying. ". . . It's rank foolishness to pass up the chance of a political career at your time of life. . . . There's no man in New York better fitted to hold office . . ."

"Looks to me as if it were your duty, Baldwin," says Densch in a deep voice, taking his tortoiseshell glasses out of a case and applying them hurriedly to his nose.

The waiter has brought a large planked steak surrounded by bulwarks of mushrooms and chopped carrots and peas and frilled browned mashed potatoes. Densch straightens his glasses and stares attentively at the planked steak.

"A very handsome dish Ben, a very handsome dish I must say. . . . It's just this Baldwin . . . as I look at it . . . the country is going through a dangerous period of reconstruction . . . the confusion attendant on the winding up of a great conflict . . . the bankruptcy of a continent . . . bolshevism and subversive doctrines rife . . . America . . ." he says, cutting with the sharp polished steel knife into the thick steak, rare and well peppered. He chews a mouthful slowly. "America," he begins again, "is in the position of taking over the receivership of the world. The great principles of democracy, of that commercial freedom upon which our whole civilization depends are more than ever at stake. Now as at no other time we need men of established ability and unblemished integrity in public office, particularly in the offices requiring expert judicial and legal knowledge."

"That's what I was tryin to tell ye the other day George."

"But that's all very well Gus, but how do you know I'd be elected. . . . After all it would mean giving up my law practice for a number of years, it would mean . . ."

"You just leave that to me. . . . George you're elected already."

"An extraordinarily good steak," says Densch, "I must say. . . . No but newspaper talk aside . . . I happen to know from a secret and reliable source that there is a subversive plot among undesirable elements in this country. . . . Good God think of the Wall Street bomb outrage. . . . I must say that the attitude of the press has been gratifying in one respect . . . in fact we're approaching a national unity undreamed of before the war."

"No but George," breaks in Gus, "put it this way. . . .

The publicity value of a political career'd kinder bolster up your law practice."

"It would and it wouldn't Gus."

Densch is unrolling the tinfoil off a cigar. "At any rate it's a grand sight." He takes off his glasses and cranes his thick neck to look out into the bright expanse of harbor that stretches full of masts, smoke, blobs of steam, dark oblongs of barges, to the hazeblurred hills of Staten Island.

Bright flakes of cloud were scaling off a sky of crushing indigo over the Battery where groups of dingy darkdressed people stood round the Ellis Island landing station and the small boat dock waiting silently for something. Frayed smoke of tugs and steamers hung low and trailed along the opaque glassgreen water. A threemasted schooner was being towed down the North River. A newhoisted jib flopped awkwardly in the wind. Down the harbor loomed taller, taller a steamer head on, four red stacks packed into one, creamy superstructure gleaming. "*Mauretania* just acomin in twentyfour hours lyte," yelled the man with the telescope and fieldglasses. . . . "Tyke a look at the *Mauretania*, farstest ocean greyhound, twentyfour hours lyte." The *Mauretania* stalked like a skyscraper through the harbor shipping. A rift of sunlight sharpened the shadow under the broad bridge, along the white stripes of upper decks, glinted in the rows of portholes. The smokestacks stood apart, the hull lengthened. The black relentless hull of the *Mauretania* pushing puffing tugs ahead of it cut like a long knife into the North River.

A ferry was leaving the immigrant station, a murmur rustled through the crowd that packed the edges of the wharf. "Deportees. . . . It's the communists the Department of Justice is having deported . . . deportees . . . Reds. . . . It's the Reds they are deporting." The ferry was out of the slip. In the stern a group of men stood still tiny like tin soldiers. "They are sending the Reds back to Russia." A handkerchief waved on the ferry, a red handkerchief. People tiptoed gently to the edge of the walk, tiptoeing, quiet like in a sickroom.

Behind the backs of the men and women crowding to the edge of the water, gorillafaced chipontheshoulder policemen walked back and forth nervously swinging their billies.

"They are sending the Reds back to Russia. . . . Deportees. . . . Agitators. . . . Undesirables." . . . Gulls wheeled crying. A catsupbottle bobbed gravely in the little groundglass waves. A sound of singing came from the ferryboat getting small, slipping away across the water.

C'est la lutte finale, groupons-nous et demain
L'Internationale sera le genre humain.

"Take a look at the deportees. . . . Take a look at the undesirable aliens," shouted the man with the telescopes and fieldglasses. A girl's voice burst out suddenly, *"Arise prisoners of starvation."* "Sh. . . . They could pull you for that."
The singing trailed away across the water. At the end of a marbled wake the ferryboat was shrinking into haze. *International . . . shall be the human race.* The singing died. From up the river came the longdrawn rattling throb of a steamer leaving dock. Gulls wheeled above the dark dingydressed crowd that stood silently looking down the bay.

II. Nickelodeon

A *nickel before midnight buys tomorrow . . .*
holdup headlines, a cup of coffee in the auto-
mat, a ride to Woodlawn, Fort Lee, Flatbush. . . . A
nickel in the slot buys chewing gum. Somebody Loves
Me, Baby Divine, You're in Kentucky Juss Shu' As
You're Born . . . bruised notes of foxtrots go limping
out of doors, blues, waltzes (We'd Danced the Whole
Night Through) trail gyrating tinsel memories. . . .
On Sixth Avenue on Fourteenth there are still fly-
specked stereopticons where for a nickel you can peep at
yellowed yesterdays. Beside the peppering shooting
gallery you stoop into the flicker A HOT TIME, THE
BACHELOR'S SURPRISE, THE STOLEN GARTER *. . .*
wastebasket of tornup daydreams. . . . A nickel before
midnight buys our yesterdays.

Ruth Prynne came out of the doctor's office pulling the fur
tight round her throat. She felt faint. Taxi. As she stepped in
she remembered the smell of cosmetics and toast and the littered hallway at Mrs. Sunderland's. Oh I cant go home just
yet. "Driver go to the Old English Tea Room on Fortieth
Street please." She opened her long green leather purse and
looked in. My God, only a dollar a quarter a nickel and two
pennies. She kept her eyes on the figures flickering on the
taximeter. She wanted to break down and cry. . . . The way
money goes. The gritty cold wind rasped at her throat when
she got out. "Eighty cents miss. . . . I haven't any change
miss." "All right keep the change." Heavens only thirtytwo
cents. . . . Inside it was warm and smelled cozily of tea and
cookies.

"Why Ruth, if it isn't Ruth. . . . Dearest come to my arms
after all these years." It was Billy Waldron. He was fatter and
whiter than he used to be. He gave her a stagy hug and kissed
her on the forehead. "How are you? Do tell me. . . . How
distinguée you look in that hat."

"I've just been having my throat X-rayed," she said with a
giggle. "I feel like the wrath of God."

"What are you doing Ruth? I havent heard of you for ages."

"Put me down as a back number, hadn't you?" She caught his words up fiercely.

"After that beautiful performance you gave in The Orchard Queen. . . ."

"To tell the truth Billy I've had a terrible run of bad luck."

"Oh I know everything is dead."

"I have an appointment to see Belasco next week. . . . Something may come of that."

"Why I should say it might Ruth. . . . Are you expecting someone?"

"No. . . . Oh Billy you're still the same old tease. . . . Dont tease me this afternoon. I dont feel up to it."

"You poor dear sit down and have a cup of tea with me."

"I tell you Ruth it's a terrible year. Many a good trouper will pawn the last link of his watch chain this year. . . . I suppose you're going the rounds."

"Dont talk about it. . . . If I could only get my throat all right. . . . A thing like that wears you down."

"Remember the old days at the Somerville Stock?"

"Billy could I ever forget them? . . . Wasnt it a scream?"

"The last time I saw you Ruth was in The Butterfly on the Wheel in Seattle. I was out front. . . ."

"Why didn't you come back and see me?"

"I was still angry at you I suppose. . . . It was my lowest moment. In the valley of shadow . . . melancholia . . . neurasthenia. I was stranded penniless. . . . That night I was a little under the influence, you understand. I didn't want you to see the beast in me."

Ruth poured herself a fresh cup of tea. She suddenly felt feverishly gay. "Oh but Billy havent you forgotten all that? . . . I was a foolish little girl then. . . . I was afraid that love or marriage or anything like that would interfere with my art, you understand. . . . I was so crazy to succeed."

"Would you do the same thing again?"

"I wonder. . . ."

"How does it go? . . . *The moving finger writes and having writ moves on . . .*"

"Something about *Nor all your tears wash out a word of it*

. . . But Billy," she threw back her head and laughed, "I thought you were getting ready to propose to me all over again. . . . Ou my throat."

"Ruth I wish you werent taking that X-ray treatment. . . . I've heard it's very dangerous. Dont let me alarm you about it my dear . . . but I have heard of cases of cancer contracted that way."

"That's nonsense Billy. . . . That's only when X-rays are improperly used, and it takes years of exposure. . . . No I think this Dr. Warner's a remarkable man."

Later, sitting in the uptown express in the subway, she still could feel his soft hand patting her gloved hand. "Goodbye little girl, God bless you," he'd said huskily. He's gotten to be a ham actor if there ever was one, something was jeering inside her all the while. "Thank heavens you will never know." . . . Then with a sweep of his broadbrimmed hat and a toss of his silky white hair, as if he were playing in Monsieur Beaucaire, he had turned and walked off among the crowd up Broadway. I may be down on my luck, but I'm not all ham inside the way he is. . . . Cancer he said. She looked up and down the car at the joggling faces opposite her. Of all those people one of them must have it. Four OUT OF EVERY FIVE GET . . . Silly, that's not cancer. Ex-lax, Nujol, O'Sullivan's. . . . She put her hand to her throat. Her throat was terribly swollen, her throat throbbed feverishly. Maybe it was worse. It is something alive that grows in flesh, eats all your life, leaves you horrible, rotten. . . . The people opposite stared straight ahead of them, young men and young women, middleaged people, green faces in the dingy light, under the sourcolored advertisements. FOUR OUT OF EVERY FIVE . . . A trainload of jiggling corpses, nodding and swaying as the express roared shrilly towards Ninetysixth Street. At Ninetysixth she had to change for the local.

Dutch Robertson sat on a bench on Brooklyn Bridge with the collar of his army overcoat turned up, running his eye down Business Opportunities. It was a muggy fogchoked afternoon; the bridge was dripping and aloof like an arbor in a dense garden of steamboatwhistles. Two sailors passed. "Ze best joint I've been in since B. A."

Partner movie theater, busy neighborhood . . . stand investigation . . . $3,000. . . . Jez I haven't got three thousand mills. . . . Cigar stand, busy building, compelled sacrifice. . . . Attractive and completely outfitted radio and music shop . . . busy. . . . Modern mediumsized printingplant consisting of cylinders, Kelleys, Miller feeders, job presses, linotype machines and a complete bindery. . . . Kosher restaurant and delicatessen. . . . Bowling alley . . . busy. . . . Live spot large dancehall and other concessions. WE BUY FALSE TEETH, old gold, platinum, old jewelry. The hell they do. HELP WANTED MALE. That's more your speed you rummy. Addressers, first class penmen. . . . Lets me out. . . . Artist, Attendant, Auto, Bicycle and Motorcycle repair shop. . . . He took out the back of an envelope and marked down the address. Bootblacks. . . . Not yet. Boy; no I guess I aint a boy any more, Candystore, Canvassers, Carwashers, Dishwasher. EARN WHILE YOU LEARN. Mechanical dentistry is your shortest way to success. . . . No dull seasons. . . .

"Hello Dutch. . . . I thought I'd never get here." A grayfaced girl in a red hat and gray rabbit coat sat down beside him.

"Jez I'm sick o readin want ads." He stretched out his arms and yawned letting the paper slip down his legs.

"Aint you chilly, sittin out here on the bridge?"

"Maybe I am. . . . Let's go and eat." He jumped to his feet and put his red face with its thin broken nose close to hers and looked in her black eyes with his pale gray eyes. He tapped her arm sharply. "Hello Francie. . . . How's my lil girl?"

They walked back towards Manhattan, the way she had come. Under them the river glinted through the mist. A big steamer drifted by slowly, lights already lit; over the edge of the walk they looked down the black smokestacks.

"Was it a boat as big as that you went overseas on Dutch?"

"Bigger 'n that."

"Gee I'd like to go."

"I'll take you over some time and show you all them places over there . . . I went to a lot of places that time I went A.W.O.L."

In the L station they hesitated. "Francie got any jack on you?"

"Sure I got a dollar. . . . I ought to keep that for tomorrer though."

"All I got's my last quarter. Let's go eat two fiftyfive cent dinners at that chink place . . . That'll be a dollar ten."

"I got to have a nickel to get down to the office in the mornin."

"Oh Hell! Goddam it I wish we could have some money."

"Got anything lined up yet?"

"Wouldn't I have told ye if I had?"

"Come ahead I've got a half a dollar saved up in my room. I can take carfare outa that." She changed the dollar and put two nickels into the turnstile. They sat down in a Third Avenue train.

"Say Francie will they let us dance in a khaki shirt?"

"Why not Dutch it looks all right."

"I feel kinder fussed about it."

The jazzband in the restaurant was playing Hindustan. It smelled of chop suey and Chinese sauce. They slipped into a booth. Slickhaired young men and little bobhaired girls were dancing hugged close. As they sat down they smiled into each other's eyes.

"Jez I'm hungry."

"Are you Dutch?"

He pushed forward his knees until they locked with hers. "Gee you're a good kid," he said when he had finished his soup. "Honest I'll get a job this week. And then we'll get a nice room an get married an everything."

When they got up to dance they were trembling so they could barely keep time to the music.

"Mister . . . no dance without ploper dless . . ." said a dapper Chinaman putting his hand on Dutch's arm.

"Waz he want?" he growled dancing on.

"I guess it's the shirt, Dutch."

"The hell it is."

"I'm tired. I'd rather talk than dance anyway . . ." They went back to their booth and their sliced pineapple for dessert.

Afterwards they walked east along Fourteenth. "Dutch cant we go to your room?"

"I ain't got no room. The old stiff wont let me stay and she's got all my stuff. Honest if I dont get a job this week I'm goin to a recruiting sergeant an re-enlist."

"Oh dont do that; we wouldn't ever get married then Dutch. . . . Gee though why didn't you tell me?"

"I didn't want to worry you Francie. . . . Six months out of work . . . Jez it's enough to drive a guy cookoo."

"But Dutch where can we go?"

"We might go out that wharf. . . . I know a wharf."

"It's so cold."

"I couldn't get cold when you were with me kid."

"Dont talk like that. . . . I dont like it."

They walked leaning together in the darkness up the muddy rutted riverside streets, between huge swelling gastanks, brokendown fences, long manywindowed warehouses. At a corner under a streetlamp a boy catcalled as they passed.

"I'll poke your face in you little bastard," Dutch let fly out of the corner of his mouth.

"Dont answer him," Francie whispered, "or we'll have the whole gang down on us."

They slipped through a little door in a tall fence above which crazy lumberpiles towered. They could smell the river and cedarwood and sawdust. They could hear the river lapping at the piles under their feet. Dutch drew her to him and pressed his mouth down on hers.

"Hay dere dont you know you cant come out here at night disaway?" a voice yapped at them. The watchman flashed a lantern in their eyes.

"All right keep your shirt on, we were just taking a little walk."

"Some walk."

They were dragging themselves down the street again with the black riverwind in their teeth.

"Look out." A policeman passed whistling softly to himself. They drew apart. "Oh Francie they'll be takin us to the nuthouse if we keep this up. Let's go to your room."

"Landlady'll throw me out, that's all."

"I wont make any noise. . . . You got your key aint ye? I'll sneak out before light. Goddam it they make you feel like a skunk."

"All right Dutch let's go home. . . . I dont care no more what happens."

They walked up mudtracked stairs to the top floor of the tenement.

"Take off your shoes," she hissed in his ear as she slipped the key in the lock.

"I got holes in my stockings."

"That dont matter, silly. I'll see if it's all right. My room's way back past the kitchen so if they're all in bed they cant hear us."

When she left him he could hear his heart beating. In a second she came back. He tiptoed after her down a creaky hall. A sound of snoring came through a door. There was a smell of cabbage and sleep in the hall. Once in her room she locked the door and put a chair against it under the knob. A triangle of ashen light came in from the street. "Now for crissake keep still Dutch." One shoe still in each hand he reached for her and hugged her.

He lay beside her whispering on and on with his lips against her ear. "And Francie I'll make good, honest I will; I got to be a sergeant overseas till they busted me for goin A.W.O.L. That shows I got it in me. Onct I get a chance I'll make a whole lot of jack and you an me'll go back an see Château Teery an Paree an all that stuff; honest you'd like it Francie . . . Jez the towns are old and funny and quiet and cozylike an they have the swellest ginmills where you sit outside at little tables in the sun an watch the people pass an the food's swell too once you get to like it an they have hotels all over where we could have gone like tonight an they dont care if you're married or nutten. An they have big beds all cozy made of wood and they bring ye up breakfast in bed. Jez Francie you'd like it."

They were walking to dinner through the snow. Big snowfeathers spun and spiraled about them mottling the glare of the streets with blue and pink and yellow, blotting perspectives.

"Ellie I hate to have you take that job. . . . You ought to keep on with your acting."

"But Jimps, we've got to live."

"I know . . . I know. You'd certainly didnt have your wits about you Ellie when you married me."

"Oh let's not talk about it any more."

"Do let's have a good time tonight. . . . It's the first snow."

"Is this the place?" They stood before an unlighted basement door covered by a closemeshed grating. "Let's try."

"Did the bell ring?"

"I think so."

The inner door opened and a girl in a pink apron peered out at them. "Bon soir mademoiselle."

"Ah . . . bon soir monsieur 'dame." She ushered them into a foodsmelling gaslit hall hung with overcoats and hats and mufflers. Through a curtained door the restaurant blew in their faces a hot breath of bread and cocktails and frying butter and perfumes and lipsticks and clatter and jingling talk.

"I can smell absinthe," said Ellen. "Let's get terribly tight."

"Good Lord, there's Congo. . . . Dont you remember Congo Jake at the Seaside Inn?"

He stood bulky at the end of the corridor beckoning to them. His face was very tanned and he had a glossy black mustache. "Hello Meester 'Erf. . . . Ow are you?"

"Fine as silk. Congo I want you to meet my wife."

"If you dont mind the keetchen we will 'ave a drink."

"Of course we dont. . . . It's the best place in the house. Why you're limping. . . . What did you do to your leg?"

"Foutu . . . I left it en Italie. . . . I couldnt breeng it along once they'd cut it off."

"How was that?"

"Damn fool thing on Mont Tomba. . . . My bruderinlaw e gave me a very beautiful artificial leemb. . . . Sit 'ere. Look madame now can you tell which is which?"

"No I cant," said Ellie laughing. They were at a little marble table in the corner of the crowded kitchen. A girl was dishing out at a deal table in the center. Two cooks worked over the stove. The air was rich with sizzling fatty foodsmells. Congo hobbled back to them with three glasses on a small tray. He stood over them while they drank.

"Salut," he said, raising his glass. "Absinthe cocktail, like they make it in New Orleans."

"It's a knockout." Congo took a card out of his vest pocket:

MARQUIS DES COULOMMIERS
IMPORTS
Riverside 11121

"Maybe some day you need some little ting . . . I deal in nutting but prewar imported. I am the best bootleggair in New York.

"If I ever get any money I certainly will spend it on you Congo. . . . How do you find business?"

"Veree good. . . . I tell you about it. Tonight I'm too busee. . . . Now I find you a table in the restaurant."

"Do you run this place too?"

"No this my bruderinlaw's place."

"I didnt know you had a sister."

"Neither did I."

When Congo limped away from their table silence came down between them like an asbestos curtain in a theater.

"He's a funny duck," said Jimmy forcing a laugh.

"He certainly is."

"Look Ellie let's have another cocktail."

"Allright."

"I must get hold of him and get some stories about bootleggers out of him."

When he stretched his legs out under the table he touched her feet. She drew them away. Jimmy could feel his jaws chewing, they clanked so loud under his cheeks he thought Ellie must hear them. She sat opposite him in a gray tailored-suit, her neck curving up heartbreakingly from the ivory V left by the crisp frilled collar of her blouse, her head tilted under her tight gray hat, her lips made up; cutting up little pieces of meat and not eating them, not saying a word.

"Gosh . . . let's have another cocktail." He felt paralyzed like in a nightmare; she was a porcelaine figure under a bell-glass. A current of fresh snowrinsed air from somewhere eddied all of a sudden through the blurred packed jangling glare of the restaurant, cut the reek of food and drink and tobacco. For an instant he caught the smell of her hair. The cocktails burned in him. God I dont want to pass out.

Sitting in the restaurant of the Gare de Lyon, side by side

on the black leather bench. His cheek brushes hers when he reaches to put herring, butter, sardines, anchovies, sausage on her plate. They eat in a hurry, gobbling, giggling, gulp wine, start at every screech of an engine. . . .

The train pulls out of Avignon, the two awake, looking in each other's eyes in the compartment full of sleep-sodden snoring people. He lurches clambering over tangled legs, to smoke a cigarette at the end of the dim oscillating corridor. Diddledeump, going south, Diddledeump, going south, sing the wheels over the rails down the valley of the Rhone. Leaning in the window, smoking a broken cigarette, trying to smoke a crumbling cigarette, holding a finger over the torn place. Glubglub glubglub from the bushes, from the silver-dripping poplars along the track.

"Ellie, Ellie there are nightingales singing along the track."

"Oh I was asleep darling." She gropes to him stumbling across the legs of sleepers. Side by side in the window in the lurching jiggling corridor.

Deedledeump, going south. Gasp of nightingales along the track among the silverdripping poplars. The insane cloudy night of moonlight smells of gardens garlic rivers freshdunged field roses. Gasp of nightingales.

Opposite him the Elliedoll was speaking. "He says the lobstersalad's all out. . . . Isnt that discouraging?"

Suddenly he had his tongue. "Gosh if that were the only thing."

"What do you mean?"

"Why did we come back to this rotten town anyway?"

"You've been burbling about how wonderful it was ever since we came back."

"I know. I guess it's sour grapes. . . . I'm going to have another cocktail. . . . Ellie for heaven's sake what's the matter with us?"

"We're going to be sick if we keep this up I tell you."

"Well let's be sick. . . . Let's be good and sick."

When they sit up in the great bed they can see across the harbor, can see the yards of a windjammer and a white sloop and a red and green toy tug and plainfaced houses opposite beyond a peacock stripe of water; when they lie down they can see gulls in the sky. At dusk dressing rockily, shakily stumbling through the mildewed corridors of the hotel out into streets noisy as a brass band, full of tambourine rattle, brassy shine, crystal glitter, honk and whir of motors. . . . Alone together in the dusk drinking sherry under a broadleaved plane, alone together in the juggled particolored crowds like people invisible. And the spring night comes up over the sea terrible out of Africa and settles about them.

They had finished their coffee. Jimmy had drunk his very slowly as if some agony waited for him when he finished it.

"Well I was afraid we'd find the Barneys here," said Ellen.

"Do they know about this place?"

"You brought them here yourself Jimps. . . . And that dreadful woman insisted on talking babies with me all the evening. I hate talking babies."

"Gosh I wish we could go to a show."

"It would be too late anyway."

"And just spending money I havent got. . . . Lets have a cognac to top off with. I don't care if it ruins us."

"It probably will in more ways than one."

"Well Ellie, here's to the breadwinner who's taken up the white man's burden."

"Why Jimmy I think it'll be rather fun to have an editorial job for a while."

"I'd find it fun to have any kind of job. . . . Well I can always stay home and mind the baby."

"Dont be so bitter Jimmy, it's just temporary."

"Life's just temporary for that matter."

The taxi drew up. Jimmy paid him with his last dollar. Ellie had her key in the outside door. The street was a confusion of driving absintheblurred snow. The door of their apartment closed behind them. Chairs, tables, books, windowcurtains crowded about them bitter with the dust of yesterday, the day before, the day before that. Smells of diapers and coffeepots and typewriter oil and Dutch Cleanser oppressed them. Ellen put out the empty milkbottle and went to bed. Jimmy kept walking nervously about the front room. His drunkenness ebbed away leaving him icily sober. In the empty chamber of his brain a doublefaced word clinked like a coin: Success Failure, Success Failure.

*

> I'm just wild about Harree
> And Harry's just wild about me

she hums under her breath as she dances. It's a long hall with a band at one end, lit greenishly by two clusters of electric lights hanging among paper festoons in the center. At the end where the door is, a varnished rail holds back the line of men. This one Anna's dancing with is a tall square built Swede, his big feet trail clumsily after her tiny lightly tripping feet. The music stops. Now it's a little blackhaired slender Jew. He tries to snuggle close.

"Quit that." She holds him away from her.

"Aw have a heart."

She doesn't answer, dances with cold precision; she's sickeningly tired.

> Me and my boyfriend
> My boyfriend and I

An Italian breathes garlic in her face, a marine sergeant, a Greek, a blond young kid with pink cheeks, she gives him a smile; a drunken elderly man who tries to kiss her . . . *Charley my boy O Charley my boy* . . . slickhaired, freckled rumplehaired, pimplefaced, snubnosed, straightnosed, quick dancers, heavy dancers. . . . *Goin souf.* . . . *Wid de taste o de sugarcane right in my mouf* . . . against her back big hands, hot hands, sweaty hands, cold hands, while her dancechecks mount up, get to be a wad in her fist. This one's a good waltzer, genteel-like in a black suit.

"Gee I'm tired," she whispers.

"Dancing never tires me."

"Oh it's dancin with everybody like this."

"Don't you want to come an dance with me all alone somewhere?"

"Boyfrien's waitin for me after."

> With nothing but a photograph
> To tell my troubles to . . .
> What'll I do . . . ?

"What time's it?" she asks a broadchested wise guy. "Time you an me was akwainted, sister. . . ." She shakes her head. Suddenly the music bursts into Auld Lang Syne. She breaks

away from him and runs to the desk in a crowd of girls elbowing to turn in their dancechecks. "Say Anna," says a
broadhipped blond girl . . . "did ye see that sap was dancin
wid me? . . . He says to me the sap he says See you later an
I says to him the sap I says see yez in hell foist . . . and then
he says, Goily he says . . ."

III. Revolving Doors

G lowworm trains shuttle in the gloaming through the foggy looms of spiderweb bridges, elevators soar and drop in their shafts, harbor lights wink.

Like sap at the first frost at five o'clock men and women begin to drain gradually out of the tall buildings downtown, grayfaced throngs flood subways and tubes, vanish underground.

All night the great buildings stand quiet and empty, their million windows dark. Drooling light the ferries chew tracks across the lacquered harbor. At midnight the fourfunneled express steamers slide into the dark out of their glary berths. Bankers blearyeyed from secret conferences hear the hooting of the tugs as they are let out of side doors by lightningbug watchmen; they settle grunting into the back seats of limousines, and are whisked uptown into the Forties, clinking streets of ginwhite whiskey-yellow ciderfizzling lights.

She sat at the dressingtable coiling her hair. He stood over her with the lavender suspenders hanging from his dress trousers prodding the diamond studs into his shirt with stumpy fingers.

"Jake I wish we were out of it," she whined through the hairpins in her mouth.

"Out of what Rosie?"

"The Prudence Promotion Company. . . . Honest I'm worried."

"Why everything's goin swell. We've got to bluff out Nichols that's all."

"Suppose he prosecutes?"

"Oh he wont. He'd lose a lot of money by it. He'd much better come in with us. . . . I can pay him in cash in a week anyways. If we can keep him thinkin we got money we'll have him eatin out of our hands. Didn't he say he'd be at the El Fey tonight?"

Rosie had just put a rhinestone comb into the coil of her black hair. She nodded and got to her feet. She was a plump broadhipped woman with big black eyes and higharched eyebrows. She wore a corset trimmed with yellow lace and a pink silk chemise.

"Put on everythin you've got Rosie. I want yez all dressed up like a Christmas tree. We're goin to the El Fey an stare Nichols down tonight. Then tomorrer I'll go round and put the proposition up to him. . . . Lets have a little snifter anyways . . ." He went to the phone. "Send up some cracked ice and a couple of bottles of White Rock to four o four. Silverman's the name. Make it snappy."

"Jake let's make a getaway," Rosie cried suddenly. She stood in the closet door with a dress over her arm. "I cant stand all this worry. . . . It's killin me. Let's you an me beat it to Paris or Havana or somewheres and start out fresh."

"Then we would be up the creek. You can be extradited for grand larceny. Jez you wouldnt have me goin round with dark glasses and false whiskers all my life."

Rosie laughed. "No I guess you wouldnt look so good in a fake zit. . . . Oh I wish we were really married at least."

"Dont make no difference between us Rosie. Then they'd be after me for bigamy too. That'd be pretty."

Rosie shuddered at the bellboy's knock. Jake Silverman put the tray with its clinking bowl of ice on the bureau and fetched a square whiskeybottle out of the wardrobe.

"Dont pour out any for me. I havent got the heart for it."

"Kid you've got to pull yourself together. Put on the glad rags an we'll go to a show. Hell I been in lots o tighter holes than this." With his highball in his hand he went to the phone. "I want the newsstand. . . . Hello cutie. . . . Sure I'm an old friend of yours. . . . Sure you know me. . . . Look could you get me two seats for the Follies. . . . That's the idear. . . . No I cant sit back of the eighth row. . . . That's a good little girl. . . . An you'll call me in ten minutes will you dearie?"

"Say Jake is there really any borax in that lake?"

"Sure there is. Aint we got the affidavit of four experts?"

"Sure. I was just kinder wonderin. . . . Say Jake if this ever gets wound up will you promise me not to go in for any more wildcat schemes?"

"Sure; I wont need to. . . . My you're a redhot mommer in that dress."

"Do you like it?"

"You look like Brazil . . . I dunno . . . kinder tropical."

"That's the secret of my dangerous charm."

The phone rang jingling sharp. They jumped to their feet. She pressed the side of her hand against her lips.

"Two in the fourth row. That's fine. . . . We'll be right down an get em . . . Jez Rosie you cant go on being jumpy like; you're gettin me all shot too. Pull yerself together why cant you?"

"Let's go out an eat Jake. I havent had anything but buttermilk all day. I guess I'll stop tryin to reduce. This worryin'll make me thin enough."

"You got to quit it Rosie. . . . It's gettin my nerve."

They stopped at the flowerstall in the lobby. "I want a gardenia" he said. He puffed his chest out and smiled his curlylipped smile as the girl fixed it in the buttonhole of his dinnercoat. "What'll you have dear?" he turned grandiloquently to Rosie. She puckered her mouth. "I dont just know what'll go with my dress."

"While you're deciding I'll go get the theater tickets." With his overcoat open and turned back to show the white puffedout shirtfront and his cuffs shot out over his thick hands he strutted over to the newsstand. Out of the corner of her eye while the ends of the red roses were being wrapped in silver paper Rosie could see him leaning across the magazines talking babytalk to the blond girl. He came back brighteyed with a roll of bills in his hand. She pinned the roses on her fur coat, put her arm in his and together they went through the revolving doors into the cold glistening electric night. "Taxi," he yapped.

The diningroom smelled of toast and coffee and the New York *Times*. The Merivales were breakfasting to electric light. Sleet beat against the windows. "Well Paramount's fallen off five points more," said James from behind the paper.

"Oh James I think its horrid to be such a tease," whined Maisie who was drinking her coffee in little henlike sips.

"And anyway," said Mrs. Merivale, "Jack's not with Paramount anymore. He's doing publicity for the Famous Players."

"He's coming east in two weeks. He says he hopes to be here for the first of the year."

"Did you get another wire Maisie?"

Maisie nodded. "Do you know James, Jack never will write a letter. He always telegraphs," said Mrs. Merivale through the paper at her son. "He certainly keeps the house choked up with flowers," growled James from behind the paper.

"All by telegraph," said Mrs. Merivale triumphantly.

James put down his paper. "Well I hope he's as good a fellow as he seems to be."

"Oh James you're horrid about Jack. . . . I think it's mean." She got to her feet and went through the curtains into the parlor.

"Well if he's going to be my brother-in-law, I think I ought to have a say in picking him," he grumbled.

Mrs. Merivale went after her. "Come back and finish your breakfast Maisie, he's just a terrible tease."

"I wont have him talk that way about Jack."

"But Maisie I think Jack's a dear boy." She put her arm round her daughter and led her back to the table. "He's so simple and I know he has good impulses. . . . I'm sure he's going to make you very happy." Maisie sat down again pouting under the pink bow of her boudoir cap. "Mother may I have another cup of coffee?"

"Deary you know you oughtnt to drink two cups. Dr. Fernald said that was what was making you so nervous."

"Just a little bit mother very weak. I want to finish this muffin and I simply cant eat it without something to wash it down, and you know you dont want me to lose any more weight." James pushed back his chair and went out with the *Times* under his arm. "It's half past eight James," said Mrs. Merivale. "He's likely to take an hour when he gets in there with that paper."

"Well," said Maisie peevishly. "I think I'll go back to bed. I think it's silly the way we all get up to breakfast. There's something so vulgar about it mother. Nobody does it any more. At the Perkinses' it comes up to you in bed on a tray."

"But James has to be at the bank at nine."

"That's no reason why we should drag ourselves out of bed. That's how people get their faces all full of wrinkles."

"But we wouldn't see James until dinnertime, and I like to get up early. The morning's the loveliest part of the day." Maisie yawned desperately.

James appeared in the doorway to the hall running a brush round his hat.

"What did you do with the paper James?"

"Oh I left it in there."

"I'll get it, never mind. . . . My dear you've got your stickpin in crooked. I'll fix it. . . . There." Mrs. Merivale put her hands on his shoulders and looked in her son's face. He wore a dark gray suit with a faint green stripe in it, an olive green knitted necktie with a small gold nugget stickpin, olive green woolen socks with black clockmarks and dark red Oxford shoes, their laces neatly tied with doubleknots that never came undone. "James arent you carrying your cane?" He had an olive green woolen muffler round his neck and was slipping into his dark brown winter overcoat. "I notice the younger men down there dont carry them, mother . . . People might think it was a little . . . I dont know . . ."

"But Mr. Perkins carries a cane with a gold parrothead."

"Yes but he's one of the vicepresidents, he can do what he likes. . . . But I've got to run." James Merivale hastily kissed his mother and sister. He put on his gloves going down in the elevator. Ducking his head into the sleety wind he walked quickly east along Seventysecond. At the subway entrance he bought a *Tribune* and hustled down the steps to the jammed soursmelling platform.

Chicago! Chicago! came in bursts out of the shut phonograph. Tony Hunter, slim in a black closecut suit, was dancing with a girl who kept putting her mass of curly ashblond hair on his shoulder. They were alone in the hotel sitting room.

"Sweetness you're a lovely dancer," she cooed snuggling closer.

"Think so Nevada?"

"Um-hum . . . Sweetness have you noticed something about me?"

"What's that Nevada?"

"Havent you noticed something about my eyes?"

"They're the loveliest little eyes in the world."

"Yes but there's something about them."

"You mean that one of them's green and the other one brown."

"Oh it noticed the tweet lil ting." She tilted her mouth up at him. He kissed it. The record came to an end. They both ran over to stop it. "That wasnt much of a kiss, Tony," said Nevada Jones tossing her curls out of her eyes. They put on *Shuffle Along.*

"Say Tony," she said when they had started dancing again. "What did the psychoanalyst say when you went to see him yesterday?"

"Oh nothing much, we just talked," said Tony with a sigh. "He said it was all imaginary. He suggested I get to know some girls better. He's all right. He doesn't know what he's talking about though. He cant do anything."

"I bet you I could."

They stopped dancing and looked at each other with the blood burning in their faces.

"Knowing you Nevada," he said in a doleful tone, "has meant more to me . . . You're so decent to me. Everybody's always been so nasty."

"Aint he solemn though?" She walked over thoughtfully and stopped the phonograph.

"Some joke on George I'll say."

"I feel horribly about it. He's been so decent. . . . And after all I could never have afforded to go to Dr. Baumgardt at all."

"It's his own fault. He's a damn fool. . . . If he thinks he can buy me with a little hotel accommodation and theater tickets he's got another think coming. But honestly Tony you must keep on with that doctor. He did wonders with Glenn Gaston. . . . He thought he was that way until he was thirty-five years old and the latest thing I hear he's married an had a pair of twins. . . . Now give me a real kiss sweetest. Thataboy. Let's dance some more. Gee you're a beautiful dancer. Kids like you always are. I dont know why it is. . . ."

The phone cut into the room suddenly with a glittering sawtooth ring. "Hello. . . . Yes this is Miss Jones. . . . Why of course George I'm waiting for you. . . ." She put up the receiver. "Great snakes, Tony beat it. I'll call you later. Dont go down in the elevator you'll meet him coming up." Tony Hunter melted out the door. Nevada put *Baby . . . Babee Deevine* on the phonograph and strode nervously about the room, straightening chairs, patting her tight short curls into place.

"Oh George I thought you werent comin. . . . How do you do Mr. McNiel? I dunno why I'm all jumpy today. I thought you were never comin. Let's get some lunch up. I'm that hungry."

George Baldwin put his derby hat and stick on a table in the corner. "What'll you have Gus?" he said. "Sure I always take a lamb chop an a baked potato."

"I'm just taking crackers and milk, my stomach's a little out of order. . . . Nevada see if you cant frisk up a highball for Mr. McNiel."

"Well I could do with a highball George."

"George order me half a broiled chicken lobster and some alligator pear salad," screeched Nevada from the bathroom where she was cracking ice.

"She's the greatest girl for lobster," said Baldwin laughing as he went to the phone.

She came back from the bathroom with two highballs on a tray; she had put a scarlet and parrotgreen batik scarf round her neck. "Just you an me's drinkin Mr. McNiel. . . . George is on the water wagon. Doctor's orders."

"Nevada what do you say we go to a musical show this afternoon? There's a lot of business I want to get off my mind."

"I just love matinees. Do you mind if we take Tony Hunter. He called up he was lonesome and wanted to come round this afternoon. He's not workin this week."

"All right. . . . Nevada will you excuse us if we talk business for just a second over here by the window. We'll forget it by the time lunch comes."

"All righty I'll change my dress."

"Sit down here Gus."

They sat silent a moment looking out of the window at the red girder cage of the building under construction next door. "Well Gus," said Baldwin suddenly harshly, "I'm in the race."

"Good for you George, we need men like you."

"I'm going to run on a Reform ticket."

"The hell you are?"

"I wanted to tell you Gus rather than have you hear it by a roundabout way."

"Who's goin to elect you?"

"Oh I've got my backing. . . . I'll have a good press."

"Press hell. . . . We've got the voters. . . . But Goddam it if it hadn't been for me your name never would have come up for district attorney at all."

"I know you've always been a good friend of mine and I hope you'll continue to be."

"I never went back on a guy yet, but Jez, George, it's give and take in this world."

"Well," broke in Nevada advancing towards them with little dancesteps, wearing a flamingo pink silk dress, "havent you boys argued enough yet?"

"We're through," growled Gus. ". . . Say Miss Nevada, how did you get that name?"

"I was born in Reno. . . . My mother'd gone there to get a divorce. . . . Gosh she was sore. . . . Certainly put my foot in it that time."

Anna Cohen stands behind the counter under the sign THE BEST SANDWICH IN NEW YORK. Her feet ache in her pointed shoes with runover heels.

"Well I guess they'll begin soon or else we're in for a slack day," says the sodashaker beside her. He's a rawfaced man with a sharp adamsapple. "It allus comes all of a rush like."

"Yeh, looks like they all got the same idear at the same time." They stand looking out through the glass partition at the endless files of people jostling in and out of the subway. All at once she slips away from the counter and back into the stuffy kitchenette where a stout elderly woman is tidying up the stove. There is a mirror hanging on a nail in the corner. Anna fetches a powderbox from the pocket of her coat on the rack and starts powdering her nose. She stands a second with the tiny puff poised looking at her broad face with the bangs across the forehead and the straight black bobbed hair. A homely lookin kike, she says to herself bitterly. She is slipping back to her place at the counter when she runs into the manager, a little fat Italian with a greasy bald head. "Cant you do nutten but primp an look in de glass all day? . . . Veree good you're fired."

She stares at his face sleek like an olive. "Kin I stay out my day?" she stammers. He nods. "Getta move on; this aint no beauty parlor." She hustles back to her place at the counter. The stools are all full. Girls, officeboys, grayfaced bookkeepers. "Chicken sandwich and a cup o caufee." "Cream cheese and olive sandwich and a glass of buttermilk."

"Chocolate sundae."

"Egg sandwich, coffee and doughnuts." "Cup of boullion." "Chicken broth." "Chocolate icecream soda." People eat hurriedly without looking at each other, with their eyes on their plates, in their cups. Behind the people sitting on stools those waiting nudge nearer. Some eat standing up. Some turn their backs on the counter and eat looking out through the glass partition and the sign HCNUL ENIL NEERG at the jostling crowds filing in and out the subway through the drabgreen gloom.

"Well Joey tell me all about it," said Gus McNiel puffing a great cloud of smoke out of his cigar and leaning back in his swivel chair. "What are you guys up to over there in Flatbush?"

O'Keefe cleared his throat and shuffled his feet. "Well sir we got an agitation committee."

"I should say you had. . . . That aint no reason for raidin the Garment Workers' ball is it?"

"I didn't have nothin to do with that. . . . The bunch got sore at all these pacifists and reds."

"That stuff was all right a year ago, but public sentiment's changin. I tell you Joe the people of this country are pretty well fed up with war heroes."

"We got a livewire organization over there."

"I know you have Joe. I know you have. Trust you for that. . . . I'd put the soft pedal on the bonus stuff though. . . . The State of New York's done its duty by the ex-service man."

"That's true enough."

"A national bonus means taxes to the average business man and nothing else. . . . Nobody wants no more taxes."

"Still I think the boys have got it comin to em."

"We've all of us got a whole lot comin to us we dont never get. . . . For crissake dont quote me on this. . . . Joey fetch yourself a cigar from that box over there. Frien o mine sent em up from Havana by a naval officer."

"Thankye sir."

"Go ahead take four or five."

"Jez thank you."

"Say Joey how'll you boys line up on the mayoralty election?"

"That depends on the general attitude towards the needs of the ex-service man."

"Look here Joey you're a smart feller . . ."

"Oh they'll line up all right. I kin talk em around."

"How many guys have you got over there?"

"The Sheamus O'Rielly Post's got three hundred members an new ones signin up every day. . . . We're gettin em from all over. We're goin to have a Christmas dance an some fights in the Armory if we can get hold of any pugs."

Gus McNiel threw back his head on his bullneck and laughed. "Thataboy!"

"But honest the bonus is the only way we kin keep the boys together."

"Suppose I come over and talk to em some night."

"That'd be all right, but they're dead sot against anybody who aint got a war record."

McNiel flushed. "Come back feeling kinder smart, dont ye, you guys from overseas?" He laughed. "That wont last more'n a year or two. . . . I seen em come back from the Spanish American War, remember that Joe."

An officeboy came in an laid a card on the desk. "A lady to see you Mr. McNiel."

"All right show her in. . . . It's that old bitch from the school board. . . . All right Joe, drop in again next week. . . . I'll keep you in mind, you and your army."

Dougan was waiting in the outer office. He sidled up mysteriously. "Well Joe, how's things?"

"Pretty good," said Joe puffing out his chest. "Gus tells me Tammany'll be right behind us in our drive for the bonus . . . planning a nation wide campaign. He gave me some cigars a friend o his brought up by airplane from Havana. . . . Have one?" With their cigars tilting up out of the corners of their mouths they walked briskly cockily across City Hall square. Opposite the old City Hall there was a scaffolding. Joe pointed at it with his cigar. "That there's the new statue of Civic Virtue the mayor's havin set up."

The steam of cooking wrenched at his knotted stomach as he passed Child's. Dawn was sifting fine gray dust over the black ironcast city. Dutch Robertson despondently crossed Union Square, remembering Francie's warm bed, the spicy smell of her hair. He pushed his hands deep in his empty pockets. Not a red, and Francie couldn't give him anything. He walked east past the hotel on Fifteenth. A colored man was sweeping off the steps. Dutch looked at him enviously; he's got a job. Milkwagons jingled by. On Stuyvesant Square a milkman brushed past him with a bottle in each hand. Dutch stuck out his jaw and talked tough. "Give us a swig o milk will yez?" The milkman was a frail pinkfaced youngster. His blue eyes wilted. "Sure go round behind the wagon, there's an open bottle under the seat. Dont let nobody see you drink it." He drank it in deep gulps, sweet and soothing to his parched throat. Jez I didn't need to talk rough like that. He waited until the boy came back. "Thankye buddy, that was mighty white."

He walked into the chilly park and sat down on a bench. There was hoarfrost on the asphalt. He picked up a torn piece of pink evening newspaper. $500,000 HOLDUP. Bank Messenger Robbed in Wall Street Rush Hour.

In the busiest part of the noon hour two men held up Adolphus St. John, a bank messenger for the Guarantee Trust Company, and snatched from his hands a satchel containing a half a million dollars in bills . . .

Dutch felt his heart pounding as he read the column. He was cold all over. He got to his feet and began thrashing his arms about.

Congo stumped through the turnstile at the end of the L line. Jimmy Herf followed him looking from one side to the other. Outside it was dark, a blizzard wind whistled about their ears. A single Ford sedan was waiting outside the station.

"How you like, Meester 'Erf?"

"Fine Congo. Is that water?"

"That Sheepshead Bay."

They walked along the road, dodging an occasional blue-steel glint of a puddle. The arclights had a look of shrunken grapes swaying in the wind. To the right and left were flickering patches of houses in the distance. They stopped at a long building propped on piles over the water. POOL; Jimmy barely made out the letters on an unlighted window. The door opened as they reached it. "Hello Mike," said Congo. "This is Meester 'Erf, a frien' o mine." The door closed behind them. Inside it was black as an oven. A calloused hand grabbed Jimmy's hand in the dark.

"Glad to meet you," said a voice.

"Say how did you find my hand?"

"Oh I kin see in the dark." The voice laughed throatily.

By that time Congo had opened the inner door. Light streamed through picking out billiard tables, a long bar at the end, racks of cues. "This is Mike Cardinale," said Congo. Jimmy found himself standing beside a tall sallow shylooking man with bunchy black hair growing low on his forehead. In the inner room were shelves full of chinaware and a round table covered by a piece of mustardcolored oilcloth. "Eh la patronne," shouted Congo. A fat Frenchwoman with red apple-cheeks came out through the further door; behind her came a *chiff* of sizzling butter and garlic. "This is frien o mine. . . . Now maybe we eat," shouted Congo. "She my wife," said Cardinale proudly. "Very deaf. . . . Have to talk loud." He turned and closed the door to the large hall carefully and bolted it. "No see lights from road," he said. "In summer," said Mrs. Cardinale, "sometime we give a hundred meals a day, or a hundred an fifty maybe."

"Havent you got a little peekmeup?" said Congo. He let himself down with a grunt into a chair.

Cardinale set a fat fiasco of wine on the table and some glasses. They tasted it smacking their lips. "Bettern Dago Red, eh Meester 'Erf?"

"It sure is. Tastes like real Chianti."

Mrs. Cardinale set six plates with a stained fork, knife, and spoon in each and then put a steaming tureen of soup in the middle of the table.

"Pronto pasta," she shrieked in a guineahen voice. "Thisa Anetta," said Cardinale as a pinkcheeked blackhaired girl with long lashes curving back from bright black eyes ran into the room followed by a heavily tanned young man in khaki overalls with curly sunbleached hair. They all sat down at once and began to eat the peppery thick vegetable chowder, leaning far over their plates.

When Congo had finished his soup he looked up. "Mike did you see lights?" Cardinale nodded. "Sure ting . . . be here any time." While they were eating a dish of fried eggs and garlic, frizzled veal cutlets with fried potatoes and broccoli, Herf began to hear in the distance the pop pop pop of a motorboat. Congo got up from the table with a motion to them to be quiet and looked out the window, cautiously lifting a corner of the shade. "That him," he said as he stumped back to the table. "We eat good here, eh Meester Erf?"

The young man got to his feet wiping his mouth on his forearm. "Got a nickel Congo," he said doing a double shuffle with his sneakered feet. "Here go Johnny." The girl followed him out into the dark outer room. In a moment a mechanical piano started tinkling out a waltz. Through the door Jimmy could see them dancing in and out of the oblong of light. The chugging of the motorboat drew nearer. Congo went out, then Cardinale and his wife, until Jimmy was left alone sipping a glass of wine among the debris of the dinner. He felt excited and puzzled and a little drunk. Already he began to construct the story in his mind. From the road came the grind of gears of a truck, then of another. The motorboat engine choked, backfired and stopped. There was the creak of a boat against the piles, a swash of waves and silence. The mechanical piano had stopped. Jimmy sat sipping his wine. He could smell the rankness of salt marshes seeping into the house. Under him there was a little lapping sound of the water against the piles. Another motorboat was beginning to sputter in the far distance.

"Got a nickel?" asked Congo breaking into the room suddenly. "Make music. . . . Very funny night tonight. Maybe you and Annette keep piano goin. I didnt see McGee about landin. . . . Maybe somebody come. Must be veree quick." Jimmy got to his feet and started fishing in his pockets. By the piano he found Annette. "Wont you dance?" She nodded. The piano played *Innocent Eyes*. They danced distractedly. Outside were voices and footsteps. "Please," she said all at once and they stopped dancing. The second motorboat had come very near; the motor coughed and rattled still. "Please stay here," she said and slipped away from him.

Jimmy Herf walked up and down uneasily puffing on a cigarette. He was making up the story in his mind. . . . In a lonely abandoned dancehall on Sheepshead Bay . . . lovely blooming Italian girl . . . shrill whistle in the dark . . . I ought to get out and see what's going on. He groped for the front door. It was locked. He walked over to the piano and put another nickel in. Then he lit a fresh cigarette and started walking up and down again. Always the way . . . a parasite on the drama of life, reporter looks at everything through a peephole. Never mixes in. The piano was playing *Yes We Have No Bananas*. "Oh hell!" he kept muttering and ground his teeth and walked up and down.

Outside the tramp of steps broke into a scuffle, voices snarled. There was a splintering of wood and the crash of breaking bottles. Jimmy looked out through the window of the diningroom. He could see the shadows of men struggling and slugging on the boatlanding. He rushed into the kitchen, where he bumped into Congo sweaty and staggering into the house leaning on a heavy cane.

"Goddam . . . dey break my leg," he shouted.

"Good God." Jimmy helped him groaning into the diningroom.

"Cost me feefty dollars to have it mended last time I busted it."

"You mean your cork leg?"

"Sure what you tink?"

"Is it prohibition agents?"

"Prohibition agents nutten, goddam hijackers. . . . Go put a neeckel in the piano." *Beautiful Girl of My Dreams*, the piano responded gayly.

When Jimmy got back to him, Congo was sitting in a chair

nursing his stump with his two hands. On the table lay the cork and aluminum limb splintered and dented. "Regardez moi ça . . . c'est foutu . . . completement foutu." As he spoke Cardinale came in. He had a deep gash over his eyes from which a trickle of blood ran down his cheek on his coat and shirt. His wife followed him rolling back her eyes; she had a basin and a sponge with which she kept making ineffectual dabs at his forehead. He pushed her away. "I crowned one of em good wid a piece o pipe. I think he fell in de water. God I hope he drownded." Johnny came in holding his head high. Annette had her arm round his waist. He had a black eye and one of the sleeves of his shirt hung in shreds. "Gee it was like in the movies," said Annette, giggling hysterically. "Wasnt he grand, mommer, wasn't he grand?"

"Jez it's lucky they didn't start shootin; one of em had a gun."

"Scared to I guess."

"Trucks are off."

"Just one case got busted up. . . . God there was five of them."

"Gee didnt he mix it up with em?" screamed Annette.

"Oh shut up," growled Cardinale. He had dropped into a chair and his wife was sponging off his face. "Did you get a good look at the boat?" asked Congo.

"Too goddam dark," said Johnny. "Fellers talked like they came from Joisey. . . . First ting I knowed one of em comes up to me and sez I'm a revenue officer an I pokes him one before he has time to pull a gun an overboard he goes. Jez they were yeller. That guy George on the boat near brained one of em wid an oar. Then they got back in their old teakettle an beat it."

"But how they know how we make landin?" stuttered Congo his face purple.

"Some guy blabbed maybe," said Cardinale. "If I find out who it is, by God I'll . . ." he made a popping noise with his lips.

"You see Meester 'Erf," said Congo in his suave voice again, "it was all champagne for the holidays. . . . Very valuable cargo eh?" Annette, her cheeks very red sat still looking at Johnny with parted lips and toobright eyes. Herf found himself blushing as he looked at her.

He got to his feet. "Well I must be getting back to the big city. Thanks for the feed and the melodrama, Congo."

"You find station all right?"

"Sure."

"Goodnight Meester 'Erf, maybe you buy case of champagne for Christmas, genuine Mumms."

"Too darn broke Congo."

"Then maybe you sell to your friends an I give you commission."

"All right I'll see what I can do."

"I'll phone you tomorrow to tell price."

"That's a fine idea. Good night."

Joggling home in the empty train through empty Brooklyn suburbs Jimmy tried to think of the bootlegging story he'd write for the Sunday Magazine Section. The girl's pink cheeks and toobright eyes kept intervening, blurring the orderly arrangement of his thoughts. He sank gradually into dreamier and dreamier reverie. Before the kid was born Ellie sometimes had toobright eyes like that. The time on the hill when she had suddenly wilted in his arms and been sick and he had left her among the munching, calmly staring cows on the grassy slope and gone to a shepherd's hut and brought back milk in a wooden ladle, and slowly as the mountains hunched up with evening the color had come back into her cheeks and she had looked at him that way and said with a dry little laugh: It's the little Herf inside me. God why cant I stop mooning over things that are past? And when the baby was coming and Ellie was in the American Hospital at Neuilly, himself wandering distractedly through the fair, going into the Flea Circus, riding on merrygorounds and the steam swing, buying toys, candy, taking chances on dolls in a crazy blur, stumbling back to the hospital with a big plaster pig under his arm. Funny these fits of refuge in the past. Suppose she had died; I thought she would. The past would have been complete all round, framed, worn round your neck like a cameo, set up in type, molded on plates for the Magazine Section, like the first of James Herf's articles on The Bootlegging Ring. Burning slugs of thought kept dropping into place spelled out by a clanking linotype.

At midnight he was walking across Fourteenth. He didnt

want to go home to bed although the rasping cold wind tore at his neck and chin with sharp ice claws. He walked west across Seventh and Eighth Avenues, found the name Roy Sheffield beside a bell in a dimly lit hall. As soon as he pressed the bell the catch on the door began to click. He ran up the stairs. Roy had his big curly head with its glassgray gollywog eyes stuck out the door.

"Hello Jimmy; come on in; we're all lit up like churches."

"I've just seen a fight between bootleggers and hijackers."

"Where?"

"Down at Sheepshead Bay."

"Here's Jimmy Herf, he's just been fighting prohibition agents," shouted Roy to his wife. Alice had dark chestnut dollhair and an uptilted peaches and cream dollface. She ran up to Jimmy and kissed him on the chin. "Oh Jimmy do tell us all about it. . . . We're so horribly bored."

"Hello," cried Jimmy; he had just made out Frances and Bob Hildebrand on the couch at the dim end of the room. They lifted their glasses to him. Jimmy was pushed into an armchair, had a glass of gin and ginger ale put in his hand. "Now what's all this about a fight? You'd better tell us because were certainly not going to buy the Sunday *Tribune* to find out," Bob Hildebrand said in a deep rumbling voice.

Jimmy took a long drink. "I went out with a man I know who's shiek of all the French and Italian bootleggers. He's a fine man. He's got a cork leg. He set me up to a swell feed and real Italian wine out in a deserted poolroom on the shores of Sheepshead Bay. . . ."

"By the way," asked Roy, "where's Helena."

"Dont interrupt Roy," said Alice. "This is good . . . and besides you should never ask a man where his wife is."

"Then there was a lot of flashing of signal lights and stuff and a motorboat loaded down with Mumm's extra dry champagne for Park Avenue Christmases came in and the hijackers arrived on a speedboat. . . . It probably was a hydroplane it came so fast . . ."

"My this is exciting," cooed Alice. ". . . Roy why dont you take up bootlegging?"

"Worst fight I ever saw outside of the movies, six or seven on a side all slugging each other on a little narrow landing the size of this room, people crowning each other with oars and joints of lead pipe."

"Was anybody hurt?"

"Everybody was. . . . I think two of the hijackers were drowned. At any rate they beat a retreat leaving us lapping up the spilled champagne."

"But it must have been terrible," cried the Hildebrands. "What did you do Jimmy?" asked Alice breathless.

"Oh I hopped around keeping out of harm's way. I didnt know who was on which side and it was dark and wet and confusing everywhere. . . . I finally did drag my bootlegger friend out of the fray when he got his leg broken . . . his wooden leg."

Everybody let out a shout. Roy filled Jimmy's glass up with gin again.

"Oh Jimmy," cooed Alice, "you lead the most thrilling life."

James Merivale was going over a freshly decoded cable, tapping the words with a pencil as he read them. Tasmanian Manganese Products instructs us to open credit. . . . The phone on his desk began to buzz.

"James this is your mother. Come right up; something terrible has happened."

"But I dont know if I can get away. . . ."

She had already cut off. Merivale felt himself turning pale. "Let me speak to Mr. Aspinwall please. . . . Mr. Aspinwall this is Merivale. . . . My mother's been taken suddenly ill. I'm afraid it may be a stroke. I'd like to run up there for an hour. I'll be back in time to get a cable off on that Tasmanian matter."

"All right. . . . I'm very sorry Merivale."

He grabbed his hat and coat, forgetting his muffler, and streaked out of the bank and along the street to the subway.

He burst into the apartment breathless, snapping his fingers from nervousness. Mrs. Merivale grayfaced met him in the hall.

"My dear I thought you'd been taken ill."

"It's not that . . . it's about Maisie."

"She hasnt met with an accid . . . ?"

"Come in here," interrupted Mrs. Merivale. In the parlor sat a little roundfaced woman in a round mink hat and a long

mink coat. "My dear this girl says she's Mrs. Jack Cunningham and she's got a marriage certificate to prove it."

"Good Heavens, is that true?"

The girl nodded in a melancholy way.

"And the invitations are out. Since his last wire Maisie's
been ordering her trousseau."

The girl unfolded a large certificate ornamented with pansies and cupids and handed it to James.

"It might be forged."

"It's not forged," said the girl sweetly.

"John C. Cunningham, 21 . . . Jessie Lincoln, 18," he read
aloud. . . . "I'll smash his face for that, the blackguard.
That's certainly his signature, I've seen it at the bank. . . .
The blackguard."

"Now James, don't be hasty."

"I thought it would be better this way than after the cere-
mony," put in the girl in her little sugar voice. "I wouldnt
have Jack commit bigamy for anything in the world."

"Where's Maisie?"

"The poor darling is prostrated in her room."

Merivale's face was crimson. The sweat itched under his
collar. "Now dearest" Mrs. Merivale kept saying, "you must
promise me not to do anything rash."

"Yes Maisie's reputation must be protected at all costs."

"My dear I think the best thing to do is to get him up here
and confront him with this . . . with this . . . lady. . . .
Would you agree to that Mrs. Cunningham?"

"Oh dear. . . . Yes I suppose so."

"Wait a minute," shouted Merivale and strode down the
hall to the telephone. "Rector 12305. . . . Hello. I want to
speak to Mr. Jack Cunningham please. . . . Hello. Is this Mr.
Cunningham's office? Mr. James Merivale speaking. . . . Out
of town. . . . And when will he be back? . . . Hum." He
strode back along the hall. "The damn scoundrel's out of
town."

"All the years I've known him," said the little lady in the
round hat, "that has always been where he was."

Outside the broad office windows the night is gray and
foggy. Here and there a few lights make up dim horizontals

and perpendiculars of asterisks. Phineas Blackhead sits at his
desk tipping far back in the small leather armchair. In his hand
protecting his fingers by a large silk handkerchief, he holds a
glass of hot water and bicarbonate of soda. Densch bald and
round as a billiardball sits in the deep armchair playing with
his tortoiseshell spectacles. Everything is quiet except for an
occasional rattling and snapping of the steampipes.

"Densch you must forgive me. . . . You know I rarely permit myself an observation concerning other people's business," Blackhead is saying slowly between sips; then suddenly
he sits up in his chair. "It's a damn fool proposition, Densch,
by God it is . . . by the Living Jingo it's ridiculous."

"I dont like dirtying my hands any more than you do. . . .
Baldwin's a good fellow. I think we're safe in backing him a
little."

"What the hell's an import and export firm got to do in
politics? If any of those guys wants a handout let him come
up here and get it. Our business is the price of beans . . . and
it's goddam low. If any of you puling lawyers could restore the
balance of the exchanges I'd be willing to do anything in the
world. . . . They're crooks every last goddam one of em . . .
by the Living Jingo they're crooks." His face flushes purple,
he sits upright in his chair banging with his fist on the corner
of the desk. "Now you're getting me all excited. . . . Bad for
my stomach, bad for my heart." Phineas Blackhead belches
portentously and takes a great gulp out of the glass of bicarbonate of soda. Then he leans back in his chair again letting
his heavy lids half cover his eyes.

"Well old man," says Mr. Densch in a tired voice, "it may
have been a bad thing to do, but I've promised to support the
reform candidate. That's a purely private matter in no way in-
volving the firm."

"Like hell it dont. . . . How about McNiel and his gang?
. . . They've always treated us all right and all we've ever
done for em's a couple of cases of Scotch and a few cigars
now and then. . . . Now we have these reformers throw the
whole city government into a turmoil. . . . By the Living
Jingo . . ."

Densch gets to his feet. "My dear Blackhead I consider it

my duty as a citizen to help in cleaning up the filthy conditions of bribery, corruption and intrigue that exist in the city government . . . I consider it my duty as a citizen . . ." He starts walking to the door, his round belly stuck proudly out in front of him.

"Well allow me to say Densch that I think its a damn fool proposition," Blackhead shouts after him. When his partner has gone he lies back a second with his eyes closed. His face takes on the mottled color of ashes, his big fleshy frame is shrinking like a deflating balloon. At length he gets to his feet with a groan. Then he takes his hat and coat and walks out of the office with a slow heavy step. The hall is empty and dimly lit. He has to wait a long while for the elevator. The thought of holdup men sneaking through the empty building suddenly makes him catch his breath. He is afraid to look behind him, like a child in the dark. At last the elevator shoots up.

"Wilmer," he says to the night watchman who runs it, "there ought to be more light in these halls at night. . . . During this crime wave I should think you ought to keep the building brightly lit."

"Yassir maybe you're right sir . . . but there cant nobody get in unless I sees em first."

"You might be overpowered by a gang Wilmer."

"I'd like to see em try it."

"I guess you are right . . . mere question of nerve."

Cynthia is sitting in the Packard reading a book. "Well dear did you think I was never coming."

"I almost finished my book, dad."

"All right Butler . . . up town as fast as you can. We're late for dinner."

As the limousine whirs up Lafayette Street, Blackhead turns to his daughter. "If you ever hear a man talking about his duty as a citizen, by the Living Jingo dont trust him. . . . He's up to some kind of monkey business nine times out of ten. You dont know what a relief it is to me that you and Joe are comfortably settled in life."

"What's the matter dad? Did you have a hard day at the office?" "There are no markets, there isnt a market in the goddam world that isnt shot to blazes. . . . I tell you Cynthia it's

nip and tuck. There's no telling what might happen. . . .
Look, before I forget it could you be at the bank uptown at
twelve tomorrow? . . . I'm sending Hudgins up with certain
securities, personal you understand, I want to put in your safe
deposit box."

"But it's jammed full already dad."

"That box at the Astor Trust is in your name isnt it?"

"Jointly in mine and Joe's."

"Well you take a new box at the Fifth Avenue Bank in your
own name. . . . I'll have the stuff get there at noon sharp.
. . . And remember what I tell you Cynthia, if you ever hear
a business associate talking about civic virtue, look lively."

They are crossing Fourteenth. Father and daughter look
out through the glass at the windbitten faces of people waiting to cross the street.

Jimmy Herf yawned and scraped back his chair. The nickel
glints of the typewriter hurt his eyes. The tips of his fingers
were sore. He pushed open the sliding doors a little and
peeped into the cold bedroom. He could barely make out Ellie asleep in the bed in the alcove. At the far end of the room
was the baby's crib. There was a faint milkish sour smell of
babyclothes. He pushed the doors to again and began to undress. If we only had more space, he was muttering; we live
cramped in our squirrelcage. . . . He pulled the dusty cash-
mere off the couch and yanked his pyjamas out from under
the pillow. Space space cleanness quiet; the words were gesticulating in his mind as if he were addressing a vast auditorium.

He turned out the light, opened a crack of the window and
dropped wooden with sleep into bed. Immediately he was
writing a letter on a linotype. Now I lay me down to sleep
. . . mother of the great white twilight. The arm of the linotype was a woman's hand in a long white glove. Through the
clanking from behind amber foots Ellie's voice Dont, dont,
dont, you're hurting me so. . . . Mr. Herf, says a man in
overalls, you're hurting the machine and we wont be able to
get out the bullgod edition thank dog. The linotype was a
gulping mouth with nickelbright rows of teeth, gulped,
crunched. He woke up sitting up in bed. He was cold, his
teeth were chattering. He pulled the covers about him and

settled to sleep again. The next time he woke up it was daylight. He was warm and happy. Snowflakes were dancing, hesitating, spinning, outside the tall window.

"Hello Jimps," said Ellie coming towards him with a tray.

"Why have I died and gone to heaven or something?"

"No it's Sunday morning. . . . I thought you needed a little luxury. . . . I made some corn muffins."

"Oh you're marvelous Ellie. . . . Wait a minute I must jump up and wash my teeth." He came back with his face washed, wearing his bathrobe. Her mouth winced under his kiss. "And it's only eleven o'clock. I've gained an hour on my day off. . . . Wont you have some coffee too?"

"In a minute. . . . Look here Jimps I've got something I want to talk about. Look dont you think we ought to get another place now that you're working nights again all the time?"

"You mean move?"

"No. I was thinking if you could get another room to sleep in somewhere round, then nobody'd ever disturb you in the morning."

"But Ellie we'd never see each other. . . . We hardly ever see each other as it is."

"It's terrible . . . but what can we do when our officehours are so different?"

Martin's crying came in a gust from the other room. Jimmy sat on the edge of the bed with the empty coffeecup on his knees looking at his bare feet. "Just as you like," he said dully. An impulse to grab her hands to crush her to him until he hurt her went up through him like a rocket and died. She picked up the coffeethings and swished away. His lips knew her lips, his arms knew the twining of her arms, he knew the deep woods of her hair, he loved her. He sat for a long time looking at his feet, lanky reddish feet with swollen blue veins, shoebound toes twisted by stairs and pavements. On each little toe there was a corn. He found his eyes filling with pitying tears. The baby had stopped crying. Jimmy went into the bathroom and started the water running in the tub.

"It was that other feller you had Anna. He got you to thinkin you didnt give a damn. . . . He made you a fatalist."

"What's 'at?"

"Somebody who thinks there's no use strugglin, somebody who dont believe in human progress."

"Do you think Bouy was like that?"

"He was a scab anyway . . . None o these Southerners are classconscious. . . . Didn't he make you stop payin your union dues?"

"I was sick o workin a sewin machine."

"But you could be a handworker, do fancy work and make good money. You're not one o that kind, you're one of us. . . . I'll get you back in good standin an you kin get a good job again. . . . God I'd never have let you work in a dancehall the way he did. Anna it hurt me terrible to see a Jewish girl goin round with a feller like that."

"Well he's gone an I aint got no job."

"Fellers like that are the greatest enemies of the workers. . . . They dont think of nobody but themselves."

They are walking slowly up Second Avenue through a foggy evening. He is a rustyhaired thinfaced young Jew with sunken cheeks and livid pale skin. He has the bandy legs of a garment worker. Anna's shoes are too small for her. She has deep rings under her eyes. The fog is full of strolling groups talking Yiddish, overaccented East Side English, Russian. Warm rifts of light from delicatessen stores and softdrink stands mark off the glistening pavement.

"If I didn't feel so tired all the time," mutters Anna.

"Let's stop here an have a drink. . . . You take a glass o buttermilk Anna, make ye feel good."

"I aint got the taste for it Elmer. I'll take a chocolate soda."

"That'll juss make ye feel sick, but go ahead if you wanter."

She sat on the slender nickelbound stool. He stood beside her. She let herself lean back a little against him. "The trouble with the workers is" . . . He was talking in a low impersonal voice. "The trouble with the workers is we dont know nothin, we dont know how to eat, we dont know how to live, we dont know how to protect our rights. . . . Jez Anna I want to make you think of things like that. Cant you see we're in the middle of a battle just like in the war?" With the long sticky spoon Anna was fishing bits of icecream out of the thick foamy liquid in her glass.

*

George Baldwin looked at himself in the mirror as he washed his hands in the little washroom behind his office. His hair that still grew densely down to a point on his forehead was almost white. There was a deep line at each corner of his mouth and across his chin. Under his bright gimleteyes the skin was sagging and granulated. When he had wiped his hands slowly and meticulously he took a little box of strychnine pills from the upper pocket of his vest, swallowed one, and feeling the anticipated stimulus tingle through him went back into his office. A longnecked officeboy was fidgeting beside his desk with a card in his hand.

"A lady wants to speak to you sir."

"Has she an appointment? Ask Miss Ranke. . . . Wait a minute. Show the lady right through into his office." The card read Nellie Linihan McNiel. She was expensively dressed with a lot of lace in the opening of her big fur coat. Round her neck she had a lorgnette on an amethyst chain.

"Gus asked me to come to see you," she said as he motioned her into a chair beside the desk.

"What can I do for you?" His heart for some reason was pounding hard.

She looked at him a moment through her lorgnette. "George you stand it better than Gus does."

"What?"

"Oh all this. . . . I'm trying to get Gus to go away with me for a rest abroad . . . Marienbad or something like that . . . but he says he's in too deep to pull up his stakes."

"I guess that's true of all of us," said Baldwin with a cold smile.

They were silent a minute, then Nellie McNiel got to her feet. "Look here George, Gus is awfully cut up about this. . . . You know he likes to stand by his friends and have his friends stand by him."

"Nobody can say that I havent stood by him. . . . It's simply this, I'm not a politician, and as, probably foolishly, I've allowed myself to be nominated for office, I have to run on a nonpartisan basis."

"George that's only half the story and you know it."

"Tell him that I've always been and always shall be a good

friend of his. . . . He knows that perfectly well. In this particular campaign I have pledged myself to oppose certain elements with which Gus has let himself get involved."

"You're a fine talker George Baldwin and you always were."

Baldwin flushed. They stood stiff side by side at the office door. His hand lay still on the doorknob as if paralyzed. From the outer offices came the sound of typewriters and voices. From outside came the long continuous tapping of riveters at work on a new building.

"I hope your family's all well," he said at length with an effort.

"Oh yes they are all well thanks . . . Goodby." She had gone.

Baldwin stood for a moment looking out of the window at the gray blackwindowed building opposite. Silly to let things agitate him so. Need of relaxation. He got his hat and coat from their hook behind the washroom door and went out. "Jonas," he said to a man with a round bald head shaped like a cantaloupe who sat poring over papers in the highceilinged library that was the central hall of the lawoffice, "bring everything up that's on my desk. . . . I'll go over it uptown tonight."

"All right sir."

When he got out on Broadway he felt like a small boy playing hooky. It was a sparkling winter afternoon with hurrying rifts of sun and cloud. He jumped into a taxi. Going uptown he lay back in the seat dozing. At Fortysecond Street he woke up. Everything was a confusion of bright intersecting planes of color, faces, legs, shop windows, trolleycars, automobiles. He sat up with his gloved hands on his knees, fizzling with excitement. Outside of Nevada's apartmenthouse he paid the taxi. The driver was a negro and showed an ivory mouthful of teeth when he got a fiftycent tip. Neither elevator was there so Baldwin ran lightly up the stairs, half wondering at himself. He knocked on Nevada's door. No answer. He knocked again. She opened it cautiously. He could see her curly towhead. He brushed into the room before she could stop him. All she had on was a kimono over a pink chemise.

"My God," she said, "I thought you were the waiter."

He grabbed her and kissed her. "I dont know why but I feel like a threeyear old."

"You look like you was crazy with the heat. . . . I dont like you to come over without telephoning, you know that."

"You dont mind just this once I forgot."

Baldwin caught sight of something on the settee; he found himself staring at a pair of darkblue trousers neatly folded.

"I was feeling awfully fagged down at the office Nevada. I thought I'd come up to talk to you to cheer myself up a bit."

"I was just practicing some dancing with the phonograph."

"Yes very interesting. . . ." He began to walk springily up and down. "Now look here Nevada. . . . We've got to have a talk. I dont care who it is you've got in your bedroom." She looked suddenly in his face and sat down on the settee beside the trousers. "In fact I've known for some time that you and Tony Hunter were carrying on." She compressed her lips and crossed her legs. "In fact all this stuff and nonsense about his having to go to a psychoanalyst at twentyfive dollars an hour amused me enormously. . . . But just this minute I've decided I had enough. Quite enough."

"George you're crazy," she stammered and then suddenly she began to giggle.

"I tell you what I'll do," went on Baldwin in a clear legal voice, "I'll send you a check for five hundred, because you're a nice girl and I like you. The apartment's paid till the first of the month. Does that suit you? And please never communicate with me in any way."

She was rolling on the settee giggling helplessly beside the neatly folded pair of darkblue trousers. Baldwin waved his hat and gloves at her and left closing the door very gently behind him. Good riddance, he said to himself as he closed the door carefully behind him.

Down in the street again he began to walk briskly uptown. He felt excited and talkative. He wondered who he could go to see. Telling over the names of his friends made him depressed. He began to feel lonely, deserted. He wanted to be talking to a woman, making her sorry for the barrenness of his life. He went into a cigarstore and began looking through the phonebook. There was a faint flutter in him when he found the H's. At last he found the name Herf, Helena Oglethorpe.

Nevada Jones sat a long while on the settee giggling hysterically. At length Tony Hunter came in in his shirt and drawers with his bow necktie perfectly tied.

"Has he gone?"

"Gone? sure he's gone, gone for good," she shrieked. "He saw your damn pants."

He let himself drop on a chair. "O God if I'm not the unluckiest fellow in the world."

"Why?" she sat spluttering with laughter with the tears running down her face.

"Nothing goes right. That means it's all off about the matinees."

"It's back to three a day for little Nevada. . . . I dont give a damn. . . . I never did like bein a kept woman."

"But you're not thinking of my career. . . . Women are so selfish. If you hadn't led me on. . . ."

"Shut up you little fool. Dont you think I dont know all about you?" She got to her feet with the kimono pulled tight about her.

"God all I needed was a chance to show what I could do, and now I'll never get it," Tony was groaning.

"Sure you will if you do what I tell you. I set out to make a man of you kiddo and I'm goin to do it. . . . We'll get up an act. Old Hirshbein'll give us a chance, he used to be kinder smitten. . . . Come on now, I'll punch you in the jaw if you dont. Let's start thinkin up. . . . We'll come in with a dance number see . . . then you'll pretend to want to pick me up. . . . I'll be waitin for a streetcar . . . see . . . and you'll say Hello Girlie an I'll call Officer."

"Is that all right for length sir," asked the fitter busily making marks on the trousers with a piece of chalk.

James Merivale looked down at the fitter's little greenish wizened bald head and at the brown trousers flowing amply about his feet. "A little shorter. . . . I think it looks a little old to have trousers too long."

"Why hello Merivale I didn't know you bought your clothes at Brooks' too. Gee I'm glad to see you."

Merivale's blood stood still. He found himself looking straight in the blue alcoholic eyes of Jack Cunningham. He bit his lip and tried to stare at him coldly without speaking.

"God Almighty, do you know what we've done?" cried out Cunningham. "We've bought the same suit of clothes. . . . I tell you it's identically the same."

Merivale was looking in bewilderment from Cunningham's brown trousers to his own, the same color, the same tiny stripe of red and faint mottling of green.

"Good God man two future brothersinlaw cant wear the same suit. People'll think it's a uniform. . . . It's ridiculous."

"Well what are we going to do about it?" Merivale found himself saying in a grumbling tone.

"We have to toss up and see who gets it that's all. . . . Will you lend me a quarter please?" Cunningham turned to his salesman. "All right. . . . One toss, you yell."

"Heads," said Merivale mechanically.

"The brown suit is yours. . . . Now I've got to choose another . . . God I'm glad we met when we did. Look," he shouted out through the curtains of the booth, "why dont you have dinner with me tonight at the Salmagundi Club? . . . I'm going to be dining with the only man in the world who's crazier about hydroplanes than I am. . . . It's old man Perkins, you know him, he's one of the vicepresidents of your bank. . . . And look when you see Maisie tell her I'm coming up to see her tomorrow. An extraordinary series of events has kept me from communicating with her . . . a most unfortunate series of events that took all my time up to this moment. . . . We'll talk about it later."

Merivale cleared his throat. "Very well," he said dryly.

"All right sir," said the fitter giving Merivale a last tap on the buttocks. He went back into the booth to dress.

"All right old thing," shouted Cunningham, "I've got to go pick out another suit . . . I'll expect you at seven. I'll have a Jack Rose waiting for you."

Merivale's hands were trembling as he fastened his belt. Perkins, Jack Cunningham, the damn blackguard, hydroplanes, Jack Cunningham Salmagundi Perkins. He went to a phone booth in a corner of the store and called up his mother. "Hello Mother, I'm afraid I wont be up to dinner. . . . I'm dining with Randolph Perkins at the Salmagundi Club. . . . Yes it is very pleasant. . . . Oh well he and I have always been fairly good friends. . . . Oh yes it's essential to stand in with the men higher up. And I've seen Jack Cunningham. I put it up to him straight from the shoulder man to man and he was very much embarrassed. He promised a full explanation within twentyfour hours. . . . No I kept my temper very well. I felt I owed it to Maisie. I tell you I think the man's a blackguard but until there's proof. . . . Well good night dear, in case I'm late. Oh no please dont wait up. Tell Maisie not to worry I'll be able to give her the fullest details. Good night mother."

They sat at a small table in the back of a dimly lighted tearoom. The shade on the lamp cut off the upper parts of their faces. Ellen had on a dress of bright peacock blue and a small blue hat with a piece of green in it. Ruth Prynne's face had a sagging tired look under the street makeup.

"Elaine, you've just got to come," she was saying in a whiny voice. "Cassie'll be there and Oglethorpe and all the old gang. . . . After all now that you're making such a success of editorial work it's no reason for completely abandoning your old friends is it? You dont know how much we talk and wonder about you."

"No but Ruth it's just that I'm getting to hate large parties. I guess I must be getting old. All right I'll come for a little while."

Ruth put down the sandwich she was nibbling at and reached for Ellen's hand and patted it. "That's the little trouper. . . . Of course I knew you were coming all along."

"But Ruth you never told me what happened to that traveling repertory company last summer. . . ."

"O my God," burst out Ruth. "That was terrible. Of course it was a scream, a perfect scream. Well the first thing that happened was that Isabel Clyde's husband Ralph Nolton who was managing the company was a dipsomaniac . . . and then the lovely Isabel wouldn't let anybody on the stage who didn't act like a dummy for fear the rubes wouldnt know who the star was. . . . Oh I cant tell about it any more. . . . It isnt funny to me any more, it's just horrible. . . . Oh Elaine I'm so discouraged. My dear I'm getting old." She suddenly burst out crying.

"Oh Ruth please dont," said Ellen in a little rasping voice.

She laughed. "After all we're none of us getting any younger are we?"

"Dear you dont understand . . . You never will understand."

They sat a long while without saying anything, scraps of lowvoiced conversation came to them from other corners of the dim tearoom. The palehaired waitress brought them two orders of fruit salad.

"My it must be getting late," said Ruth eventually.

"It's only half past eight. . . . We dont want to get to this party too soon."

"By the way . . . how's Jimmy Herf. I havent seen him for ages."

"Jimps is fine. . . . He's terribly sick of newspaper work. I do wish he could get something he really enjoyed doing."

"He'll always be a restless sort of person. Oh Elaine I was so happy when I heard about your being married. . . . I acted like a damn fool. I cried and cried. . . . And now with Martin and everything you must be terribly happy."

"Oh we get along all right. . . . Martin's picking up, New York seems to agree with him. He was so quiet and fat for a long while we were terribly afraid we'd produced an imbecile. Do you know Ruth I don't think I'd ever have another baby. . . . I was so horribly afraid he'd turn out deformed or something. . . . It makes me sick to think of it."

"Oh but it must be wonderful though."

They rang a bell under a small brass placque that read: Hester Voorhees INTERPRETATION OF THE DANCE. They went up three flights of creaky freshvarnished stairs. At the door open into a room full of people they met Cassandra Wilkins in a Greek tunic with a wreath of satin rosebuds round her head and a gilt wooden panpipe in her hand.

"Oh you darlings," she cried and threw her arms round them both at once. "Hester said you wouldnt come but I just knew you would. . . . Come wight in and take off your things, we're beginning with a few classic wythms." They followed her through a long candlelit incensesmelling room full of men and women in dangly costumes.

"But my dear you didn't tell us it was going to be a costume party."

"Oh yes cant you see evewything's Gweek, absolutely Gweek. . . . Here's Hester. . . . Here they are darling. . . . Hester you know Wuth . . . and this is Elaine Oglethorpe."

"I call myself Mrs. Herf now, Cassie."

"Oh I beg your pardon, it's so hard to keep twack. . . . They're just in time. . . . Hester's going to dance an owiental dance called Wythms from the Awabian Nights. . . . Oh it's too beautiful."

When Ellen came out of the bedroom where she had left her wraps a tall figure in Egyptian headdress with crooked rusty eyebrows accosted her. "Allow me to salute Helena Herf, distinguished editress of *Manners*, the journal that brings the Ritz to the humblest fireside . . . isnt that true?"

"Jojo you're a horrible tease. . . . I'm awfully glad to see you."

"Let's go and sit in a corner and talk, oh only woman I have ever loved . . ."

"Yes do let's . . . I dont like it here much."

"And my dear, have you heard about Tony Hunter's being straightened out by a psychoanalyst and now he's all sublimated and has gone on the vaudeville stage with a woman named California Jones."

"You'd better watch out Jojo."

They sat down on a couch in a recess between the dormer windows. Out of the corner of her eye she could see a girl dancing in green silk veils. The phonograph was playing the Cesar Franck symphony.

"We mustnt miss Cassie's daunce. The poor girl would be dreadfully offended."

"Jojo tell me about yourself, how have you been?"

He shook his head and made a broad gesture with his draped arm. "Ah let us sit upon the ground and tell sad stories of the deaths of kings."

"Oh Jojo I'm sick of this sort of thing. . . . It's all so silly and dowdy. . . . I wish I hadnt let them make me take my hat off."

"That was so that I should look upon the forbidden forests of your hair."

"Oh Jojo do be sensible."

"How's your husband, Elaine or rathah Helenah?"

"Oh he's all right."

"You dont sound terribly enthusiastic."

"Martin's fine though. He's got black hair and brown eyes and his cheeks are getting to be pink. Really he's awfully cute."

"My deah, spare me this exhibition of maternal bliss. . . . You'll be telling me next you walked in a baby parade."

She laughed. "Jojo it's lots of fun to see you again."

"I havent finished my catechism yet deah. . . . I saw you in the oval diningroom the other day with a very distinguished looking man with sharp features and gray hair."

"That must have been George Baldwin. Why you knew him in the old days."

"Of course of course. How he has changed. A much more interesting looking man than he used to be I must say. . . . A very strange place for the wife of a bolshevik pacifist and I.W.W. agitator to be seen taking lunch, I must say."

"Jimps isnt exactly that. I kind of wish he were. . . ." She wrinkled up her nose. "I'm a little fed up too with all that sort of thing."

"I suspected it my dear." Cassie was flitting selfconsciously by.

"Oh do come and help me. . . . Jojo's teasing me terribly."

"Well I'll twy to sit down just for a second, I'm going to dance next. . . . Mr. Oglethorpe's going to wead his twanslation of the songs of Bilitis for me to dance to."

Ellen looked from one to the other; Oglethorpe crooked his eyebrows and nodded.

Then Ellen sat alone for a long while looking at the dancing and the chittering crowded room through a dim haze of boredom.

The record on the phonograph was Turkish. Hester Voorhees, a skinny woman with a mop of hennaed hair cut short at the level of her ears, came out holding a pot of drawling incense out in front of her preceded by two young men who unrolled a carpet as she came. She wore silk bloomers and a clinking metal girdle and brassières. Everybody was clapping and saying, "How wonderful, how marvelous," when from another room came three tearing shrieks of a woman. Everybody jumped to his feet. A stout man in a derby hat appeared in the doorway. "All right little goils, right through into the back room. Men stay here."

"Who are you anyway?"

"Never mind who I am, you do as I say." The man's face was red as a beet under the derby hat.

"It's a detective." "It's outrageous. Let him show his badge."

"It's a holdup."

"It's a raid."

The room had filled suddenly with detectives. They stood in front of the windows. A man in a checked cap with a face knobbed like a squash stood in front of the fireplace. They were pushing the women roughly into the back room. The men were herded in a little group near the door; detectives were taking their names. Ellen still sat on the couch. ". . . complaint phoned to headquarters," she heard somebody say. Then she noticed that there was a phone on the little table beside the couch where she sat. She picked it up and whispered softly for a number.

"Hello is this the district attorney's office? . . . I want to speak to Mr. Baldwin please. . . . George. . . . It's lucky I knew where you were. Is the district attorney there? That's fine . . . no you tell him about it. There has been a horrible mistake. I'm at Hester Voorhees'; you know she has a dancing studio. She was presenting some dances to some friends and through some mistake the police are raiding the place . . ."

The man in the derby was standing over her. "All right phoning wont do no good. . . . Go 'long in the other room."

"I've got the district attorney's office on the wire. You speak to him. . . . Hello is this Mr. Winthrop? . . . Yes O . . . How do you do? Will you please speak to this man?" She handed the telephone to the detective and walked out into the center of the room. My I wish I hadnt taken my hat off, she was thinking.

From the other room came a sound of sobbing and Hester Voorhees' stagy voice shrieking, "It's a horrible mistake. . . . I wont be insulted like this."

The detective put down the telephone. He came over to

Ellen. "I want to apologize miss. . . . We acted on insufficient information. I'll withdraw my men immediately."

"You'd better apologize to Mrs. Voorhees. . . . It's her studio."

"Well ladies and gents," the detective began in a loud cheerful voice, "we've made a little mistake and we're very sorry. . . . Accidents will happen . . ."

Ellen slipped into the side room to get her hat and coat. She stood some time before the mirror powdering her nose. When she went out into the studio again everybody was talking at once. Men and women stood round with sheets and bathrobes draped over their scanty dancingclothes. The detectives had melted away as suddenly as they came. Oglethorpe was talking in loud impassioned tones in the middle of a group of young men.

"The scoundrels to attack women," he was shouting, red in the face, waving his headdress in one hand. "Fortunately I was able to control myself or I might have committed an act that I should have regretted to my dying day. . . . It was only with the greatest selfcontrol. . . ."

Ellen managed to slip out, ran down the stairs and out into drizzly streets. She hailed a taxi and went home. When she had got her things off she called up George Baldwin at his house. "Hello George, I'm terribly sorry I had to trouble you and Mr. Winthrop. Well if you hadnt happened to say at lunch you'd be there all the evening they probably would be just piling us out of the black maria at the Jefferson Market Court. . . . Of course it was funny. I'll tell you about it sometime, but I'm so sick of all that stuff. . . . Oh just everything like that æsthetic dancing and literature and radicalism and psychoanalysis. . . . Just an overdose I guess. . . . Yes I guess that's it George . . . I guess I'm growing up."

The night was one great chunk of black grinding cold. The smell of the presses still in his nose, the chirrup of typewriters still in his ears, Jimmy Herf stood in City Hall Square with his hands in his pockets watching ragged men with caps and earsflaps pulled down over faces and necks the color of raw steak shovel snow. Old and young their faces were the same color, their clothes were the same color. A razor wind cut his ears and made his forehead ache between the eyes.

"Hello Herf, think you'll take the job?" said a milkfaced young man who came up to him breezily and pointed to the pile of snow. "Why not, Dan. I dont know why it wouldnt be better than spending all your life rooting into other people's affairs until you're nothing but a goddam traveling dictograph."

"It'd be a fine job in summer all right. . . . Taking the West Side?"

"I'm going to walk up. . . . I've got the heebyjeebies tonight."

"Jez man you'll freeze to death."

"I dont care if I do. . . . You get so you dont have any private life, you're just an automatic writing machine."

"Well I wish I could get rid of a little of my private life. . . . Well goodnight. I hope you find some private life Jimmy."

Laughing, Jimmy Herf turned his back on the snowshovelers and started walking up Broadway, leaning into the wind with his chin buried in his coatcollar. At Houston Street he looked at his watch. Five o'clock. Gosh he was late today. Wouldnt be a place in the world where he could get a drink. He whimpered to himself at the thought of the icy blocks he still had to walk before he could get to his room. Now and then he stopped to pat some life into his numb ears. At last he got back to his room, lit the gasstove and hung over it tingling. His room was a small square bleak room on the south side of Washington Square. Its only furnishings were a bed, a chair, a table piled with books, and the gasstove. When he had begun to be a little less cold he reached under the bed for a basketcovered bottle of rum. He put some water to heat in a tin cup on the gasstove and began drinking hot rum and water. Inside him all sorts of unnamed agonies were breaking loose. He felt like the man in the fairy story with an iron band round his heart. The iron band was breaking.

He had finished the rum. Occasionally the room would start going round him solemnly and methodically. Suddenly he said aloud: "I've got to talk to her . . . I've got to talk to her." He shoved his hat down on his head and pulled on his coat. Outside the cold was balmy. Six milkwagons in a row passed jingling.

On West Twelfth two black cats were chasing each other. Everywhere was full of their crazy yowling. He felt that something would snap in his head, that he himself would scuttle off suddenly down the frozen street eerily caterwauling.

He stood shivering in the dark passage, ringing the bell marked Herf again and again. Then he knocked as loud as he could. Ellen came to the door in a green wrapper. "What's the matter Jimps? Havent you got a key?" Her face was soft with sleep; there was a happy cozy suave smell of sleep about her. He talked through clenched teeth breathlessly.

"Ellie I've got to talk to you."

"Are you lit, Jimps?"

"Well I know what I'm saying."

"I'm terribly sleepy."

He followed her into her bedroom. She kicked off her slippers and got back into bed, sat up looking at him with sleep-weighted eyes.

"Dont talk too loud on account of Martin."

"Ellie I dont know why it's always so difficult for me to speak out about anything. . . . I always have to get drunk to speak out. . . . Look here do you like me any more?"

"You know I'm awfully fond of you and always shall be."

"I mean love, you know what I mean, whatever it is . . ." he broke in harshly.

"I guess I dont love anybody for long unless they're dead. . . . I'm a terrible sort of person. It's no use talking about it."

"I knew it. You knew I knew it. O God things are pretty rotten for me Ellie."

She sat with her knees hunched up and her hands clasped round them looking at him with wide eyes. "Are you really so crazy about me Jimps?"

"Look here lets get a divorce and be done with it."

"Dont be in such a hurry, Jimps. . . . And there's Martin. What about him?"

"I can scrape up enough money for him occasionally, poor little kid."

"I make more than you do, Jimps. . . . You shouldnt do that yet."

"I know. I know. Dont I know it?"

They sat looking at each other without speaking. Their eyes burned from looking at each other. Suddenly Jimmy wanted terribly to be asleep, not to remember anything, to let his head sink into blackness, as into his mother's lap when he was a kid.

"Well I'm going home." He gave a little dry laugh. "We didn't think it'd all go pop like this, did we?"

"Goodnight Jimps," she whined in the middle of a yawn. "But things dont end. . . . If only I weren' so terribly sleepy. . . . Will you put out the light?"

He groped his way in the dark to the door. Outside the arctic morning was growing gray with dawn. He hurried back to his room. He wanted to get into bed and be asleep before it was light.

A long low room with long tables down the middle piled with silk and crêpe fabrics, brown, salmonpink, emeraldgreen. A smell of snipped thread and dress materials. All down the tables bowed heads auburn, blond, black, brown of girls sewing. Errandboys pushing rolling stands of hung dresses up and down the aisles. A bell rings and the room breaks out with noise and talk shrill as a birdhouse.

Anna gets up and stretches out her arms. "My I've got a head," she says to the girl next her.

"Up last night?"

She nods.

"Ought to quit it dearie, it'll spoil your looks. A girl cant burn the candle at both ends like a feller can." The other girl is thin and blond and has a crooked nose. She puts her arm round Anna's waist. "My I wish I could put on a little of your weight."

"I wish you could," says Anna. "Dont matter what I eat it turns to fat."

"Still you aint too fat. . . . You're juss plump so's they like to squeeze ye. You try wearing boyishform like I told an you'll look fine."

"My boyfriend says he likes a girl to have shape."

On the stairs they push their way through a group of girls

listening to a little girl with red hair who talks fast, opening her mouth wide and rolling her eyes. ". . . She lived just on the next block at 2230 Cameron Avenue an she'd been to the Hippodrome with some girlfriends and when they got home it was late an they let her go home alone, up Cameron Avenue, see? An the next morning when her folks began looking for her they found her behind a Spearmint sign in a back lot."

"Was she dead?"

"Sure she was. . . . A negro had done somethin terrible to her and then he'd strangled her. . . . I felt terrible. I used to go to school with her. An there aint a girl on Cameron Avenue been out after dark they're so scared."

"Sure I saw all about it in the paper last night. Imagine livin right on the next block."

"Did you see me touch that hump back?" cried Rosie as he settled down beside her in the taxi. "In the lobby of the theater?" He pulled at the trousers that were tight over his knees. "That's goin to give us luck Jake. I never seen a hump back to fail. . . . if you touch him on the hump . . . Ou it makes me sick how fast these taxis go." They were thrown forward by the taxi's sudden stop. "My God we almost ran over a boy." Jake Silverman patted her knee. "Poor ikle kid, was it all worked up?" As they drove up to the hotel she shivered and buried her face in her coatcollar. When they went to the desk to get the key, the clerk said to Silverman, "There's a gentleman waiting to see you sir." A thickset man came up to him taking a cigar out of his mouth. "Will you step this way a minute please Mr. Silverman." Rosie thought she was going to faint. She stood perfectly still, frozen, with her cheeks deep in the fur collar of her coat.

They sat in two deep armchairs and whispered with their heads together. Step by step, she got nearer, listening. "Warrant . . . Department of Justice . . . using the mails to defraud . . ." She couldnt hear what Jake said in between. He kept nodding his head as if agreeing. Then suddenly he spoke out smoothly, smiling.

"Well I've heard your side Mr. Rogers. . . . Here's mine. If you arrest me now I shall be ruined and a great many people who have put their money in this enterprise will be ruined. . . . In a week I can liquidate the whole concern with a profit. . . . Mr. Rogers I am a man who has been deeply wronged through foolishness in misplacing confidence in others."

"I cant help that. . . . My duty is to execute the warrant. . . . I'm afraid I'll have to search your room. . . . You see we have several little items . . ." The man flicked the ash off his cigar and began to read in a monotonous voice. "Jacob Silverman, alias Edward Faversham, Simeon J. Arbuthnot, Jack Hinkley, J. J. Gold. . . . Oh we've got a pretty little list. . . . We've done some very pretty work on your case, if I do say it what shouldnt."

They got to their feet. The man with the cigar jerked his head at a lean man in a cap who sat reading a paper on the opposite side of the lobby.

Silverman walked over to the desk. "I'm called away on business," he said to the clerk. "Will you please have my bill prepared? Mrs. Silverman will keep the room for a few days."

Rosie couldnt speak. She followed the three men into the elevator. "Sorry to have to do this maam," said the lean detective pulling at the visor of his cap. Silverman opened the room door for them and closed it carefully behind him. "Thank you for your consideration, gentlemen. . . . My wife thanks you." Rosie sat in a straight chair in the corner of the room. She was biting her tongue hard, harder to try to keep her lips from twitching.

"We realize Mr. Silverman that this is not quite the ordinary criminal case."

"Wont you have a drink gentlemen?"

They shook their heads. The thickset man was lighting a fresh cigar.

"Allright Mike," he said to the lean man. "Go through the drawers and closet."

"Is that regular?"

"If this was regular we'd have the handcuffs on you and be running the lady here as an accessory."

Rosie sat with her icy hands clasped between her knees swaying her body from side to side. Her eyes were closed. While the detectives were rummaging in the closet, Silverman took the opportunity to put his hand on her shoulder. She opened her eyes. "The minute the goddam dicks take me out phone Schatz and tell him everything. Get hold of him if you have to wake up everybody in New York." He spoke low and fast, his lips barely moving.

Almost immediately he was gone, followed by the two detectives with a satchel full of letters. His kiss was still wet on her lips. She looked dazedly round the empty deathly quiet room. She noticed some writing on the lavender blotter on the desk. It was his handwriting, very scrawly: Hock everything and beat it; you are a good kid. Tears began running down her cheeks. She sat a long while with her head dropped on the desk kissing the penciled words on the blotter.

IV. Skyscraper

The young man without legs has stopped still in the middle of the south sidewalk of Fourteenth Street. He wears a blue knitted sweater and a blue stocking cap. His eyes staring up widen until they fill the paperwhite face. Drifts across the sky a dirigible, bright tinfoil cigar misted with height, gently prodding the rainwashed sky and the soft clouds. The young man without legs stops still propped on his arms in the middle of the south sidewalk of Fourteenth Street. Among striding legs, lean legs, waddling legs, legs in skirts and pants and knickerbockers, he stops perfectly still, propped on his arms, looking up at the dirigible.

Jobless, Jimmy Herf came out of the Pulitzer Building. He stood beside a pile of pink newspapers on the curb, taking deep breaths, looking up the glistening shaft of the Woolworth. It was a sunny day, the sky was a robin's egg blue. He turned north and began to walk uptown. As he got away from it the Woolworth pulled out like a telescope. He walked north through the city of shiny windows, through the city of scrambled alphabets, through the city of gilt letter signs.

Spring rich in gluten. . . . Chockful of golden richness, delight in every bite, THE DADDY OF THEM ALL, spring rich in gluten. Nobody can buy better bread than PRINCE ALBERT. Wrought steel, monel, copper, nickel, wrought iron. *All the world loves natural beauty.* LOVE'S BARGAIN that suit at Gumpel's best value in town. Keep that schoolgirl complexion. . . . JOE KISS, starting, lightning, ignition and generators.

Everything made him bubble with repressed giggles. It was eleven o'clock. He hadnt been to bed. Life was upside down, he was a fly walking on the ceiling of a topsyturvy city. He'd thrown up his job, he had nothing to do today, tomorrow, next day, day after. Whatever goes up comes down, but not for weeks, months. Spring rich in gluten.

He went into a lunchroom, ordered bacon and eggs, toast and coffee, sat eating them happily, tasting thoroughly every mouthful. His thoughts ran wild like a pasture full of yearling colts crazy with sundown. At the next table a voice was expounding monotonously:

"Jilted . . . and I tell you we had to do some cleaning. They were all members of your church you know. We knew the whole story. He was advised to put her away. He said, 'No I'm going to see it through'."

Herf got to his feet. He must be walking again. He went out with a taste of bacon in his teeth.

Express service meets the demands of spring. O God to meet the demands of spring. No tins, no sir, but there's rich quality in every mellow pipeful. . . . SOCONY. One taste tells more than a million words. The yellow pencil with the red band. Than a million words, than a million words. "All right hand over that million. . . . Keep him covered Ben." The Yonkers gang left him for dead on a bench in the park. They stuck him up, but all they got was a million words. . . . "But Jimps I'm so tired of booktalk and the proletariat, cant you understand?"

Chockful of golden richness, spring.

Dick Snow's mother owned a shoebox factory. She failed and he came out of school and took to standing on streetcorners. The guy in the softdrink stand put him wise. He'd made two payments on pearl earrings for a blackhaired Jewish girl with a shape like a mandolin. They waited for the bankmessenger in the L station. He pitched over the turnstile and hung there. They went off with the satchel in a Ford sedan. Dick Snow stayed behind emptying his gun into the dead man. In the deathhouse he met the demands of spring by writing a poem to his mother that they published in the *Evening Graphic.*

With every deep breath Herf breathed in rumble and grind and painted phrases until he began to swell, felt himself stumbling big and vague, staggering like a pillar of smoke above the April streets, looking into the windows of machineshops, buttonfactories, tenementhouses, felt of the grime of bedlinen and the smooth whir of lathes, wrote cusswords on typewriters between the stenographer's fingers, mixed up the pricetags in departmentstores. Inside he fizzled like sodawater into sweet April syrups, strawberry, sarsaparilla, chocolate, cherry, vanilla dripping foam through the mild gasolineblue air. He dropped sickeningly fortyfour stories, crashed. And suppose I bought a gun and killed Ellie, would I meet the demands of

April sitting in the deathhouse writing a poem about my mother to be published in the *Evening Graphic*?

He shrank until he was of the smallness of dust, picking his way over crags and bowlders in the roaring gutter, climbing straws, skirting motoroil lakes.

He sat in Washington Square, pink with noon, looking up Fifth Avenue through the arch. The fever had seeped out of him. He felt cool and tired. Another spring, God how many springs ago, walking from the cemetery up the blue macadam road where fieldsparrows sang and the sign said: Yonkers. In Yonkers I buried my boyhood, in Marseilles with the wind in my face I dumped my calf years into the harbor. Where in New York shall I bury my twenties? Maybe they were deported and went out to sea on the Ellis Island ferry singing the International. The growl of the International over the water, fading sighing into the mist.

DEPORTED

James Herf young newspaper man of 190 West 12th Street recently lost his twenties. Appearing before Judge Merivale they were remanded to Ellis Island for deportation as undesirable aliens. The younger four Sasha Michael Nicholas and Vladimir had been held for some time on a charge of criminal anarchy. The fifth and sixth were held on a technical charge of vagrancy. The later ones Bill Tony and Joe were held under various indictments including wifebeating, arson, assault, and prostitution. All were convicted on counts of misfeasance, malfeasance, and nonfeasance.

Oyez oyez oyez prisoner at the bar. . . . I find the evidence dubious said the judge pouring himself out a snifter. The clerk of the court who was stirring an oldfashioned cocktail became overgrown with vineleaves and the courtroom reeked with the smell of flowering grapes and the Shining Bootlegger took the bulls by the horns and led them lowing gently down the courthouse steps. "Court is adjourned by hicky," shouted the judge when he found gin in his waterbottle. The reporters discovered the mayor dressed in a leopard skin posing as Civic Virtue with his foot on the back of Princess Fifi the oriental dancer. Your correspondent was leaning out of the window of the Banker's Club in the company of his uncle, Jefferson T. Merivale, wellknown clubman of this city and two lamb chops well peppered. Meanwhile the waiters were hastily organizing an orchestra, using the potbellies of the Gausenheimers for snaredrums. The head waiter gave a truly delightful rendition of *My Old Kentucky Home*, utilizing for the first time the resonant bald heads of the seven directors of the Well Watered Gasoline Company of Delaware as a xylophone. And all the while the Shining Bootlegger in purple running drawers and a blueribbon silk hat was leading the bulls up Broadway to the number of two million, three-hundred and fortytwo thousand, five hundred and one. As they reached the Spuyten Duyvil, they were incontinently drowned, rank after rank, in an attempt to swim to Yonkers.

And as I sit here, thought Jimmy Herf, print itches like a rash inside me. I sit here pockmarked with print. He got to his feet. A little yellow dog was curled up asleep under the bench. The little yellow dog looked very happy. "What I need's a good sleep," Jimmy said aloud.

"What are you goin to do with it, Dutch, are you goin to hock it?"

"Francie I wouldnt take a million dollars for that little gun."

"For Gawd's sake dont start talkin about money, now. . . . Next thing some cop'll see it on your hip and arrest you for the Sullivan law."

"The cop who's goin to arrest me's not born yet. . . . Just you forget that stuff."

Francie began to whimper. "But Dutch what are we goin to do, what are we goin to do?"

Dutch suddenly rammed the pistol into his pocket and jumped to his feet. He walked jerkily back and forth on the asphalt path. It was a foggy evening, raw; automobiles moving along the slushy road made an endless interweaving flicker of cobwebby light among the skeleton shrubberies.

"Jez you make me nervous with your whimperin an cryin. . . . Cant you shut up?" He sat down beside her sullenly again. "I thought I heard somebody movin in the bushes. . . . This goddam park's full of plainclothes men. . . . There's nowhere you can go in the whole crummy city without people watchin you."

"I wouldnt mind it if I didnt feel so rotten. I cant eat anythin without throwin up an I'm so scared all the time the other girls'll notice something."

"But I've told you I had a way o fixin everythin, aint I? I promise you I'll fix everythin fine in a couple of days. . . . We'll go away an git married. We'll go down South. . . . I bet there's lots of jobs in other places. . . . I'm gettin cold, let's get the hell outa here."

"Oh Dutch," said Francie in a tired voice as they walked down the muddyglistening asphalt path, "do you think we're ever goin to have a good time again like we used to?"

"We're S.O.L. now but that dont mean we're always goin to be. I lived through those gas attacks in the Oregon forest didnt I? I been dopin out a lot of things these last few days."

"Dutch if you go and get arrested there'll be nothin left for me to do but jump in the river."

"Didnt I tell you I wasnt goin to get arrested?"

Mrs. Cohen, a bent old woman with a face brown and blotched like a russet apple, stands beside the kitchen table with her gnarled hands folded over her belly. She sways from the hips as she scolds in an endless querulous stream of Yiddish at Anna sitting blearyeyed with sleep over a cup of coffee: "If you had been blasted in the cradle it would have been better, if you had been born dead. . . . Oy what for have I raised four children that they should all of them be no good, agitators and streetwalkers and bums . . . ? Benny in jail twice, and Sol God knows where making trouble, and Sarah accursed given up to sin kicking up her legs at Minski's, and now you, may you wither in your chair, picketing for the garment workers, walking along the street shameless with a sign on your back."

Anna dipped a piece of bread in the coffee and put it in her mouth. "Aw mommer you dont understand," she said with her mouth full.

"Understand, understand harlotry and sinfulness . . . ? Oy why dont you attend to your work and keep your mouth shut, and draw your pay quietly? You used to make good money and could have got married decent before you took to running wild in dance halls with a goy. Oy oy that I've raised daughters in my old age no decent man'd want to take to his house and marry. . . ."

Anna got to her feet shrieking "It's no business of yours. . . . I've always paid my part of the rent regular. You think a girl's worth nothin but for a slave and to grind her fingers off workin all her life. . . . I think different, do you hear? Dont you dare scold at me. . . ."

"Oy you will talk back to your old mother. If Solomon was alive he'd take a stick to you. Better to have been born dead than talk back to your mother like a goy. Get out of the house and quick before I blast you."

"All right I will." Anna ran through the narrow trunkobstructed hallway to the bedroom and threw herself on her bed. Her cheeks were burning. She lay quiet trying to think. From the kitchen came the old woman's fierce monotonous sobbing.

Anna raised herself to a sitting posture on the bed. She caught sight in the mirror opposite of a strained teardabbled face and rumpled stringy hair. "My Gawd I'm a sight," she sighed. As she got to her feet her heel caught on the braid of her dress. The dress tore sharply. Anna sat on the edge of the bed and cried and cried. Then she sewed the rent in the dress up carefully with tiny meticulous stitches. Sewing made her feel calmer. She put on her hat, powdered her nose copiously, put a little rouge on her lips, got into her coat and went out. April was coaxing unexpected colors out of the East Side streets. Sweet voluptuous freshness came from a pushcart full of pineapples. At the corner she found Rose Segal and Lillian Diamond drinking coca-cola at the softdrink stand.

"Anna have a coke with us," they chimed.

"I will if you'll blow me. . . . I'm broke."

"Vy, didnt you get your strike pay?"

"I gave it all to the old woman. . . . Dont do no good though. She goes on scoldin all day long. She's too old."

"Did you hear how gunmen broke in and busted up Ike Goldstein's shop? Busted up everythin wid hammers an left him unconscious on top of a lot of dressgoods."

"Oh that's terrible."

"Soive him right I say."

"But they oughtnt to destroy property like that. We make our livin by it as much as he does."

"A pretty fine livin. . . . I'm near dead wid it," said Anna banging her empty glass down on the counter.

"Easy easy," said the man in the stand. "Look out for the crockery."

"But the worst thing was," went on Rose Segal, "that while they was fightin up in Goldstein's a rivet flew out the winder an fell nine stories an killed a fireman passin on a truck so's he dropped dead in the street."

"What for did they do that?"

"Some guy must have slung it at some other guy and it pitched out of the winder."

"And killed a fireman."

Anna saw Elmer coming towards them down the avenue, his thin face stuck forward, his hands hidden in the pockets of his frayed overcoat. She left the two girls and walked towards him. "Was you goin down to the house? Dont lets go, cause the old woman's scoldin somethin terrible. . . . I wish I could get her into the Daughters of Israel. I cant stand her no more."

"Then let's walk over and sit in the square," said Elmer. "Dont you feel the spring?"

She looked at him out of the corner of her eye. "Dont I? Oh Elmer I wish this strike was over. . . . It gets me crazy doin nothin all day."

"But Anna the strike is the worker's great opportunity, the worker's university. It gives you a chance to study and read and go to the Public Library."

"But you always think it'll be over in a day or two, an what's the use anyway?"

"The more educated a feller is the more use he is to his class."

They sat down on a bench with their backs to the play-ground.The sky overhead was glittering with motherofpearl flakes of sunset. Dirty children yelled and racketed about the asphalt paths.

"Oh," said Anna looking up at the sky, "I'd like to have a Paris evening dress an you have a dress suit and go out to dinner at a swell restaurant an go to the theater an everything."

"If we lived in a decent society we might be able to. . . . There'd be gayety for the workers then, after the revolution."

"But Elmer what's the use if we're old and scoldin like the old woman?"

"Our children will have those things."

Anna sat bolt upright on the seat. "I aint never goin to have any children," she said between her teeth, "never, never, never."

Alice touched his arm as they turned to look in the window of an Italian pastryshop. On each cake ornamented with bright analin flowers and flutings stood a sugar lamb for Easter and the resurrection banner. "Jimmy," she said turning up to him her little oval face with her lips too red like the roses on the cakes, "you've got to do something about Roy. . . . He's got to get to work. I'll go crazy if I have him sitting round the house any more reading the papers wearing that dreadful adenoid expression. . . . You know what I mean. . . . He respects you."

"But he's trying to get a job."

"He doesnt really try, you know it."

"He thinks he does. I guess he's got a funny idea about himself. . . . But I'm a fine person to talk about jobs . . ."

"Oh I know, I think it's wonderful. Everybody says you've given up newspaper work and are going to write."

Jimmy found himself looking down into her widening brown eyes, that had a glimmer at the bottom like the glimmer of water in a well. He turned his head away; there was a catch in his throat; he coughed. They walked on along the lilting brightcolored street.

At the door of the restaurant they found Roy and Martin Schiff waiting for them. They went through an outer room into a long hall crowded with tables packed between two greenish bluish paintings of the Bay of Naples. The air was heavy with a smell of parmesan cheese and cigarettesmoke and tomato sauce. Alice made a little face as she settled herself in a chair.

"Ou I want a cocktail right away quick."

"I must be kinder simpleminded," said Herf, "but these boats coquetting in front of Vesuvius always make me feel like getting a move on somewhere. . . . I think I'll be getting along out of here in a couple of weeks."

"But Jimmy where are you going?" asked Roy. "Isnt this something new?"

"Hasnt Helena got something to say about that?" put in Alice.

Herf turned red. "Why should she?" he said sharply.

"I just found there was nothing in it for me," he found himself saying a little later.

"Oh we none of us know what we want," burst out Martin. "That's why we're such a peewee generation."

"I'm beginning to learn a few of the things I dont want," said Herf quietly. "At least I'm beginning to have the nerve to admit to myself how much I dislike all the things I dont want."

"But it's wonderful," cried Alice, "throwing away a career for an ideal."

"Excuse me," said Herf pushing back his chair. In the toilet he looked himself in the eye in the wavy lookingglass.

"Dont talk," he whispered. "What you talk about you never do. . . ." His face had a drunken look. He filled the hollow of his two hands with water and washed it. At the table they cheered when he sat down.

"Yea for the wanderer," said Roy.

Alice was eating cheese on long slices of pear. "I think it's thrilling," she said.

"Roy is bored," shouted Martin Schiff after a silence. His face with its big eyes and bone glasses swam through the smoke of the restaurant like a fish in a murky aquarium.

"I was just thinking of all the places I had to go to look for a job tomorrow."

"You want a job?" Martin went on melodramatically. "You want to sell your soul to the highest bidder?"

"Jez if that's all you had to sell. . . ." moaned Roy.

"It's my morning sleep that worries me. . . . Still it is lousy putting over your personality and all that stuff. It's not your ability to do the work it's your personality."

"Prostitutes are the only honest . . ."

"But good Lord a prostitute sells her personality."

"She only rents it."

"But Roy is bored. . . . You are all bored. . . . I'm boring you all."

"We're having the time of our lives," insisted Alice. "Now Martin we wouldn't be sitting here if we were bored, would we? . . . I wish Jimmy would tell us where he expected to go on his mysterious travels."

"No, you are saying to yourselves what a bore he is, what use is he to society? He has no money, he has no pretty wife, no good conversation, no tips on the stockmarket. He's a useless fardel on society. . . . The artist is a fardel."

"That's not so Martin. . . . You're talking through your hat."

Martin waved an arm across the table. Two wineglasses upset. A scaredlooking waiter laid a napkin over the red streams. Without noticing, Martin went on, "It's all pretense. . . . When you talk you talk with the little lying tips of your tongues. You dont dare lay bare your real souls. . . . But now you must listen to me for the last time. . . . For the last time I say. . . . Come here waiter you too, lean over and look into the black pit of the soul of man. And Herf is bored. You are all bored, bored flies buzzing on the windowpane. You think the windowpane is the room. You dont know what there is deep black inside. . . . I am very drunk. Waiter another bottle."

"Say hold your horses Martin. . . . I dont know if we can pay the bill as it is. . . . We dont need any more."

"Waiter another bottle of wine and four grappas."

"Well it looks as if we were in for a rough night," groaned Roy.

"If there is need my body can pay. . . . Alice take off your mask. . . . You are a beautiful little child behind your mask. . . . Come with me to the edge of the pit. . . . O I am too drunk to tell you what I feel." He brushed off his tortoiseshell glasses and crumpled them in his hand, the lenses shot glittering across the floor. The gaping waiter ducked among the tables after them.

For a moment Martin sat blinking. The rest of them looked at each other. Then he shot to his feet. "I see your little smirking supercil-superciliosity. No wonder we can no longer have decent dinners, decent conversations. . . . I must prove my atavistic sincerity, prove. . . ." He started pulling at his necktie.

"Say Martin old man, pipe down," Roy was reiterating.

"Nobody shall stop me. . . . I must run into the sincerity of black. . . . I must run to the end of the black wharf on the East River and throw myself off."

Herf ran after him through the restaurant to the street. At the door he threw off his coat, at the corner his vest.

"Gosh he runs like a deer," panted Roy staggering against Herf's shoulder. Herf picked up the coat and vest, folded them under his arm and went back to the restaurant. They were pale when they sat down on either side of Alice.

"Will he really do it? Will he really do it?" she kept asking.

"No of course not," said Roy. "He'll go home; he was making fools of us because we played up to him."

"Suppose he really did it?"

"I'd hate to see him. . . . I like him very much. We named our kid after him," said Jimmy gloomily. "But if he really feels so terribly unhappy what right have we to stop him?"

"Oh Jimmy," sighed Alice, "do order some coffee."

Outside a fire engine moaned throbbed roared down the street. Their hands were cold. They sipped the coffee without speaking.

Francie came out of the side door of the Five and Ten into the six o'clock goinghome end of the day crowd. Dutch Robertson was waiting for her. He was smiling; there was color in his face.

"Why Dutch what's . . ." The words stuck in her throat.

"Dont you like it . . . ?" They walked on down Fourteenth, a blur of faces streamed by on either side of them. "Everything's jake Francie," he was saying quietly. He wore a light gray spring overcoat and a light felt hat to match. New red pointed Oxfords glowed on his feet. "How do you like the outfit? I said to myself it wasnt no use tryin to do anythin without a tony outside."

"But Dutch how did you get it?"

"Stuck up a guy in a cigar store. Jez it was a cinch."

"Ssh dont talk so loud; somebody might hear ye."

"They wouldnt know what I was talkin about."

Mr. Densch sat in the corner of Mrs. Densch's Louis XIV

boudoir. He sat all hunched up on a little gilt pinkbacked chair with his potbelly resting on his knees. In his green sagging face the pudgy nose and the folds that led from the flanges of the nostrils to the corners of the wide mouth made two triangles. He had a pile of telegrams in his hand, on top a decoded message on a blue slip that read: Deficit Hamburg branch approximately $500,000; signed Heintz. Everywhere he looked about the little room crowded with fluffy glittery objects he saw the purple letters of *approximately* jiggling in the air. Then he noticed that the maid, a pale mulatto in a ruffled cap, had come into the room and was staring at him. His eye lit on a large flat cardboard box she held in her hand.

"What's that?"

"Somethin for the misses sir."

"Bring it here. . . . Hickson's . . . and what does she want to be buying more dresses for will you tell me that. . . . Hickson's. . . . Open it up. If it looks expensive I'll send it back."

The maid gingerly pulled off a layer of tissuepaper, uncovering a peach and peagreen evening dress.

Mr. Densch got to his feet spluttering, "She must think the war's still on. . . . Tell em we will not receive it. Tell em there's no such party livin here."

The maid picked up the box with a toss of the head and went out with her nose in the air. Mr. Densch sat down in the little chair and began looking over the telegrams again.

"Ann-ee, Ann-ee," came a shrill voice from the inner room; this was followed by a head in a lace cap shaped like a libertycap and a big body in a shapeless ruffled negligée. "Why J. D. what are you doing here at this time of the morning? I'm waiting for my hairdresser."

"It's very important. . . . I just had a cable from Heintz. Serena my dear, Blackhead and Densch is in a very bad way on both sides of the water."

"Yes ma'am," came the maid's voice from behind him.

He gave his shoulders a shrug and walked to the window. He felt tired and sick and heavy with flesh. An errand boy on a bicycle passed along the street; he was laughing and his cheeks were pink. Densch saw himself, felt himself for a second hot and slender running bareheaded down Pine Street years ago catching the girls' ankles in the corner of his eye. He turned back into the room. The maid had gone.

"Serena," he began, "cant you understand the seriousness . . . ? It's this slump. And on top of it all the bean market has gone to hell. It's ruin I tell you. . . ."

"Well my dear I dont see what you expect me to do about it."

"Economize . . . economize. Look where the price of rubber's gone to. . . . That dress from Hickson's. . . ."

"Well you wouldnt have me going to the Blackhead's party looking like a country schoolteacher, would you?"

Mr. Densch groaned and shook his head. "O you wont understand; probably there wont be any party. . . . Look Serena there's no nonsense about this. . . . I want you to have a trunk packed so that we can sail any day. . . . I need a rest. I'm thinking of going to Marienbad for the cure. . . . It'll do you good too."

Her eye suddenly caught his. All the little wrinkles on her face deepened; the skin under her eyes was like the skin of a shrunken toy balloon. He went over to her and put his hand on her shoulder and was puckering his lips to kiss her when suddenly she flared up.

"I wont have you meddling between me and my dressmakers. . . . I wont have it . . . I wont have it. . . ."

"Oh have it your own way." He left the room with his head hunched between his thick sloping shoulders.

"Ann-ee!"

"Yes ma'am." The maid came back into the room.

Mrs. Densch had sunk down in the middle of a little spindlelegged sofa. Her face was green. "Annie please get me that bottle of sweet spirits of ammonia and a little water. . . . And Annie you can call up Hickson's and tell them that that dress was sent back through a mistake of . . . of the butler's and please to send it right back as I've got to wear it tonight."

Pursuit of happiness, unalienable pursuit . . . right to life liberty and. . . . A black moonless night; Jimmy Herf is walking alone up South Street. Behind the wharfhouses ships raise shadowy skeletons against the night. "By Jesus I admit that I'm stumped," he says aloud. All these April nights combing the streets alone a skyscraper has obsessed him, a grooved building jutting up with uncountable bright windows falling onto him out of a scudding sky. Typewriters rain continual nickelplated confetti in his ears. Faces of Follies girls, glorified by Ziegfeld, smile and beckon to him from the windows. Ellie in a gold dress, Ellie made of thin gold foil absolutely lifelike beckoning from every window. And he walks round blocks and blocks looking for the door of the humming tinselwindowed skyscraper, round blocks and blocks and still no door. Every time he closes his eyes the dream has hold of him, every time he stops arguing audibly with himself in pompous reasonable phrases the dream has hold of him. Young man to save your sanity you've got to do one of two things. . . . Please mister where's the door to this building? Round the block? Just round the block . . . one of two unalienable alternatives: go away in a dirty soft shirt or stay in a clean Arrow collar. But what's the use of spending your whole life fleeing the City of Destruction? What about your unalienable right, Thirteen Provinces? His mind unreeling phrases, he walks on doggedly. There's nowhere in particular he wants to go. If only I still had faith in words.

"How do you do Mr. Goldstein?" the reporter breezily chanted as he squeezed the thick flipper held out to him over the counter of the cigar store. "My name's Brewster. . . . I'm writing up the crime wave for the *News*."

Mr. Goldstein was a larvashaped man with a hooked nose a little crooked in a gray face, behind which pink attentive ears stood out unexpectedly. He looked at the reporter out of suspicious screwedup eyes.

"If you'd be so good I'd like to have your story of last night's little. . . . misadventure . . ."

"Vont get no story from me young man. Vat vill you do but print it so that other boys and goils vill get the same idear."

"It's too bad you feel that way Mr. Goldstein . . . Will you give me a Robert Burns please . . . ? Publicity it seems to me is as necessary as ventilation. . . . It lets in fresh air." The reporter bit off the end of the cigar, lit it, and stood looking thoughtfully at Mr. Goldstein through a swirling ring of blue smoke. "You see Mr. Goldstein it's this way," he began impressively. "We are handling this matter from the human interest angle . . . pity and tears . . . you understand. A photographer was on his way out here to get your photograph. . . . I bet you it would increase your volume of business for the next couple of weeks. . . . I suppose I'll have to phone him not to come now."

"Well this guy," began Mr. Goldstein abruptly, "he's a well-dressed lookin feller, new spring overcoat an all that and he comes in to buy a package o Camels. . . . 'A nice night,' he says openin the package an takin out a cigarette to smoke it. Then I notices the goil with him had a veil on."

"Then she didnt have bobbed hair?"

"All I seen was a kind o mournin veil. The foist thing I knew she was behind the counter an had a gun stuck in my ribs an began talkin . . . you know kinder kiddin like . . . and afore I knew what to think the guy'd cleaned out the cashregister an says to me, 'Got any cash in your jeans Buddy?' I'll tell ye I was sweatin some . . ."

"And that's all?"

"Sure by the time I'd got hold of a cop they vere off to hell an gone."

"How much did they get?"

"Oh about fifty berries an six dollars off me."

"Was the girl pretty?"

"I dunno, maybe she was. I'd like to smashed her face in. They ought to make it the electric chair for those babies. . . . Aint no security nowhere. Vy should anybody voirk if all you've got to do is get a gun an stick up your neighbors?"

"You say they were welldressed . . . like welltodo people?"

"Yare."

"I'm working on the theory that he's a college boy and that she's a society girl and that they do it for sport."

"The feller vas a hardlookin bastard."

"Well there are hardlooking college men. . . . You wait for the story called 'The Gilded Bandits' in next Sunday's paper Mr. Goldstein. . . . You take the *News* dont you?"

Mr. Goldstein shook his head.

"I'll send you a copy anyway."

"I want to see those babies convicted, do you understand?

If there's anythin I can do I sure vill do it . . . Aint no security no more. . . . I dont care about no Sunday supplement
publicity."

"Well the photographer'll be right along. I'm sure you'll
consent to pose Mr. Goldstein. . . . Well thank you very
much. . . . Good day Mr. Goldstein."

Mr. Goldstein suddenly produced a shiny new revolver
from under the counter and pointed it at the reporter.

"Hay go easy with that."

Mr. Goldstein laughed a sardonic laugh. "I'm ready for em
next time they come," he shouted after the reporter who was
already making for the Subway.

"Our business, my dear Mrs. Herf," declaimed Mr. Harpsicourt, looking sweetly in her eyes and smiling his gray
Cheshire cat smile, "is to roll ashore on the wave of fashion
the second before it breaks, like riding a surfboard."

Ellen was delicately digging with her spoon into half an alligator pear; she kept her eyes on her plate, her lips a little
parted; she felt cool and slender in the tightfitting darkblue
dress, shyly alert in the middle of the tangle of sideways
glances and the singsong modish talk of the restaurant.

"It's a knack that I can prophesy in you more than in any
girl, and more charmingly than any girl I've ever known."

"Prophesy?" asked Ellen, looking up at him laughing.

"You shouldnt pick up an old man's word. . . . I'm ex-
pressing myself badly. . . . That's always a dangerous sign.
No, you understand so perfectly, though you disdain it a little
. . . admit that. . . . What we need on such a periodical, that
I'm sure you could explain it to me far better."

"Of course what you want to do is make every reader feel
Johnny on the spot in the center of things."

"As if she were having lunch right here at the Algonquin."

"Not today but tomorrow," added Ellen.

Mr. Harpsicourt laughed his creaky little laugh and tried to
look deep among the laughing gold specs in her gray eyes.
Blushing she looked down into the gutted half of an alligator
pear in her plate. Like the sense of a mirror behind her she
felt the smart probing glances of men and women at the tables round about.

*

The pancakes were comfortably furry against his ginbitten tongue. Jimmy Herf sat in Child's in the middle of a noisy drunken company. Eyes, lips, evening dresses, the smell of bacon and coffee blurred and throbbed about him. He ate the pancakes painstakingly, called for more coffee. He felt better. He had been afraid he was going to feel sick. He began reading the paper. The print swam and spread like Japanese flowers. Then it was sharp again, orderly, running in a smooth black and white paste over his orderly black and white brain:

Misguided youth again took its toll of tragedy amid the tinsel gayeties of Coney Island fresh painted for the season when plainclothes men arrested "Dutch" Robinson and a girl companion alleged to be the Flapper Bandit. The pair are accused of committing more than a score of holdups in Brooklyn and Queens. The police had been watching the couple for some days. They had rented a small kitchenette apartment at 7356 Seacroft Avenue. Suspicion was first aroused when the girl, about to become a mother, was taken in an ambulance to the Canarsie Presbyterian Hospital. Hospital attendants were surprised by Robinson's seemingly endless supply of money. The girl had a private room, expensive flowers and fruit were sent in to her daily, and a well-known physician was called into consultation at the man's request. When it came to the point of registering the name of the baby girl the young man admitted to the physician that they were not married. One of the hospital attendants, noticing that the woman answered to the description published in the *Evening Times* of the flapper bandit and her pal, telephoned the police. Plain-clothes men sleuthed the couple for some days after they had returned to the apartment on Seacroft Avenue and this afternoon made the arrests.

The arrest of the flapper bandit . . .

A hot biscuit landed on Herf's paper. He looked up with a start; a darkeyed Jewish girl at the next table was making a face at him. He nodded and took off an imaginary hat. "I thank thee lovely nymph," he said thickly and began eating the biscuit.

"Quit dat djer hear?" the young man who sat beside her, who looked like a prizefighter's trainer, bellowed in her ear.

The people at Herf's table all had their mouths open laughing. He picked up his check, vaguely said good night and walked out. The clock over the cashier's desk said three o'clock. Outside a rowdy scattering of people still milled about Columbus Circle. A smell of rainy pavements mingled with the exhausts of cars and occasionally there was a whiff of wet earth and sprouting grass from the Park. He stood a long time on the corner not knowing which way to go. These nights he hated to go home. He felt vaguely sorry that the Flapper Bandit and her pal had been arrested. He wished they could have escaped. He had looked forward to reading their exploits every day in the papers. Poor devils, he thought. And with a newborn baby too.

Meanwhile a rumpus had started behind him in Child's. He went back and looked through the window across the griddle where sizzled three abandoned buttercakes. The waiters were struggling to eject a tall man in a dress suit. The thickjawed friend of the Jewish girl who had thrown the biscuit was being held back by his friends. Then the bouncer elbowed his way through the crowd. He was a small broadshouldered man with deepset tired monkey eyes. Calmly and without enthusiasm he took hold of the tall man. In a flash he had him shooting through the door. Out on the pavement the tall man looked about him dazedly and tried to straighten his collar. At that moment a policewagon drove up jingling. Two policemen jumped out and quickly arrested three Italians who stood chatting quietly on the corner. Herf and the tall man in the dress suit looked at each other, almost spoke and walked off greatly sobered in opposite directions.

V. The Burthen of Nineveh

Seeping in red twilight out of the Gulf Stream fog, throbbing brassthroat that howls through the stiff-fingered streets, prying open glazed eyes of skyscrapers, splashing red lead on the girdered thighs of the five bridges, teasing caterwauling tugboats into heat under the toppling smoketrees of the harbor.

Spring puckering our mouths, spring giving us gooseflesh grows gigantic out of the droning of sirens, crashes with enormous scaring din through the halted traffic, between attentive frozen tiptoe blocks.

Mr. Densch with the collar of his woolly ulster up round his ears and a big English cap pulled down far over his eyes, walked nervously back and forth on the damp boat deck of the Volendam. He looked out through a drizzly rain at the gray wharfhouses and the waterfront buildings etched against a sky of inconceivable bitterness. A ruined man, a ruined man, he kept whispering to himself. At last the ship's whistle boomed out for the third time. Mr. Densch, his fingers in his ears, stood screened by a lifeboat watching the rift of dirty water between the ship's side and the wharf widen, widen. The deck trembled under his feet as the screws bit into the current. Gray like a photograph the buildings of Manhattan began sliding by. Below decks the band was playing *O Titin-e Titin-e*. Red ferryboats, carferries, tugs, sandscows, lumber-schooners, tramp steamers drifted between him and the steaming towering city that gathered itself into a pyramid and began to sink mistily into the browngreen water of the bay.

Mr. Densch went below to his stateroom. Mrs. Densch in a cloche hat hung with a yellow veil was crying quietly with her head on a basket of fruit. "Dont Serena," he said huskily. "Dont. . . . We like Marienbad. . . . We need a rest. Our position isnt so hopeless. I'll go and send Blackhead a radio. . . . After all it's his stubbornness and rashness that brought the firm to . . . to this. That man thinks he's a king on earth. . . . This'll . . . this'll get under his skin. If curses can kill I'll be a dead man tomorrow." To his surprise he found the gray drawn lines of his face cracking into a smile. Mrs. Densch lifted her head and opened her mouth to speak to him, but the tears got the better of her. He looked at himself in the glass, squared his shoulders and adjusted his cap. "Well Serena," he said with a trace of jauntiness in his voice, "this is the end of my business career. . . . I'll go send that radio."

Mother's face swoops down and kisses him; his hands clutch her dress, and she has gone leaving him in the dark, leaving a frail lingering fragrance in the dark that makes him cry. Little Martin lies tossing within the iron bars of his crib. Outside dark, and beyond walls and outside again the horrible great dark of grownup people, rumbling, jiggling, creeping in chunks through the windows, putting fingers through the crack in the door. From outside above the roar of wheels comes a strangling wail clutching his throat. Pyramids of dark piled above him fall crumpling on top of him. He yells, gagging between yells. Nounou walks towards the crib along a saving gangplank of light. "Dont you be scared . . . that aint nothin." Her black face grins at him, her black hand straightens the covers. "Just a fire engine passin. . . . You wouldn't be sceered of a fire engine."

Ellen leaned back in the taxi and closed her eyes for a second. Not even the bath and the halfhour's nap had washed out the fagging memory of the office, the smell of it, the chirruping of typewriters, the endlessly repeated phrases, faces, typewritten sheets. She felt very tired; she must have rings under her eyes. The taxi had stopped. There was a red light in the traffic tower ahead. Fifth Avenue was jammed to the curbs with taxis, limousines, motorbusses. She was late; she had left her watch at home. The minutes hung about her neck leaden as hours. She sat up on the edge of the seat, her fists so tightly clenched that she could feel through her gloves her sharp nails digging into the palms of her hands. At last the taxi jerked forward, there was a gust of exhausts and whir of motors, the clot of traffic began moving up Murray Hill. At a corner she caught sight of a clock. Quarter of eight. The traffic stopped again, the brakes of the taxi shrieked, she was

thrown forward on the seat. She leaned back with her eyes
closed, the blood throbbing in her temples. All her nerves
were sharp steel jangled wires cutting into her. "What does it
matter?" she kept asking herself. "He'll wait. I'm in no hurry
to see him. Let's see, how many blocks? . . . Less than
twenty, eighteen." It must have been to keep from going
crazy people invented numbers. The multiplication table better than Coué as a cure for jangled nerves. Probably that's
what old Peter Stuyvesant thought, or whoever laid the city
out in numbers. She was smiling to herself. The taxi had
started moving again.

George Baldwin was walking back and forth in the lobby of
the hotel, taking short puffs of a cigarette. Now and then he
glanced at the clock. His whole body was screwed up taut like
a high violinstring. He was hungry and full up with things he
wanted to say; he hated waiting for people. When she walked
in, cool and silky and smiling, he wanted to go up to her and
hit her in the face.

"George do you realize that it's only because numbers are
so cold and emotionless that we're not all crazy?" she said
giving him a little pat on the arm.

"Fortyfive minutes waiting is enough to drive anybody
crazy, that's all I know."

"I must explain it. It's a system. I thought it all up coming
up in the taxi. . . . You go in and order anything you like.
I'm going to the ladies' room a minute. . . . And please have
me a Martini. I'm dead tonight, just dead."

"You poor little thing, of course I will. . . . And dont be
long please."

His knees were weak under him, he felt like melting ice as
he went into the gilt ponderously ornamented diningroom.
Good lord Baldwin you're acting like a hobbledehoy of seventeen . . . after all these years too. Never get anywhere that
way. . . . "Well Joseph what are you going to give us to eat
tonight? I'm hungry. . . . But first you can get Fred to make
the best Martini cocktail he ever made in his life."

"Tres bien monsieur," said the longnosed Roumanian
waiter and handed him the menu with a flourish.

Ellen stayed a long time looking in the mirror, dabbing a
little superfluous powder off her face, trying to make up her

mind. She kept winding up a hypothetical dollself and setting it in various positions. Tiny gestures ensued, acted out on various model stages. Suddenly she turned away from the mirror with a shrug of her toowhite shoulders and hurried to the diningroom.

"Oh George I'm starved, simply starved."

"So am I" he said in a crackling voice. "And Elaine I've got news for you," he went on hurriedly as if he were afraid she'd interrupt him.

"Cecily has consented to a divorce. We're going to rush it through quietly in Paris this summer. Now what I want to know is, will you . . . ?"

She leaned over and patted his hand that grasped the edge of the table. "George lets eat our dinner first. . . . We've got to be sensible. God knows we've messed things up enough in the past both of us. . . . Let's drink to the crime wave." The smooth infinitesimal foam of the cocktail was soothing in her tongue and throat, glowed gradually warmly through her. She looked at him laughing with sparkling eyes. He drank his at a gulp.

"By gad Elaine," he said flaming up helplessly, "you're the most wonderful thing in the world."

Through dinner she felt a gradual icy coldness stealing through her like novocaine. She had made up her mind. It seemed as if she had set the photograph of herself in her own place, forever frozen into a single gesture. An invisible silk band of bitterness was tightening round her throat, strangling. Beyond the plates, the ivory pink lamp, the broken pieces of bread, his face above the blank shirtfront jerked and nodded; the flush grew on his cheeks; his nose caught the light now on one side, now on the other, his taut lips moved eloquently over his yellow teeth. Ellen felt herself sitting with her ankles crossed, rigid as a porcelain figure under her clothes, everything about her seemed to be growing hard and enameled, the air bluestreaked with cigarettesmoke, was turning to glass. His wooden face of a marionette waggled senselessly in front of her. She shuddered and hunched up her shoulders.

"What's the matter, Elaine?" he burst out. She lied:

"Nothing George. . . . Somebody walked over my grave I guess."

"Couldnt I get you a wrap or something?"

She shook her head.

"Well what about it?" he said as they got up from the table.

"What?" she asked smiling. "After Paris?"

"I guess I can stand it if you can George," she said quietly.

He was waiting for her, standing at the open door of a taxi. She saw him poised spry against the darkness in a tan felt hat and a light tan overcoat, smiling like some celebrity in the rotogravure section of a Sunday paper. Mechanically she squeezed the hand that helped her into the cab.

"Elaine," he said shakily, "life's going to mean something to me now. . . . God if you knew how empty life had been for so many years. I've been like a tin mechanical toy, all hollow inside."

"Let's not talk about mechanical toys," she said in a strangled voice.

"No let's talk about our happiness," he shouted.

Inexorably his lips closed on to hers. Beyond the shaking glass window of the taxi, like someone drowning, she saw out of a corner of an eye whirling faces, streetlights, zooming nickelglinting wheels.

The old man in the checked cap sits on the brownstone stoop with his face in his hands. With the glare of Broadway in their backs there is a continual flickering of people past him towards the theaters down the street. The old man is sobbing through his fingers in a sour reek of gin. Once in a while he raises his head and shouts hoarsely, "I cant, dont you see I cant?" The voice is inhuman like the splitting of a plank. Footsteps quicken. Middleaged people look the other way. Two girls giggle shrilly as they look at him. Streeturchins nudging each other peer in and out through the dark crowd. "Bum Hootch." "He'll get his when the cop on the block comes by." "Prohibition liquor." The old man lifts his wet face out of his hands, staring out of sightless bloodyrimmed eyes. People back off, step on the feet of the people behind them. Like splintering wood the voice comes out of him. "Don't you see I cant . . . ? I cant . . . I cant."

When Alice Sheffield dropped into the stream of women

going through the doors of Lord & Taylor's and felt the close smell of stuffs in her nostrils something went click in her head. First she went to the glovecounter. The girl was very young and had long curved black lashes and a pretty smile; they talked of permanent waves while Alice tried on gray kids, white kids with a little fringe like a gauntlet. Before she tried it on, the girl deftly powdered the inside of each glove out of a longnecked wooden shaker. Alice ordered six pairs.

"Yes, Mrs. Roy Sheffield. . . . Yes I have a charge account, here's my card. . . . I'll be having quite a lot of things sent." And to herself she said all the while: Ridiculous how I've been going round in rags all winter. . . . When the bill comes Roy'll have to find some way of paying it that's all. Time he stopped mooning round anyway. I've paid enough bills for him in my time, God knows." Then she started looking at fleshcolored silk stockings. She left the store her head still in a whirl of long vistas of counters in a violet electric haze, of braided embroidery and tassels and nasturtiumtinted silks; she had ordered two summer dresses and an evening wrap.

At Maillard's she met a tall blond Englishman with a coneshaped head and pointed wisps of towcolored mustaches under his long nose.

"Oh Buck I'm having the grandest time. I've been going berserk in Lord & Taylor's. Do you know that it must be a year and a half since I've bought any clothes?"

"Poor old thing," he said as he motioned her to a table. "Tell me about it."

She let herself flop into a chair suddenly whimpering, "Oh Buck I'm so tired of it all. . . . I dont know how much longer I can stand it."

"Well you cant blame me. . . . You know what I want you to do. . . ."

"Well suppose I did?"

"It'd be topping, we'd hit it off like anything. . . . But you must have a bit of beef tea or something. You need picking up." She giggled. "You old dear that's just what I do need."

"Well how about making tracks for Calgary? I know a fellow there who'll give me a job I think."

"Oh let's go right away. I dont care about clothes or anything. . . . Roy can send those things back to Lord & Taylor's. . . . Got any money Buck?"

A flush started on his cheekbones and spread over his temples to his flat irregular ears. "I confess, Al darling, that I havent a penny. I can pay for lunch."

"Oh hell I'll cash a check; the account's in both our names."

"They'll cash it for me at the Biltmore, they know me there. When we get to Canada everything will be quite all right I can assure you. In His Majesty's Dominion, the name of Buckminster has rather more weight than in the U.S."

"Oh I know darling, it's nothing but money in New York."

When they were walking up Fifth Avenue she hooked her arm in his suddenly. "O Buck I have the most horrible thing to tell you. It made me deathly ill. . . . You know what I told you about the awful smell we had in the apartment we thought was rats? This morning I met the woman who lives on the ground floor. . . . O it makes me sick to think of it. Her face was green as that bus. . . . It seems they've been having the plumbing examined by an inspector. . . . They arrested the woman upstairs. O it's too disgusting. I cant tell you about it. . . . I'll never go back there. I'd die if I did. . . . There wasnt a drop of water in the house all day yesterday."

"What was the matter?"

"It's too horrible."

"Tell it to popper."

"Buck they wont know you when you get back home to Orpen Manor."

"But what was it?"

"There was a woman upstairs who did illegal operations, abortions. . . . That was what stopped up the plumbing."

"Good God."

"Somehow that's the last straw. . . . And Roy sitting limp over his damn paper in the middle of that stench with that horrible adenoid expression on his face."

"Poor little girl."

"But Buck I couldn't cash a check for more than two hundred. . . . It'll be an overdraft as it is. Will that get us to Calgary?"

"Not very comfortably. . . . There's a man I know in Montreal who'll give me a job writing society notes. . . . Beastly thing to do, but I can use an assumed name. Then we can trot along from there when we get a little more spondulix as you call it. . . . How about cashing that check now?"

She stood waiting for him beside the information desk while he went to get the tickets. She felt alone and tiny in the middle of the great white vault of the station. All her life with Roy was going by her like a movie reeled off backwards, faster and faster. Buck came back looking happy and masterful, his hands full of greenbacks and railway tickets. "No train till seven ten Al," he said. "Suppose you go to the Palace and leave me a seat at the boxoffice. . . . I'll run up and fetch my kit. Wont take a sec. . . . Here's a fiver." And he had gone, and she was walking alone across Fortythird Street on a hot May afternoon. For some reason she began to cry. People stared at her; she couldnt help it. She walked on doggedly with the tears streaming down her face.

"Earthquake insurance, that's what they calls it! A whole lot of good it'll do 'em when the anger of the Lord smokes out the city like you would a hornet's nest and he picks it up and shakes it like a cat shakes a rat. . . . Earthquake insurance!"

Joe and Skinny wished that the man with whiskers like a bottlecleaner who stood over their campfire mumbling and shouting would go away. They didn't know whether he was talking to them or to himself. They pretended he wasnt there and went on nervously preparing to grill a piece of ham on a gridiron made of an old umbrellaframe. Below them beyond a sulphurgreen lace of budding trees was the Hudson going silver with evening and the white palisade of apartmenthouses of upper Manhattan.

"Dont say nutten," whispered Joe, making a swift cranking motion in the region of his ear. "He's nuts."

Skinny had gooseflesh down the back, he felt his lips getting cold, he wanted to run.

"That ham?" Suddenly the man addressed them in apurring benevolent voice.

"Yessir," said Joe shakily after a pause.

"Dont you know that the Lord God forbad his chillun to eat the flesh of swine?" His voice went to its singsong mumbling and shouting. "Gabriel, Brother Gabriel . . . is it all right for these kids to eat ham? . . . Sure. The angel Gabriel, he's a good frien o mine see, he said it's all right this once if you dont do it no more. . . . Look out brother you'll burn it." Skinny had got to his feet. "Sit down brother. I wont hurt you. I understand kids. We like kids me an the Lord God. . . . Scared of me cause I'm a tramp aint you? Well lemme tell you somethin, dont you never be afraid of a tramp. Tramps wont hurt ye, they're good people. The Lord God was a tramp when he lived on earth. My buddy the angel Gabriel says he's been a tramp many a time. . . . Look I got some fried chicken an old colored woman gave me. . . . O Lordy me!" groaning he sat down on a rock beside the two boys.

"We was goin to play injuns, but now I guess we'll play tramps," said Joe warming up a little. The tramp brought a newspaper package out of the formless pocket of his weathergreened coat and began unwrapping it carefully. A good smell began to come from the sizzling ham. Skinny sat down again, still keeping as far away as he could without missing anything. The tramp divided up his chicken and they began to eat together.

"Gabriel old scout will you just look at that?" The tramp started his singsong shouting that made the boys feel scared again. It was beginning to get dark. The tramp was shouting with his mouth full pointing with a drumstick towards the flickering checkerboard of lights going on up Riverside Drive. "Juss set here a minute an look at her Gabriel. . . . Look at the old bitch if you'll pardon the expression. Earthquake insurance, gosh they need it dont they? Do you know how long God took to destroy the tower of Babel, folks? Seven minutes. Do you know how long the Lord God took to destroy Babylon and Nineveh? Seven minutes. There's more wickedness in one block in New York City than there was in a square mile in Nineveh, and how long do you think the Lord God of Sabboath will take to destroy New York City an Brooklyn an the Bronx? Seven seconds. Seven seconds. . . . Say kiddo what's your name?" He dropped into his low purring voice and made a pass at Joe with his drumstick.

"Joseph Cameron Parker. . . . We live in Union."

"An what's yours?"

"Antonio Camerone . . . de guys call me Skinny. Dis guy's my cousin. His folks dey changed deir name to Parker, see?"

"Changing your name wont do no good . . . they got all the aliases down in the judgment book. . . . And verily I say unto you the Lord's day is at hand. . . . It was only yesterday that Gabriel says to me 'Well Jonah, shall we let her rip?' an I says to him, 'Gabriel ole scout think of the women and children an the little babies that dont know no better. If you shake it down with an earthquake an fire an brimstone from heaven they'll all be killed same as the rich people an sinners,' and he says to me, 'All right Jonah old horse, have it your own way. . . . We wont foreclose on em for a week or two.' . . . But it's terrible to think of, folks, the fire an brimstone an the earthquake an the tidal wave an the tall buildings crashing together."

Joe suddenly slapped Skinny on the back. "You're it," he said and ran off. Skinny followed him stumbling along the narrow path among the bushes. He caught up to him on the asphalt. "Jez, that guy's nuts," he called.

"Shut up cant ye?" snapped Joe. He was peering back through the bushes. They could still see the thin smoke of their little fire against the sky. The tramp was out of sight. They could just hear his voice calling, "Gabriel, Gabriel." They ran on breathless towards the regularly spaced safe arclights and the street.

Jimmy Herf stepped out from in front of the truck; the mudguard just grazed the skirt of his raincoat. He stood a moment behind an L stanchion while the icicle thawed out of his spine. The door of a limousine suddenly opened in front of him and he heard a familiar voice that he couldnt place.

"Jump in Meester 'Erf. . . . Can I take you somewhere?" As he stepped in mechanically he noticed that he was stepping into a Rolls-Royce.

The stout redfaced man in a derby hat was Congo. "Sit down Meester 'Erf. . . . Very pleas' to see you. Where were you going?"

"I wasnt going anywhere in particular." "Come up to the house, I want to show you someting. Ow are you today?"

"Oh fine; no I mean I'm in a rotten mess, but it's all the same."

"Tomorrow maybe I go to jail . . . six mont' . . . but maybe not." Congo laughed in his throat and straightened carefully his artificial leg.

"So they've nailed you at last, Congo?"

"Conspiracy. . . . But no more Congo Jake, Meester 'Erf. Call me Armand. I'm married now; Armand Duval, Park Avenue."

"How about the Marquis des Coulommiers?"

"That's just for the trade."

"So things look pretty good do they?"

Congo nodded. "If I go to Atlanta which I 'ope not, in six mont' I come out of jail a millionaire. . . . Meester 'Erf if you need money, juss say the word. . . . I lend you tousand dollars. In five years even you pay it back. I know you."

"Thanks, it's not exactly money I need, that's the hell of it."

"How's your wife? . . . She's so beautiful."

"We're getting a divorce. . . . She served the papers on me this morning. . . . That's all I was waiting in this goddam town for."

Congo bit his lips. Then he tapped Jimmy gently on the knee with his forefinger. "In a minute we'll get to the 'ouse. . . . I give you one very good drink. . . . Yes wait," Congo shouted to the chauffeur as he walked with a stately limp, leaning on a goldknobbed cane, into the streaky marble hallway of the apartmenthouse. As they went up in the elevator he said, "Maybe you stay to dinner." "I'm afraid I cant tonight, Con . . . Armand."

"I have one very good cook. . . . When I first come to New York maybe twenty years ago, there was a feller on the boat. . . . This is the door, see A. D., Armand Duval. Him and me ran away togedder an always he say to me, 'Armand you never make a success, too lazy, run after the leetle girls too much.' . . . Now he's my cook . . . first class chef, cordon bleu, eh? Life is one funny ting, Meester 'Erf."

"Gee this is fine," said Jimmy Herf leaning back in a highbacked Spanish chair in the blackwalnut library with a glass of old Bourbon in his hand. "Congo . . . I mean Armand, if I'd been God and had to decide who in this city should make a million dollars and who shouldnt I swear you're the man I should have picked."

"Maybe by and by the misses come in. Very pretty I show you." He made curly motions with his fingers round his head. "Very much blond hair." Suddenly he frowned. "But Meester 'Erf, if dere is anything any time I can do for you, money or like dat, you let me know eh? It's ten years now you and me very good frien. . . . One more drink?"

On his third glass of Bourbon Herf began to talk. Congo sat listening with his heavy lips a little open, occasionally nodding his head. "The difference between you and me is that you're going up in the social scale, Armand, and I'm going down. . . . When you were a messboy on a steamboat I was a horrid little chalkyfaced kid living at the Ritz. My mother and father did all this Vermont marble blackwalnut grand Babylonian stuff . . . there's nothing more for me to do about it. . . . Women are like rats, you know, they leave a sinking ship. She's going to marry this man Baldwin who's just been appointed District Attorney. They're said to be grooming him for mayor on a fusion reform ticket. . . . The delusion of power, that's what's biting him. Women fall for it like hell. If I thought it'd be any good to me I swear I've got the energy to sit up and make a million dollars. But I get no organic sensation out of that stuff any more. I've got to have something new, different. . . . Your sons'll be like that Congo. . . . If I'd had a decent education and started soon enough I might have been a great scientist. If I'd been a little more highly sexed I might have been an artist or gone in for religion. . . . But here I am by Jesus Christ almost thirty years old and very anxious to live. . . . If I were sufficiently romantic I suppose I'd have killed myself long ago just to make people talk about me. I havent even got the conviction to make a successful drunkard."

"Looks like," said Congo filling the little glasses again with a slow smile, "Meester 'Erf you tink too much."

"Of course I do Congo, of course I do, but what the hell am I going to do about it?"

"Well when you need a little money remember Armand Duval. . . . Want a chaser?"

Herf shook his head. "I've got to chase myself. . . . So long Armand."

In the colonnaded marble hall he ran into Nevada Jones. She was wearing orchids. "Hullo Nevada, what are you doing in this palace of sin?"

"I live here, what do you think? . . . I married a friend of yours the other day, Armand Duval. Want to come up and see him?"

"Just been. . . . He's a good scout."

"He sure is."

"What did you do with little Tony Hunter?"

She came close to him and spoke in a low voice. "Just forget about me and him will you? . . . Gawd the boy's breath'd knock you down. . . . Tony's one of God's mistakes, I'm through with him. . . . Found him chewing the edges of the rug rolling on the floor of the dressing room one day because he was afraid he was going to be unfaithful to me with an acrobat. . . . I told him he'd better go and be it and we busted up right there. . . . But honest I'm out for connubial bliss this time, right on the level, so for God's sake dont let anybody spring anything about Tony or about Baldwin either on Armand . . . though he knows he wasnt hitching up to any plaster virgin. . . . Why dont you come up and eat with us?"

"I cant. Good luck Nevada." The whisky warm in his stomach, tingling in his fingers, Jimmy Herf stepped out into seven o'clock Park Avenue, whirring with taxicabs, streaked with smells of gasoline and restaurants and twilight.

It was the first evening James Merivale had gone to the Metropolitan Club since he had been put up for it; he had been afraid, that like carrying a cane, it was a little old for him. He sat in a deep leather chair by a window smoking a thirtyfive cent cigar with the *Wall Street Journal* on his knee and a copy of the *Cosmopolitan* leaning against his right thigh and, with his eyes on the night flawed with lights like a crystal, he abandoned himself to reverie: Economic Depression. . . . Ten million dollars. . . . After the war slump. Some smash I'll tell the world. BLACKHEAD & DENSCH FAIL FOR $10,000,000. . . . Densch left the country some days ago. . . . Blackhead incommunicado in his home at Great Neck. One of the oldest and most respected import and export firms in New York, $10,000,000. *O it's always fair weather When good fellows get together.* That's the thing about banking. Even in a deficit there's money to be handled, collateral. These commercial propositions always entail a margin of risk. We get 'em coming or else we get 'em going, eh Merivale? That's what old Perkins said when Cunningham mixed him that Jack Rose. . . . *With a stein on the tabul And a good song ri-i-inging clear.* Good connection that feller. Maisie knew what she was doing after all. . . . A man in a position like that's always likely to be blackmailed. A fool not to prosecute. . . . Girl's crazy he said, married to another man of the same name. . . . Ought to be in a sanitarium, a case like that. God I'd have dusted his hide for him. Circumstances exonerated him completely, even mother admitted that. *O Sinbad was in bad in Tokio and Rome* . . . that's what Jerry used to sing. Poor old Jerry never had the feeling of being in good right in on the ground floor of the Metropolitan Club. . . . Comes of poor stock. Take Jimmy now . . . hasnt even that excuse, an out and out failure, a misfit from way back. . . . Guess old man Herf was pretty wild, a yachtsman. Used to hear mother say Aunt Lily had to put up with a whole lot. Still he might have made something of himself with all his advantages . . . dreamer, wanderlust . . . Greenwich Village stuff. And dad did every bit as much for him as he did for me. . . . And this divorce now. Adultery . . . with a prostitute like as not. Probably had syphilis or something. Ten Million Dollar Failure.

Failure. Success.

Ten Million Dollar Success. . . . Ten Years of Successful Banking. . . . At the dinner of the American Bankers Association last night James Merivale, president of the Bank & Trust Company, spoke in answer to the toast 'Ten Years of Progressive Banking.' . . . Reminds me gentlemen of the old darky who was very fond of chicken. . . . But if you will allow me a few serious words on this festive occasion (flashlight photograph) there is a warning note I should like to sound . . . feel it my duty as an American citizen, as president of a great institution of nationwide, international in the better sense, nay, universal contacts and loyalties (flashlight photograph). . . . At last making himself heard above the thunderous applause James Merivale, his stately steelgray head shaking with emotion, continued his speech. . . . Gentlemen you do me too much honor. . . . Let me only add that in all trials and tribulations, becalmed amid the dark waters of scorn or spurning the swift rapids of popular estimation, amid the still small hours of the night, and in the roar of millions at noonday, my staff, my bread of life, my inspiration has been my triune loyalty to my wife, my mother, and my flag.

The long ash from his cigar had broken and fallen on his knees. James Merivale got to his feet and gravely brushed the light ash off his trousers. Then he settled down again and with an intent frown began to read the article on Foreign Exchange in the *Wall Street Journal*.

They sit up on two stools in the lunchwaggon.

"Say kid how the hell did you come to sign up on that old scow?"

"Wasnt anything else going out east."

"Well you sure have dished your gravy this time kid, cap'n 's a dopehead, first officer's the damnedest crook out o Sing Sing, crew's a lot o bohunks, the ole tub aint worth the salvage of her. . . . What was your last job?"

"Night clerk in a hotel."

"Listen to that cookey . . . Jesus Kerist Amighty look at a guy who'll give up a good job clerkin in a swell hotel in Noo York City to sign on as messboy on Davy Jones' own steam yacht. . . . A fine seacook you're goin to make." The younger man is flushing. "How about that Hamburgher?" he shouts at the counterman.

After they have eaten, while they are finishing their coffee, he turns to his friend and asks in a low voice, "Say Rooney was you ever overseas . . . in the war?"

"I made Saint Nazaire a couple o times. Why?"

"I dunno. . . . It kinder gave me the itch. . . . I was two years in it. Things aint been the same. I used to think all I wanted was to get a good job an marry an settle down, an now I dont give a damn. . . . I can keep a job for six months or so an then I get the almighty itch, see? So I thought I ought to see the orient a bit. . . ."

"Never you mind," says Rooney shaking his head. "You're goin to see it, dont you worry about that."

"What's the damage?" the young man asks the counter-man.

"They must a caught you young."

"I was sixteen when I enlisted." He picks up his change and follows Rooney's broad shambling back into the street. At the end of the street, beyond trucks and the roofs of ware-houses, he can see masts and the smoke of steamers and white steam rising into the sunlight.

"Pull down the shade," comes the man's voice from the bed.

"I cant, it's busted. . . . Oh hell, here's the whole business down." Anna almost bursts out crying when the roll hits her in the face. "You fix it," she says going towards the bed.

"What do I care, they cant see in," says the man catching hold of her laughing.

"It's just those lights," she moans, wearily letting herself go limp in his arms.

It is a small room the shape of a shoebox with an iron bed in the corner of the wall opposite the window. A roar of streets rises to it rattling up a V shaped recess in the building. On the ceiling she can see the changing glow of electric signs along Broadway, white, red, green, then a jumble like a bub-ble bursting, and again white, red, green.

"Oh Dick I wish you'd fix that shade, those lights give me the willies."

"The lights are all right Anna, it's like bein in a theater. . . . It's the Gay White Way, like they used to say."

"That stuff's all right for you out of town fellers, but it gives me the willies."

"So you're workin for Madame Soubrine now are you Anna?"

"You mean I'm scabbin. . . . I know it. The old woman trew me out an it was get a job or croak. . . ."

"A nice girl like you Anna could always find a boyfriend."

"God you buyers are a dirty lot. . . . You think that be-cause I'll go with you, I'd go wid anybody. . . . Well I wouldnt, do you get that?"

"I didnt mean that Anna. . . . Gee you're awful quick tonight."

"I guess it's my nerves. . . . This strike an the old woman trowin me out an scabbin up at Soubrine's . . . it'd get anybody's goat. They can all go to hell for all I care. Why wont they leave you alone? I never did nothin to hurt anybody in my life. All I want is for em to leave me alone an let me get my pay an have a good time now and then. . . . God Dick it's terrible. . . . I dont dare go out on the street for fear of meetin some of the girls of my old local."

"Hell Anna, things aint so bad, honest I'd take you West with me if it wasnt for my wife."

Anna's voice goes on in an even whimper, "An now 'cause I take a shine to you and want to give you a good time you call me a goddam whore."

"I didnt say no such thing. I didnt even think it. All I thought was that you was a dead game sport and not a kewpie above the ears like most of 'em. . . . Look if it'll make you feel better I'll try an fix that shade."

Lying on her side she watches his heavy body move against the milky light of the window. At last his teeth chattering he comes back to her. "I cant fix the goddam thing. . . . Kerist it's cold."

"Never mind Dick, come on to bed. . . . It must be late. I got to be up there at eight."

He pulls his watch from under the pillow. "It's half after two. . . . Hello kitten."

On the ceiling she can see reflected the changing glare of the electric signs, white, red, green, then a jumble like a bubble bursting, then again white, green, red.

"An he didn't even invite me to the wedding. . . . Honestly Florence I could have forgiven him if he'd invited me to the wedding," she said to the colored maid when she brought in the coffee. It was a Sunday morning. She was sitting up in bed with the papers spread over her lap. She was looking at a photograph in a rotogravure section labeled Mr. and Mrs. Jack Cunningham Hop Off for the First Lap of Their Honeymoon on his Sensational Seaplane Albatross VII. "He looks handsome dont he?"

"He su' is miss. . . . But wasn't there anything you could do to stop 'em, miss?"

"Not a thing. . . . You see he said he'd have me committed to an asylum if I tried. . . . He knows perfectly well a Yucatan divorce isn't legal."

Florence sighed.

"Menfolks su' do dirt to us poor girls."

"Oh this wont last long. You can see by her face she's a nasty selfish spoiled little girl. . . . And I'm his real wife before God and man. Lord knows I tried to warn her. Whom God has joined let no man put asunder . . . that's in the Bible isnt it? . . . Florence this coffee is simply terrible this morning. I cant drink it. You go right out and make me some fresh."

Frowning and hunching her shoulders Florence went out the door with the tray.

Mrs. Cunningham heaved a deep sigh and settled herself among the pillows. Outside churchbells were ringing. "Oh Jack you darling I love you just the same," she said to the picture. Then she kissed it. "Listen, deary the churchbells sounded like that the day we ran away from the High School Prom and got married in Milwaukee. . . . It was a lovely Sunday morning." Then she stared in the face of the second Mrs. Cunningham. "Oh you," she said and poked her finger through it.

When she got to her feet she found that the courtroom was very slowly sickeningly going round and round; the white fishfaced judge with noseglasses, faces, cops, uniformed attendants, gray windows, yellow desks, all going round and round in the sickening close smell, her lawyer with his white hawk nose, wiping his bald head, frowning, going round and round until she thought she would throw up. She couldn't hear a word that was said, she kept blinking to get the blur out of her ears. She could feel Dutch behind her hunched up with his head in his hands. She didnt dare look back. Then after hours everything was sharp and clear, very far away. The judge was shouting at her, from the small end of a funnel his colorless lips moving in and out like the mouth of a fish.

". . . And now as a man and a citizen of this great city I want to say a few words to the defendants. Briefly this sort of thing has got to stop. The unalienable rights of human life and property the great men who founded this republic laid down in the constitootion have got to be reinstated. It is the dooty of every man in office and out of office to combat this wave of lawlessness by every means in his power. Therefore in spite of what those sentimental newspaper writers who corrupt the public mind and put into the head of weaklings and misfits of your sort the idea that you can buck the law of God and man, and private property, that you can wrench by force from peaceful citizens what they have earned by hard work and brains . . . and get away with it; in spite of what these journalistic hacks and quacks would call extentuating circumstances I am going to impose on you two highwaymen the maximum severity of the law. It is high time an example was made. . . ."

The judge took a drink of water. Francie could see the little beads of sweat standing out from the pores of his nose.

"It is high time an example was made," the judge shouted. "Not that I dont feel as a tender and loving father the misfortunes, the lack of education and ideels, the lack of a loving home and tender care of a mother that has led this young woman into a life of immorality and misery, led away by the temptations of cruel and voracious men and the excitement and wickedness of what has been too well named, the jazz age. Yet at the moment when these thoughts are about to temper with mercy the stern anger of the law, the importunate recollection rises of other young girls, perhaps hundreds of them at this moment in this great city about to fall into the clutches of a brutal and unscrupulous temper like this man Robertson . . . for him and his ilk there is no punishment sufficiently severe . . . and I remember that mercy misplaced is often cruelty in the long run. All we can do is shed a tear for erring womanhood and breathe a prayer for the innocent babe that this unfortunate girl has brought into the world as the fruit of her shame. . . ."

Francie felt a cold tingling that began at her fingertips and ran up her arms into the blurred whirling nausea of her body. "Twenty years," she could hear the whisper round the court, they all seemed licking their lips whispering softly "Twenty years." "I guess I'm going to faint," she said to herself as if to a friend. Everything went crashing black.

*

Propped with five pillows in the middle of his wide colonial mahogany bed with pineapples on the posts Phineas P. Blackhead his face purple as his silk dressing gown sat up and cursed. The big mahogany-finished bedroom hung with Javanese print cloth instead of wallpaper was empty except for a Hindu servant in a white jacket and turban who stood at the foot of the bed, with his hands at his sides, now and then bowing his head at a louder gust of cursing and saying "Yes, Sahib, yes, Sahib."

"By the living almighty Jingo you goddam yellow Babu bring me that whiskey, or I'll get up and break every bone in your body, do you hear, Jesus God cant I be obeyed in my own house? When I say whiskey I mean rye not orange juice. Damnation. Here take it!" He picked up a cutglass pitcher off the nighttable and slung it at the Hindu. Then he sank back on the pillows, saliva bubbling on his lips, choking for breath.

Silently the Hindu mopped up the thick Beluchistan rug and slunk out of the room with a pile of broken glass in his hand. Blackhead was breathing more easily, his eyes sank into their deep sockets and were lost in the folds of sagged green lids.

He seemed asleep when Gladys came in wearing a raincoat with a wet umbrella in her hand. She tiptoed to the window and stood looking out at the gray rainy street and the old tomblike brownstone houses opposite. For a splinter of a second she was a little girl come in her nightgown to have Sunday morning breakfast with daddy in his big bed.

He woke up with a start, looked about him with bloodshot eyes, the heavy muscles of his jowl tightening under the ghastly purplish skin.

"Well Gladys where's that rye whiskey I ordered?"

"Oh daddy you know what Dr. Thom said."

"He said it'd kill me if I took another drink. . . . Well I'm not dead yet am I? He's a damned ass."

"Oh but you must take care of yourself and not get all excited." She kissed him and put a cool slim hand on his forehead.

"Havent I got reason to get excited? If I had my hands on that dirty lilylivered bastard's neck. . . . We'd have pulled through if he hadnt lost his nerve. Serve me right for taking such a yellow sop into partnership. . . . Twentyfive, thirty years of work all gone to hell in ten minutes. . . . For twenty-five years my word's been as good as a banknote. Best thing for me to do's to follow the firm to Tophet, to hell with me. And by the living Jingo you, my own flesh, tell me not to drink. . . . God almighty. Hay Bob . . . Bob. . . . Where's that goddam officeboy gone? Hay come here one of you sons of bitches, what do you think I pay you for?"

A nurse put her head in the door.

"Get out of here," shouted Blackhead, "none of your starched virgins around me." He threw the pillow from under his head. The nurse disappeared. The pillow hit one of the posts and bounced back on the bed. Gladys began to cry.

"Oh daddy I cant stand it . . . and everybody always respected you so. . . . Do try to control yourself, daddy dear."

"And why should I for Christ's sake . . . ? Show's over, why dont you laugh? Curtain's down. It's all a joke, a smutty joke."

He began to laugh deliriously, then he was choking, fighting for breath with clenched fists again. At length he said in a broken voice, "Don't you see that it's only the whiskey that was keeping me going? Go away and leave me Gladys and send that damned Hindu to me. I've always liked you better than anything in the world. . . . You know that. Quick tell him to bring me what I ordered."

Gladys went out crying. Outside her husband was pacing up and down the hall. "It's those damned reporters . . . I dont know what to tell 'em. They say the creditors want to prosecute."

"Mrs. Gaston," interrupted the nurse, "I'm afraid you'll have to get male nurses. . . . Really I cant do anything with him. . . ." On the lower floor a telephone was ringing, ringing.

When the Hindu brought the bottle of whiskey Blackhead filled a highball glass and took a deep gulp of it.

"Ah that makes you feel better, by the living Jingo it does. Achmet you're a good fellow. . . . Well I guess we'll have to face the music and sell out. . . . Thank God Gladys is settled. I'll sell out every goddam thing I've got. I wish that precious son-in-law wasnt such a simp. Always my luck to be surrounded by a lot of capons. . . . By gad I'd just as soon go to jail if it'll do em any good; why not? it's all in a lifetime. And afterwards when I come out I'll get a job as a bargeman or watchman on a wharf. I'd like that. Why not take it easy after tearing things up all my life, eh Achmet?"

"Yes Sahib," said the Hindu with a bow.

Blackhead mimicked him, "Yes Sahib. . . . You always say yes, Achmet, isn't that funny?" He began to laugh with a choked rattling laugh. "I guess that's the easiest way." He laughed and laughed, then suddenly he couldnt laugh any more. A perking spasm went through all his limbs. He twisted his mouth in an effort to speak. For a second his eyes looked about the room, the eyes of a little child that has been hurt before it begins to cry, until he fell back limp, his open mouth biting at his shoulder. Achmet looked at him coolly for a long time then he went up to him and spat in his face. Immediately he took a handkerchief out of the pocket of his linen jacket and wiped the spittle off the taut ivory skin. Then he closed the mouth and propped the body among the pillows and walked softly out of the room. In the hall Gladys sat in a big chair reading a magazine. "Sahib much better, he sleep a little bit maybe."

"Oh Achmet I'm so glad," she said and looked back to her magazine.

Ellen got off the bus at the corner of Fifth Avenue and Fiftythird Street. Rosy twilight was gushing out of the brilliant west, glittered in brass and nickel, on buttons, in people's eyes. All the windows on the east side of the avenue were aflame. As she stood with set teeth on the curb waiting to cross, a frail tendril of fragrance brushed her face. A skinny lad with towhair stringy under a foreignlooking cap was offering her arbutus in a basket. She bought a bunch and pressed her nose in it. May woods melted like sugar against her palate.

The whistle blew, gears ground as cars started to pour out of the side streets, the crossing thronged with people. Ellen felt the lad brush against her as he crossed at her side. She shrank away. Through the smell of the arbutus she caught for a second the unwashed smell of his body, the smell of immigrants, of Ellis Island, of crowded tenements. Under all the nickelplated, goldplated streets enameled with May, uneasily she could feel the huddling smell, spreading in dark slow crouching masses like corruption oozing from broken sewers, like a mob. She walked briskly down the cross-street. She went in a door beside a small immaculately polished brass plate.

MADAME SOUBRINE

ROBES

She forgot everything in the catlike smile of Madame Soubrine herself, a stout blackhaired perhaps Russian woman who came out to her from behind a curtain with outstretched arms, while other customers waiting on sofas in a sort of Empress Josephine parlor, looked on enviously.

"My dear Mrs. Herf, where have you been? We've had your dress for a week," she exclaimed in too perfect English. "Ah my dear, you wait . . . it's magnificent. . . . And how is Mr. Harrpiscourt?"

"I've been very busy. . . . You see I'm giving up my job."

Madame Soubrine nodded and blinked knowingly and led the way through the tapestry curtains into the back of the shop.

"Ah ça se voit. . . . Il ne faut pas trravailler, on peut voir dejà des toutes petites rrides. Mais ils dispareaitront. Forgive me, dear." The thick arm round her waist squeezed her. Ellen edged off a little. . . . "Vous la femme la plus belle de New Yorrk. . . . Angelica Mrs. Herf's evening dress," she shouted in a shrill grating voice like a guineahen's.

A hollowcheeked washedout blond girl came in with the dress on a hanger. Ellen slipped off her gray tailored walking-suit. Madame Soubrine circled round her, purring. "Angelica look at those shoulders, the color of the hair. . . . Ah c'est le rêve," edging a little too near like a cat that wants its back rubbed. The dress was pale green with a slash of scarlet and dark blue.

"This is the last time I have a dress like this, I'm sick of always wearing blue and green. . . ." Madame Soubrine, her mouth full of pins, was at her feet, fussing with the hem.

"Perfect Greek simplicity, wellgirdled like Diana. . . . Spiritual with Spring . . . the ultimate restraint of an Annette

Kellermann, holding up the lamp of liberty, the wise virgin," she was muttering through her pins.

She's right, Ellen was thinking, I am getting a hard look. She was looking at herself in the tall pierglass. Then my figure'll go, the menopause haunting beauty parlors, packed in boncilla, having your face raised.

"Regardez-moi ça, cherrie;" said the dressmaker getting to her feet and taking the pins out of her mouth "C'est le chef-dœuvre de la maison Soubrine."

Ellen suddenly felt hot, tangled in some prickly web, a horrible stuffiness of dyed silks and crêpes and muslins was making her head ache; she was anxious to be out on the street again.

"I smell smoke, there's something the matter," the blond girl suddenly cried out. "Sh-sh-sh," hissed Madame Soubrine. They both disappeared through a mirrorcovered door.

Under a skylight in the back room of Soubrine's Anna Cohen sits sewing the trimming on a dress with swift tiny stitches. On the table in front of her a great pile of tulle rises full of light like beaten white of egg. *Charley my boy, Oh Charley my boy*, she hums, stitching the future with swift tiny stitches. If Elmer wants to marry me we might as well; poor Elmer, he's a nice boy but so dreamy. Funny he'd fall for a girl like me. He'll grow out of it, or maybe in the Revolution, he'll be a great man. . . . Have to cut out parties when I'm Elmer's wife. But maybe we can save up money and open a little store on Avenue A in a good location, make better money there than uptown. La Parisienne, Modes.

I bet I could do as good as that old bitch. If you was your own boss there wouldn't be this fightin about strikers and scabs. . . . Equal Opportunity for All. Elmer says that's all applesauce. No hope for the workers but in the Revolution. *Oh I'm juss wild about Harree, And Harry's juss wild about me*. . . . Elmer in a telephone central in a dinnercoat, with eartabs, tall as Valentino, strong as Doug. The Revolution is declared. The Red Guard is marching up Fifth Avenue. Anna in golden curls with a little kitten under her arm leans with him out of the tallest window. White tumbler pigeons flutter against the city below them. Fifth Avenue bleeding red flags, glittering with marching bands, hoarse voices singing Die

Rote Fahne in Yiddish; far away, from the Woolworth a banner shakes into the wind. 'Look Elmer darling' ELMER DUSKIN FOR MAYOR. And they're dancing the Charleston in all the officebuildings. . . . *Thump. Thump. That Charleston dance.* . . . *Thump. Thump.* . . . Perhaps I do love him. Elmer take me. Elmer, loving as Valentino, crushing me to him with Dougstrong arms, hot as flame, Elmer.

Through the dream she is stitching white fingers beckon. The white tulle shines too bright. Red hands clutch suddenly out of the tulle, she cant fight off the red tulle all round her biting into her, coiled about her head. The skylight's blackened with swirling smoke. The room's full of smoke and screaming. Anna is on her feet whirling round fighting with her hands the burning tulle all round her.

Ellen stands looking at herself in the pierglass in the fitting room. The smell of singed fabrics gets stronger. After walking to and fro nervously a little while she goes through the glass door, down a passage hung with dresses, ducks under a cloud of smoke, and sees through streaming eyes the big workroom, screaming girls huddling behind Madame Soubrine, who is pointing a chemical extinguisher at charred piles of goods about a table. They are picking something moaning out of the charred goods. Out of the corner of her eye she sees an arm in shreds, a seared black red face, a horrible naked head.

"Oh Mrs. Herf, please tell them in front it's nothing, absolutely nothing. . . . I'll be there at once," Madame Soubrine shrieks breathlessly at her. Ellen runs with closed eyes through the smokefilled corridor into the clean air of the fitting room, then, when her eyes have stopped running, she goes through the curtains to the agitated women in the waiting room.

"Madame Soubrine asked me to tell everybody it was nothing, absolutely nothing. Just a little blaze in a pile of rubbish. . . . She put it out herself with an extinguisher."

"Nothing, absolutely nothing," the women say one to another settling back onto the Empress Josephine sofas.

Ellen goes out to the street. The fireengines are arriving. Policemen are beating back the crowds. She wants to go away but she cant, she's waiting for something. At last she hears it tinkling down the street. As the fireengines go clanging away, the ambulance drives up. Attendants carry in the folded stretcher. Ellen can hardly breathe. She stands beside the ambulance behind a broad blue policeman. She tries to puzzle out why she is so moved; it is as if some part of her were going to be wrapped in bandages, carried away on a stretcher. Too soon it comes out, between the routine faces, the dark uniforms of the attendants.

"Was she terribly burned?" somehow she manages to ask under the policeman's arm.

"She wont die . . . but it's tough on a girl." Ellen elbows her way through the crowd and hurries towards Fifth Avenue. It's almost dark. Lights swim brightly in night clear blue like the deep sea.

Why should I be so excited? she keeps asking herself. Just somebody's bad luck, the sort of thing that happens every day. The moaning turmoil and the clanging of the fireengines wont seem to fade away inside her. She stands irresolutely on a corner while cars, faces, flicker clatteringly past her. A young man in a new straw hat is looking at her out of the corners of his eyes, trying to pick her up. She stares him blankly in the face. He has on a red, green, and blue striped necktie. She walks past him fast, crosses to the other side of the avenue, and turns uptown. Seven thirty. She's got to meet some one somewhere, she cant think where. There's a horrible tired blankness inside her. O dear what shall I do? she whimpers to herself. At the next corner she hails a taxi. "Go to the Algonquin please."

She remembers it all now, at eight o'clock she's going to have dinner with Judge Shammeyer and his wife. Ought to have gone home to dress. George'll be mad when he sees me come breezing in like this. Likes to show me off all dressed up like a Christmas tree, like an Effenbee walking talking doll, damn him.

She sits back in the corner of the taxi with her eyes closed. Relax, she must let herself relax more. Ridiculous to go round always keyed up so that everything is like chalk shrieking on a blackboard. Suppose I'd been horribly burned, like that girl, disfigured for life. Probably she can get a lot of money out of old Soubrine, the beginning of a career. Suppose I'd gone with that young man with the ugly necktie who tried to pick me up. . . . Kidding over a banana split in a soda fountain, riding uptown and then down again on the bus, with his knee pressing my knee and his arm round my waist, a little heavy petting in a doorway. . . . There are lives to be lived if only you didn't care. Care for what, for what; the opinion of mankind, money, success, hotel lobbies, health, umbrellas, Uneeda biscuits . . . ? It's like a busted mechanical toy the way my mind goes brrr all the time. I hope they havent ordered dinner. I'll make them go somewhere else if they havent. She opens her vanity case and begins to powder her nose.

When the taxi stops and the tall doorman opens the door, she steps out with dancing pointed girlish steps, pays, and turns, her cheeks a little flushed, her eyes sparkling with the glinting seablue night of deep streets, into the revolving doors.

As she goes through the shining soundless revolving doors, that spin before her gloved hand touches the glass, there shoots through her a sudden pang of something forgotten. Gloves, purse, vanity case, handkerchief, I have them all. Didn't have an umbrella. What did I forget in the taxicab? But already she is advancing smiling towards two gray men in black with white shirtfronts getting to their feet, smiling, holding out their hands.

Bob Hildebrand in dressing gown and pyjamas walked up and down in front of the long windows smoking a pipe. Through the sliding doors into the front came a sound of glasses tinkling and shuffling feet and laughing and *Running Wild* grating hazily out of a blunt needle on the phonograph.

"Why dont you park here for the night?" Hildebrand was saying in his deep serious voice. "Those people'll fade out gradually. . . . We can put you up on the couch."

"No thanks," said Jimmy. "They'll start talking psychoanalysis in a minute and they'll be here till dawn."

"But you'd much better take a morning train."

"I'm not going to take any kind of a train."

"Say Herf did you read about the man in Philadelphia who was killed because he wore his straw hat on the fourteenth of May?"

"By God if I was starting a new religion he'd be made a saint."

"Didnt you read about it? It was funny as a crutch. . . .
This man had the temerity to defend his straw hat. Somebody
had busted it and he started to fight, and in the middle of it
one of these streetcorner heroes came up behind him and
brained him with a piece of lead pipe. They picked him up
with a cracked skull and he died in the hospital."

"Bob what was his name?"

"I didnt notice."

"Talk about the Unknown Soldier. . . . That's a real hero
for you; the golden legend of the man who would wear a
straw hat out of season."

A head was stuck between the double doors. A flushfaced
man with his hair over his eyes looked in. "Cant I bring you
fellers a shot of gin. . . . Whose funeral is being celebrated
anyway?"

"I'm going to bed, no gin for me," said Hildebrand
grouchily.

"It's the funeral of Saint Aloysius of Philadelphia, virgin
and martyr, the man who would wear a straw hat out of season," said Herf. "I might sniff a little gin. I've got to run in
a minute. . . . So long Bob."

"So long you mysterious traveler. . . . Let us have your
address, do you hear?"

The long front room was full of ginbottles, gingerale
bottles, ashtrays crowded with halfsmoked cigarettes, couples
dancing, people sprawled on sofas. Endlessly the phonograph
played *Lady . . . lady be good*. A glass of gin was pushed into
Herf's hand. A girl came up to him.

"We've been talking about you. . . . Did you know you
were a man of mystery?"

"Jimmy," came a shrill drunken voice, "you're suspected of
being the bobhaired bandit."

"Why dont you take up a career of crime, Jimmy?" said the
girl putting her arm round his waist. "I'll come to your trial,
honest I will."

"How do you know I'm not?"

"You see," said Frances Hildebrand, who was bringing a
bowl of cracked ice in from the kitchenette, "there is something mysterious going on."

Herf took the hand of the girl beside him and made her

dance with him. She kept stumbling over his feet. He danced her round until he was opposite to the halldoor; he opened the door and foxtrotted her out into the hall. Mechanically she put up her mouth to be kissed. He kissed her quickly and reached for his hat. "Good night," he said. The girl started to cry.

Out in the street he took a deep breath. He felt happy, much more happy than Greenwich Village kisses. He was reaching for his watch when he remembered he had pawned it.

The golden legend of the man who would wear a straw hat out of season. Jimmy Herf is walking west along Twentythird Street, laughing to himself. Give me liberty, said Patrick Henry, putting on his straw hat on the first of May, or give me death. And he got it. There are no trollycars, occasionally a milkwagon clatters by, the heartbroken brick houses of Chelsea are dark. . . . A taxi passes trailing a confused noise of singing. At the corner of Ninth Avenue he notices two eyes like holes in a trianglewhite of paper, a woman in a raincoat beckons to him from a doorway. Further on two English sailors are arguing in drunken cockney. The air becomes milky with fog as he nears the river. He can hear the great soft distant lowing of steamboats.

He sits a long time waiting for a ferry in the seedy ruddylighted waiting room. He sits smoking happily. He cant seem to remember anything, there is no future but the foggy river and the ferry looming big with its lights in a row like a darky's smile. He stands with his hat off at the rail and feels the riverwind in his hair. Perhaps he's gone crazy, perhaps this is amnesia, some disease with a long Greek name, perhaps they'll find him picking dewberries in the Hoboken Tube. He laughs aloud so that the old man who came to open the gates gave him a sudden sidelong look. Cookoo, bats in the belfry, that's what he's saying to himself. Maybe he's right. By gum if I were a painter, maybe they'll let me paint in the nuthouse, I'd do Saint Aloysius of Philadelphia with a straw hat on his head instead of a halo and in his hand the lead pipe, instrument of his martyrdom, and a little me praying at his feet. The only passenger on the ferry, he roams round as if he owned it. My temporary yacht. By Jove these are the doldrums of the night all right, he mutters. He keeps trying to explain his gayety to himself. It's not that I'm drunk. I may be crazy, but I dont think so. . . .

Before the ferry leaves a horse and wagon comes aboard, a brokendown springwagon loaded with flowers, driven by a little brown man with high cheekbones. Jimmy Herf walks round it; behind the drooping horse with haunches like a hatrack the little warped wagon is unexpectedly merry, stacked with pots of scarlet and pink geraniums, carnations, alyssum, forced roses, blue lobelia. A rich smell of maytime earth comes from it, of wet flowerpots and greenhouses. The driver sits hunched with his hat over his eyes. Jimmy has an impulse to ask him where he is going with all those flowers, but he stifles it and walks to the front of the ferry.

Out of the empty dark fog of the river, the ferryslip yawns all of a sudden, a black mouth with a throat of light. Herf hurries through cavernous gloom and out to a fogblurred street. Then he is walking up an incline. There are tracks below him and the slow clatter of a freight, the hiss of an engine. At the top of a hill he stops to look back. He can see nothing but fog spaced with a file of blurred arclights. Then he walks on, taking pleasure in breathing, in the beat of his blood, in the tread of his feet on the pavement, between rows of otherworldly frame houses. Gradually the fog thins, a morning pearliness is seeping in from somewhere.

Sunrise finds him walking along a cement road between dumping grounds full of smoking rubbishpiles. The sun shines redly through the mist on rusty donkeyengines, skeleton trucks, wishbones of Fords, shapeless masses of corroding metal. Jimmy walks fast to get out of the smell. He is hungry; his shoes are beginning to raise blisters on his big toes. At a cross-road where the warning light still winks and winks, is a gasoline station, opposite it the Lightning Bug lunchwagon. Carefully he spends his last quarter on breakfast. That leaves him three cents for good luck, or bad for that matter. A huge furniture truck, shiny and yellow, has drawn up outside.

"Say will you give me a lift?" he asks the redhaired man at the wheel.

"How fur ye goin?"

"I dunno. . . . Pretty far."

CHRONOLOGY

NOTE ON THE TEXTS

NOTES

Chronology

1896   Born John Roderigo Madison on January 14 in a Chicago hotel, the natural son of Lucy Addison Sprigg Madison of Petersburg, Virginia, and John Randolph Dos Passos, a prominent New York corporation lawyer. (Father, known as "John R." or "The Commodore," was born John Rodrigues Dos Passos in Philadelphia in 1844, the son of an immigrant Portuguese cobbler; he worked as office boy in a law firm and briefly served as a drummer in a Pennsylvania regiment in the Civil War before opening his own law firm in New York City in 1867. He achieved prominence in 1873 by successfully appealing the murder conviction of Edward S. Stokes, who had shot financier Jim Fisk. Later that year he married socialite Mary Dyckman Hays; they had a son, Louis Hays Dos Passos. Dos Passos moved into brokerage and corporation law, became known for his success in establishing several large commercial trusts, and wrote several books on law. Mother Lucy Sprigg was born in 1854 in Cumberland, Maryland; her family moved to Petersburg, Virginia, before the Civil War. In 1872 she married Ryland Randolph Madison with whom she had a son, James Madison, the following year; the couple never lived together for any length of time and soon separated; James was left in the care of Lucy's mother when Lucy went to Washington, D.C., to work in her father's surveying office. Lucy may have met John Randolph, a business associate of her father, as early as 1883, and their liaison had begun by the early 1890s.)

1897–1900   Travels through Europe with his mother, staying in Brussels, Wiesbaden, Paris, and London (will later remember having had a "hotel childhood"). Learns French as his first spoken language. Father visits Europe frequently on business and travels openly with mother; during his father's visits, is often left in the care of friends of his mother. In 1899 mother's health begins to fail when she suffers the first of a series of strokes and is diagnosed with Bright's disease.

1901   Returns with mother to America and enrolls in the Sid-
            well Friends School in Washington.

1902   Returns to Brussels with his mother, who had felt isolated
            in America. Father continues to visit three or four times a
            year.

1903   Suffers an attack of what is probably rheumatic fever (ill-
            ness will recur throughout his life); after spending a month
            in bed, accompanies his parents to Madeira to recuperate.
            Mother's husband, Ryland Randolph Madison, dies. Fa-
            ther publishes a political treatise, *The Anglo-Saxon Cen-
            tury and the Unification of the English Speaking People.*

1904–06   Attends boarding school at Peterborough Lodge in
            Hampstead, England. Returns to the U.S. with his
            mother in the summer of 1906.

1907–09   Enters Choate School in Wallingford, Connecticut, in
            January 1907. Does well academically but is hazed by
            other students because of his foreign accent and lack
            of athletic ability. Edits school newspaper, to which he
            contributes fiction and articles. Visits father during sum-
            mers at his farmhouse at Sandy Point, Westmoreland
            County, Virginia (part of extensive Virginia land hold-
            ings) and on board his yacht, *Gaivota.*

1910   Father's wife, Mary Hays Dos Passos, dies March 10. Par-
            ents marry on June 21.

1911   Begins using name John Roderigo Dos Passos, Jr. Having
            enough credits to graduate, does not return to Choate for
            senior year. Passes Harvard entrance examination, then
            sails to Europe in November with tutor Virgil Jones. Trav-
            els in France and Italy.

1912–14   Visits Egypt, Turkey, and Greece. Returns to the U.S. in
            May 1912 and enters Harvard in September. Studies Euro-
            pean languages and literature under teachers including
            Bliss Perry, Charles T. Copeland, and George Lyman Kit-
            tredge. Forms friendships with fellow students E. E.
            Cummings, Robert Nathan, Gilbert Seldes, and Dudley
            Poore, and contributes fiction, poetry, and reviews to the
            Harvard Advocate and *Harvard Monthly.* Keeps diaries in

which he makes critical comments on books he reads (entries for September 1914, for example, include remarks on Fielding, Stendhal, Goldsmith, de Quincey, Chekhov, O. Henry, Lafcadio Hearn, Henry James, Stevenson, George Sand, Turgenev, and William Morris); major literary influences include *Vanity Fair* and *Don Quixote*. Attends opera and ballet and is interested in modern art; exhilarated by the Armory Show.

1915   Joins editorial board of *Harvard Monthly*. Mother dies on May 15; Dos Passos is devastated and does not want to go back to school, but father insists that he return. Travels across country during summer to visit World's Fair in San Francisco; in San Diego meets Walter Rumsey Marvin, who becomes lifelong friend and correspondent. At Harvard, becomes member of newly formed Poetry Society along with Cummings, Robert Hillyer, S. Foster Damon, R. Stewart Mitchell, and John Wheelwright.

1916   Begins autobiographical novel (later published as *Streets of Night*). After taking final examinations, visits Cape Cod for first time and is enthralled by Provincetown. Graduates cum laude from Harvard in June. Attempts to join Herbert Hoover's Commission for Relief in Belgium, but is rejected as being too young. Publishes essay "Against American Literature" in *The New Republic*: "We find ourselves floundering without rudder or compass, in the sea of modern life, vaguely lit by the phosphorescent gleam of our traditional optimism." Sails to Bordeaux in October and travels to Madrid to study Spanish and architecture. Meets poet Juan Ramon Jimenez and university student Jose Robles, who becomes a close friend. Travels extensively in Spain during his stay.

1917   Stunned by news of father's sudden death from pneumonia on January 27, Dos Passos returns to the U.S. in February and becomes involved in disposition of father's estate, which is encumbered with debt. Authorizes his maternal aunt, Mary Lamar Gordon, to collect his share of interest on Virginia property of which he is now co-owner (over the next two decades, she and her family receive but do not pass on to Dos Passos income totaling approximately $100,000). Settles temporarily in New York City in an apartment on East 33rd Street. Observes rallies against

American participation in World War I; is almost arrested when police raid a party in Greenwich Village. Expresses radical sentiments to a friend: "Every day I become more red." Takes lessons in driving, automobile maintenance, and medical techniques as preparation for volunteer service with Norton-Harjes volunteer ambulance unit, made up of Harvard graduates and serving under the auspices of the Red Cross. Contributes seven poems to anthology *Eight Harvard Poets*, published by Laurence J. Gomme; publishes article "Young Spain" in August issue of *Seven Arts*. Sails to France June 20 on the *Chicago*. Aboard ship forms friendship with playwright and left-wing activist John Howard Lawson. In Paris, reunites with college friends Robert Hillyer, Frederic van den Arend, and Dudley Poore. After several weeks of training at Sandricourt north of Paris, serves at Verdun front during French offensive in late August, where he undergoes German shelling with high explosives and poison gas. Writes to friend Rumsey Marvin: "The war is utter damn nonsense—a vast cancer fed by lies and self seeking malignity on the part of those who don't do the fighting . . . none of the poor devils whose mangled dirty bodies I take to the hospital in my ambulance really give a damn about any of the aims of this ridiculous affair." Collaborates with Hillyer on unpublished novel "Seven Times Round the Walls of Jericho." Returns to Paris and in November drives into northern Italy; remains in Milan for most of December before going to Dolo.

1918   Arrives January 17 in Bassano, headquarters for ambulance unit; town undergoes frequent bombings and shellings. On leave in March, travels to Bologna, Rome, Naples, and Florence. Meets Ernest Hemingway. Accused of disloyalty by Red Cross authorities who disapprove of his rowdy and insubordinate attitude, and of criticism of "stupidities" of modern war expressed in an intercepted letter. Returns to Paris in June after his enlistment ends and is forced by Red Cross authorities to return to the U.S. Sails home in August and enlists in the U.S. Army Medical Corps. On November 12, the day after the armistice, sails with his unit for England, and on arrival is assigned to an American base at Fèrrieres-en-Gatinais, south of Paris.

1919   Reassigned in January to a camp in Alsace, where his light duties enable him to explore the region; in March is re-

leased from active service with Medical Corps. Returns to
Paris to attend classes in anthropology at the Sorbonne.
Sent for several weeks in June to Gièvres for further military service; goes absent without leave to Tours and per-
suades a top sergeant to issue delayed discharge orders.
Returns to Paris in July, then travels to London to arrange
publication by Allen and Unwin of *One Man's Initiation—
1917*, a novel derived from "Seven Times Round the Walls
of Jericho." Goes to Spain with Dudley Poore; travels in
Basque country; arrives in Madrid at end of August and remains there for most of September. Rents house in
Granada; travels briefly to Lisbon to report on a rumored
revolution which does not take place, then returns to
Granada, where he becomes ill for a month with rheumatic
fever. Returns to Madrid at the end of November and
works on novel *Three Soldiers*, also based on World War I
experiences.

1920   Moves to Barcelona in March. Returns to Paris by first of
May and completes manuscript of *Three Soldiers* in June.
Novel is rejected by Allen and Unwin. Sails for America in
August and settles in New York City, on East 15th Street
off Stuyvesant Square; writes to a French friend, "New
York—after all—is magnificent—a city of cavedwellers,
with a frightful, brutal ugliness about it, full of thunderous
voices of metal grinding on metal and of an eternal sound
of wheels which turn, turn on heavy stones." Takes art
classes with Adelaide Lawson, sister of John Howard Lawson. Sees E. E. Cummings frequently, and takes long walks
with him through the city. Publishes essays, poems, and reviews in *The Dial*, *The Nation*, and *The Freeman*, to which
he contributes a series of articles about Spain. *One Man's
Initiation—1917* is published in England in October by
Allen and Unwin, after Dos Passos agrees to make cuts in
allegedly offensive passages.

1921   *Three Soldiers* is accepted for publication by George H.
Doran (after being rejected, according to Dos Passos, by
14 other publishers). Sails with Cummings in March from
New Bedford, Massachusetts, to Lisbon; they travel together in Spain and France, visiting Seville and hiking in
the Pyrenees before moving on to Paris. With the help of
Paxton Hibben, an American friend working in Paris for
the Red Cross's Near East Relief organization, Dos Passos

is able to travel in July to Constantinople and to sail aboard an American destroyer in the Sea of Marmara, observing the devastation of the Turkish-Greek War. Sails on Italian steamer to Batum and then travels through Georgia, Armenia, and Azerbaijan, which had recently come under Soviet rule. Later writes of journey: "Where starving people weren't dying of typhus they were dying of cholera. The flatcars and boxcars that made up our train were packed with refugees escaping from what? Where bound? Nobody seemed to know. In one station corpses were stacked like cordwood behind the stove." After crossing the Persian border, goes by horse-drawn carriage to Teheran, where he suffers from malaria for several weeks before traveling by car and train to Baghdad in October. During three weeks in Baghdad makes arrangements with help of British intelligence officer Gertrude Bell to travel by camel caravan across desert to Damascus.

1922   Arrives in Damascus shortly after New Year's after 39-day journey, then goes to Beirut. Gratified by letters congratulating him on the success of *Three Soldiers*, published September 1921. Travels to Paris, where he meets up again with Cummings before returning to America in February. Publishes three books with George H. Doran: *Rosinante to the Road Again*, a collection of essays on Spain (March), an American edition of *One Man's Initiation* (June), and *A Pushcart at the Curb*, a poetry collection (October). Works seriously at painting as well as writing. Begins close friendship with Edmund Wilson and associates with many writers, including F. Scott and Zelda Fitzgerald, Dawn Powell, John Peale Bishop, Elinor Wylie, Donald Ogden Stewart, and Sherwood Anderson. At funeral in August of Wright McCormic, a Harvard friend killed in an accident, meets Crystal Ross and forms close friendship with her.

1923   Exhibits paintings at Whitney Studio Club in January. Completes first play, *The Moon Is a Gong*, and writes an introduction to John Howard Lawson's play *Roger Bloomer*. Travels to Paris in March, remaining in Europe until August and making a trip to Spain; in Paris becomes close friends with wealthy expatriates Gerald and Sara Murphy, whom he helps paint sets for the Ballet Russe. Through the Murphys meets painter Fernand Léger, poet Blaise

Cendrars, and other leading figures of the modernist movement; is impressed by backdrop of newspaper headlines designed by Gerald Murphy for Cole Porter ballet *Within the Quota*. Returns to the U.S. in the fall and stays in a boarding house in Far Rockaway, Long Island, to work on new novel *Manhattan Transfer*, which he describes to a friend as "utterly fantastic and New Yorkish." *Streets of Night*, autobiographical novel begun at Harvard, is published in November by George H. Doran.

1924   During the winter lives at Columbia Heights in Brooklyn, in building overlooking the Brooklyn Bridge. Travels in February to New Orleans where he stays until early March, and then travels through Florida to Key West. Becomes friends with Hart Crane after he moves into Columbia Heights building in the spring. Goes in June to France, where he meets again with Crystal Ross, now studying at the University of Strasbourg, and forms close friendship with Ernest Hemingway. Travels to Pamplona in July with Crystal and becomes engaged to her. Attends Fiesta of San Fermín with Hemingway and other friends including Donald Ogden Stewart and Robert McAlmon; afterward takes two-week walking trip across the Pyrenees to Andorra before rejoining the Murphys in Antibes. Sees Crystal several more times in Strasbourg, Bruges, and London, but she resists his wish to marry quickly. Returns to New York in September and devotes the fall to working on *Manhattan Transfer*.

1925   Joins executive board of left-wing journal *New Masses*. *The Moon Is a Gong* is performed by the Harvard Dramatic Club in May. After completing *Manhattan Transfer*, suffers bout of rheumatic fever and is hospitalized several times, May–July. Visited by Crystal Ross, who is still reluctant to marry him. Returns to France in late summer, spending time with Hemingway in Paris and cruising on a yacht in the Mediterranean with the Murphys. *Manhattan Transfer* is published in November by Harper & Brothers, receiving mixed reviews; Dos Passos is pleased by praise in *The Saturday Review of Literature* from Sinclair Lewis, who calls the book "a novel of the very first importance . . . the foundation of a whole new school of novel-writing." Sails to Morocco in December.

1926   Travels in Morocco, January–February. Receives cable from John Howard Lawson asking him to become a director of the New Playwrights Theatre; accepts and returns to New York in March, in time to see a production of his play *The Garbage Man*, revised version of *The Moon Is a Gong* (published in July by Harper & Brothers). Receives letter from Crystal Ross in the spring announcing her engagement to another man. First issue of *New Masses* appears in May. Becomes increasingly involved with radical causes, including the textile strike in Passaic, New Jersey, but expresses concern about the influence of the Communist Party. Travels to Boston in June to gather information about the case of Italian anarchists Nicola Sacco and Bartolomeo Vanzetti, who were sentenced to death in 1921 for robbery and murder. Interviews Sacco and Vanzetti and becomes convinced of their innocence; publishes preliminary report on case in August *New Masses* and returns to Boston for further investigation. Later in the year travels in the South and West, spending time in Louisville, St. Louis, and Dallas, and arriving in Mexico City in mid-December.

1927   Travels extensively in Mexico, where he meets young Mexican artists whose work interests him; also spends time with journalist Carleton Beals and former IWW member Gladwin Bland (on whom he models character of Mac in *The 42nd Parallel*). Returns to New York in March to continue work with New Playwrights Theatre. *Orient Express*, an account of his 1921–22 travels in the Near East, is published in March by Harper & Brothers (with a number of Dos Passos' paintings as illustrations). Continues to work on efforts to procure a new trial for Sacco and Vanzetti; his pamphlet *Facing the Chair: Story of the Americanization of Two Foreignborn Workmen* is published in the spring by the Sacco-Vanzetti Defense Committee. Arrested and briefly jailed after protest march in Boston on August 21; Sacco and Vanzetti are electrocuted August 23. Writes "They Are Dead Now," prose poem which is published in *New Masses* (it is later incorporated in altered form in *The Big Money*). Begins work on *The 42nd Parallel*, the first novel in what will become the *U.S.A.* trilogy.

1928   Goes to Key West in April to visit Hemingway; meets Katharine (Katy) Smith, a childhood friend of Hemingway's from Michigan. Sails to Europe in May. Visits friends in London, Paris, Antibes, and Berlin before going to Helsinki in July. Travels to Leningrad where he meets Dr. Horsley Gantt, an American scientist working with Pavlov. Meets theater director Vsevolod Meyerhold and filmmakers Sergei Eisenstein and Vsevolod Pudovkin in Moscow, as well as American publicist Ivy Lee (on whom Dos Passos models character of J. Ward Moorehouse in *U.S.A.*); impressed by "Living Newspapers," improvisational plays performed in workers' clubs and unions. Takes a steamer down the Volga to Astrakhan, then travels through the Caucasus region, visiting Grozny and Tiflis. Spends two months in Moscow before returning to New York at year's end, taking an apartment on Washington Square South.

1929   Dos Passos' second play, *Airways, Inc.*, opens in February at New Playwrights Theatre for unsuccessful four-week run; he resigns from theater group in March, troubled by ineffective organization and internal dissension. Travels in March to Key West, where he sees Katy Smith again, then visits her in June at her home in Provincetown. They marry on August 19 in Ellsworth, Maine, and spend September in Wiscasset, Maine, before moving to her house in Provincetown. In early December they sail to France; they see Hemingway, the Fitzgeralds, Léger, and Cendrars, and spend Christmas skiing in Switzerland with Gerald and Sara Murphy.

1930   Travels with Katy in Austria, France, England, and Spain, before sailing across the Atlantic, arriving in Havana in April. Visits Hemingway in Key West before returning to Provincetown to work on *1919*; is pleased to learn of many good reviews of *The 42nd Parallel*, published in February by Harper & Brothers. Travels in Mexico, May–June. Buys small farm in Truro, near Provincetown (he and Katy will live partly on income from renting out this and two other properties they own). Declares to Edmund Wilson that he is becoming "a middle-class liberal" but continues to support some left-wing causes. Visits Hemingway in Montana in October; escapes unharmed from an automobile accident in which Hemingway breaks an arm.

1931   Dos Passos' translation of *Panama, or The Adventures of My Seven Uncles*, a poem by Blaise Cendrars, is published in January, illustrated with his paintings. Travels with Katy in Mexico, February–March, before returning to

Provincetown to complete *1919*. Harper's balks at publishing satirical profile of J. P. Morgan included in the novel, and Dos Passos arranges for Harcourt, Brace to publish it. Travels to Harlan County, Kentucky, with Theodore Dreiser and others on behalf of National Committee for the Defense of Political Prisoners to investigate situation of striking miners; appalled by conditions there, contributes to *Harlan Miners Speak* (published in March 1932). Refuses to return to Kentucky to stand trial after being indicted for "criminal syndicalism" despite urgings of Communist leader Earl Browder.

1932   Travels with Katy in Mexico and southwestern United States, February–April, visiting Hemingway in Key West en route. *1919* is published in March and receives excellent reviews. Reports on public events, including the "Bonus Army" of protesting veterans camped in Washington, D.C., and the Republican and Democratic national conventions, for *The New Republic*; works on *The Big Money*. Votes for Communist candidate William Z. Foster in November presidential election.

1933   Suffers serious recurrence of rheumatic fever in April. Sails to Europe in May with Katy, a trip financed in part by Hemingway and the Murphys, at whose Antibes home they stay through June. Travels through Spain and, although still convalescing from rheumatic fever, conducts interviews which will form part of travel book *In All Countries*; returns to Provincetown in October.

1934   Signs open letter protesting Communist disruption of a Socialist Party meeting in Madison Square Garden in February. Responds to criticism in *New Masses* by stating that he signed the letter to oppose "the growth of unintelligent fanaticism." Spends much of the spring with Katy in Key West, where they are visited by Dawn Powell. Writes to Edmund Wilson in March that "the whole Marxian radical movement is in a moment of intense disintegration." *In All Countries* and *Three Plays: The Garbage Man, Airways, Inc., and Fortune Heights* are published in the spring by Harcourt, Brace. Flies to Hollywood in July to work on screenplay for Josef von Sternberg's film *The Devil Is a Woman*, starring Marlene Dietrich (little of his work is used). Has another attack of rheumatic fever and is bedridden until Katy's arrival in mid-August. They remain in Hollywood until October, then sail for Havana; while Katy returns to Massachusetts for medical tests (she had suffered several miscarriages), Dos Passos goes to Key West where Katy joins him at Christmas. Criticizes the Soviet Union in letters to Edmund Wilson ("From now on events in Russia have no more interest—except as a terrible example—for world socialism. . . . The thing has gone into its Napoleonic stage") and remarks: "It would be funny if I ended up an Anglo Saxon chauvinist—Did you ever read my father's Anglo Saxon Century? We are now getting to the age when papa's shoes yawn wide."

1935   Visits Jamaica and New York in January, then stays in Key West, with occasional trips to Bimini and Havana, before returning to Provincetown in June. Continues to correspond with Edmund Wilson about his disillusionment with Stalinist Communism: "I'm now at last convinced that means cant be disassociated from ends and that massacre only creates more massacre and oppression more oppression and means become ends." Works steadily on *The Big Money*, the third volume of the *U.S.A.* trilogy, whose completion has been delayed by lingering health problems.

1936   Completes *The Big Money* by March. With Katy and their guest Sara Murphy, visits Hemingway in Havana; returns to Provincetown in May. Embarks on a course of reading in American history. *The Big Money* is published in August and receives major attention; Dos Passos is pictured on the cover of *Time* on August 10, and the book is widely praised despite complaints by some left-wing reviewers about its pessimism. Seeks way to participate in a news service reporting the Spanish civil war. Writes to Malcolm Cowley in December: "A fascist Spain will mean a fascist France and more violent reaction here & in England."

1937   Learns in early January that he has been elected to the National Institute of Arts and Letters. Works with Archibald MacLeish, Lillian Hellman, Hemingway, and others in organizing Contemporary Historians, a group formed to produce a documentary film about Spain (later released as *The Spanish Earth*, directed by Joris Ivens and with commentary by Hemingway). Disagrees with Hemingway about the film's content, seeking to concentrate on the

Spanish land and people while Hemingway wishes to emphasize the war. Sails with Katy to Europe in early March, and after several weeks in France arrives by early April in Valencia, now the capital of the Spanish Republic. Becomes aware of internecine struggles among political factions fighting for the Republic; learns that his friend Jose Robles, an official in the Republican government, has been arrested by Republican security forces, and seeks information about him. Goes to Madrid and stays at Hotel Florida with Hemingway, who berates him for not bringing in food, and accuses him of cowardly behavior. Learns that Robles has been secretly shot by Communists for alleged spying. Rift with Hemingway worsens when Hemingway argues that Robles would not have been executed without justification. Leaves Madrid in April and visits Fuenteduena, a village to be filmed for *The Spanish Earth*. In Barcelona and Valencia others, including English writer George Orwell, further convince him of Communist duplicity and brutality. Returns in May to Paris, where he again argues with Hemingway about Spain. After his return with Katy to the U.S., writes article "Farewell to Europe!" for *Common Sense*, in which he praises the American spirit of individual liberty in contrast to the "stifling cellar" of Europe; criticized by leftist friends such as John Howard Lawson, he responds that "Anglo-Saxon democracy is the best political method of which we have any . . . I have come to believe that the CP is fundamentally opposed to our democracy." Revises and adds a prologue to *The 42nd Parallel* for a Modern Library edition published in November.

1938   *U.S.A.*, uniting *The 42nd Parallel, 1919*, and *The Big Money* in one volume, is published in January by Harcourt, Brace; sales are indifferent, exacerbating chronic financial difficulties. *Journeys Between Wars*, a compilation of excerpts from earlier travel books along with new material about Spain, is published in April by Harcourt, Brace. Goes to New Orleans in the spring; works on a new novel, *Adventures of a Young Man* until he and Katy depart for Europe in June. They cruise the Mediterranean with the Murphys, visit Rome, Pisa, Florence, and Paris, before returning to Provincetown.

1939   *Adventures of a Young Man* is published in June and receives generally weak reviews, particularly from critics sympathetic to the Communist Party (*New Masses* calls it "a crude piece of Trotskyist agitprop"); sales are poor. Travels with Katy in the Southwest during the spring. Despite receipt of Guggenheim grant for book on American history (later published as *The Ground We Stand On*), continues to suffer from financial difficulties. Begins to help care for two boys whose mother, a neighbor, had died suddenly (the boys will sometimes live with Dos Passos and his wife during the early 1940s).

1940   Contributes lengthy introduction to *The Living Thoughts of Tom Paine*, an anthology published in February. Lives in Alexandria, Virginia, from February to April while conducting research at the Library of Congress. Investigates Virginia property held in trust for him by his aunt's family, and discovers that they have withheld income from the land (initiates civil suit in 1941 which is not resolved until 1944). On behalf of New World Resettlement Fund, visits Ecuador and Haiti to help with resettlement of Spanish Republican refugees.

1941   Agrees during summer to serve with Italian anarchist Carlo Tresca as a vice-chairman of Civil Rights Defense Committee in the case of 29 truckers and union members (some of them members of the Trotskyist Socialist Workers' Party) accused of conspiracy by the Justice Department. *The Ground We Stand On*, historical study celebrating the American heritage of "selfgovernment," is published in August. Travels to England in September for a P.E.N. Club conference at which he meets H. G. Wells. Writes articles for *Harper's Magazine* praising the British war effort and emphasizing need for American industrial strength.

1942–43   In late 1942 and throughout 1943 makes a series of trips around the U.S. gathering information for series of *Harper's* articles titled "People at War." *Number One*, a novel based on the career of Huey Long, is published by Houghton Mifflin, his new publisher, in March 1943. Sells house in Truro; despite literary fame, finances continue to be shaky.

1944   Receives favorable judgment in April in lawsuit over Virginia property. *State of the Nation*, book version of the "People at War" articles, is published in July. Works on a biography of Thomas Jefferson, which will occupy him for the next decade. Leaves in December for the West Coast and the Pacific to begin research for series of articles on the war; spends Christmas on Kwajalein in the Marshall Islands.

1945   Continues Pacific tour, visiting Eniwetok, Saipan, and Ulithi, and witnesses preliminary bombardment of Iwo Jima in January; enters Manila on February 5, shortly after arrival of American troops; interviews General Douglas MacArthur. Rests from trip in Australia in March; survives, without major injury, a freak accident in which he is struck on head by wing-tip of low-flying airplane; returns to U.S. in April. Travels in Europe, October–December, to report on postwar conditions for *Life*; attends Nuremberg trials, and is depressed by conditions in Europe and what he views as Russian threat: "Never felt so much sadder and wiser in my life as after this trip to Europe. . . ."

1946   Expresses political fears in January *Life* article, "Americans Are Losing the Victory in Europe." Travels with Katy in March and April, visiting Florida and Mexico; they also make periodic visits to Virginia property to supervise restoration of colonial home at Spence's Point where they intend to live. *Tour of Duty*, collecting his war articles, is published in August. *U.S.A.* is reissued by Houghton Mifflin in a deluxe three-volume edition with illustrations by Reginald Marsh.

1947   Travels with Katy to Key West, February–March. In England, July–August, researches articles on British politics for *Life*. Collides with rear of parked truck near Wareham, Massachusetts, on September 12; Katy is killed instantly and Dos Passos loses his right eye. While recovering from injuries, tells friends of his intention to move to Virginia: "If I tried to avoid all the places I'd been happy with Katy I'd have to get off the earth because there's nothing lovely in life that doesn't make me think of her, but I find it perhaps a little less painful to be down here than in P'-town." Travels to Iowa in mid-October for a month's stay to research another *Life* article; on his return stays with friends Lloyd and Marion Lowndes in Snedens Landing, New York, with whom he spends much time over next several years. Learns in November that he has been elected to American Academy of Arts and Letters.

1948 Article "The Failure of Marxism" published in *Life* in January. Travels, February–March, to Bermuda and Haiti, spending time with friends including writers John P. Marquand and Dawn Powell. Settles ownership of the Virginia property with his half-brother Louis, taking 2,100 acres which he hopes to develop as a farm. Travels in September to South America to report on social and political conditions; visits briefly with Hemingway in Cuba before going to Colombia, Brazil, Argentina, Uruguay, Chile, and Peru; returns to U.S. in December.

1949 *The Grand Design* is published in January. Travels extensively through the U.S. in April and May to research series of articles for *Modern Millwheels*, publication of the General Mills Corporation. Meets Elizabeth (Betty) Holdridge when she visits the Lowndes in Snedens Landing in May (Holdridge, b. 1909, had lost her husband in an automobile accident in 1946). Marries Betty Holdridge on August 6 in Maryland and moves with her and her seven-year-old son Christopher to the restored house at Spence's Point. Travels in September to Italy for a P.E.N. conference.

1950 Daughter Lucy Hamlin Dos Passos is born May 15. *The Prospect Before Us*, a collection of political essay incorporating material on England, South America, and American business and agriculture, is published in October to generally poor reviews. Contributes text to *Life's Picture History of World War II*, also published in October.

1951 *Chosen Country* is published in the fall; the novel, which features a character modeled on Katy, receives positive response from reviewers including Edmund Wilson and Archibald MacLeish, but provokes an enraged reaction from Ernest Hemingway at his own fictionalized portrait. Visits Cape Cod briefly during summer.

1952 *District of Columbia*, one-volume edition of the trilogy consisting of *Adventures of a Young Man*, *Number One*, and *The Grand Design*, is published.

1953   Despite his support for anti-Communist hearings led by
            Senator Joseph McCarthy, comes to the defense of old
            friend Horsley Gantt, whose loyalty has been questioned
            by government investigators. Works to complete biog-
            raphy of Thomas Jefferson which has occupied him for
            many years.

1954   Travels to New York in January for publication of *The
            Head and Heart of Thomas Jefferson*. *Most Likely to
            Succeed*, whose central character is in part a satirical por-
            trait of John Howard Lawson, is published in September
            by Prentice-Hall. Experiences renewed financial difficul-
            ties due to weak sales of recent books and insufficient re-
            turns from farming; undertakes a lecture tour, traveling
            through the Midwest and Pacific Northwest in October
            and November.

1955–56   *The Theme Is Freedom*, another collection of political
            essays, is published in March 1956. Devotes much time to
            farming, and writes to Edmund Wilson that he has "al-
            most ceased to think of myself as a literary gent." Visits
            Mexico in the fall to attend a meeting of the Congress for
            Cultural Freedom. Corresponds with William Faulkner
            about Faulkner's proposal for a writers' conference de-
            signed to encourage support for the U.S. among foreign
            intellectuals.

1957   *The Men Who Made the Nation*, a historical study of Amer-
            ica from the Revolution to the second Jefferson adminis-
            tration, is published in February. Travels to New York in
            May to accept Gold Medal for Fiction from National Insti-
            tute of Arts and Letters, and comments on his own work:
            "Satirical writing is by definition unpopular writing. Its aim
            is to prod people into thinking. Thinking hurts." Travels to
            Japan for two weeks in September to attend P.E.N. confer-
            ence; visits Mexico with his family in November.

1958   Spends much time researching article on labor unions for
            Reader's Digest (published in September as "What Union
            Members Have Been Writing Senator McClellan"). *The
            Great Days*, an autobiographical novel dealing with the
            period before and during World War II, is rejected
            by Prentice-Hall and Doubleday; after considerable revi-
            sion, it is published in March by Sagamore Press, receiving

generally poor reviews. In July and August travels in Brazil; visits Brasilia, then under construction, and meets its architect, Oscar Niemeyer, and Brazilian president Juscelino Kubitschek.

1959   *Prospect of a Golden Age*, another study of early American history, is published by Prentice-Hall. With family and friends, cruises on chartered boat in the Bahamas for two weeks during the summer. In collaboration with Paul Shyre, adapts *U.S.A.* for stage; it opens in October at the Hotel Martinique in New York City and has a successful run.

1960   Works on a new novel, *Midcentury*, which applies the same narrative techniques as *U.S.A.* to the postwar period. Vacations in Europe during August, traveling in Italy, Switzerland, France, and Portugal.

1961   *Midcentury* is published in the spring by Houghton Mifflin and becomes a bestseller; the reviews are the best he has received since *U.S.A.* Travels in Spain in August and September.

1962   Receives award in Madison Square Garden in March from conservative group Young Americans for Freedom, sharing podium with Senator Strom Thurmond and actor John Wayne. Visits Peru, Brazil, and Argentina, August–September; lectures at Brazilian-American Institute in Rio de Janeiro and addresses P.E.N. conference in Buenos Aires. *Mr. Wilson's War*, a historical survey covering the period 1901–21, is published in November.

1963   Serves as writer in residence at the University of Virginia for three weeks in February. Travels in Canada and the American West in August, and in September flies briefly to Rome at the invitation of Centro di Vita Italiana, an anti-Communist organization. *Brazil on the Move* is published in September.

1964   Attends Republican convention in San Francisco in July, and writes enthusiastically of Barry Goldwater's nomination for *The National Review*; travels in Alaska in August. *Occasions and Protests*, a collection of political essays, and *Thomas Jefferson: The Making of a President*, a biography for children, are published.

1965   Receives Alumni Seal Prize from Choate School in May. Suffers mild heart seizure (possibly related to earlier bouts of rheumatic fever) in June.

1966   *Shackles of Power: Three Jeffersonian Decades* is published in March. Travels in Yucatan in March, and in Brazil, July–August. In November publishes *World in a Glass: A View of Our Century* and *The Best Times*, a memoir.

1967   Travels in Portugal, July–August, to research a study of Portuguese history. Flies to Rome in November to receive $32,000 Antonio Feltrinelli Prize for fiction.

1968   Visits old friend Dudley Poore in Florida in February, then goes to California in March. Travels in the Midwest during the summer.

1969   Visits Easter Island in January, continuing on to Chile and Argentina. *The Portugal Story* is published in April; works on *Easter Island: Island of Enigmas*, which is published posthumously in 1971. Travels to Florida in May to watch the launching of Apollo 10 from Cape Kennedy. Suffers minor heart attack while visiting friends in Maine during the summer. Works on final novel, *Century's Ebb* (published posthumously in 1975).

1970   Hospitalized briefly at Johns Hopkins in January for heart problems. Travels with Betty to Tucson, Arizona, in March. Returns to Johns Hopkins in July and August. Dies of congestive heart failure in Baltimore on September 28. Buried at Yeocomico Church near Spence's Point on October 7.

Note on the Texts

This volume collects three novels by John Dos Passos: *One Man's Initiation: 1917* (1920), *Three Soldiers* (1921), and *Manhattan Transfer* (1925).

While serving in France with a Red Cross ambulance unit during the summer of 1917, Dos Passos and his college friend Robert Hillyer wrote alternate chapters of a novel titled "Seven Times Round the Walls of Jericho." Dos Passos continued to work on the novel after Hillyer left France in September 1917, finishing two sections and outlining a third by April 1918. After returning to the United States in August 1918, he completed a draft of the novel shortly before he reported for duty with the U.S. Army Medical Corps at Camp Crane in Pennsylvania in late September 1918. The following spring, while revising the manuscript in Paris, Dos Passos wrote to his friend Dudley Poore that the fourth and final section of the novel "has been amputated and has become something else. . . . I'm going to enlarge it and put in steam heat and call it France 1917 or something of that sort and try to publish it that way." He completed the expanded fourth section by the summer of 1919 and submitted it to the London publishing house of Allen & Unwin under the title *One Man's Initiation—1917*. When the firm told him that they would publish the novel if he would help defray the cost of publication, Dos Passos initially refused, but decided several months later to accept their offer. After the page proofs were set, the printers demanded that several passages be revised because they feared legal action against them, presumably on grounds of indecency and blasphemy. Allen & Unwin sent the proofs to Dos Passos with recommendations for changes, and he eventually agreed to the alteration of the passages deemed objectionable by the printers.

One Man's Initiation—1917 was published by Allen & Unwin on October 20, 1920. It was brought out in the United States in 1922 by George H. Doran, using 500 sets of unbound sheets from the Allen & Unwin printing. A new edition was published in 1945 by the Philosophical Library under the title *First Encounter*, but apart from the change of title and the addition of a preface, Dos Passos made no revisions to the novel. In 1969 Cornell University Press published a "complete and unexpurgated" edition of the book, titled *One Man's Initiation: 1917*, based on a set of uncorrected page proofs of the Allen & Unwin edition acquired by the Cornell University Library in 1959. Dos Passos read and approved final proof for the

Cornell edition, which restored the passages that had been rewritten in 1920. The present volume prints the text of the 1969 Cornell University Press edition of *One Man's Initiation: 1917*. Significant variant passages from the 1920 Allen & Unwin edition are included in the notes to this volume.

Dos Passos began writing "The Sack of Corinth," the original title of *Three Soldiers*, in Paris in May 1919. He worked steadily on the novel over the next several months while traveling in Spain and submitted a completed draft of *Three Soldiers* to Allen & Unwin in the spring of 1920. The novel was rejected by them and by several other publishers before it was accepted by George H. Doran. While preparing *Three Soldiers* for publication, Doran advised Dos Passos to soften some of the language and alter passages that might offend readers, but Dos Passos appears to have resisted making most of these changes.

Three Soldiers was published in New York by George H. Doran on September 27, 1921. The novel was brought out in 1922 in England by Hurst & Blackett and in Canada by Doubleday, and was published in the Modern Library series in 1932. In his introduction to the Modern Library edition, Dos Passos wrote that he reread the book looking for "misprints" to correct, although his changes were not limited to the correction of typographical errors. For example, the spelling of "Wild Dan Cohen" is changed to "Cohan" throughout; when Chrisfield and Andrews leave their tent at 199.33–34, "to make water" is added in the Modern Library edition; the sentence at 231.9–10 ("He crumpled it up suddenly in his fist and shoved it down between her breasts.") did not appear in the Doran edition; at 319.2–3, "God, Lord, Lord, Lord, Lord" in the Doran edition is changed to "The sons of bitches . . . the sons of bitches," in the Modern Library version. It is not known whether these changes restore passages that were altered for the Doran edition. Dos Passos did not subsequently revise *Three Soldiers*. The present volume prints the text of the 1932 Modern Library edition of *Three Soldiers*.

Manhattan Transfer, which Dos Passos began in the fall of 1923 and competed in May 1925, was published by Harper & Brothers on November 12, 1925. Dos Passos did not subsequently revise the novel. An English edition published by Constable appeared in 1927. The 1925 Harper & Brothers edition of *Manhattan Transfer* is the text printed here.

This volume presents the texts of the original printings chosen for inclusion here, but it does not attempt to reproduce features of their typographic design, such as display capitalization of chapter openings. The texts are presented without change, except for the correction of

typographical errors. Spelling, punctuation, and capitalization are often expressive features and are not altered, even when inconsistent or
irregular. The following is a list of typographical errors corrected,
cited by page and line number: 22.35, Wounded; 42.11, hold; 57.26, ¶
"Damn; 58.6, material; 96.12, board-; 101.3, typewriter. . . . Sen;
108.40, Chris!"; 136.26, voice,; 136.27, on;; 150.7, Cohen; 156.13, sing-
sing; 172.15, butter with; 172.21, she; 172.29, americain; 183.30, of;
186.12, partitions waiting; 208.8, J'ai; 220.18, soldier.; 230.17 where
was; 230.30, way?"; 231.20, dunno,' "; 235.15, pigeon-cot; 262.1, slip.";
273.10–11, everyone; 275.16, Brown; 275.25, room; 332.33, Said; 332.39,
major?"; 337.23, Gasgogne; 343.3, table."; 350.11, on a rug; 350.27,
way; 355.33, God;; 355.35, here,"; 357.35, convusively; 358.5, mouillè;
360.19, Walters,"; 363.9, Rod?"; 370.25, that; 373.16, "Ô; 379.30, rest
leaning; 381.13, Restaurant; 381.14, Terte; 395.6, better; 433.26, He;
434.30, it."; 452.37, *Pelleas and Melisande*; 453.5, *doits*; 454.30, but;
463.31, Come; 464.37, Germans,; 468.38, windmill; 472.30, He;
489.3, *colums*; 497.16, Its; 503.8, slivvers; 505.5, often. . . . He . . .
glass. An; 511.6, Marco; 512.18, Emile; 514.14, rotton; 563.19, tatooed;
571.38, Scotchman;; 582.8, hand, 584.24, parsely; 589.27, on a; 601.7,
mirrors,; 618.12, past; 620.19, eyes; 621.11, oughnt; 624.33, said be;
628.22, that; 629.20, year.; 630.1, hi minto; 632.31, I; 640.30, It's;
641.29, Cecily"; 656.26, What'll; 659.10, been?; 660.28, McNeil;
665.6, Oh; 670.6&10, dressingown; 675.10, pleas.; 686.7, psychoana-
lyist; 722.1, tables; 726.8, minature; 736.17, pull-; 736.20, Sunderlands;
742.31, your; 745.6, they; 754.20, tone; 764.2, Thank's; 773.26, Mari-
anbad; 780.27, Frank; 790.14, Pulizter; 791.22, earings; 812.21, nick-
leglinting; 818.24, drink."; 818.35, much. . . . ; 823.13, face,

Notes

In the notes below, the reference numbers denote page and line of this volume (the line count includes headings). No note is made for material included in standard desk-reference books. Biblical quotations are keyed to the King James Version. Quotations from Shakespeare are keyed to *The Riverside Shakespeare*, ed. G. Blakemore Evans (Boston: Houghton Mifflin, 1974). For references to other studies, and further biographical background than is contained in the Chronology, see John Dos Passos, *One Man's Initiation: 1917* (Ithaca: Cornell University Press, 1969); John Dos Passos, *The Fourteenth Chronicle: Letters and Diaries of John Dos Passos* (Boston: Gambit, 1973), edited by Townsend Ludington; John Dos Passos, *The Best Times: An Informal Memoir* (New York: New American Library, 1966); Townsend Ludington, *John Dos Passos: A Twentieth Century Odyssey* (New York: E. P. Dutton, 1980); Virginia Spencer Carr, *Dos Passos: A Life* (New York: Doubleday & Co., 1984).

ONE MAN'S INITIATION: 1917

1.1   ONE MAN'S INITIATION: 1917]   In 1945 the novel was reprinted as *First Encounter* (New York: Philosophical Library) with "A Preface Twenty-Five Years Later":

It just happens that I'm looking over this little book with a view to its publication at a time when I'm in the middle of writing up the notes of another tour to another front in another war. This narrative was written more than a quarter of a century ago by a bookish young man of twenty-two who had emerged half-baked from Harvard College and was continuing his education driving an ambulance behind the front in France. The young man who wrote it was about the same age as so many of the young men I was seeing and talking to last winter in the Pacific. All the time I was trying to imagine how I'd be thinking and feeling if I were that young man again, really in the war up to my ears, instead of being a middle-aged literary man getting a couple of quick looks at it as a correspondent.

There would be a number of differences.

For one thing I think the brutalities of war and oppression came as less of a shock to people who grew up in the thirties than they did to Americans of my generation, raised as we were during the quiet afterglow of the nineteenth century, among comfortably situated people who were confident that industrial progress meant an improved civilization, more of the good things of life all around, more freedom, a more humane and peaceful society. To us, the European war of 1914–1918 seemed a horrible monstrosity, something outside of the normal order of things like an epidemic of yellow fever in some place where yellow fever had never been heard of before.

The boys who are fighting these present wars got their first ideas of the world during the depression years. From the time they first read the newspapers they drank in the brutalities of European politics with their breakfast coffee.

War and oppression in the early years of this century appeared to us like stinking slums in a city that was otherwise beautiful and good to live in, blemishes that skill and courage would remove. To the young men of today those things are inherent deformities of mankind. If you have your club foot you learn to live with your club foot. That doesn't mean they like the dust and the mud and the fatigue and the agony of war or the oppression of man any better than we did. But the ideas of these things are more familiar.

Looking back it is frightening to remember that naïve ignorance of men and their behavior through history which enabled us to believe that a revolution which would throw the rascals out of the saddle would automatically, by some divine order of historical necessity, put in their places a band of benign philosophers. It was only later that some of us came to understand that when you threw out King Log you were like as not to get King Stork in his place.

Nobody had given a thought to educating us in the traditional processes of self-government or in the rule that individual liberty, wherever it has existed in the world, has come as the result of a balance between the rights and duties of various contending individuals or groups, every man standing up for himself within the framework of a body of laws and customs. Having no knowledge of the society we had grown up in, or of the traditional attitudes that had produced in us the very ethical bent which made war and tyranny abhorrent to us, we easily fell prey to the notion that by a series of revolutions like the Russian the working people of the world could invent out of their own heads a reign of peace and justice. It was an illusion like the quaint illusion the early Christians had that the world would come to an end in the Year One Thousand.

In reporting a conversation we had with a congenial bunch of Frenchmen one night in a little town where the division was *en repos*, I tried to get some of this down on paper. As an American unaccustomed to the carefully articulated systems of thought which in those days were still part of the heritage of the European mind, I remember being amazed and delighted to meet men who could formulate their moral attitudes, Catholic, Anarchist, Communist, so elegantly. Reading it over I find the chapter scrappy and unsatisfactory, but I am letting it stand because it still expresses, in the language of the time, some of the enthusiasms and some of hopes of young men already marked for slaughter in that year of enthusiasms and hopes beyond other years, the year of the October Revolution.

It was this sanguine feeling that the future was a blank page to write on, focusing first about the speeches of Woodrow Wilson and then about the figure of Lenin, that made the end of the last war so different from the period we are now entering. Perhaps the disillusionments of the last quarter of a century have taught us that there are no short cuts to a decent ordering of human affairs, that the climb back up out of the pit of savagery to a society of even approximate justice and freedom must necessarily be hard and slow. We can only manage one small step at a time. The quality of the means we use will always determine the ends we reach.

Last winter, talking to the young men out in the Pacific I found that most of them just hoped that what they would return to after the war would not be worse than what they had left. This was not an age of illusions. We can only hope that it will become an age of clear thinking.

                                                                    JOHN DOS PASSOS

Provincetown, Mass.
April 26, 1945

2.2–3   *Erize-la-Petite and Erize-la-Grande*]   Two villages along the road between Bar-le-Duc and Verdun.

9.11–14   "Why didn't you . . . though, isn't it?"]   In the 1920 Allen & Unwin edition this passage was changed to:
    "Gee, these Frenchwomen are immoral. They say the war does it."
    "Can't be that. Nothing is more purifying than sacrifice."
    "A feller has to be mighty careful, they say."

11.5   permissionaires.]   Soldiers on leave.

12.39   camions]   Trucks.

15.2   ravitaillement]   Provisions.

15.38   bidons]   Metal water-bottles.

19.26   Etat-Major]   Headquarters.

19.27   embusqués]   Shirkers.

19.31   abris]   Dugouts.

19.37   boyau]   Communication trench.

20.38   brancardiers]   Stretcher-bearers.

22.8–9   Anyway, she lays . . . ready for business.]   In the 1920 Allen & Unwin edition: Anyway, she comes up to me with a funny look in her eyes an' starts makin' love to me.

22.29   peste]   Plague.

23.3–4   "Not exactly, but . . . amounted to the same. . . ."]   This passage did not appear in the 1920 Allen & Unwin edition.

23.5   Athos, Porthos, and d'Artagnan]   Protagonists of Alexandre Dumas' *The Three Musketeers* (1844).

23.14–17   "*Au plein . . . fait bon dormir.*"]   "Full of my cognac / How good it is, good it is, good it is, / Full of my cognac / How good it is to sleep."

23.18   the 'Internationale'] Socialist anthem, with words (1871) by Eugène Pottier and music (1888) by Adolphe Degeyter.

23.28–31   "*Auprès de ma . . . fait bon dormir.*"] "Beside my blonde / How good it is, good it is, good it is, / Beside my blonde, / How good it is to sleep."

26.25   seventy-fives] French field artillery guns. Each gun fired a 16-pound shell 75 millimeters in diameter and had a maximum range of almost five miles (8,600 yards).

29.22   popote] Field mess.

32.21   singe and pinard] Bully beef and wine.

35.10   Entente Cordiale] Diplomatic agreement signed by Great Britain and France on April 8, 1904, that resolved several colonial disputes and resulted in closer relations between the two countries in the decade before the outbreak of World War I.

36.3   *Madelon*] Song (1914) about a barmaid, with words by Louis Bousquet and music by Camille Robert, that became very popular among French soldiers.

36.38   mangai, mangai.] Eat, eat.

37.34–35   I'll sleep without a man. . . .] In the 1920 Allen & Unwin edition: I have not made a sou. . . .

38.6   Louise in the opera] *Louise*, opera by Gustave Charpentier (1860–1956), first performed in Paris in 1900.

38.16–30   The girls had two rooms . . . only you and me."] In the 1920 Allen & Unwin edition this passage was changed to:
    They stopped under a broken sign of black letters on greyish grass, within which one feeble electric light bulb made a red glow. The pavement was wet, and glimmered where it slanted up to the lamp-post at the next corner.
    "Here we are. Come along, Janey," cried the Australian in a brisk voice.
    The door opened and slammed again. Martin and the other girl stood on the pavement facing each other. The Englishman collapsed on the doorstep, and began to snore.
    "Well, there's only you and me," she said.
    "Oh, if you were only a person, instead of being a member of a profession——" said Martin softly.
    "Come," she said.

43.17   aspirant] An officer candidate in the French army.

44.37   part of Virgil] In the *Inferno* the poet Virgil guides Dante through Hell.

46.11–13   He smiled, asking . . . that barbed wire?"]   In the 1920 Allen & Unwin edition this passage was changed to:

He smiled, and asked the swaying figure in his mind:
"And You, what do You think of it?"
For an instant he could feel wire barbs ripping through his own flesh.

47.7–8   *Camp des Pommiers*]   Camp of the Apple Trees.

49.29   poste de secours]   First-aid post.

49.38–39   piece of éclat]   Shell splinter.

52.37–53.6   *"Ah, sunflower . . . wishes to go."*]   Cf. William Blake, "Ah, Sun-flower," *Songs of Experience.*

56.16   the Eroica]   Beethoven's Third Symphony (1804).

61.27   aumonier]   Chaplain.

64.17   gniolle]   Brandy.

67.4   copain]   Pal.

72.24   Shelley's *Hellas*]   Verse drama (1822) by Percy Bysshe Shelley, written in support of the Greek war of independence.

74.27–29   people in Boccaccio . . . at Florence]   Giovanni Boccaccio's *Decameron* (1348–53) is narrated by characters who have fled to Fiesole to escape the Black Death in Florence.

THREE SOLDIERS

87.1   THREE SOLDIERS]   In 1932 Dos Passos wrote an introduction for the Modern Library edition of *Three Soldiers*:

It is thirteen years since I finished writing this book. Reading it over to correct misprints in the original edition has not been exactly a comfortable task. The memory of the novel I wanted to write has not faded enough yet to make it easy to read the novel I did write. The memory of the spring of 1919 has not faded enough. Any spring is a time of overturn, but then Lenin was alive, the Seattle general strike had seemed the beginning of the flood instead of the beginning of the ebb, Americans in Paris were groggy with theatre and painting and music; Picasso was to rebuild the eye, Stravinski was cramming the Russian steppes into our ears, currents of energy seemed breaking out everywhere as young guys climbed out of their uniforms, imperial America was all shiny with the new idea of Ritz, in every direction the countries of the world stretched out starving and angry, ready for anything turbulent and new, whenever you went to the movies you saw Charlie Chaplin. The memory of the spring of 1919 has not faded enough yet to make the spring of 1932 any easier. It wasn't that today was any finer then than it is now, it's perhaps that tomorrow seemed vaster; everyone knows that growing up is the process of pinching off the buds of tomorrow.

Most of us who were youngsters that spring have made our beds and lain in them; you wake up one morning and find that what was to have been a springboard into reality is a profession, the organization of your life that was to be an instrument to make you see more and clearer turns out to be blinders made according to a predestined pattern, the boy who thought he was going to be a tramp turns out a nearsighted middleclass intellectual, (or a tramp; it's as bad either way). Professional deformations set in; the freeswimming young oyster fastens to the rock and grows a shell. What it amounts to is this: our beds have made us and the acutest action we can take is to sit up on the edge of them and look around and think. They are our beds till we die.

Well you're a novelist. What of it? What are you doing for it? What excuse have you got for not being ashamed of yourself?

Not that there's any reason, I suppose, for being ashamed of the trade of novelist. A novel is a commodity that fulfills a certain need; people need to buy daydreams like they need to buy icecream or aspirin or gin. They even need to buy a pinch of intellectual catnip now and then to liven up their thoughts, a few drops of poetry to stimulate their feelings. All you need to feel good about your work is to turn out the best commodity you can, play the luxury market and to hell with doubt.

The trouble is that mass production involves a change in the commodities produced that hasn't been worked out yet. In the middleages the mere setting down of the written word was a marvel, something of that marvel got into the words set down; in the renaissance the printing press suddenly opened up a continent more tremendous than America, sixteenth and seventeenth century writers are all on fire with it; now we have linotype, automatic type-setting machines, phototype processes that plaster the world from end to end with print. Certainly eighty percent of the inhabitants of the United States must read a column of print a day, if it's only in the tabloids and the Sears Roebuck catalogue. Somehow, just as machinemade shoes aren't as good as handmade shoes, the enormous quantity produced has resulted in diminished power in books. We're not men enough to run the machines we've made.

A machine's easy enough to run if you know what you want it to do; that's what it's made for. The perfection of the machinery of publication (I mean the presses; obviously smalltime boom finance has made a morass of the booktrade) ought to be a tremendous stimulant to good work. But first the writer must sit up on the edge of his bed and decide exactly what he's cramming all these words into print for; the girlishromantic gush about self-expression that still fills the minds of newspaper critics and publishers' logrollers, emphatically won't do any more. Making a living by selling daydreams, sensations, packages of mental itchingpowders, is all right, but I think few men feel it's much of a life for a healthy adult. You can make money by it, sure, but even without the collapse of capitalism, profit tends to be a wornout motive, tending more and more to strangle on its own power and complexity. No producer, even the producer of the shoddiest five and ten cent store goods, can do much about money any more; the man who wants to play with the power of money has to go out after it straight, without any other interest. Writing for money is as silly as writing for selfexpression. The nineteenth century brought us up to believe in the dollar as an absolute like the law of gravitation. History has riddled money value with a relativity more scary than Einstein's. The pulpwriter of today writes for a meal ticket, not for money.

What do you write for then? To convince people of something? That's preaching, and is part of the business of everybody who deals with words; not to admit that is to play with a gun and then blubber that you didn't know it was loaded. But outside of preaching I think there is such a thing as straight writing. A cabinet maker enjoys cutting a dovetail because he's a cabinet maker; every type of work has its own vigor inherent in it. The mind of a generation is its speech. A writer makes aspects of that speech enduring by putting them in print. He whittles at the words and phrases of today and makes of them forms to set the mind of tomorrow's generation. That's history. A writer who writes straight is the architect of history.

What I'm trying to get out is the difference in kind between the work of James Joyce, say, and that of any current dispenser of daydreams. It's not that Joyce produces for the highbrow and the other for the lowbrow trade, it's that Joyce is working with speech straight and so dominating the machine of production, while the daydream artist is merely feeding the machine, like a girl in a sausage factory shoving hunks of meat into the hopper. Whoever can run the machine runs it for all of us. Working with speech straight is vigorous absorbing devastating hopeless work, work that no man need be ashamed of.

You answer that Joyce is esoteric, only read by a few literary snobs, a luxury product like limited editions, without influence on the mass of ordinary newspaper readers. Well give him time. The power of writing is more likely to be exercised vertically through a century than horizontally over a year's sales. I don't mean either that Joyce is the only straight writer of our time, or that the influence of his powerful work hasn't already spread, diluted through other writers, into many a printed page of which the author never heard of *Ulysses.*

None of this would need saying if we didn't happen to belong to a country and an epoch of peculiar confusion, when the average man's susceptibility to print has been first enflamed by the misty sentimentality of school and college English teachers who substitute "good modern books" for the classics, and then atrophied by the bawling of publishers' barkers over every new piece of rubbish dished up between boards. We write today for the first American generation not brought up on the Bible, and nothing as yet has taken its place as a literary discipline.

These years of confusion, when everything has to be relabeled and catchwords lose their meaning from week to week, may be the reader's poison, but they are the writer's meat. Today, though the future may not seem so gaily colored or full of clanging hopes as it was thirteen years ago when I quit work on this novel that should have been worked over so much more, we can at least meet events with our minds cleared of some of the romantic garbage that kept us from doing clear work then. Those of us who have lived through have seen these years strip the bunting off the great illusions of our time, we must deal with the raw structure of history now, we must deal with it quick, before it stamps us out.

JOHN DOS PASSOS.

Provincetown,
June, 1932.

90.1–4 *"Les contemporains . . . lire un conte."*] *The Red and the Black* (1830), book I, chapter 27: "The contemporaries who suffer from certain things can only remember them with a horror which paralyzes every other pleasure, even that of reading a story."

103.12 "Arbeit und Rhythmus"] "Work and Rhythm," title of book by German economist Karl Bucher (1847–1930).

106.6 "Y" man] A civilian employed by the YMCA and assigned to build morale and maintain good morals among servicemen.

110.27 Kubelik] Jan Kubelik (1880–1940), Czech violinist and composer.

117.3 the Exposition ground] The Panama-Pacific International Exposition, held in San Francisco from February 20 to December 4, 1915, in what is now the Marina district.

117.5 "When It's Apple . . . Normandy."] Song (1912) by Harry Gifford, Huntley Trevor, and Tom Mellor.

119.6–11 "Beautiful Katy . . . kitchen door."] "K-K-K-Katy" (1918), song by Geoffrey O'Hara.

134.26 a torpedo] A mortar shell.

140.7–8 "There's a long . . . France."] A wartime version of the song "The Long, Long Trail" (1914) by Stoddard King (words) and Zo Elliot (music).

141.20 'Twentieth Century.'] A high-speed deluxe-service train that operated between New York and Chicago, beginning in 1902.

141.30 'Sunset Limited,'] A train that operated between New Orleans and San Francisco.

144.13 the Oregon forest,"] The Argonne Forest, about 15 miles west of Verdun.

148.11 mame shows] *Même chose*: same thing.

148.16 Voulay vous couchay aveck moy] Do you want to sleep with me?

150.24–25 "Ban swar . . . allez vous?"] Good night, my dear, How are you?

161.8 mackabbies] Dead bodies, from "macabre."

161.9   poilus] *Poilu* (hairy, shaggy) was the slang term for French infantrymen in World War I.

165.29   Demain] Tomorrow.

168.18   Vin blank,] White wine.

168.28–29   moving picture of "Quo Vadis,"] Directed by Enrico Guazzoni, the film (1912) was based on the novel (1897) by Henryk Sienkiewicz (1846–1916).

170.33   S.O.L.] Shit Out of Luck.

172.25   "Sale bête,"] Filthy beast.

177.10   "Je mourrais de cafard."] I was dying from tedium.

177.14–15   Avant . . . le cafard.] Before the war nobody knew what tedium was.

207.3   vin rouge, vite] Red wine, quickly.

208.8   j'ai un ami,] I have a friend.

208.11   Joli garçon] Handsome boy.

208.15   mon ami vous . . . vous admire,] My friend admires you.

210.25   Avions boches] German airplanes.

217.35   time of the Marne] The battle of the Marne was fought from September 5 to September 10, 1914.

229.11   *Make the world safe for Democracy*] In his address to Congress on April 2, 1917, asking for a declaration of war against Germany, President Woodrow Wilson said: "The world must be made safe for democracy."

242.9–10   "Dites-donc . . . lapins?"] Tell me, do the Germans run like rabbits?

254.24–25   "There's a girl . . . to mee."] Song (1913) with words by Ballard MacDonald and music by Harry Carroll.

263.11–12   Poor Miss Cavell] Edith Cavell (1865–1915), a British nurse who taught at a nursing school in Brussels, was shot by the Germans on October 12, 1915, for helping Allied soldiers escape to Holland.

267.25–28   "The world . . . game anew."] From *A Shropshire Lad* (1896), Verse LXII, by A. E. Housman (1859–1936).

267.29–30   "*Tentation de Saint Antoine*,"] *The Temptation of St. Anthony* (1874) by Gustave Flaubert.

269.12   the Argonne offensive] American troops attacked the Germans along a line running from the Meuse River to the western edge of the

Argonne Forest on September 26, 1918, and reached the northern end of the Argonne on October 11. The offensive continued until the Armistice on November 11, 1918.

272.2–3   "Yanks are Coming,"] From the song "Over There" (1917), words and music by George M. Cohan.

276.2   Army of Occupation in Germany] Under the terms of the Armistice, American troops moved into Germany and by December 17, 1918, had occupied a section of the west bank of the Rhine as well as a zone on the east bank extending for 30 kilometers around Coblenz. The last American occupation troops were withdrawn from Germany in January 1923.

277.4   changed the name of their institutions] A republic was proclaimed in Berlin on November 9, 1918, after it was announced that Kaiser William II had abdicated.

277.21   Conference at Paris] The Paris Peace Conference formally opened on January 18, 1919, under the leadership of the "Big Four": President Woodrow Wilson, French premier Georges Clemenceau, British prime minister David Lloyd George, and Italian premier Vittorio Orlando.

281.6   Sale Américain] Dirty American.

281.34   Ronsard] Pierre de Ronsard, French poet (1524–85).

282.16–17   *Red wine . . . the rose*] Cf. Edward Fitzgerald, *The Rubáiyat of Omar Khayyám* (1859).

282.24   *The lion . . . courts where*] Cf. Edward Fitzgerald, *The Rubáiyat of Omar Khayyám* (1859).

288.28   V'là un gars . . . vin] There's a boy who is wasting good wine.

288.30   Pour vingt . . . bouteille] For twenty sous I'll eat the bottle.

289.1   M'en fous, c'est mon métier] I don't give a damn, it's my business.

292.7   loukoumi] A sweet paste, also known as Turkish delight.

292.37   Nous rions . . . gris] We're laughing because we're drunk on vin gris.

294.36   prunelle] A sweet liqueur flavored with wild plums.

297.30   R.T.O.] Regimental Transport Officer.

306.12   Locksley Hall] Poem (1842) by Alfred Tennyson.

307.1   Nevin's] American composer Ethelbert Nevin (1862–1901).

307.27   Puvis de Chavannes] Pierre-Cécile Puvis de Chavannes (1824–98), French painter known for his murals.

311.7   Mais quelle gaieté] Such gaiety.

329.5   Gare de l'Est] Station of the East, the railroad station in Paris for train service to eastern France.

329.31–32   Flatiron Building . . . Eiffel Tower] The 20-story Flatiron Building was built at Fifth Avenue and 23rd Street in 1902; the Brooklyn Bridge was completed in 1883; the Eiffel Tower was built in 1889.

333.22   the Schola Cantorum] Music school founded in Paris in 1895 by the composers Vincent d'Indy, Charles Bordes, and Alexandre Guilmant as an alternative to the Paris Conservatory.

335.38   sole meunière] Sole that is rolled in flour, fried in butter, and served with parsley, melted butter, and lemon.

336.10   Lucullus] Lucius Licinius Lucullus (c. 114–57 B.C.), a wealthy Roman famous for giving lavish banquets.

337.24   ivrogne and sans vergogne] Drunken and shameless.

338.29   explosion of a Bertha] "Big Bertha" was the popular Allied name for the long-range gun used by the Germans to shell Paris from March 23 to August 12, 1918. During the bombardment 367 shells were fired over a distance of 70 miles, killing 256 people.

339.3   Manon's songs] *Manon*, opera (1884) by Jules Massenet (1842–1912).

339.6   Catonian] Austere, severe, harsh. The term refers to the Roman politicians Cato the Elder (234–149 B.C.) and his great-grandson, Cato the Younger (95–46 B.C.).

339.10   Jean-Jacques] Jean-Jacques Rousseau.

341.11   Oh, oui . . . la nature.] Oh yes, sir, directly from life.

341.16–17   de matière . . . l'accapareur] From making it to selling it (literally, from raw material to the hoarder's profit).

344.8   Rien de plus?] Nothing more?

344.11   Que . . . l'armistice.] What do you want, mister, it's the armistice.

344.26   Dee-dong . . . Bourgogne] Say, a little Burgundy wine.

344.35–36   America . . . prohibition?] Ratification of the Eighteenth Amendment was completed on January 16, 1919. Under its terms, prohibition would begin one year after the amendment was ratified.

346.11   Lui est Sinbad] He is Sinbad.

346.23   O, qu'il est drôle, celui-là.] Oh, he's funny, that guy.

347.10   O qu'il est rigolo]   Oh, he's so funny.

347.14   Eh bien . . . le camp]   Well, Jeanne, it's time to get out of here.

349.15   'Internationale.']   See note 23.18.

350.34   *Depuis . . . donnée*]   Song from the opera *Louise* (see note 38.6).

358.5   O ce pauvre . . . mouillé]   Oh that poor soldier! He must be soaking wet.

358.11   Mais ça ne vaut pas la peine.]   But it's not worth the trouble.

358.21   Et celui-la! . . . rigolo]   And that one! Oh, he was funny.

359.10–11   tigress . . . Mme. Clemenceau]   George Clemenceau (1841–1929), premier of France 1906–9 and 1917–20, was known as "the Tiger" for his combativeness.

359.14   *l'Humanité*]   Socialist newspaper founded in 1904.

368.13   MacDowell who went mad]   American composer Edward Alexander MacDowell (1860–1908) began showing signs of mental illness in 1904 and suffered a complete collapse in 1905.

368.27–28   paintings . . . Fayum]   Naturalistic Greco-Roman portraits dating from the first three centuries A.D. that were found in tombs in the Fayum district of upper Egypt.

373.17   la jeunesse]   The young.

373.21   an 1870 look]   The siege of Paris during the Franco-Prussian War began on September 20, 1870, and continued until an armistice was signed on January 28, 1871.

382.31   Bien. Tu peux venir]   Fine. You can come.

385.25   Pelléas]   *Pelléas et Mélisande*, opera (1902) by Debussy, based on the play (1892) by Maurice Maeterlinck.

386.5   Emile Faguet]   Faguet (1847–1916) was a French literary critic and the author of a critical study (1899) of Flaubert.

394.18   vous voulez monter?]   Do you want a ride?

420.2   OH, QU'IL . . . blanche!]   Oh, how clean he is! Oh, his skin is so white!

421.3   Il va mieux]   He's doing better.

421.27–28   Sont . . . salauds-là]   Those bastards are royalists.

422.24   Les bourgeois . . . nom de dieu!]   Hang the bourgeoisie from the lampposts, for God's sake!

422.25   Oh, qu'il est malin, ce Coco!]   Oh, he's sly, that Coco!

433.17   Et toi . . . mai?]   And you, are you going to take off work on May Day?

435.35   Mais . . . étrange]   But, Mr André, how strange you seem.

443.2–3   the war with Russia]   In December 1918 a French expeditionary force landed at Odessa and the Crimea to assist the southern White army fighting the Bolsheviks in the Russian Civil War. The French evacuated their troops in April 1919, but continued to provide limited aid to the Whites until the end of the Civil War in November 1920.

453.3   château . . . très profond,]   Very cold and very deep castle.

453.5–7   *Je les . . . la tour*]   "I hold it in my fingers, I hold it in my mouth . . . All your hair, all your hair, Mélisande, has fallen from the tower." Lines from the Debussy opera.

462.6–7   "Qu'il a . . . revolutionnaire,"]   "How interesting he seems." "Ferocious, isn't he? The revolutionary type."

462.10   Mais ne vous dérangez pas,]   But don't disturb yourself.

MANHATTAN TRANSFER

488.9–10   King C. Gillette]   King Camp Gillette (1855–1932), American co-inventor and first manufacturer of safety razors and blades.

489.24   MORTON SIGNS . . . BILL]   Governor Levi P. Morton signed the bill consolidating Manhattan, Brooklyn, Queens, the Bronx, and Staten Island into a single city on May 11, 1896. The consolidation went into effect on January 1, 1898.

493.25   PARKER'S FRIENDS]   Alton B. Parker (1852–1926), chief justice of the New York court of appeals, was the Democratic presidential nominee in 1904. He was defeated in a landslide by Theodore Roosevelt.

493.35   RELIEVE PORT ARTHUR]   The Russian naval base at Port Arthur (now Lüshun), Manchuria, was besieged by the Japanese during the Russo-Japanese War from May 26, 1904, until its surrender on January 2, 1905.

494.16   the Mosquito Parade]   Probably "The Mosquito's Serenade" by the songwriter H. W. Loomis (1865–1930).

496.19   J'te dis . . . à New York]   I'm telling you, man, I'm jumping ship in New York.

497.27   merde v'la l'heure.]   Shit, it's time.

498.25   Chicago theater fire]   A fire at the Iroquois Theater in Chicago on the afternoon of December 30, 1903, killed 602 people.

499.1   Maude Adams]   American actress (1872–1953), famous for her performances in the plays of James M. Barrie, including *Peter Pan* (1904).

506.20   Bob Ingersoll]   Robert G. Ingersoll (1833–99), American orator and lawyer who was known as "the great agnostic" for his views on religion.

511.35   Dio cane]   God is a dog.

511.40   les bourgeois . . . dieu.]   See note 422.24.

512.35–36   Errico Malatesta]   Italian anarchist Errico Malatesta (1853–1932).

530.15–16   Faut faire . . . dieu!]   Got to make like a wedding party, for God's sake!

530.21   Tu m'emmerdes . . . manières]   You know you give me a pain with your ways.

530.37   Tieng . . . ami-es,]   That's the way people forget their friends.

532.3–7   Just a birrd . . . seems to be]   From "A Bird in a Gilded Cage," song (1900) with words by Arthur J. Lamb (1870–1928) and music by Harry Von Tilzer (1872–1946).

547.17–18   Non posso leggere,]   I can't read.

557.2   Ingersoll]   A watch, named after its manufacturer Robert H. Ingersoll (1859–1928), that was introduced in 1892 and priced at one dollar.

566.37   *The Coral Island*]   Adventure novel (1857) by Scottish author R. M. Ballantyne (1825–94).

582.4–5   Cherie . . . du feu.]   Darling that shakes me up . . . I'm terribly afraid of fire.

582.33–34   Behold thou art . . . thy locks.]   Song of Solomon 4:1.

583.11–12   stay me with . . . of love]   Song of Solomon 2:5.

596.10–11   Thy navel . . . with lilies]   Song of Solomon 7:2.

598.31–32   DANDERINE]   A scalp tonic.

599.24   Sherman in gold]   Augustus Saint-Gaudens' gold-leafed equestrian statue of General William Tecumseh Sherman and the Winged Goddess of Victory at Fifth Avenue and 60th Street. The statue was unveiled on May 30, 1903.

616.8–9   Forbes Robertson]   British actor Sir Johnston Forbes-Robertson (1853–1937).

616.37   The Stag at Bay]   Painting (1846) by Sir Edwin Henry Landseer (1802–73).

623.36–37   *Youth's Encounter . . . Chansons de Bilitis*]   Novel (1913) by Compton Mackenzie; philosophical work (1883–92) by Friedrich Nietzsche; novel (2nd-century A.D.) by Apuleius; *Imaginary Conversations of Literary*

Men and Statesmen (1824–29) by Walter Savage Landor; novel (1896) by Pierre Loüys; collection of prose poems (1894) by Loüys.

628.21–24   White . . . Thaw] Harry K. Thaw (1880–1947), the wealthy son of a Pittsburgh industrialist, fatally shot architect Stanford White (1853–1906) in the rooftop theater at Madison Square Garden on June 25, 1906. At trial Thaw claimed the shooting was in revenge for White's alleged rape in 1901 of Evelyn Nesbit (1884–1967), the showgirl Thaw had married in 1905. After his first trial ended in a deadlocked jury, in 1908 Thaw was found not guilty for reasons of insanity and was committed to a mental hospital. In 1913 he walked away from the asylum and fled to Canada. He was extradited to the United States, but was set free in 1915.

631.26   *La Revolte des Anges*] *The Revolt of the Angels* (1914), novel by Anatole France.

632.40   "City of orgies walks and joys. . ."] Cf. Walt Whitman, "City of Orgies," in the sequence "Calamus" from *Leaves of Grass.*

638.36–37   the *General Slocum*] A wooden excursion steamer that burned in the East River on June 15, 1904, with the loss of 1,021 lives.

640.38–39   ASSASSINATION OF ARCHDUKE] Austrian Archduke Ferdinand was assassinated in the Bosnian capital of Sarajevo on June 28, 1914, by Gabriel Princip, a Bosnian Serb nationalist who acted as part of a plot organized by Serbian army officers. Austria-Hungary broke diplomatic relations with Serbia and partially mobilized its army on July 25, then declared war on July 28, 1914.

649.5   *Jean Christophe*] A *roman–fleuve* in ten volumes (1906–12) by Romain Rolland.

653.7–8   *Lucia . . . The Quaker Girl.*] *Lucia di Lammermoor,* opera (1835) by Gaetano Donizetti, with a libretto by Salvatore Cammarano; musical (1910) with music by Lionel Monckton, lyrics by Adrian Ross and Percy Greenbank, and book by James T. Tanner.

653.11   *Town Topics*] A weekly New York magazine, edited from 1891 to 1920 by Colonel William d'Alton Mann (1839–1920), that purveyed society gossip.

658.24–25   *He's a Ragpicker*] Song (1914) by Irving Berlin.

661.23   *Sweet Rosy O'Grady*] Song (1896) by Maude Nugent.

670.4   *He's a devil in his own home town*] Song (1914) with words by Irving Berlin and Grant Clarke and music by Berlin.

672.21   *Everybody's Doing It*] Song (1911) by Irving Berlin.

675.24   Black Hand] Secret Italian-American criminal society that engaged in extortion in immigrant neighborhoods.

676.12 They've killed Jaures.] Jean Jaurès (1859–1914), a leading French Socialist, was assassinated in Paris on July 31, 1914, by an extreme nationalist.

678.10–11 J'ai fait . . . mes voyages,] I've been around the world three times in my travels.

680.32 Guillaume and Viviani] Kaiser William II and René Viviani, premier of France 1914–15.

684.27 Dies like . . . he said] Cf. John Greenleaf Whittier, "Barbara Frietchie" (1864), line 42.

684.29–30 And they left . . . his glory.] Cf. Charles Wolfe, "The Burial of Sir John Moore" (1817), line 32.

684.30–31 where the embattled . . . heard round] Ralph Waldo Emerson, "Hymn: Sung at the Completion of the Concord Monument" (1836), lines 3–4.

684.33–34 shame on . . . his home when] Thomas Babington Macaulay, "Horatius," stanza 2, from *Lays of Ancient Rome* (1842).

687.37 Vive le sang] Long live blood.

687.38–39 *And three times . . . went*] Cf. the traditional song "The Mermaid."

688.8 mondiale.] Worldwide.

688.13–14 The stars look . . . world, unite.] Cf. John Greenleaf Whittier, "Barbara Frietchie" (1864), lines 59–60; Karl Marx and Friedrich Engels, *The Communist Manifesto* (1848).

690.16 the Agadir incident."] A German gunboat anchored at Agadir on July 1, 1911, escalating the rivalry between France and Germany for economic and political influence in Morocco. Fears of war increased after Britain sided with France, but the crisis was resolved on November 4, 1911, when France ceded approximately 100,000 square miles of the Congo to Germany in return for German recognition of a French protectorate over Morocco.

693.33 battle of the Marne] See note 217.35.

694.31 Booth, Jefferson, Mansfield] American actors Edwin Booth (1833–93), Joseph Jefferson (1829–1905), and Richard Mansfield (1854–1907).

695.14 Wallack's] New York theater company founded in 1852 by the actor-manager James William Wallack (1794–1864) and continued by his son Lester Wallack (1819–88) until his retirement in 1887.

696.7 *In My Harem*] Song (1913) by Irving Berlin.

705.36–37 Fitzgerald's contraction] The contraction or foreshortening of a moving body in the direction of its motion, first suggested in 1892 by

George Francis Fitzgerald (1851–1901) and elaborated in 1895 by the Dutch physicist Henrik Lorentz.

709.8   The shadow of white Death]   Percy Bysshe Shelley, "Adonais" (1821), stanza VIII.

709.9–10   And at . . . Corruption]   "Adonais," stanza VIII.

709.13–14   Far from the . . . tempest given]   "Adonais," stanza LV.

711.21   The Lilac Domino]   Musical (1912; English version, 1914) composed by Charles Cuvillier.

733.39   Wall Street bomb outrage]   A bomb hidden in a horse-drawn cart exploded near 23 Wall Street on September 16, 1920, killing or fatally wounding 40 people. No one was ever arrested for the crime.

735.9–10   C'est la lutte . . . genre humain.]   From the "Internationale," Socialist anthem with words (1871) by Eugène Pottier and music (1888) by Adolphe Degeyter. In an American version of the song, these lines are: "'Tis the final conflict; / Let each stand in their place! / The international working class / Shall be the human race."

736.5–6   *Somebody Loves Me*]   Song (1924) with music by George Gershwin and lyrics by Buddy DeSylva and Ballard MacDonald.

736.6–7   *You're in Kentucky . . . Born*]   Song (1923) by George A. Little, Haven Gillespie, and Larry Shay.

737.23–24   The Butterfly on the Wheel]   *A Butterfly on the Wheel*, play (1911) by Edward G. Hemmerde and Francis Neilson.

737.38–39   *The moving finger . . . moves on*]   Cf. Edward Fitzgerald, *The Rubáiyat of Omar Khayyám* (1859).

737.40   *Nor all your . . . word of it*]   Cf. Edward Fitzgerald, *The Rubáiyat of Omar Khayyám* (1859).

738.17–18   Monsieur Beaucaire]   Play (1901) by Booth Tarkington and Evelyn Greenleaf Sutherland, adapted from the novella (1900) by Tarkington about an 18th-century French aristocrat.

740.19   Hindustan]   Song (1917) with music by Harold Weeks and lyrics by Oliver Wallace.

742.25   Château Teery]   Château Thierry, a town on the Marne River 40 miles east of Paris where American troops helped stop a major German offensive in June 1918.

747.1   I'm just wild about Harree]   Song (1921) by Eubie Blake and Noble Sissle.

754.9   *Shuffle Along*]   Song (1921) by Eubie Blake and Noble Sissle.

762.19–20   *Yes We Have No Bananas*]   Song (1923) by Frank Silver and Irving Cohn.

762.38   *Beautiful Girl of My Dreams*]   Song (1875) by A. P. Wyman.

780.32–33   let us sit . . . deaths of kings.]   *Richard II*, III, ii, 155–56.

781.27   songs of Bilitis]   See note 623.36–37.

793.24   the Sullivan law.]   New York State law, passed in 1911, that prohibits possession of a handgun without a police permit.

794.13   the Oregon forest]   See note 269.12.

803.18   City of Destruction]   The city that Christian flees in *Pilgrim's Progress* (1678) by John Bunyan.

810.8   Coué]   Émile Coué (1857–1926), French advocate of psychotherapy through autosuggestion; his methods included the repetition of the phrase "Every day, and in every way, I am becoming better and better."

820.39–821.1   *O it's always . . . get together*]   Cf. Richard Hovey, "A Stein Song" (1898), stanza 1.

821.6–7   *With a stein . . . ri-i-inging clear*]   Cf. Richard Hovey, "A Stein Song" (1898), stanza 1.

830.22–23   Ah ça se voit . . . ils dispareaitront]   You can tell. . . . You must not work, your little wrinkles are already showing. But they'll disappear.

830.31–32   c'est le rêve]   It's perfect.

830.39–831.1   Annette Kellermann]   Kellermann (1887–1975) was an Australian swimmer and film actress.

831.6   boncilla]   A cosmetics brand whose products included a clay pack used for skin cleansing.

831.40–832.1   Die Rote Fahne]   "The Red Flag," socialist anthem written in 1889 by Jim Connell.

834.26–27   *Running Wild*]   Song (1922) with words by Joe Grey and Leo Wood and music by A. Harrington Gibbs.

835.27   *Lady . . . lady be good.*]   From "Oh, Lady Be Good," song (1924) with words by Ira Gershwin and music by George Gershwin.

Library of Congress Cataloging-in-Publication Data

Dos Passos, John, 1896–1970.
  [Novels, Selections]
  Novels, 1920–1025 / John Dos Passos.
        p.   cm. — (The Library of America; 142)
Contents: One man's initiation, 1917 — Three soldiers — Manhattan transfer.
ISBN 1–931082–39–1 (alk. paper)
    I. Title. II. One man's initiation, 1917. III. Three soldiers.
      IV. Manhattan transfer. V. Series.
PS3507.O743 A6 2003b
813′.52 dc21   2003047529

THE LIBRARY OF AMERICA SERIES

The Library of America fosters appreciation and pride in America's literary heritage by publishing, and keeping permanently in print, authoritative editions of America's best and most significant writing. An independent nonprofit organization, it was founded in 1979 with seed money from the National Endowment for the Humanities and the Ford Foundation.

This book is set in 10 point Linotron Galliard,
a face designed for photocomposition by Matthew Carter
and based on the sixteenth-century face Granjon. The paper
is acid-free Domtar Literary Opaque and meets the requirements
for permanence of the American National Standards Institute. The
binding material is Brillianta, a woven rayon cloth made by
Van Heek-Scholco Textielfabrieken, Holland. The compo-
sition is by The Clarinda Company. Printing and
binding by R.R.Donnelley & Sons Company.
Designed by Bruce Campbell.

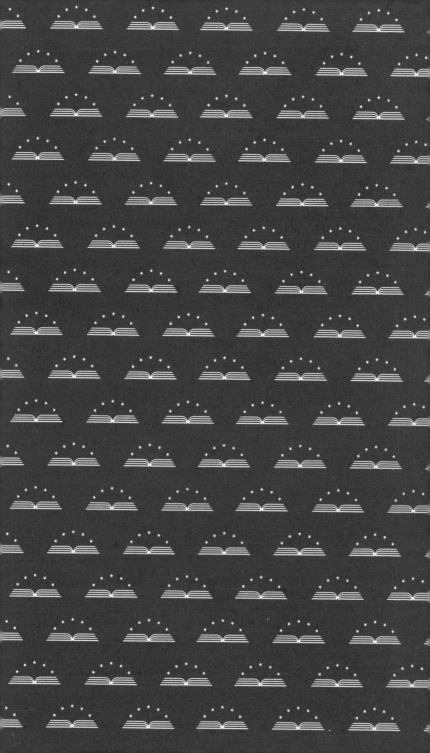